WINGS

STORIES OF RAF II

CHARLES ANTHONY
PETER LESLIE

BLITZ EDITIONS

This edition published in Great Britain 1997

Published by Blitz Editions
an imprint of Bookmart Limited
Registered Number 2372865
Trading as Bookmart LTD
Desford Road, Enderby
Leicester, LE9 5AD

Copyright © 1997 by 22 Books

A CIP record for this book is available from the British Library

ISBN 1 85605 381 4

10 9 8 7 6 5 4 3 2 1

Typeset by Hewer Text Composition Services, Edinburgh
Printed in Great Britain by Clays Ltd, St Ives plc

WINGS 4

FERRET FLIGHT

Charles Anthony

1

North Korea, April 1951

Osipovsky knew he was not going to make it back to base. He was OK, but the MiG-15 was definitely not. It still flew – just – and while it continued to do so, he was getting deeper into friendly territory and away from the Sabres. Those damned Blue Fins had been everywhere.

After being fleetingly hit by the six guns of a blue-finned F-86 Sabre, he'd considered himself very lucky indeed not to have been wounded; but though it was not an immediate killing shot by the American pilot, it was still a kill as far as the MiG was concerned.

The trail of billowing smoke had grown spectacularly, and Osipovsky began to worry about getting roasted if he tried to make it back. He would have to eject. At least he was well into friendly territory now.

Osipovsky began to think of his future prospects after ejecting. He did not relish being the only survivor of the special 'Green Ringer' squadron that had been commanded by the Great Patriotic War ace Major Valentina Nerova. From the snatches of radio conversations he'd picked up, he realized to his horror that she was gone, as was Beryev, the deputy commander. The squadron had been wiped out.

He knew that the squadron had been operating under quite different orders from those of the other Soviet squadrons, all of which operated clandestinely, under 'North Korean' colours. Stalin did not want the world to know he was using the Korean War to give Soviet pilots combat experience in the jet age, and to blood the formidable MiG-15.

The Green Ringer squadron had been far more special. It had been given the best aircraft and the best pilots, whose main task was to take on the best the Americans could offer, and win. But it had not worked out that way. The best, the Blue Fins, had triumphed.

The MiG squadron's patron had been a top KGB general, who had no doubt hitched his own star to its eventual success. Given Stalin's notorious dislike for failure, Osipovsky reasoned that the general's star would soon be in serious jeopardy. That general would want a scapegoat.

'Me!' Osipovsky said aloud as the fire warning light began to blink.

He came to a decision about his own future. He would go missing in action, presumed dead. His mother originally came from one of the USSR's Asian republics and he reasoned he could just about pass himself off as a border Korean from the north-east. He was going to disappear.

Having made his decision, Osipovsky reached for the knob by his left thigh to first jettison the canopy; then he ejected.

The now-burning MiG-15 spiralled towards the ground 3000 feet below, and exploded on impact.

Osipovsky eventually landed gently, and quite unhurt.

Arizona, USA, April 1996, 10.00 hours
The two-lane blacktop undulated in a straight line across a terrain that looked more like the moon than the earth. There was a single car cruising along it, but in the far distance behind, currently in a dip in the road, was another vehicle, travelling fast to catch up.

The cruiser was a Ford Mustang. It was not new, but a '69 fast-back model. Despite its vintage, there was something purposeful about the way it powered along on its fat new wheels. This was in no small measure due to the spanking, newly rebuilt Shelby Cobra engine lurking beneath its scooped bonnet, the large tailpipes at the rear betraying the existence of the non-standard motor.

The paint job still needed attention, as evidenced by the extensive amount of primer coating parts of the bodywork. The driver's door was all primer, as was the boot lid. The bonnet carried smears that made it seem like a bad attempt at camouflage. Diagonal streaks adorned the passenger door, and the roof looked as if someone had been playing noughts and crosses on it but had forgotten how to draw the grid.

But Captain Milton Garner, USAF, dressed casually in T-shirt and jeans, didn't care how the car looked from the outside. The Cobra engine he'd lovingly worked on grumbled with latent power, hinting at the massive surge on tap, should he need it. The upholstery also left much to be desired but that, too, would eventually be taken care of.

He'd been working on the car in his spare

time for nearly three years now, ever since he'd spotted it neglected and forlorn, in a corner at the back of a used-car lot in Atlanta. He could not believe, when he first saw it, that anyone could have given the Boss 429 Mustang such shabby treatment. It was the Boss of all the Boss models as far as he was concerned, and its erstwhile owner had either gone broke or was just too rich to care and had at the time seen the Mustang as just a fashionable set of wheels.

The astonished salesman had been so shocked that Garner was actually serious about buying the dilapidated car and was so pleased to be simply rid of it that he'd almost forgotten himself and nearly paid him to take it away. But the god of commerce had intervened and had soon brought him back to his senses. Even so, in the end Garner had got it for little more than the price for scrap.

It brought down the tone of his place, the salesman had said with evident relief, waving expansively at the gleaming, nearly new cars parked neatly on display. He had even offered to have the sorry Mustang transported to Garner's home.

Garner had thought the man wouldn't have

known a good car if it ran him over, but had accepted the offer.

For his part, the salesman had clearly thought Garner had taken complete leave of his senses, but was quite happy to sell a sucker a non-runner. On his wedding anniversary, he bought his mistress a present with Garner's money, while trying to persuade his wife that pressure of work had made him think of the wrong date.

When Garner eventually got the car home, he discovered that perhaps the original owner was not such a fool, after all. Though the Mustang did not have the triple-scoop Shelby bonnet and restyled nose, it had all the special equipment. He then realized that the previous owner must have once loved the car to have acquired such a special model and wondered what had dragged it to such a low station. Then the real work began.

Every leave he got, Garner worked on that car. But eventually all the hard graft and the substantial amount of money inevitably spent, paid off. This was the very first time he'd actually got it licensed and on the road once more, since its sad days with the used-car firm.

He listened in air-conditioned splendour to a track of *Mainstreet* by Bob Seger on the expensive CD system he'd installed, and enjoyed a great sense of achievement as the open road stretched before him.

He patted the steering wheel affectionately. 'That's my baby. Eat up the miles.'

He glanced in his mirror and frowned. A speck had appeared there. He was no longer alone. He was still some fifty miles from the base, and wondered if this was someone else heading for the same destination.

The bright-red, fat-wheeled, high-sitting pick-up truck roared in pursuit of the Mustang. The truck, a '96 Dodge Ram with extended cab and a heavily modified 5.2-litre V8 engine, was driven by a pig-faced man of about twenty-five who had a fixed, humourless grin stamped upon his mean features. His mean little eyes stared into the distance, malevolence seeping out of their opaque depths.

His companions, about the same age, were also male. Two of them were just as nasty-looking, with expressions of ugly anticipation on their faces. Their shirt sleeves were rolled tightly up their thick arms, almost to their shoulders.

The driver's third companion, sitting alone in the back, looked slightly younger, and was not at all happy with the situation. All four had brought pump-action shotguns.

'Look,' the unhappy one began. 'I thought we were going after rattlers. That's why I said I'd come.'

'What's the matter, boy?' the driver said disparagingly. 'This is much better than blowing the heads off rattlesnakes. You 'fraid your pappy's gonna find out?'

'Why worry, Billy?' another of the men said with a laugh. 'Hell. It's good to have a pappy who's the local sheriff.'

They all laughed, except Billy.

'Hell, Billy,' the driver was saying, 'my pappy and your pappy did this all the time when they was our age. They crossed into other states, looking for this kind of sport. You think your old man's changed that much, just because he's the sheriff?'

'Hell, no!' the three all said together, laughing raucously.

Billy looked even more unhappy.

Garner watched the speck in his mirror continue to grow, its trail of rising dust betraying its fearsome speed. He turned off the music and lowered the windows. The desert heat rolled in. After the incredible winter that had seen even Florida shivering, April in the Arizona vastness was nowhere as baking as June could be, but the temperature was high enough to get the air-conditioning working itself up furiously in an attempt to compensate. He turned it off. The warmth with the windows down and the slipstreamed breeze entering the car was quite pleasant at this time of day.

'Someone in a real hurry,' he said to himself.

He did not increase speed. There was plenty of time before he was due at the base. With the windows down, he savoured the deep growl of the cruising Cobra engine.

'And all my own work too,' he added with satisfaction.

Though he'd used the main highways on the long east-west cross-country trip, he'd deliberately begun using the back roads once he'd crossed out of Texas and into New Mexico, so as to better enjoy from time to time, with the windows down, the wonderful burble of that engine against the emptiness all around him. Only the powerful roar of the F-15 Eagle on full afterburner at take-off got to him as much.

A nighthawk, one of the whippoorwill family that confusingly liked to hunt during the day, fluttered off the side of the road as the Mustang

9

passed, darting skywards and performing a neat barrel roll as it went.

Garner felt a slight annoyance that someone else had encroached on his solitude, but consoled himself with the fact that, given the speed the other vehicle was doing, it would soon be gone and he'd be alone again.

He thought whoever was driving was taking a chance. This was not Montana, way up north on the Canadian border, where speed limits on the open road had recently been abolished. Even in this apparently featureless place the highway patrol had a nasty habit of materializing, as if out of nowhere. He knew of at least one pilot who'd been clocked doing 140mph in a Viper on another lonely and totally empty road, by a motorcycle patrolman who'd been hiding behind a boulder. The cop had issued the ticket with a huge grin. They loved catching fast-jet aircrew.

'You're on the ground now,' the patrolman had said to the hapless pilot gleefully. 'My territory. Have a nice day.'

There was no record of what the pilot had remarked, if anything, but Garner could imagine the fury of that jet jockey's thoughts.

He glanced again at the growing speck. 'It's your licence, buddy,' he said aloud.

*　　*　　*

The vast airbase was many things, among which were: training unit, operational conversion unit, operational unit and, occasionally, specialist operational unit. All these identities existed concurrently within the whole and tucked away in a far corner, some distance from prying eyes, were four brand-new McDonnell-Douglas F-15 Eagles whose presence involved that specialist role.

These formidably capable two-seat aircraft could turn and fight as lethally as the single-seat version; but their real territory was in the strike arena, where they could deliver an astonishingly varied selection of weaponry, day or night, in all weathers.

But this was not their reason for being there.

'Give me an E!' Hands came together. Clap.
  'Give me an E!' came the chorus. Clap-clap.
  'Give me an A!' Clap.
  'Give me an A!' Clap-clap.
  'Give me a G!' Clap.
  'Give me a G!' Clap-clap.
  'Give me an L!' Clap.
  'Give me an L!' Clap-clap.
  'And give me an E!' Clap.
  'And give me an E!' Clap-clap.

'And give me *another* E!' Clap.

'And give me *another* E!' Clap-clap.

'We are the Eagle *Ego* drivers!' they all chorused.

The four men who made up two of the Eagle E crews were in the officers' club, 'singing' their litany in loud homage to their much-loved aircraft.

They were being observed, with barely concealed disgust, by two F-16 pilots.

'You guys are dicks,' one of them said. 'You know that?'

'Yeah,' an unrepentant back-seat occupier retorted. 'Don't you wish you had one?'

The pilot who had spoken bristled.

Doug Herlihy, a captain and one of the Eagle E pilots, sensing possible trouble, cut in quickly.

'Hey now, ladies!' he began lightly. 'Let's not forget we're all officers and gentlemen.' He had the crisp, staccato accents of a Boston patrician.

'Could have fooled me,' the F-16 pilot grumbled. 'We'll see how well you do upstairs.'

'A *challenge*?' the second back-seat man, Hal 'Computer' Mossman, remarked with fake awe. 'I *like* challenges.'

'Your itsy-bitsy toy against *ours*?' the cheerleader, a Californian named Lancer, asked in mock dismay. He clutched at his chest. 'Oh no! I'm terrified!' Lancer was a first lieutenant, and also a pilot. 'You'll give my poor lil' ol' wizzo heart failure!' He turned to the weapons systems officer who normally occupied the back seat of his aircraft. 'Say you're afraid, Johnny, boy.'

'I'm afraid, I'm afraid!' Johnny Hershon said dutifully. 'I'm really terrified.' It was Hershon who had cast doubt upon their anatomical endowment. He didn't look terrified.

'There you go,' Lancer, seeming almost too tall to get into any fighter cockpit, said to the F-16 pilot. 'We're all afraid.'

'You guys won't think it's so funny when you come up against us,' the F-16 jockey grated. 'C'mon, Norm,' he added to his companion. 'Let's leave these jokers to their fantasies.'

'"Norm",' Lancer mouthed to Hershon with a straight face. 'Aren't you pretty, Norm!' he said aloud, watching them leave the room. 'Fantasies?' he went on with a soft snarl. 'We'll show you fantasies!'

'Perhaps we shouldn't needle them,' Mossman suggested lightly. 'They're tender souls.'

'I like them needled,' Lancer retorted. 'Perhaps they'll fight better.' He turned once more to Hershon. 'You reckon these guys're Tactical

Adversary jocks? Or just regular F-16 drivers talking big?'

Among the Adversary force on the base – aircraft and pilots playing the part of the enemy during mock air combat – were many F-16 Falcons.

'Who knows?' Hershon replied. 'They're not wearing any Adversary badges that I could see.'

'Who cares?' Mossman said. 'We'll still whup 'em, but good.'

They laughed.

Just then another Eagle pilot turned up. Captain Matt Sukowinsky came from New York and sounded like it.

'Anyone heard from the Jazz Couple?' he asked. 'It's getting close to briefing time.'

'You worry too much, Sukowinsky,' Mossman said. He was Sukowinsky's WSO. 'It's two and a half hours yet. Have a coffee and sit down.'

'What's the Jazz Couple?' Lancer asked.

Sukowinsky gave him a jaded look. 'I keep forgetting you're our new tenderfoot, plucked fresh from the selfish Eagles.' It was his way of describing the pilot-only, single-seat versions of the aircraft. 'Captains Nathan "The Ball" Adderly, and Milton "The Sax" Garner. We call them the Jazz Couple because they've got the names of two of the greatest jazzmen that ever lived: Cannonball Adderley, and Errol Garner. Sometimes, we also call them Nate and Milt. You should wait till you know them better before doing that.'

It was a testament to Lancer's and Hershon's success as a crew that they had made it into the special unit while Garner and Adderly had been away.

'They're related to these guys?' Lancer asked.

'No,' Herlihy began patiently. 'They're just namesakes. The Jazz Couple also hate each other's guts.'

Lancer stared at him. 'You're kidding. And the Air Force put them in the *same* plane?'

'Ah well, you see,' Herlihy told him, 'they're like a married couple. Can't live with each other, but can't live without each other. In short, they chew all comers in the air. Whatever it is we're here for, they're the ones to beat.'

'We can beat them. Can't we, Johnny?'

'Sure,' Hershon replied, not looking as if he believed it.

'What I like,' Sukowinsky said, favouring Lancer with a sceptical stare, 'is confidence in the air. In your dreams, buddy. You're not in single-seaters any more. This is a whole

15

new ball game, as you should've learned by now.'

'We'll see.' But Lancer's curiosity was aroused. 'Why do they hate each other?'

Silence greeted the question.

'Aw c'mon,' Lancer persisted. 'If it's such a big secret, why tell me about them in the first place?'

'You'd have noticed sooner or later, I guess,' Sukowinsky remarked with mild resignation.

'So . . . tell me the rest.'

Herlihy decided to do the telling; but he uttered the sigh of a man who had travelled too far and dreaded continuing.

'By some bizarre twist of fate, as they say,' he began, taking over from Sukowinsky, 'Sax Garner discovered that Adderly's family once owned slaves, Garner's ancestors among them.'

'You've got to be kidding.'

'As someone whose own forebears sailed with the Pilgrims to escape the King's minions, I don't kid about such things. Adderly's people really did own slaves, and those out of whose loins sprang the modern-day Garners were indeed among them. According to the documents, the Adderlys were not the nicest of the Southern slave owners. In fact, if they gave Oscars for being bastards, then the slaver Adderlys would have won every time. Today's supremacists would love them.'

Fascinated, Lancer stared at him. 'So now the Adderlys are rich white folk and the Garners are poor black? That's why Garner still hates them?'

Someone gave a chuckle.

'I said something funny?'

'Got it all wrong, tenderfoot,' Mossman said. 'Garner hates them all right. From what we've heard, they did some terrible things to his kinfolk, even by slave-owner standards. But the Garners are *rich* black folk and the Adderlys, for their sins, while not down there in the dirt, are the *poor* white folk by comparison. Seems sometime in the last century the market went out of slavery,' he added, straight-faced.

'You're kidding,' Lancer said for the third time.

'He likes using those words, doesn't he?' Sukowinsky murmured.

Lancer ignored his remark and looked to Hershon for help. Hershon shrugged.

'You could almost say,' Mossman went on, 'under different circumstances, Adderly could easily have been Garner's chauffeur . . .'

'Which of course,' Herlihy began mildly, 'is

17

what he really is.' He smiled at Lancer. 'If you get my meaning.'

'I get it. You guys are having some fun with me. Well, thank you for nothing.'

Sukowinsky shook his head solemnly. 'It is true about the slaves, and Garner really is rich – kind of. Word is, his father's a financial wizard. The old man was in financial circles when a black face in that line of business was scarcer than snow on a hot day. Moved to New York from the South, but they've still got family and a home down there. He bought one of those Southern mansions that had been a wreck for years, and built it right up again. Some kind of historical justice, huh?'

'The Adderlys' home?'

'No, Lieutenant Lancer. *That* would be too much coincidence.'

'Talking of wrecks,' Herlihy said. 'Didn't Garner say he'd finished that wreck he's been working on for nearly three years? That Mustang no one's ever seen.'

'Like father like son,' Sukowinsky commented drily. 'If he is driving that thing, he probably won't get here at all.'

'We don't even know for sure he's a . . .' Billy began, then stopped.

'C'mon, Billy!' the driver of the pick-up urged. 'Say it, say it!' he encouraged, as if at some initiation. 'Goddamit! Are you your daddy's boy, or some peckerwood? He and my pappy had some rare ol' times across in Alabama and Georgia way back in the sixties. "Nigger weekends" they used to call it, my pappy said.'

'We don't know he's . . . black.'

'That's not the word, Billy,' the driver said coldly.

'Oh leave me be, Amos!'

'Leave him be, he says. Goddamit, Billy! Nigger's the word. *Nigger!*'

The other men giggled slyly.

'Didn't you see that car go by just before we came to that corner just out of town? The way it looked? Hell, it wasn't even painted. That was a nigger car for sure. No pride in anything, niggers. Give 'em welfare every week. That's all they want.'

'I got a bad feeling about this, Amos.'

Amos turned to look at the younger man. 'Don't you go cissy on me, Billy.'

'Jesus!' one of the men yelled. 'Watch the damn road, Amos!'

The pick-up had veered alarmingly.

'Hold on to your balls, Yannock. I was

driving pick-ups since I was a tick in my daddy's porker. Don't you tell me how to drive this damn thing.'

Garner was again checking his mirrors. The speck had metamorphosed into a red pick-up truck. It came on without slackening pace. It would soon catch up and pass him, he reasoned. Then he'd be all alone once more to enjoy the vastness about him.

After several moments had gone by and the truck made no move to pull out to overtake, Garner began to wonder what the other driver was up to, and felt a strange tension rise within him. Perhaps it was nothing. He was just being jumpy, he persuaded himself. The otherwise empty road was suddenly spooking him. There was nothing to worry about.

But the truck was almost filling the mirrors, and it made no move to overtake.

Garner kept his nerve and did not accelerate. 'Pass, damn you!' he hissed.

The truck stayed put. Then it began to get closer still. Soon its image had spilled out beyond the edges of the mirrors.

It was now nearly crawling up the back of the Mustang.

'Wha'd I tell you?' Amos crowed. 'A nigger!'

Suddenly he pulled out and matched speeds with the Mustang. He began to blow the loud air-horns.

The two vehicles travelled side by side for a while.

Garner glanced across and saw the men grinning down at him from the high cab, and felt a weary resignation.

He'd travelled right across the country without the slightest problem of this kind, and this was the last place he'd expected it. But that particular boil was still so deep within the guts of the nation it leaked its poison anywhere, and any time. This bunch of retards had decided he was their sport for the day.

But he should have expected it, he told himself angrily. There were all sorts of gun-happy white supremacists inhabiting the desert backcountry. He should have known.

The occupants of the pick-up were yelling and whooping. He couldn't see the person in the back properly, but he didn't appear to be joining in the fun.

'Hey, boy!' one of them yelled from the cab. 'That's some car you got there! What's the matter? The pimping business not going too good? Not enough welfare?'

The truck had now come so close that if they

had stopped, neither door on the opposing sides would have opened fully.

Garner gave Yannock a cold glance.

'Hey! See that? He's got grey eyes! You've got grey eyes, boy! There's a lil' bit of white in you! Some nice white man porked your mammy, boy?' Yannock gave him an ugly grin, deliberately goading. 'An' don't give me one of them looks. I'd just as soon blow your damn fool head to kingdom come, right here!'

This, Garner decided, could get seriously dangerous. It was time for some discretion over valour.

He changed down a gear and stamped on the accelerator.

The Mustang squealed its rear wheels and suddenly rocketed away, a powerful roar echoing in its wake. The pick-up rapidly became a pinprick once more.

'Sweet Jesus!' Yannock exclaimed, gaping. 'What the hell has he got under that hood?'

'I don't like this,' Billy said from the back.

'*Shut up!*' Amos snarled at him, humiliated by the Mustang's easy escape. He floored the accelerator. Though the pick-up took off with alacrity, even its modified engine was no real match for the Mustang. But he kept going, driving at the edge of control. 'No nigger's gonna make a fool out of me, *goddamit*!' He thumped the steering wheel twice.

Amos had become what those stupid enough to be his friends called 'killing mean'.

The red Dodge pick-up raced after the fleeing Mustang.

Some distance away, Deputy Sheriff Zack Milson focused his powerful binoculars on a fast-moving shape that had come round a wide bend in the road, and into view. He was standing on an escarpment, looking down on the otherwise empty black ribbon that fed its way across the parched landscape.

'Got us a race driver here, Sheriff!' he called eagerly to his superior. 'Must be doing a hundred, at least. Maybe more.'

He stepped back slightly to look behind him. About fifty feet down at the bottom of a gentle, shale and rock-strewn slope, the patrol car was hidden behind one of those tall rock sculptures that had graced many a Western.

The sheriff, a grey-haired, thickset man, had removed his hat and was dabbing at his forehead with a handkerchief. He was leaning against the car.

'How long before he gets close enough?'

Sheriff Jess Newberg, Billy's father, called up.

'We got some time.' Milson was once more focusing on the road. He tracked the binoculars rearwards from the speeding Mustang. 'Hey! What the hell's this?'

Newberg put his hat back on. 'You tell me, Zack,' he said wearily. 'You're the one looking.'

'There's another car . . . no it's a pick-up . . . and it's racing too. Those nuts are having a race, Sheriff!'

'Well now . . . we'll just have to spoil their fun.'

'Hell, Sheriff,' Milson continued, the binoculars clamped to his eyes. 'I know that pick-up. It's Amos Brant's.'

'Goddam that idiot!' the sheriff growled. 'Probably got his idiot friends with him too.'

Milson was hurrying down. 'He's not gonna catch that Mustang. That thing's *moving*. It'll be hitting the county line soon.'

Newberg eased himself off the car. 'How far are *we* from the county line, Zack?'

Milson reacted by glancing involuntarily to his left. A few yards away a sign informed travellers they were leaving the county.

'Well come *on*, Zack. Get into the car and

put it across the road. Our fast man in the Mustang's going nowhere before we've had a little talk with him.'

'Yes, sir!' Milson hurriedly got into the patrol car.

'And get those lights moving. Better bring out one of the shotguns too.'

'Yes, sir!' Milson repeated, started the car and lurched towards the road to place the vehicle broadside on, straddling the centreline. The roof lights began to flash.

Milson grabbed one of the shotguns, and quickly climbed out. Feet planted apart, he positioned himself at the ready near the patrol car, as Newberg joined him.

They waited, looking down the road in the direction from which the Mustang and the pick-up would be coming.

Newberg did not draw his own sidearm.

'Shit!' Garner exclaimed softly as he saw the lights of the police car. 'I don't need this.'

He began to slow down.

'He's slowing down!' Yannock chortled. 'He's busted his goddam engine! We got you now, niggerboy!' Then he saw the lights. 'Oh hell!' he added.

'I knew it!' Billy Newberg said. 'Goddamit, Amos!'

'*Shut the fuck up, Billy!*' Brant snarled. 'You hear me?'

'Well, well,' the sheriff said to his deputy as the Mustang came towards them at a crawl, then stopped. 'What have we here. Georgia plates and a nigger at the wheel. You cover me, Zack. I'm gonna have me a talk with the fast nigger.'

'You got it, Sheriff,' Milson acknowledged with a smirk, bringing the shotgun up but staying by the car.

The sheriff walked stiff-legged towards the Mustang.

The pick-up had slowed down and had also stopped, some distance behind.

'Damn!' Billy cried. 'It's my father! Turn this thing round, Amos!'

'You think he's blind? He's already seen us. Relax. Your daddy doesn't like niggers any more than we do. He'll take him in, and we can have him later. Let's watch this.'

Garner watched neutrally as the sheriff stopped a short distance away.

'Out of the car, boy!' Newberg ordered, and

placed a precautionary hand on the gun at his hip.

Garner complied expressionlessly.

'What's a Georgia boy doing way out here, racing on the public highway?' Newberg demanded.

'I wasn't racing,' Garner replied calmly. 'Those morons in that pick-up tried to run me off the road. They're looking for trouble. I was just getting away from them.'

Newberg didn't like the way Garner had responded. His face clouded over.

'Let's hear some respect in your voice, boy, when you talk to me. *Hands on the car!* You know the drill. And no funny moves. My deputy back there's got a nervous disposition. The last time he got nervous he blew some guy's face clean off with that pump gun. Now I'm gonna search you for weapons . . .'

'I think you should see my ID, Sheriff, before this gets worse . . .'

'Don't interrupt me, boy! You hear what I'm saying?'

'I hear you.'

'And you talk funny for a black Georgia boy. You sound like a Yankee.'

'My family moved to New York,' Garner told him, still keeping calm. 'But we've got a home in

27

Georgia.' Jumpy backcountry sheriffs and their deputies tended to have 'accidents'. He wasn't keen to add to the number. 'Please check my ID, Sheriff. Holding me here is against the national interest, as you will soon see.'

Newberg paused. 'You telling me you're one of them fancy black FBI agents?' he began sceptically, an unpleasant grin on his face. 'You know . . . fancy-talking college boys – like you sound – in sharp suits. Only you got no sharp suit on. You one of them?' The sneer in his voice fairly leapt at Garner.

'No, Sheriff.'

There was another pause.

'Well, then,' Newberg drawled. 'Better let me see that ID you're so all fired up about.' He was clearly having fun, and did not believe Garner. 'And if you're messing with me, you're going to be one sorry black boy. You got that? You'll wish that pick-up had run you off the road. No funny moves now. Remember my nervous deputy.'

Garner slowly reached into his jeans for his USAF ID, then handed it to Newberg.

There was a long silence as Newberg studied it.

'No shit.' Another silence followed. 'Captain Garner,' Newberg continued at last to himself.

'Yeah, yeah.' He glanced up at the sky, and sighed. He looked as if he wanted to spit. 'United States Air Force. Straighten up, Captain.' He spat on to the edge of the road.

Garner obeyed, and turned round.

Newberg handed back the ID, then cleared his throat. It was obvious he hated what he was going to have to say.

'Uh, look. Sorry, Captain . . . I . . .'

'Forget it, Sheriff,' Garner interrupted coolly. With all the bases in the area, he'd expected that even a local sheriff would have been less quick to jump to the wrong conclusions. But prejudice was like that. 'We all make mistakes,' he added.

He got back into the Mustang and started the engine. It burst into powerful life and grumbled at idle. 'I'm expected at my base soon,' he continued. 'Got to get going. Could you please ask your man to move the patrol car?'

Newberg's eyes danced briefly. He gnawed at his lower lip, hating even more the fact that he was forced to do Garner's bidding.

'Sure. *Zack!*'

He didn't turn to look at his deputy. His eyes continued to stare at Garner, as if in thrall.

'Sheriff?'

'Move the car! We don't want to delay the Captain . . .'

'*Captain* . . .'

'Goddamit, Zack. Get the damn car out of the way!'

'Yessir, Sheriff!'

Milson hurried back into the patrol car to carry out his superior's orders.

As the patrol car lurched out of the way, Garner eased the Mustang slowly forward.

'Thank you, Sheriff.' Garner gave Newberg a casual salute.

Involuntarily, Newberg responded before he realized what he was doing. He brought his hand back down guiltily, and turned to watch as the Mustang roared across the county line.

'*Shit, shit, shit!*' Yannock fumed. 'I don't get it. He's let him go! What the hell do you make of that?'

Amos Brant gripped at the wheel and said nothing.

'Perhaps he was police,' Billy suggested. 'He gave my father something. Must've been an ID. My father even saluted him. You all saw.'

'Now I've seen it all,' Yannock said. 'Sheriff Newberg, terror of the niggers, salutin' one. That sure beats all.'

'*Are you two assholes going to stop yammering?*' Amos Brant yelled.

By the police car, Newberg was still staring after the rapidly receding Mustang. He looked like a man who'd been cheated, and he wanted to vent his frustration on something, or someone.

'Get on the speakers, Zack,' he said at last to his deputy, 'and get those peckerheads in that pick-up down here.'

'I think your son's with them, Sheriff,' Milson announced tentatively. 'I've been watching the truck . . .'

'Goddamit, Zack! Quit arguin' with me! I don't give a shit if the President himself's in that truck. You think I'm going up to them and say please? *Get them here!*'

'Yes, sir!' Zack acknowledged quickly, and turned on the patrol car's loudspeakers to order the pick-up to approach.

When the Dodge had arrived Newberg glared at the occupants, reserving the hardest look for his son.

'Amos Brant,' he began formally, 'I'm arresting you for speeding on the public highway . . .'

Brant refused to believe it at first. 'C'mon, Uncle Jess. It was just a bit of fun . . .'

Newberg shut him up with a baleful stare. 'You're going to lose that licence, Amos.'

Brant was scandalized. 'You can't . . .'

'I can, and I will. I'm the sheriff. Remember?'

'But Uncle Jess . . . I drive a truck for a living. What am I gonna do without my licence?'

'Should've thought about that, boy, before you decided to go on a coon hunt. Now come on out. Get into the car with Zack. C'mon. *Move!*'

Brant climbed reluctantly out, still wanting to believe that Newberg would only go so far. But it was the wrong day for favours.

Newberg's eyes searched out his son. 'Billy!' There was no warmth in them.

'Yes, sir!'

'You get behind that wheel and drive the pick-up back to town. Go on.'

'Yes . . . yes, sir!'

WINGS

2

Garner did not enjoy the remainder of the
journey to the base. The incident with the
pick-up and the sheriff had soured the pleasure
the long drive had given him. Worse, it had
reminded him of his continuing antipathy for
his pilot.

As a man and an officer in the United States
Air Force, he felt secure within himself. As an
American, he felt secure in his rights as a citizen.
As a black American, he felt the burden of his
nation's history weighing heavily upon him. As
one of the crew pair of his F-15 Eagle E, for
him that burden had become sharply focused.

The aircraft, he felt, symbolized all the
contradictions of the powerful country that had
become the United States; but like the aircraft,
there was an almost omnipotent capability,
accompanied by an unmistakable tension. The
potential of this tension for disaster – which

was on all the streets of the nation – could only be guessed at, and was thus to be much feared. There was the constant awareness that the glue that held the country together could come unstuck at any moment.

Garner loved his country, and loved his profession. It was a calling. Clinically, he knew that Adderly was an excellent pilot. He knew they worked well together, as long as he did not allow his own personal feelings to surface while in the air. On the ground, it was another matter altogether; but in the interests of discipline, he kept that in check. However, there was still a discernible tension between pilot and back-seater, when they were not flying. They kept their social contact within strict limits.

Not for the first time, he cursed the fate that had brought the two of them together.

Throughout the States, the descendants of slaver and enslaved crossed one another's paths every day. But how many not only personally *knew* the descendant of his family's slavers, but actually *worked* with one in the confined cockpit space of one of the world's most technically advanced combat aircraft?

Perhaps, defying the odds, there were many such; but he would always consider his own situation unique.

Half an hour later he pulled up at the wide gates to the base. A young air force policeman he did not recognize came up to the car, studying it with more than passing interest.

The policeman looked at the ID that Garner held up to him, but his eyes were really for the car.

'Yes, sir, thank you, Captain,' he said, saluting smartly. 'You've got one hell of a car there, sir,' he continued. 'A 429. Best of all the Boss Mustangs. You working on her, sir?'

Garner was impressed. He had not yet remounted the badging on the car.

'Yes. I am. You know your Mustangs,' he added to the air policeman.

The younger man grinned. 'Sure love those cars, sir. Last of the great Americans. I know Corvette crazies would hate to hear that but for me, the Mustang's the thing . . . the Boss 429 most of all. Got me a '66 convertible back home. She's not running yet but when I'm done she's gonna look like a GT350. I've already got me a four-barrel Holly carb on the 289 engine, and some big-finned wheels. She's gonna look real good, sir.'

'I'll bet.' Garner looked at the enlisted man's name tag. 'Is that a Georgia accent I'm listening to, Lyle?'

'It sure is, sir. Mason Lyle, from Macon, GA, like in the song.'

'That was Philadelphia, PA.'

Lyle grinned. 'Nobody comes from Philadelphia.'

'Except Philadelphians.'

'Like I said, nobody.'

'Well, don't let any Phillies on this base hear you,' Garner advised the smiling air policeman. 'I'm a Georgia man, born, but bred elsewhere,' he continued. 'My folks come from just outside Olympic City.'

'Atlanta, huh?'

'Queen of the South, herself. Spent my youth in New York, so the accent's taken a beating.'

'They can take the man out of the South, sir, but they sure can't take the South out of the man.'

'Amen to that, Lyle,' Garner agreed, for many reasons, as he prepared to drive off.

'Excuse me, sir.'

Garner paused.

'I was thinking, sir,' Lyle continued, 'if you'd like some help with the car I'd . . . well . . . I'd like to offer . . . I'm pretty good, sir.'

Garner smiled at him. 'I might just take you up on that.'

'Sir, thank you, sir!'

Lyle saluted once more as Garner drove on. Their friendly talk went some way towards removing some of the sourness from the day after the encounter with the hick sheriff and the men in the pick-up.

There it was again, he thought wryly: the contradictions inherent within the nation. Lyle was pure Georgia and probably even came from a family that had made life hell for the blacks during the sixties. Yet Lyle, despite the fact that Garner was an Eagle crewman and an officer, still looked upon the captain simply as a fellow Georgian; a compatriot with whom a bond had been formed, sharing the love of the classic Mustang.

Garner felt appreciably better.

Colonel Robert E. Dempsey, a Texan, had a voice which, even when used softly, tended to fill the space about him irrespective, it sometimes appeared, of the size of the room he happened to be in at the time. However, for anyone seeing him for the first time the truly remarkable thing about him was his stature. For Dempsey was a small man; so small, he was frequently mistaken for a boy ... until one saw the colonel's eagles on his shoulders, or his lapels; or looked into his eyes. A tall, slim

major stood next to him, vividly accentuating
the difference in height.

Looking so much younger than his real
age tended to cause confusion in others; but
the colonel was a veteran of many combat
missions, and legend had it that he could fly
any aircraft with his eyes shut. Even allowing
for the exaggeration, there was no doubt that
he had an impressive flying history. The stack
of medal ribbons beneath the pilot's wings on
his left breast when he was in full uniform were
more than sufficient testimony. Among other
things on the base, he was responsible for
bringing the special Eagle E unit up to speed,
for the as-yet-unknown mission.

Dempsey, inevitably nicknamed Robert E.
Lee, stood before the assembled crews, legs
parted, hands gripping his hips. His cropped,
grey-flecked black hair seemed incongruous
atop the baby-like features.

'Can you all see me properly?' the booming
voice demanded.

'Yes, sir!' they chorused. No one would dare
make a joke about his height.

'Good.' His lively blue eyes raked his audi-
ence. 'We seem to be one officer light. Where is
Mr Adderly?' The eyes fastened upon Garner.
'Mr Garner . . . where's your pilot?'

'Er . . .' Garner began.

'Sir!' Someone had entered the room. Adderly came briskly to attention. 'Sorry I'm late, *sir*!'

Dempsey stared at him for long moments. 'Don't do it again, Captain,' the deep voice said quietly. It was almost as if he had pronounced sentence.

'No, sir!'

'Sit down, Mr Adderly.' Dempsey did not ask for an explanation and in a way this was a far more effective censure.

'Yes, sir!' Adderly took an empty chair next to Garner. He did not look at his back-seater.

'Now that we're all here,' Dempsey continued, without a trace of sarcasm, 'we can commence this briefing.'

They watched him intently.

'For the past six weeks,' he went on, 'your training missions have been in competition with each other. The four crews remaining are those who have, in my estimation, merited getting this far. This is not a downer on the capabilities of the crews that have not made it. They will return to their units without a stain on their confidential records. The quality of all those who made it for this contest was commendably high.'

Dempsey briefly scratched the tip of his nose with a little finger. Those who knew him well understood this to be a signal that he had a small bomb to drop somewhere along the line, always unexpectedly.

'The mission for which you are being tested will require an exceptional team in the cockpit. This crew will carry out the mission, with one more as a back-up should, for any reason, whoever has made the top spot be unable to continue. I know Eagles like to prowl in pairs, but this is a very special mission. It requires just the one ship.

'The winning Echo Eagle's pilot and wizzo will be told the mission on the day of take-off for the forward base. The back-up will not be informed, unless it becomes necessary to carry out the mission in place of that first airplane. From today, we go into a new phase. If you thought things were tough before, think again. This is crunch time. Each crew will fly two hops today. One this afternoon and one tonight. On each of these flights you will be bounced at any time, by the Tactical Adversary Falcons. How you cope will decide your eventual position at the finish.

'Oh yes, gentlemen,' Dempsey added, as if the thought had just come to him. The bomb was coming. 'I'll be flying one of the Falcons. You won't know which, so stay alert. If you find me crawling all over your six, God help you.'

There were subdued groans at this.

Dempsey looked at his crews and didn't smile. 'Take over, Major Carter.'

'Sir,' the major acknowledged. 'Right, gentlemen,' he went on as Dempsey left. 'You know what's expected of you. Weather for today is perfect as usual.' He gave a wicked grin. 'Nice for us to see you by.'

'Don't tell us you're going hunting as well, sir,' Hershon pleaded.

Robert E. *and* Carter. Crapville.

Carter's smile was feral. 'It's bad news day, Hershon.' Carter was known as 'Killer'; with good reason.

'This is just great,' Lancer began after Carter had followed Dempsey. 'Just great. Old Robert E. Lee himself *and* the nasty neighbourhood major, playing at bogeys. Dempsey hates staying on the ground, and as for Carter, he *enjoys* taking out Eagle jocks. The man's a sadist. They'll cream *all* our asses.'

'Worse,' Hershon joined in, 'we won't know if we're tangling with one of those Falcon jocks we saw in the club, or the old man himself, or Carter. Until it's way too late.'

'If Robert E. decides to fly on all the adversary missions,' Sukowinsky began tentatively, 'he'll be tired. That might give us a chance.' There was more hope than belief in those words.

'You wish,' Mossman commented drily. 'He *never* gets tired. That guy's so fit, I feel weak just looking at him. We'll wear him out, he'll be laughing so much.'

'Well, *any* F-16 we see,' Adderly said, 'I'm going to assume it's him, or Carter, and act accordingly. Better safe.'

Garner nodded. 'I agree. They're both going to be out to get us. It's the mean season, guys.' He turned to his pilot. 'We'd better get suited up. We've got the first hop.'

Adderly nodded. 'Yeah. Just our luck.'

'I'll pray for you turkeys,' Lancer called after them as they left the room together. 'Robert E. Lee will be good and fresh, and just hungry for suckers! And if he doesn't get you, the sadist will!' He gave a loud and passable imitation of the gobbling sound of the hapless bird in a blind panic. 'And if they don't, *we* will in the fly-off.'

Lancer clearly believed his aircraft would be in the last two to survive the predations of the colonel and the major.

'Pray for yourselves!' Garner retorted. 'You'll need it more than us.'

Lancer's laughter followed them out.

'We're going to have to teach that guy a lesson he'll never forget,' Garner went on to Adderly. 'He thinks he can beat us.'

'That'll be the day,' Adderly said.

They walked on in silence for a while, then Garner said, 'What happened?'

'Why was I late?'

Garner nodded.

'Small problem at home. I missed the earlier flight back.' Adderly did not elaborate.

Garner did not press the issue, but he knew it was more than a 'small' problem. He knew what had caused Adderly to be late for the start of the briefing.

Adderly was married, with a baby boy. It was not his first child. The earlier one, a girl, had died during birth, nearly killing her mother as well. Arlene Adderly, previously a sparkling, outgoing person, had become very introverted after that. When Garner and Adderly had been sent on temporary assignment from their base in North Carolina to Arizona, she had been very unhappy. The new baby had just arrived. Adderly could have cited the situation and requested removal from the assignment; but his commitment to his career was such that he would never have contemplated making such a request.

Garner also knew that a now very much changed Arlene would like her husband to leave the air force, though she would never admit this publicly, even in her current state. But flying fast jets was all that Adderly knew, and all that he wanted to do. To take him away would be like depriving him of a great part of his life. He would not be the same man she had fallen in love with, and subsequently married. But for the moment, she was not the woman he'd married either.

Though not married himself, Garner could well sympathize with Adderly's situation. His own dreams of marriage had foundered upon the rocks of a disastrous love affair. The woman in question had been someone from his school days. He'd fallen for her from the first day he'd seen her at school. Then her family had moved to California and they'd lost touch for years. But he'd never forgotten her.

One day, during vacation with his family to celebrate his brand-new commission, he'd unexpectedly bumped into her – literally – in a New York department store.

Then a budding financial whiz-kid, she'd

joined a New York firm. They continued where they'd left off, as if the years had not intervened. The affair was intense, but something was wrong. The years *had* changed things. An officer in the air force was small beer, and a husband with a military career was not high on her list of priorities. She would never become an air force flyer's wife, she'd told him bluntly. Airline, maybe. Why hadn't he gone into finance, like his father? But despite this personal downgrading, he'd still felt a powerful physical attraction to her. She'd reciprocated with an almost consuming enthusiasm.

Garner had hung on to that dream for two years; but the damage had long been done. One weekend he arrived in New York from his North Carolina base to spend the time with her. That first night they had a romantic dinner in a fashionable restaurant, followed by long bouts of ferocious lovemaking in her apartment, for the remainder of the weekend. She'd dropped the bombshell on the morning of his last day in town. She was going to marry someone from Wall Street.

Benumbed, he'd walked out and checked into a hotel, waiting out the time before his return flight by making a close acquaintance with a bottle of bourbon. He'd found it hard to equate the person who'd had the dinner with him, who had made such fantastic love during the weekend, with the one who had acted with such clinical ruthlessness. The condemned man had eaten a hearty dinner, enjoyed hearty, wild sex, and eaten a hearty breakfast. Then dropped through the trapdoor.

Astonishingly, he'd made it back to his quarters on the base without disgracing himself. But that night the pain of the loss hit him with a vengeance and he'd vomited until there was nothing left to bring up. The bourbon had not been solely responsible.

He didn't see her again.

To compensate, he concentrated single-mindedly on his job and became an even better wizzo than he already was. For recreation, he spent most of his spare time visiting relatives in Georgia, and working on the Mustang. That way, he'd managed to keep her out of his mind. She sent letters, asking him to be happy for her. Driven by guilt, he'd reasoned coldly. He'd ripped the letters to shreds, and never replied. Eventually they had stopped coming.

Then the air force teamed him up with Adderly.

It was during that dark period that he discovered the history of the Adderly family and, as with so many things in life, it had occurred innocuously. Adderly had introduced him to Arlene, herself a Southern beauty from Arkansas. One evening, during a dinner at the Adderlys' home near the base, he and Arlene had found themselves alone and she'd said something quite casually, never dreaming of the repercussions.

'It's kinda great,' she'd said, 'the air force putting you and Nate together in the same plane. Who'd have thought that before the Civil War, Nate's family owned slaves who were part of your family?'

Stunned by the revelation, he'd made no big deal about it at the time, keeping his true reactions to himself.

'How do you know that?' he'd asked her as calmly as he could.

Quite unaware of the effect the news had had on him, she'd replied easily, 'Oh, Nate's got some of the family papers among his junk. He told me.'

'He never told me.'

'Well, he wouldn't, would he? He's kinda embarrassed about that part of the family history. But just before the Civil War, the last Adderly to inherit the plantation freed all the slaves. *He* was against slavery. Nate reckons that's when the family started to get poor. He's proud about that.'

'I guess.'

Garner never forgave Adderly for not telling him and decided to do some investigation of his own. Perhaps if the woman he'd loved so deeply had not dumped him, he would not have channelled his pain into finding out about the Adderlys and their slaves. From his own family, he'd known of the slave history, but no one had ever told him of the Adderly connection, even when he'd introduced his then new pilot. The reason had been simple enough. The existence of the branch of the Garner family who'd been Adderly slaves had been unknown.

Garner had started dividing his spare time between the trips to Georgia to work on the Mustang, and digging into the past. During his researches, he discovered a personal journal in an obscure library in West Virginia, of all places. How it had got there from Georgia was anyone's guess. No one at the library had seemed to know. The book itself was of little importance to them. They'd looked upon it as just another account among the countless number of written words about slavery.

The Journal of Nathan Adderly, had been

written on the soft, faded cover, in neat copperplate. It was dated 1837.

That particular Nathan Adderly had been the last of the real slave owners of the family, before Josiah Adderly had turned everything on its head and freed the human beings he'd inherited. Nathan Adderly had also been a master of unspeakable cruelty and his thoughts had been set down in the journal, in an almost businesslike way. There was no feeling for the suffering he had caused in his fellow human beings.

Garner had found no discernible emotion in the narrative as the facts, noted down by Nathan Adderly, had screamed their horror at him.

An entry, dated and timed, had grabbed Garner's attention: 'Caught a runaway. Enoch by name. Punished him to teach others a lesson. Tied him to a tree and slit his nose. He squealed like a hog. He won't be going anywhere now.'

The matter-of-fact tone had sickened Garner and brought the sharp taste of nausea into his mouth. He'd forced himself to continue reading, scanning through the many other entries, each vying with the rest for horrific content.

By the time he'd perused Nathan Adderly's

personal record as much as he'd wanted to, he'd also discovered something even more horrific in that precise account of one man's capacity for inhumanity.

The entry in question spoke of a rape – as recorded by Nathan Adderly – by a young black male slave, of a teenage daughter of the family. She had been made pregnant as a result.

'Mercifully,' Adderly's ancestor had written, 'the wretched animal that issued out of her loins was dead at birth. She has been confined, as during the pregnancy, to keep our shame from other eyes. None, except her servant, will cast eyes upon her. She is not to be visited by any of the family. I am no longer father to this daughter. The slaves mutter among themselves, a dreadful calumny upon her. They say she was not raped! How dare these savage beasts of the fields cast such aspersions! That my daughter Helena would willingly consort with a young buck is beyond imagining! But, as I have written, she is no longer my daughter.'

Nathan Adderly had taken a terrible revenge.

He'd had the young slave, himself a teenager, eviscerated alive. And he'd written it all down, describing the terrible process in full, almost loving detail. He'd watched from beginning to end. There'd been no law to stop him and in any case, no one would have. Slaves were not human.

Garner had walked out of the genteel little library feeling soiled, and for a while had stood outside in the warmth of a bright day gulping for air as he tried to regain his emotional equilibrium. He'd looked at the faces passing by, and had wondered how many of them knew of the dark horrors confided to that faded, innocent-looking journal. Had any of them ever come upon it? And would they have cared even if they had?

Then, as now, he doubted it.

My country, my pain, he'd thought as he stood there watching the oblivious people walk past.

He'd told no one about what he'd found; not even his father who, even now, knew nothing of it. He'd also wondered whether Nathan Adderly knew anything about those particular pastimes of his nineteenth-century namesake.

For Garner, the poisoned knowledge made him hate the Adderly family even more.

But he was genuinely concerned about Arlene's health. He had nothing against her

51

and before the miscarriage she'd always been pleasant company, humorous and sometimes quite daring.

'In certain lighting, you and Nate look alike,' she'd once said to him one warm evening, in sultry Arkansas tones laced with Louisiana and oiled by Southern Comfort. 'You know that? You got the same grey eyes too.'

Before she'd married Adderly, her name had been Labouchere. Her family had moved from Louisiana to Arkansas before she was born, but their accents had been grafted on to those of the state of her birth. The blend had given her a devastatingly sensuous voice.

'Would I know the difference in the dark?' she'd added mischievously.

'You'd better!' her husband had warned drily, coming up to them with replenished drinks. 'Behave yourself, Arlene. Quit hitting on my wizzo. I might get jealous.'

But that had been before Garner had discovered about the first Nathan Adderly. Days of innocence. Fun times.

'How's Arlene doing?' he now asked.

'She's OK,' Adderly replied, just short of being curt. 'She's going to be all right. Plenty of family to spend time with her.'

'That's good.'

They walked on in silence, to get kitted up. Fun times.

For a fighter, the standard single-seat F-15 Eagle was a huge beast. If anything, the F-15E, also known as the Echo Eagle or Eagle E, looked subtly bigger but was in fact of roughly the same dimensions. It was the conformal tanks – allowing extra fuel and thus range – tucked inboard beneath the wing on either side of the airframe, that served to give the F-15E an aggressive, broad-shouldered and awesome presence. Its vital statistics were no less awesome. Many people swore that the huge wing was as big as a tennis court. At nearly sixty-four feet long and close to eighteen and a half feet high to the tips of the vast sails of its twin fins, the aircraft was no midget.

The F-15E was not pretty in the ordinary sense of the word; but to those lucky enough to fly it, that big wing – all 608 square feet of it – made the Eagle E so agile that in the hands of a pilot who knew his stuff, few existing fighter aircraft could cope with it.

So it bounced about a bit at very low altitudes because of that playing field of a wing, and was not a smooth ride down there. So what? Garner thought. It made up for that drawback in many other ways. A dual-role aircraft, it was devastatingly effective against ground as well as air targets. It could pull more positive G than even the standard F-15 – 9 to the single-seater's 7.2 – and certainly more than its crew, even with their suits to help them, could. Even in the most violent of manoeuvring combat they couldn't break it, unless they slammed into something. It would break them first.

Many fast-jet crews would kill to get into its roomy, air-conditioned cockpits, Garner knew, and he felt highly privileged to be one of the fortunate few who'd actually made it.

As in all things, it was not without its detractors. The single-seat crews had various derogatory names for it: 'mudhen' and 'pregnant duck' were among the more polite epithets. To Garner, it was all sour grapes. Sheer jealousy.

The Echo Eagle could carry a formidable array of weaponry, from various air-to-ground munitions to three types of air-to-air missiles. For close-in work there was the internal Vulcan 20mm, six-barrelled rotary cannon. She could fly in all weathers, and her LANTIRN navigation and attack pods enabled her to find the enemy, irrespective of conditions outside. In the dark, an infrared image superimposed on the head-up display gave the crew a window on the night.

Today, Garner decided, he and Adderly were going to ruin an F-16 jock's entire day. Two or three, if they could also get the colonel and the major.

They would not be carrying bombs but inert air-to-air missiles, making the aircraft considerably lighter than normal. This meant their Eagle E was virtually configured for air combat, despite the fact that they would be making a low-level run to dodge the fully functioning radars dotted out there on the desert weapons range. The object of the exercise was not to be caught by them, or to so jam their opponents' sensors that in a hot situation in a real theatre of war the surface-to-air-missiles would not get off the ground, or miss altogether if they did.

The people waiting in the desert for them to make mistakes loved catching out hot-shot Eagle crews, as Garner knew only too well. He also knew Robert E. would be assessing their performance, even as the wily colonel prepared to catch them napping, and he was determined they would not be caught out.

As for the inert air-to-air missiles they carried, these dummy weapons would perform as if in real combat, without actually firing; but they would record the results as if they had been. If the Echo Eagle killed, it would be there for all to see. No Adversary jock would be able to argue his way out of the evidence.

Trussed up in their olive-green flight gear, they walked out towards their Eagle. As he strode next to Adderly, Garner suddenly remembered an instructor from the early days of conversion training on the F-15E. The instructor had put on display a life-sized illustration of the full kit necessary for flying an Eagle.

'What the well-dressed pilot or wizzo should wear,' he'd begun drily, then gone on to point out the various items that went to make up the entire outfit. 'Without this piece of tailoring you're a dead duck up there. *Always* check to make sure you've got it right. Check for the full integrity of your survival gear. Punching out is not the time to discover something is missing, or not working properly.

'Note this, people . . . nobody's going to give you a replacement while you're up in the wide blue; and though I know Ego drivers and back-seaters think they've got a direct line to the big Chief upstairs, *He* has not yet given you the ability to walk on air. You cannot leap buildings with a single bound. Thou art not God. Soft mortals like us need assistance to survive in His environment. A lot of very smart people have constructed your fashionable outfits. *Take care of them. Check them, and check again.* When I was somewhere near the age of you eager tenderfeet, I made a mistake. I was lucky to survive. You may not be.'

Garner had taken the warning to heart. Unconsciously, he ran a hand over his suit, checking for anomalies.

Arlene, with her well-honed intuition, had been right about the similarity between them. Both were roughly the same height at two inches under six feet. Both had slim, muscled frames with strong shoulders. Both had grey eyes and both, if one looked closely enough, had remarkably similar features. They even walked with a recognizable and indeed similar gait. But neither would accept it, if this was pointed out.

Their crew chief was waiting, in khaki T-shirt, camouflaged trousers and soft-soled boots. He would have already done his customary fine-toothcomb, pre-flight inspection; but it was still up to the aircrew to satisfy themselves with their own inspection. Standing next to the crew chief was a member of the ground crew, similarly dressed, attached to the aircraft by the umbilical cord of his headphones and mike. Through this, the ground crewman would talk to the aircrew while they went through their internal checks. But to begin with, the vital externals had to be done.

Garner glanced up at the stencil of their names, beneath the left rim of the one-piece curved windscreen. The cartoon profile of the head of an eagle was attached to an oblong box of a body. Within the box was the legend:

CAPT NATHAN ADDERLY
CAPT MILTON GARNER

Adderly began the walk-round of the aircraft while Garner climbed up to get on to the wing to ensure no items of maintenance equipment had been left there. It was not unknown with other aircraft – despite the inspections – for a forgotten spanner to slide its way between the slots of a flap or aileron, a possible guarantee of a hasty exit at altitude, or perilously close to the ground, later on.

This had never happened to Garner and Adderly, and they had no intention of letting it. Garner checked the wing surface for distortions, missing panels and so on. He checked that the huge blade of the dorsal air brake fitted its slot properly, and that there were no distortions that might affect its smooth deployment. Every minute detail had to be checked out for the safe operation of the aircraft.

On the ground, Adderly's inspection had taken him to the tail. He looked up at the huge engine nozzles looming above him. Grabbing a rim, he jumped briefly upwards to peer inside for loose articles. People tended to forget things in there too. He repeated the action with the second engine, looking for all the world as if doing a pre-flight workout.

Each cavernous circle of the Pratt and Whitney F-100 turbofans, as wide as half a man, could, on full afterburning thrust, hurl the massive aircraft vertically towards the heavens at 50,000 feet per minute: 570 miles an hour straight up. The Eagle E could do standing on its tail what the average airliner struggled to reach in level flight; faster than a cruising 747. If need be, it could hit Mach 2.5, yet it could also dawdle at 200 knots.

'All that,' Garner was fond of saying, 'and as agile as hell. Flyer heaven.'

They eventually completed their inspections and, satisfied, signed the 781 on the crew chief's clipboard. They were now accepting the aircraft. From now on until they brought it back in one piece and handed it over, it was their responsibility.

Garner climbed into the rear cockpit and settled into the zero-zero ejection seat. If for any reason he needed to eject, as with the front seat he could make his exit at high altitude, or at ground level. High-altitude ejection was not a choice he ever wanted to face.

In the front seat, Adderly began to swiftly do his cockpit checks. It was quite a cockpit. Roomy and bristling with the latest high-tech equipment, it was a fighter pilot's dream. The advanced head-up display, mounted at eye-level, was the widest HUD he'd ever seen. Its many modes would display all the essential information he would need at any given time, to enable him to fly the aircraft to the limits of his and its ability.

Below the head-up display were four flat panel displays. These were multi-function units and were virtually the instrument panel itself; a far cry from the relatively cluttered cockpit of the standard F-15. The two main displays, each with several menus, flanked the central control panel with its alphanumeric keypad sited directly beneath its vertically arranged, six-line data read-out strips. This was the up-front control panel through which virtually everything was programmed. It was the brains of the aircraft.

There was another item that was not so welcome for the crew: a voice. It was a female voice – chosen, it seemed, to be deliberately annoying – that warned them when things were getting too close for comfort. They called it Bitching Betty, and could do nothing about it.

Beneath the 'up-front' was another display, full colour and smaller than the main ones. This was currently showing the horizontal display map with the aircraft's position marked at the beginning of the programmed waypoint diagram. As the aircraft moved, so would its position on the map change in response.

An instrument's width over to the right of that display was the smallest of all. This contained the digital read-outs for the engines, among which were rpm, temperature and nozzle positions.

Adderly's left and right hands fell easily upon the throttles and stick. Covered in a plethora of buttons and switches, they would enable him to operate all the essential controls during hard-manoeuvring combat, without once having to remove them from there, even to change a page on one of the displays or arm a weapon. Convenient when your hands would at times weigh several times the norm, usually in a situation where you'd need to move them swiftly.

He rapidly checked the few analogue stand-by instruments that still remained from the older versions of the aeroplane, then prepared for engine start.

In the back seat, Garner also had four displays to occupy him. These were arranged horizontally: the two main ones in the centre, flanked by a slightly smaller display on either side. All the multi-page menus were interchangeable, between displays, and between cockpits.

Across the top of his cockpit, just forward of the instrument glare shield, was a solid grab bar that roughly followed the contours of the instrument panel, a shallow U-shape mounted upside down. The rear cockpit also had an up-front control, but this was positioned over on the forward section of the right console.

Immediately to the right of that was the black and yellow, T-shaped handle for the eject-mode seat control. It had three positions: normal was vertical. This enabled both seats to leave the aircraft, whoever pulled the handle. Forty-five degrees left position, was solo. This would mean that only the person wanting to leave the aircraft would go. Bad news for whoever was left behind.

The third position – aft initiate – ninety degrees to the left, gave the back-seater the command. In a situation where the pilot was incapacitated, or the aircraft was too low for him to let go of the controls and grab at the seat handles, the wizzo could still get him out.

Garner, in addition to his two hand controllers for the operation of his displays, also had a full set of controls to enable him to fly the aircraft, again in case of pilot incapacitation. He called them his security blanket.

3

Harnesses secured, helmets comfortable, masks on, gloves on, visors down.

Adderly reached to his right on the console by the edge of the seat, and moved the right engine generator switch to the ON position. He then reached forward for the T-shaped handle of the jet fuel starter lever on the bottom right of the instrument panel, and pulled. Almost simultaneously, his left hand moved the right throttle lever forward past the IDLE detent. He watched the engine display screen as the engine spooled up to fifty per cent rpm. The JFS disengaged and recharged. He repeated the procedure for the left engine. The Eagle woke up and was alive.

In the back seat, Garner initiated the built-in test sequence and began to set up his screens. The aircraft went through its BITE checks and on one of the main displays the read-outs began to show the status of the various systems by listing them as the Echo Eagle checked itself out.

Garner watched all this on his multi-function displays, which the air force liked to call CRTs – cathode ray tubes – and got all his systems on-line. He had his own less-than-respectful interpretation of the term; so he called the CRTs 'crits' and sometimes 'critters', as the mood took him. He now checked them out thoroughly, ensuring the inertial navigation system knew where it was starting from, meticulously working through all the aids that enabled him to operate the aircraft, in conjunction with the man in the driving seat up front. Adderly's own CRTs would be carrying repeated displays.

Adderly continued with his own programme in the front office, checking the flying controls for full and free movement, opening and closing the huge air brake to ensure its smooth operation. They checked the flying controls of both cockpits. Very bad news indeed if something were to happen to Adderly and Garner found he could not control the aircraft because they'd omitted to ensure everything worked while still safely on the ground.

The ground crewman unplugged himself from the aircraft and came to attention to give a smart salute. Adderly responded. They were ready to roll.

He began taxiing, lowering the big clamshell canopy as he did so. The noise of the engines was immediately muted, but their smoothly powerful vibrations coursed through the airframe.

Adderly looked left and right, ensuring the Eagle was clear of obstructions as they rolled forwards. In the back, Garner followed suit, double-checking their freedom of passage. They stopped a short distance later as attendant ground crew made final visual checks. No leaks, no loose missiles. People had been known to take off with loose ordnance, only to have them drop off in very embarrassing – and sometimes dangerous – circumstances.

But in their case everything was OK. Now they really were clear. They taxied out to the runway threshold. In the Arizona heat a haze seemed to rise from the surface of the vast 'road' as it stretched into the distance.

Then Adderly shoved the throttles into 'burner.

The Echo Eagle began to surge forwards, accelerating rapidly as twin tongues of flame seared into the baking air thirty feet behind them. The big E roared down the wide concrete.

Because of the relative lightness of armament load, the main wheels left the runway at 165 knots – instead of closer to 185 with a full warload – and Adderly reached ahead of the throttles for the small, red-wheeled lever to raise the gear swiftly, as speed increased relentlessly. He watched as the numerals in the oblong airspeed box on the HUD whirled themselves upwards dementedly.

'Gear up and locked,' he heard Garner confirm on the headphones.

'Roger. Gear locked.'

Adderly gave a firm pull on the stick then centred it, holding the attitude.

Momentarily punishing them with a sudden slam of increased G, the Eagle pointed its nose to the clear, bright sky, stood on its tail and headed for the upper reaches.

Garner always enjoyed these take-offs. As he stared past the back of Adderly's ejection seat to the deep blue of the sky, seemingly impaled on the nose of the aircraft, Garner reflected upon how accomplished a pilot the man in that seat really was. When it came to driving the Echo Eagle, Adderly was very hard to beat. If there was any pilot likely to ruin both Robert E.'s and 'Killer' Carter's day, it would be Adderly.

*　　　*　　　*

Fifty miles south of the base, they were approaching the northern boundary of the weapons range.

'Waypoint two in one minute,' Garner said. 'On your screen.'

'Roger,' Adderly acknowledged as the entire waypoint diagram appeared on one of his displays, superimposed on the moving map. On another CRT, the green waypoint diagram appeared by itself then expanded until only the current waypoint showed, with time to destination counting down at the top of the screen. 'Confirm.'

He knew that Garner's manipulation of the systems was exceptional and left all the navigation, planning and pre-merge battle tactics to him in the air-to-air role; and in the attack role, all the way to target. Garner had never let him down. He just wished there was a way to resolve the slavery business between them.

Adderly felt no guilt about the fact that he was descended from a slave-owning family. He was proud of his ancestor Josiah, who'd taken a radical step without even realizing it. Josiah had responded to his conscience and had simply brought to an inevitable conclusion the events that had put their mark upon him from boyhood. On a fateful day ten years before the

Civil War, he had been forced by his father to watch the gutting of the young slave who had been accused of raping his sister. Tears streaming down his cheeks, he had been a mere twelve years old at the time.

Always wanting a son but cursed – as Nathan Adderly had seen it – by a succession of daughters, Josiah had arrived late on the scene to a father who had grown too old to be a sympathetic parent during his son's childhood years. A true nineteenth-century patriarch with all the rigid attitudes of the time, he would not have tolerated any views other than his own. It was thus doubtful whether he would ever have been an understanding father.

Josiah's grooming to become a slave owner had thus begun very early. The pressure-cooker treatment had only succeeded in filling the boy with revulsion for the practice, turning him for ever against slavery; but he'd been smart enough to keep it well hidden from his brutal father. He'd done other things, too, that his father never suspected.

Josiah had never forgotten the experience of that appalling execution. When his father had been killed years later, by vengeful slaves whose suffering had driven them beyond despair and care for their own fate, he'd responded, on inheriting the plantation, by freeing them all. It had been just a year before the Civil War brought devastation upon the South. None of the former slaves had gone away, but had instead remained to continue working for him as free people. But the inexorable nature of war had destroyed the plantation, and the Adderlys had lost all the wealth that had taken generations to build. Josiah had looked upon the outcome as a kind of justice, before the Civil War had claimed him too. He'd succumbed to a wound, years after it had ended.

Adderly banked hard on to the new heading, as the next waypoint appeared on screen. It would soon be time to descend towards the barren Arizona peaks, thousands of feet below.

'I've been thinking,' came Garner's voice in his ear.

'I'm listening.'

'I don't think ol' Robert E.'s going to let us make the low run first. I think that sucker's going to bounce us *before* we descend. He's going to reckon we'll be too occupied, and won't be expecting it.'

'I agree. So what do we do?'

'We look below. He's down there somewhere. I can feel it.'

Adderly did not argue. He trusted Garner's instincts completely.

'Let's have a look,' he said.

It was Garner who made the first sighting.

'Got him!' he called. 'Low, low down. Five o'clock.'

He had seen the barest flitting of something down among the peaks off his right shoulder, in their five o'clock position. Whoever it was clearly intended to manoeuvre behind them, hoping to slide unnoticed into the six o'clock position behind the tail, before racing upwards for a sneaky kill. Dempsey had decreed that the air-to-air exercise would be simulated guns only, in the first engagement. This meant they did not have the benefit of an arm's-length kill with a missile shot. It was thus going to be a knife fight.

The tricky colonel obviously intended to make it as hard as possible for them. A knife fight in the big Eagle versus the much smaller, agile F-16 would be stacking the odds against them. A knife fight forced you to go slow, and slower still. In the Eagle, it was much better to be able to use all that power, to maximize the assets, and to take the opponent in very quick order.

Turning and burning wasted time and fuel, and tied you up for the bogey's friend to stand back and zap you while you were thinking you had his pal snarled up. Laughing all the way to a hole in the ground in real combat, in admiration of your fantastic flying, was not an option if his friend had got you in the meantime.

Dempsey, Garner knew, was well aware of that and wanted to drag them into a box where the F-16's considerable talents would begin to gain the upper hand, and perhaps set them up for a shot by the sadistic Major 'Killer' Carter. One of Carter's favourite sayings was 'gun their brains out'. Many a hot-shot, single-seat F-15 jock had been routinely taken by the old Aggressor F-5 pilots. The F-5 was a small, and basically simple, advanced trainer that had made it to fighter status in many air forces of smaller countries. The fact that the very able pilots who flew them could trounce more advanced machines was graphic proof of their deadliness.

Garner was thus very well aware of the even more deadly nature of the F-16s being flown by two of the hottest of the hot pilots around, as was Adderly. Garner also felt certain that the aircraft shadowing them at low level was piloted by Dempsey.

The colonel hadn't said they couldn't use their radar. However, in a hostile environment too much use of the radar would leave a calling card no self-respecting surface-to-air missile crew could afford to ignore. It was another lesson the colonel was forcing upon them, making them use their instincts instead of relying too much on all the technical wizardry at their fingertips. The technical aids were just that.

'Technology is your handmaiden,' Dempsey had pounded into their heads. 'Not your boss. Use them to *augment* your God-given instincts, and the training you have received. Become too dependent and if you should suffer even light battle damage, you become useless, and we lose a $44-million airplane; and possibly, two expensive crewmen. Airplanes we can build. Aircrews . . .' There had never been any need for him to continue.

So it would have to be mainly eyeball stuff in the coming fight, Garner reasoned.

'Happy to oblige,' he now murmured.

He briefly checked the radars to see if anything else was stooging around out there; but nothing showed. He put the radars on stand-by, leaving them ready for use, but not transmitting.

'OK,' Adderly was saying. 'I've got the systems. Let me know what he does.'

'You got it.'

Now that close-in combat was about to be joined, Adderly had command of the aircraft systems for that regime. Everything would now depend on his skills and instincts as a fighter pilot. Garner, meanwhile, would also be keeping his eyes out of the cockpit, sharing the lookout with Adderly, watching out for the Adversary, making sure that Adderly had full awareness of what the threat was doing. Four eyes were always better than two.

'Whoever is down there,' Adderly said, 'is going to have a buddy up top.'

Garner had already come to that conclusion and was surveying the air above them.

'Looking,' he said, 'but so far, diddly squat. But someone's up there all right.'

'OK. How's the low boy doing?'

Garner looked. 'He's still playing possum. Reckon he thinks we haven't seen him. My scalp says it's the colonel.'

'Your scalp may be right.'

Adderly had not yet given any overt indication that the sneaky F-16 had been spotted. He wanted to be sure of where the second, or perhaps even a third, might be.

Garner did another swift check of the sky above. He grabbed at the sturdy bar above the instrument panel for support, leaned forward to allow the inertia reel system to extend his harness, then twisted slightly round to check above and behind the tail. The exceptional vision afforded by the big canopy and the vast space between the fins enabled him to have a perfect view of the danger area.

Something flashed minutely, high up, then was gone.

'Oh yeah!' he said, still twisted round.

'Something?'

'Oh yes, indeed. *Some*thing. Company. Six o'clock and pretty high. Bet he thinks he's smart.'

'What's he doing?'

'Nothing yet, but I think he's going to be the decoy. He'll try a bounce and when he believes we're spooked and focused on him, the guy below will come up for a bite of our ass.'

'Or the other way round.'

'Yeah.' Garner agreed. He had turned round again, and had settled back in his seat.

'OK,' Adderly repeated. 'Let's see how smart they are.'

Adderly lit the 'burners suddenly and hauled the Eagle into a steep climb. The aircraft's phe- nomenal power had it standing on its tail once more. But Adderly kept a firm back pressure on the stick and the F-15E began to bring its nose past the vertical, until it was climbing at a steep angle in a reverse direction, upside down. He eased the pressure then rolled upright. They were now hurtling towards where Garner had seen the flash.

Garner's four CRTs had twenty push buttons each, arranged around each screen, in groups of five. Additionally, there were three rocker switches – again on the borders of each display – controlling on-off, brightness and contrast. But much of the work was done via the two fixed controllers – one on each side console – which looked like joysticks, housing their own plethora of buttons and switches. This made life easier and enabled Garner to work his screens, even under heavy manoeuvring conditions.

He could have gone for a brief flash of the radar for a quick scan, but had no wish to warn whoever was up there by setting off in response the Falcon's radar warning receiver. He decided to occupy himself by keeping his eyes out of the cockpit, hunting out their still-invisible adversary.

Something flashed in the distance once more, this time heading earthwards.

'He's made us,' Garner announced. 'He's

decided not to commit for now, and is heading for the deck.'

'Got him. What's his buddy doing?'

Garner had a quick look. A nimble shape was in a fast climb. 'Coming up.'

'Going for the sucker punch, are they? Well, not this kid. Going down!'

Adderly rolled the big fighter and pulled hard towards the primeval spines of the parched mountains far beneath them.

Garner continued to resist the desire to give a quick sweep of the powerful radar. The colonel wanted it the tough way. That was what the colonel was going to get.

He looked at the olive-brown terrain expanding towards him; saw the large tract of a dried river-bed with the familiar etchings of paths that crossed each other in wild patterns, reminding him of a child's first attempts at drawing. Almost like his own, he thought detachedly. He saw a paved road curving gently through the mountains. Here and there, tiny clusters of buildings branched haphazardly off it.

Then the Eagle was being wrenched to the right and the world pivoted as Adderly turned hard on to the tail of the ascending Falcon. But the move had been spotted early and the Falcon was twinkling away to the left, seemingly to fall out of the sky as it flashed out of the targeting box on the Eagle's HUD.

'Where ... where's his buddy?' Adderly grunted as he went into a body-punishing turn to follow.

Garner saw 7.5G registered on the meter for the briefest of instants. Even without that information, the sudden, giant-hand pressure on his body would have told him.

The G-forces went back to normal, but that would not last for long. When Adderly's air-fighting blood was up, being in a state of 1G for any appreciable length of time was a luxury.

'Down among the rocks,' Garner replied. 'Three o'clock. Through that valley, there.'

A shape, camouflaged to blend with the desert scenery, was fleeing along a narrow cleft. The other F-16 seemed to have disappeared ...

'*Break hard left!*' Garner shouted.

Adderly did not question the call and reacted instantly. The world tumbled. Earth changed places with sky, then back again. The big Eagle was in a steep climb on the 'burners, then it was hauling itself off the top of a loop. As the nose began to come down once more, Adderly rolled ninety degrees and pulled tightly into another left turn.

The Falcon he had broken away from flashed by at a shallow angle just off the nose, going the other way.

'Holy shit!' Garner exclaimed as the shape hurtled past. 'That was close! Speed of light!'

'You wish. That was a good call.'

'Aim to please. He nearly suckered us though. He was real sneaky.'

'"Nearly" is a miss. Good enough for me. Now let's put this joker out of his misery. Keep an eye on the guy down there in the dirt.'

'I got him . . . and he's on his way up. I guess they're talking to each other, trying to corral us. We'd better get his buddy quick before he gets here.'

'I'm on him.'

Adderly had hit the air brake as he'd banked into another punishing turn to follow the Falcon. The huge panel on the spine had deployed, slowing the Eagle as if it had slammed against a brick wall, and allowing Adderly to reef the aircraft round on a wingtip. Then the air brake was going back in and the 'burners came on. The Eagle leapt after its prey.

The Falcon, meanwhile, was already into its own turn, aiming to get back on the Eagle's tail. But Adderly had gone high and the Echo Eagle was now upside down and both he and

Garner were looking through the top of the canopy, down at the Falcon, which was by now wrenching round into its turn, looking for the fat Eagle.

Adderly eased the stick gently backwards. The Eagle's nose began to inch down, following the Falcon precisely. The symbology on the HUD began to indicate that he was getting close to a gun solution.

Don't rush it, he said in his mind. Easy. Easy.

It wouldn't do to miss the shot now, after having sweated to get into a nice position for the kill.

To someone standing outside with a God's-eye view, the entire manoeuvre was unfolding with astonishing rapidity. But in the cockpit it was as if the Eagle and the Falcon were standing still as in a split second Adderly matched momentum with the aircraft beneath him.

The tone sounded just as he squeezed the trigger. A perfect kill. In a real shoot, the Falcon would have been straddled from nose to tail. The Falcon pilot made no comment over the air, but both felt certain his cockpit was probably blue with expletives.

'Yes!' Garner exulted. 'We got him!'

Adderly did not waste time gloating but had

already broken off the attack, to hunt out the second Falcon.

'Where's his buddy now?' he asked tersely.

Garner had again swivelled round. 'Trying to waltz into our six. He's not there yet. Seven o'clock, coming down.'

Adderly glanced over his left shoulder even as he was again reefing the Eagle into a hard left-hander, and spotted the F-16 curving down. Its chance spoiled, the Falcon rolled out of the turn and disappeared to their right, still going down.

Adderly fell after him and began to gain. But the Falcon had leapt into a rocket-like climb and shot past their nose, going straight up. Adderly kept going down.

'*What are you doing?*' Garner was once more looking at the ground rushing up. 'He's going to come over the top and follow us down!'

'Yep.'

'*Yep?* What if it's old Robert E. himself?'

'We've either just got him, or the crazy major. Either way, our chances have improved.'

'You reckon whoever's in that bird knows that? And does he care? He's out for a piece of our butt.'

'And I'm after his head. What's he doing now?'

Garner glanced back and up at the receding sky. 'We've got a tail, and it's Falcon-shaped. Gawd! That bird looks mean as hell from this angle.'

Adderly rolled a full 180 degrees in the dive and began to pull. The Eagle continued to drop, but the nose was beginning to curve through, though with some reluctance as the phenomenal momentum continued to drag them earthwards. Soon they were plunging vertically; then the nose was creeping past the vertical. Yet ground still seemed to be rushing straight at them, still on the nose.

Those damn mountain peaks are beginning to look very, very hungry, Garner thought calmly.

He stared at the brown earth, and said nothing. He forced his head round. The Falcon was still hanging on, but was not close enough for guns.

The ground was beginning to look close enough to touch. A peak to the right was definitely too close. The Eagle's nose had now crept upwards, making the dive shallow. Adderly was still hauling on the stick. The G-forces were squeezing at them. The Eagle itself seem quite happy to hit them with as much as they could stand – and more.

They flashed past the mountain peak and hurtled, in level flight now, into its valley.

Garner let out his breath slowly and caught a sudden, great mouthful of oxygen as he instinctively inhaled, unaware he'd been holding his breath.

'What's he doing?' Adderly grunted.

Garner had taken another look behind the tail. The Falcon had pulled away just above the peak, over whose spine it was now skimming.

'He's bugged out! He's on that peak. Go get him!'

Adderly grinned, without humour, in his mask. He'd been hoping for that. He brought the throttles briefly back, hit the air brake and, as the big aircraft slowed, hauled the nose slightly up and curved towards the peak, closing the air brake as he did so, and increasing speed to slide neatly into the Falcon's six.

The tone came almost immediately.

The Falcon rolled frantically, but it was far too late.

'Goddamit!' they heard. It was 'Killer' Carter.

'Hell,' Adderly exclaimed softly in wonder. 'We got the colonel first. Wow!'

'Good stuff, Nathan. Good stuff.'

'You weren't so bad yourself.'

'Yeah.'

As if afraid of this sudden rush of bonhomie, they fell silent. In the air, however, despite the antipathy generated by their ancestral histories, there was a contract between them. Each knew that neither would let the other down, no matter what. This covered all aspects of their flying. To break that unwritten contract would be beyond the pale.

Then Garner began working the screens. 'I'm setting up the low-level run now,' he told Adderly briskly. 'We'll do RAF altitudes, instead of standard TF. That OK with you?'

'It's OK with me.'

Though the normal Echo Eagle low-level attack altitude under terrain-following control was 350 feet, Garner and Adderly tended to emulate the RAF Tornado crews and go as low as they dared. If they were not doing a stand-off attack, fifty feet was their usual above-ground-level height, which Adderly flew manually. This gave them an added bonus. No TF at ultra-low AGL meant no returns to alert the bad boys. It allowed them to sneak up on the target and do the dirty, before being picked up on radar; by which time they'd be well away out of the hot area. Today they were going to do the ultra-low run. The intention was to beat the training SAMs and the eager anti-aircraft crews, waiting for them out there in the desert and among the mountains.

'Waypoints on your screen,' Garner said.

Adderly saw the new waypoint pattern appear, with symbols where each SAM and anti-aircraft artillery was expected to be. Their route in and out should take them safely past all the known threat areas.

That still left mobile and hand-held missiles, as well as mobile triple-A. They'd just have to be quick with the electronic countermeasures and jam any searching radars that tried to snare them. The trouble with flooding the frequencies with ECM was that in a real situation, even if the enemy couldn't locate you he'd still know you were out there somewhere.

This was not to be an attack run. The colonel had been quite specific. The task they were training for was not an attack mission. The prime requirement was *avoidance*. The radar and SAMs were not supposed to know they were there; or at the very least, be unable to get a lock on them while they flashed through.

'Let's do it,' Adderly said, and took the Eagle low.

'So far so good,' Garner said moments later.

Adderly banked the Eagle to thread their way between two claw-faced, reddish-brown perpendicular walls and wondered whether the storm of their passage would start a rock slide. Then they were through and coming out over wide, open ground.

'Hope it stays that way,' Adderly said.

They were heading for waypoint four on the plan that Garner had programmed, and had managed to avoid being detected. Four more to go and they'd be home and dry. But the wide, flat valley they were now hurtling over was a risk. He'd inserted that particular waypoint because, according to the information supplied at the briefing, this section of the range was clear of anti-aircraft weaponry. That did not mean it was *absolutely* clear. Simulated threat or not, the unexpected was always to be expected.

As with all things to do with combat, intelligence received could be out of date less than a minute after receipt. The cunning people manning the training radars were justly famous for their nasty little tricks. They could easily have positioned a mobile SAM out there, somewhere, just for the hell of it; just nicely positioned to catch out overconfident, hot-shot Echo Eagle crews.

Garner did not want to call a pop-up, so that

he could flash the Eagle's exceedingly powerful APG-70 radar to make a quick grab at anything that might have sneaked into the area. Doing that would inevitably send the lurking SAM crews' own warning systems berserk, and these would in turn swiftly start hunting for the interloper. One more fish in the net.

'Not us,' Garner muttered.

'Say what?'

'Just wondering if there's a sneaky SAM out there,' he replied.

The waypoints he'd set up had nicely avoided all attention – so far. They had slid between mountains, roared along dried river-beds, squeezed between rock faces, putting solid ground between them and the hopeful radars – until now.

'We'll soon find out if there is,' Adderly said.

'Yeah.'

Garner had gambled on the route, knowing that at the mouth of at least one canyon, someone would have had the bright idea to position a SAM site. He'd pored over the topo map of the area and had made his choices. For waypoints four to five he'd decided to risk open ground. They'd never expect something so crazy. He hoped.

Adderly was considering the same odds. 'Hope you guessed right,' he said.

'Yeah,' he repeated.

To anyone watching, they appeared to be skating along the desert floor at suicidal speed, so low had Adderly taken the aircraft. If a radar was indeed hiding out there, it would find it very difficult to acquire the Eagle E.

Because of the extremely low altitude, Bitching Betty was going crazy in their ears, warning them of their perilous proximity to the ground. She castigated them every time she thought her precious Eagle was being put at risk by its crazy crew, and she *always* sounded pissed off.

They ignored her.

The Eagle's big wing made the ride a little rough as it raced through the heavy air. This low down, it could never compete for ride quality with the likes of the variable sweep F-111, or the Tornado. But both Garner and Adderly had long ago accepted that. Better a rough ride low down coupled with astounding power and agility at virtually all altitudes, than the reverse, with – relatively speaking – the turning capability of a truck in mud.

Five miles ahead of them was a slot in the high terrain, within which they could hide once more. From waypoints five to six the run was through a deep valley that ran straight from point to point.

Garner willed the aircraft on. Despite their high speed, he felt exposed. The short distance to the safety of the mountain range seemed inordinately long.

But the radar warners stayed resolutely quiet. There were no lurking SAM radars trying to hook them. The naked ground was clear.

At last, they reached waypoint five and plunged into the hidden recess of the deep canyon.

Garner felt relief. It should be a milk run to home base from now on.

Then the radar warners gave a frantic beeping.

Goddamit! he thought.

The worst had happened. Someone had been smart enough to plant a SAM site right at the exit.

Damn! Damn! Damn!

Even as these thoughts hit him, he was shouting, 'Go *up the left wall and over the top! Now, now, now! I'm hitting ECM!'*

Adderly did not waste valuable energy in acknowledgement.

As Garner began jamming the offending

radar, he reacted instantly and hauled the Eagle steeply up, rolled over the top of the canyon and dropped breathtakingly down the other, equally steep wall, to curve into another deep gorge. Then he rolled the aircraft upright.

The beeping had stopped.

Garner's heart was pounding. 'You big beautiful bird!' he said to the Eagle exultantly, patting the instrument panel as he would a favourite horse, or even his Boss Mustang. 'I'm modifying the other waypoints,' he went on to Adderly. 'Sheee-it! That was close. They didn't get a lock-on. Good stuff. Good stuff there, driver.'

'Sharp call,' Adderly responded. 'That was pretty hot too.'

'Yeah. Not bad, if I say so myself. New waypoint pattern coming up. On your screen.'

'Got it. Was that some nasty little surprise. Reckon they've got more rigged up for us?'

'Could be. Could be.'

But Garner's new waypoints did the trick. The remainder of the run was clear, all the way back to base.

4

The colonel and the major were waiting for them in debriefing. They were the only Eagle crew in the room. The major was in flight overalls, but Dempsey was in uniform.

Dempsey looked thoughtfully at them, stroking the tip of his nose with a forefinger. He stopped, and placed both hands on his hips.

'Gentlemen,' the deep voice began. 'You did good up there. Very impressive.' He glanced at Carter. 'You got Major Carter, and the other bogey.'

Carter did not look pleased.

Dempsey stared at them. 'You seem surprised, *and* disappointed, gentlemen. Am I to believe you hoped for a kill on me? Did you think I was up there too?'

'Well, sir . . .' Adderly began. 'You did say . . .'

'I don't remember specifying which aircraft I'd be flying.'

'Yes, sir . . . I mean, no, sir.'

'Exactly. As I was saying, you did good but . . .' The eyes stared hard at them. 'My little surprise with the SAM caught you out. I contacted the range personnel and set it up once you were airborne, just in case. You entered the trap. In a real situation you would have been caught in that canyon and even if you had managed to evade as successfully as you did out there today, every fighter airfield within a hundred miles would have sent the hunters out. In short, gentlemen, you would have been compromised, and in deep doo-doo.'

'Sir,' Garner and Adderly said together.

Then Dempsey relented. 'As it was the only mistake – which, I accept, you quickly rectified – all things considered, you had a good day, gentlemen. But don't go sitting on your laurels, or giving them a good polish. Get some rest and be ready for your next hop. Who knows? You might come up against me tonight. Thank you, gentlemen.'

'Sir,' they again said together, and went out.

When they'd left, Carter said, 'Why didn't you tell them they'd got you too?' He sounded aggrieved.

'Keeps them on their toes,' Dempsey replied

unrepentantly. 'They thought they'd scored a major victory. Knowing they got the colonel's head would have caused them to relax. I can't allow that. Your head's trophy enough for now.'

'Gee. Thanks!'

'Don't take it so hard, Major. You got hit by a pair of real stars. Nearly put you into that mountain, didn't they? These boys play hard. I like that. We've got our first team. The only other crew who come close are our Californian beach god, Lancer, and his wizzo, Hershon. Unless, of course, they foul up today. So for the moment, assuming things don't change, they're our stand-by if something goes wrong with the Jazz Couple.'

'Seems like your mind's already made up. So we're cancelling the night hop?'

'No, we're not. The programme continues until there's absolutely no doubt we've got what we're looking for. The night hop's the most important of all.'

'Nice man,' Garner said drily, as they walked away from the briefing room.

'Look at it this way . . . he didn't chew us out for getting tagged by that SAM radar. Still, I'd hoped we'd got him.'

'We got him,' Garner said quietly.

Adderly glanced at him, not quite certain whether to give any serious credence to the remark. 'What do you mean? He hasn't been up. He's in uniform.'

'Yeah. He's throwing us a curve. Didn't you see his feet?'

'Why should I look at his feet?'

'He was in uniform, but he was wearing flying boots.'

'Perhaps he's getting ready . . .'

'Aw, c'mon. The *colonel*? Mr Every-button-in-the-right-place? Give me a break.'

Adderly paused. 'If you're right . . . Of all the low-down . . .'

'You got it,' Garner said with a tight smile as they continued walking.

'Well, I'll be . . . So we did get the head of Robert E. Hah! Wonder if he'd ever tell us.'

'I suggest we tell no one until this is over. *He* won't realize we already know. That gives us an edge. He's going to try something sneaky again tonight. I can feel it.'

'Well, then, let's see if we can get us a bird colonel twice in one day.'

'You're playing my tune.'

*   *   *

Garner spent much of the time before their next flight working on the Mustang. The air policeman, Mason Lyle, was very eager to help.

Adderly made a long call to his wife. After they'd been speaking for half an hour or so, she wanted to know when he'd be coming home.

'Can't say for sure, sweetheart,' he told her. 'You know how it is.'

'Sure I know, but I want you home, Nate.' She sounded petulant.

It was not like the old Arlene at all. He'd hoped that after the birth of the new baby she'd start getting back to her old self and stop feeling so guilty. But that didn't seem to be happening. Perhaps it was still too soon. She now watched the infant like a hawk, and was most reluctant to let anyone else hold him.

The only people she seemed happy to pass him to without hesitation were Adderly and, strangely, Garner.

But Garner did not come visiting so often any more.

As if she'd read what was going on in Adderly's mind, she said, 'You and Milt getting on OK?'

'We're OK. We did pretty well today. Tell you all about it when I get back.'

'It would be nice to see him come round again.'

'You'll have to take that up with him. He won't take an invite from me. You know that.'

'It's so foolish, Nate.'

'I guess he's got to work things out for himself.'

'I guess.'

There was the faint hum of electronics as they both fell silent for some moments.

'I love you, sweetheart,' he told her softly.

'I love you too, Nate.'

'Your mama with you?'

'She's here.'

'Need anything?'

'I need you with me.'

'I know.'

'Call me tonight?'

'I might be late . . .'

'I don't mind. Call as late as you want. You know I'll be here.'

'OK, sweetheart. I call tonight. Love you.'

'Love you, Nate.'

He waited for her to hang up, then hung up with a sigh.

* * *

Night time with the Echo Eagle was a whole new ball game. That was when the other aspects of its wondrous equipment came into their own. The Eagle had many eyes in the night and Garner loved trying to get the maximum out of the various modes of the aircraft's optical, radar and infrared systems.

The LANTIRN targeting and navigation pods gave him the ability to get to and see his targets on the blackest of nights. Up front, Adderly would be looking at the world through the FLIR's infrared window, superimposed on the HUD.

Low-altitude navigation and targeting infrared for night. A mouthful. LANTIRN was a lot easier to say.

Garner smiled in his mask as he thought of the acronym-speak necessary in the fighter jock world. FLIR. Forward-looking infrared. TACAN. Tactical air navigation. HSD. Horizontal situation display . . .

'You having fun back there?' came Adderly's voice.

'What?'

'Sounds like you're doing some kind of recitation.'

He hadn't realized he'd voiced his thoughts. 'Er . . . no. Just muttering while I move one of the waypoints.'

They were flying a little higher on this hop. Two hundred feet. On the far-left screen, he had put on the repeated HUD display, complete with infrared image. He could see the patch of the outside world that Adderly was looking at, as they hurtled through the Arizona night. They were not using the terrain-following radar, in order to minimize 'signature', and were again flying manually. Every so often, a warning would appear on the HUD, giving steering commands. At the moment, it was telling them to pull up.

Adderly eased the stick back slightly and the Eagle breasted a mean-looking outcrop whose infrared image was clearly seen.

'Wonder what Robert E. has planned for us this time,' Adderly said.

'Whatever it is, it won't be nice.'

'Amen to that.'

'At least we're allowed to go to missiles, so perhaps we'll zap him before he gets us. I think he'll come at us sometime during the run – maybe when we think we're home and dry he'll try to shut the door. He's sure mean enough to pull that one. Waypoint three. On screen.'

'Got it. All quiet,' Adderly went on, as the radar warning receiver stayed silent. 'So far, no tags. Looks like we've got another good pattern.'

'Yeah . . . but we're not out of the woods yet.' Garner glanced up through the canopy. 'Nice bright starlight and . . .' He paused.

'What? What?'

'*Climb! Climb!*' Garner shouted. 'And go 180. Select AMRAAM.'

''Burners in! Going up!' Adderly did not hesitate. Tongues of flame lit the night as the Echo Eagle roared skywards, streaking away from the rocks below. Then he pulled further on the stick. The aircraft began to curve into the beginnings of a loop. 'AMRAAM selected. So much for quiet! Every SAM will be on to us now. What did you see?'

The Eagle was now going in the opposite direction, on its back. Adderly rolled upright. He was ready for the simulated advanced medium-range missile shot, if things worked out.

Garner had switched on the air-to-air radar. 'Take a look at your screen.'

Adderly looked. 'Where did *he* come from?'

Using his sidestick controllers, Garner had moved the cursor to frame the target aircraft neatly, designating it; then he pressed the radar auto-acquisition switch. Almost immediately, the radar locked up the target.

'And we've got lock.'

On the HUD repeater, the target designator box appeared at top right.

Adderly had already begun to manoeuvre to bring the box within the missile's wide steering circle. Once in there, he'd get the shoot cue.

'How did you know he'd be there?' Adderly enquired.

'My scalp itched.'

'You didn't see him?'

'No. Watch him! He's heard the tone and is trying to break out.'

'I've got him. He's not getting away.'

Whoever was out there in the night was manoeuvring frantically, and jamming for all he was worth. Twice, the targeting box disappeared, only to appear once more at a different location on the HUD. Adderly was as good as his word. He had no intention of losing the target aircraft.

Then the radar warning went.

'Shit!' he muttered. 'A SAM's painting us! Break him!'

'You hang on to that guy,' Garner said as he began to jam the SAM radar. 'I've got those dead-beats down there trying to read the snow on their screens.'

'I'm hanging on! He's dancing all over the place.'

'Don't you lose him!'

Then another sound came. Ominous. A SAM had been 'fired'. Bitching Betty was also telling them all about it.

'Launch!' Garner called.

'I hear! Damn it!' Adderly continued, venting his frustration. Then their missile at last achieved full shooting parameters.

Adderly fired.

There was no need to keep radar lock now. The simulated missile would do its own thing and chase the target independently, as if it had been really fired. The computers – both on the aircraft and on the range – would have calculated the firing parameters, come to a precise conclusion about the result and relayed the information to the core of the simulation system back at the base, in real time.

'We're out of here!' Adderly said, flung the Eagle on to its back and headed earthwards. 'How's that SAM doing?' he grunted.

'You can hear it. It's still coming. Find us a nice mountain while I spoil its dinner.'

'You got it.'

As Adderly sent the Eagle rushing towards a peak he could see clearly on the infrared HUD display, Garner worked at jamming the missile. Then they were rushing through the darkness of a canyon and the missile warner abruptly went quiet. Bitching Betty sulked off.

Adderly sighed with relief. 'Well, we lost it, and maybe got whoever was out there too.'

'And we're compromised, as Robert E. would say.'

'Yeah. Damn it!'

'Back to the waypoint pattern,' Garner said. 'Let's see if we can get home without alerting any more SAMs, *or* the fighters.'

They made it back without further excitement, to discover they had indeed got the colonel a second time. But it was a pyrrhic victory.

'Good shooting, gentlemen,' he told them drily in the debriefing room. He stroked his nose briefly. 'Shame you got the SAMs all excited. What's wrong with that picture?'

Carter was standing to one side. Both senior officers were in their flying overalls.

'We're compromised?' Garner suggested tentatively.

'Indeed, Mr Garner. You are.'

Major Carter looked on with a smirk. He was also very pleased he was not the one who had taken their missile shot.

'Why did you turn to attack me?' Dempsey was asking. 'I had not swept you with my radar. For all you knew, I might have had no idea you were there, until you initiated the attack.'

'I called the attack, sir,' Garner said.

Dempsey fixed him with an unblinking stare. 'Why?'

Garner stood his ground. 'You were about to become a threat, sir.'

'But I gave no indication, Captain. I did not use my radar.'

'Only because we got to you first, sir.'

There was a sudden silence. Even Carter had stopped smirking, as they all waited for Dempsey's reaction.

Dempsey said nothing for some moments, his eyes never leaving Garner's. Then still without saying anything, he turned to a computer behind him which had a screen saver running, and tapped a key. Immediately, a generated image of the flight began to run on the large monitor.

'Download from the main debrief,' Dempsey explained. 'Watch carefully, gentlemen.'

All aspects of the flight were shown, with all the aircraft involved, and the terrain, displayed in wireframe. The Echo Eagle was outlined in blue, the pursuing Falcons in orange. The mountains, the desert floor, the SAM sites and radar units, all came up as the flight progressed. Each aircraft had wingtip trails, so that their manoeuvres could be graphically depicted.

One of the F-16s had clearly begun to stalk the Eagle and just as the latter pulled into its sudden climb, a coned pulse shot from the stalking F-16, missing the target altogether. Dempsey had used his radar an instant too late; but he'd used it.

The Eagle's completed manoeuvre then put it in a perfect position to get a fast lock on the by now desperately evading Falcon. The F-16's efforts were to no avail.

Then came the SAM lock, and the surface-to-air missile 'fired' at the Eagle. Soon after, the Eagle's own shot at the Falcon was displayed as a trail with the 'missile' at its head. It 'hit' the Falcon squarely, turning it into a little orange coffin. The colonel had bought it. This was then followed by the Eagle's own energetic avoidance manoeuvres as Adderly had lost height rapidly, to make for the safety of the canyon, towing the hungry SAM in its wake.

But Garner's jamming, plus Adderly's inspired manoeuvres, had worked and the 'missile' had impacted on high ground.

The replay ended.

Dempsey exited the programme and faced them once more.

'Good work,' he said, astonishing them. 'You used your instincts and caught me out. But you still alerted the SAMs. You'll have to think of a way to look after your butts, without exciting the SAMs. On the mission itself, *avoidance* is the key. Thank you, gentlemen. I'll give you my decision in the morning. Back here at 10.00 hours, on the button.'

They came to attention. 'Sir!' they said together, and to Carter, 'Major.'

Carter nodded at them.

As they began to leave, Dempsey said, 'By the way. I was up this afternoon. You got me.'

'We know,' Adderly said. 'You still had your flying boots on, sir.'

'I'll be damned,' Dempsey said to Carter as the two captains left. He smiled fleetingly, then slowly drew forefinger and thumb along his jawline. 'I'll be damned.'

Carter looked smug, and said nothing.

Adderly made his promised call to Arlene. She'd been eagerly waiting for it and they talked for a good hour. The baby was peacefully asleep. He knew that Arlene would be watching the child even as she spoke, alert to anything that might go wrong. He didn't think she was getting enough sleep herself.

He told her so.

'I'm OK,' she said. 'I don't need much.'

He wasn't convinced, but said nothing more about it. If the colonel picked him and Garner for the mission, he hoped he'd be able to spend a day or two with her before setting off.

But he wouldn't ask for special treatment. He didn't want anyone to think he was sloping off in order to attend to his family problems.

In the event, there was no need.

When they'd turned up at the briefing room, Dempsey surprised them by giving them three days off. Lancer and Hershon had also been called in.

'I want you all back on base, gentlemen,' Dempsey said to them, 'three days from now. Captain Adderly, Captain Garner, you get the first crack, and will be told the mission on your return. Are you happy with that?'

'Yes, sir!' they replied.

'Good. I want you both in here, at 10.00 hours, on day four. I do not expect you to be late. Mr Lancer, Mr Hershon,' Dempsey went on to the second crew, 'you will be on stand-by in case for any reason Garner and Adderly can't make it. You will be given details of the mission only when the situation arises. However, both ships will fly as a pair to the forward base. Mr Adderly.'

'Sir?'

'I've assumed you'd like to see your family, back at your home unit. There's an AFRes MAC flight heading in that direction in one hour. You've got a seat on it. Be there.'

A very surprised Adderly could not hide his pleasure. 'Yes, sir. Thank you, sir!'

'Just don't be late back.'

'That's a roger, sir,' Adderly vowed.

'I'll hold you to it. You've all done well,' Dempsey continued. 'As the requirement is for two crews, those who didn't get to this point are heading back to their units, knowing a little more about themselves. You were all good. It's been a privilege to work with you. And that's all, gentlemen. Enjoy your three days.'

Adderly caught the Air Force Reserve military airlift command flight Hercules C-130, to his base in North Carolina. Lancer and Hershon took a civilian flight north-west across the state border into Nevada, bound for Las Vegas for some serious entertainment. Garner decided to spend the free time working on the Mustang.

The air policeman, Lyle, would put in an

appearance from time to time, when he was off duty.

It was early evening when Adderly arrived home.

Arlene rushed to the door, wrapped her arms about him and hung on for several moments. He held her tightly. Her long and fine hair, bunched against his cheek, smelled fresh and intoxicating.

'I'm here, sweetheart,' he said gently. 'I'm here.' He held her face in his hands, kissed both her eyelids, then the full lips that had so captivated him when he'd first set eyes on her.

'Do you really have to go back so soon?' she asked, inclining her head back slightly, to look at him.

He nodded. 'Yes.'

She stiffened abruptly as the sound of Eagle Es taking off from the nearby base came to them. She relaxed again as the sounds faded.

She's still so jumpy, he thought.

'It's all right,' he soothed. He held her close, one arm about her waist as they moved further into the house.

She flashed him a quick smile. 'I'm OK. Really.'

'Come on. Show me the boy.'

'Mama's with him. He's asleep right now. He sleeps a lot.'

'That's good, isn't it?'

'I guess.'

They went up to their bedroom. Arlene had put the baby's cot right next to her side of the bed. Her mother, a very handsome woman who looked astonishingly like her, greeted Adderly with a warm smile.

'Nate,' she said, giving him a quick hug and a kiss on the cheek. 'Your boy's been good. He's fast asleep.' She even sounded like her daughter. 'Saving all that energy for when he grows up and becomes a fighter pilot, just like his daddy.'

'My son's not going to be a fighter pilot,' Arlene said sharply.

Adderly glanced urgently at his mother-in-law and signalled that she should make no comment. Nadine Labouchere nodded barely perceptibly, and left the bedroom.

'No one's going to make him do what he doesn't want to,' he said to Arlene as they approached the cot. He smiled proudly down at the infant boy. 'He's so beautiful,' he went on. 'Just like you. I can't believe it. Sometimes, I think I'm dreaming it all.'

'Are you happy with him, Nate? Really happy? There's nothing wrong with him, is there?' She frowned uncertainly at the baby. Her hand gripped his tightly, then relaxed.

'Happy? What do you think? I'm crazy about him. I'm crazy about you. And no, there's nothing wrong with him. He's perfect.' He continued to smile foolishly down at the baby, forcing himself not to pick up the child and so wake him. 'Hi there, John Milton,' he whispered. 'Daddy's home.'

Watching him touch a small hand very lightly, Arlene said, 'How's Milt?'

'He's OK.' Adderly stroked the baby's hand once more, then took his finger away. 'Working on that car of his.'

'It really exists?' She now seemed less anxious, as if talking about the car was a safer subject.

Adderly smiled at her. 'It really exists, and it really is a Boss Mustang. For a while there, I thought it was all part of his imagination and I was never going to see that thing for real. He's done a good job too, so far. He's even got himself an AP from the base – another Georgia man, and a certified Mustang nut – to help him. When I left, they were making like they were tuning it for a NASCAR race.'

'Have you told him yet, Nate?' She was

looking at him intently, her hand still loosely in his.

Adderly knew what she meant. He shook his head slowly.

'You should,' she insisted. 'He should know we named the baby after him.'

'I promise to tell him,' Adderly said after a pause. 'And I'll bring him here when we get back, whatever he says. This time, I won't take no for an answer. OK?'

She put her arms about him and leaned back, her pelvis pressed against him. It was something she used to do quite often before the first baby. It usually drove him wild, and was beginning to work.

'Good enough,' she said.

'And now,' he said, feeling a growing heat where their bodies met, 'can a man have a real welcome around here?'

'The baby,' she demurred half-heartedly. 'And there's Mama.'

'Somehow, I don't think your mama's going to come looking for us for a while. And as for young John here, he sleeps a lot, you said.'

Her smile came close to the way he remembered it used to be, when she was feeling sexy. 'I guess I did.'

He stroked her cheek. 'Are you going to be

OK with this?' His concern, despite his desire for her, was genuine.

After the death of the first baby, she'd once told him something was wrong with her down there. It had killed her little girl and therefore *she* was really responsible for what had happened. She hadn't said that since having the new baby but, even so, he'd always had the feeling she was primed to go off at any moment. He'd talked to the base MO about it.

'What she needs,' the doctor had said, 'is a lot of understanding, and plenty of loving. Deep within her mind, she believes you might be blaming her, just as she blames herself. She may get over it quickly, or it may take some time. Let her get through it. She'll sometimes think you don't find her attractive any more.

'You're going to have to show her you don't blame her, and that you do still find her very attractive. Just give her the love and reassurance she needs. From what I know of both your families, she has all the support she requires, and more. So just give her some time, and keep letting her know you're still crazy about her.'

Adderly had no problem with that. As he'd just said, he was crazy about her.

'What I mean . . .' he continued.

But she was kissing him, interrupting whatever he'd been about to say. 'Why don't you find out?'

He fell asleep that night a very happy man, with Arlene's moist and satisfied, naked body partially lying across his.

The baby slept all night.

'Mason,' Garner said on the second free day at the Arizona base.

The enlisted man was under the car, checking the hydraulics on a front brake calliper.

'Sir?' Lyle's smudged face peered up at him.

'Can I trust you to look after my wheels when I'm away?'

'You surely can, sir!' Lyle said eagerly.

'You certainly don't sound reluctant,' Garner remarked drily. 'All right. I'll leave you the keys whenever I'm not here. Take the Boss for a run if you want, but Lyle . . .'

'Sir?'

'One scratch, and you're history.'

Lyle grinned. 'I'll treat the Boss like my own, sir . . . only better.'

'See that you do.'

'Yessir!'

Lyle ducked back under the car.

5

Both Adderly and Garner were precisely on time for the briefing, though each had arrived independently.

For Adderly, it was a traumatic return.

Everything had gone beautifully. It had been a joy to play with the baby. The child had made precious few demands. He'd howled when he needed to be fed and changed, but that had virtually been it. In between takes, he'd been as content and happy as anyone could have wished for, and had slept when he needed to. Friends who had visited had said they'd never seen such an accommodating baby.

Things between him and Arlene had been great – until the last night. In the middle of lovemaking, she had suddenly begun to weep.

'Take it out!' she'd cried. '*Take it out!* It's all your fault. You put it in there and made me pregnant. You made me lose my baby!'

Shocked, he'd withdrawn from her and lain on his back staring up at the ceiling, while she had bunched herself into a protective ball and continued weeping. He'd had no idea how long he'd remained like that, listening to her, feeling the gluey dampness from within her on his inner thigh, all lust having unceremoniously vanished.

He'd tried to take her in his arms, to comfort her, but she had flinched from him. The baby had slept through it all.

He'd woken up in the early hours, to find Arlene's lips on his.

'I'm so sorry about last night,' she'd said, voice full of remorse.

But she'd been looking twitchy again. She hadn't wanted him to leave.

In order to spend as much time with her and the boy as possible, he'd opted for the latest MAC flight he could find *en route* to the Arizona base which would still enable him to arrive in time for the briefing. The flight west would get him back on the base a good half-hour early, local time.

'You're not the only pilot around,' she'd said. 'Why can't they let you off for a while?'

'It's my job, Arlene. I can't let someone else take my duty.'

'And what about your family? Don't you have a duty to us too?'

'Sure I do. This is all part of it. Arlene . . . you knew what I was when you married me.'

She had fallen silent, and he'd found himself wondering if he shouldn't pay another visit to the MO when he returned from the mission. Hours before, he had been enjoying the best sex with her since the new baby; then it had all changed. Back to square one. They had barely kissed when he'd said goodbye.

'It's because she doesn't want you to go back,' Nadine had told him quietly, out of Arlene's earshot. 'Give her the time, Nate. She'll come out of it. I know what I'm talking about. I've lost a baby too.'

He had stared at his mother-in-law. 'I never imagined . . .'

'Why should you? Arlene doesn't know.'

He had taken some small hope from that, but he was still very worried.

He now pushed these thoughts from his mind as footsteps tramped into the room. Both he and Garner came to attention.

'At ease, gentlemen!' ordered the familiar deep voice as Dempsey came up to position himself before them. 'Please resume your seats. Punctual,' he went on approvingly. 'Mr Garner.

I hear you've got yourself a classic Mustang. Been working on it?'

'Yes, sir.'

'Is it any good?'

'The best, sir. A Boss 429.'

'When you get back, I want a ride in that thing.'

Garner smiled. 'Consider your seat booked.'

'I do. And you, Mr Adderly. Did you enjoy your time with the family?'

'Yes, thank you, sir. And thanks for getting me the flights at such short notice.'

Dempsey's eyes studied him closely. 'Everything OK back there?'

'Yes, sir.'

'The question's a serious one, Captain. I want your mind very clear on this mission.'

'My mind *is* clear, sir.'

'Then we'd better begin.'

Dempsey had brought company. Major Carter stood to one side, legs slightly apart, hands behind his back.

The other person was a woman, also in a major's uniform. She was tall, with a finely chiselled face. Gleaming red hair, drawn tightly and secured in a bun at the back, showed beneath her air force hat. Hers was an athletic-looking body that gave an impression of latent and

vibrant power. Her eyes, a strikingly bright
green, were very hard to look away from.
They demanded that you look at her.

She was, Garner thought, a beauty, and
probably had a lot of trouble with men;
mainly trying to keep out of their clutches.
She had a body that made you want to sit on
your hands, in case they betrayed you. He was
equally certain she was no pushover. This was
not a woman who took any crap from anyone,
unless she chose to. He guessed her age at about
the late twenties; which meant she was moving
fast up the ranks. A real high-flyer.

'This is Major Hoag, gentlemen,' Dempsey
was saying. 'Major Hoag is an Intelligence
officer. She has relevant information about
your mission. Listen very carefully to what she
has to say. Major.' He stood aside to allow her
to step forward.

A projector with a large screen had been set
up next to the debriefing workstation. Next to
the projector was a small table, and Major Hoag
placed her briefcase on it. She then removed her
hat and placed it carefully by the case. Now
fully uncovered, the red hair was even more
lustrous. She did not pat at it reassuringly.
This woman had enough self-assurance for an
entire squadron of ego-rich fighter jocks. She

turned towards them, green eyes commanding their attention.

'I'm Shelley Hoag,' she began, introducing a note of informality, in a voice that was warm and friendly. 'My grandfather was Colonel Hoag, also in Intelligence. I make the point only because there is a connection with your mission. During the war in Korea, my grandfather was responsible for handling a very sensitive incident in 1951. As the world outside now knows, but only suspected during that war, the Soviet Union rotated whole squadrons of jets and their pilots to fight alongside the North Koreans, even ordering these pilots to pretend they were themselves North Koreans.

'Their aircraft all carried the NK insignia . . . all, that is, except for one unit. This was a special squadron, equipped with the very best of the MiG-15s, and ostensibly set up by a KGB general who appears to have had a very wide jurisdiction. It's job was intended to be the decimation of Allied aircraft, with special attention to the F-86 Sabre. For a while, they did just that. The pilots were all Second World War veterans, some of whom were aces. They were commanded by a woman.'

Major Hoag paused, her voice clearly indicating approval of a female appointment to

119

command, as well as carrying an air of reproach. Her secondary message was that she felt there should be more female fighter pilots in the air force. Dempsey remained impassive, but Carter's face showed clearly what *he* thought of that idea.

Shelley Hoag glanced at each of the senior officers, the tiniest of smiles teasing at the corners of her mouth. She understood only too well precisely what Dempsey and Carter really thought.

'The special unit,' she went on, 'was unofficially called the Green Ringers. They seem to have had a kind of needle match with one particular US Air Force squadron. This was commanded by a Royal Air Force Squadron Leader, who was seconded to the USAF at the time. This unit flew F-86s, and was one of the most successful squadrons out there.

'It completely destroyed the Green Ringer squadron. The squadron commander himself shot down the Russian commander. Her body was recovered by our people. A very bizarre incident took place after the recovery. The RAF officer discovered that not only had he met her previously in Berlin, but they had actually danced together during the end-of-war celebrations.'

Her disclosures had them riveted. Even Carter, who'd never heard this before, could not prevent himself from being fascinated by the tale.

'Shit,' Garner said involuntarily.

The green eyes seemed to twinkle at him. 'Shit is right, Captain. My grandfather took charge of the body and had it shipped out. Years later, it came to our attention that not all members of that special unit had been killed. One pilot had ejected safely, but never returned to the Soviet Union.

'He was from one of the Asian Soviet republics and he stayed in North Korea, successfully passing himself off as a border Korean. He clearly had no intention of facing the wrath of Stalin all by himself, after the catastrophic failure of his squadron. It was a time for scapegoats, and I don't blame him. He is still alive, which is more than he could have expected had he gone back home. His sideways defection was our gain. Let us simply say he's been of use to us for many years.'

Major Hoag now turned to the projector and switched it on. Using a remote control, she brought a map up on the screen, showing the border region that covered North Korea, China and Russia. Each border was outlined in a different colour, so that the demarcation between the three countries was clearly visible. With the device, she drew a white circle about the area where the borders were closest to each other.

'This part of the world,' she said, 'is either going to be one of the most hotly contested pieces of real estate in the not too distant future, or it's going to be the basis of a new alliance. For the moment, we favour the alliance scenario.'

Dividing her attention between the screen and her audience, she continued, 'The world is supposed to have changed. We think not. North Korea and China are still communist countries and as for Russia . . . the recent elections have shown that old habits die very hard indeed.'

She clicked the remote and the area within the circle expanded to fill the entire screen. She clicked it once more and a small arrow appeared. Using the arrow, she first moved it along the North Korean border with China.

'From Musan,' she said, 'the border meanders and loops up here in the north-east, before doubling back southward, following this river here, all the way down to the Sea of Japan. For about twenty kilometres up from the coast, the border is with Russia. Then here, at Namjungsan, it splits – with the Russian border now moving eastward as it goes north – to create a forty-kilometre corridor to Nanhua as part of China, before opening out from there and into the rest of that country.

'According to our information, somewhere within that three-country sector is a very special site.' She turned from the screen to look at them. 'There are three possibilities: a nuclear facility, a chemical weapons programme or . . . a secret fighter base *dug into the mountains*, where pilots from *all* three countries are being trained on advanced fighters.

'I personally favour the last option. I believe that something close to the alliance of the Korean War may be taking shape again. Apart from this airfield here, just inside the North Korean border at Kyonhung, and this unnamed one forty kilometres directly south, there are no others in either country within that area, except for a minor field south-east of Kraskino, Russia. At least, none that we are currently aware of. We have been unable to spot any aerial activity from this mountain base, if it exists.' Using the remote, Major Hoag drew a small square on the map. 'Our information puts the most likely location of the site within this box. We'd like to know what's really in there.' She stopped, and looked at the colonel.

'Thank you, Major,' Dempsey said.

She inclined her head slightly. 'Sir.'

'May I have the remote?'

'Yes, sir.' She handed it over, and moved to one side.

'Thank you.' Dempsey looked at Garner and Adderly. 'I think, gentlemen, you have begun to grasp the nature of the mission: a low-level reconnaissance. In effect, a ferret flight, to sniff out whatever they've got hidden in there. As Major Hoag has said, we don't *know* for sure; but if there's some kind of international fighter-pilot training facility in those mountains, we've got to plug that gap in our intelligence data. If that base does exist, it becomes a target *if and when* such a need arises.

'With the excitement going on down in the Taiwan Straits, we've got to know whether at some future date if Korea erupts again, or the Taiwan situation goes really hot, what kind of stuff we're going to be facing. According to the major, the news is that the very latest versions of the MiG-29 and the Su-27 are being flown by those pilots.'

Dempsey turned to the map on the screen. 'Take a good look at the topography. We cannot give you much in the way of suspected SAM sites, so any such information displayed will be speculative; but you can bet your shirt the area *will* be protected. Use every scrap of cover you can find, to hide yourselves from their radars. Ingress to target will be as low as you can hack it.'

He turned to face them, eyes seeming to drill into their very souls. 'Remember what I said about avoidance. We're not looking for a war, and we don't want a downed Eagle out there, gentlemen – and we certainly don't want captured aircrew. That would be very bad news indeed – for us and most particularly for you. Do not expect kind treatment if you are captured. If the worst comes to the worst, you will therefore make every effort to avoid being taken.

'If this doomsday scenario does occur, you must try to get the aircraft as close as possible to this point.' Dempsey pointed to a lake which was skirted by a railway line, not far from the coast. A road ran parallel to the rail line. 'A rescue mission will be on stand-by should there be a need.

'The Taiwan Straits party is good cover. Not only has it got attention focused down there, but Navy ships in the area around where you'll be going in will not arouse undue interest. It will appear to be just another muscle-flexing exercise, to guard our assets up that way. With the shadow-boxing going on down near Taiwan, a battle group on manoeuvres up here will be almost expected as par for the course. They would be more suspicious if there *wasn't* one. At this time they have no reason to suspect we have any knowledge of their little mountain hide-out.

'Our information is that there is no habitation in the area for several miles around. Don't take that for granted and, of course, there's always the risk of a patrol, particularly if the ether is humming with news of a damaged foreign aircraft looking for somewhere to set down. So use that road only if necessary, but knowing where it is will help with your bearings. If you have made it to the RV point, a helicopter will be waiting.

'If you're forced to walk a long way to the rendezvous, a chopper will come every day at a specific time, which you will be given before you take off from the forward base. If you arrive early, you must find a way to secure yourselves until the rescue chopper makes it. There will be special forces aboard a second helicopter, to give the rescue mission cover. Both choppers will be heavily armed, in order to sanitize the area, if need be.

'At no time will you engage in radio communication if you're down. Just leave your beacon on just long enough to let us know you're down OK. Thirty seconds. No more. We'll pick it up by satellite. Then get well away from the aircraft.

'Once your aircraft has been abandoned, charges placed in every piece of sensitive equipment aboard will detonate, ensuring nothing of use will be left for the enemy. If you eject, the detonators will go off once the seats are well clear. Your aircraft will carry no unit markings, and your names will have been removed from beneath the cockpit rim. This will be done in Japan, before you take off on the mission. You will, of course, be carrying handguns and enough ammo to see you through until the rescue. The hope is that you will not have to use them. Optimum result is that no rescue will become necessary.

'Rules of engagement: you will not attack *any* ground target. You will not attack any air target *unless* this is in self-defence. In short, you *wait* until he has launched at you. Even at that stage, it is better that you bug out. I know, I know, gentlemen. It's a tough break, but there it is. However, after he has initiated that first launch, he or any buddies he may have with him, are fair game. Use your initiative, but *always* remember: hang around only long enough to punch your way out of there.'

At last Dempsey paused. 'Questions?'

Garner and Adderly looked at each other, then looked at Dempsey. They shook their heads.

He turned to Shelley Hoag. 'Major?'

'I'm done here, sir.'

Dempsey again turned to Garner and Adderly. 'The mission is designated Organ Pipe, and your waypoint pattern will approximately follow the boundaries of the Organ Pipe cactus national monument, down on the Mexican border. You are Cactus One. The pattern is roughly kite-shaped. Position it so that the tail straddles the RV point. Modify that basic shape to your mission requirements, but remain *within* it. If for any reason you can't make the RV, we'll know the area within which to conduct a major search. Let's hope we won't have to, because by then the shit will really be *in* the fan.

'Clock's ticking as of now, gentlemen. Remain here and set up your waypoints. You will not be disturbed. You will take off at 14.00 hours for Alaska. Lancer and Hershon will accompany you, but will not know the mission. From

Alaska, both aircraft will stage to Japan. You will fly the mission from there. Thank you, gentlemen.'

While the colonel had been speaking, Major Hoag had picked up her hat and put it back on. She now picked up the briefcase and walked out, followed by Dempsey and Carter. Then the door to the room opened again, and she was standing in the doorway.

'Is it really a Boss Mustang?' she asked Garner. 'A 429?'

'It is.'

The green eyes smiled at him. 'I'd like to try it when the mission's done.'

'Then your seat's booked too.'

'I mean *drive* it.'

'It's a date.'

The eyes were speculative, and amused. 'A *date*?'

'A date. Take it or leave it, Major.'

'I'll take it.' She beamed at him and backed out of the door, closing it softly.

'That was quick work,' Adderly remarked lightly, introducing a note of friendliness between them. 'Your Boss Mustang must be bringing you luck.'

'She's quite a lady.'

'Careful. You'll make Arlene jealous.'

'Arlene's already got her man,' Garner said easily. 'You. And how is she?' he added.

'You really asking? Or making polite conversation?'

'I'm really asking.'

'She's OK.'

'Just OK?'

'She'd like to see you, Milt. She specifically asked me to invite you. I promised her I wouldn't take no for an answer.'

Garner fell silent.

'Look,' Adderly went on. 'I think it would help her if you did visit. Sometimes blood family can be too close to the problem. You know how she used to enjoy having you around. She feels as if you're making her pay for your beef with me. Don't do it for my sake. Do it for Arlene's. That's always assuming you really do care about her, and you're not just making polite talk.'

'That was a low blow, Nathan.'

'Yeah. It was, wasn't it?' Adderly did not sound repentant.

Garner passed a thoughtful hand across his eyes and said nothing. He looked as if he'd been boxed into a corner.

'We work well together in the air,' Adderly said, pressing home his advantage, 'but if you want another pilot when this mission is over, go right ahead. I won't stop you. Just remember, we used to be friends. I'd like it back that way. So would Arlene.'

'Then why didn't you trust me enough to tell me about that wonderful human being, old Nathan Adderly, the slave-owning ancestor whose name you carry?'

'Do you think it was *easy* for me? I would have told you eventually . . .'

'*Eventually?*'

'Milt . . . listen . . . throughout these United States we have sworn to defend, there must be . . . God knows how many families with a history like ours . . .'

'And it's still poisoning the damn country.'

'Don't you think I know that? Look. What say we concentrate on the mission and have a good long talk about this afterwards? Everything out in the open. As I've said, I want us to be friends again.'

Garner looked at his pilot for some moments. 'After the mission,' he agreed at last.

'OK. You got it.'

At exactly 14.00 hours, the two Echo Eagles lifted off in tight formation on the first leg of their flight, to the base near Anchorage, Alaska. They took off with a load of a centreline tank

each, plus a full complement of four AIM-9L
Sidewinder short-range heat-seeking missiles,
and four AIM-120 AMRAAMS for longer-
range kills.

Fully tanked up, the Echo Eagle had a ferry
range of over 2700 miles; but they would be
using the flight to do some air-to-air refuelling
practice. For the stage from Alaska to Japan,
they would need to refuel.

As Dempsey had indicated, Lancer and
Hershon were totally unaware of the nature
of the mission, but all mission data was ready
for a fast and complete briefing, should the
occasion arise. In the event of the first aircraft
being compromised without first locating the
secret base, the mission would be postponed.
With the area on full alert as a result of the
first Eagle's incursion, a second flight would
be suicidal in the short term. But options
were open.

Garner had programmed the entire mission
waypoint data into the system, ready to be
called up when needed. This started from the
base in Japan. They would use separate data,
copied to Lancer's aircraft, for the flight from
Arizona to Japan. Everything that could be done
to ensure a successful mission had been attended
to. They had also double-checked their survival

vests, ensuring that all was as it should be. An omission could mean the difference between life and death; between rescue and capture.

Garner ran through the list in his mind, as the Eagles climbed to high altitude for the fast transit to Anchorage: radio, mirror, flares, pencil flare gun, smoke, food, water bottle, fish hooks, knife, torch, strobe, pistol and ammo, and more. He would again double-check before take-off from the Alaskan base, and yet again from Japan, at the start of the mission proper. He knew Adderly would have done and would do the same, with his own kit. They were leaving nothing to chance.

He looked across to where Lancer's and Hershon's aircraft was keeping perfect station, and remembered Lancer's challenge.

'You guys may be kings of the walk,' Lancer had said as they had sauntered towards their waiting Echo Eagle, 'getting both Robert E. and killer, but you haven't come up against us. Reckon you can take us in a turning fight?'

Adderly had looked at him. 'This is a joke. Right?'

Garner had smiled, waiting for Lancer's reaction. Adderly could chew Lancer to pieces up there, any day of the week.

'Come on, guys,' Lancer had said. 'Not scared, are you?'

Garner had given Hershon a quick glance.

'Don't look at me,' Hershon had said, ducking out from under. 'I only fly with him.'

'When we get back,' Adderly had told Lancer, 'you're in for a sharp lesson. There will be weeping, and the gnashing of teeth.'

'Says who?'

'Says the man you can never beat, boy.'

Garner had given Hershon another surreptitious glance.

'Don't look at me,' Hershon had pleaded.

Garner smiled as he remembered. Lancer really should have known better.

Before leaving, Garner had also given Mason Lyle permission to look after the Mustang and to drive it, backing that up by giving the air policeman written authorization, just in case Lyle was stopped for any reason.

He relaxed in his seat as they settled out of the climb at 50,000 feet. Everything was done. The mission was on.

Let's get in, and get out quickly, he said to himself in his mind.

'You OK back there, Milt?' came Adderly's voice on the headphones.

'I'm fine.'

'This is it, huh?'

'It is.'

'In and out. Greased lightning.' Adderly was clearly having the same thoughts.

'Greased lightning,' Garner agreed.

After that, there was very little conversation between them. The aircraft flew on smoothly, all its systems fully operational, its technology working as it was meant to. Its crew, for the time being, had been relegated to the role of systems managers, watching like hawks to ensure that nothing went wrong or, if it did, to take swift remedial action. Highly trained and skilled individuals, they sat astride their potent steeds, marking the thin air with their passage.

Garner took a quick look at Lancer's and Hershon's aircraft. The Californian beach god was keeping faultless station.

About a thousand miles into the flight, they made a rendezvous with the KC-10 tanker at 20,000 feet above the Pacific, off the coast of Newport, Oregon.

'Anyone see a gas station around here?' Lancer quipped at the tanker aircraft.

'Be nice, sir,' the boom operator answered, 'or you'll go thirsty.' A woman's voice.

'I'm nice, I'm nice!'

Everyone could sense the operator grinning as she said, 'Then come on to mama for some refreshing JP4!'

Adderly had instructed Lancer to go first. The long boom, with its steerable fins close to the tip, extended as Lancer moved the Echo Eagle into position. Carefully, he eased forward, the aircraft weaving slightly in the tanker's wake. The KC-10's operator helped by steering the boom towards the fuel intake receptacle on the Eagle's left shoulder blister, next to the rear quarter of the engine intake's upper housing. The boom slid in, connected. Fuel rushed through the metallic umbilical cord at speed, giving the Eagle a generous drink.

Off to one side, Garner watched the process, checking out the wingman's aircraft as it drank. He knew that Hershon, in the back seat, would be eyes-out-of-cockpit, ready to warn Lancer of any impending danger. It was not unknown for customer and tanker to merge into an all-consuming fireball. All it needed was one bad mistake from either aircraft.

But everything went smoothly and Lancer had decoupled, and was banking the Eagle gracefully away.

Garner now checked out their own aircraft as Adderly swung into position. The boom came

towards him, looking as if it was about to stab
him between the eyes. Then it wavered slightly
and clunked neatly into place, just past his left
shoulder. The fuel pulsed through and soon
they too were banking away, fully topped up.

'Nice to do business with you!' the operator
called in parting. 'Y'all come again, now.
Y'hear?'

'How about a phone number?' Lancer
suggested.

'Never give ma number to strange men
in airplanes. Out.' A giggle sounded before
transmission was cut.

'Life's tough, Lancer,' Garner said.

'Looking forward to trashing you guys,'
Lancer retorted.

'Dream on.'

Garner had selected Channel 81 on the Tacan.
The right CRT was diplaying the main
navigation format, with the steering bug on
the compass rose showing five degrees off track.
He compared that with the waypoint on the
left-hand display. On the top right of the nav
display, distance to the base showed forty-five
nautical miles and was counting down.

'Come left three-three-zero . . .' he began.
'Now!'

'Roger. Three-three-zero.'

Adderly eased the Eagle on to the new heading. As if glued to them, Lancer's aircraft kept perfect station, matching the manoeuvre.

'Three-five miles to touchdown.'

'Roger. Three-five miles.'

Garner looked out upon the grey and white-streaked slopes of the snowy Alaskan peaks. Beautiful, he thought, but only if they stayed where they were. Still, it was a breathtaking sight.

Now that they'd descended in preparation for landing, clouds wisped past them. Despite the brightness of what was left of the day this far north, spring would be a lot colder than in Arizona; an average of 46° Fahrenheit during the day, to Arizona's 84°. It wouldn't do to go down among these mountains. Minimum temperatures would be well below zero.

But the Eagle flew smoothly on, with not the slightest hiccup in her systems.

The landing was carried out in formation.

The fighter break was made snappily over the runway and held as a tight pair, as they curved round on the downwind leg. Adderly throttled back to maintain 250 knots. Gear down, flaps down. Three greens above the red wheel, confirming gear down and locked. The little oblongs with their green lettering announcing 'NOSE', 'LEFT', 'RIGHT'.

'Gear down and locked,' he heard Garner say in further confirmation.

All was well.

He executed a descending turn, lining up nicely on the runway. They were now a mile out, and at 300 feet. Lancer was right there, keeping station.

Runway numbers centred on the HUD. One hundred and sixty knots now, descending. Air brake extended. Touchdown. Speed 130 and decreasing. Hold nose up. Big wing giving excellent aerodynamic braking. Ninety knots. Nose is down. Rolling, slowing down. Tap brakes. Slowing right down. Taxi to parking slot.

'Cheated death again,' Garner said.

'Yep. Don't know how I do it.'

6

They spent the night and took off again at 08.00 hours the following morning, for the stage to Japan. They made a rendezvous with another tanker over the Aleutians, and crossed the dateline while tanking. Making a dog-leg to avoid the Kamchatka Peninsula in far eastern Russia, they touched down at the forward base on the southern tip of the north Japanese island of Hokkaido. The high-cruise flight, including time out for tanking, had taken six hours. It was 09.00 hours the next day.

'West is east,' Lancer remarked as the four of them walked away from their aircraft to the ubiquitous little Volkswagen van that ferried crews around the base. 'We went west and, hey presto, we're in the east. Welcome to Japan. Who's for sushi?'

'Did you learn all that at school?' Garner said as they began to climb aboard the van.

'Oh ho!' Lancer said, unabashed. 'Who's a sourpuss?'

Garner shook his head pityingly.

When they were all in, the driver set off at seemingly breakneck speed.

'Hey!' Lancer called to the driver. 'You trying to kill us?'

'Sorry, sir!' the driver called back cheerfully. He didn't slow down.

Lancer looked aggrieved. 'I fly over miles of ocean in an Eagle for the privilege of being killed on the ground by a nut of an enlisted man? Do something, Captains,' he went on to Garner and Adderly. 'You're the senior men here.'

Garner and Adderly just looked at him. Garner then gave Hershon a long-suffering glance.

'I just fly with him,' Hershon said.

Once they'd been installed in the officers' club, Garner and Adderly decided to catch up on some sleep. Lancer decided he was not ready for sleep and persuaded Hershon to stay up with him. Neither crew would be going off the base until the mission was over. For Garner and Adderly, take-off on the mission was 02.00 hours.

The four men were not to see each other again.

* * *

A secure briefing room had been set aside for Garner and Adderly, within which to make final checks on their planning. They found two surprises waiting.

'Gentlemen,' Colonel Dempsey said.

'Colonel!' they both exclaimed.

'And the major,' Garner added, looking pleased. 'The Mustang's not over here, sir,' he said to Shelley Hoag.

She smiled at him. 'Colonel Dempsey wanted to be here for when you got back. I persuaded him to take me along. I've also got some extra information. Should the worst happen, our contact will be at the RV to help get you under cover.'

'Isn't he old for that kind of thing?' Adderly commented sceptically. 'He must be what . . . seventy? Eighty?'

'Sixty-eight. He's been doing plenty of mountain walking over the last forty years. He's a lot younger than the Republican nominee, and probably fitter than either of you.'

'Well,' Garner said. 'That puts us in our place.'

'Your aircraft has been prepared,' Dempsey cut in. 'To keep you as light as possible, the centreline tank has been removed. When you find the target, send the details via secure

datalink, and get the hell out of there. In case
you're forced to turn and burn before you get
out, there'll be a tanker waiting on station. You
will rendezvous with the tanker on egress, 300
miles from the coast. Make sure you've got at
least bingo fuel to get you there. So watch that
fuel flow if you've got to engage in combat, or
you'll be going for a swim.'

Bingo fuel state was their safety margin,
enough to get them to the tanker with still
sufficient left, in case they had to look around
for it. There had been cases during the Gulf War
of aircraft returning thirsty from their missions
and either finding dried-out tankers, or missing
their rendezvous points. Luckily, other tankers
had come to their rescue.

This was a different situation. There would
be just the one tanker. But even without the
centreline tank, they would be carrying sufficient fuel for the mission, and still be able to
make it back to base at bingo state; but that
excluded fuel-consuming combat.

'We certainly don't want to swim,' Adderly
said.

'Didn't think so.' Dempsey stared at them.
'Good luck, gentlemen.'

'Sir,' they both said.

Major Hoag hung around as the colonel

left. 'Not as tough as he likes to think, is he?' she began.

'What do you mean?' Garner asked.

'He tries not to show it, but he's not going to relax until you two are back.' She gave his arm a brief squeeze. 'Good luck. Both of you.'

She hurried out.

'"Good luck",' Adderly mimicked. '"Both of you". Notice that afterthought?'

'What afterthought?'

Adderly made a scoffing noise. '"What afterthought?" he says. She's after your balls. I mean that literally. That kind of woman is dangerous.'

'Bull.'

'Oh yeah? She doesn't want just a ride in your Mustang. She wants to *drive* it.'

'So?'

'You don't get it, do you?'

'So tell me.'

'That kind of woman likes to be on top . . .'

'I'm liking it already. She can ride my mustang anytime . . .'

'Forget your dick and where you'd like to put it. She's a control freak. You'll always be fighting her for control. Take my word for it. That one's grief on legs. Or have you forgotten what happened to you in New York?'

'I thought you said my lucky Mustang brought the sexy major to me. You've changed your mind about her so suddenly?'

'I haven't changed my mind. She's exactly what I expect her to be.'

Garner said nothing to that.

'Know what really hooks me about Arlene, even with our current problem?' Adderly went on. 'It's not just because she looks great, and it's not only because she's great at sex. She *needs* me, as much as I need her. That's what makes it work for me; for us. A woman doesn't need you, you're headed for trouble. Major Shelley Hoag doesn't need anybody. She's going places, and picks up little amusements along the way. But you already know about that, don't you? Remember New York?

'I don't know how far you're hoping to get with the major with the body to kill for; but a lover should also be a friend. You don't crap on a friend. That girl in New York was not your friend, even during schooldays. She crapped on you. Shelley Hoag's nobody's friend . . . 'cepting maybe her own. Perhaps you've got a thing about such women. Watch your six, buddy.'

145

'Finished?'

Adderly gave a worldly smile. 'Sure.'

'Let's get on with the planning,' Garner said.

'Sure.'

The darkness, speckled by the runway lights, was something insubstantial beyond the environs of the base. The Echo Eagle was at the threshold, engines spooling up to take-off thrust.

Garner looked about him and paused as his gaze fell upon the control tower. Both Dempsey and Shelley Hoag, he knew, were in there to watch their departure.

Was she really the single-minded power babe that Nathan Adderly had painted? He put Adderly's comments about her out of his mind. Time enough to consider them when they returned. He glanced down at the nav display. The time was 01.59.55 . . . 02.00.00.

'We're out of here,' came Adderly's voice, and the Eagle began to roll, accelerating in an enormous rush as the 'burners came on.

Then the nose was rising and almost immediately the main wheels left the runway. They were airborne, hurled forward on twin tongues of blue-white flame.

Adderly raised the wheels swiftly.

'Gear locked,' Garner confirmed.

'Roger. Gear locked.'

Adderly banked hard out of the circuit and settled on to the heading of the first waypoint, in a shallow climb. He cut the afterburners.

Garner had watched the map display rotate until it steadied, now moving as the aircraft position marker traversed its surface. He cross-checked with the waypoint display. All OK.

They would be covering the first 460 miles at high altitude. Any interested snooping radars and satellites would log just another standard flight from the many training missions of either Japanese or US aircraft. At 460 miles the Echo Eagle would head steeply for the lower levels until, at 300 feet, it would turn towards the target area.

With the FLIR on the HUD, they would go as low as they dared and head towards where Major Hoag's people had indicated the site was likely to be. Then it would be all up to how matters developed from then on.

Garner's mind went back to the moment when they had been just about to board the aircraft. Adderly had put a hand on his shoulder.

'We grab ourselves a coffee at the O-Club and have that talk when we get back.'

'We'll do it.'

'OK.'

Garner looked out at the night and wondered what was waiting for them out there.

'Waypoint two. Five miles. Three-zero-zero feet,' Garner announced.

'Two. Five miles. Three-zero-zero,' Adderly confirmed.

They were coming to the end of their steep descent and nearly at the required altitude. All active radar was on stand-by, closing down emissions. The passive radar warning receivers had remained silent. No one was currently taking overt interest in them. Waypoint three could change all that. By then, they would have intruded into potential enemy airspace.

'Waypoint two. Two-five seconds.' Garner watched as the remaining seconds counted down. 'Waypoint three, right two-nine-one degrees.'

'Two-nine-one.' Adderly took the Eagle into a gentle right turn. He watched as the compass numerals at the top of the HUD slid from right to left until the new course, marked by the small vertical line beneath it, was centred on the head-up display. 'On course.'

Garner thought he could sense his breathing

quickening slightly. This was it. They were about to poke their heads into the open jaws of the tiger. The trick would be to get them out again without having them bitten off.

'Going low,' Adderly said.

The Echo Eagle began to descend until it reached 100 feet. Adderly flew on at that altitude.

Garner had repeated the HUD display combined with the FLIR navigation overlay, on his left CRT. The infrared image showed him lots of water rushing past beneath them. He had done a quick radar scan while still well out, but nothing had shown in their path. The route he had chosen was so far devoid of shipping, and even if some radar post somewhere had managed to catch the fleeting sweep, it had been far too brief to allow any chance of pinpointing. In any case, they were now a long way from that last position.

'Waypoint three . . . ten miles,' he called. Then, 'Five, four, three, two, one . . . Waypoint four . . . two-eight-zero. Twenty miles.' He had modified the kite-shaped pattern of the waypoints, but had remained within the area covered by it, as he had been instructed by Dempsey.

'Two-eight-zero. Twenty.'

Adderly confirmed the change of course and put the Eagle into a steep left bank and on to the new heading. He stayed at 100 feet.

The twenty miles was soon covered.

'Waypoint four . . . three-zero seconds. Waypoint five . . . right, two-nine-six . . . thirty-five miles.'

'Two-nine-six. Three-five.'

'And here's the coast.' Garner had spoken in a hushed voice as they crossed into Russian territory. They flashed over several bodies on enclosed water. Nothing screamed on the radar warning. Even Bitching Betty seemed to be holding her breath.

Adderly had found a path through rising ground. They kept going. Sixteen miles later, they were into Chinese territory. Still nothing squawked at them. Then the convoluted border had them crossing the meandering river, and into North Korean airspace. Still nothing on the radar warner.

'Jesus,' Garner began softly. 'Are we going to get away with it?'

'It ain't over till the radar sings,' Adderly said drily.

They crossed the river again as it looped and were once more over the territory of the People's Republic of China, this time within

the six-mile corridor bounded by North Korea
and Russia.

The ground was rising quickly now and twice,
Betty called out altitude warnings.

'Target ten miles,' Garner warned. 'I'll leave
all systems on stand-by until the last moment.
Somebody must have heard us by now, even if
they haven't picked us up yet.'

They were not on 'burners, so there were no
tell-tale plumes of fire to mark their passage.

'According to this enhanced map,' Garner
continued, 'we've got a nice low-level run on
approach, then everything turns into a wall.
So watch it. We'll need a real fast pull-up
to clear. I'll hit the systems on the pull-up.
If this isn't a wild-goose chase, anything out
there will show.'

'Roger that.'

'It's just too damn quiet,' Garner muttered.
He searched the darkness about him, as if
expecting to see fighter aircraft bearing down
on them. 'I've got this horrible feeling of being
watched by a million pairs of eyes.'

'Quit that. You're getting itchy.'

'Better itchy than sleeping our way into
a trap.'

'That bad?'

'Listen ... my scalp wants to leave my

skull.' Garner searched the darkness once more.

'*Jesus!*' Adderly suddenly shouted and the Eagle was standing on its tail, 'burners coming on as it reached for altitude.

Several things were happening at once and it was a testament to both men's astonishingly quick reaction times that not only was disaster averted, but Garner had actually managed to trigger the systems just *before* the pull-up, as the aircraft hauled itself up to clear what looked, on the infrared, like a never-ending cliff face. Then they were over and heading rapidly down for the nearest valley.

Adderly killed the 'burners as they swooped for the welcoming valley.

'Sweet Jesus!' Adderly said, sounding very shaken. 'Did you see it?'

'I saw,' Garner replied, his own voice none too steady. 'That was a goddam big airplane. As big as our bird, I'm sure.'

'Where the hell did it come from?'

'Let's not worry about where it came from. There's another one and they're out there, and looking for us now – with maybe an extra buddy, or two.'

'That scalp of yours was right. They were waiting. Did you get anything?'

'Got it and sent it while you were trying not to commit suicide. Should be a good picture. I don't think they were waiting. I think we surprised the hell out of them. We were certainly not expected.'

'Dig whatever it was out of the memory. Let's see what we got.'

Garner called up the 'picture' that the radar-enhanced infrared sweep had taken in that terrifying moment. What they saw was astonishing.

'Jesus!' Adderly exclaimed softly when Garner had repeated it on one of the front cockpit displays.

What they had caught was an aircraft in the very act of taking off from what seemed like a huge hole in the mountain. There was a perfect overhead plan view of the aeroplane, clearly following the one that had nearly slammed into them.

'Shit,' Adderly said. 'I know an Su-27K when I see one. That's a mean fucking airplane. I'm not arguing with them. I'm taking the fuckers out.'

'I'm with you.'

The beautiful, flowing lines and canard foreplanes of the so-called 'Sea Flanker' stood out clearly.

'Well, we know the sexy major's information was right,' Garner went on. 'But Sea Flankers coming *out of a mountain*?'

'It makes sense. Those foreplanes make it manoeuvre even better. They've probably got to turn pretty tight once they've got off that mountain runway. Hell, it's a land-based aircraft carrier. Smart stuff. They've gone one better than the Swiss. Thank Shelley Hoag's mole. Satellites could look for years and never find it. Imagine, there could be others like it.'

'Nightmare time.'

Back at the forward base in Japan, both Dempsey and Shelley Hoag were having the same thoughts.

The 'picture' had been flashed, at the instant of its taking from the Eagle, up to the repositioned satellite, and sent by the satellite to a receiving unit in the States and to a waiting intelligence-gathering aircraft well out into international airspace, simultaneously. The intelligence-gathering Boeing had then relayed it to the room where Dempsey and Shelley Hoag were waiting.

They were staring at the same image that Garner and Adderly had been looking at.

'I'll be damned,' Dempsey said quietly. 'Will

you just look at that thing? Those boys are good. Now just get the hell out, you guys,' he added fervently. He turned to Shelley Hoag. 'Well, Major . . . looks like your people were right. This is not a good thing to see.'

'No, sir.'

'What do you make of it?'

She stared at the image on the screen before turning to look at him. 'First, the airplane. Su-27K. From what my department knows, and adding that knowledge to this picture, I would say we are looking at something that's like a huge, land-based aircraft carrier. They have tunnelled a large runway through that mountain, wide enough to take three airplanes in a loose V on take-off and maybe even on landing. Like a carrier, you take off and land in one direction. You're always into wind; but better than an aircraft carrier or even ordinary runways, there are no crosswinds strong enough to cause problems.

'Almost immediately on landing, you're into the tunnel. Out of sight quickly. On take-off, you're in the tunnel until the wheels leave the ground. Then you're over the lip at the end – just like on a carrier – but with plenty of drop to gain flying speed if you screw up. The Su-27K's canards enable it to manoeuvre tightly and also give it extra lift for such operations. I'm certain they'll have arrester wires in there for rapid stops, instead of the normal braking parachutes. With the hook and that big speed brake on the spine, stopping will be no problem.

'The airplane's sturdy landing gear enables it to use indifferent surfaces, so it can take off and land even on stony ground. This means they don't have to build a pool-table-smooth runway. Its engine intakes are protected by gridded debris guards, so even a rough runway will present no problems with foreign object damage. No ingested debris, no FOD. The tunnel runway is also practically weatherproof. No snow, ice or rainwater to worry about.

'The exposed parts are so short, it would be no trouble to keep them clear at all times; and importantly for spotting, very little heat traces for the infrared cameras on satellites or recce aircraft to pick up; which is why we needed that close look. They've probably got some surface cooling systems for the exposed sections of the runway, to keep infrared signatures down.

'They're also bound to have filtration systems to keep the fumes out. I'd say via long tunnels that exit the gases a long way from the base, and well camouflaged. They could also have all their administration, accommodation and engineering scattered within that mountain area, mostly underground. The Su-27K's folding wings would also enable them to store more airplanes in there, just like on a carrier. Sir, this could be the first of a proposed system of airfields. And they've got the best camouflage in the world. Nature.'

Dempsey was silent for long moments, impressed by her very extensive and detailed knowledge.

'This is a nightmare,' he said at last. 'If we ever get into a scenario where we've got to take those assets out, finding them first will be one hell of a job. Attacking them would be another nightmare. Hell, I could hold off a potentially overwhelming force with a wing of Eagles, SAM sites and triple-A saturating the area and, as a third line of defence, specialist combat troops to deter a ground assault. I'm certain whoever commands that unit has the same idea. You'd have to launch stand-off weapons *into* that hole in the mountain. That would not be easy. They've probably even got huge blast doors at each end.'

Major Hoag leaned against a table, and slowly crossed one glorious leg over the other.

'There's always another way, Colonel,' she said calmly, 'if we're in a bad shooting war and we can't seal off those bases, or neutralize them enough to make them inoperative.'

Dempsey looked at her. 'And that is?'

'Decapitate the whole damn mountain.'

Dempsey was staring at her now. 'Excuse me?'

Shelley Hoag allowed a tiny smile to play about her tempting lips, and said nothing.

'Nuke 'em, you mean?' Dempsey asked disbelievingly.

She still said nothing, but the smile continued to play about her mouth.

'Jesus, Major,' Dempsey said. 'You scare the shit out of me. You know that?'

'It is an idea, sir. And one that may have to be seriously looked at one day. Or perhaps the tunnel runway is the trend of the future. We'll all be burying our airfields.'

'And then we'll start – how did you put it? – *decapitating* mountains all over the goddam planet. We'll be burying our airfields all right,' Dempsey added drily. 'You'll be suggesting this idea to your superiors?'

'Yes, sir. All options must be reviewed.'

'Some advice from an old warrior, Major Hoag. Put that one back in cold storage. Bury *that* for good. The object of this exercise, I *hope*, is to let them know we're on to them, so that they'll think twice about constructing more of those underground airfields. They'll know we'll be keeping a close watch from now on, and that it's all going down in the target data. We're trying to prevent a potential war scenario here.'

'Bet the Taiwanese think differently.'

'We're not the Taiwanese, Major. That's a different ball game down in the Straits.'

'Yes, sir.'

Shelley Hoag didn't sound as if she thought it was. To her, it was all part of the same picture. The posturings in the Taiwan Straits were a few small brush strokes being added in a far corner of that picture. The mountain airfield was another in a different part of the same thing. One day, it would all come together. Decisions would have to be made.

'Right now,' the colonel said, 'I'm more worried about those boys getting the hell out of there.'

'So am I, sir,' she said. 'What response will we make if they do get brought down, sir?'

'Response? We don't want them brought down, Major. We don't want them captured and used in propaganda displays on TV, or forced to sign papers saying they're imperialist dogs and all that crap. We don't want Korean War, Version Two.'

'But if they are shot down?' she insisted.

'I'm sure you haven't forgotten our contingency plan. We rescue them. We do not respond.'

'Yes, sir.'

Dempsey looked at her warily. Jesus, he thought.

'Anything?' Adderly enquired.

'Nope,' Garner replied. 'Same answer as thirty seconds ago. Nothing on the warner. All our radars are off, so there's nothing for them to acquire. But they can hear us, and somebody must be talking to those guys we saw.'

He looked about him. This was not like most areas in the West, where there was always some residual glow from a city or town below, or even on the horizon. Even over the desert back in Arizona, something showed. But here, a hundred and fifty perilous feet above a strange landscape, there was no light showing anywhere.

'Look at it this way,' he went on. 'The longer we remain undetected, the closer to home we're getting. Waypoint seven. Three miles. Then it's zero-nine-five for waypoint eight . . . forty miles. Home stretch to the coast.'

'Roger. I . . .'

'*Launch! Launch!*' Garner bawled. 'We have a heat-seeker! Go for height, but leave the 'burners alone! I'm spoofing!' He cranked his head round. He could see a bright flame searing the darkness, coming from above. 'Holy shit. It's his infrared tracking ball and sight. That's how he acquired us. Must be. These guys are usually ground-controlled intercept and never work independently.'

'Well, he hasn't read that book,' Adderly grunted as he hauled the Eagle into a punishing avoidance manoeuvre.

Or he's disobeyed his GCI, Garner thought. Or he let one loose on spec. Whatever, we've still gotten ourselves a missile on our butts. This isn't the colonel, or the major out there. This is for real, and these guys are out to kill us!

The dark world, seen only in infrared, tumbled disorientatingly as Adderly did his stuff.

Then an ominous tone sounded.

'The goddam thing's got a lock on us!' Garner shouted. 'Get out of the fucker's way, Nate! Lose it!'

He fired off another decoy. A bright sunburst turned a patch of darkness into temporary day.

Adderly flung the big Eagle on to its back and plunged from the 10,000 feet he'd rapidly gained, towards the ground. He watched the AGL altitude on the infrared HUD as it counted down. There was a difference of 1000 feet between height above ground and above sea level. Many pilots had gone in, reading the wrong set of numerals. A thousand feet between life and death.

A valley opened up before him. He took the Eagle into it. Something bloomed brightly in the distance.

'There goes his missile,' Garner said with relief.

'All right,' Adderly said. 'We've obeyed the rules of engagement. I don't think this guy's going to let us get away without a fight. His buddy, or buddies, may already be trying to close the door on us. Let's kick ass if we want to get out of here.'

'You got it. Radars going on. Auto acquisition.'

'OKayyyy. Let's go to the party.'

Adderly hauled the Eagle into another steep climb, heading for altitude. Control the vertical before you go vertical, was the instructors' mantra; but there was no choice tonight. He needed some elbow room. The dive had given him plenty of energy, without need of the 'burners. He used that to convert to height.

Garner was making brief sweeps of the radar as the Eagle came over on to its back and began to drop its nose once more.

There!

'Got one!' he called. 'Got two!'

'Going to AIM-120,' Adderly said as he selected AMRAAMS.

Almost immediately, the targeting box appeared and began hunting. Then the seeker acquired. The box was solid. He began to manoeuvre to bring the box into the steering circle.

This would have to be quick. No time for fancy moves. Kill them and get out. Fast. Get him first before he manages to get another one off, forcing you to break your own lock, so as to manoeuvre out of his shot's killing envelope.

Range decreasing rapidly.

Shoot cue on. *Fire.*

Adderly pressed the release. The missile went off the rails in a blaze of fire that lit up the aircraft starkly, as it streaked towards the target.

See us for miles, Garner thought.

Then it was dark again as Adderly racked the Eagle into a diving spiral, to spoil any attempt by the opposing aircraft for another lock.

Would they get the kill? Garner wondered. Or was the other pilot, out there in the dark, already into his own ferocious avoidance manoeuvres? Was he jamming and spoofing like mad to escape being killed? Was he going to make it?

A flash in the distance.

A kill? Or had the missile expired uselessly on a decoy?

Major Konstantin Ilyich Udlov felt a deep sense of helpless frustration as he watched Captain Yeung die. The North Korean had disobeyed his advice and had not waited, and had paid the ultimate price for his haste.

Udlov had first heard Yeung's startled cry, followed by an excited rush of words. Yeung had reported that he'd nearly collided with another aircraft. At first, Udlov had thought the North Korean was still shaky from his first night take-off in the aircraft. He must have lost height rapidly, and had nearly gone into the trees far below the cliff face, Udlov had concluded.

Then twin plumes of flame had nearly scorched his own Su-27K, as he had followed Yeung into the air. The unknown aircraft had missed him but, experienced pilot though he was, the incident had left him temporarily shaken. It was then that he'd understood the reason for Yeung's sudden torrent of words.

But he'd recovered quickly. Who was the unauthorized maniac out there? He'd angrily demanded answers from those on the ground. There were no other friendly aircraft around, authorized or unauthorized, they'd told him. Then a message had come through of the noise of a low-flying aircraft coming up from the coast. It had not been challenged.

'*Why not?*' he'd barked furiously.

He would not have authorized the take-off if that piece of information had been received in time.

'We wanted to see where he was headed before shooting him down.'

Well, he's just shot down one of us, Udlov thought bitterly. And we know where he was headed.

Udlov was a tactics instructor, who knew the high value of patience. Had the excited Yeung not been so hasty with a missile release, they might have trapped the unknown aircraft in a classic pincer. Instead, the intruder had reacted very swiftly indeed. The pilot, whoever he was, was playing for keeps now. But how had he locked up Yeung so quickly? It had been a remarkably fast response.

Udlov could not know he was facing a two-man crew.

He did not call for another aircraft to be sent up. He'd been assured there was definitely just the one hostile target, and was certain he could handle it without the distraction of another insufficiently experienced pilot – even in a superb aircraft like the Su-27K – blundering about in the dark. He was determined to bring this intruder down by himself.

Then GCI began speaking to him.

Dempsey sat in the briefing room staring at the phone. He both wanted and dreaded to hear its ring. The news he wanted was that Cactus One was out. The other . . .

'Get some rest, sir,' Shelley Hoag advised. 'Why don't you? I'll wait here for the call.'

'Thank you, Major, but I think I'd better hang around. They should be on their way back, heading for the tanker rendezvous. We'll hear soon enough.'

'Yes, sir.'

But the colonel did not look at her. He was looking at the phone.

7

Major Udlov had a great liking for his Su-27K. He would even go so far as to say he loved it. It was, as far as he was concerned, a magnificent aircraft. It was potent, and the basis of this potency was the massive pair of Lyul'ka AL-31F afterburning turbofans that could hurl it through the air with astonishing speed. Its comparatively light weight, owed in no small measure to the incorporation of aluminium-lithium alloys in its construction, contributed greatly to this remarkable performance. It could turn very tightly indeed for such a big aeroplane, even at low altitudes and low speeds. It could also do its famous 'cobra' and snatch its nose round, while virtually appearing to be standing still in the air.

The first basic Su-27 had startled the West out of its complacency, just as the MiG-15 had done during the Korean War. It was a constant source of amusement to him, whenever the West thought it had discovered something new about the aircraft. Their interpretations of the uses for the various modifications they saw generated much hilarity among his fellow pilots back home in Russia. He thought it very ironic that here he now was, in one of the most accomplished variants of the Sukhoi, hunting out a Western intruder in the dark Korean sky.

He was in full agreement with the new and tentative friendship pact between the three countries, and the experiment of teaching the pilots of the two partners how to fly the advanced fighter. Many of them were still awed by its power, instead of revelling in it and making it work for them. Yeung had been one of those he would have marked down as being a top student; but the captain had made the worst mistake of a combat rookie. He had reacted hastily, underestimating his opponent. He had paid the inevitable price.

Udlov had no intention of making such an error, especially after what had just occurred. He was going to stalk this unknown enemy, prevent him from escaping, and shepherd him into the killing zone.

I'm going to drive him into coffin corner, Udlov decided grimly.

He would not use his radar, with its 240-kilometre long range for search, and 185-kilometre tracking range. This would alert the target and, in any case, he had little need of it. His infrared search and track system could spot a target from nearly 70 kilometres, and would give no warning. The missiles would be off the rails before the target aircraft even suspected he'd been tagged. The night was no hindrance.

GCI was speaking to him again, and directed him to where the intruder was heading.

Udlov opened the throttles but stayed out of 'burner to avoid visual detection. His present course would take him on a perfect intercept.

He was closing the door.

Then Udlov decided to reverse his earlier decision not to call up another aircraft. There was another of his students, who possessed an altogether more stable attitude: Captain Ling, of the People's Republic of China air force.

Though Ling did not appear to have the late Captain Yeung's flair, he was rather more than an efficient stick and rudder man. Ling was more precise in his flying than the flamboyant North Korean had been.

But he's just the kind of pilot I need right now,

169

Udlov thought, to help me trap this cunning bird out there.

He requested that Ling be sent aloft quickly.

In the tunnel, the alarm klaxons reverberated as the blast doors at each end were opened to the night. The runway lights were dimmed and all unnecessary illumination cut or switched to low-level red.

Captain Ling Chiu-Hua, secured within the enclosed world of his Su-27K's cockpit, waited for the slamming push of the catapult that would hurl him into the waiting darkness.

He moved the throttles smoothly to their full travel. The tunnel was suddenly bathed in a surreal glare of vivid light, as the 'burners speared their fire rearwards. He kept his head firmly, but without undue pressure, against the concave of the ejection seat's headrest as, with the familiar body-squeezing shove, the catapult hurled him into the night. He knew that even as he went into a steep accelerating climb, the blast doors were already being shut.

Ling felt proud to have been selected in the first place as a candidate for the new tri-national force and marvelled – as he continually did – at the ability of the aircraft to leap for altitude, even when pointing straight up. He cut the 'burners, not wanting to telegraph his position visually, and headed in the direction given by GCI.

He was also very proud of having been singled out by Major Udlov to aid him in this very important combat. Ling possessed utter respect for the Russian; as far as he was concerned, the major could do no wrong. He had listened avidly to every instruction Udlov had given him, throughout his conversion to this superb fighting aircraft. He had learned to stop being afraid of it, and to become at ease with its formidable capabilities. He had learned to look on the night as a friend, despite his limited experience. And it had all been due to the major's teaching and flying skills.

Ling's loyalty to Udlov was so great that it was touch-and-go whether he would back the Russian tactically, against the dictates of his own countrymen.

The American pilot – Ling was certain the intruder was American – would regret this incursion. Americans were always reckless. They thought they were omnipotent. He would show the imperialists that the price for such irresponsibility was very high indeed. This airspace violator and his imperialist compatriots would also one day discover to their cost – in the not too distant future – when the Korean comrades inevitably went on to reclaim the South, just how high it could be. It was only a matter of time. He was sure of it.

And he'd be right there in the thick of it with his fellow countrymen, supporting the comrades when the time came.

Ling banked the Sukhoi hard towards where Udlov was stalking the Eagle.

'We're in NK airspace,' Garner said as their track took them into North Korea.

He checked the threat display. It did not light up like a Christmas tree, and the audio warning had again relapsed into silence. It had been like that for some minutes now. He'd put the radars back on stand-by, to cut emissions.

'How's your scalp?' Adderly enquired.

'Still trying to leave my skull, and I've got an itch between my shoulder blades. They're still out there. One, two . . . who knows how many. We're definitely being stalked, even though there's no radar warning.'

'Infrared?'

'That's the baby. It's infrared search-and-track time. He, or they, are hunting us down with their night torch. If we got the other guy, there's maybe just one of them now and he'll be mean as hell. He wants our butts. We're going to have to be real fast and slick to get him first. We're going nowhere till we do.'

Though they were still heading in the general direction of the next waypoint, Adderly frequently altered course, never travelling on the same heading for long, and keeping as low as he dared.

'OK,' Adderly said. 'I'm going to try something. We're not going to wait for him to rope us, so let's hit him with the unexpected. I've got AIM-120 selected, and I'm going to give him two to play with. He should have a real party trying to dance the night away with those two babies after his ass. Meanwhile, we hightail it out of here. If he survives, we'll be well out to sea. Too late for him to come looking.'

'Sounds good to me. How do we do it?'

'We've been changing course all the time, so if GCI's been trying to guide him to us they can't be using radar, or we'd have known it . . .'

Then the radar warner clamoured for attention in his headphones. He threw the Eagle into a violent series of manoeuvres to break the scan, while its auto jammers went to work. The noise stopped. The probing radar no longer probed.

'You were saying?' Garner remarked drily. 'That was just long enough to set him on our tail. But they're not sure if we've got anti-radar missiles, so they've shut down pretty quick.'

'So he knows where we are at this time . . . or *thinks* he knows. OK. Here's the deal. I believe he may be in trail now, trying to sneak up for a close kill. It could be tricky, but I'm going for a sudden reversal. Head shot, if he's behind us. Get ready to hit the radars. If he's really there, we'll have him before he can use his gizmo. OK?'

'I'm ready to roll. I also have a thought.'

'Will I like it?'

'You might not.'

'Shoot.'

'What if,' Garner began, 'he's called up another buddy to replace the one we may just have splashed? What if there's a bunch of them out there?'

'It's a thought to give us nightmares. But that's the deck we've got, and we play the cards as they've been dealt. So we'd better get the sucker, and quick.'

'No complaints from me. You have full auto-acquisition.'

'Let's do it.'

Adderly suddenly pulled the Echo Eagle into a hard and tight turn, reversing on to a reciprocal heading. He was careful not to light the 'burners.

At the instant of the turn, Garner had used the side controllers to give Adderly the radars.

On the HUD, Adderly saw the targeting box come on, hunt briefly, then fix itself on the upper-left quadrant of the head-up display. He needed only a slight adjustment to ease the Eagle round until he got the box nicely into the missile steering circle. Almost immediately, he got the shoot cue.

He fired. Twice.

The night was lit doubly bright, as the two AIM-120s flashed off the rails and streaked into the far darkness.

'Let's get the hell out of here!' Adderly rasped, hauling the aircraft tightly round, to head for the waypoint.

Though they were rushing away at high speed, he desperately wanted to light the 'burners, so that they could extend the distance travelled at an even greater velocity. He disciplined himself not to push the throttles that much further, in order to demand full afterburning thrust. They would be lighting up the night for every heat-seeking SAM in the area. Not a smart move.

Garner had turned off the radar as soon as the missiles had gone. Now, as the infrared image of the HUD on his CRT whirled again, he glanced over at the waypoint display. He was very gratified to note that they were only six miles from the ground RV. He felt a great relief. They wouldn't be needing it.

The bogey would have his hands full by now, trying to disentangle himself from a pair of implacable AMRAAMS after his blood. They were going to make it home after all. The hope was that there was not a third bogey out there.

'Five miles to waypoint,' he announced.

'Roger. Five.'

Udlov felt sick. When he'd seen the pair of bright stars suddenly lighting up the sky, he knew instantly what had happened. The other pilot had correctly arrived at the conclusion that as his radar warning systems had been so conspicuously silent, he was being tracked by infrared. When the ground control had scanned for a position update, he had also correctly worked out what was happening. Although not certain of how many adversaries he faced, the intruder had done that most potent thing in combat: the unexpected.

Even as he watched the bright stars hurtling toward him, Udlov felt a chagrined admiration for the other pilot. *He leaves me to* cope with his missiles while he escapes, he reflected.

Udlov was already furiously ejecting decoys and heading earthwards to drag the missiles into a position where their great speed would force them into collision with the ground, when they tried to turn to follow him. Countermeasures would also make life very difficult for them.

One missile veered off, chasing a decoy. The other came on inexorably.

Udlov felt the sweat pop from his brow, making the helmet feel damp as he tried to evade the second missile. He flung the big, agile aircraft into seemingly impossible manoeuvres.

He had again gone for height, not wanting to make a terminal acquaintance with the ground.

The missile was still following.

The unknown pilot had been smart. Assuming that another adversary could be on the scene, he'd taken drastic action to lessen the odds as quickly as possible. No adversary remaining, and he was OK. Another, and it was still down to one-on-one.

'A smart move,' Udlov grunted as he continued to throw the big fighter into a furious series of evasive manoeuvres. 'Bastard!'

Ling was on his own now and at this rate

would probably be making a rapid exit. The Chinese pilot's chances of continuing survival did not look at all good.

Udlov swore at the missile, and at the American pilot who had fired it. Then he realized that unless he wanted to be roasted, it was time to get out.

'*He's getting away!*' he yelled at GCI. '*Ejecting! Ejecting!*'

He grabbed at the double-looped red handle between his knees and gave it a firm pull.

He ejected cleanly.

As he left the aircraft, he was aware of the rapid passage of something very hot. Fractions of a second later the missile's fire curved to the left and a violent sunburst smeared itself against the backdrop of the night, as it hit the abandoned aircraft. He'd got out just in time.

He would live to fight another day.

He experienced a feeling of sour pleasure as he floated towards the treetops. The SAMs had held back while the first two Sukhois were in the air, not wanting to hit them by mistake. Now they would be after the intruder with a vengeance. They would be less restrained, even with Ling around.

'Hope they get you, you bastard!' he said

in his native tongue, and cursed the unknown pilot again.

It was now up to Ling, and the SAMs.

Continuing down in the darkness, Udlov felt even less secure about Ling's chances. Despite his undoubtedly growing skills, the Chinese was still a long way from being independently capable of handling a fight like this; he still needed the guiding hand of a combat leader. Now out there on his own, he might as well be trapped in a darkened room with a vengeful cobra.

Udlov found that he now regretted having called out his pupil. He had sent the young pilot to certain death.

'Think we got him?' asked Adderly.

'He's either the best damn dodger there is with *two* 120s on his tail,' Garner replied, 'or he's toast. At least his airplane is. He could have got out, if he didn't leave it too late. Waypoint three miles.'

'Three miles.'

'Uh oh!' Garner said.

'What? *What?* Speak to me!'

'More company. Definitely more company.'

'*Goddamit!*'

'He must have called up another buddy, after

all. Best assume it's another of those hot Su-27K ships. But this guy's not as good. He's all over the radar warner. One-three-zero at thirty miles. He's too keen.'

'Then let's sock the dude in the teeth before he launches at us, and get out of here. I'm getting homesick.'

'You got it,' Garner said. 'He's now at two-three-nine, and still playing with his radar. I don't get it. He might as well say come and get me. He's still at thirty miles. Someone should have warned you about that radar, boy,' he added to the Sukhoi pilot.

'If he's not as good,' Adderly said tentatively, 'you reckon we can get him with the same trick?'

'Don't see why not. He's probably still in shock from watching the lead go down, and is wondering what the hell happened. I hope.'

'Perhaps we just splashed another rookie and it's the sharp one still out there, trying to sucker *us*.'

'Maybe,' Garner conceded, 'but I wouldn't go to the bookie's with it. The other guy might have tried that trick if the *two* of them were still out there, getting his wingman to corral us with the radar while he sneaked in for an infrared shoot. I think that's what they planned. I think we just ruined their day.'

'OK. We'll go with that.'

Ling was indeed in a state of shock.

Major Udlov shot down!

He didn't want to believe it. Even if he'd chosen to ignore the shocking news that had been relayed by GCI, he could not deny the evidence of his own eyes. He'd seen the brilliant flaring in the night, twelve kilometres away from his last position. He hoped the major had managed to escape injury. He had not picked up the Russian's eject cry, but GCI had given him as detailed a picture of the incident as they could. The only cheering aspect of the whole thing was the fact that the major appeared to have ejected cleanly.

Ling heard himself breathing deeply in his mask as he manoeuvred for a missile shot. He tightened his lips. This intruder was not going to get away with such impertinence. First Yeung, now Udlov.

It was time to collect from the American.

The missile warner was going crazy again.

'*Launch!*' Garner called. 'We've got a radar sniffer incoming, and it's got our names on it!'

'Too soon,' Adderly grunted, then groaned against the sudden onset of G-forces as he pulled the Eagle into a punishing turn, to reverse direction. 'He should have . . . waited a mite . . . longer. Lock not solid.'

They were now head on to the incoming missile.

Garner knew it was going to be close, but calmly set up the radar for auto-acquisition as Adderly manoeuvred for an AMRAAM shot. He watched the targeting box on the HUD repeater, watched as the missile seeker hunted then stabilized on the box; watched as Adderly manoeuvred so that the symbols drifted into the steering circle; saw the shoot cue come on; saw the sunburst in the night as the missile hurled itself off the rails to scar the darkness with its fiery wake.

Then the unseen world was again tumbling as Adderly threw the Echo Eagle into another set of frantic gyrations, as he fought to escape the impending terminal clutches of the radar homer that was seeking them out.

And all the while, the warning of the incoming missile filled their headphones.

Ling was occupied with his own avoidance manoeuvres.

At the moment that he'd launched his missile, his own warners had bayed at him. As he tried to escape the American missile, he thought grimly that both aircraft were now totally defensive, both so occupied with trying not to get shot down that neither could find the time to continue the attack.

And meanwhile, Ling thought furiously, he's getting away!

That pilot out there was very good. He hadn't wasted any time. Even within the barest of windows of opportunity, the speed of his reactions had enabled him to make certain of his lock, before missile release.

The American missile seemed implacable.

Ling threw the Su-27K into the series of manoeuvres he'd so assiduously learned from Major Udlov, breathing hard against the forces that mercilessly squeezed at him, but remaining calm throughout. He wasn't going to panic. The major had warned him about panic.

'Panic is a win for the enemy,' he remembered the major saying bluntly. 'Your tactical thinking is gone. You might as well fly straight and level, and give him the kill. Always think, *then* react. Do this so swiftly that it merges to become a single act. Thinking and reaction *must* be a seamless join.

Don't react and then think. By that time, you're dead.'

Ling heard the words pounding in his mind as he too fought to avoid the flaming nemesis that reached for him. He wondered whether he'd achieved a decent lock on the intruder. He hoped so. It would make up for Yeung and the major. It would be good to land with that kill to his credit.

But first, he had to get away from this determined missile.

'It's still with us!' Garner said, as calmly as he could. 'What was that about a solid lock?'

'So it didn't hear me,' Adderly grunted. 'What do you want? Miracles?'

'That would help.'

'OK. One miracle coming up.'

Adderly flung the Eagle on to its back and headed earthwards.

On the infrared display, Garner watched the image of some very ugly high ground reaching for them. He said nothing. Adderly knew what he was doing.

He'd better, he thought, staring at the image.

Then the terrifying image was receding and his body felt as if it wanted to fuse into the seat,

as the Eagle was again reaching for the upper
levels in a steep climb.

As the G-forces faded with seeming reluctance, Garner looked over his left shoulder and
saw a flaring far below. The missile had been
too close to the ground when it had tried to
turn to follow them, and had impacted.

He shut his eyes briefly, sensing a great
relief.

'Good enough for a miracle?' Adderly was
saying.

'Give the man a nickel. Can we go home
now?'

'Took the words right out of my mouth.'

I'm not going to get away, Ling thought
clinically.

The American missile was still with him,
trailing him with a single-mindedness that made
him feel the thing had a mind of its own. It was as
if the seeker head had become sentient and knew
every manoeuvre he was capable of executing,
before he went into them. It even ignored the
decoys.

Surely it would run out of fuel soon?

Time seemed to stretch for ever. The missile
appeared to be infernally happy to follow him
for just as long.

I've got to do something!

Following Udlov's diktat of thinking and reacting seamlessly, Ling chopped the throttles and hauled the Sukhoi's nose into the vertical. The aircraft lost speed rapidly.

Without looking, he knew the missile was hurtling inexorably towards him, now in a flat trajectory. In his fevered mind he imagined he could hear it yelp for joy, knowing it had him cornered. The impact, he reasoned, would be at the precise point where the top of his head now was.

Please, please.

He waited, as the aircraft seemed to hang in the air as speed bled off and gravity began to take over.

Please, please.

Then the Su-27K seemed to drop like a stone, tail first.

A cone of fire hurtled past, several metres above as the missile punched through the space where the aircraft had been. But it was not to be thwarted. It began curving round, hunting out the prey that had dared to fool it.

Ling's immediate problem now was loss of both energy and control. His manoeuvre had been one of inspired desperation. Had the opposing aircraft been in the vicinity, letting himself hang in the air like that would have been suicidal. A fat target going nowhere. But against the missile, it had proved to be a life-saver, if only somewhat temporary. But any extra time was a bonus; a chance to get away.

The missile was coming back.

Ling shoved the throttles forward as he fell. Power returned smoothly. Power brought flying speed. He rolled the Suhkoi into a ninety-degree bank and hauled into a turn that would force the missile to alter course, as it tried to reacquire him.

It came close. Then as if fed up with being continually balked, it exploded.

What sounded like a shower of hail rattled against the aircraft. It jolted severely, like a horse that had been jabbed by viciously applied spurs. It shuddered, seemed to shake itself as if brushing off the blow, and flew on.

But damage had been done. Power on one engine was falling rapidly. But there seemed to be no further damage. Ling was astonished to find he was still alive. There seemed to be a pool of sweat encasing his face, as he silently thanked the Fates for his good fortune.

He forced himself not to take deep gulps of oxygen as he did a swift check of his systems. The left engine appeared to be the only truly serious damage, but with it, some systems would eventually go.

Even so, he would make it back. He called the base to warn them he was damaged and coming in.

'Glad we got that bozo off our backs,' Adderly said. 'Man, I could use some coffee.'

'I could use something. It's got oak leaves on its shoulders.'

Adderly gave a resigned chuckle. 'You're not thinking of the sexy major, are you? After all I said? Some people just like living dangerously.'

'Have you *seen* that body? I'm not talking about a life-long commitment here. I know her game.'

'Don't fool yourself. When you *think* you know, that's when she'll throw you a big curve.'

'Hey . . . it's just a little rock 'n' roll. No big deal.' Even as he'd been talking, Garner was moving his head around, checking the night about him. 'Hold.'

The tenseness in his voice made Adderly say, 'What? What?'

'Thought I saw something flash way over at three o'clock. Low . . . *shit! Break right! Break right! SAM launch!*'

The flash had turned into a long stream of flame, and it was headed towards them. There had been no radar warning, so it was a heat-seeker, probably launched willy-nilly across their path in the hope of a kill.

Garner had begun his countermeasures even as Adderly again threw the Eagle into a series of avoidance turns.

'We must have got that third 27,' he said between grunts to Adderly as the G-forces came pressing at him intermittently, in response to the hard turns the aircraft was making. 'Or damaged him enough to send him back to his carrier in the mountain. So they've woken up the SAMs. Shit, shit, *shit!*'

The surface-to-air missile consumed itself violently in one of the flares from the Eagle.

'OK,' Adderly said, relaxing slightly. 'That's gone. Any more?'

'None so far ... *Launch! Launch! Six o'clock!* Jesus! Those bastards want our hides real bad.'

The radar warning went crazy. Bitching Betty joined it. The ECM systems went into their routines, and Adderly again did his daredevil stuff, keeping a sharp eye on the threat display. Again they managed to evade the missile. This one tried to follow the reflecting decoy, and went back towards the ground.

They were now four miles away from the waypoint.

'I think they're trying to herd us back,' Garner said grimly.

'No way,' Adderly said, and returned to course.

Garner was right about the intentions of those on the ground.

'*Launch! Launch!*' he called yet again. 'Two! Six o'clock and nine o'clock. These dudes are really after a kill tonight. Find a valley. Get away from the waypoint!'

For a third time the Eagle was flung about and the countermeasures went to work in an effort to deny the missiles their kill.

Adderly found a valley in which to temporarily hide. One missile followed, but took the turn into the valley too wide, and slammed into the opposite slope. The other seemed to have disappeared.

'We've got to get out of here,' Garner said, 'or we'll hit bingo fuel long before we make it to the tanker.'

They both knew that the combat manoeuvring had gone on for much longer than had been anticipated. If they didn't get away soon, they would be going for a swim. They tried to put the thought of being shot down out of their minds and concentrated on making their escape.

Garner was running the map through, looking for a route out. Mindful of the colonel's remarks about remaining within the kite-shaped pattern, he quickly set up new waypoints that would take them back to the egress point, but from a new direction that still gave them ground cover.

'New waypoints on your screen,' he said to Adderly. 'Old four is now eight. New four two-seven-zero at five miles. We should have the fuel if nothing else happens.'

'Roger,' Adderly confirmed.

They went through waypoints five, six and seven without any more attention from the SAMs.

'Nice going,' Adderly said. 'Looks like they lost us.'

'Don't bring out the champagne yet,' Garner cautioned. Waypoint eight . . . one-six-five . . . ten miles.'

'One-six-five. Ten.'

They were again approaching the ground RV point. The coast was just a little way ahead, and then the open sea.

*   *   *

Ling had shut down the damaged engine to lessen the risk of an in-flight fire. Hook down, wheels down, flaps down, ailerons drooping. He gingerly made a long, straight approach to the runway, holding the aircraft steady as it descended.

Though generally blacked out, they had put on the red horizontal lights that marked out the threshold of the section of the runway that was outside the tunnel.

His approach was steady, his speed good. He needed only the slightest of corrections on the rudder, in order to neutralize the natural tendency of the good engine to swing the aircraft slightly. There was no crosswind to give him extra trouble.

Then the almost sedate approach gave the impression of speeding up suddenly, as he got closer. He kept his nerve. If he panicked and jerked at the controls, the aircraft would swing or rise, and he'd be ploughing into the mountain itself.

He brought the Sukhoi steadily down. The wheels hit the runway, just ahead of the lights. The hook squealed as it scraped along then grabbed one of the four arrester cables. The Su-27K was jerked to an abrupt halt.

Ling quickly shut down the engine and

allowed himself a sigh of relief. He was down! He'd made it.

He was still alive.

The squad of soldiers had been told to look out for a foreign aircraft crashing but they'd neither seen nor heard anything. They were working their way in the dark, down a steep incline which was about fifteen miles from the ground RV point as the crow flew, but was a good thirty or more on foot, over rough terrain. If they were heading there, it would take them at the very least until the next night to make it. But they weren't headed there.

At least, not yet.

They came into a tiny clearing. Suddenly, they paused, listening. There was a sound; definitely the sound of an aircraft.

The squad leader shouted to one of the men to make his man-portable SAM launcher ready. It was a Chinese-made version of the old Soviet Strela, in use from the days of the Vietnam War, but still very effective. It even possessed a filtering capability, allowing the seeker to screen out flares that might be released as decoys, and still home in on the target aircraft.

The man worked quickly. Another soldier helped him load the plastic tube with the heat-seeking missile. He brought the launcher to his shoulder, and waited. He had no idea what he would be aiming at and judged the target by sound.

The launcher had an open sight only, which was of little use to him in the dark. But his hearing was acute, and he aimed where he thought the sound was coming from. However, a red light would come on in the sight when the infrared seeker was energized, and would change to green when it had achieved lock-on. All he then had to do was squeeze the trigger in the pistol grip.

As the sound grew louder, the soldier saw the red light come on. He waited patiently for the green; and it came. He fired, still without seeing his target.

The missile shot out of the tube, propelled by its booster motor, then when it was about twenty feet away the sustainer ignited, hurling the missile towards its target. Without this two-stage system, operators of that particular missile launcher would be toasted by their own weapon.

The squad watched as their missile flew.

*　　*　　*

'*Launch!*' Garner bawled in his mask. 'Six o'clock! Shit, shit, shit! Another heat-seeker! Where did *he* come from?'

Once again, he began countering the missile, feeding it the searingly hot flares, while Adderly threw the Eagle into punishing manoeuvres.

The missile came on.

'It's not taking the flares!' Garner said. 'Damn!'

He fed it some more. Adderly pulled out all the stops.

The missile followed.

'Shit,' Garner said. 'This thing looks like it's got our names on it.'

He kept turning his head, hunting out the missile's flaming plume, as Adderly used every move he knew in an attempt to beat the slavering fire on their tail.

Still the missile came on.

'Man, this is . . .' Garner began.

Then the missile exploded.

It didn't actually hit the aircraft, but it was close enough to do considerable damage. Its dying pieces ripped through the Eagle, most going through the front cockpit and the engines. Miraculously, the canopy was intact, as was the rear cockpit. Many systems remained on-line, and there was no fire. Yet. But the master caution was blinking like mad, and the warning tone was going. Bitching Betty added to the fun.

Garner did a rapid check of his systems.

The double row of the twenty-six lights of the aircraft systems warning panel, across the top of the two main CRTs, had begun to come on immediately after the missile explosion. But now, red lights started appearing in the group of eight on the left of the master caution light and, on the right, more captions were winking on.

The Eagle had pitched upwards, as if it had really felt the pain of the near impact.

Garner was unhurt. 'You OK?' he called to Adderly.

There was a long pause.

'*Nathan!* You OK? Talk to me!'

At last Adderly said, 'Take control.'

'*What?*'

'Right arm . . . right arm's useless. Take . . . take control.'

Jesus! Garner thought.

But he did not argue, and immediately assumed control of the aircraft and brought it back to level flight, roughly on course. He was no fighter jock, but he was sure he could fly it back to base. The problem was, there was not enough fuel to make it all the way back to Japan. And certainly, there was no way he could tank *at night*, without turning both their aircraft and the tanker into a fireball.

It looked like a swim, after all. Time to let them know. He dialled up the guard channel.

'Cactus One to Organ Pipe ... *mayday, mayday, mayday*. Cactus One to Organ Pipe ... *mayday, mayday, mayday*.'

No one replied.

'Cactus One to Organ Pipe ... *mayday, mayday, mayday* ...'

Still no response.

The warning panel had the story. All comms were out.

Great.

Two of his screens went blank and stared back at him like socketless eyes. The aircraft began to shake violently and he was having difficulty keeping it steady. It felt ready to roll over at any moment. A coarse rumble told him the engines were no longer happy. Engine RPM was dropping alarmingly. He worried about fire, every flyer's nightmare. Remarkably, the infrared HUD was still working and it was repeated on his left-hand display.

They were low enough for him to see that they were currently above reasonably open ground, and their heading showed they were still pointing the right way.

It was time to leave while he could still see roughly where they were, and the aircraft was still in level flight.

'Nathan! Can you hear me?' Garner spoke rapidly, urgently.

'Yes . . . yes . . .'

He sounded very weak, Garner thought anxiously.

'Nathan . . . we've got some bad ju-ju here. We're losing fuel, RPM's tumbling, radio's down, and the systems are going off-line. We're not going to make it. We're going to have to eject. I'm moving to aft initiate. You got that?'

'Yes . . .'

'All right. Here we go!'

They left the Eagle cleanly. It flew steadily in the dark for a good thirty seconds, then a vivid brightness lit up the night as it exploded. Secondary explosions followed.

'They'll have seen that for miles,' Garner said to himself as he floated down.

He hoped Adderly had made it without further injury. Ejection was not always the end of your problems, even over friendly territory.

By the time he'd landed, his eyes had adjusted themselves to the gloom. He came down just a few yards from the road that Dempsey had told them about. He quickly got free of his chute, then rolled it and hid it with his helmet as best he could. He kept on his G-suit and survival vest. After activating his beacon for the length of time specified by the colonel, he went to look for Adderly.

About five minutes later, he found him. Adderly had landed at the edge of the lake. His chute was in the water, with Adderly himself still attached to it, but his body was actually on dry land.

Before he risked touching him, Garner wanted to be certain there were no spinal injuries from the ejection.

'Nathan,' he began. 'Can you talk? Can you move?'

Adderly groaned softly. 'If . . . you're worried . . . about my back . . . it's OK. My arm . . . and my left ankle . . . are not so hot.'

Relieved there were no spinal problems, Garner began to work quickly to free his pilot from the chute, then eased away from the edge. He toyed with the idea of hauling the chute out, but it had filled with water. Then, even as he watched, its amorphous form began to disappear. It was sinking. He wondered where their seats had landed. Any troops within a thirty-mile radius might well stumble across those tell-tales within the next hours, and that would sharply focus the area of search, as they hunted for the users of those seats.

We've got to make it to the RV, he thought urgently.

Garner found that he could now see appreciably well, but knew it would take another thirty minutes or so before he acquired full night vision. He returned his attention to Adderly, whose injuries he could not yet examine properly, but whose right arm felt strange. Adderly had somehow managed to remove his helmet, for it was next to his good arm.

Expecting that the pilot would be suffering from some degree of shock because of his injuries, Garner began to gently check by feel. The facial skin was not cold or damp, pulse was strong, and breathing was regular. He couldn't check the eyes, but as far as shock was concerned, Adderly seemed to be OK for the moment.

'We've got to get out of here, Nathan,' he said. 'I don't know what other injuries you may have, but we're kind of exposed if we stay. I've got to move you. We'll find a hide-out, then I'll check you out with my torch. I've already sent the signal, so they'll know we're down. But we'll have to move during the night to get as close to the RV as we can. It's only about four miles from here, along this road. All we've got to do is follow it.'

He glanced along the road in both directions. There was not even a pinprick of light.

'We're in luck,' he continued. 'It doesn't look as if this road is the busiest in the world. But that can easily change. This may not be a car-owning democracy, but it's got plenty of soldiers. Soldiers mean military traffic. Come daylight, we go into the bush. Can you walk?'

'I . . . think so . . .'

'OK. Let's have a try.'

'Arrggh!'

'Sorry, sorry . . .'

'It's not you. It's the ankle. I don't think it's broken, but I'll keep off it as best I can. Let's . . . get . . . out of here.'

Garner helped Adderly to his feet, and they staggered across the road. He took the helmet with him.

There was a wide strip of ground between the road and the single-track railway. They found a clump of bushes that would suit their purposes. Within the clump, there was enough room for Adderly to recline. Garner got out his pencil torch and began to check out his pilot.

There didn't seem to be as much blood as he'd feared, but Adderly's right arm seemed a mess above the elbow. Missile splinters had chewed through it, although there appeared to be no arterial bleeding. At least that was something.

He ran the torch over the whole of Adderly's body, and decided it would be best to leave his boot on. A fracture would need the support and a sprain – if the boot were removed – would cause the foot to swell so much they'd never get it back on again.

Probably landed badly after ejection, Garner decided.

He checked Adderly's eyes. No dilation, and though he was in pain, Adderly was fully alert. The shock had either not hit him as yet, or he was over it.

There was also a slight swelling by Adderly's right temple. He reached into Adderly's survival kit and got out painkilling tablets and gave him two with sips of water from his bottle. He checked the arm once more. The blood seemed to have formed its own seal and he thought it best not to mess around with it. With a bandage from his own kit he bound the arm carefully, then made a sling out of Adderly's bandage to keep the pilot's forearm across his body.

'How do you feel?' Garner asked. He switched

off the torch and waited for his eyes to get reaccustomed to the dark.

'Keep the day job,' Adderly said with a weak chuckle.

'So I'm no doctor.'

'You've done OK. Thanks for getting us out, and for coming back for me.'

'What makes you think I'd leave you out there?'

'Don't . . . don't mind telling you that I used to think if we ever got into this situation you'd sure be glad to see the last of me.'

Garner thought about that before saying, 'I've had the idea from time to time.'

'You hate me that much?'

'I don't hate you, Nathan. I hate what your family did.'

'That's not *me*. I'm Nathan Adderly, twentieth-century version . . . not . . . not the nineteenth . . .'

'It's your heritage. *My* heritage. It's responsible for the shit that's still in our country.'

Adderly felt silent for a long time.

'Hey!' Garner said. 'Nathan!'

'It's OK. I . . . haven't . . . died on you. Seems we're having our little talk earlier than expected . . . and in a very different place. Wonder what your . . . ball-chewing . . . major's doing right now. Wishing you were with her?' The pain was now making Adderly pause frequently.

'I'm wishing we'll get out of this piece of real estate real soon. I have no taste for a prison camp. Whoever shot at us will have called the dogs out. We'd better try to move on to the RV.'

If troops came on the scene, Garner decided, he'd try to evade and if that failed, they had two pistols between them, and plenty of ammo. There was no way he was going to let either of them go into captivity. He could only hope rescue arrived before matters got that desperate. Things were already bad enough.

'A minute . . . or two,' Adderly was saying '. . . and I'll be . . . ready. Just a . . . minute . . . or two.'

The ball-chewing major had stalked around the room twice and was again leaning against the table, watching the colonel.

The colonel was watching the phone.

'What I need,' Shelley Hoag said, 'is a pool.'

Dempsey stared at her. 'A *swimming* pool?'

'I could do with twenty lengths.'

Wondering if he'd heard correctly, Dempsey went back to looking at the phone.

It rang.

Dempsey stared at it for a moment, then grabbed the receiver. 'Dempsey.'

Shelley Hoag eased herself slowly off the table, a big, sleek cat coming to the alert.

Dempsey got the message he didn't want to hear.

'Cactus down,' he heard.

His hand tightened round the phone. Watching closely, Shelley Hoag knew it was bad news.

'Where?' Dempsey asked.

'According to the position of the short signal, just four miles from the RV. They should make it easy.'

'If they're not hurt. If there are no troops on their trail.'

'We'll have to hope not. Are your boys smart enough to head for cover during the day?'

'They're smart enough.'

'It will be daylight by the time we get to the RV. We'll go in tonight.'

'They'll have to wait the *whole day* out there?'

'If we go in at daylight, Colonel, we're sure as hell going to have a major fire-fight. We'll need air cover, the works. We do this the quiet way, we should get away with it. All they've got to do is stay put.'

'And evade troops.'

'We can't go in earlier.'

'I guess not, Colonel,' Dempsey said to the senior Marine officer responsible for dispatching the rescue mission. 'Keep me informed.'

'I'll do that.'

Dempsey put down the phone. The man with whom he'd been speaking on the secure line was on the ship aboard which the two assault helicopters waited.

He looked at Shelley Hoag. 'No need to tell you what's happened, Major.'

'No, sir. I'm very sorry.'

'So am I, Major. So am I.'

'I've . . . I've got to stop,' Adderly gasped.

'Sure.'

Garner eased him down by the side of the road. This was the fourth time Adderly had called a halt. They had been moving for a while, but had not covered much distance. Adderly would appear to be moving along nicely, then would suddenly gasp and plead to stop. Garner was worried there were other injuries he didn't know about, which were perhaps being exacerbated by his trying to get the pilot to the RV.

Yet leaving him behind, even to get to the RV and bring help back, was not an option. Four miles still meant eight miles there and back, even if the helicopters were waiting. Adderly on his own would be easy meat for any troops that came along in the meantime.

Garner also felt that as the darkness would begin to give way to daylight in about an hour, it was very likely that the helicopters would wait for night, making hiding out for the day necessary. They had to get closer to the RV. Perhaps the old man that Shelley Hoag had spoken about would be there to help.

'Here,' Garner said. He broke a piece of chocolate from his kit and put it into Adderly's mouth. 'Some energy.'

'Thanks,' Adderly said, chewing.

'Need a drink?'

'OK . . . for now. Let . . . let's do it.'

'Are you sure you're ready?'

'Ready as I'll ever be. Come on. Help me up. Aarrghh *shit!* No. No. Don't stop. I've . . . got to . . . do it.'

Garner helped him up, and they stumbled on.

8

The squad had watched their missile chase its
target all over the night sky and had seen its
explosion in the distance, beyond the tops of
the trees. Then some time later a vivid flash,
much brighter, had lit the night once more. It
had been a long way from them, well beyond
the trees, but they'd had no doubt what had
caused it.

They were jubilant. The squad leader spoke
urgently into his radio. He received orders to
go and find the wreck.

When the sky began to lighten, Garner took
Adderly off the road, across the strip of ground,
over the railway track and deep into some woods
beyond it. He laid Adderly down, then went
in search of a good place to hide out for
the day.

After what had seemed ages of looking, he

found something that would do. It was a small cave in a steep, well-wooded section of rising ground. It was still gloomy in the trees, and the cave entrance was heavily screened by thick undergrowth.

He remembered an incident from his childhood when his grandfather had taken him hunting in Georgia.

'Lie on your belly,' Grandpa Garner had said, 'and look along the ground. What do you see?'

It had taken his eyes a long time to focus on what he'd been looking at. It had been a small burrow.

'See it?'

'Yes, Gran'pa.'

'The game's in there, boy. Now let's flush him out.'

Garner had employed the same trick when looking for the cave, and after the third try the thin beam from his pencil torch at last seemed to hit nothing but empty space, between two intertwined, and corded stems in the foliage. He'd struggled his way through, and had found it.

Wondering about wild animals and snakes, he used his torch to cautiously check it out. There was neither, and the place was dry. It looked as if nothing had been in there for years. Perhaps the almost solid screen of undergrowth had made home-hunting animals pass it by. Perhaps it just wasn't suitable. Whatever the reasons for its current vacancy, it was a welcome sight for humans on the run.

He made his way back to where he'd left Adderly. The pilot was lying very still.

'Nathan!' he whispered.

'Don't bust your breeches,' Adderly responded in a surprisingly strong voice. 'Conserving energy.'

'You had me worried.'

'For a man who hates my guts . . .'

'I told you. I don't hate *you* . . . although I still think you shouldn't have waited for me to find out all those things. You could have told me. We were supposed to be friends. Come on. I've found us a place to hide.'

'OK. I'm . . . I'm ready.'

'Getting in there might hurt a little. The bush is almost solid, so we've got to work our way in; but it's a good screen.'

'Like I said . . . I'm ready.'

Garner reached down for him.

'Christ!' Adderly said in horror, leaning heavily against his back-seater. 'I'm . . . I'm never going to get through that!'

The effort to work their way through the

wood to get to the hide had been so great, and had taken so long – despite the short distance involved – that the light was appreciably stronger, and Adderly could clearly see the obstruction.

'You've got to,' Garner told him. 'It's our best chance. The cave is about twelve feet behind that . . .'

'Je . . . Jesus! I'll never make it.'

'You must,' Garner insisted. '*I* can't see it from here, and I know it is there. It's covered from all sides. What better place to hide? It's dry, and there are no animals.'

'But how . . . do I get in?'

'The same way I did. I'll lift some of those bushes to make a sort of tunnel for you while you crawl through on your good elbow and shoulder. I'll go in before you to make the hole. The screen will drop on you as you move in, so try and keep your bad ankle away from it, if you can. When you're in, I'll go back out and make sure we've left no signs for anyone to read out there.'

Adderly stared at the tightly packed foliage. 'I feel like we need one . . . of those . . . machetes you see . . . in all jungle films.'

'No knives. We cut nothing, we break nothing.'

'OK. OK. Let's do it.'

It took some time. Adderly's progress was painfully slow, but he did not complain. At last he got into the cave. There was plenty of room for him to stretch out along its length, with plenty of space between his feet and the entrance. There was also enough room for one other person to lie the same way. Additionally, in the space between him and the entrance, there was sitting room for one, well inside the mouth of the cave. It was still very dark within.

'Hell, you're . . . right,' Adderly said. 'Can't even see . . . daylight from here.'

'It's still a sort of twilight out. We'll be able to see what it's like when the sun's really up. Good thing this isn't one of those wet and wintry Korean days. They would have been able to follow our footprints all the way from that lake. Something to eat? A drink?'

'I'm OK. Just resting . . . after that little . . . workout.'

'All right. I'm going back out to check our trail. I won't be long. You going to be OK?'

'Yes . . . yes.'

'Fine. Just hang in there.'

Garner went back out, spent some time retracing their steps from the time they'd left the railway track. He lay on his stomach behind a screen of low bushes and studied the area for about five minutes. The light was very much brighter now and he could see beyond the track and the road, to the lake. Nothing moved on either the road or the railway. There were no boats on the lake. He could hear no man-made sounds. It was as if there was no one else on the entire planet. A high cloud base of cirrocumulus promised a fine day to come.

He looked at his watch. It was 05.45. They had perhaps gone just one mile since ejecting; a mile – or more realistically, even less – in over two hours. He would have preferred to be closer to the RV. On the other hand, there was probably not such a good location within which to sit out what was going to be a long, fraught day. He wondered where the seats had fallen.

After checking as best he could that they'd left no obvious signs, he worked his way back to the cave. Adderly was dozing

'How're you doing?' Garner asked.

'OK,' Adderly replied drowsily. 'Tired though.'

Garner tested him again for shock, checking the pupils with the torch angled away a little, so that it was not shining in his eyes. He still appeared not to be in shock.

'More chocolate?'

Adderly nodded.

Garner gave him another piece, and some water.

'I could . . . use that coffee,' Adderly said.

'You and me both.'

'Is it light . . . out there yet?'

Despite the increasing light outside, none had so far penetrated into the cave.

'It's daylight.'

'None . . . here. Good find, Milt.'

'As the day gets brighter and our eyes adjust, we should be able to see a twilight in here.'

'Something . . . to tell you.'

'I'm listening.'

'You . . . you're an . . . Adderly. Well . . . sort of.'

Garner was sitting with his back against the curve of the cave. He went perfectly still.

'Say what?'

'You . . . are . . . an Adderly.'

His pilot was getting delirious, Garner concluded. There must be other, more serious injuries, probably internal . . .

'You're . . . thinking, his mind's gone . . . ballistic. Am I . . . right?'

'If not,' Garner began carefully, 'what kind of sick game are you playing with me?'

'No . . . game. What you found out . . .

about Nathan Adderly . . . and his daughter's
baby . . .'

'You *know* about that?'

'Sure . . . my father . . . gave that journal . . .
away. There was . . . is another journal . . . at
home. My home. Wait. Let . . . me finish. That
baby . . . didn't die. Josiah Adderly, as a boy . . .
helped fool . . . his father. With the . . . help of
household . . . slave women, he . . . put a . . .
dead slave baby . . . in its place. His father . . .
never bothered . . . to check. He just . . . wanted
it out . . . out of the way. A black baby . . . was
a black baby.

'The boy . . . grew up on the . . . plantation.
His light . . . skin was passed off as his . . . being
the son . . . of one of . . . the white overseers
and . . . and a slave woman. It . . . worked . . .
because this . . . particular overseer . . . used
. . . used to rape . . . her often . . .'

'Jesus. And you wonder why blacks feel the
way they do?'

'Are . . . you going . . . to listen . . . or what?
You've waited . . . a long time . . . to hear . . .
and I . . . to tell.'

'Go on. I'm listening. I'm going nowhere.'

'The boy was . . . called John,' Adderly continued. 'He and Josiah were . . . secret friends
until . . . Nathan was killed. Then they became

open . . . friends and . . . of course, Josiah was
also . . . John's uncle. John was not . . . involved
in . . . the killing.'

'What surname did John have?'

'The . . . the . . . overseer's. Unusual name.
Melthorp.'

Garner fell into a stunned silence.

'But that's my . . .' he began at last.

But Adderly interrupted him. 'Your mother's
family . . . name. All over . . . the States . . .
things like that happen. Bound to . . . given
our . . . history. John's father never . . . raped
Helena . . . you know. She . . . loved him. As I've
said . . . you're an Adderly. You're descended
from . . . Helena . . . cousin.'

Adderly gave a weak sigh, and was silent.

'Nathan!'

'Don't shout! I'm . . . OK. Just tired . . .
with all that . . . talking. Good to have
got this . . . off my mind . . . at last. We
named our baby . . . John Milton Adderly.
No more . . . Nathans. Now I want . . . some
rest. OK?'

'Yeah,' Garner said vaguely. 'Sure.'

He was going through an emotional over-
load. Thoughts tumbled one after another as
he tried to come to terms with what Adderly
had said.

Did the pilot's words owe anything to reality? Or was he in the grip of a delirium brought on by his injuries?

But it had sounded like a confession of sorts. And Adderly had called him *cousin*, and had meant it.

In Arizona the previous evening Mason Lyle had been feeling very pleased with himself. It was really neat of the captain to have given him permission to drive the Mustang. He enjoyed working on it, and appreciated being given the opportunity.

What a car! The sound of that engine was totally fantastic. It was the first time he had taken it out since the captain had gone, and he'd wanted to enjoy it all by himself. He had promised the captain he'd look after it even better than his own, and that was exactly what he would do. This was not a joy wagon for his buddies, some of whom had wanted to come with him.

The captain was not like some officers he knew; officers who thought you could gain respect by pulling rank all the time. Captain Garner was different. You could respect a guy who treated you like a human being. When the captain came back, he'd suggest it was time to paint the car. The captain had said he liked metallic blue. Lyle thought that was an excellent colour for the Boss.

He floored the accelerator, and savoured the roar of the 429 engine as the big exhaust pipes echoed in the Arizona night. Then he glanced at the fuel gauge.

'Uh oh. Better put some gas in that tank before I get back to base.'

The base was just thirty miles away, but it was a measure of Mason Lyle's desire to do things the right way that he was reluctant to return the car with less fuel than he'd found in it.

Five miles later he pulled into a service station, just off the minor road he'd been using. There was also a diner, so he decided he might as well grab a bite.

He filled the tank then parked, and went in to eat.

Yannock's pick-up truck pulled in at the station about five minutes later. Amos Brant and Billy Newberg were with him.

Brant jerked upright like a gundog. 'Ain't that the nigger Mustang?'

'Where?' Yannock asked, peering through the windscreen.

'Been at your pecker again? You that blind? Shit, it's over there. By that little yellow, or some faggot colour, foreign sedan. See it?'

'You can't be sure . . .' Yannock began uncertainly.

'Sure I'm sure! Billy! You go look.'

'Amos . . . I don't think . . .'

'Goddamit, Billy! You your daddy's boy, or what? Or maybe a nancy . . .'

'Amos,' Billy said, 'leave it!'

Brant twisted round to glare at Billy. '*Leave* it? *Leave it?* That nigger cost me my licence, boy! I can't drive my truck. You hear me? I can't drive my truck, I got no business. Nobody takes my business from me. I got no fucking licence! Because of that nigger, your pappy took it away!'

It never occurred to Brant to consider that it had all been his own fault.

'I'm not with you on this, Amos . . .'

'Not with me? You scared of your pappy the sheriff? We ain't in your daddy's jurisdiction, Billy. Now go on out and check that car.'

Billy stayed where he was in the back seat while Brant remained twisted round, and continued to glare at him.

The station attendant was looking at them. 'You after some gas? Or you're staying there all night?'

'Smart-ass!' Brant snarled, turning his glare on the attendant.

'Hey! All I asked was if you wanted gas.'

Yannock said, 'Yeah. We want gas. Fill her up.'

'That's all I want to hear.'

Brant poked his head out of the cab. 'You serve that Boss Mustang over there?'

'Nope.'

'Then who?' Brant demanded in exasperation.

The attendant paused. 'What's this? Twenty questions?' He resumed what he was doing.

'Smart-ass!' Brant growled once more, then got out and walked over to where the Mustang was parked.

He made a close inspection of it.

'What's biting your buddy?' the attendant asked.

Both Yannock and Billy were watching Brant.

'Aw . . . he thinks that car belongs to a friend,' Billy replied eventually.

'Sure doesn't act like it,' the attendant said as he completed the fill-up.

He put the hose away, and Yannock got out

to go over to the cashier. When Yannock got back, Brant was standing by the pick-up. The attendant was nowhere to be seen.

'It's the damn car,' Brant said tightly. He glanced up at the sky. 'Good night for a hunt.'

'Amos . . .' Billy began.

'Shut up, Billy! Shut the fuck up! Yannock, you with me?'

Yannock hesitated.

'*You with me, Yannock?*'

After a moment's hesitation, Yannock said, 'I'm with you.'

He got back in behind the wheel, reached behind him, and patted the shotgun clamped in its rack.

Brant gave a nasty smile. 'Good. Now I'm going in there to see if he's eating. You watch to see if he gets into the car.' Brant looked at Billy. 'I don't want to hear it.'

He turned away and walked belligerently towards the diner entrance. They watched him go in.

'I don't like this,' Billy said. 'My father said the guy's an air force officer . . .'

'Out here, in the night, he's just another nigger to me.' Yannock started the pick-up and drove

to park in shadow, from where they could keep
an eye on the Mustang.

'You guys are crazy. This is gonna go
bad . . .'

'Here's Amos.'

Brant was returning. He paused to look
around until he saw the pick-up. He didn't
look pleased as he approached.

'No niggers in there,' he said as he came up.
'Must be in the john.' He spat. 'Goddam niggers
using the same john as white folk. Time we had
us a white homeland in this country.'

'How much of it?' Yannock asked.

'*All* of it!' Brant snapped. 'Get rid of anyone
who ain't white, and Aryan.'

'What about the Indians, Amos?' Billy
Newberg put in. 'They were here long before . . .'

Brant stopped him with a glare. 'You trying
to be funny?'

'I just thought . . .'

'Don't think, peckerhead!'

Then the sounds of movement by the diner
entrance made them stop to look. People were
coming out. None of them was black.

Brant turned to the pick-up once more.
'Must be trying to empty that big black
dong of his.'

They all laughed at the coarse joke, Billy

doing so reluctantly. For brief moments, their attention was focused on each other.

The sudden and powerful roar of the Mustang startled them into staring in its direction.

'*Goddamit!*' Amos Brant shouted. 'He must have seen us and waited for a chance to get away!' He hauled himself into the cab. '*Get going, Yannock!* You want him to get away?'

By the time Yannock had got the pick-up moving, the Mustang was on the road and accelerating away.

'We've lost him,' Yannock said. 'That thing's too fast. He beat us last time, and this pick-up is not as fast as yours.'

But Brant was not about to give up. 'We're not beat yet. I know this place. There's a short cut. We can head him off.'

Yannock glanced at him. 'You want me to take *my* pick-up off the road out here, *at night*?'

'I told you I know this place, didn't I? I'll give you directions. Now get this heap moving, goddamit, or we'll lose him for sure. C'mon, c'*mon, Yannock!*'

'What did I tell you?' Brant was triumphant.

They were waiting just beyond a bend, off the road, lights out, ahead of the Mustang.

Yannock and Brant were outside, shotguns in their hands. Billy remained inside.

Then they saw the lights.

'Here he comes,' Brant said softly, as if the driver of the Mustang could hear.

Then the lusty roar reached them.

'Enjoy your last ride, nigger.' Brant raised his shotgun.

Yannock did the same with his own weapon.

Mason Lyle saw the two men in the glare of the headlights and had barely time to register the pump-action shotguns in their hands before the windscreen shattered. There were several rapid explosions, and a terrible pain followed.

Then the world began to tumble.

'*We got him!*' Brant crowed as the Mustang careered off the road.

The spinning car tipped on to its side, then rolled completely three times, its headlights describing crazy arcs as it went. Then the gyrations stopped as it again finished on its side, the headlights pointing accusingly towards the pick-up. It did not catch fire.

Through the pick-up's windscreen, Billy's face looked whitely out on the horrific scene.

'Better finish him off,' Brant said. 'Billy! Give me the flashlight.' He took a couple of paces back and reached with one hand towards Billy Newberg.

Billy did nothing.

'*Get me the goddam flashlight!*' Brant yelled.

Billy jerked out of his stupor and mechanically pulled the powerful torch from its clip, and passed it over.

'Thank *you*!' Brant said with biting sarcasm as he took it. He began walking towards the wreck.

'Watch yourself there, Amos,' Yannock warned. 'Damn-fool thing might explode!'

Brant ignored the advice and was now trotting over to the stricken Mustang, shotgun held ready in one hand, and braced beneath his arm. The twin beams of light from the car seemed to flutter briefly, as he walked through them.

The upper flank of the Mustang was the driver's side, and Brant now slowed as he approached it. He raised the torch, holding it away from his body as he walked cautiously across the remaining distance. He stopped, peered in.

'Oh shit,' he said.

*　　*　　*

'What do you mean: he's *white*?' Yannock asked fearfully, his agitation raising his voice and turning it into a muted squeal.

Blow away a black and mostly, a white jury would not convict. But this was very different. Yannock did not like what the future promised at all.

'*What do you mean: he's white?*' he repeated, panic in his voice now. 'You said . . .'

'I *know* what I said!' Amos Brant cut in sharply 'He *is* white. Can't change that. Maybe that nigger spotted us and got this guy to switch . . . Come see for yourself.'

'I knew this was not good . . .' Billy Newberg began.

'Shut . . . your . . . *mouth*, Billy! You hear? And don't you go telling me you told me so! We're all in this together. Come see for yourself, Yannock. C'mon.'

The fearful, reluctant Yannock went over to the Mustang.

'Oh my God!' he said when he saw Mason Lyle's shattered face. 'Oh my God! Amos, this is big, big shit. Boy! Are we in it! And who the hell is he?'

'How in hell should I know?' was Brant's savage response. 'We'll burn it.'

'*What?*'

'Your ears gone too? We'll burn it! He had an accident.'

'Jesus, Amos! What good will that do? They'll still find all those buckshot holes . . .'

'Get out of the way! I'm gonna torch the tank.' Brant had moved back from the car and was pointing his gun at the rear of the car. 'Get the hell out of there, Yannock!'

Yannock scurried out of harm's way, then stopped to watch apprehensively.

The single shotgun blast made him jump.

Yannock watched with a mind made blank by the fear of the probable repercussions, as Garner's many years of hard work on his pride and joy went up in flames.

And Mason Lyle with it.

'That's strange,' Garner said.

'What's strange?' Adderly enquired in a low voice from within the gloom of the cave.

'I just thought of the Mustang.'

A weak chuckle followed this. 'What do . . . you . . . miss most? The car? Or . . . or the . . . sexy, ball-grabbing major?'

'She hasn't grabbed my balls.'

'Yet. I hear . . . a yet in there some . . . somewhere. And . . . anticipation.'

'You hear too much.'

Another weak chuckle, ending in a single, low cough.

'You all right?' Garner asked anxiously.

'Yes, yes. It's just a . . . slight cough. To a cigarette smoker . . . this would be just . . . a tickle.'

'You don't smoke.'

'Quit it, mother hen.' There was not a second cough.

Garner looked out at the screen of bushes. It was so thick that even though it was now a bright day outside, within the cave a deep twilight remained. Anyone passing would be doing so more than twelve feet away; and as the cave entrance was at foot level before belling out into the chamber itself, he was certain that even someone that close would not realize it was there.

They would be safe until nightfall, when it would be time to try for the RV. He looked across to where Adderly was lying. There was enough difference between the light levels to enable his gloom-adjusted vision to make out his companion quite clearly. He had recently checked Adderly's arm, which had showed no extra sign of bleeding. The ankle was no doubt painful, but the pilot continued to make no complaint.

He had also given Adderly a tablet ration. Garner had decided to conserve the foodstuffs they each carried in their survival vests, in case they had to remain in hiding longer than anticipated. The area would be too hot because of certain pursuit to allow foraging or fishing and still enable them to evade discovery.

Though not strictly a food item, just the one tablet possessed high nutritive value. In addition to relieving thirst and reducing hunger, it produced energy by metabolizing body fat. One of the concentrated tablets – even if that was all that was available – delivered sufficient energy for a man for an entire day. The tablet rations were of particularly immense value if ejection was over the sea.

Garner was glad he had chanced upon the cave. Had he not done so, Adderly would have found the going extremely difficult, perhaps ensuring their eventual discovery by the troops who were undoubtedly searching for them. He again toyed with the idea of leaving his wounded colleague while he struck out for the RV. It was safe enough in the cave.

But again he was reluctant to do so. What if Adderly coughed loudly, just as someone was passing? The cave would act like an echo chamber, and discovery would be inevitable.

Worse, it was virtually certain that jumpy and eager soldiers would simply empty their weapons into the foliage, shredding it, and eventually filling the cave with a barrage of lead and explosives.

I won't leave him, Garner thought.

But there had been times when he'd asked himself what he would have done in such circumstances. He had run the whole gamut: from their current situation, to simply walking out on the man whose family had so brutalized his ancestors. Adderly had been closer to the truth than even he had thought.

But Garner's powerful sense of discipline and responsibility had not let him. He would not have left his pilot to the brutal fate that would certainly be waiting, even if he had not been made aware of the missing section of the astonishing secret history of the Adderly family.

And besides, Arlene would never have forgiven him. *He* would never have forgiven himself.

Garner frowned. But why had he so suddenly thought of the Mustang?

9

'Take . . . a woman . . . like Arlene.'

Adderly had begun to speak so suddenly that Garner, momentarily taken unawares, gave an involuntary start.

'Take . . . someone like . . . Arlene,' Adderly repeated. 'I know . . . I know that some . . . people think . . . she's just a . . . Southern bimbo . . .'

'Nobody thinks that, Nathan.'

'Oh yes . . . some . . . do. Some do. I . . . heard a visiting . . . Falcon jock . . . back at our home . . . base . . . who didn't know shit . . . about her, who'd been . . . looking at her . . . and . . . who didn't realize . . . I was close . . . by. He . . . went on about . . . her . . . her tits and . . . her ass . . . that she was . . . sex on legs . . . but nothing much . . . on top.'

'Take it easy, Nathan. You don't have to

think about this. So some guy was flapping his big mouth . . .'

'Listen! I'm trying . . . to tell you . . . something.'

The sudden intensity in Adderly's voice alarmed Garner. He moved over to where the pilot was lying.

'Nate! You OK, buddy?'

'Sure . . . I'm OK. *Listen* . . . will you?'

'OK, OK. I'm all ears.'

Must be mild delirium, Garner decided. If Adderly wanted to talk about Arlene, let him. It probably helped him to cope with the situation.

'She's . . . she's not . . . like that . . . at all,' Adderly continued. 'Sure, she's got . . . a real . . . nice ass and legs . . . that even . . . Major Hoag would . . . kill for. Hey . . . I married . . . the gal. I know . . . a good thing . . . when I see it. But . . . there's so much . . . more to her. You know . . . what she was . . . like before . . . before we . . . lost the . . . the . . . the baby. You . . . remember?'

'I remember,' Garner said quietly. 'You told me once she looked like a million dollars, and made a man *feel* like a million dollars.'

'Yeah. I . . . remember . . . that.' Adderly gave his weak chuckle, followed by another of the slight coughs. As if knowing what was going on

in Garner's mind, he added, 'Don't ask . . . if I'm
. . . OK. I . . . am, all things . . . considered.'

There was a slight pause, then Adderly
continued. 'Remember . . . something else . . .
I said?'

Garner nodded in the gloom. 'You said I
needed someone like Arlene.'

'Yeah. I did . . . didn't I? Now . . . you take
Major Hoag. Everybody looks . . . at her and
they . . . think . . . razor. There's . . . a woman
. . . with razors for . . . brains, she's so . . . sharp.
She's got . . . that . . . in-your-face . . . don't-fuck
. . . with-me-unless . . . I-say-so look. But I'll . . .
tell you, Milt . . . Arlene's got real . . . guts.
Good, good . . . woman. And . . . she'll still
look . . . as . . . beautiful when . . . she's gone
. . . eighty. The . . . major now . . . the major
. . . will look . . . kind of hard. A man . . . *needs*
. . . a woman like . . . Arlene.'

'What are you saying to me there, Nate?'

'Anything should . . . should happen . . .'

'Nothing's going to happen.'

'*Anything* . . . should happen!' Adderly
insisted, 'you've got . . . to promise me . . .
you'll see that . . . she and young . . . John are
OK. You *must* . . . promise.'

'Will you stop that kind of talk? Nothing's
going to happen. You're going to go home to

233

your wife and son, if I have to drag you all the way. *They* need *you*. You got that?'

'Promise!' Adderly insisted once more.

'Nathan . . .'

'*Promise!*'

Garner sighed. 'If it means you'll quit this crazy talking, I promise.'

'You'll look . . . after them? Arlene's going . . . to need you . . . there.'

Believing it must be the delirium, Garner decided to humour the pilot. 'I'll look after them.'

'OK.'

'And Nate . . .'

'Yeah?'

'If you go dying on me, I swear I'll beat you to death.'

Adderly chuckled.

It was about 13.00 hours when an airman brought in a single sheet of paper to the colonel.

Dempsey had left the room just once, for a call of nature. Shelley Hoag had also remained. Coffees had been brought to them; but neither had gone to breakfast. Neither seemed keen to go to lunch either.

Dempsey read the message and handed it,

without speaking, to Shelley Hoag, who looked as fresh as if she'd had a full night's sleep.

She read it silently.

'My God,' she then said as she handed it back. 'They've gone public.'

'Good propaganda,' Dempsey commented with dry resignation. '"American imperialists",' he quoted without looking at the sheet of paper, '"invaded our airspace during the night. Our glorious comrades have shot them down and are now hunting out the criminal pilot. He will be found and tried for crimes against the people". How'd I do?'

'Word-perfect.'

'At least they still haven't found the wreckage; or the seats. They said "pilot". One crew member. They don't know it's an Echo Eagle. That's something.'

'They could be lying, to keep us guessing.'

'They could. But whatever the real situation, we don't let them get their hands on those boys.' Dempsey paused. 'We've got to hope that Adderly and Garner are not injured. At least, not seriously enough to cause incapacitation.'

'What if they've already got them?'

Dempsey shook his head. 'They couldn't have stopped themselves from crowing about it. They're holding back on something, but not

235

this. A capture would have been too much to keep quiet about. They need the propaganda, especially with Taiwan shaping up to be the next flashpoint.

'Even if there have been injuries,' the colonel went on, 'they're still mobile, or they've managed to hole up somewhere, to wait till nightfall. As for the three countries involved with the mountain base, they sure as hell won't want too much public light on that little secret. There's going to be some horse-trading, so they badly need to make a capture. They want another TV show, like that time with the helicopter on the southern border. We must make damn sure they don't get it.'

'You know the insertion team's recommendations, sir,' Shelley Hoag reminded him. 'We can't mount the rescue mission till tonight.'

'I know, Major,' Dempsey admitted, curbing his frustration. 'I know. The worst of it is, I have to agree. But if we do . . . *when* we get them out, our friends across the water will suddenly go mighty quiet. They know we've caught them with their pants down. As I've said, there'll be some horse-trading . . . but not with those two boys for bargaining chips. We *must* get them out of there.'

Dempsey rubbed at his nose in quiet agitation. Then as he saw Shelley Hoag watching him, he stopped, looking slightly sheepish.

'Sir,' she began solicitously. 'Why don't you go get some rest? Not much you can do right now but wait.'

'I'm not going down till I know those boys are safe. *They're* not in some cosy bed. What kind of a commander would I be?'

'One who conserves his strength?'

'I'm fine, Major. You go get some sleep.'

She shook her head. 'The colonel stays, I stay.'

Dempsey gave her a tight smile. 'Stubborn too. You worried about Garner?'

'I'm worried about both of them, sir.'

'Now that's a good answer.'

The old man, dressed in the ubiquitous peasant-style jacket and trousers, rode the bicycle slowly along the empty road. There was a covered bamboo basket secured to the pillion. He kept going until he came to the general area where Adderly had landed, then stopped, got off the cycle, and wheeled it to where the pilot had been lying when Garner had found him.

After carefully laying the cycle against a small tree, the old man simply stood there, perfectly still, looking out across the lake. Then he began turning very slowly so that he appeared not to be moving at all, his position altering fluidly.

He studied the ground about him as he turned. When he had finished, he retrieved the bicycle and once more stood for a few seconds, as if waiting for something to happen. His head again turned slowly, his eyes missing nothing.

Then once again he stood still. His gaze was locked upon the high, wooded ground beyond the railway track. He seemed convinced of something.

He mounted the bicycle, and rode back the way he had come.

'You know . . . Helena had the . . . most beautiful . . . grey eyes.'

'Hell, Nathan! Quit startling me like that! I never know when you're going to start talking. I thought you were grabbing some zees.'

The familiar soft chuckle came out of the gloom, and Garner primed himself for the cough to follow, but there wasn't one.

'As I said . . . Helena . . . your ancestor . . . had grey eyes . . . like yours . . . like mine. Arlene noticed that . . . straight off . . . first time she . . . saw you . . . and me . . . together. And here . . . we are in this . . . in a cave . . . in a country . . . far from ours . . . where . . . no one can . . . see our . . . eyes. Crazy life . . . huh?'

Then the cough arrived. It was more prolonged than any of the previous ones and when
it was over, Adderly sounded short of breath.

Garner switched on his torch to look at
him.

'Hey!' Adderly said. 'Trying . . . to blind . . .
me? Put . . . the darned thing . . . out.'

'Just checking you out.'

'I'm OK. Just . . . a cough.'

Garner put out the torch. He had checked
round Adderly's mouth, but could see nothing
amiss. He went back to his sitting position by
the mouth of the cave.

Long before, he'd removed his G-suit, and
had folded it so as to make a pillow for Adderly's
head to rest upon. The pilot had now moved off
it, during the bout of coughing, so Garner slid
it gently back beneath his head.

'Want something to drink – or eat?' he
asked.

'No . . . thanks. Not hungry. Not thirsty. Did
I tell you . . . about Arlene?'

'You told me.'

'Hell of . . . a woman. I ever . . . told you
. . . she once knocked . . . a guy flat on . . .
his ass?'

'Haven't heard that one. When did this
happen?'

Better to let him continue to talk about Arlene, Garner decided. It was obvious that thinking about her kept him in good spirits.

'I think we . . . were in some . . . shopping mall . . . somewhere,' Adderly said. 'Can't . . . can't quite . . . remember. I'd left . . . her by a perfume counter . . . and this . . . jerk came up . . . to her and put . . . his hand on . . . her ass. She was . . . wearing . . . short shorts.' A soft chuckle as he remembered. 'Boy! She zapped that . . . guy right in . . . the kisser. I mean . . . *zap*!'

'What did she use?'

'Use? Her *fist*! She's got . . . a mean right . . . hand. Remember that. The guy went . . . down. I don't mean . . . staggered. He went . . . *down*. Right on his . . . ass. I was . . . proud of . . . her. That's my . . . Arlene.'

Adderly was suddenly quiet, as if the talking had exhausted him. Garner, again anxious, began to move back to check on him. But Adderly sensed the movement.

'You're . . , fussing again, Milt. Sit down. I'm just . . . having another rest.'

'OK.'

Arlene had woken suddenly without quite knowing why.

240

A weak night light was on, near the baby's cot. She looked anxiously at the infant, wondering if perhaps he had whimpered in his sleep, triggering her mothering instincts. Her highly alert state was another legacy of the loss of the first baby.

But he was peacefully sleeping the night away, as always.

She glanced at the digital alarm clock. It was 1.30. So why had she woken, if not for the baby?

She sat up in bed, pondering upon it for some moments, trying not to think it was anything to do with Nathan. She always worried about him.

But what wife of the fighter crews didn't?

Every wife and girlfriend she'd spoken to about it when she had first got married had told her essentially the same thing in her own way. Each coped according to her own personality. Some looked upon it as part of the territory, and had long come to terms with the fact that they knew what they had been getting into, before they'd done the deed. There was little point in making a big deal about it. But one thing Arlene was certain of: they all worried.

There was a small television set on a bedside table, with headphones attached. She propped herself up against the pillows, turned on the set, and put on the headphones. She switched on the TV. It came on in the middle of a newsflash.

'. . . and they claim . . .' the anchorman was saying, 'to have shot down a Western military aircraft, in the early hours of the morning, local time. There is as yet no confirmation. I'll repeat that: *no* confirmation. We'll bring you more news about this incident directly. But now, to Joanne Marr in Washington for a Pentagon comment, and Don Yamuchi in Tokyo . . .'

Arlene raised her hand to her mouth slowly. 'Oh no,' she whispered, dreading to hear more. 'Please don't let it be Nate and Milton. Please, God. Not them.'

When they went on their various deployments, Nathan did not always call if, for operational reasons, it was not feasible to do so. As far as she knew, he was still out there in Arizona. So why should she worry if something had happened way out in the Far East?

She could always call to check with the base. But she was reluctant to do anything that might reflect badly on Nathan.

She turned off the TV, as if suddenly repelled by it. Removing the headphones, she placed them with exaggerated care on top of the set, before folding her arms tightly across her chest.

She remained propped up against the pillows, staring at the baby's cot, hugging herself, and shaking.

At the mountain base, Major Udlov strode towards the room where he was to be interviewed by the three commanders of the unit.

Colonel Peng was Senior Officer Commanding. Colonel Krashinev was First Deputy Commander and Colonel Ongg, North Korean, Second Deputy Commander. All were experienced fighter pilots. Though officially of equal status, everyone, especially the Russian aircrew and ground personnel, knew this was a face-saving exercise. In reality, Krashinev was the true commander. Russian personnel irreverently called them the Troika. Udlov was well aware of this, having heard the term used by some of his own fellow officers.

Udlov had been picked up by helicopter within forty-five minutes of being shot down. Unlike Garner and Adderly, he'd had the luxury of being able to keep his location beacon continuously transmitting, without fear of being captured.

But Udlov was not feeling particularly happy. He had already been grilled by the unit's three intelligence officers – another troika, he mused sourly – and the general consensus was that he should not have allowed himself to be shot down.

You should have been there, he'd thought grimly, listening to their waffle. How well would you have done?

None of the intelligence officers – one of whom was a woman and the North Korean representative – had any flying experience. It had galled him to listen to them questioning tactics they clearly knew very little about.

He enjoyed the reputation of being the ace of the base. He was also the senior fighter instructor. But the fact that he had not only lost his best pupil among the Koreans, but had himself been vanquished by the as-yet-unknown Westerner, was doing that reputation no good at all. Last night's events, he knew, would seriously dent it. He would have to do some rapid retrieval, and he believed he knew how best to accomplish that. It helped to know that Ling had made it back.

He would be pleased when the Western pilot, if still alive, was eventually caught. He would like to meet the man who had cost him two Su-27Ks, a promising student, *and* dealt his reputation such a blow, face to face. There was one way to ensure it.

Udlov was in a foul temper. The only thing that alleviated this was the fact that the other pilot had not yet escaped, and was even now endeavouring to avoid capture; if he had survived the hit by the surface-to-air missile.

Ready for anything, Udlov marched into the room and saluted smartly.

'We will not stand on ceremony, Comrade,' Colonel Peng began immediately, speaking Russian. 'Please sit down.'

Udlov knew that Peng's rapid opening of the proceedings had less to do with putting him at ease than with establishing the pecking order over his fellow colonels. As representative of the base's host country, he clearly felt this was the correct state of affairs.

'Thank you, Comrade Colonel,' Udlov said respectfully and sat down on the straight-backed chair that had been placed there for him.

'We have the intelligence report on your combat,' Peng continued, clearly intent on keeping the initiative over the others. 'Now we would like to hear of it from you.'

Udlov glanced at Krashinev, who gave him the barest perceptible sanction. Peng caught the glance and for the most fleeting of seconds, he looked annoyed.

Then Udlov gave a factual account of what

had occurred, making no embellishments. When he had finished, it was the Korean who looked offended.

'Are you blaming Captain Yeung for this . . . fiasco?' he demanded.

Fiasco, Udlov thought contemptuously.

There was another North Korean senior officer, a lieutenant colonel, who sometimes deputized for Ongg. Udlov had a lot of time for him. The lieutenant colonel would have understood the situation, without waving national dignity in everybody's face. Udlov frequently thought the appointments were in the wrong order. Ongg should have been the underling.

'With great respect, Comrade Colonel,' he now said, 'I strongly advised him against precipitate action. As both my student and my wingman, he was under my orders.'

'Captain Yeung cannot speak for himself.'

'He brought about his own death.' Udlov was unrepentant.

The North Korean colonel bristled, but Udlov steamrollered through the possible interruption.

'When you have listened to the cockpit recordings, sir,' Udlov continued, 'you'll hear me clearly forbidding him to attack while he was still out of position. He was to follow my lead. I believe he wanted to make a kill over the border, for glory.'

'*How dare you!*' Ongg snapped. 'You are besmirching a noble comrade!'

Udlov was still irritated by the interview with the intelligence officers, and was in no mood to be lectured by anyone, particularly Ongg. He was the best Su-27K pilot around and if they wanted to relieve him of his command, that was their affair. The entire training programme would grind to a halt, as the other instructors would not be happy with the change.

'I *dare*, Comrade Colonel,' he now said, 'because I have spent several weeks pounding the correct procedures into the dead noble comrade's head! It was his *first* night flight, and the first time he was carrying live weapons. No one expected to find a hostile fighter right on our doorstep. Ground control didn't warn us until too late! In such circumstances, it was insane of him not to have listened to someone of experience; to have ignored his superior officer and senior instructor! Perhaps he even panicked. I *won't* accept the blame for someone who disobeys orders, and is then killed by his own folly! Compare *that* with Captain Ling, who brought back his severely damaged aircraft.'

Udlov stopped, eyes unflinchingly holding on to the Korean colonel's. It was Peng who stepped in to cool things down.

'Yet you, an experienced fighter pilot, were shot down.' The Chinese colonel spoke softly, clearly impressed by Ling.

'I make no excuses,' Udlov said. 'He surprised me, and he was good.' He knew his comments about Ling had gone down well.

'You sound as if you admire the intruder.'

'If an opponent is good, there is no disgrace in honouring him, even if you want his destruction.'

Peng inclined his head slightly. 'A commendable attitude which finds favour with me. Nevertheless, this foreigner has done us considerable damage and cannot be allowed to get away with it. If he is still alive, he must be found before the imperialists attempt to rescue him.'

'If I may be permitted,' Udlov said, 'I would like to lead the hunt. During the recent rapprochement with the West, I had the opportunity to visit some of their units and talk with their pilots. I believe I have a general idea of how they would behave under these circumstances. I may know what to look for. I also want the squad who fired the missile that brought down the foreigner to be placed under my command.'

Peng looked at Krashinev, who had not spoken at all but had been observing the entire proceedings keenly. The Russian's eyes now held his compatriot's gaze.

Still looking at Udlov, Krashinev gave another of his barely perceptible signals.

'I think it's a good idea,' he remarked.

The North Korean colonel looked outraged, but chose not to raise any objection.

The old man did not look up when he heard the helicopter. He was sitting at the edge of the lake, his bicycle lying on its side next to him. The woven bamboo basket was close to hand.

The helicopter, a huge predatory insect bearing the insignia of the three allied countries, touched down a hundred yards away.

A squad of soldiers leapt out.

The helicopter rose into the air once more, almost before the last man hit the ground. The aircraft, a Mil Mi-24 assault gunship, originally dubbed the Hind by NATO, was heavily armed and armoured. This was an advanced version with a full complement of radar and infrared sensors, and carried four rocket pods beneath its mid-mounted stub wings. It also had fixed twin 23mm guns mounted on the right side of its nose. Wheeling about within its own length, it headed off the way it had come.

The soldiers approached the old man at a fast trot. When they had come to within a few yards, they stopped and fanned out. The junior NCO leading them strode arrogantly towards him. They were the same North Korean squad who had shot down Adderly and Garner.

'*You!* Old man! What are you doing here?'

'Fishing,' the old man replied calmly, 'as you can see. I have been fishing here for years. And have you no respect for your elders?' He reached into his peasant's jacket and took out a small document. 'I am permitted.'

'And have you caught anything?'

'Alas . . . so far today, the fish are smarter than I am.' The old man gave a deprecating shrug.

'What's in that basket?'

'Food. You may look if you wish.'

'I do not need your permission!'

The squad leader stared at the old man coldly, but made no move to check the basket. At last, he deigned to look at the document.

While he was doing so the soldier who had fired the missile stared quizzically at the old man.

The squad leader handed back the document,

and was slightly less belligerent. 'Have you seen anyone else around here?'

'Should I have?'

'Just answer me!'

'But what kind of person?'

'That is none of your affair!'

'Then how am I to know if I have seen the right person?'

'I said *anyone*! That is all you need to know!'

'Then I have seen no one. I have been here all alone.'

'Why did you not say so in the beginning?' the squad leader demanded crossly.

'You confused me,' the old man replied apologetically.

'You are very far from your village.'

'I often go long distances on my bicycle,' the old man explained. 'The people of my village know this. I have done this for years also.'

The squad leader made a dismissive sound and went back to his men. The one who had fired the missile spoke urgently to him. The squad leader stiffened, then strode back to the old man.

'One of my men believes he knows you.'

The old man turned to peer at the other soldiers, squinting against the bright sun.

'My eyes . . .' he began. 'They are not as they used to be . . .'

'He says you come from his village, and that you are the father of a comrade, a glorious fighter pilot.'

'I do have a son who flies one of those machines, yes. I don't know how he does it. I would not go into one of these things . . .'

'He is doing good work protecting us against the imperialist dogs. He is protecting you so that you can fish in freedom!'

'I am very proud of him.'

The squad leader had become respectful now. He stood to attention as he spoke. 'You should have told me who you are.'

'One should not boast. We all serve our glorious country in our own way.'

'Yes. Yes. You are correct. We must now be on our way. We are hunting enemies of the people.'

'Then I wish you success.'

'Thank you, respected Comrade.'

The squad leader was now courtesy itself. He saluted the old man and went back to his men. He bawled out orders and the entire group trotted off. They did not go across the railway track, towards the woods.

The old man watched them leave, then

glanced in the direction of the high ground. He looked down at the basket and made no move to take anything to eat from it.

He calmly went back to his fishing.

In the cave, both Garner and Adderly had heard the sound of rotors.

'Ours?' Adderly asked in a sharp whisper.

'Not a chance,' Garner replied. 'They wouldn't be crazy enough to do this in daylight. The hunting dogs have been let loose.' He cocked his automatic pistol as softly as he could, and waited. 'Sounds like it's moving away.'

'Perhaps . . . they've dropped . . . troops.'

'Could be.'

'If that . . . chopper's got . . . heat sensors . . .'

'We're safe in here. Those sensors would have to try to see right through this mountain. And we've been in here long enough not to have left any traces outside.'

'As long as . . . they don't . . . use real . . . dogs.'

'Yeah,' Garner agreed. 'That could give us a problem. But first, they've got to have an idea of where we may be. If they haven't found the airplane, they won't know how many people they're looking for. Hell, pieces of the bird must be all over the place anyway.

It could take them months, maybe years, to find it all.'

'Did I . . . just hear . . . you cock . . . that pistol?'

'You did. They won't take us. Not alive, that's for sure. But we will be getting out of here. I'm going to get you back to Arlene, and to your boy.'

'That's a promise . . . is it?'

'It is. Besides, she'd never forgive me if I didn't.'

'She'd . . . understand . . . if she knew . . . what really happened.'

'She won't have to, because you're going to be right there.'

'Not . . . trying to be . . . a VF-32 . . . hero . . . in reverse, are you?'

'What? VF-32? That's *Navy*.'

Was Adderly going into another bout of delirium? Garner wondered. What was all this about a Navy squadron? And what was happening in reverse?

'The Swordsmen,' Adderly was saying. 'Korea, 1953. They had . . . a black Ensign. First black . . . Navy aviator. He was . . . giving air support . . . to the Marines . . . at Chosin. Hit by . . . ground fire. He crash . . . landed on . . . a rough-as-hell . . . mountain . . . slope. He got down . . . OK . . . but was trapped . . . in cockpit. His white . . . buddy force . . . landed his . . . own plane . . . to try . . . rescue. Tried to . . . put out the fire . . . on his buddy's . . . plane with bare . . . hands. The black . . . guy died in . . . the end. They both . . . got medals. The guy . . . who died . . . got the post . . . posthumous DFC. The other guy . . . got the . . . Medal of Honour . . . from the President . . . too . . .'

Adderly lapsed into silence.

For a while, Garner too was silent as he thought about Adderly's story of the Navy pilots.

'The only medal I want,' he eventually said in a quiet voice, 'is the smile on Arlene's face when she sees you. OK?'

'But what if . . .'

'*OK?*'

'Sure.'

Udlov was in a second Mi-24. As heavily armed and comprehensively equipped as its sister machine, it clattered low over the dense covering of a mountainside. It was thirty-five kilometres from where Garner and Adderly lay hidden, and going away from them.

In the cabin of the helicopter, Udlov was strapped to his seat staring at one infrared, and one radar monitor that had been specially rigged up for him. Everything that the co-pilot gunner in the forward of the two bulbous cockpits saw would be relayed to him. As yet, nothing of interest had appeared on either screen.

In the seven other seats were three Russian and four Chinese soldiers. The crews of both helicopters were also Russian. All were under Udlov's overall command, but with a Russian captain in charge of the combined assault troops.

If the pilot who had shot him down had managed to get out before being hit by the missile, Udlov now reasoned, the ejection seat should be within the area. If the hit had been too quick to allow ejection, then pieces of the aircraft would soon come to light. In the case of the first scenario, he hoped to get to that pilot well before a rescue was mounted.

On the ground, some two kilometres from Garner and Adderly, the squad passed within twenty feet of where Adderly's seat lay, half buried in an abundantly overgrown gully. It had thumped itself down there, even as the Echo Eagle was being consumed by its fuel and the detonated charges.

The squad kept going.

10

'*Arlene!*'

The loudly whispered name had Garner scrabbling over to Adderly's side. 'Nate! You OK?'

'Wh . . . what? Oh. Yeah. Sure. What did . . . I do?'

'You called Arlene. Louder than normal. I kind of wondered if . . .'

'No sweat. I'm . . . I'm OK. Must have . . . dreamed . . . I guess.'

'Here. Let me check you over.'

'No . . . need. I'm fine.'

'I'll do it, anyway. I won't move you. Just a routine inspection.'

'Did I say . . . you were . . . a mother . . . hen?'

'Yeah, yeah. You did.'

'That's not . . . going to . . . stop you . . .'

'Nope.'

257

A sigh. 'I guess.'

Garner had got out his torch and was looking Adderly over even as they spoke. The arm still did not seem to have bled further. He looked at the booted, damaged ankle. Little point in unlacing it until they had access to proper medical attention.

He checked Adderly's head, but did not touch it. Adderly seemed comfortable enough. However, Garner was worried about the swelling by the temple, which seemed to have grown slightly.

He put out the light.

'Is . . . is it me?' Adderly began. 'Or . . . does this . . . cave seem darker?'

'The day's nearly done. It's just after 17.00 hours. Soon be night, and we can get out of here. They haven't found us, so just hang in there a little longer. Need a drink, or a bite?'

'No. That tablet's . . . still working.'

'All right. Look . . . I'm going to grab me a little shut-eye. But I'll be right here by the entrance. Just sing out if you want anything. I'll just be having a catnap.'

'Go right ahead. You've been . . . awake all this . . . time while I've been getting all . . . the sleep. Go . . . go on. I'll yell . . . if I hurt too . . . much.'

'Not a yell. Please! Think of the neighbours!'

Adderly chuckled. The cough didn't sound.

'See?' he said triumphantly. 'No cough.'

Garner smiled in the gloom and shut his eyes, to try and get some sleep.

It was the Hind that had dropped the Korean squad that made the first discovery.

The co-pilot/gunner, searching with both radar and infrared sensors, caught something motionless on radar. They went closer to investigate. Hovering close to some treetops, they were astonished to discover the Echo Eagle's completely intact tailplane. It was lying on the top branches, twenty-five kilometres from the cave, and its only blemish was a large scorch mark on its upper surface. It was 18.00 hours local time.

They informed Udlov immediately.

The second Mi-24 arrived on the scene within twenty minutes and stood off to one side. Sliding down from their helicopter, two Russian soldiers hung by their ropes from their hovering aircraft, and secured the tailplane in a harness. With the two men and the captive tailplane now dangling beneath it, the helicopter, in company with Udlov's, moved away from the trees to a patch of open ground about a kilometre away.

Udlov's machine touched down, while the soldiers hanging from the other Mi-24 dropped the few feet to the ground. Then the tailplane was put gently down, and the harness released. The Mi-24 then landed.

Udlov hurried to inspect the find. Light was fading in the clearing, and he used a torch to do so.

'This is from an Eagle,' he said. 'See that dog-tooth here at the leading edge? An Eagle,' he repeated.

So that's what he'd been up against. Had the pilot survived? He had a sudden thought. An Eagle. What if it had been the advanced *Eagle E*? There could be *two* crew members. An even bigger coup.

He glanced up at the darkening sky. 'Everybody gather round,' he ordered and when they had done so, went on, 'The light's going, but that does not matter. We're going to work all night, and all day tomorrow and beyond, if necessary. We'll give our search area a radius of thirty kilometres from this point. Look for the ejection seat. There may also be two crew members, so you may find two seats. Look for more bits of the aircraft, parachutes, helmets, discarded flight clothing . . . anything that points to the downed American.'

He stopped and got out a map of the area from his flight overalls, then walked over to the port stub wing of the nearest helicopter and laid the map on it.

They followed, forming a loose group about him.

He drew a rough circle, using their current position as its centre. He then quartered the circle and numbered each segment clockwise.

He looked at the Russian captain. 'Arkady, you and your men take sector one.'

Arkady Litiniev nodded.

'I'll take sector two,' Udlov continued, 'using the squad that was dropped off by that small lake. We'll pick them up when we leave here, so you can have their chopper. I'll be calling up two more 24s, each with troops, and give them the information for sectors three and four. They can go directly to their assigned area.

'I want you all to look for *anything* and *everything*. As I've said, we may actually have two of them out there, if they survived the SAM. You've got your night-sights. Find him, or them. We want a prisoner, or prisoners. Not dead bodies . . . unless we find them that way. And we want them *before* the Americans come for them.'

'And if we can't do that?' In the gathering gloom, Litiniev's eyes were shadows. 'If we can't take him . . . them alive?'

'*Alive*, Arkady,' Udlov said quietly. 'All right, everybody. Go to it!'

They ran to their machines. Soon, the predator insects were lifting off the ground. From his helicopter, Udlov called up the Korean squad and made a rendezvous.

The cave where Garner and Adderly were hiding fell neatly into sector three.

Garner awoke suddenly. He looked at the glow on his watch: 19.00 hours. He'd been down longer than he'd intended.

'Nathan!'

'I'm here.'

Garner felt a huge relief, and moved over. 'How are you feeling?'

'OK. But my . . . head's . . . slipped off the . . . speed jeans.'

'Soon fix that.'

Garner shone the torch briefly to find the rough pillow, then placed it back beneath Adderly's head.

'Thanks,' the pilot said.

'It's going to be time to be heading to the RV soon, Nate,' Garner said. 'I've thought hard about this and I want you to tell me if you can move. The truth now. I don't want to leave you here in case that chopper comes back. But when we're out there, we could be sitting ducks for night-sights. Our choppers will have a doctor and a medic aboard. It might make better sense for me to go out and bring them back, instead of my doing you more damage by dragging you three or four miles . . .'

'Could you . . . love someone . . . like Arlene?' Adderly posed the question instead of replying to Garner.

'*What?* What are you saying now, Nathan?'

'Could . . . you . . . love someone . . . like Arlene?'

'Any man with red blood . . .'

'Could *you*? I know . . . you . . . understand the . . . question.'

'What is this? You're passing your wife on to me now?'

'I want you . . . to look . . . after her. She's . . . going to need . . . you.'

'Hey, man. You're scaring me. Don't talk like that.'

'Makes . . . makes . . . sense.'

'That kind of talk does *not* make sense! You just hang on in there, Nathan Adderly. You hear me?'

'I . . . hear . . .'

'And before you know it we'll be on that chopper, heading away from this place. Like that.'

Garner clicked the fingers of his right hand. Only there was no clicking sound. The fingers felt sticky. He must have touched a bug and squashed it, he decided, and tentatively sniffed at them in the dark. He expected a pungent smell. What he got made his heart suddenly beat faster.

He shone the torch on the folded G-suit, and felt as if he'd been hit in the stomach. A smear of bright blood was on the fabric. But where from?

Then he saw the corners of Adderly's mouth. Internal bleeding. The worst. Lungs.

Even as he watched, Adderly coughed and the blood welled out of him.

'Jesus, Nate! Why didn't you tell me?'

Heart in mouth, Garner gently removed the G-suit pillow, enabling Adderly to lie flat, then moved the pillow to the legs, to raise them off the floor of the cave. Keeping the legs higher would help the heart pump blood upwards, but short of wiping Adderly's mouth periodically, there was very little else he could do. Adderly needed urgent medical care.

'Tell . . . you . . . what?'

'You're hurt inside . . .'

Garner stopped. Adderly *had* been telling him. All that stuff about Arlene . . .

Adderly sensed Garner's realization. 'Now . . . now you . . . know.'

'I'm getting you out!'

'Move me . . . and you . . . kill me . . . anyway . . .'

Garner was distraught. 'Nate! You can't do this.'

'I . . . didn't . . . the SAM . . . did . . .' Adderly's voice faded.

Garner sat in the dark cave, listening to his friend die and felt the tears in his eyes.

This just isn't right, he thought helplessly.

Adderly had needed urgent medical attention, virtually from the moment he'd landed after ejection. Internal injuries were enemies of time.

What was Nathan Adderly doing so far from home, dying in a cave on a Korean hillside? What of the baby boy he should be watching grow up?

'And what am I going to say to Arlene?' he said aloud.

'Tell . . . her . . . you love . . . her . . .'

'Nathan! You're going to be OK!'

'Shh . . . !'

Garner felt a hand groping for his, and held on to it.

'Gentlemen!'

Garner jerked at the sound of the voice outside the cave, then remained absolutely still. It was then that he realized there was an abnormal heaviness about Adderly's hand.

He felt for a pulse. There was none. When had Adderly died?

'Gentlemen!' came the voice again.

Garner drew his pistol.

'I know you are in there,' the voice said pleasantly. 'No need to cock your weapons. I am a friend.'

Garner said nothing.

'I will give you a short history. Perhaps you will then believe me. In 1951, a pilot was shot down. He did not return to his homeland, but remained here. Is this a help?'

Garner still waited. North Korean Intelligence might easily know that story.

'I will say a name,' the voice continued. 'Green Ringer. Please hurry. The helicopter and the troops will be back. Perhaps with reinforcements. I have been waiting all day to make contact.'

Garner still waited.

'How about Cactus?'

That got Garner's attention.

What the hell, he thought after a while. I can't stay in here for ever.

He began to make his way out of the cave. When he was eventually outside, his gloom-accustomed eyes made out the figure of an old man.

'At last!' the man said. 'You can put away your gun. I am a friend. Where is your colleague? We must hurry. I have brought food. You can eat on the way. This is a very good hiding place that you have found. I once used it myself, a long time ago.'

'He's dead,' Garner said flatly.

'Ah. I am sorry . . .'

'I'm not leaving him in there.'

The old man was silent and Garner knew he was being scrutinized.

'I understand,' the old man said at last. 'I, too, once lost many close friends. I have a bicycle. We shall manage.'

With some difficulty, they finally got Adderly's body out of the cave. The old man had brought more than food in the basket. They used lengths of light rope to tie Adderly to the bike and, supporting it on either side, they walked down the slope and on to the road.

They began walking towards the RV.

*   *   *

The squad had found nothing by the time Udlov's helicopter had picked them up.

As it beat across its designated area of search, the squad leader spoke to Udlov.

'We saw an old man by the lake today, Comrade Major.'

Udlov looked at him. 'Why did you not mention this on the radio?'

'He was fishing. He frequently fishes there. He has papers of authority.'

'What has that got to do with it? He might have seen something, or someone.'

'I interrogated him. He had seen no one. I also discovered . . .' The squad leader paused, clearly uncomfortable.

'Yes?'

The NCO cleared his throat, looked round at his men.

'Are you addressing me? Or them?'

'You, Comrade Major.'

'Then please continue.'

'The old man has a son in the People's Air Force.'

'I see. What is this son's status?'

'He is a lieutenant colonel.'

Udlov stared at the NCO. 'I see,' he repeated. 'And this officer's name?'

The NCO told him.

It was the name of the deputy to Colonel Ongg.

'My son is also a fighter pilot,' the old man was saying conversationally.

'Like you used to be.'

'Yes.'

'Isn't what you're doing against what he stands for?'

'On the contrary. He wants a democratic nation, and does not want this country to be involved in another war. The only way is to eventually merge with the South, democratically. A war would bring suffering far worse than the one which first brought me here. We desire the same thing. He believes that for real change to occur, you must be on the inside. He is a lieutenant colonel at the base.'

Garner nearly lost his grip on the bicycle. '*He* gave you the information?'

'Oh no. He is not involved in this. My squadron was wiped out by your Sabres,' the old man went on. A sad note had crept into his voice. 'It is ironic to meet you, an American airman, here. Our squadron commander, a fierce pilot in combat, was killed. Such a beautiful woman, our Valentina.' He paused, remembering. 'I believe she was in love with one of your pilots.'

Garner remembered the strange story Shelley Hoag had told. It seemed incredible; but in wartime many strange things happened. The old man's own history was a case in point.

'How can you be sure?' he asked.

'They met during the end-of-war celebrations,' the old man said. 'I believe they even kissed.' He sighed. 'Life is sometimes most cruel. In a better world, they might have become man and wife. Who knows? He was the only one who could have beaten her in combat. And he did.'

For a while they walked the bicycle, with its dead rider, in silence.

'You were close?' the old man began once more. 'You and your friend?'

'He is family,' Garner said.

If the old man thought that strange, he made no comment about it.

'It is even harder,' he said, 'when the lost one is family.'

Garner nodded in the darkness and said nothing. He walked on, feeling the weight of Adderly's body against his left shoulder.

The rescue mission was on its way.

The two Blackhawk helicopters skimmed the water, escorted by two Apache gunships spread out on either side, and holding station. They were there to deter any interference with the mission. The Blackhawks' crews were, like the troops they carried, and the doctor and medical assistant, US Marines. The Apaches were also flown by Marines.

Before they'd left, the briefing had been to the point.

'Go in,' their colonel had said. 'Get them, and get out. We're not looking for a fight, but if anyone tries to stop the mission . . . waste him.'

They had cheered loudly. Soon, they would be crossing ultra-low, over the coast.

Udlov's gunship made the next find. They spotted a big chunk of the Echo Eagle lying half-submerged in a fast-flowing stream, some fifteen kilometres north of the cave.

The gunship settled down near a bank and Udlov and his Korean troops climbed out. Using night-vision binoculars, he studied what looked like a long piece of the side of the cockpit.

The squad leader started moving towards the stream.

'Stay where you are!' Udlov ordered in Korean. He kept looking at the piece of the aircraft, then he took the glasses away from his eyes and spoke into the radio attached to his flight suit. 'Turn on your landing lights,' he said to the pilot.

The lights came on, shining clearly on the chunk of aircraft in the water.

'All right,' he said to the NCO. 'Take a man and get it out. Be careful of booby-traps.'

'Yes, Comrade Major.'

The NCO called to one of his men and together, they waded into the stream. They had to struggle to get it out, because it had embedded itself into the bottom of the stream.

Udlov sent a third man to help. Eventually they managed it, and dragged the piece of wreckage to the bank.

Udlov saw the two inverted black triangles with the word 'DANGER' stencilled along each side, and within the triangles the white stencilled captions 'EJECTION SEAT' and 'CANOPY'.

'And now we know,' Udlov remarked softly. 'Two cockpits. An Eagle E. There are *two* of them!' he went on to the troopers. 'We'll note the location and leave this for the salvage teams. Now back on board! Let us find these Americans!'

'Now all we have to do,' the old man said, 'is wait.'

They had arrived at the RV, which was a kilometre beyond the road and the southern shore of the lake; it was virtually on the coast.

From where he stood, Garner could make out distant lights, way out to sea. He knew those lights did not belong to the ships from which the rescue was being mounted. They would be well out of harm's way, beyond the horizon.

Then he heard rotors, coming from inland.

'This is not good,' he said. 'You should get away from here,' he went on to the old man. 'If they should find you . . .'

'I shall leave when your people arrive.'

They had untied Adderly, and laid him gently behind a screen of bushes large enough to hide them all.

But for how long?

'I can't ask you to do that,' Garner said.

'You're not asking me. It is my wish. If you listen, you may hear something on the breeze from the sea.'

Garner could hear nothing. 'I have perfect hearing, but . . .' He paused, listening. 'Yes! I hear rotors.'

'I shall leave now. You no longer need me.'

Not knowing what else to do, Garner stuck

out a hand. 'I cannot thank you enough. I am very sorry about your Valentina.'

The old man took the hand and shook it. 'That is the tragedy of our profession. I am sorry about your . . .'

'Cousin,' Garner said.

'Your cousin.'

'I hope your son succeeds.'

'It would be a worthwhile thing.'

Then the old man was leaving as the sound of rotors grew louder. In moments, he seemed to have disappeared.

Garner turned on his beacon briefly.

In the lead Blackhawk, a crewman said, '*Beacon!* They're at the RV!'

'OK, hogs!' the mission commander said into his radio. 'In and out. Fast.'

Then he heard from one of the Apaches. 'We have company! Moving to intercept.'

'Don't fire unless they do!'

'Roger. No engagement unless attacked.'

'Let's hope they feel the same way,' the rescue mission commander said to himself.

The Blackhawks crossed the coast.

'I've got helicopters!' the pilot of the Mi-24 in sector three called to Udlov's helicopter urgently, as he studied his radar. 'Four! Two are moving on an intercept course. Probably Apaches.'

Udlov fully understood what that meant. The Americans would fight to rescue their men. And the Apaches could make life exceedingly difficult. But would they attack first?

'On our way! Get the others to join us as quickly as they can,' he added to his pilot. 'They must *not* engage.'

'No engagement. Understood.' The pilot relayed the new orders to the remaining Hind gunships. 'They're on their way.'

Udlov considered his options. Shooting down an intruder was one thing. Attacking a rescue mission was another.

Had he got to the men first, the Americans' hands would have been tied. They would have had to have been prepared to follow inland, exposing themselves to the SAMs. This was different.

'Do not fire unless attacked.'

'Understood,' the pilot repeated.

While the Apaches and the Hinds stood off against each other in the dark, the Blackhawks landed.

The Marines jumped off and fanned out quickly, forming a protective screen about the RV.

*   *   *

'Captain Adderly?' a Marine lieutenant said to Garner. 'Lieutenant Corinni, sir. We've come to take you home.' Another Marine was with him. 'This is the doc.'

'Very pleased to see you, gentlemen. I'm Garner,' Garner was thankful for the darkness, so they wouldn't see his sorrow. 'Captain Adderly's just here. He's dead.'

The doctor immediately went to Adderly's body to check it.

'I'm sorry, sir,' Corinni said with deep sympathy. 'A fire-fight?'

'No. The SAM got him.'

The six gunships, monstrous dragonflies in the night, hung motionless, their rotors beating an ominous war cry at one another.

'What are they doing?' Udlov asked the pilot.

'Just sitting there,' came the response in his helmet. 'They're out of gun range, so they must have missiles. We are carrying none. They have almost certainly already picked their targets. We'd be out of the sky before we got near. What should we do?'

'Can you get an infrared picture? See if they really are carrying missiles.'

'I can,' It was the co-pilot/gunner who replied.

Seconds later Udlov was viewing the expanded picture of one of the Apaches. It bristled with missiles.

'Well, we know,' Udlov commented drily. 'We do exactly what they're doing. It's a stand-off. As they're carrying missiles, it's obvious they don't want to start a fight any more than we do in this situation. No one wants to escalate. They got there first. We stay here until they leave, just in case.'

Udlov still felt admiration for his opponents in the Eagle. They were an excellent and combative crew. He wouldn't have minded a return match one day.

Whoever they were, they'd managed to evade capture during the day, and were now about to make it back.

From the Americans' point of view, it had been a good haul. Two Su-27Ks down, one damaged; the base compromised, a student pilot dead, and a reputation severely dented.

From my point of view, he thought grimly, it's all downhill if I let Ongg have his way.

But Ongg would not have it his own way. It was time to talk seriously to the lieutenant colonel.

'The Apaches are leaving,' the pilot announced.

'They've picked up their people,' Udlov said. 'Nothing more we can do here. Back to base.'

Dempsey grabbed the phone as soon as it rang.

'We got them!' the Marine colonel's voice said in his ear.

'Good news! Good news!'

'It's not all good, Colonel.'

Dempsey went very still.

Shelley Hoag watched him closely, attempting to gauge the nature of the rest of the news by his reaction. But he was remaining impassive. When he'd finished, he put the phone down so slowly that she feared the worst.

'They've picked them up,' Dempsey told her.

She began to beam; then the beam faltered, then vanished altogether as she saw the pain in his eyes.

'Adderly's dead,' he said bluntly.

He thrust his hands in his pockets and went to stand by a window to look out at the lights of the airfield.

'Garner is totally wrecked by it,' he continued without looking round. 'He did his best to save him, but Adderly had serious internal injuries. They were holed up in a cave that Garner found.

If they hadn't been forced to stay in that damn hole all day, medical attention would have saved Adderly. Goddamit! I didn't want to lose that boy. I didn't want to lose either of them.'

'This is not your fault, sir.'

'It's somebody's. Might as well be me.'

Shelley Hoag did not argue with him, knowing it would be the very worst thing she could do. Like all strong commanders, he outwardly gave the impression he would mercilessly push his men to their limits and beyond. Inside, they always feared losing them. Like those same commanders, he would come to terms with it eventually, and in his own way. But for now, this was his time to give vent to his pain and anger.

'They got *two* Su-27s,' Dempsey went on, sounding as if it was a private conversation with himself. A note of pride had crept in. 'Maybe even a third. And they did the job they were sent out to do. Knew those boys were good. Hell, they got me and Carter in one hop. We lost one hell of a pilot today. We'd better make sure we don't lose one of the best damn wizzos around too. Those boys deserve medals. I'll see that they get them.'

Suddenly, Dempsey whirled and Shelley

Hoag was shocked by the haunted look in his eyes.

'Damn it, Major. We could have saved him! We *should* have!' The haunted eyes remained fastened upon Shelley Hoag. 'I'd like to be alone.'

'Sir,' she said, saluted him, and left the room.

In one of the Blackhawks, Garner sat with his hand on Adderly's body. The Marine doctor had gently tried to move the hand. In the subdued internal lighting the doctor had taken one look at Garner's eyes and had left well alone.

As the Blackhawk, leading the other three helicopters, headed back for the ship, they heard him speaking to the body.

'I'm going to transfer to the front seat,' they heard him say softly. 'I hope I can be as good a pilot as you. And I'll take good care of Arlene, cousin. And young John. I promise.'

He looked up from the body of his friend and kinsman, and saw the others staring at him.

He stared right back until eventually they were forced to look away.

The helicopters skimmed the darkened sea, taking their warriors away from the hostile shore.

WINGS 5

NORWEGIAN FIRE

Charles Anthony

1

Laerdal, Norway. May 1941

Per Ålvik lay flat against the steep slope, keeping
his head below the skyline. The laboured whine
of the engine of the German troop carrier, as it
made its way up the winding mountain road,
came distantly to him. He would have plenty
of time to set his ambush, he reasoned, and
to get away before they knew what hit them.
The troop carrier was still some way down the
mountain.

As he lay there he reflected upon how radically
his life had changed from what it had been
exactly a year earlier. Then, despite the war
storms further south in mainland Europe and
the increasing anxieties of the whole nation, he'd
still been hoping to continue his career as an
architect. True, he'd just been starting, but he'd
had ideas with which he'd hoped to revolution-
ize modern architecture, and not just in Norway.

He'd been looking forward to launching his designs internationally. Perhaps he could have been a new Frank Lloyd Wright.

Perhaps, he now thought grimly. How quickly dreams foundered against the rough seas of reality.

He'd been fooling himself. Nazi Germany had been crushing entire countries beneath its heel. It had only been a matter of time before it would be Norway's turn. Despite all the conciliatory propaganda about wanting to trade with a neutral Norway, the enemy had been preparing for invasion. But still he'd hung on to his dream of creating beautiful buildings; constructions for a benign civilization.

Instead, the barbarians had not only arrived at the gate but had comprehensively breached it, and were now in control. On the night of 8–9 April the year before, while everyone had still been vainly hoping that war would not come, the invasion had begun. The undermanned and under-armed national forces had not been able to cope. But the fight continued in the mountains.

The Allies should have seen it coming, he now thought. There had certainly been warning enough. We should have seen it coming. Then he raged at himself. *I* should have seen it coming.

Despite the passage of the year, he was still disgusted with the way he'd allowed his dreams to blind him. He had paid dearly for that folly; and something else had been added to the disgust. Guilt. He now carried enough to last a lifetime, although that might not prove long under the circumstances.

The Allies, with Norwegian forces, had wrested control from the enemy at Narvik, by 28 May, soundly beating him in the process. The French Foreign Legion had even captured Bjervik, thirty-two kilometres further north, in a pincer movement. All in vain. A brave, but woefully ill-prepared adventure had ended within a fortnight. The Allies, needing their troops in other theatres, had been forced to withdraw, and Norway had been left to watch the hope of a swift dispatch of the enemy comprehensively extinguished. The Germans had marched back into the battered town with its precious iron ore up for grabs, and had met no resistance. Instead, it was going to be a long, painful fight-back against the brutal invader, with no certainty of the outcome.

With the legitimate government-in-exile safely in England and the Quisling puppet serving the invaders, it was up to the members of the resistance – the Milorg and disparate underground groups – along with clandestine Allied forces, to continue the fight.

The fortunes of war had put Ålvik in command of such a group. There were just thirty in his command – including four women – but what they lacked in numbers, they more than made up for in impact. Of all the groups, they were among the most ruthless, and therefore the most feared by the enemy soldiers. They were also the most hunted.

Ålvik's transformation from dreaming creator of beautiful buildings to fearsome destroyer had begun the day he had travelled down to Bergen to visit his family, after six months in the mountains. He had taken the appalling risk because word had come that his mother had fallen dangerously ill and was not expected to live.

In the house that evening had been his father, who once had his own business and was himself not in the best of health, having been pressed into a local forced-labour group; his sixteen-year-old sister, Marianne, allowed to stay home to look after his mother; his fiancée, Elle, a teacher who now worked in a bakery; and his ten-year-old brother. And their neighbour.

Until that day Ålvik had been a reasonably courageous fighter; but there was nothing particularly special about him to distinguish him from the many other brave Norwegians who were fighting back any way they could. The events at the house, however, would eventually turn him into the sort of killer that would soon give him command of his own special team and, in turn, make him a man hunted with passion by the local SS.

The family's neighbour was a friend of many years, a man trusted by them all. What no one suspected at the time was that he was a Quisling who had been making reports about everyone who lived in the street. The arrival of Ålvik that night, smuggled into the house under the noses of the frequent patrols, was meant to have been his major coup.

A trap had been set for Ålvik's capture; but it was the young boy, Christer, who would save his older brother.

Christer had become restless and had found it difficult to come to terms with the fact that his mother was going to die. He had gone outside to sit alone, and to weep. It was then that he had seen surreptitious movement. With a wisdom beyond his years, he had given no sudden indication that he was aware of what was happening. He had remained sitting, loudly giving vent to his grief, then had gone back in as if he'd seen nothing. Once safely back in the house, he had pulled his brother to one side and whispered urgently to him.

Just then Ålvik had picked up a nervous glance in their direction, from the trusted neighbour. He had shown no reaction, but the survival instincts that had rapidly come to him during his still-limited experience in the field had made Ålvik realize instantly what was going on.

Feigning an urgent call of nature, he had sauntered out of the room as calmly as he could; but instead of making for the toilet, he had quickly headed for the cellar. There was a ground-level window down there, hidden by a high wall, and it would allow him to make his escape in the darkness. He was fortunate in that the SS troopers waiting to spring their ambush had not yet closed in on the house. He would not have made it if they had already been in place. Had it not been for Christer's impulsive rush outside . . .

Meanwhile, the boy had managed to place himself by the door to block the neighbour, in case the man should decide to follow and check if Ålvik had really gone to the toilet.

Continuing to play the picture of innocence, the neighbour had remained where he was.

However, he'd cast frequent worried glances at the door, waiting for Ålvik's return.

Ålvik had made good his escape, but his entire family and his fiancée had paid a dreadful price. His mother was shot where she lay, by the frustrated troopers who had stormed into the house. Christer was brought down by sub-machine-gun fire while trying to run. Elle and Marianne were taken away, raped repeatedly and then shot. The SS did not kill his father immediately. They made Henrik Ålvik work continuously, gradually reducing his meal rations until one day his broken heart simply gave up. He never betrayed his son.

Ålvik had then taken a searing revenge on the treacherous neighbour. He had kept well away from Bergen for several months, until the bodyguards that the terrified man had demanded from his masters were withdrawn. The underground network got the news to Ålvik that very day.

He made his last foray into Bergen one night, entered the neighbour's house and shot the man before his family, at the dinner table. He touched no one else. The man's wife, a woman who'd held Ålvik in her arms as a baby, could only stare at him with a deep sadness, shock and profound shame. She'd raised no alarm, until long after he'd gone. Ålvik had just turned twenty-one.

The local German troop commander, *Oberst* Helmut Delsingen, had himself gone to the scene. It was rumoured that he'd stared with contempt at the body, then said, 'I would have done the same.' Then he'd turned on the heels of his highly polished jackboots and walked out crisply without a backward glance or a word to the recently widowed woman.

When that story had eventually reached Ålvik, it had also carried the news that Delsingen had arrived that very night, to replace the previous commander, *Obersturmbannführer* Hans-Otto Brucht. A Waffen-SS veteran, Brucht had been put in local command of the mainly Wehrmacht, regular army, troops, to stiffen them during the initial months of the occupation. He had also brought with him a small cadre of SS officers, who were given precedence over all the Wehrmacht officers. Brucht and his SS personnel controlled the whole show.

The Wehrmacht NCOs and soldiers had not liked the idea of being under the command of an SS fanatic and his cronies, but none had possessed the courage to say so openly. The officers felt the same but they too had said nothing. They had loved ones back in

Germany who were all too vulnerable. Even at that relatively early stage of the war, they had no illusions. They had therefore followed Brucht's orders.

It had been during Brucht's term of command that the Ålvik family had met their horrific deaths. What the Milorg did not realize at the time was that Delsingen – a proper Wehrmacht officer – had been posted in because Brucht had been killed. The SS officers, however, would remain.

Brucht's staff aeroplane – a Blohm and Voss Bv138C1 – had been travelling north from Holland, where he'd been attending a high-level SS staff meeting.

Originally intended for long-range ocean recce, the Bv138 was a strange-looking beast. It was a high-wing aircraft with a flying-boat hull, and three high-mounted Junkers Jumo 205D diesels. It was slow, with a maximum speed of 171 mph. It looked like two different aeroplanes glued together, with the flying-boat hull suspended beneath the triple-engined, tail-boomed wing. It had rudimentary defensive armament. A 20mm turreted cannon was positioned ahead of the cockpit, with a similar weapon in the rear. A dorsal 13mm machine-gun was also installed behind the central engine. The Bv138 had a long range of over 2500 miles and was capable of carrying depth charges. Its service ceiling was a little over 16,000 feet; but it was in the transport role that it was most widely used, particularly in the Norwegian theatre.

Brucht had three under his command, and two of these were used in a multi-role capacity. Their hulls enabled them to be used as fast transports between the fiords, giving him the capability to quickly insert specialist teams over a wide area, to hunt out the resistance. He also used them as spotters.

The third Bv138 was reserved specifically for staff use. Brucht's aircraft was thus rigorously serviced and always in perfect operational condition. It was his great misfortune that it attracted the attentions of a pair of marauding Spitfires. The two fighters, on a daring intruder mission, had chanced upon the much slower aircraft as it had flown northwards, hugging the coastline and low over the war, clearly considering itself safe so deep within occupied airspace. The Spitfire pilots, on their way home, could hardly believe their luck when they'd come across the unescorted sitting duck.

Both aircraft had gone into the attack and within seconds the Bv138, desperately making for shallower water near the shoreline, had spiralled on to coastal rocks with explosive and fiery impact. There had been no survivors.

One of the Spitfire pilots was Johnny 'Jo-Jo' Kearns, an Australian. It would be nearly three years before the paths of Ålvik and Kearns would cross; but on that day the link that would one day bring them together had been forged.

The labouring troop carrier was rounding one of the many hairpin bends in the narrow, unmetalled mountain road. One side of the road was bordered by high earthen walls that had been hacked into the rock; the other dropped away precipitously towards the fiord far below.

Ålvik inched his head above the crest, until his eyes were exposed. He was well in cover, but he saw no reason to take chances. An alert soldier with a pair of binoculars could still spot him. He therefore ensured that his movements were infinitesimal. When he was at last satisfied with his vantage-point, he saw the half-track carrier clawing its way round another bend. It was now close enough and at its most vulnerable, as the driver became more worried about toppling off the road than about ambushes.

The rest of his body still hidden from the

enemy by the slope, Ålvik raised his left hand slowly towards the crest, then chopped it down sharply. This same action rippled through his team. When the ripple reached the last position – a mortar team – the firing began.

The hapless troop carrier, caught at the moment of negotiating the dangerous bend, came to a sudden stop as mortar shells rained down on it. Automatic fire joined the hellish noise, mercilessly raking it from nose to tail. Then came an explosion that tore great gouges out of the cliff-like border of the road as the vehicle was ripped apart. Charred, shattered bodies mingled with cascading pieces of the troop carrier as they were flung into the air and over the edge, to tumble towards the waters of the fiord. Other pieces landed in the trees or littered the ground near the burning remnants of the vehicle. Small tongues of flames, like alien creatures, licked at bits of metal and flesh. It was all over in seconds.

Swiftly but cautiously, a group of four resistance members worked their way towards the carnage, covered by their colleagues. They checked that all the troopers were dead, then laid booby-traps by the wreck before hurrying back.

As he moved down the slope to regroup with

his personnel, Ålvik did not pause to wonder about the people who had just died on his orders. Part of his mind clinically accepted that the enemy had loved ones somewhere who would mourn their passing. But he had not asked them to invade his country.

He had not asked them to do what they were doing to his own people. He had not asked them to kill his family, or to abuse and then kill the two young women who had meant so much to him. He had not asked them to destroy his dreams. He had not asked them to bring him so much grief. He would continue killing them, until every one was gone from his homeland. There was no conflict within him. As long as the war lasted he would continue to kill them, and would suffer no pangs of conscience as a result.

'The usual split,' he now said as the members of his group gathered around him. 'They'll soon come looking, but the road will be blocked for some time while they deal with our booby-traps. Watch out for the spotter planes. We'll meet at rendezvous Geiranger.'

They were going nowhere near Geiranger. It was a code for their next target. They split into smaller teams of five and headed off in different directions, into the forest and away from Laerdal.

He had spoken to them in *landsmål*, the language of the land, the tongue of the late nineteenth century, as opposed to *bokmål*, the literary language. There was a very good reason for this. Norwegian-speaking enemy agents had tried to infiltrate some of the Milorg teams. They could speak 'correct' Norwegian flawlessly. But *landsmål* trapped them every time. Even genuine Norwegians had been caught out.

Ålvik set off with the four who would be travelling with him. One was Inge Jarl.

Inge was from Tromsø, well within the Arctic Circle, and nearly two thousand kilometres from where she now was. She had *walked* from Tromsø, somehow managing to stay out of German hands during the journey. She had set off after her family had been killed in a bombing raid, not quite knowing where she was headed. She had simply wanted to get away and had eventually joined the Milorg, more by accident than by design.

On her marathon walk, she had blundered into an ambush set by a small sabotage team. A wounded German soldier, unable to move but clutching a pistol, had pointed it directly at her. She'd simply stood transfixed, staring back at him. He had died staring at her, and the pistol had fallen out of his lifeless hand.

A resistance fighter had come out of the undergrowth. 'You'd better pick that up,' he'd said to her, pointing at the pistol. 'It's yours now, and you'd better learn pretty fast how to use it.' He'd peered at her. 'I can't understand why he didn't shoot you. He must have thought you were an angel.'

That was how she'd first met Per Ålvik.

She attached herself to his team and as no one had bothered to tell her to get lost, each then seemed to have adopted the other.

Ålvik's comment about the soldier mistaking her for an angel had not been entirely grimly frivolous. Though strappingly built, her figure was richly curved. She was tall, and her very pale skin and fine blonde hair were enhanced by widely spaced, oval and slightly angled eyes of deep blue. It was a strikingly beautiful face. There was the blood of the Lapps in her veins.

When the German, a young lieutenant, had been pointing his pistol at her, the sun was at her back. Perhaps in his dying moments, the soldier had seen something no one else had. Perhaps with the sun gleaming through her golden hair, she had indeed looked like an angel to him. Whatever the reason, it had saved her life.

As Inge's stay with Ålvik's group continued to last longer than anyone expected, her performance in the field became more impressive. She learned quickly, and soon became very accurate with a mortar launcher. She was both quick and devastating. Before long, if anyone needed a good mortar on a mission they asked for Inge. On one such occasion she was wounded and nearly captured. Remembering what had happened to his sister and Elle, Ålvik had a nightmare vision of what would have happened to her.

'Her body screams for sex,' one of his men had once confided to him, waxing lyrical. 'I could just lie between those great thighs, and stay there for ever. The problem is,' he'd gone on ruefully with a sigh of deep regret, 'she's not interested. At least, not in me. She must be saving it for someone . . .' The man had looked at Ålvik. 'It's you, of course. Why don't you put the poor girl out of her misery? Probably still a virgin. You know it's you she's after.'

'Don't be ridiculous,' Ålvik had said. 'She's a child!'

'And I suppose you're an old man? More to the point, do you think you'll make it to ripe old age? You should live that long. *We* should live that long, at the rate we're going.'

After that scare, Ålvik had refused to let anyone else take Inge out on further missions. She was happy with that arrangement. Where he went, she went.

It was Inge's mortars that had pulverized the troop carrier. She was barely eighteen.

The commandeered building by the waterfront was the headquarters building of Colonel Delsingen's command.

He stood by a window looking out on the waters of the Vågen, Bergen's inner harbour. Directly in his line of vision were the sea-grey, shark-like shapes of the E-boats that prowled the fiords and frequently went out to sea to hunt out any Tommis foolish enough to cross the water from England to help the Norwegian resistance. Sometimes both Norwegian and British commandos were caught.

A knock sounded.

'*Hierein!*'

A bareheaded Wehrmacht captain came in, and snapped to attention. He carried a sheet of paper.

'Information on that troop carrier that set out from Aurland, *Herr Oberst*,' he barked.

Delsingen turned slowly. A slim, athletic-looking man with close-cropped, greying hair, he had the eyes of a tolerant schoolmaster. They were eyes that had fooled many people into believing he was soft.

'How long have I been here, Geissler?'

Put slightly off balance by the unexpected question, Geissler looked uncertain, then said, 'Two months, sir.'

'Two months. In that time, what have I told you about stamping into my office and barking at me like one of those overdressed, mechanical creatures out there?'

Geissler's eyes crinkled with worry. 'Sir!' he said in a low voice. 'One of them's waiting to see you!'

'Is he? Which one?'

'*Sturmbannführer* Mindenhof, sir.' Geissler looked as if even mention of the name was a forbidden act.

Delsingen stared at him. The tolerant eyes had become less so. 'You are an officer of the Wehrmacht, man! I will not have any member of the Wehrmacht under my command being terrorized by these ... these mannequins in black. I expect you to lead by example to your men.'

'Sir ...'

'You are not married, are you, Geissler?'

Again the captain was momentarily caught out by this new, unexpected question. He knew the colonel would already have known that from his service file.

'No, *Herr Oberst*.' Then before he could stop himself, he added, 'I was smart.'

Delsingen studied him closely. 'Do I detect some bitterness in those words? What happened? Did she walk away?'

'I did.'

Delsingen waited.

'If the *Herr Oberst* permits, I would prefer not to talk about it.'

After a while, Delsingen said quietly, 'Very well, Geissler. We'll leave it for now. But if there is something on your mind that prevents you from giving your full attention to your duties, I expect you to tell me about it. We'll continue this later.'

'Yes, sir.'

'Now give me that message.'

Geissler handed it over.

Delsingen read it silently, then turned to look out of the window once more.

'Who found them?' he asked without turning round.

'The 138 from Aurlandsfjord spotted the

19

wreckage. A salvage troop is up there now. The wreck is booby-trapped.'

'He's tying us up.'

'Mountain patrols are out . . .'

'They won't find anything.'

'You said "he", sir . . . You think this is Ålvik's work?'

'I'm sure of it.' Delsingen turned to face his subordinate. 'After what was done to his family, he's carrying his own war to us. And his rage, Geissler, is of great use to the resistance movement.'

Geissler cleared his throat.

Delsingen stared at him. 'You've got something to say?'

'*Sturmbannführer* Mindenhof . . .'

'The major can wait.'

'It's Ålvik he wants to talk about, sir.'

'What you really mean, Captain, is that he believes I am not doing enough to catch these people. Presumably he wants me to take severe reprisals on the civilian population. It's this very type of reaction that has brought us this problem,' Delsingen continued in a hard voice. 'All right, Geissler. Send him in. I'm just in the mood for his nonsense.'

Geissler hesitated.

'Well?' Delsingen demanded. 'What are you waiting for?'

'Just be careful of him, sir,' Geissler advised cautiously. 'He's already managed to sneak in some SS troopers. He'll try for more.'

'Himmler's black angels don't frighten me. Send him in.'

'Yes, *Herr Oberst*.'

Geissler went out.

Seconds later, loud heels sounded outside Delsingen's door. Then it was opened by Geissler, after a discreet knock. The captain stood back for someone to enter.

Sturmbannführer Reinhardt Mindenhof, resplendent in black SS uniform, marched into the office and clicked his heels as he came to ramrod attention. Despite the control he exerted over his expression, it was clear he had not liked being made to wait.

The man seemed to gleam. His jackboots gleamed. His cross-belt gleamed. The pistol holster on his left hip, with the gun inside nestling butt forwards, gleamed. Soft, black-leather gloves were tucked into the belt, next to it. They gleamed. His cap, with its death's-head insignia, gleamed. His face gleamed. Even the very material of his back uniform seemed to gleam; and the red, white and black strip of

21

ribbon that peeped out of his tunic drew the eye like a magnet. Iron Cross, Second Class. His hair, savagely pruned in the Himmler fashion, was a white-blond, giving the impression that he had none at all. When his cap was removed, he appeared to have a gleaming bald head. His eyes were like the night.

The dark eyes stared with evangelical fervour at the regulation portrait of Hitler that glared balefully back at him from the wall. It had been put there by Brucht. There was an even larger portrait in Mindenhof's own office.

Mindenhof was not a happy man. He was almost pathologically ambitious and, at twenty-eight, had hoped that with Brucht's death he would have received the command and the promotion that went with it. When he'd learned of his former commander's demise, he had felt an initial and very private sense of elation. In his mind, he had thanked the Tommi pilots. The command, and the promotion, were his! Now he would really show these Norwegians who was master.

But it had not turned out as he'd expected. It galled him that the decision-makers had chosen instead to send in a *full* colonel, from the *Wehrmacht*, of all things. *Two* ranks up, and still barely thirty. One more step and the man would be a general. This appointment was obviously intended to be the next stage towards general officer rank, if he did well in the post. Even worse, the Wehrmacht colonel wore the Iron Cross, *First* Class.

Ever since Delsingen had arrived, Mindenhof had been cursing the wretched Tommi pilots who had intervened so disastrously in his life. It did not occur to him to consider, even briefly, the notion that the effect on Brucht's own life had been even more disastrous – terminal, in fact.

'*Sturmbannführer* Mindenhof, *Herr Oberst!*' Geissler announced with snappy formality.

'Thank you, Geissler,' Delsingen acknowledged.

'Sir!' Geissler said as he withdrew with obvious relief, shutting the door as he did so.

Mindenhof's right arm shot out. '*Heil Hitler!*'

'What?' Oh yes. *Heil Hitler*. At ease, Major.'

Mindenhof's obsidian eyes were poisonous as he regarded his superior officer. He made no effort to disguise his disapproval of Delsingen's off-hand response to the salute.

'*Sturmbannführer!*' Mindenhof corrected him sharply, reminding the Wehrmacht officer of the preferred Waffen-SS rank.

Delsingen's eyes appeared to change in intensity as he stared back at Mindenhof.

'Don't shout, Mindenhof,' he remonstrated mildly, before going on, 'In my office, you're a major. In your office . . .'

'May I remind the colonel that as the senior Waffen-SS officer in this command . . .'

'You are my subordinate! And as far as I am aware, majors do *not* outrank colonels of *any* grade, whatever the military organization. That goes for the security police. The SS may be responsible for security in occupied areas, but here you are under *my* command. Don't you *ever* . . . interrupt me again. Is that clear, *Major*?'

For one brief and astonishing moment, Mindenhof actually quivered as he tried to control his fury. Like a gleaming black tuning fork with his feet seemingly riveted to the floor, his upper body vibrated, as if in response to a blow across the face from Delsingen.

Mindenhof, a member of the Allgemeine-SS, also belonged to the 6th SS-Totenkopfverband – one of the SS Death's-Head Units – and though these had been disbanded and amalgamated into the Waffen-SS in February that year, he and his fellow SS officers, like others in similar units, continued to swan around in their black uniforms. They liked people to know who they really were. They also relished the fact that the black outfits were very intimidating, even to other Germans. But this Wehrmacht colonel didn't seem to realize that.

'Is that clear, Major?' Delsingen repeated, stressing each word.

Mindenhof, his face pale with stifled anger, at last replied stiffly, 'Yes, sir.'

'Good. Now let's get down to business. You may remove that hat. And please take a seat.'

'I prefer to stand.' Mindenhof planted his legs apart and placed his hands behind his back. The cap stayed on. He faced Delsingen squarely, his black eyes empty.

'As you wish,' said Delsingen, who also remained standing. 'I hear you want to speak to me about the resistance fighter Ålvik.'

'The *terrorist*,' Mindenhof corrected. 'If I may be allowed to inform the *colonel*,' he continued, skirting the edges of insolence, 'when *Obersturmbannführer* Brucht was in command we had a perfect way of handling these people. The Norwegian resistance cannot properly function without help from the outside. The English send them agents, and weapons; but we have had many successes. It will not take much longer to pacify this area completely. The *Obersturmbannführer* and I –

as I have already said – did have a perfect way of attending to this.'

'I know your "perfect" way. Slaughter the civilians.'

'Their people are killing German soldiers!'

'Tell me, Mindenhof,' Delsingen began softly. 'What would you do if the Tommis – or anyone else – invaded Germany? How would you react to them?'

Mindenhof stared at him as if he had gone mad. 'That will *never* happen!'

'I am impressed by your certainty.'

'To think otherwise is not only defeatist, but unpatriotic! The Reich will prevail for . . .'

'Yes, yes. I know the rest. Happily, we do not have to worry about an invasion of the Fatherland.' Delsingen paused. The unspoken 'yet' was almost palpable. 'So let us concentrate on the problem at hand. If we were to follow the line of action you clearly favour, we would soon find ourselves receiving unwelcome attention from Berlin.'

Mindenhof stared at him.

'You don't see what I'm getting at, do you, Major?' Delsingen said.

'You are correct, Colonel. I do not.'

'Why are we here, Major?'

'You . . . *we* are here to suppress terrorist

activity while the district command secures, rebuilds and expands industry, to enable the Reich to pursue its aims. We also convert the population – who are supremely Nordic – to the German way.

'I can see you were well briefed.' Delsingen kept the irony out of his voice. 'And what do we require, to enable us to secure and expand this industry *and* convert the population?'

Again, Mindenhof looked at Delsingen as if at someone whose faculties were not quite all there. 'The area command pacifies the area. We . . . have the specific duty of hunting out the terrorists. We have specialist Wehrmacht mountain troops for this purpose. Waffen-SS mountain troops would be better, but none have been allocated to us so far. The industrial work is carried out by the defeated people, under German direction, of course . . . until they have all learned the way. Some have already done so. Quisling's Nasjonal Samlig has given us many recruits to the cause, as have the other sympathetic organizations.'

'Indeed.' Delsingen chose to ignore the pointed remark about mountain troops; and as for Quisling and the various 'sympathetic' organizations . . . 'Therefore in our specific area, we use the local populace as our labour force.'

'But naturally, Colonel.' Mindenhof was again flirting with insolence. He clearly felt Delsingen was a bit slow, and not at all equal to the important command he'd been given.

Delsingen nodded thoughtfully. 'Naturally. So how long do you think it would take for us to run out of people to supply this workforce, and to convert, if we continued with your methods? Five for every German soldier killed? Ten? Fifteen? You do not need to be a mathematical genius to realize that before long we would have no one left to do the work required – or to be converted, for that matter. What would *you* say to Berlin?'

Delsingen waited, while he secretly enjoyed watching the SS man's attempts to wriggle his way out without losing face.

'I think, Major,' Delsingen went on, before Mindenhof could say anything, 'we should call a temporary halt to the reprisals. We should concentrate on stopping the ambushes, the assassinations, the sniper attacks and the sabotage. I believe that the more victims we create, the more we feed the flames of resistance. We're giving them martyrs. If they're as ineffectual as you seem to believe, let's not give them their martyrs. Let us try another way. My way.'

'Which is?'

'I will let you have your orders in due course.'

'And, in the meantime, these attacks will continue.'

Delsingen's eyes were no longer tolerant. 'They can't sustain it for much longer. I have your word on that.'

Mindenhof clamped his jaws together. It was obvious he did not want to back down, but chose not to voice his feelings. He would fight another day.

'Very well, *Herr Oberst*,' he eventually accepted tightly. 'But if your methods do not work, I shall recommend to the High Command . . .'

'Through channels, of course. Through me, in fact.'

Mindenhof clamped his mouth shut again. His nostrils flared as he pondered his next move.

Finally he said, 'The High Command, *Waffen-SS*.' He spoke with relish. The SS High Command would sort out this upstart army man. 'May I be dismissed, Colonel?'

'You are.'

Mindenhof snapped to attention with a sharp

click of the heels. The right arm shot out. '*Heil Hitler!*'

'*Heil Hitler*,' Delsingen responded. He did not raise his arm, and his eyes surveyed the other man neutrally.

Mindenhof strutted out, face still pale with fury.

'And you, my dear Delsingen,' the colonel said to himself as Mindenhof banged the door shut behind him, 'have just made yourself a dangerous enemy.'

But he did not feel unduly disturbed by this as he turned to look at the Führer's portrait.

'I must take that thing down one day,' he muttered.

2

Delsingen walked into the outer office with his cap on. Geissler was talking to a sergeant who was seated at a desk but who got smartly to his feet as the colonel entered.

'Hat on, Captain,' Delsingen said. 'We're going on a surprise inspection. At ease, Sergeant.'

The sergeant sat down again.

Geissler ended his conversation with the NCO and hurried to take his cap off a wall hook.

'I'll warn your driver, *Herr Oberst*,' the sergeant said, reaching for the phone on his desk.

Delsingen paused. 'No. Captain Geissler will drive. Have you the spare keys?'

'Yes, *Herr Oberst*.' The sergeant unlocked a drawer and took out the spares.

'Give them to the captain. And where is *Leutnant* Kahler?'

The sergeant cleared his throat awkwardly. 'In . . . in the toilet, *Herr Oberst*.' He was sitting to attention now.

'Again? That man spends his life in there.'

'Yes, *Herr Oberst*,' the sergeant said, then correcting himself hastily, '. . . I mean, no, *Herr Oberst*!'

'I'd give up, if I were you, Sergeant. You're digging yourself in deeper.'

'Yes, *Herr Oberst*!'

'Tell *Leutnant* Kahler where we've gone when he finally gets out of there. If anything of operational urgency occurs while we're out, he is to contact me immediately on the radio, then inform Major Mindenhof.'

'Yes, *Herr Oberst*! May I ask where the inspection is to be? So we know where . . .'

'It would not be a surprise, would it, Sergeant? And you never know, someone might warn the unit concerned.'

'No one would, *Herr Oberst*!' the sergeant protested.

'I'm sure of it,' Delsingen said mildly, knowing better as he continued on his way out. 'And stop sitting to attention.'

'Yes, *Herr Oberst*.'

Geissler grabbed the keys from the sergeant,

shrugged in reply to the NCO's raised-eyebrow query and hurried after the colonel.

Delsingen said nothing until they had left the building and were walking towards the Mercedes staff car.

'You are full of questions, Geissler?'

'The colonel will tell me when he is ready.'

'Very diplomatic.'

'I take it we're not going on an inspection.'

'Not immediately. Has Kahler always been prone to going to the toilet?'

'He was at Narvik, sir.'

'Yes, I know. I've studied his file. I was at Narvik too. I was a major then. That first German defeat was a psychological shock for many. But then the enemy was rather more ferocious than those we had previously been accustomed to. Do you think Kahler is now permanently frightened? Is that why he visits the toilet so often?'

'I would not like to say, Colonel,' Geissler offered cautiously.

'I understand.'

'Shouldn't we have a motorcycle escort, sir?' Geissler went on, wanting to keep away from the subject of Kahler's fading courage. 'For wherever it is we're going?'

The colonel did not seem to mind the change

of subject. 'We're not going far. Besides, I don't think Ålvik and his gang are close enough to shoot at us. Do you?'

Geissler looked about him. There were more soldiers about than civilians. Sandbagged gun emplacements were dotted all over the place. Some were anti-aircraft cannon.

A four-man squad of Mindenhof's newly arrived SS men, all in black uniforms, marched towards Bryggen, Bergen's old Hanseatic quarter, weapons slung. They carried brand-new MP40 sub-machine-guns, with the 'broom handle' folding stock. Hanging at each hip from the black leather belts about their waists was a leather triple-pocket ammunition pouch. Each pocket held a spare thirty-two-round magazine, to complement the one already loaded into the gun.

Because of the antipathy which existed between the Wehrmacht and the SS – the former was determined to retain military control over the latter – much of the equipment passed on to the SS tended to be of inferior quality. The SS, however, had other ideas. Already running what was virtually its own shadow industry, the organization was beginning to manufacture its own equipment. It also modified and improved upon captured enemy weaponry, which was sometimes of a better standard.

Looking at the squad's new guns, Geissler wondered where Mindenhof had 'acquired' them. He was certain they had not come through normal channels.

He glanced at Delsingen to check his superior's reaction; but the colonel appeared not to mind.

The SS men ignored every Wehrmacht uniform they passed, including junior officers. They took notice only when they saw the colonel as they stomped past. Four arms shot out.

'*Heil Hitler!*' they barked in chorus.

Delsingen raised a hand to them. They marched on.

'They still refuse to salute you properly, sir,' Geissler observed.

'Let them have their day,' the colonel said mysteriously.

He glanced to his right, at the commandeered hotel that served both as headquarters and sleeping accommodation for the SS contingent. It was festooned with swastika banners and emblems. In its immediate vicinity, a rash of posters had been put up. Some were portraits of Hitler. Others carried exhortations to greater effort for the glory of the Reich, or warnings of severe punishment for those who gave aid and comfort to the resistance movements.

One, particularly ominous, was in Norwegian, but carried the date and originating department in German. *Oslo, den 22 Juni 1941. Der Reichskommissar für die besetzten norwegischen Gebiete.* It was a brand-new poster, and was signed 'Terboven'.

Most of these warnings promised the penalty of death.

Another poster, also in Norwegian, exhorted young men to join the SS. The ghostly head and shoulders of a helmeted Norseman was flanked by the modern one of a soldier in an SS helmet, looking suitably square-jawed.

Nordmenn, it seemed to shout. *Kemf for Norge!* Norsemen. Fight for Norway!

A swelling roar made Geissler look up. A pair of Messerschmitt Me-109s hurtled past, coming from the direction of Mount Fløien, which overlooked the city, and heading out along the fiord. Soon, they had disappeared.

'Hunting for straying Tommis, no doubt,' Delsingen remarked without looking up. 'If they're mad enough to come all the way here.'

Geissler hurried on ahead as they approached the car, to open the passenger door, but Delsingen stopped him.

'Get behind the wheel,' the colonel said, then opened the passenger door himself and got in.

'How far is "not far", sir?' Geissler asked, as they shut the doors. He put the key in the ignition.

'Just follow my directions.'

Geissler started the car and they moved off.

'Here. This will do. Stop here.'

Geissler brought the car to a halt, in response to Delsingen's command.

'Let us walk,' the colonel said, and climbed out. 'Bring the radio.'

Geissler pulled the bulky handset out of its base unit beneath the instrument panel. The radio was in a camouflaged canvas pouch with a rolled sling tucked into a side pocket. He got out, unrolled the sling and slipped it over his left shoulder.

They had stopped at the end of a road that had coursed its way up Mount Fløien. Close by, was the penultimate stop of the funicular railway that began on the Øvregaten and went up to a mountain-top restaurant. The upward car, full of off-duty soldiers, had stopped. But they did not make for it.

The colonel strode off up the mountain, with

Geissler in tow. They passed gun emplacements, several of which were multi-barrelled
anti-aircraft cannon. The soldiers and junior
officers manning them snapped to attention,
clearly wondering whether the colonel had
come on a sudden inspection. He was not
their commander but, like soldiers everywhere,
they had long ago come to the conclusion that
the presence of any senior officer always meant
a disruption of their daily routine. Then they
relaxed as he went on, relieved to discover they
were not the object of his visit.

Delsingen and Geissler kept walking until
they reached the last stop. The restaurant,
looking like a miniature palace of crystal and
wood, came into view. It sat atop the mountain,
looking down on the city spread below. It was
doing good business. The uniformed diners
were all officers from the various services.
Two of the anti-aircraft weapons were sited
in the grounds.

'This mountain is bristling,' Delsingen
remarked. 'Hartmann and his boys intend
to shred any enemy aircraft that ventures
this way.'

Hartmann, also a Wehrmacht colonel, was
in command of the local area artillery.

A path which skirted the restaurant led to its

terrace. Delsingen paused there by the safety railing, and stared out over the city. They were now just over a thousand feet up. He looked down at the E-boats moored in the inner harbour, and at the other craft further out. An E-boat was going out on patrol, streaming a white, boiling wake that churned the surface of the water.

'The city among the seven hills,' he began quietly. 'Before the war, my wife and I came here for our honeymoon. Germans have been coming here for a long time. Since the early thirteenth century there have been German traders in Norway, followed a century later by the Hanseatics. And now . . .' Abruptly, he continued walking, crisply returning a salute from two passing soldiers. 'Come, Geissler.'

They continued beyond the restaurant, using an easy trail that took them further up the mountain. At last Delsingen stopped. They were well clear of the restaurant, with a spectacular view of Bergen, the surrounding mountains and the fiord and skerries. There were no soldiers or gun emplacements within 300 yards.

'We can talk,' the colonel said. He did not look at his subordinate.

Geissler took a nervous glance about him, as

if expecting to see Mindenhof suddenly materialize. He waited for the colonel to continue.

'Don't look so worried, Geissler,' the colonel said, his eyes still on the city below. 'Mindenhof's snoopers are a long way from us.' Delsingen placed his hands behind his back as he stared down at the city. 'We are going to lose this war. We began losing it the day *Adler Tag* failed. The Tommis, as you know, call it the Battle of Britain.'

Out of the corner of his eye, he observed the startled turning of the captain's head, as Geissler stared at him.

'It is true, Geissler. I know if our fanatical *Sturmbannführer* could hear me, he would choke on his oath to Hitler, denounce me, then do his best to have me shot as a defeatist traitor. That idiot truly believes in the thousand-year Reich. We have sown the wind and one day the whirlwind will be upon us. And then, Geissler, we shall pay. How we shall pay.' The colonel spoke softly as he continued to look down on the city, given a cloak of peace by the distance. 'My wife and I were truly happy here.'

Geissler said nothing.

'Mindenhof has an unsavoury past in the SS,' Delsingen continued, 'even by their own standards. I am quite aware that he is ruthlessly

40

ambitious, and will do *anything* to advance himself.'

Uncertain of how to deal with the colonel's dangerous frankness, Geissler said uncertainly, 'Strictly speaking, *Herr Oberst*, he is your second in command.'

'And a difficult one he's proving to be.' Delsingen spoke as if to himself. 'He wants nothing less than full command of the unit. I could thwart his ambitions by giving you a field promotion to major.'

Geissler's eyes twitched beneath the peak of his cap. 'If the *Herr Oberst* would permit . . . I would very much like to be a major – but not at the expense of *Sturmbannführer* Mindenhof.'

'It would not be at his expense. You'd be of equal rank.'

'He would not see it like that.'

The colonel smiled tightly. 'You are a cautious man, Geissler. Good.'

'Was that a test, *Herr Oberst*?'

But Delsingen made no reply. Instead, he continued, 'Today, Geissler, Operation Barbarossa has begun. It is madness, of course. We are striking at the Soviets, hoping for a swift blitzkrieg victory, while still heavily engaged in the west. When the Japanese attack the Americans – as they most certainly will –

we shall have the Yankees fully in the war, with all the weight of their industrial might against us.

'It is what Churchill hopes for, and he will get it. I tell you, Geissler, we shall truly pay a terrible price for our folly, no matter how long it takes. The thousand-year Reich will be expensive in blood, and will not last beyond this war. I am not the only one who has come to that conclusion.'

Delsingen at last turned to look at the dumbstruck captain.

'You are wondering,' the colonel said, 'whether I am mad to talk to you like this. You are perhaps asking yourself: how do I know I can trust you?' He paused. 'I know more about you than you think. Mindenhof is not the only person out here with powerful contacts. I have a close friend in the SS. We were at school together. He now holds general rank – *Gruppenführer-SS*. When he heard I had been given this command, he came to see me. He wanted me to keep an eye on you.'

Geissler's expression had turned to one of alarm. 'On *me*?'

'Don't worry, Geissler. You are safe with me. You will receive no attention from the SS. But perhaps *you* can now feel you can trust me sufficiently, and can tell me about that young woman you walked away from.'

For several moments, Geissler said nothing. 'The *Gruppenführer* you mentioned, sir,' he was at last able to say quietly. 'He *knows*?' There was a tinge of real fear in his voice.

'You know what the SS are like. They check up on everybody. However, as a favour to me, the information he gave me is not listed in your files.'

'So Mindenhof . . .'

'Knows nothing of it.'

Geissler gave a hesitant sigh of relief. 'I do not feel proud of what I did,' he began, a sense of guilt now in his voice. 'She was so beautiful. The most beautiful . . .' He stopped, remembering. 'This is what they have done to us,' he continued bitterly. He shook his head. 'No. This is what we have done to ourselves. We allowed it. Her father was my music professor. I frequently dined at their house. That was how I met her. I could not believe anyone could be so beautiful. She was . . . ethereal . . .'

'And you stopped seeing her, because she was a Jew.'

Geissler turned to look out on the city below. There was a suspicious glisten to his eyes. 'To my eternal shame, yes, *Herr Oberst*.'

'Do you know where she is now?'

Geissler shook his head slowly.

'Perhaps you will find her again,' Delsingen suggested.

'She may already be dead.'

'Will you look for her? Is there enough of the man left in you to try? Just in case?'

Geissler was again silent for several moments. 'If I ever get the chance, I shall,' he vowed eventually. 'I might never find her again. I'm . . . I'm not sure I deserve to. But I will at least try to find out what happened. I owe that to her – and to myself.'

'Good,' the colonel said. 'Now I shall tell you what I intend to do about Ålvik. First, we will prevent Mindenhof from taking out his frustrations on the local populace.'

'He won't like that. He'll bring in more SS personnel.'

'He'll try. He does not know I have my own big gun in the SS. All his requisitions will be seen by my old classmate.'

'He won't give up.'

'I am well aware of that. However, I intend to have Ålvik neutralized, before our *Sturmbannführer* can whip up sufficient support for his requests. There will be plenty of people out for revenge on us, when this war is over. As long as I am responsible for this unit, no one under my command will be allowed to abuse the locals. I will be ruthless in hunting out Ålvik's gang, even though I fully understand his reasons for attacking us. He is fighting for his country, and it is our job to stop him; but I will not use the local civilians as hostage fodder.'

'Many of them support him, and others like him.'

'If they're caught with weapons they are no longer civilians but soldiers, and must accept the fortunes of war. Until that occurs, none of the locals will be terrorized.'

'What about the members of the Nasjonal Samlig, the Hird, and the Bergen detachment of the Germanske-SS Norge? Mindenhof calls them his "sympathetic" Norwegians.'

'He's used that same description to me.'

'These particular Norwegians, sir, are sometimes harder on their own than even Mindenhof.'

'The convert always wishes to prove himself, and is frequently more brutal. The classic lesson of occupying a country, Geissler. Caesar employed the tactic centuries ago. When he had raised his legions among the conquered, he sent them out to pacify other nations. His Teutonic legionaries did their fair share.

Nothing is new, Geissler. Only the methods, and their implementation, change.'

'*Herr Oberst* . . .' Geissler said, '. . . do you really think Barbarossa will . . .?'

'Fail?' Delsingen supplied. 'It is inevitable. The Führer and his advisers have seriously miscalculated. Oh, our blitzkrieg will certainly stun the Russians and we shall make great advances – initially. I also suspect that our troops, and their Waffen-SS comrades, will not be gentle with the populace, whom they will look upon as sub-human. More acts to be avenged by the Russians. When the enemy finally rallies, he will come at us in great hordes.

'They will get better and better, Geissler. They will be fuelled by a great hatred and anger; and to help them, they will have the force that took such severe toll of Napoleon's troops: Generals January and February. Some leaders never seem to study history closely. If they did, it might help them avoid the more glaring of their mistakes; and people like us would not have to be sacrificed to their vanity. Our forces are fighting on several fronts, against a mass of enemies who will eventually overwhelm us. The people of the countries we have occupied will have their revenge one day; perhaps sooner than our great Führer and his Mindenhofs think.

The Fatherland, inevitably, will suffer gravely for this madness. A few of our countrymen can see it; a very, very few.'

Geissler was again looking anxiously about him.

Noting this, Delsingen said, 'You are disturbed by my comments. More than ever you think I am mad to say these things, even up here on this mountain.'

'I am worried for your safety, Colonel. Ålvik's people are not the only snipers.'

'Even Mindenhof would not be so blatant as to attempt to assassinate me openly. The man is an appalling example of German manhood, but he is not stupid.'

'He would blame it on terrorists.'

Delsingen waved an arm briefly, indicating the immediate area about them. 'This mountain is crawling with Wehrmacht troops. Ålvik's people would not be so insane as to come within five kilometres. If Mindenhof has something in mind, he will be far more subtle. When I called him an idiot earlier, I meant it as a comment on his philosophy, such as it is.

'He is dangerous, but he is also sly. When he was a captain, he got rid of a rival of equal rank by sleeping with the man's wife. The enraged husband, not knowing the identity of the man who had cuckolded him, shot the wife. He was executed for the murder. It was his great misfortune that the wife had also been the daughter of the local *Gauleiter*.'

'If you know so much of Mindenhof's personal history, sir, it's all the more reason for you to be careful. He will be constantly seeking ways to discredit you.'

'I have been given command of a unit,' Delsingen said calmly, 'that is distinct from the other forces in the area. This gives me a certain degree of autonomy. Don't worry, Geissler. I know my enemy – both the Norwegian and the German. And I will face both, when the time comes.'

They set off back down the mountain.

'We had better inspect some poor unit,' Delsingen said, 'to satisfy Mindenhof's inevitable curiosity.'

The radio remained silent.

Whitehall, London, the same day

In a small office whose shabbiness belied its importance, two men in crumpled suits sat facing each other, at two desks that had been pushed together. One was staring with open disbelief at a sheet of paper he had picked up from a pile that a secretary had recently brought in. He pursed his lips thoughtfully.

'Look at this,' he said to his companion, passing him the sheet.

The other man took it, read slowly, then read it again.

'Well?' demanded his colleague.

'I find that hard to believe . . .'

'My feelings precisely.'

'However, it would be prudent to keep an eye on developments. The source appears to be one of our more reliable ones.'

'He could have been compromised, and Jerry's put that out to confuse us.'

'He would have slipped in a warning with the code. If he had been unable to transmit himself, he would have left something out. That would also have warned us. And yet . . .'

'And yet?'

'One can't really hide a battleship, even when it's only just being built. According to this, the keel's barely laid. It could be a hoax. They may not intend to build it at all, assuming the keel-laying is the real thing.'

'What should we do?'

'Wait and see if anything further comes in on this.'

But the men in the shabby room would

hear nothing further of the phantom pocket battleship – the *Graf von Hiller* – for another three years. During that time, with other, vitally urgent matters constantly vying for their attention, they would forget all about it.

Until it was too late.

An envelope with a bright-red seal was waiting for Delsingen when he returned to his office after his perfunctory troop inspection. He stared at it as he placed his cap, with studied deliberation, on his desk. He picked up the square, buff envelope. Apart from his address, there were no markings except for the dried wax of the seal. He recognized the stamped insignia.

He inspected the envelope minutely, checking it for tampering, then smiled grimly. No one would be daring or suicidal enough to interfere with the *Gruppenführer's* communications.

Delsingen began to unseal the envelope. He took the single sheet of paper out of it, then went round to his chair and sat down. He began to read:

My dear Rüdi,

A request from Mindenhof has landed on my desk. He has asked for an additional two SS officers, two *Unteroffiziere*, and 20 men. Do you approve of this? It is clear he has not informed you, for the request came through SS channels. I will do nothing until I hear from you.

   Max

The colonel gave another grim smile as he finished reading. Mindenhof was already attempting to bolster his forces.

'*Geissler!*' Delsingen shouted.

The door opened almost immediately. '*Herr Oberst?*'

'Come in, Geissler. And shut the door.'

The captain obeyed and walked towards the desk.

'Read this,' Delsingen said, handing him the letter.

Geissler took it wordlessly and began to read. His eyes grew round as he took in its meaning.

'My God, sir,' he said, returning the paper. 'He must have put in that request some time ago. Everyone knows how long it takes for something like this to get through.'

'Obviously not in the SS,' Delsingen said drily. 'Not one for letting the grass grow under his feet, our *Sturmbannführer*. He is greedy, but sly. He's trying to build up his own SS forces. However, he's doing it gradually, hoping that by the time he feels he has a sufficient number it will be too late for the poor fools in the Wehrmacht to do anything.'

'Is this from the, er, person you spoke of, sir?'

'Yes.'

'What are you going to do?'

'Promote you to major. I need two deputy commanders.'

Geissler looked white around the gills. 'Is that such a good idea, Colonel?'

'Calm yourself, Major. Your record shows you're an excellent man in combat. Mindenhof is only human.'

'There are many descriptions in my mind for him,' Geissler said. 'Human isn't one of them.' He was quite serious.

'All the same, you are now a major. I'll see that the promotion goes rapidly to the High Command, for approval. With my recommendation tagged to it, consider the rank confirmed. Before this war is over, Ernst,' Delsingen went on, 'you will see many terrible things – perhaps do some yourself – and face up to terrible nightmares. If Mindenhof is one of those nightmares, so be it. Any objections, Major?'

'Er . . . no, *Herr Oberst*,' replied a stunned Geissler.

'Good. Get yourself some new insignia. Tomorrow, I shall be calling a special meeting, with certain officers from both the Luftwaffe and the Kriegsmarine in attendance. You and Mindenhof will be there. I expect to see you in major's uniform.'

'Yes, sir!'

'Thank you, Major.'

South-east England

The two Spitfires came in fast and low over the grass strip, flitting shadows in the late-afternoon sun. The wingman performed two slow rolls.

'Oh dear,' remarked a pilot, lounging on the ground with his Mae West on. 'Jo-Jo hasn't scored, while young Bede has. This will not please our Antipodean.'

'It's not that he isn't good,' another said thoughtfully, as they watched the Spitfires come in to land. 'We've all seen him in a fight. He's ferocious . . .'

'But a terrible shot,' a third put in.

'It's just bad luck,' the first pilot said. 'I once saw him glued to the tail of an Me-109. Whatever that Jerry did, he couldn't shake off old Kearns. He was a dead duck. No more *sieg heiling* for him. No more *"Jawohl, mein Führer!"* or whatever it is they say to that lunatic with the toothbrush moustache. But poor old Jo-Jo's guns just wouldn't fire. For a moment, I thought Jo-Jo was going to ram him in frustration. In the end, I had to put the Jerry sod out of his misery, when Jo-Jo called for me to administer the old *coup de grâce*. When we landed, Jo-Jo was fit to bust, as our Yank friends would say.'

'Well, it can't be his bad luck,' the second pilot joined in. 'He's never been shot down, while all of us have.'

The three of them, on standby, were sprawled close to their machines. None had yet reached his twenty-first birthday.

'Twice for me,' said the first pilot gleefully.

'I think you bale out just for the fun of it,' one of his companions said. The third pilot. 'Anyway, I think Jo-Jo's lucky. No one who flies with him is ever shot down.'

'A flying rabbit's foot,' the first pilot said.

They laughed.

'He did get one,' the second pilot recalled. 'Some weeks ago.'

'Ah yes,' confirmed the first pilot. 'I remember. A fat old sitting duck of a flying boat, off the Dutch coast somewhere. Had to share it, though, didn't he? Who was with him that day?'

'Spots Spottiswood.'

'Alas, poor Spots. Knew him well. Bought the farm, poor devil.'

Spottiswood had been nineteen and a half years old.

'He wasn't flying with Jo-Jo that day,' the third pilot said triumphantly, seeing that as confirmation of Kearns's luck. 'He would still have been alive if he had.'

'If you say so, old son,' the first pilot said.

'I do say so. Old Spots is dead, isn't he?'

'We don't always fly with Jo-Jo. We're still here.'

'But for how long?'

No one laughed.

The mark of Spitfire flown by Jo-Jo Kearns's squadron was the Vb. The V was eventually to become the most numerous Spitfire and the Vb version, powered by a 1440-horsepower Merlin 45 engine, was armed with two 20mm cannon and four .303 machine-guns. While it took its toll of the Messerschmitt Bf-109, the Focke-Wulf Fw-190 gave it a tough time indeed. The radial-engined Fw-190 was smaller, lighter, stronger, even more powerfully armed, and highly agile. At that period of the war it was ahead of its time. A Spitfire V pilot who won against it either had to be very good, be lucky enough to catch an enemy rookie, or come up against an indifferent pilot.

Kearns had previously come up against good pilots but as his colleagues knew, he was an exceptional flyer. Most importantly, he was also very good at looking after his wingmen. There was an added bonus. They tended to score when in his company and, not surprisingly, everyone wanted to fly with him.

Pilot Officer Kearns was almost too old for the rank at twenty-one, and a bit of an enigma. Unlike the other pilots in his flight, he had begun as a sergeant, then moved up a rank to flight sergeant, before receiving a commission as a pilot officer. Though there were others on the squadron a year or two older than he was, in combat terms he was among the veterans. A Queenslander, he came from a family who were uncompromising in their hostility towards his decision to travel all the way to Britain to join the Royal Air Force.

This hostility had its roots in the family history.

The ancestor whose name he bore had been transported to Australia nearly two centuries earlier, for the heinous crime of stealing a chicken to feed his starving wife and child, who had then subsequently died during his enforced exile. He had willed himself to survive the appalling harshness of the penal colony and on eventually gaining his release in that vast, unforgiving land, had started a new family to replace the one he had lost. He never again set foot on British soil.

His descendants, who were now prosperous, were never allowed to forget how they came to be in Australia. It was burned into the family psyche. So when Johnny Kearns had announced that he was going to the old country to offer his services to the Crown, it was looked upon as the worst kind of treachery. Cutting him off from the family wealth was threatened. But Kearns had had no intention of changing his mind. With a small, secretly given sum from a sympathetic grandfather, the lonely and ostracized youngster had made his way to England.

If asked, he would not have been able to properly explain why he had been so stubborn and had chosen to estrange himself from his family, except to say that he believed in what he was doing. The family, had they so wished it, would have recognized in him the strong will of the man who had been the founder of the Kearns Australian tribe. They would have seen the spirit of the man who had not been defeated by his terrible experiences. They would have recognized a certain irony that might have given them pause for thought. But, having benefited from the wealth whose creation had begun with the reluctant convict all those hard years ago, they had chosen not to do so. Cushioned in moneyed comfort, they found it easier to milk the ancestral cross they bore for all it was worth.

Needless to say, the young Kearns's distant forebear would have recognized himself in his stubborn descendant.

As he taxied towards the waiting ground crew, family problems were not on Kearns's mind. He was fuming. His guns had jammed yet again after one burst, just when he'd had the Fw-190 pilot where he'd wanted him. The enemy aircraft had spiralled away trailing smoke, but had recovered sufficiently to scuttle back to its base in France.

Kearns's wingman, Pilot Officer James Bede – whom everyone had taken to calling 'Venerable' – had scored two kills. One had been against a Ju-87 Stuka that had been damaged during an anti-shipping strike in the Channel. The other kill had been the Me-109 that had been shepherding it home.

Kearns, having set Bede on the Stuka, had gone for the 109; but the Fw-190 had made an unexpected appearance, very determined to join in the fun. Kearns had broken off his attack on the Messerschmitt, to turn to face the more dangerous enemy. Bede, having mortally wounded the Ju-87, had then engaged the 109 that Kearns had been forced to abandon. By the time Kearns had given the pilot of the Fw-190 the fright of his life, Bede had dispatched the 109.

'*Bloody guns!*'

Kearns's frustration was unmistakable in the yell that rose above the sounds of the dying engine as the aircraft came to a stop and he slid back the canopy. He got out and made his way to the ground in a fury.

'Jesus, blokes!' he went on to the curious ground crew who had gathered. 'What the bloody hell's going on with these guns? And don't blame it on gremlins. There's a Nazi that's alive and well today, when he bloody well should be dead! I had him. One fart from the guns, then *nothing*.'

Kearns looked as if he had the enemy pilot by the throat. His hands were curved into claws round an invisible neck which he shook once, to emphasize the last word.

'I'd have got more action from a dried-up wallaby's tits!' he went on, teeth bared in a humourless grin. 'Find out what the hell happened!' He began to stomp away from them, then stopped and turned round. 'Look,' he said more calmly. 'I know it's not your fault; but how would you feel if you'd had a 190 so close you could see the scared bastard's head in the cockpit looking back at you, scared enough to shit? Then your guns don't work.'

'Bloody annoyed, sir,' one of the mechanics ventured.

'*Annoyed?*'

'Bloody fucked-off, sir,' another suggested.

'That's more like it. I want these things

working next time I'm up. Give it a go, will you?'

'We will, sir. Bad luck, sir.'

Kearns slowly removed his helmet. 'Yeah,' he sighed. 'Bad luck.'

Bergen, Norway. 0800 the next day
Geissler, resplendent in major's uniform,
knocked on Delsingen's door.

'*Hierein!*'

Geissler entered and saluted smartly.

'Ah, Geissler,' the colonel greeted him. 'So,
how does it feel to be a major?' He'd been
putting some papers into a thin blue folder.

'Getting used to it, *Herr Oberst*.'

'Thought you might,' Delsingen commented,
the fasteners on the folder clicking sharply as he
snapped it shut. 'Take off your hat. Relax. We
have a little time before the others get here.'

Geissler removed his cap and tucked it
beneath an arm. 'Didn't see you at breakfast, sir.'

'I had an early coffee. Terrible stuff. I hear
the Norwegian resistance sometimes manages
to get the real thing. Interesting, isn't it,
Geissler? We have all the weaponry and the

men. We're in control. But we can't get proper coffee.' Delsingen paused, as if remembering what good coffee was like.

'The restaurant on the mountain sometimes has the real stuff,' Geissler said.

'Yes,' the colonel said drily. 'And I wonder where *they* get their supplies from.'

'Nobody asks. Not even Mindenhof. We all like to taste the real thing now and then.'

'You see? He does have a human side.'

'I doubt it, sir. He'd close that place down out of spite, if it suited his purposes.'

'Speaking of which, has he seen your new rank yet?'

'No, sir. He'll know soon enough, if one of his cronies hasn't already passed on the news.'

'I've had the order posted.'

'I can see his face now.'

'Looking forward to that?'

'Not really, sir.'

Delsingen glanced at a clock on the wall. 'Time for the briefing.' He got up from behind his desk, picked up the folder and went to get his cap off its hook. 'They should all be there. Hat on, Geissler.'

The new major followed his colonel out of the room.

*   *   *

Two officers were waiting: a Luftwaffe lieutenant colonel and a navy lieutenant commander.
They snapped to attention when Delsingen
entered the room, and saluted in the standard
military manner.

'*Oberstleutnant* Gustav Mölner, Luftwaffe.'

'Korvettenkapitän Ulrich Fröhmann, Kriegsmarine.'

Delsingen returned their salutes. 'At ease,
gentlemen. Please sit down.'

Five chairs had been arranged at a large,
round table. Each visiting officer removed his
cap and placed it on the table before him, then
took his designated seat. Delsingen removed his
own cap, placed it on the table at his position,
put the folder down next to it, but remained
standing.

He looked at Geissler. 'It would appear that
Major Mindenhof is late. Find him, will you,
Geissler?'

Geissler's eyes gave nothing away. 'Sir,' he
acknowledged, and went out to find the SS
officer. He turned a corner into a short
corridor, and saw the gleaming black uniform
striding towards him. He stopped, waiting for
Mindenhof to draw near.

The SS major slowed his pace, then came to
a halt, his face expressionless.

'You're late,' Geissler said firmly.

The black eyes stared pointedly at Geissler's new insignia of rank.

'Don't feel too bold with those on, Geissler,' Mindenhof said coldly. 'I'm still senior to you.'

Geissler did not react to the taunt. 'The colonel's waiting. He is not pleased that you are late. The others are already there.'

Mindenhof's eyes glared beneath the peak of his spotless black cap. 'Don't push your luck, Geissler.'

He brushed past the army major, and continued on his way.

Geissler followed.

When they got to the door of the briefing room Mindenhof stood aside, expecting Geissler to knock.

Geissler watched him and did nothing.

Mindenhof's eyes hardened as he hesitated slightly. Then, seeing that Geissler had no intention of moving, he knocked sharply.

'*Hierein!*' came from within.

Mindenhof opened the door and stamped in, heels clicking sharply as he snapped to attention. His right arm shot out. '*Heil Hitler! Sturmbannführer* Mindenhof reporting as ordered, *Herr Oberst!*'

Mölner and Fröhmann began to get to their feet in response to the Hitler salute, but Delsingen indicated that they should remain seated.

The colonel stared at Mindenhof. 'You are late, Major. Please take your seat.'

Mindenhof stood uncertainly for a moment, temporarily confused by Delsingen's reaction. It was clear from his demeanour that the lack of response to his salute had not gone down well with him. He was also irritated by Geissler's sudden promotion, and annoyed by the public censure in front of the off-unit officers. However, he had expected a demand from the colonel that he explain himself for being late for the briefing. He had been deliberately late, and knew that Delsingen knew it. It was the colonel's low-key response to this that was confusing him.

Well aware of his own nature, Mindenhof expected everyone to be involved in a plot of some kind, and was convinced that Delsingen was planning something. This made him wary of things he could not foresee. He was beginning to realize that Delsingen was made of far sterner stuff than he had originally imagined. No matter. A Wehrmacht officer was no match for a dedicated member of the Waffen-SS.

'Major?' Delsingen was saying mildly.

'*Herr Oberst.*'

Mindenhof slowly removed his cap, walked to the table and carefully placed it among the others. The black cap, with its death's-head insignia and sweeping prow, was starkly different. Its presence dominated. Mölner and Fröhmann, glancing at it warily, appeared morbidly fascinated.

Even with an expressionless look on his face, Mindenhof still appeared to be smirking. He took his seat in a studied manner, fully enjoying the impact his presence had on the visiting officers.

'Lieutenant Colonel Mölner,' Delsingen began, introducing them, 'and Lieutenant Commander Fröhmann. Gentlemen, Major Mindenhof.'

Mindenhof nodded with cold detachment. The other two nodded at him, as they would at a dangerous beast they hoped would not attack them.

'Take your chair, Major,' Delsingen now said to Geissler, who had entered and was pushing the door shut. 'Then we can begin.' The colonel sat down.

'Sir,' Geissler said. He went to the last empty chair and placed his cap with the others on the table, then he too sat down.

Delsingen got straight down to business.

'I have been authorized,' he began, 'to form a unit whose specific task is to hunt out the resistance movements in the area. If this unit proves to be successful, it will form the basis for more units which will be deployed throughout the occupied countries. The unit which we're forming here will be the prototype. Success will mean more units in Norway. When these have also proved to be successful, the work on forming the others for the remaining occupied countries will then begin.' Delsingen paused to look at Mindenhof, whose face had gone pale and stiff. 'You have a comment, Major?'

'With respect, *Herr Oberst*,' Mindenhof said tightly, 'you also mean *future* occupied territories. Also, the SS is already responsible for . . .'

'Yes, yes,' Delsingen interrupted mildly. 'I know what you're going to say. Do not worry, Major. The normal SS role is not being usurped. As for future occupied territories, we shall know in the fullness of time what transpires. So, if you'll bear with me, I'll explain the specific role of the new unit. May I have your indulgence?'

Mindenhof's eyes tracked round, looking into the faces of the others at the table. They all had neutral expressions. The black eyes snapped back to the colonel.

'Please excuse the interruption, *Herr Oberst*.' It was not a climb-down.

'I have already forgotten about it.'

If anything, Delsingen's magnanimity annoyed Mindenhof even more. It had established the fact that the colonel was in such complete command that he could afford to be generous. Someone other than Mindenhof would have been grateful for not being bawled out in company; but to him, it was an even greater put-down, in front of everyone at the table. A knot of anger tightened in his stomach. It was an anger that would bide its time, determined to exact its revenge at the appropriate moment.

Delsingen gave no indication that he was aware of the SS officer's true feelings. Geissler, however, shot Mindenhof a wary glance, before returning his neutral gaze to Delsingen.

'To continue,' the colonel said evenly, 'we shall be forming a unified command for the unit, which is to be called *Sondergruppe-Norwegen* [Special Group-Norway] and will have the specific duty of hunting out resistance units like the Per Ålvik gang. It will deploy four-man hunter teams, and these will each have an officer, or senior non-commissioned officer, in command.

Each member will be a specialist of some kind: explosives expert, mountain trooper, sniper and so on. All will be expert in concealment.

'Each team must be able to operate independently of home base for long periods. Once deployed, they should expect to be in the field for as long as is required, to achieve an objective. There will be considerable danger. If discovered by members of the resistance, they should expect ferocious and implacable combat. In such circumstances, the options will be clear: a fighting withdrawal, and vacation of the area. While it will be hoped that such withdrawal can be achieved with the team remaining intact, it would be irresponsible of me not to warn you that this may not always be possible. If captured, *no* information – of any kind – must be given to the enemy. The general opinion is that our adversaries do not interrogate prisoners as . . . rigorously as we do.'

Delsingen paused, leaving the rest unspoken. But everyone knew exactly what he meant. If captured, the teams could expect far better treatment from their captors than any member of the resistance could hope to receive from the SS. All the military officers felt a private revulsion for the methods of the SS. None of them looked at Mindenhof. This was an act which, if anything, served to betray their thoughts more nakedly.

Mindenhof tightened his lips briefly, knowing exactly what the others were thinking. He studiously avoided looking at them, keeping his dark eyes firmly on the colonel.

'The teams' greatest effectiveness,' Delsingen went on, 'will be in remaining as difficult to spot as possible. Once discovered, their usefulness in that particular area will have been compromised. The psychological impact of these killer teams operating in the countryside will be immense. The resistance gangs will themselves feel threatened. They won't know where the next blow might come from. In short, we'll be doing to them what they've been doing to us.

'No contact must be made with the local populace at *any* time. The teams must not betray their presence, whatever area they may be operating in; but at least one member should be able to understand Norwegian, for eavesdropping purposes. The teams will not only be hunter-killers, but also intelligence gatherers. They will do this by observation and eavesdropping. Whenever they return to base, the information they have obtained will be absorbed into the general intelligence picture.

'If any member is injured and requires more

than basic medical attention, the team involved will contact base by a coded radio signal. Each team will have a casualty evacuation rendez-vous. These are the *only* conditions under which the rendezvous will be used and the radio operated for transmission. The radio is primarily for receiving and listening in on the Norwegian field frequencies. At all other times the teams will make their own way back to base, or to a prearranged pick-up point. There will be no exceptions to this rule.'

Delsingen now spoke directly to Mindenhof. 'Each team will have at least one member of the Waffen-SS. He may be the officer in command, or one of the team. Like the others, he will have an expert skill. No captures must be made and no interrogations will be undertaken in the field. As with the arrangements I have just mentioned, there will be no deviation from these orders.'

Mindenhof, at first surprised by what he saw as an olive branch from the colonel, was not at all happy about being forbidden to take prisoners and carry out interrogations.

'Then how are we to get information?' he asked.

'The teams will be operating in designated areas, basing their approach on information supplied by our intelligence network. Some of this will come from SS security operations. As you've also just heard me say, they themselves will be covert intelligence gatherers.'

'We all know that intelligence can change from day to day, hour to hour, minute to minute. The teams cannot transmit. Someone captured in the field . . .'

'Will, and can lie. A prisoner's information can also be out of date, or false.'

'There are ways . . .'

'We all know of those ways, Major,' Delsingen interrupted calmly. '*Sondergruppe-Norwegen* will be known for its ruthlessness in combat, *not* for its prowess at torture. I hope I have made this quite clear. I expect any SS personnel in the *Sondergruppe* to follow my orders. As the senior SS officer in my command, I also expect your support in this. You will instruct your fellow members of the SS accordingly.'

Mindenhof's eyes danced briefly. 'May we speak privately after we are finished here, Colonel?'

'Of course.'

Mindenhof gave a curt nod of thanks.

The others at the table continued to keep their expressions neutral.

Delsingen now opened the folder he had brought with him, and took out two sealed envelopes. He handed one each to the Luftwaffe and Kriegsmarine officers.

They opened the envelopes carefully, then read the contents.

Mölner looked up when he had finished. 'I have been ordered to place six fighters at your disposal. For the purposes outlined in here, I would prefer to have the Focke-Wulf 190. At the moment, we are using the Me-109.'

'Put in a requisition,' Delsingen told him. 'I am certain we can find six 190s, and their pilots, from somewhere.'

'If I can get those 190s, I'll find the pilots.'

'Then put in that requisition. I'll have it attended to.'

Mölner gave a tight smile. 'I'll do it as soon as we have finished.'

'Good. And you, Commander?' Delsingen went on to Fröhmann.

'I am to command a flotilla of four E-boats and, like Colonel Mölner, place them at your disposal.'

'Do you need anything special for them?'

'No, sir. They are well armed.'

'Including anti-aircraft?'

'Yes, sir. We have multi-barrelled cannon.'

'Good,' Delsingen repeated. 'I now come to other aspects of *Sondergruppe-Norwegen*. First, the air element. In addition to the six fighters, I have requested a Blohm and Voss 138, to replace the one in which my predecessor so tragically lost his life. His work for the Fatherland will not be forgotten.' Delsingen paused. 'Yes, Major?' he added to Mindenhof, who looked as if he wanted to say something.

'His work for the Führer and the Reich!' Mindenhof corrected.

Everyone at the table seemed to hold his breath, waiting for Delsingen's reply. His benevolent eyes looked squarely at the SS major. 'The Führer and the Reich *are* the Fatherland,' he said quietly, his tone clearly indicating that the other man should have been aware of that.

'That's what I meant,' Mindenhof said gruffly.

'Of course. Now where was I? Ah. Yes. The 138. This aircraft will belong to *Sondergruppe-Norwegen* and will be allocated specifically for the hunter-killer teams. It will be used to put them in place rapidly.' Delsingen looked at Fröhmann. 'A task it will share with your E-boats, Commander.'

Fröhmann nodded in acknowledgement.

'The remaining two 138s,' Delsingen went on, 'will continue with their normal duties.' His lips moved in a faint, brief smile. 'Despite the overwhelming successes of blitzkrieg operations – with the air elements working in support of the ground forces – we all know in our heart of hearts that, in a general sense, communications between the armed forces are limited. I am being polite.

'The Luftwaffe does not talk to the Kriegsmarine, the Wehrmacht does not talk to the SS and all four barely talk to each other. The point I'm making, gentlemen, is that poor communications have hampered many operations, as we all know. When the Royal Navy or the RAF attacks a ship, it takes a long time before that ship can receive air cover. I know of at least one that was sunk due to the fact that the Luftwaffe went in the wrong direction.'

He turned to Mölner. 'Please do not misunderstand me, my dear Mölner. I am not here to waste time scoring points off the Luftwaffe. The enemy, I am sure, has such problems too. However, I intend to show that close co-operation *can* yield spectacular results. I do not pretend that this will become as common a practice as I would like, throughout our forces. But I do hope we'll achieve some measure of it within our small group. Our various forces all jealously guard their independence; but remember, gentlemen, this is a war that will build to a terrible climax. We talk of blood and iron. There will be plenty of that to give us our fill. This is not the time for fighting among ourselves.'

Mölner nodded slowly. It was obvious from his expression that he was all too aware of the incident that had cost the ship.

Mindenhof looked as if he wanted to butt in, but made a great effort not to. The strain of that effort showed clearly on his face. The cold, glassy eyes seemed glued to Delsingen.

'We are all aware,' the colonel continued, 'that under normal circumstances anti-resistance and anti-partisan units do not receive the best equipment. They are not considered true front-line forces. Fortunately for us our *Sondergruppe*, as a new type of unit, will receive special attention. We *will* get the equipment we need. You, Colonel Mölner, will get your six 190s and you, Commander Fröhmann, will receive additional equipment as and when you decide you need it.'

Delsingen looked at Mindenhof. 'Major, in order to give us the right mix of personnel, I feel we may need a few more of your SS. Any ideas?'

Delsingen was aware that Geissler was staring at him with a wide-eyed expression that telegraphed dismay.

'Well, Major?' he urged a suddenly thoughtful Mindenhof.

'One officer of *Hauptsturmführer* rank,' Mindenhof began, the barest touch of hesitation in his voice, 'a senior NCO, and ten men should do it.'

'Good,' Delsingen said affably. 'You shall have your captain, your NCO and your men. Let me have the paperwork as soon as you can, and I'll have it sent through quickly.'

'Very well, *Herr Oberst*.' Mindenhof looked as if he expected a catch to be lurking in there somewhere.

Geissler was still giving Delsingen glances that, although covert, clearly indicated that he was wondering if his colonel had suddenly gone mad.

Delsingen ignored them.

'Our air cover,' he went on, 'will be for the benefit of any Tommi aircraft that choose to pay us a visit during operations. But we shall also use the 190s in the bombing role, whenever we find a resistance target. This could be a mountain cabin, an arms dump – anything whose destruction will hurt. The E-boats, in addition to their task of landing the teams, will also continue to hunt down commando vessels and submarines.' Delsingen paused briefly. 'The unit will go into immediate training. A programme has already been created, and within a month I expect to see the first teams go out. Our friend Ålvik has a nasty shock coming. Let us make sure he realizes that very soon.'

Delsingen paused again, then slowly looked at each man in turn.

'Finally, I am authorized to pass on to you information that very few people are aware of. It will not go beyond this room. There will be a field court martial for *anyone* who disobeys this order. The penalty will be as severe as you can already imagine. If any of you has any doubts, you may ask to be relieved of your command and your responsibilities before I continue.'

The kindly eyes had become so cold that even Mindenhof appeared to sit more upright.

No one spoke. Each man knew that even asking to be relieved of his command would have a disastrous effect on his career. The worst of postings would follow, as sure as night followed day.

Delsingen nodded and continued, 'This is what I expect of German officers. I can now tell you that a new pocket battleship is being built. She will be lighter but faster and more powerful than her sister ships already at sea. Her armament will be formidable. The enemy knows nothing of her existence. When complete, she will be coming here to Norway, to Sognefjord. Before that occurs, all the resistance groups in the area must be wiped out or neutralized. Security over her arrival and presence will be extreme. If we carry out our duty successfully, the Reich's most secret ship will remain secure and be able to strike at the enemy at will. The enemy must continue to be ignorant of her existence. She is the *Graf von Hiller*.'

'When will she arrive?' the Lieutenant Commander asked.

'I cannot tell you, because I don't know. It could be months. It could be years. Her deployment schedule is a matter for the Naval Staff, and is highly secret. Now, gentlemen. Questions?'

There were none.

Delsingen carefully put his cap on its hook and walked back to his desk. As he sat down he looked up at Mindenhof, who stood before him stiffly, legs apart, cap still on.

'All right, Major,' Delsingen began. 'I know

you've been bursting to have your say. Let's hear it.'

'There are many things that disturb me, *Herr Oberst*.'

'I've no doubt. Let's have them.'

Mindenhof seemed to pause for thought. 'At the briefing you appeared to suggest that we may not win this war.'

'I don't remember having said so.'

'You said this war would reach a terrible climax. We shall have our fill of blood and iron.'

'Yes, Major. I did say that. But I'm equally certain you did not hear me say we would lose.'

'It suggests that you expect us to fight for a long time. I do not agree. Our blitzkrieg will . . .'

'Have you ever been in combat, Major? I mean *real* combat. Not just suppressing an occupied populace, chasing a few saboteurs or manning concentration camps. I am talking about having your face in the mud while the world explodes around you. Or putting a hand out where a friend should be and touching what feels like a soft, warm and runny pie. Or seeing a helmet and turning it round to check who's lying next to you, to find a head in it but no body attached. Have you?'

Mindenhof was looking as if he was about to vomit. This, Delsingen thought, was odd for a man who had spent some time running the camps.

The SS major swallowed. 'I have not had that honour,' he said tightly. 'I have asked many times to be posted to the front; but I have been assured that my work is here.'

Delsingen made no comment. He knew that Mindenhof had no intention of going anywhere near a front if he could possibly help it.

'What other objections do you have?' the colonel asked.

'I do not believe that being soft with these people is the answer. One regiment of Waffen-SS would sweep these mountains of the likes of Ålvik and his kind. At the very least, it should not be difficult to perhaps have a unit of the *Germanske-SS Norge* deployed . . .'

'That is not an option,' Delsingen interrupted firmly. 'When dealing with people like Ålvik, try to remember this: they have lost everything that was dear to them. Their one driving force is a monumental hatred that pervades the very blood in their veins. Bludgeoning them will not make them easier to deal with. You merely fuel the hatred – and the determination.

'They will not be frightened of you and

sending in the *Germanske-SS Norge* will enrage them even further. They hate us; but they hate these particular countrymen – whom they look upon as the worst of traitors – even more. They will despise you and dedicate themselves to your destruction. You will not win that way, Major.

'The structure of the *Sondergruppe* has been approved by the General Staff. If you have objections, I would suggest you put them in writing and, I promise you, I will have them forwarded to the highest level. Who knows? Perhaps they will require your presence, in order that you may make those objections in person.'

The black eyes held a cold fury. 'May I speak frankly, Colonel?'

'You may, Major.'

'You have not won this. I know why you've shoved Geissler up a rank and made him a deputy commander. I'm not blind. I know what you're up to.'

'You misunderstand me, Major,' Delsingen said evenly. 'That can be a serious mistake. I am indulging you by allowing you to speak to me like this. As you've heard me say at the briefing, I believe that co-operation between the forces is vital to success. I believe we can show

how this can be of great benefit to our cause. As one of my deputy commanders, I expect you to show loyalty rather than try to undermine my command. I gave you a chance to get out. You chose not to. As you have chosen to stay I will demand, and expect, your full support. I do not intend to repeat this conversation with you.'

Mindenhof went through his vibrating routine. The eyes beneath the peak of his cap were malevolent; but he was trapped, and knew it.

'You will have my request for the additional men,' he said at last.

'Thank you, Major.'

Mindenhof's heels clicked sharply. The right arm shot out. '*Heil Hitler!*'

Delsingen nodded at him.

Mindenhof wheeled, and stamped out.

Delsingen gave a low sigh and shook his head slowly as the door shut behind the SS major. Within seconds there was a knock.

'In!'

Geissler entered, carrying a strip of paper.

'Ah, Geissler,' Delsingen began. 'You have a tortured expression on your face. What is it? Apprehension? Confusion?'

'Both, sir.'

'You think I've gone mad because I've given

Mindenhof a chance to bring even more of his SS into our midst?'

'I'm just puzzled,' Geissler replied diplomatically.

'Don't be. I know what I'm doing.'

'You do realize, Colonel, that Mindenhof really expects to have more SS than the requirement he'll submit to you.'

'Of course. That was why he asked for so few. He expects to have the others as well. The man's an empire builder. His own. The trick, Geissler, is to feed your enemy; but only enough to ease his hunger. Never make him strong enough to devour you.'

'So he won't be getting those he asked for through the SS High Command.' Geissler smiled. 'And, of course, he can't blame you. A flanking movement of some finesse, if I may say so, Colonel.'

'You may.'

'But you do know he won't give up. Don't you, sir?'

'I would be very surprised if he did,' Delsingen replied calmly. 'There are many ways of fighting a war, Geissler. Remember that.'

'Yes, sir.'

'Now what's that thing you're waving about like a white flag? A signal?'

Geissler handed over the piece of paper.

Delsingen read the signal, then put it down on the desk. A platoon of mountain troops had been wiped out.

He stood up, and went over to a large map of south-western Norway with its myriad fiords, islands, inlets and mountains. Various locations had been circled in red. He stared at them silently for a long time.

'He is clever, our Ålvik,' the colonel remarked softly. 'He knows we'll be noting the location of each attack. There's no logical pattern for us to follow. No way of knowing where he'll strike next. I'm certain he's got a map of his own on which he's putting his own marks. He'll be seeing the pattern we see. The trouble is, Geissler, we can only react to his moves – for the moment.

'Our teams must gather intelligence, to give us an edge. It will take some time to build a picture from which we can predict his movements with reasonable accuracy; but we shall do so. Your time is coming, Per Ålvik.'

For the briefest of moments, Geissler had the strangest feeling that Delsingen was actually in conversation with the Norwegian resistance man.

Delsingen turned to face his subordinate.

'Oh, and tell *Leutnant* Kahler he has command of one of the teams. Show him the training schedule. That should cure his visits to the toilet.'

Geissler's face broke into a slow grin. 'Or make it worse.'

'You never know, Geissler. This might be the making of him.'

The major's grin widened. 'Yes, sir.'

4

The small hut had been built into the rock-face. The narrow strip of roof that protruded from the towering wall was lushly covered with grass and moss. It was high up the mountain and, before war had come, might have been used as a refuge for mountain hikers and skiers. But this one was on no hiker's or skier's map. Access to it was via a secluded track that took a meandering and precipitous route.

The resistance movement had the comprehensive details of such refuges throughout Norway, many of which were unknown to the occupying forces.

Those suspected to have been discovered by the enemy, or whose sites had been betrayed by collaborators, were given a wide berth by members of the resistance. New huts, at secret locations, had also been constructed. The compromised refuges had sometimes been used by the invading forces. On such occasions many had been destroyed by the resistance – an inevitable consequence of the ambushes sprung on the soldiers who had foolishly taken shelter in them.

The hut that Ålvik and his small team now entered had, like many others, been presciently constructed, just before the war. One of the men, Olav Skjel, had remained outside to stand the first watch among the trees that totally concealed the refuge from view, even from someone watching through binoculars from the other side of the fiord which it overlooked. Skjel, having taken up his position, was equally well hidden.

Though basic, the hut was surprisingly comfortable and well stocked. There was plenty of room for four people to move around without crowding. Sleeping was done on the floor, on mattresses that looked like padded blankets but were also surprisingly comfortable.

There were two bench seats at a pine table big enough to accommodate six diners. There were also two low stools. The sleeping area was separated from the dining area by a partition that ended in a doorway, but there was no door. Instead, a heavy, lined curtain of plain, rough material hung from a pine rail. At the back of the hut a flush-fitting, removable panel in the pine wall led to an escape exit. There was no way of telling at first, or even second and third glances, that such a way out existed.

The rock-face behind the hut contained the entrance to a natural tunnel, created by an ancient fissure. This continued through the mountain for just over half a mile, until its exit opened out on to a steeply inclined, shrub-pocked scree that went down to a river. No roads or tracks led to that section of the river, which was heavily wooded on both sides. A powerful radio, used to communicate with Britain, was kept hidden in the tunnel.

Ålvik removed his flat cap, unslung his Sten gun and placed them both on the table. The sub-machine-gun was one of the many that had been supplied from Britain to virtually all the resistance movements within occupied Europe.

Although among captured weaponry many of his comrades prized the SS's MP40, he preferred to stick with the simple Sten. Despite some of its drawbacks, it was easy to repair in the field. He knew there were occasions when the Sten was prone to jam, usually at the very worst of moments; but it had never happened to him. He looked after the weapon scrupulously. His life depended on it.

Inge had followed him in. She carried one section of the mortar launcher in a backpack, a rifle in one hand and a pistol in a holstered belt. The 50mm launcher was little more than a tube with a base plate. She could assemble and dismantle it quickly, and was able to shift firing positions with a speed that always surprised her colleagues. She seldom required a ranging shot, rarely missing a target with the first round. Ammunition, she maintained, was precious and should not be wasted.

The remaining two men trailed in after her. one had the second section of the dismantled mortar in his backpack. In a hand-held pack, he carried the mortar rounds. Slung from his shoulder was a liberated MP40, for which he had plenty of ammunition. The last man carried a heavy machine-gun, as well as the team's field radio, which he had taken from Skjel, who normally carried it. Skjel, a fantastic shot, was also the team's sniper. He kept his superbly maintained rifle with him at all times.

They put their equipment down on the floor, then took seats at the table.

Ålvik remained standing. He unbuttoned his dark-green jacket of rough wool and pulled a map out of a concealed lining. They watched as he spread it on the table. Had Delsingen been there to see, he would have smiled grimly.

With a pencil that he took from a pouch on his left sleeve, Ålvik circled a spot on the map. It was the location where the mountain troops had been killed.

'If this map should ever fall into their hands,' he said, 'it will tell them where we've been, which is old news – not where we're going to strike next. I think we should stay here for a few days. Keep them guessing. In any case, we could do with a rest.'

The others nodded.

Throughout the area, the rest of his group would also be going to ground.

Ålvik looked at the faces of his fellow-fighters, who had also become his friends. Before the war, none of them had known each other. So far, the luck had been with them. Not one had even been injured while under his leadership. He wondered how long it would be before he suffered his first casualty. It was, he knew, only a matter of time before that happened.

He tried not to imagine who would be first. His eyes fell upon Inge, who was smiling at him.

Please don't let it be Inge, he prayed silently.

Then he felt guilty, and slightly disloyal. He would hate to lose any of them.

The man who had carried the heavy machine-gun, Morgens Morgensen, stood up and said, 'I need a cigarette.' He looked at the one with the MP40. 'Coming, Henrik?'

Henrik Arendt, who didn't smoke, first looked puzzled, then got up as he understood the other's motives.

'All right. Just to make sure you keep that smoke under control. You never know who might be watching.'

'They went out together, taking their personal weapons with them.

A charged silence fell as they left.

'You know why they did that, don't you?' Inge eventually said to Ålvik. She did not look at him.

He cleared his throat. 'I do?'

'Of course you do. They are leaving us together.'

'Inge, I . . .'

Without warning, she stood up in a rush and launched herself at him. He staggered back, nearly falling as her hands reached for his face, the palms clamping themselves against his cheeks. She drew the face close and kissed him urgently, almost devouring him. Then abruptly, she stopped and stood back, breathing hard, bosom heaving with the effort, her eyes burning with a wild intensity. A red bloom had appeared on both her own cheeks. She seemed barely under control.

Ålvik stared at her, mouth slightly open.

'A . . . a German patrol could come up this track at any time,' she began, the words tumbling over each other, 'and . . . we could be fighting for our lives. I have had my feelings for you for a long time, Per. We have been through many fights with the Germans. Once I saw a soldier take aim at you from behind a tree, and I knew if he got the chance to fire, you would be dead. All I could think of was that if you were killed, you would die without ever having made love to me. I couldn't bear to think about it. I brought up my rifle and shot him before he could pull the trigger. You didn't even know what had happened. Nobody did. Nobody else had seen that soldier.'

Her words ended suddenly, as if she had decided she'd said too much. Her eyes remained fastened on him.

Then she began to remove her clothes.

'What . . . are you doing?' he asked in a voice that had suddenly become hoarse. 'The others . . .' But his eyes followed each item of clothing as she dropped it to the floor.

'Getting undressed, as you can see.'

'The others . . .' he heard himself repeat, as if taking refuge in the words.

'They will have moved far enough way from . . .'

'They planned this? You all planned this?'

She continued to undress. 'Oh, Per!' It was almost as if she had spoken to a child. 'No one planned anything. They know how you feel, even if you pretend . . .'

'How do they know how I feel? They're not me.'

With the necessarily dowdy clothes of resistance warfare now completely removed, he was at last able to see how truly magnificent a body she possessed. He watched, mesmerized, as she walked slowly up to him, the movements of the muscles in her legs and thighs sending a tingling sensation through him. She stopped, standing very close, but without touching. She didn't need to. He could feel the heat of her reaching out, caressing him.

'Now tell me you don't feel anything for me,' she said in a soft voice.

Then she reached for his mouth with her lips and kissed him gently. She drew back, eyes searching his face, before turning away to push through the rough curtain as she entered the other room.

He remained irresolutely where he was, listening as she moved around. Then the sounds of her movements stopped. After a short while, he went to the curtain and pushed it slightly aside. She was lying on one of the thin mattresses, flat on her back. Her legs were pressed tightly together, as if, having gone this far, she was now unsure of how to continue.

He entered the room and looked down at her. As his eyes roamed over her body, he felt a powerful arousal being born within him. It was the first time he had felt this way since he had lost Elle.

'You don't have to do this,' he said.

'I know you still love her,' she told him softly. 'But I don't mind.' Her eyes had begun to glisten. 'And now, I have made a fool of myself.'

'No, no,' he told her gently. He went over to her and eased himself to the floor. 'You haven't.'

A small trickle had appeared at the corner of her left eye. He wiped it away, then kissed the corner.

'What has happened to my brave mortar lady?'

'I . . . I don't know,' she replied in a small voice.

He kissed her at the corner of her right eye, then on the forehead. He kissed the tip of her nose, then each cheek and finally her lips.

She gave a shuddering little sigh as her mouth opened in response. Her lips and tongue began working at first hesitantly, then with increasing passion. Her hands were once more holding on to his face, keeping his lips fiercely attached to hers.

Her body had begun to move.

With frantic hands, Ålvik began to remove his own clothes. It was not an easy task, as Inge would not let go. So he had to do it all while seemingly glued to her mouth. But somehow, he managed to get everything off and when at last he was able to bring his body against hers, she gave a little squeal that expressed both delight and eager anticipation.

He felt the burning heat of her as he lay himself gently on her soft body. But soon his own desires were bringing with them a very urgent need to enter her. He felt the legs he had surreptitiously admired for so long opening beneath him, in readiness for his entry.

And when he did, she gasped; and he felt resistance.

He stopped. My God, he thought, astonished. She really is!

'*No!*' she cried. 'Don't stop, Per! *Please!*'

'I don't want to hurt you.'

'You won't hurt me.' There was a touch of exasperation in her voice. She spread her thighs wider. 'Please,' she said softly. 'Come in.'

Sensing he would still hesitate, she placed both hands on his buttocks and pulled firmly. Already fully aroused, Ålvik felt himself responding and he plunged into her. Now driven by his own body's desires he found he could no longer stop, even if he'd wanted to. His need for her went beyond all other considerations.

She gave a sharp cry as he broke through. Then the cry turned into a squeal that turned into a sobbing little chuckle of pleasure that again turned into a squeal. From then on, they seemed to be frantically trying to fuse into each other's body. They rolled off the mattress and on to the floor, thrusting so hard at each other that they appeared in imminent danger of damaging themselves. They were oblivious to the world about them; to the hard floor of the hut; to the noises that were being forced out of them. Inge seemed engulfed by a series of continuing squeals, while he grunted like some primeval beast as he felt himself pounding uncontrollably into her. Their bodies became damp with the searing frenzy of their exertions.

Perhaps it was because they lived constantly with fear; or because of the things they had seen and done. Perhaps it was because of a deep longing for something other than the harsh realities of warfare. Whatever the reason, the passions that raged within sent them rolling and undulating all round the room.

At last, a great shudder seized her and she arched beneath him like a tautened bow, remaining in the tensed position for long, delicious moments. Then with a great lash of her body she hauled back, then slammed against him, stiffening and holding him fast within her. He strained at the wild, energetic body, feeling as if the very energies which gave him life were emptying into her. The breath rushed out of him in a tortured rasp that left him so completely spent, it was as if all his muscles had been turned into jelly. Then he collapsed on her in halting stages as, slowly, she too began to relax.

'You wanted me,' she said gently, a sense of wonder in her voice. She stroked his damp hair lovingly. 'You wanted me.'

'Yes,' he said. 'I did . . . and I do.'

She moved a thigh slightly beneath him.

The brief movement reminded him of the new stirrings she had generated within him when he'd first seen her lying on the mattress, waiting. He felt desire returning.

Some way down the track, but still in cover, Morgensen said to the others, 'I hope he's finally doing what he should have done ages ago.' He smoked his second cigarette, in cupped hands.

'He's still got Elle on his mind,' Skjel commented. 'And you shouldn't smoke any more. That stink will last for a while. Do you want some German mountain trooper smelling it?'

'They don't know about this place,' Morgensen retorted.

'Olav is right, Morgens,' Arendt said placatingly. 'Anyway, after what happened,' he went on swiftly before Morgensen could say anything, 'it's not surprising Per feels the way he does, is it?'

'I don't want to sound hard,' Morgensen said, ignoring the comments about his smoking, 'but he's not the only one to have lost. The living must go on, so we can make the bastards pay. If a new woman is in love with him, he should be smart enough to grab with both hands. Inge is a little younger, but under all those clothes I'll bet you she's one hell of a woman. He can't bring Elle back, no matter how much he loved her. But he can continue to make those animals pay a very high price for what they did. If Inge can prevent him from turning into a dried stick, that's good for us.'

'What are you talking about?' Arendt demanded. 'He's a good leader. Do you have complaints?'

'Of course he's a good leader,' Morgensen said defensively. 'But I've seen people go strange when something like this happens to them. They begin to take chances. They don't care if they die. The problem is, they risk other lives too.'

'Per's not like that. Not one member of our group has been killed.'

'I didn't say he's like that. But I don't believe in all that crap about war leaving no time for love. In war, time is precious. You should take everything you can get out of it. We've each got someone we care about. Per *needs* someone. It's not healthy for him to be feeding on himself like that. Not good for us, either, because one day . . .'

'I wonder how many people have been killed in this war while doing it,' Arendt said thoughtfully, deliberately veering off at a tangent.

'Plenty,' Skjel said, as if he'd been present on

each occasion. 'Maybe he thinks about that, and feels loving someone will make him vulnerable. Look what happened to his family.'

'As I have just said,' Morgensen told them, returning to his theme, 'he's not the only one to have lost people to the Germans. There is nothing wrong in being vulnerable. You know what you're fighting to protect.'

'So what do you want to do?' Skjel demanded. 'Go back up there and tell him to take Inge to bed?'

Arendt gave a chuckle. 'I'd love to hear his response to that one.'

They eventually returned to the hut, leaving Morgensen to take his turn on watch. He lit his third cigarette as he went to his position.

'Those cigarettes will kill you one day,' Arendt called softly after him.

'The war will probably do it first,' the unrepentant Morgensen countered. 'So why should I worry?'

'It's your funeral.'

'Lot's of funerals these days, but more dead bodies.'

Arendt shook his head, giving up on Morgensen and his smoking.

They entered the hut to find Ålvik and Inge

fully dressed and in the final stages of preparing a meal. There was nothing about the hut to suggest anything had happened. But though everyone took turns at preparing meals when they used the refuges, it was the first time they could remember seeing Ålvik helping Inge. They also noted there was quite a glow to her cheeks.

Arendt glanced at Skjel, who had a neutral expression on his face.

'Morgens will be pleased with what you've done,' Arendt said to Inge.

Colour rose from her neck to join the bloom on her cheeks as her head darted round to look at him. 'What?'

He pointed to the food. 'Cake. He likes cakes.'

'Oh,' she said faintly. 'I found some in the supplies.'

'Arendt again glanced at Skjel, who was looking at Ålvik.

But the leader had his eyes on Arendt. 'Not a word from you, Henrik,' he said sternly.

Arendt put a finger to his lips.

Two weeks later Geissler entered Delsingen's office.

The colonel was standing before the map,

looking at the circles he'd made. No new ones had been added.

'Still no information about attacks any-where?' the colonel asked.

'No, sir,' replied Geissler.

'Hmm,' Delsingen said.

'It's been remarkably quiet out there in the mountains,' Geissler went on, 'and it's giving me the shivers.'

'It's giving *us* time to get on with our training,' said Delsingen, still staring at the map. 'What are you up to, Per Ålvik?' he said to it. He turned to his subordinate. 'I can almost enjoy this. Our young Norwegian is a worthy adversary. The man *thinks*. I like that in an enemy.'

'Speaking of enemies, sir. Major Mindenhof is walking around with a face like thunder. It seems that his request for those extra SS men was turned down by the SS High Command.'

'War moves in mysterious ways, Geissler.'

'Yes, sir,' Geissler said, hiding a smile.

There were no attacks in the area for an entire month, and Delsingen's new teams completed their high-pressure training schedule.

Mindenhof's new SS additions had arrived

after all, but he was still fuming over SS High Command's initially negative response to his request. *Oberstleutnant* Mölner got his six Focke-Wulf 190s and Delsingen's replacement Blohm and Voss 138 had arrived.

Fröhmann's E-boats had practised fast deployments and had carried out random search-and-destroy missions in the fiords. One of those had actually borne fruit when they had surprised two agents from England, paddling to shore in a rubber boat. The operatives had clearly been brought over by submarine and had disembarked just off the mouth of one of the fiords. There had been an exchange of fire. Both agents were killed, and Fröhmann had lost one of his own crew. However, papers had been found which Delsingen thought would be useful in the fight against the resistance.

After studying them closely, he had sent the papers under secure cover to his friend in Berlin, the SS *Gruppenführer*. The major-general would know how to make the best possible use of the information.

Mindenhof had wanted to use the papers for his own purposes, insisting that as he was the SS senior officer on the spot, security matters concerning enemy agents were his responsibility.

'All right, Major,' Delsingen had said. '*You* explain to the *Gruppenführer* in Berlin why you thought it best to keep these papers to yourself.'

Mindenhof's objections had miraculously vanished, like snowflakes on a hot day. But he took being thwarted yet again with unconcealed bad grace.

'That man does not like you at all, sir,' Geissler said afterwards.

'Tell me something new, Major.'

'*Leutnant* Kahler.'

'If it's about his toilet training, I don't want to hear.'

'That's just it, sir,' Geissler said. 'Kahler has discovered new resources within himself. If I hadn't written his fitness report myself, I would scarcely have believed it. He's been transformed into a keen leader. He wants his team to be the first into operations.'

'And are you prepared to entrust him with it?'

'He'll surprise you. He certainly surprised me.'

'All right, Ernst. We'll follow your recommendation. Tell him to be ready to go within two days. He can have the honour of carrying out the *Sondergruppe*'s first mission.'

'I'll tell him.'

Delsingen smiled thinly. 'Perhaps I was right, after all. This could be the making of our toilet-happy lieutenant.'

'He doesn't go so often now.'

'You see? An improvement already.'

Within three weeks *Sondergruppe-Norwegen* had its first success, and first blood went to the team led by Kahler. They returned without prisoners, but with captured weapons as evidence of the kill. They had caught four members of the resistance. None, however, was from Ålvik's group. Even so, Delsingen held a small celebration.

Kahler's team had been in the field for most of the three weeks, patiently gathering intelligence and biding their time. The Waffen-SS sergeant attached to the team as his second in command had given no trouble and had supported him loyally. The sergeant, Heinz Eiche, was even fulsome in his praise of Kahler's behaviour in combat, when reporting to Mindenhof. This did not please the SS major, who came close to accusing Eiche of disloyalty to the SS.

But Mindenhof could not deny the fact that Delsingen's ideas appeared to have worked.

'So far,' he muttered to himself.

Barely a week later a second team, this time led by an SS captain, carried out a successful ambush. Again no prisoners were taken, as the resistance fighters never surrendered. The captain suffered one casualty: a man badly wounded. They got him back safely.

Five days later Delsingen got a summons from Berlin. He called Mindenhof to his office.

'I'm going to Berlin,' he said as soon as Mindenhof had gone through his usual routine of striding in on hard heels, clicking to attention and barking out his '*Heil Hitler*'. 'I'm leaving you in command, Major.' Delsingen fixed his subordinate with a hard stare. 'I expect you to carry out my orders without the slightest deviation. If any of the teams bring in prisoners, they are to be interrogated *without* torture. Major Geissler will be present at all interrogations to ensure that this rule is obeyed.'

'You're ordering him to spy on me, *Herr Oberst*?'

'No, Major. To ensure that our work is not jeopardized by any misguided policies. We are having success. This will continue. The way we handle our prisoners will pay dividends. Brutalizing them will not.'

'May I ask why the colonel is being summoned to Berlin?'

'You may. I have been summoned to discuss future developments of the *Sondergruppe* idea. Berlin is pleased with our initial successes. Let us not spoil the picture, eh?'

Mindenhof appeared to take a deep breath, as if biting back the words he really wanted to speak. His dark eyes were opaque.

'I wish you a safe journey, *Herr Oberst*. Watch out for those Tommi Spitfires.'

'Thank you, Major, I will. As of tomorrow, you have command until my return.'

After Mindenhof had gone, Delsingen called Geissler into the office.

'Keep an eye on him, Ernst. I don't want this to go to his head.'

'Yes, sir. What if you're away for longer than a week?'

'The same applies, no matter how long I'm away. Don't allow him to get his SS ordering the Wehrmacht around. He'll be tempted.'

'And if he tries to force the issue?'

'Restrain him.'

'Use *force*, sir?'

'One of the reasons I have not allowed him to build up the SS strength is for just such an eventuality. There's not enough of them around to give you serious trouble in a shooting match. The training we have put our men through has transformed them. Look at the change in Kahler. Our men can now give a good account of themselves against Mindenhof's SS. Besides, I believe those SS who are in the teams may not necessarily support any such moves he might try during my absence. Just keep on your toes, Geissler.'

'Yes, sir.'

'And I'll back up whatever action you may be forced to take, should the situation demand it.' Delsingen handed Geissler a sealed envelope. 'Keep this in a safe place. Your authority – which I've signed – is in there, should you need it.'

Geissler took it reverently.

'I'm counting on you, Major, to look after things until I return.'

Geissler nodded. 'I will.'

'Good.' Delsingen gave a grim chuckle. 'Mindenhof wished me a safe journey and urged me to watch out for Tommi fighters. I had the strongest feeling he was wishing I would meet them and nor survive the encounter. What do *you* think, Geissler?'

'I think you're right, sir.'

*　　　*　　　*

Delsingen's 138 made the flight to Berlin safely. On arrival, he was taken straight to the office of his friend, the *Gruppenführer*.

A tall, well-built man with fine blond hair and deep-blue eyes stood up from behind a huge ornate desk as Delsingen was ushered in. The room was big enough to make the desk look small. Quite a contrast with his own office in Bergen, Delsingen thought drily.

The SS major-general grinned in welcome. 'Rüdi!' He held out a hand as he came forward to greet Delsingen. 'Good to see you!'

They shook hands warmly.

'Good to see you too, General.'

'Call me Max, for God's sake, Rüdi.

'Max, you're looking fit.'

Max Honnenhausen shrugged. 'By the grace of the Royal Air Force, who sends a bomber or two or a high-flying reconnaissance Spitfire, I survive.'

They laughed.

'So, Rüdi. You seem to have excited some people in the High Command with your ideas.' Honnenhausen went to a drinks cabinet. 'Can I offer you something? I have a fine selection of "liberated" stuff: from France, Holland, Poland, Belgium, Denmark, Norway, even from Spain during the days of the Condor Legion. Plus, of course, our own good German schnapps.'

'Quite a list of countries.'

'Yes. Isn't it? Sometimes, I wonder how we were able to accomplish so much, so quickly. Quite unbelievable how easy it was, and how swiftly they all tumbled like dominoes in a row.'

'They were asleep.'

'And we were very much awake!'

They laughed again, loudly.

'Now come on, Rüdi,' Honnenhausen urged. 'Make your choice. What is it to be.'

'I seem to remember, Max, you used to like something you called nectar from Kentucky – whiskey with an 'e' for excellent, to quote you. You wouldn't still be jealously guarding an ancient bottle of the stuff, would you?'

Honnenhausen feigned a pained look. 'My secret!' Then he gave another laugh. 'Same old Rüdi.'

'And the same old Max.'

The SS general reached into the back of the cabinet to take out a full bottle of the Kentucky nectar. 'A present from an American newspaperman, in 1937. How the world has moved since then. Yes. Today is a good day to open it. We'll toast your *Sondergruppe* for its successes, and for many more to come.'

Honnenhausen opened the bottle with a flourish and poured two generous helpings into crystal tumblers, then went back to the desk, leaving the bottle on top of the cabinet.

He put the glasses down and pointed to a comfortable leather armchair. 'Pull that up to the desk. You can put your hat there.' He tapped a corner of the desk.

When Delsingen had complied, Honnenhausen raised his glass. Delsingen did the same.

'To friendship,' the SS general began, 'and to the confusion of our enemies.'

'Friendship, and the confusion of our enemies.'

They drank.

'Aaahh!' Honnenhausen said appreciatively. 'Let us hope the Amis don't make war as well as they make this.'

'You believe they'll come in? Officially?'

'Don't you?'

Delsingen nodded. 'I do.'

The deep-blue eyes looked squarely at the Wehrmacht colonel. 'I would say this to no one but you. I believe it is inevitable, no matter how hard we may try to avoid it. But . . .'

There was a knock on the big double doors.

'Come in!'

Both doors opened and a very beautiful young woman entered. She wore an SS uniform, but no badges of rank.

'Oh! I'm sorry, sir. I didn't realize . . .'

'Come in, my dear,' Honnenhausen said expansively. 'May I present Colonel Delsingen. Colonel Delsingen, Fräulein Trudi Deger. She is in the documentation section, with direct access to me. I would be lost without her superb work.'

Trudi Deger showed a fetching pair of dimples in her cheeks as she smiled at the compliment.

She held out a hand, which Delsingen shook. 'Colonel.'

'Fräulein Deger, a pleasure.'

'The *Gruppenführer* is, of course, being very kind.'

'Nonsense, my dear,' Honnenhausen said warmly. 'Your work is quite exceptional. Now, what can I do for you?'

She passed him the thin buff file she had brought with her. 'A family of Jews, sir.

They were hiding in a disused farmhouse near Stolpe.'

Honnenhausen studied the file. 'Remarkable. Stolpe,' he went on to Delsingen, 'is just north-west of the city. You wouldn't think there'd be any Jews left hiding so close to Berlin.' He put down the file. 'All right, Trudi. I'll attend to it. Thank you for bringing this in.'

She smiled at him, pleased that he was pleased. 'Thank you, sir. I am happy to be of service to the Reich.'

She went out, beaming.

'I call her my *kleine Hilferin*,' Honnenhausen said when she had gone.

'You do realize, Max,' Delsingen began, 'that your little helper is absolutely crazy about you? Did you see the look in her eyes? If that wasn't adoration, I don't know what is.'

'Oh rubbish,' Honnenhausen said gruffly. 'I'm old enough to be her father.'

'If you say so. But the way she brought you that file was almost like a child bringing teacher an apple, or a kitten bringing in a mouse to lay at your feet.'

'Don't let that pretty face fool you. She's a zealous worker.'

'I don't doubt it.'

Honnenhausen took his place behind his desk and indicated that Delsingen should also sit down.

'But you didn't bring me all the way out here,' Delsingen continued, 'so we could talk about your female staff.'

'Indeed not. As I've said, your *Sondergruppe* is beginning to impress many people. Its importance to operations in Norway will increase during the coming months and possibly years. We have many secret projects that our enemies know absolutely nothing about. Naturally, we expect them to employ every effort in their attempts to discover these secrets. They will also try to destroy those that become operational, or attempt to prevent their deployment. But we will astonish them when we put some of these weapons into action. The *Graf von Hiller* is one.

'It is most definitely being built, but will not be put into service immediately and is being held in reserve, to strike at the Allies when they least expect it. It will be a formidable ship, Rüdi. It will also be a precious ship. And yours will be the task of ensuring it remains secure when it eventually moves to Norway.

From a security point of view, I have the authority to give you its projected deployment schedule. You are to plan your operations accordingly. However, you cannot discuss it with anyone, including your most trusted officers. They must carry out your orders on the understanding that you are working to a specific purpose, about which they have no further need to know. It is sufficient that your senior officers already know that the *Graf von Hiller* will be deployed to Norway. That is as far as their knowledge of this will extend, for the time being. The work of your *Sondergruppe* is therefore most important. Sabotage teams must *never* get near that ship.'

'I understand.'

'I repeat, your ideas are pleasing many people on the General Staff.' Honnenhausen's lips twitched in what could have been a smile. 'It also helps, of course, that you've got a friend high in the SS. Do this well, and you'll be a general before long.'

'General Delsingen sounds very good to my ears,' the colonel admitted, 'but at present I'm more interested in getting the job done – and doing it properly.'

'You must not fail, Rüdi,' Honnenhausen

117

told him gravely. 'High rank or not, I may not be able to do much to help you, if such a thing were to happen.'

'I understand that too.'

The blue eyes studied Delsingen. 'I'm handing you what the English would call a very hot potato.'

'My hands can take the heat.'

'I hope so, Rüdi. Now tell me: are you still having trouble with Mindenhof?'

'I'll always have trouble with him. Here's one person who would dearly love to see me fail. But for the moment he's containable. I've left him in command.'

'You've *what*?'

'If he makes a mess of things in my absence, it's his head.'

Honnenhausen gave a smile that developed slowly. 'You're sure you wouldn't like a transfer to the SS? You've got the kind of mind we like. People like Mindenhof are blunt-edged instruments, but you . . .'

'Oh no you don't. I'm a Wehrmacht man.'

'By that criterion, we shouldn't really be friends at all.'

'Yes. Crazy, isn't it?'

Honnenhausen raised his glass once more. 'To friendship.'

Delsingen raised his. 'May it last a long time.'

The precious American liquor slipped smoothly down their throats.

5

September 1941

The two Spitfire Vbs flew low across the
Channel. Jo-Jo Kearns, newly promoted to
Flying Officer, was leading. He was still
lucky and Bede, also a Flying Officer, was
still his wingman. One of the three pilots
who had watched them return to the airfield
that afternoon months before was no longer
with the squadron. Two Messerschmitts had
caught him, and though he'd shot down one,
he had not made it back.

Kearns was still not getting as many kills as
he would have liked, but at least no one had as
yet shot him down. Bede's score, on the other
hand, was mounting inexorably. He'd reached
six, while Kearns had been forced to work hard
for his three.

Bede had been offered the chance to lead his
own pair, but turned it down. Kearns's luck,

he reasoned, was rubbing off on him. As long as he continued to fly on the Australian's wing, he'd continue to return from missions.

Kearns was still cursed by the periodic jamming of his guns, but he had refused to change his aircraft. Despite the recurrent problem, he considered himself lucky with that particular aeroplane. It had never been hit in all the time he'd been flying it.

'She's looking after me,' he'd said when turning down the chance to fly a different Spitfire. 'I never change a good thing.'

Kearns now tracked his head upwards, checking that no enemy fighters were high up and planning to bounce them.

They were on convoy patrol, but with a flexible mission brief. Instead of having to fly a constant pattern over what looked like a traffic jam of ships, they had been given a freer hand than was customary. In reality it was a sort of loose search-and-destroy mission. They were hoping to catch a bomber or two on anti-shipping strikes. Keeping a tidy distance from the continental coast in order to avoid tangling with an entire squadron of 109s or 190s that might be sent to see what they were about, they prowled northwards. In addition to the fighters, there were also the fierce coastal flak batteries to consider.

Kearns preferred such mission autonomy. Beating a fixed pattern over the convoys was not without its own hazards. Trigger-happy naval gunners – either with poor eyesight, shattered nerves or weak recognition skills – were known to punch holes into the very aircraft that had been sent to protect them, despite having given the recognition code of the day to the ship controlling the convoy. Many a surprised pilot had landed with pieces missing from his aeroplane, even when he'd never tangled with the enemy.

Another hazard was sleep. The combination of flying the fixed pattern, the drone of the engine and the warmth of the cockpit sometimes conspired to induce drowsiness. People had been known to fly towards their death in a gentle descent into the water, before waking up in time to spot the approaching danger.

Kearns glanced over his right shoulder, to see Bede holding perfect station. They were keeping radio silence.

Bede, he thought, was a born natural; a natural pilot and a natural shooter. Give him real wings and he'd be a hawk.

Bede gave him a thumbs up.

He could imagine the younger pilot grinning in his mask. Then Bede was vigorously waggling his wings and jabbing a hand that pointed forwards and downwards.

Kearns looked to his one o'clock position. Two fleeting shapes, even lower down, virtually skimming the waves. Focke-Wulf 190s, heading up the Channel. But why so low?

There were three possibilities. They were keeping low to avoid radar and were on their own marauding mission; they were on a reconnaissance probe and staying low until it was time to climb to mission altitude; or they were ship hunting.

Kearns decided on the third possibility. This would mean they were carrying bombs – which meant they'd be temporarily slower and less manoeuvrable. Sitting ducks.

He realized that the 190 pilots had probably not seen the Spitfires, because the pursuing aircraft were themselves already so low. At that altitude there was a general greyness that served to hide the two RAF aircraft, hopefully until it was too late to be of any help to the Focke-Wulf pilots.

Still keeping off the radio, Kearns signalled the attack to Bede. Like a well-oiled machine, Bede extended station behind his leader as the

Spitfires increased speed to pursue. They were so low down that they were not getting the best out of their engines. Nevertheless, they were definitely creeping up on the enemy aircraft. At times the 190s seemed to disappear into the greyness of the water. Kearns found he had to force himself to maintain vigilance in the same direction until the indistinct shapes solidified once more.

He knew if he shifted his attention, it might take him too long to reacquire them, and that could prove fatal. If, in the interim, the 190 pilots became aware of their danger and dumped the 1000lb bombs they were carrying on ventral racks, it could turn very ugly indeed. Thus lightened and therefore regaining their agility, the 190s would climb for height while splitting right and left, to curve screaming round into a six o'clock attack from above. Definitely very bad news.

'But not today,' Kearns grunted.

He forced himself to get in very close until he could clearly see the bombs beneath the bellies of the German fighters.

He opened fire.

The guns didn't jam. The combined onslaught of cannon and machine-gun fire ripped into one of the 190s and almost immediately it began to pour smoke and pieces flew off it. It dropped sickeningly a few feet, and tipped on to a wing which drove into the water. The sudden jerk pivoted it about the wingtip, slamming the aircraft into the sea. It exploded on impact, but almost in the same instant the incipient flames were doused by a huge geyser of foaming water that rose into the air to fall back, a great white drooping curtain that collapsed suddenly about itself.

The second 190 pilot was very quick. He dumped his bomb and hauled for altitude for all he was worth. Bede shot off after him.

Curving round, Kearns went after his wingman to give him cover. Already both the Spitfire and the Focke-Wulf were rocketing to altitude.

Kearns followed, making sure he kept sight of the other two. He hoped the 190 pilot was not, even now, calling for reinforcements.

But Bede was not wasting time. He was all over the 190. Soon a plume of darkening flame was telling the story as it plunged seawards. By reacting instantly to the 190's escape manoeuvre, Bede had robbed the German pilot of the chance to settle down into the new situation. He had retained the psychological advantage rather than let it go to his adversary.

Kearns was impressed by Bede's consummate artistry as he watched the Spitfire heading back towards him. Bede approached with a flourish, doing a complete roll before once again closing up nearly on his wing. Again, Bede gave a thumbs up.

Kearns responded, and they continued their roving.

The two Fw-190s had failed to carry out their mission and would not be returning to base.

It was not a bad start to the patrol.

They came to land an hour and a half later, having found just one more target: a Ju-88. The twin-engined ship killer had been sneaking up on the convoy when Kearns and Bede had pounced.

Kearns went in first, his opening burst raking the rear fuselage and killing the radio operator-gunner in the back of the glasshouse cockpit. Then his guns had jammed.

In his frustration he'd called on Bede to finish off the bomber. Bede made two, devastating diagonal attacks which sent the enemy aircraft seawards in an expanding fireball. No one had got out. They chalked it up as a shared kill.

Kearns walked away from his aircraft, fuming

as he always did whenever he'd suffered a gun jam.

A sympathetic ground-crew corporal ran up to him. 'Look, sir. We've got some nice new Spits in. Perfect guns. Why don't you take one?'

'No!' Kearns growled. 'I'm not leaving her!'

'Yes, sir,' the corporal said, and went back to his mechanics.

'Well, Corp?' one of the mechanics began. 'What'd he say?'

'Same as usual. He's keeping his old kite.'

The mechanic shook his head in resignation. 'Crazy digger, if you ask me.'

'No one's asking you.'

'Steady on, Corp! Didn't mean anything by that. But we've taken those guns of his to pieces and put them back together again so many times, they must be the best-serviced guns in the whole RAF.'

'Yeah, I know,' the corporal agreed thoughtfully, watching as Bede caught up with Kearns and they walked on together. 'If it wasn't for the fact that everyone who's seen him in a fight says he's always in the thick of it, I'd say he had "bad finger" trouble. He even tried to ram a Jerry, once.'

'He's no coward, that's a fact.'

'So what do we do, Corp?' another asked. 'Check the guns again?'

'Check them again,' the corporal said wearily. 'Let's see what we find this time.'

They did a thorough check, and found nothing wrong.

'This bloody kite has a mind of its own,' the mechanic, smeared with oil and grease from his diagnostic probings, said with bemused frustration.

'It knows how to look after itself too,' the corporal said quietly. 'It's never been hit.'

'No wonder he doesn't want to change it. I wouldn't, in his place. Jammed guns or no jammed guns.'

'It's a funny thing, though,' the corporal said, staring at the aircraft.

'You still wouldn't get me up in one of these crates,' the mechanic said. 'Mad, all of them.'

'And how would you make Jerry pay for what he's doing?'

'That lot are *all* mad over there,' the mechanic said dismissively. 'Got to be, to follow someone like old Stickelgruber.'

'It's Schickelgruber,' the corporal corrected.

'Who cares,' the mechanic said. He stroked the aircraft as he would a household pet. 'Now be good to that nice Mr Kearns next time you go up. *Fire* those bloody guns!'

'Now who's crazy?' the corporal sniffed.

'We all are, what with this bloody war.'

'Mind what you say,' the corporal admonished sternly.

'Yes, Corp.'

The corporal fixed the mechanic with a hard gaze. 'Not some sort of Bolshie, are you?'

'Just a mechanic, Corp. Just a mechanic.'

Bergen, Norway. The same day

Delsingen was in his office, studying reports of more successes by his *Sondergruppe* teams. Since his trip to Berlin close on two dozen members of the resistance had been killed and valuable pieces of intelligence gathered. This information was being fed into the wider intelligence network, to see what patterns were beginning to emerge.

Many teams were now deployed in the field and, like a spreading infestation, were being dotted throughout the area. They were giving the resistance groups a hard time, but so far there was still no evidence that they had managed to catch any of Ålvik's people.

However, the resistance group had scored some notable successes, despite the virtual twenty-four-hour daylight of the summer, when spotting them should have been easier. With the days beginning to cool and shorten, and the first chill breezes of the winter to come making their presence felt, hunting them down would be that much harder.

The onset of winter would not hamper E-boat operations in the fiords. The natural heat field of the Gulf Stream ensured that they were kept ice-free throughout the year. This, Delsingen considered, was a valuable asset that would be of vital importance when the *Graf von Hiller* finally made it to the Sognefjord.

The one good thing, as far as he was concerned, was that Ålvik had not yet struck at any of the *Sondergruppe* teams. It was still a kind of stalemate. But the time would come. There was an inexorable momentum that made this inevitable.

Delsingen wondered – not for the first time – whether Ålvik was deliberately avoiding contact with the teams, until he was quite ready.

'It's what *I* would do,' he said to himself.

He was certain the Norwegian would by now be well aware that anti-resistance operations had become sharper.

Geissler knocked on the door and entered

carrying some papers. There was a smile on his face.

Delsingen looked up. 'More good news?'

'There's some good news, sir. But that's not what I'm smiling about.'

'Oh?'

'From time to time, I still remember the expression on Major Mindenhof's face when I told him you'd returned in one piece. He was just beginning to enjoy the taste of command.'

'But not long enough for him to do any damage,' Delsingen put in drily.

'I have to admit, Colonel, when I feel down, just remembering his face that day cheers me up again.'

'Whatever you do, don't bait him. He'll always find a way to pay you back. Now, give me the good news.'

Geissler placed the papers neatly before Delsingen. 'More successful contacts with the resistance. Four killed – theirs. Two wounded – ours. The team responsible is led by *Leutnant* Hartnitz, Waffen-SS.'

'Are they back?'

'No, sir. They made contact with Sergeant Stahlberg's team at a rendezvous, and passed on the information. The men are only lightly wounded, so they decided to remain for the full period of their mission time.'

'So Stahlberg's back.'

'Yes, sir. He has some intelligence I think you'll find interesting. It's with the other reports I've just brought in. They also captured some interesting weapons: a British Sten, a Luger pistol – most likely taken off a German officer's body – and another pistol which is of the type issued to officers of the former Norwegian Army. None of the dead carried identification.'

'That's to be expected. It's no surprise that many of their military men are resistance fighters. Such people would have no stomach for Quisling. This is the Hartnitz team's second successful intercept, isn't it?'

'Yes, Colonel.'

'That ought to please Mindenhof.'

'I'm not so sure.'

'What do you mean?'

'As one of our newer arrivals, Hartnitz doesn't seem too impressed with Mindenhof. He was already a combat veteran before he came here. Wounded in battle. He was also a sergeant before he received his commission.'

'Of course. I remember seeing that in his file. Officers do not generally impress him.'

'At least, not those like Mindenhof,' Geissler
suggested. 'Do you think, sir,' he went on,
'that perhaps someone had a hand in the
selection?'

Delsingen looked coolly at the major. 'What
are you getting at, Geissler? Are you suggesting
his posting was deliberate?'

'Well, Colonel . . . I just wondered whether
someone, somewhere, might have decided to
send us less fanatical members of the SS when
Major Mindenhof made his request.'

'Are there such animals?'

'Who knows, sir.'

'Who indeed, Major. Hartnitz has an excellent combat record. The SS may well hate each
other individually; but they hate everybody else
much more. Remember that.'

'But what about your . . . friend, sir?'

'To everything in life, Geissler, there are
exceptions. Remember that, too.'

'Yes, sir.'

The position had been well chosen. The lake
on the northern edge of southern Norway's
great high plateau, the Hardangervidda, was
seventy-five miles east of Bergen. The lake itself
was about three miles across at its greatest
extent: small by Norwegian standards. On its

western shore great towers of basalt provided perfect cover for the waiting ambushers.

They had been in place for some time, watching as the dots in the distance had grown into four perceptible shapes. The shapes were now close enough to be identified as four German soldiers.

Ever since news had come that the specially trained hunter-killer teams were operating in the area, Ålvik had responded by splitting his own group of thirty into six five-man units, widely dispersed, to hunt out the hunters. He had deliberately waited before committing them. This was the first such ambush, and it had been laid after days of shadowing the four men who now approached the water's edge.

From his position, Ålvik could not see the other members of his team. Skjel, the sniper, would give the signal with his first shot. The whole thing would have to be very quick. Skjel's job was to take out the leader with that first round. This would be followed by Inge's mortars, and they in turn would be immediately joined by combined sub-machine-gun fire, to complete the job.

As he watched, Ålvik could see that, though the soldiers moved alertly, it was clear they were not expecting an ambush at this point.

But they were not taking any chances. They walked well spread out, their guns ready for instant use. Every so often one of their number would do a scan, turning completely round as he walked, to check every quarter.

These were no amateurs.

He brought up his binoculars, making sure there would be no flash of sunlight on the lenses to give his position away. He focused on the leader, an SS officer. This was to be Skjel's target.

Ålvik watched as the officer stopped abruptly and raised a hand to chest height to halt the others. The SS man stood perfectly still, as if listening for something.

As he continued to watch, Ålvik saw the man's mouth move as he snapped out an order. Still too far away to be heard, the silent mouthings had an electrifying effect on the other soldiers. They darted in different directions and dropped flat to the ground.

What had the SS officer seen? Ålvik wondered. He was certain none of his own team had betrayed their position. Perhaps it was simply a soldier's instinct, warning the German that something was wrong.

Ålvik hoped Skjel would be patient and not give the game away by firing too soon.

Tense minutes passed. The very air seemed to be holding its breath.

The Hardangervidda was full of wildlife, from the lemmings to the owls that fed on them, to reindeer. But Ålvik had chosen a location where there were no deer, whose skittishness could have warned the soldiers that there were other presences in the vicinity. There were no lemmings, or owls either. So what had spooked the soldiers?

The wait continued.

A good half-hour passed before the soldiers cautiously got to their feet. They came on, but this time they ran at the crouch, darting for cover one at a time, making it difficult for Ålvik's group to catch all four exposed.

The SS officer was not sure there was anything amiss, Ålvik decided; but the man, a lieutenant and clearly a veteran, was taking no chances.

Ålvik was relieved that Skjel was being patient. The ambush site had been chosen with several options in mind. The tactics now being employed by the soldiers had been envisaged. It would merely mean that the attack, when launched, would have to be overwhelming in its surprise and devastation. The men out there would be exceedingly dangerous close in, and if one escaped being hit he would be close enough to inflict some damage.

There was a point of no return when they would have to cross open ground, and at that time it would be equally dangerous for them to retreat. That was the moment that Ålvik expected Skjel to open fire.

The soldiers continued to dart forward, never running in one direction for more than a second.

Still no firing came to crack across the stillness of the Hardangervidda.

Then the SS officer began his dash across the short stretch of open ground that skirted the edge of the lake, from where he'd begun his run.

The sharp bark of Skjel's rifle coincided with the officer's sudden jerk into an upright position. The man's arms flew outwards, his MP40 flying out of his hands and high above his head. His helmet sailed after the gun, while his legs continued to propel him forward until they suddenly lost motive power. He pitched forward brokenly, folding as he did so, and tumbled to the ground. He did not move again.

Even before the SS man had begun to crumple, Inge's mortars straddled a low rock behind which another soldier had taken cover and was in the act of rising to his feet. He disappeared in a starburst of flame and pieces of shattered stone.

Ålvik, having already picked his own target, raked the position of the third soldier. But the man had moved and was in the act of darting for new cover.

Skjel's rifle barked again, across the roar of a second mortar barrage. The soldier kept running and Ålvik thought Skjel had somehow missed.

Then the soldier stopped, stood for a moment and finally toppled.

Ålvik swung his gun to where he knew the last soldier was hiding. He was joined by Morgensen and Arendt. In the midst of all that confusion, the last man suddenly stood up and began firing back at them.

However, this astonishing display of bravery ended very suddenly as he became the focal point of the fire from the three sub-machine-guns. He was thrown rearwards, back-pedalling as he went, until he was stopped abruptly as he slammed into a large boulder. His body slid tiredly down to a sitting position, and remained where it had fallen.

The sounds of firing died in a perfect cut-off, as if a conductor had waved a baton. No one moved. Moments passed as from their positions they all stared at the bodies, waiting to see if there would be any surreptitious movement.

But there was none.

Whitehall, London

At the very moment that Ålvik's people were wiping out SS Lieutenant Hartnitz's team, the two men in shabby suits were studying a signal that had come to them via agents in France. The signal informed them that news had come from Germany of a highly secret ship that was being built.

'Do you think Jerry's having us on?' one said. 'This is the second mention of this so-called ship.'

'We feed him duff gen. His intelligence boys do the same to us. The trick is knowing when it's duff.'

'That's why we get these things. Our job is to spot the duff ones.'

'I say we file it until we get some more. There's no location mentioned. Which shipyard, for example? We can't ask for a PR Spit to wander across the Fatherland and get some poor chap shot down for nothing. PR Spits are worth their weight in gold. Can't waste them, old boy. Can't waste pilots, either. We need more specifics. Where is it being built? What class?

How far advanced is its construction? Where will it be deployed? And so forth.'

'Perhaps we'll hear from our man again.'

'If he's still alive.'

Bergen, Norway

Five days later Geissler entered Delsingen's office. He looked sombre.

'Hartnitz's team did not make the rendezvous, Colonel. Of course, they could be making their own way back independently.'

Delsingen rose slowly from behind his desk and went over to the map. Blue circles had joined the red ones, marking the locations where the *Sondergruppe* had scored kills. There were several, and they were rapidly encroaching on the red ones of the resistance strikes.

Delsingen drew a large circle with a forefinger. 'They were operating in this area. They met up with Sergeant Stahlberg's team here . . .' He paused. 'I wonder.'

'Wonder what, sir?'

'Whether they ran into Ålvik.'

'The last we heard of Ålvik,' Geissler said, 'he was nowhere near that area.'

'That was some time ago,' Delsingen said, continuing to study the map. 'He's been biding his time, as we know. In his place, I would strike where least expected.' He turned to face Geissler. 'We expect to take casualties. But I'd like to think this has not happened to Hartnitz. Keep me informed.'

'Yes, sir.'

Kiel, Germany

A senior officer in the Intelligence branch of the Kriegsmarine was in a small, dimly lit office, studying the projected plans of the formidable new pocket battleship, the *Graf von Hiller*. It was, he decided, even more powerful than the massive *Tirpitz*, which was much bigger and a ship of the full battleship class.

Though the vessel was heavily armoured, the *von Hiller*'s sleek design and potent new engines could, according to the plans, propel it through the water at thirty-eight knots. This was faster than the *Tirpitz* and almost matched the speeds of the best of the Allied destroyers, the only ships which would be able to chase her.

This would hardly do them any good, as she would be able to blast them out of the water before they could come within the range of their own puny guns. Torpedoes wouldn't be of much use, either, for in a straight dash at high speed she would outrun anything they currently had in their stocks. Hunting her down would thus be a hopeless task for either torpedo-launching surface ships or submarines. She would first have to be ambushed; but even here, the Allied forces would face supreme difficulty. The *Graf von Hiller* would have the most advanced submarine-detection equipment ever seen.

That left aerial attack.

The naval officer smiled grimly. Again, the Allies would be in trouble. The *von Hiller*'s armament was awesome. To handle surface vessels, shore targets and aircraft, she had six fifteen-inch and fourteen 5.9-inch guns; sixteen 105mm cannon; sixteen 37mm cannon; twelve Oerlikon cannon; and to round it all off, a further thirty-six 20mm cannon. Any aircraft foolish enough to come within range of the barrage that she could put up would be vaporized in the hell it would be flying into. Submarines would be no better off, for the *von Hiller* would also carry a huge supply of depth charges more powerful than anything currently available to either side.

Deployment plans were for the ship to use the Sognefjord in Norway as its base, from where it would emerge, a fast predator of the seas, to wreak havoc upon Allied shipping before returning to its lair to restock and start all over again.

The naval officer felt pleased with himself. Much of the ship's armament fit had been the result of his own proposals.

'God help you, Tommi,' he said quietly, 'if you try to destroy this ship.'

He could almost feel sorry for them.

6

Jo-Jo Kearns was lounging in the September sun, outside the squadron hut. An unfamiliar sound made him look up alertly. Was this an attack? He was not due to fly and did not have his Mae West to hand. Even so, he instinctively glanced towards his aircraft, wondering how long it would take him to sprint for it.

But the sirens weren't going, and no one was yelling 'Scramble'.

Then a sleek, twin-engined shape banked steeply as it went into a fighter break, displaying its RAF roundels, its Merlins roaring exhilaratingly.

'What the hell's that?' Kearns yelled to no one in particular.

'A Mosquito, you ignorant colonial,' someone replied cheerfully from within the hut. 'I'd love one of those.'

'Good luck to you,' Kearns retorted. 'Give

me my Spit any day. Anyway, what's this . . .
Mosquito doing here?'

'Hang on. I'll just ask my friend the Air
Marshal at the Air Ministry. He always tells
me what the brass are planning.'

'Funny man.'

'You did ask.'

'I'm regretting it already.'

Laughter came back at him.

The Mosquito didn't land. It did a few circuits,
then went on its way. Later Kearns was told that
it had been on a training flight. Despite himself,
he found his mind lingering on the elegance of
that shape and the sound of its engines.

Within a day he'd forgotten about it, never
imagining that just under three years later he
would find himself flying one, on one of the
most terrifying missions of his life.

Bergen, Norway. Two days later, 0900 hours
Delsingen strode into his office wearing a
camouflaged combat smock over his tunic.
In one hand he carried his steel helmet; the
other held an MP40 sub-machine-gun. His
pistol was belted over the smock. A pair of
binoculars hung by its strap from his neck.
He went across to his desk and put down
the helmet and the gun. He then removed

his cap and hung it up, before walking over to the map.

Geissler, in standard uniform, came in soon after.

Delsingen tapped at the small lake where Hartnitz's team had been ambushed.

'This is the nearest body of water big enough,' he said, as Geissler approached. 'It's also within the area that Sergeant Stahlberg's team made final contact with Hartnitz. The 138 can land there.'

'I still think you shouldn't be going, sir,' Geissler advised. 'The place could be crawling with resistance fighters. You don't need the risk.'

Delsingen turned. 'I've got to go, Ernst. It's been a week. I'm certain this one's Ålvik's.'

'But sir, you can't go into the field every time we lose a team . . .'

'That's not my purpose. I want to see where Hartnitz was ambushed. I want to see if my theory is correct. I believe I understand how this Norwegian's mind works. This is a man who is not only very daring, but also extremely professional in the tactics he employs. Whatever his pursuits before the war, he has learned very quickly how to apply his mind to the current situation. A man who can enter the very heart of enemy territory to exact his revenge on the man who betrayed his family, and get out again, is no ordinary fighter. Once I have seen the site of the battle, I'll know whether it was Ålvik or not.'

Geissler decided he was never going to change Delsingen's mind.

'I don't expect this to take very long,' Delsingen continued into Geissler's silence. 'We should be back by 1500 hours. You have the command in my absence.'

'Yes, *Herr Oberst*.'

Delsingen studied his subordinate closely. 'You don't look very happy, Major.'

'It's not a good idea to take Major Mindenhof . . .'

'He ought to get out into the field once in a while. He needs to see there's more to warfare than parading about in a fancy black uniform.'

'He's not happy about being hauled into this, sir.'

'Mindenhof is never happy about anything unless he's the one initiating it. Hartnitz was SS. Mindenhof should at least show solidarity, even if he didn't like the man.'

'Just be very careful out there, sir.'

'I'm taking four men, all Wehrmacht. I don't think the major will try a field assassination.

By the way, I appreciate your worry, but it is completely unnecessary.'

A sharp knock interrupted them.

'Speaking of the devil,' Delsingen remarked softly. '*Hierein!*'

The door opened and Mindenhof, in full, camouflaged Waffen-SS combat gear and helmet, stomped in. He too carried, in addition to his ever-present pistol, an MP40. He'd also strapped on an ammunition harness to carry six spare magazines. On him, the familiar shape of the helmet looked even more menacing.

The boots clicked, the right hand shot out. '*Heil Hitler!* Reporting for combat duty as ordered, *Herr Oberst!*'

'We're not going into combat, Major,' Delsingen told him mildly, staring at the harness. 'You've got enough magazines to take on a small army. We're simply going to inspect what I believe to be the site of an ambush carried out by Ålvik's people.'

'The terrorists may still be out there.'

'I very much doubt it. It would be stupid of them to remain where they could easily attract an air strike. Not worried, are you?'

'I'm never worried about the enemies of the Reich, Colonel,' Mindenhof snapped.

'Aren't you? I know I am. A man who isn't

worried about his adversaries can make serious tactical errors of judgement.'

Mindenhof's eyes stared lifelessly from beneath the rim of his helmet. 'I am not afraid of a terrorist,' he insisted coldly.

'That's comforting to know.' Delsingen went over to his desk and picked up his helmet and the MP40. 'Come on, Major. The aircraft is waiting. See you by 1500 hours, Geissler,' he added.

'Yes, sir.'

Delsingen put the helmet on as he went out.

Mindenhof gave Geissler an empty stare, before following.

Geissler strode slowly into the outer office, to find the headquarters sergeant peering in the direction Delsingen and Mindenhof had taken.

'Shame about old Hardnuts, sir,' the sergeant began.

' "Hardnuts"?'

'*Leutnant* Hartnitz, sir. For an SS man, he wasn't a bad sort. The men respected him. A tough one, and a real soldier. Not political at all. He used to spend more time with *our* men than with his lot. It's never the shits who go first,' the sergeant finished with sudden vehemence.

Geissler knew he was talking about Mindenhof.

'I didn't hear that, Sergeant,' he remarked sternly.

'No, sir,' the sergeant acknowledged, with due deference to Geissler's rank. 'You didn't.'

'Even if I might have happened to agree.'

'Yes, sir.'

The B138, with an all-Luftwaffe crew, was piloted by a captain. It had landed in the outer harbour, then cruised under its own power to the Vågen, where it now waited. Moored to a floating pier that had been built by Wehrmacht engineers soon after the Occupation had begun, it rode gently on the placid water.

The four-man squad, carrying rifles, marched along the pier, followed by Delsingen and Mindenhof. Two sailors were standing by the mooring lines.

The two officers waited until the men had climbed into the hull of the flying boat, before themselves climbing aboard. The lines were released and a crewman secured the door, then returned to his station.

The triple engines were started. The 138 began to cruise out of Bergen's inner harbour. When it reached open water it increased speed, planed on its stepped hull, then lifted into the air. It banked left to head eastwards, making for the small lake on the Hardangervidda.

Half an hour later, as it was circling low over the lake, the crewman who had secured the door approached Delsingen.

'We have arrived, *Herr Oberst. Hauptmann* Sachsenmüller says he can see bodies.'

Delsingen gave a curt nod, expression neutral. 'Tell him to land, and to try to get us as close to shore as he's able to.'

'Yes, *Herr Oberst.*'

The crewman relayed the message, then once more returned to his station for the landing.

Sachsenmüller carried out a smooth touch-down, then brought the flying boat right up to a part of the shoreline that sloped gently.

'Looks as if you'll be getting your boots wet, Major,' Delsingen said to Mindenhof.

'I'm sure my boots can handle it, Colonel,' Mindenhof responded evenly.

'That was intended as a mild joke,' Delsingen said, then he continued to the soldiers before Mindenhof could say anything further, 'All right, men. As soon as that door opens, I want you out there *fast*.'

'Yes, *Herr Oberst*,' acknowledged the sergeant who led the squad.

The crewman opened the door.

'You heard the colonel,' the sergeant barked at his men. '*Move it!*'

They got out swiftly, followed by Delsingen and Mindenhof.

Sachsenmüller had positioned the aircraft perfectly and his passengers had to wade through water that came only halfway up their boots.

As soon as they were clear, two crewmen jumped out and pushed the 138, which moved easily off the shore. They climbed back aboard before it had gone too far.

Sachsenmüller then took it into deeper water, where a sea anchor was deployed to hold it on station. The engines were shut down, bringing a silence so sudden, it sounded deafening.

They found all four bodies.

There was not much left of three of them. Delsingen ordered the sergeant to get them all ready for burial.

He walked some distance away, taking an openly reluctant Mindenhof with him. He stopped to study the area closely, looking at the high rocks from where Ålvik had sprung the devastating ambush. He raised the binoculars to his eyes, searching out the most likely positions for concealment.

'That's the only place they could have been waiting,' he said to Mindenhof. 'It's perfect. Good cover. They must have remained there, waiting for the team to come into range. They used mortars, a sniper and sub-machine-guns.'

'You can tell by just looking around, Colonel?' Mindenhof, looking about him and holding his MP40 ready, clearly did not believe it.

'You saw Hartnitz's body.' Delsingen still held the binoculars to his eyes. 'A single, clean shot. Straight to the heart. The bullet went right through. Hartnitz was dead before he hit the ground. That's the work of a high-powered rifle. The other bodies are either full of holes or shredded. Mortar and machine-gun. Some of these boulders have been shattered. They stood no chance of getting out of the trap, once it had been sprung. This is Ålvik's work. He may even have shadowed them for days.'

'How can you know that?'

Delsingen lowered the binoculars, and turned to the SS major. 'It's what I would have done.'

Mindenhof looked as if he wasn't sure whether to be shocked by the admission, or angered.

'We should make them pay severely for this,'

he said grimly. 'They should be made to learn that an SS officer's life does not come cheaply.' The snout of his MP40 kept tracking round, as if he expected the resistance fighters to appear at any second.

'There are three Wehrmacht bodies here as well,' Delsingen reminded him gently.

'Of course, Colonel. I meant the life of any German.'

'Of course.'

'We should take severe reprisals,' Mindenhof insisted.

'Reprisals. They won't do much good.' Delsingen glanced down at Mindenhof's MP40. 'That won't be of much use, either, if a sniper's still out there.'

The MP40 abruptly stopped moving with a sharp jerk, as if the barrel had been slammed against an invisible wall.

'Relax, Major,' Delsingen said drily. 'If there had been a sniper around, we would all have been dead by now. Or at least some of us would have been. I've seen enough. Time to get back.'

He began walking back to where the squad, with tools from the aircraft, were preparing to bury the dead.

After a moment's hesitation a tight-lipped Mindenhof followed him.

The burial was completed without drama. As they stood silently over the graves, it was as if there were no other people in the world, so still did the very air about them feel.

The two officers saluted the rough mounds. Even here, Mindenhof gave the outstretched arm salute.

Each grave was marked at the head by the combat knife that had belonged to each soldier, and which had been thrust into the earth to the hilt.

They were making their way back to the shore of the lake, when Mindenhof said, 'We should have taken them back. They should not have been left here, in this empty place.'

'Before this war is over, Major,' Delsingen began evenly, 'many Germans will be without any graves at all, in places much further away from Germany than here.'

Being some distance from the soldiers, they could not be overheard.

'Those sound like words of defeat,' Mindenhof said.

'No, Major. Words of reality. People die in war, and, believe it or not, even conquerors.'

'Sometimes,' Delsingen said, after he'd told Geissler of the events by the lake, 'I despair of that man, even beyond what I expect of him.'

Once again in standard uniform, he leaned back in his chair with a sigh.

Geissler cast a quick glance at the map. 'As there was no hostile contact up there, Colonel, where do you think Ålvik will strike next?'

'Your guess is as good as mine. However, the more teams we have out in the field, the less room he is going to have for manoeuvre. We'll eliminate his people by attrition, while keeping our own casualties down. He was very lucky to catch Hartnitz the way he did. We all need luck sometimes. But sooner or later, he'll put in an appearance where we'll be waiting for him. Then we'll have him.

'You know, Geissler, one has to admire the man. He will not give up. I wonder if we shall be as good when our turn comes.'

'You expect us to be fighting on the roads and streets of Germany?'

'It's the natural consequence of things, Major.'

'But Barbarossa is doing well. The Luftwaffe destroyed nearly two thousand Russian aircraft on the first day.'

'On 22 June,' Delsingen said thoughtfully. 'I wonder what future historians will make of that date. We are only in September. There's plenty of time for things to go wrong.' Delsingen got to his feet and went over to the map. He stared at it for long seconds. 'And they will.'

Kearns and Bede were again over the Channel, forty-five minutes into their patrol.

The two Spitfires sped low over a surface that was choppy enough to display white horses. As usual, Bede was keeping perfect formation on his leader. He searched the tufted patchwork of clouds above him for enemy aircraft. Nothing flitted between them.

Then, seconds later, he spotted two shapes, ahead and above. Big enough at that distance to be bombers. He glanced across at Kearns.

Kearns had also seen the enemy bombers and, catching Bede's glance, nodded to show he was aware of them. Checking for fighters and spotting none in the immediate vicinity, he opened the throttle and gave chase, staying low.

Bede was right there with him, already understanding how the attack was going to develop. They now worked so well together that Kearns felt it was as if their nerve ends were linked together. Bede always seemed to know what was needed of him.

They began to gain on the bombers, which

turned out to be two Ju-88s. Despite the fact that Spitfires lost some performance at such low level, Kearns chose not to gain altitude. He continued the pursuit, inexorably drawing closer to the bombers. He also made a periodic check of the sky above, just in case any fighters made an appearance. So far, none had. The thing to hope for was that the bombers would not spot them before they were close enough to attack, and so have enough time to call in either any high-flying escorts that might be lurking upstairs or any free-ranging fighters in the vicinity.

Kearns reasoned that the bomber crews would be keeping a primary lookout above, as their own altitude, though greater than that of the closing Spitfires, was still low enough for them to expect an attack from a higher level.

He glanced at Bede's aircraft. His wingman was right there, holding his usual perfect station as the choppy waters rushed past beneath them.

They had got closer still and yet there continued to be no evidence of alarm from the enemy bombers. The gunner in the ventral gondola beneath the cockpit, with its rearwards-facing twin guns, must be asleep, he reasoned. So much the better. He'd soon be waking up, just in time for a more permanent slumber.

The 1440hp Merlin 45 roared exultantly as the range closed.

Please don't jam, Kearns prayed over and over in his mind to the guns.

He eased the rudder slightly to the left to get into position for the left-hand target. As if in seamless choreography, he saw Bede's aircraft shift slightly to the right, taking up position for an attack on the second aircraft.

Yet still the gunners on both Ju-88s appeared not to notice anything.

Kearns then came to the conclusion that their approach, so close to the water, must somehow be managing to keep them undetectable. All that would change once they began to rise for the shark-like attack. They would be discovered and three things would immediately occur: the gunners would fire; their warning to their pilots would cause the bombers to take immediate evasive action; and they would call out the fighters.

'We must get them before any of these things happens,' Kearns muttered to himself.

Or at least in time to make any of the above actions purely academic.

It was time.

Kearns gently pulled the stick back. The rushing Spitfire went into a high-speed, shallow climb.

Bede was following suit, as if tied to Kearns's Spitfire.

Then the gunners woke up.

But it was already too late. Even as the tracers began reaching out for him and the bomber seemed to have suddenly become large, Kearns was squeezing the button on the spade grip of the control stick.

The guns did not let him down. The six weapons hurled their combined fire-power of cannon shell and bullets in a ferocious, two-second barrage at the Ju-88. Forty 20mm shells and 133 machine-gun rounds, a combined weight of 25lb, slammed with terrific force into the gondola, chewing its way through to rage into the cockpit above, killing both the gunner and the pilot. It was enough.

Kearns had to yank the Spitfire into a hard left-hand avoidance turn as the bomber suddenly tipped over and headed downwards. By the time he'd rolled upright again and was into the climb, the Ju-88 was plunging steeply. Even if someone else had been able to get at the controls, there was not enough time for a pull-out. The aircraft slammed into the sea, spreading a great circle of foaming water.

Kearns looked round for Bede. He need not have worried. A bright Roman candle of flame gave him the answer as the second bomber plunged in a terminal dive.

'That boy *is* good,' Kearns said to himself.

'*Fighters!*' he heard suddenly. 'Downhill! Six o'clock!'

So the bombers had found time to raise the alarm.

He checked out Bede's warning call. And there they were: two rapidly expanding dots hurtling towards them.

The Spitfire had not yet lost appreciable speed in the climb and he curved round for a head-on pass. He saw that Bede had done the same.

The two enemy fighters turned out to be Messerschmitt 109s.

Either because their diving speed was already too great for ease of manoeuvring, or their pilots had misinterpreted the Spitfires' own manoeuvre, they went right past the climbing RAF fighters without firing a single shot.

'What the hell . . . ?' Kearns muttered. He rolled the Spitfire on to its back and went back down.

The 109 had a neat trick. Because of its

injected engine, the pilot could push the stick forward and go into a high-speed dive, streaking away from a pursuing Spitfire. In the Spitfire's case, its carburetted engine prevented it from doing likewise, as the negative Gs would starve the engine of much-needed fuel, causing it to cut out. There could be worse ways of losing the fight in air combat than with a faltering engine, but caught in such a situation not many pilots would think so if the adversary was concentrating on putting as many holes into you as he could in the shortest possible time.

Before the Spitfire could dive with its engine on full song, it was necessary to first roll inverted to keep positive G on the carburettors, and pull into the dive, before rolling upright again. The problem with that was that it took enough time to allow the quarry to scoot away as he went downhill.

Kearns, however, preferred the Spitfire way. He also had a method of slicing into the turn, shaving fractions off the time it took to complete the manoeuvre. He hated negative gravity, which was what happened when the stick was pushed forward in such a move. The pilot would be forced off his seat and into his harness, with the blood trying its best to send a tidal wave into his brain, giving him 'red-out'. Kearns called the condition the 'morning-after-a-bad-booze-night', because of the bloodshot eyes the phenomenon tended to induce.

As the Spitfire flipped on to its back, Kearns looked up through the inverted canopy and spotted a 109 far below. He pulled into the dive, rolled upright and hurtled towards the enemy fighter. As he fell towards the water, it occurred to him that something relatively simple may have happened to create the present situation.

'The bastards misjudged it!' he said to himself in happy surprise.

It happened. One moment you thought you had all options covered, then you made a silly mistake. If he was right, both the 109 pilots had grossly miscalculated and would try to recover the initiative. On such small things could the tide of a battle turn.

'Better you than me,' he grunted as he closed rapidly on the 109.

Then he realized why the closure rate was so high. The Messerschmitt was pulling out of the dive. Its speed had been so great that its initial recovery was slow as the pilot hauled on the stick, straining against the punishing G forces.

Kearns throttled back and began to ease the stick towards him, bringing the nose up early. By doing this, he was matching his momentum to that of the 109 and was keeping the gunsight positioned on a spot just behind the 109's birdcage cockpit.

But he was not close enough.

He kept falling upon the German fighter, continuously flattening the dive as the target aircraft began to curve upwards. Kearns knew that if the enemy pilot looked behind him at any moment, he would spot the descending Spitfire and roll out of the way. Kearns wanted him to keep concentrating on pulling out for just a while longer.

He drew closer. The black crosses were well within the sights now. Closer still.

'Easy, easy,' Kearns said to himself softly. 'Don't rush it.' Please, guns, he added mentally. Don't let me down.

They didn't.

When he fired, they roared out a song of fiendish glee. Twenty-five pounds of hellish metal tore into the Messerschmitt, ripping the entire tail completely off. Thus destabilized, the remainder of the aircraft gyrated wildly in response to the powerful torque of its still-racing engine.

Kearns stared wide-eyed as the canopy flew off and the pilot was sucked out of the cockpit. The parachute didn't open.

He banked away, looking for Bede.

A silent explosion in a relatively cloudless part of the sky caught his attention. He saw with relief that it wasn't Bede because not far from the scene a Spitfire was performing an exuberant roll. It could only be the irrepressible Bede.

Kearns did a quick scan of the air about him. You never knew who could be waiting ready to pounce on a pilot enjoying his victory. But no enemy fighters were in sight.

Bede rejoined formation and they continued the patrol, completing it without further combat.

When they landed, the mechanic who had once spoken to Kearns's aircraft came up to them.

'Any trouble with the guns today, sir?'

'None,' Kearns said. 'She's really behaving herself. I've seen you speak to her once or twice, just before I taxi. What do you say?'

'I tell her she'd better fire those guns or I'll cut her up for scrap.'

'You *what*?' Kearns stared at the mechanic as if the man had taken leave of his senses. 'Are you pulling my leg? You're talking as if she could hear you.'

'Your guns worked, didn't they, sir? Who knows with these things.'

'Well,' Kearns said after some moments, 'keep talking to her.'

The mechanic grinned. 'If you say so, sir.'

'I do say so.'

As they walked away from their aircraft, Bede said, 'You don't really believe that, do you, Jo-Jo? An *aircraft* being scared of being turned into scrap? That's a line.'

'The guns worked, didn't they?'

7

September 1943

Flight Lieutenant (Acting Squadron Leader) John Kearns, DSO, DFC, was no longer at his original station. His squadron had been posted to East Anglia for the past year. But he still flew his original Spitfire Vb, and it continued to look after him. He had never been shot down, and the aircraft continued to go serenely through the war without a scratch. Jo-Jo's luck had become the stuff of legend.

A peculiar thing had occurred on the day before the squadron was due to move. The mechanic who used to look after the aircraft was killed when the truck in which he was a passenger skidded on a wet road and careered into a ditch. The skid had been relatively mild, and the ditch shallow. But it was not the skid that had killed him. The incident had taken place at night, in rain. The mechanic had climbed unhurt up to the side of the road, to flag down some help – and was hit by another truck.

Kearns had enjoyed an unbroken spell of jam-free guns. The very next day, while on patrol, he had closed in nicely on a Focke-Wulf 190. The guns had refused to fire.

In desperation after landing, he had yelled the mechanic's threat at the aircraft.

The guns had once again begun to work properly. He made no attempt to explain the phenomenon to himself. The guns worked when he needed them, and that was that.

Many of the old faces had gone. The remaining two of the three young pilots who had been commenting about his luck were all gone. Shot down. James Bede had been posted to the desert theatre, where he had continued his single-minded determination to shoot down as many aircraft as he possibly could. He was now a flight lieutenant, DSO and Bar, DFC and Bar, with twenty victories. He had been shot down twice, but had only once been slightly wounded. He complained bitterly at the time it was because he was no longer flying on Kearns's wing that he kept getting shot down.

As a flight commander, Kearns now had an office of sorts, in a Nissen hut. He was staring out of a window at a particularly bleak Norfolk day, bleak in mood himself, when there was a knock on the door. The squadron commander entered.

Squadron Leader Harry Luwzinsky's Polish father had come to Britain just before the First World War, only to die in it after volunteering, in 1915. He never saw his son.

Luwzinsky, a veteran of several missions and survivor of a Spitfire crash, had an unmarked face; but his body was a mass of scars as a result of the crash, when his disintegrating aircraft appeared to have flung most of itself at him. It was still a wonder to many that he had not broken a single bone.

A short, stocky man with a severe, short-back-and-sides haircut and deep-grey eyes, he always seemed full of humour. It was hard to equate him with the person who so ruthlessly tore into the enemy in the air at every opportunity. He was also an excellent commander. He had been shot down five times – on one occasion twice in the same day – but never wounded.

'Well, Jo-Jo,' he said to Kearns. 'Sad day.'

'Yes, sir. I'll hate leaving my old kite.'

'She's served you well. Perhaps she'll look after whoever takes her over from now on.'

'I'll really miss her.'

'Cheer up, old chap. You're getting a fabulous, brand-new Mossie.'

'And an extra crew member. I'm a single-seater man.'

'The powers that be obviously think otherwise. They've got plans for you.'

'What do they know?' Kearns was not to be comforted.

'I dare say we'll soon find out. After all, I'm going too. At least, it won't be all strangers.'

'But *Scotland*! My God, sir. What's it going to be like up there in the winter? I come from Queensland. I hate winters.'

'You'll cope,' Luwzinsky said cheerfully. 'This news might brighten your day. You're going to be the deputy CO.'

Kearns stared at Luwzinsky. 'You're joking . . . er, sir.'

'No joke. You're my number two. So you see? The brass do know something, after all. They can spot a good man at fifty paces . . . when they're looking.' He grinned, seeming unexpectedly boyish. 'We'll be doing our conversion training in Sussex, then fly our aircraft up to the new posting.'

'Any idea as yet what the posting's about.'

The squadron leader shook his head. 'All I can tell you is that this is a new squadron being formed from scratch, for a specific task. I've no idea what that task is supposed to be. Well, I'd better be getting on. Got to hand over to the new chap who's replacing me. Just popped in to see how you were doing, and to give you the glad news.'

'I've already handed over to Jock Peebles.'

'Good show. See you in the mess later?'

'Yes, sir.'

Luwzinsky peered out at the weather. 'Nasty stuff. Hope the Yanks are not sending their bombers out in this. Took a terrible pasting last month on that Schweinfurt raid, poor blighters. Who'd fly a bomber, no matter how well armed?'

'Someone has to do it, I suppose.'

'Yes. Lucky we don't. See you later.'

Kearns nodded. 'Yes, sir.'

He turned once more, to look out at the bleak day. Deputy squadron commander.

Now there was something.

In Bergen, Delsingen, now a senior colonel, was still in command of *Sondergruppe-Norwegen*, which had proved to be extremely successful at suppressing the resistance. The teams had gained fresh impetus from the deaths of Hartnitz and his men. For a period immediately following the incident, they had scored several successes. A team led by Geissler had wiped out a group as far away as Ålesund. What was more, many of these defeated resistance fighters had turned out to be from Ålvik's group. But Ålvik himself had never been caught; nor had those closest to him.

Resistance in the area, however, had virtually disappeared. There were still sporadic attacks, but these had now become so few and far between that Delsingen believed only one small group was still operating.

But the tide of war was changing for the Reich, and not for the better. To begin with, the promised expansion of the *Sondergruppe* idea had not come. All efforts were now being concentrated on making the Sognefjord, proposed lair of the *Graf von Hiller*, a virtual fortress. As far as the Führer was concerned, the war was far from lost. It would go on. As Delsingen had long thought bitterly, until the eventual destruction of Germany. Like many others, he had seen it coming.

But we did nothing, he reminded himself. And we'll pay for that.

Von Arnim had surrendered earlier in the year in North Africa. Now Montgomery and the Americans were pounding up from Italy.

The Russians were rolling back Barbarossa. Bomber raids were frequent over the Fatherland, despite the severe punishment they took from the Luftwaffe. The enemy could take the punishment and still come back with even more aircraft. The Luftwaffe could not. Inevitably, the constant attrition would whittle the fighters and their pilots down to the point where the skies over Germany would belong to the Allies.

'And even up here in Norway,' he said to himself, 'the enemy's aircraft have been increasingly active.'

Mindenhof had got his promotion to *Obersturmbannführer* and had become even more insufferable. From his point of view, the war was still being won.

A knock interrupted Delsingen's reverie and Geissler entered, carrying a folder.

The Wehrmacht major had been decorated with the Iron Cross, First Class, for extreme bravery under fire. During a fight in which his team had been facing far superior numbers, he had held on for three days in a running battle towards a rendezvous point, losing just one man. The route to the rendezvous had been strewn with the bodies of his pursuers.

Geissler had changed. His eyes held secrets he hated. The news of what had been really going on in the concentration camps could no longer be ignored. He had met a wounded veteran from the Eastern Front in a local hospital when on one of his rare visits to his parents, and what the man had said to him had sickened him. If only half of what that veteran had told him were true, it would still be a terrible curse upon the name of Germany that would last for generations. He had seen the devastation wrought by Allied bombing and fully understood that the reckoning was only a matter of time. And in his heart was the shaming weight of the love he had betrayed.

Was she, he asked himself continually, even now dying in a camp somewhere? Was she long dead?

'Well, Geissler,' Delsingen was saying. 'The whirlwind is coming.'

'Don't let Mindenhof hear you, sir. He still believes we're winning.'

'Yes, I know. Now that he's a lieutenant colonel it will become more difficult to keep him in check. The SS are already blaming the Wehrmacht for every defeat. He sees his star in the ascendant.'

'You still have your *Gruppenführer* friend.'

'*Obergruppenführer* now. See, Geissler? The SS are getting all the promotions.'

'At least, that's a good thing for you. *He* will hold Mindenhof in check.'

'Perhaps,' Delsingen said philosophically. 'Mindenhof sees me as the epitome of all he hates about the Wehrmacht. According to him, we have betrayed the Reich. Goering blamed the Luftwaffe for not beating the British, back in 1940. Now people like Mindenhof blame the Wehrmacht for what is happening on the ground. He's been waiting a long time for my head. The time of the scapegoat is upon us, and it will get worse as the war continues. But I've got bad news for our SS lieutenant colonel. He won't get my head. Now what's that you've brought?'

Geissler passed the folder to Delsingen. 'Coded, urgent priority. I decoded it myself. No one else has seen it.'

'You don't look very happy, Ernst.'

'Read it first, sir.'

'That bad, is it?'

Delsingen slowly opened the folder. A sealed envelope was on top of the decoded message. The SS seal on the envelope was a clear indication of its origin. He read the message first. Twice.

'So,' he said quietly. 'It would appear that the *Graf von Hiller* is nearly complete, and the Allies still have no idea of its existence. It's expected in Norway early next year and our job is to provide anti-aircraft protection. We're to leave Mindenhof in charge of security.' Delsingen passed a hand over his eyes. 'God help us, and God help the local people. The worse the war gets for us, the more excesses he will commit. I must stop this.'

He picked up the sealed letter and opened it. It read:

Rüdi,

I know this will come as a shock to you, but you are now a brigadier general! The documentation will come via the usual channels. You may not like the new appointment, but look at it this way. You are not being sent into harm's way, but being taken out of it. If you think a while on this, you will understand. Take what personnel you wish, to establish your new headquarters. You will still have a certain degree of autonomy. In other words, you can still keep a check on the security arrangements for the area. As usual, I will back you if you need to rap a few knuckles.'

Max

Delsingen folded the letter slowly. 'It seems as if I may have been wrong about the SS and their promotions.'

Geissler waited.

'I seem to have been made a brigadier general, Ernst.'

Geissler's face creased into a huge grin. 'Congratulations, General!' He held out his hand. 'This will kill Mindenhof.'

The newly promoted General Delsingen shook the hand. 'Thank you, Ernst. As you will have seen by that signal, we have a new posting.'

' "We", sir?'

'We.' Delsingen tapped at the letter. 'According to this, I have the authority to set up my new headquarters with whatever staff I require. I can't have a major as my number two. I need a lieutenant colonel. At the very least.'

'I understand, sir.'

'No you don't, Lieutenant Colonel Geissler.'

Geissler's eyes widened. '*Me?*'

'Is there another Geissler in this room?'

'Er, no, sir.'

'Good. I can't think of anyone else better suited. By the time we have set up the new HQ, your file will have been amended accordingly and the promotion officially sanctioned. In the meantime, we had better get to work. There's plenty to do.'

'Yes, sir! And what about Mindenhof?'

Delsingen gave a tight smile. 'I'll still be able to keep a check on him.' He tapped the letter again. 'The *Obergruppenführer* says so.'

Geissler still had the grin pasted on his face. 'This will really kill Mindenhof.'

'It will also make him more dangerous. I think my friend,' Delsingen continued, 'wanted me away from here, to prevent Mindenhof from yielding to temptation.'

'What temptation?'

'To put a bullet in me, of course.'

Geissler has been quite correct about Mindenhof's possible reaction to the news of the promotions.

The SS lieutenant colonel had come to Delsingen's office, still unaware of the double upgrading, but eager to assert his newly established authority. The shock was yet to come.

He had stomped into the office, barked his usual '*Heil Hitler*', and was standing glowering at Delsingen. Geissler stood in a corner, watching in anticipation.

'I have a copy of the signal,' Mindenhof began. 'I am now in command here.'

'Not just yet, Colonel . . .'

'*Obersturmbannführer!* Address me by my correct rank!'

'Not just yet, Colonel,' Delsingen repeated calmly. 'You're not quite in command. And I ought to remind you that you really should observe protocol when addressing an officer of general rank.'

The dark eyes seemed to pop. '*What?*' Mindenhof demanded weakly, the chagrin plain on his face. 'You have been promoted to general?' He could not have helped himself.

' "Sir", Colonel. Promoted to general, "sir".'

Mindenhof swallowed. 'Sir,' he got out at last, nearly choking on the word.

'Yes, Colonel. Amazing, isn't it? And Geissler is now a lieutenant colonel. Just like you, in fact.'

Mindenhof's head snapped round to look at Geissler, eyes venomous. 'A lieutenant colonel,' he said tightly.

Geissler smiled thinly at him.

Mindenhof jerked his head round again to look at Delsingen. 'When do I take command . . . sir?'

'When I tell you. We have plenty of work to do, so let's all get on with it. And Colonel, what I said long ago still stands. You will not abuse the locals. I'll still be able to check on you.'

Mindenhof's eyes gave one of their more malevolent dances. He took a deep breath. His right arm shot out.

'*Heil Hitler!*' he snarled, wheeled and stomped out.

'There goes a very desperate man, Geissler,' Delsingen said when Mindenhof had gone. 'He would burn the whole of Norway if he thought he could get away with it.'

'Perhaps there might come a time when even that might not restrain him.'

'Let us hope the war will be over before he reaches that stage,' Delsingen said.

Whitehall, London

Delsingen had been wrong when he'd said that the Allies did not know of the existence of the *Graf von Hiller*; but the knowledge had come almost perilously close to being too late.

The shabby-suited men were still in their job, in their shabby office, but now they had been galvanized by more information that had recently come to them about the ship. As a result, they had begun to cross-refer to the first snippets of information they had received so long ago.

They had stared, shocked, at both the

supposed specifications of the ship and the purpose for which it had been constructed. In trying to make up for their earlier mistake, they were commendably swift in initiating the kind of action that would subsequently cause the paths of Jo-Jo Kearns and General Delsingen to cross in conflict. Per Ålvik and Delsingen would also cross paths, but not in the way either might have expected.

The men were now studying the latest information that had come in. The ship was still being deployed to Norway, but there was no indication of when. A high-flying photo-recce Spitfire had been sent to take pictures, and though a veritable swarm of fighters had risen to meet it, they had not been able to catch the unarmed PR aircraft. However, the pictures it had taken had been of the wrong location. It was obvious that many dummy ships had been built, and costly bombing raids to try to destroy the real one had been suspended after three dummies had been hit.

A different strategy had thus been planned. It had been decided to wait until the ship had actually been deployed and then to destroy it in its Norwegian lair.

The latest information indicated that deployment was now imminent.

Sussex, England

The Spitfire Vb came sweeping low over the airfield at Merston, in weather than was far better than in Norfolk. It banked steeply, wingtip seeming almost to touch the ground as it performed two complete rolls, then rose in a flashing climb. It pulled into a half loop, flew upside down, then squared the loop by pulling into the dive once more. As it dropped, it began to level out, slowing down as it did so. It arrived over the threshold at the right speed and height for a smooth touchdown.

'One day,' said someone watching, 'he's going to misjudge that.'

'Crazy Norwegian,' another commented pleasantly. 'Got another two today, by the looks.'

When he'd taxied to the flight line and had come to a stop, the pilot found the squadron CO waiting for him.

'Flight Lieutenant Ålvik,' the CO began as Ålvik climbed down from the aircraft.

'Sir?'

'Don't look so worried, man. I'm not going

to bawl you out for that ridiculous display . . . even if it's quite, er, impressive.'

'Yes . . . no, sir.'

'Quit while you're head, Ålvik.' The CO was Canadian.

'Yes, sir.'

'Right, Mr Ålvik, it seems some high-up people require your services . . .'

'I'm *leaving*? I don't want to . . .'

'Don't interrupt me again, Flight Lieutenant.'

'No, sir!'

'All right. You've been asked for, and I've got to let you go. I've no choice in the matter. Your immediate posting is not far from here. You'll be converting to a new aircraft. Whatever it is they want you to do, don't let the squadron down.'

'I won't, sir.'

'That's the stuff, Mr Ålvik. Now I guess you'd better check with the Movements people.'

'Yes, sir.'

The CO saluted. 'Good luck, Mr Ålvik.'

'Thank you, sir.'

Two weeks later, after some leave, Luwzinsky and Kearns arrived at their new unit. Some of the people who were to crew the Mosquitoes were already there. Others had still to arrive.

The incredible de Havilland Mosquito was an aircraft that was a departure from standard aircraft construction. From the outset in 1938, it was planned to be constructed in wood, with the added bonus that it would ease the demand on metals much needed for other wartime construction. The twin-engined aircraft had turned out to be even better than its designers had dared hope. Built in an astonishing number of variants, those allocated to Kearns's new unit came in three marks.

The F Mk 2 was essentially the fighter version, with an armament of four .303 Browning machine-guns and four 20mm Hispano cannon. The FB Mk 6 was classed as a fighter-bomber and based on the Mk 2. Specifically for intruder missions, it carried the same armament as the fighter version, but could also carry bombs either within its bomb bay or externally; or eight 60lb rockets – four under each wing.

The third variant was a monster. This was the FB Mk XVIII. The 'Eighteen', as some of the unit's crews would call it, or the Tse-Tse Fly, as it was more commonly known, had a good reason for the nickname. The four-cannon fit in its shark-like jaw beneath the cockpit had been replaced by a single, awesome cannon, a 57mm six-pounder Molins gun. This was the Tse-Tse's true proboscis. It was a tank gun and, on the Mosquito, was a terrifying weapon. Like its African namesake, it brought with it an explosive and permanent sleeping sickness. This double-identity, Merlin-engined 'insect' could also be fully tooled up with the additional eight rocket projectiles, or externally carried bombs. The four .303 Brownings in the nose were retained.

These were the aircraft that greeted Kearns on his arrival. There were eighteen in all, six of each variant.

'Well,' he said to Luwzinsky, 'they're a bit bigger than the Spit.'

'And you've got two lovely Merlins instead of one.'

'Even so.'

'There's no satisfying some people,' Luwzinsky remarked drily. 'This is the Wooden Wonder. Come on. Let's report to the Station Commander.'

'Before going to the mess?'

'Before the mess.'

'Welcome, gentlemen,' the group captain greeted them. A wing commander navigator

with a chestful of ribbons and a thin moustache was with him. 'This is Wing Commander
Smythe. The wing commander has some information to which you should listen very closely.
Wing Commander, if you please.'

'Sir.'

Smythe, a man of average height, had sleek
black hair parted in the middle. His eyes glowed
the deepest blue that Kearns had ever seen. The
Australian thought he looked like a matinée idol
and half expected to see a long, white silk scarf
hanging from his neck. The decorations beneath
the navigator's half-wing proved that film-star
looks or not, this man was no pampered softie
in combat.

'We are forming this unit for a specific purpose,' Smythe began. 'To eliminate a battleship.'
He looked at each face as he said that. 'I can see
by your expressions you may be going into an
advanced state of shock. I'm afraid you heard
me correctly. The ship in question, a pocket
battleship to rival all the other heavy German
ships, is called the *Graf von Hiller*, and she
outperforms – according to her specifications
– everything else afloat – on either side.

'We know she has not yet been deployed, but
she soon will be. This means she has not yet
had her shake-down cruise. Her intended safe

186

haven is to be the Sognefjord. This is Norway's biggest fiord. It is longer and deeper than any of the others. The vital statistics are these: 127 miles long and nearly 4,300 feet deep. That's deeper than the North Sea.

'This great depth means the *von Hiller* might well be at sea herself, for all the worries her captain will have about grounding. It also means we can't hope to force her aground, unless she can be made to try to run for it, going too close to the shore and doing so too fast for the narrower sections of the fiord or the many islands and skerries which abound. The risk in that option, of course, is that she might well manage to escape into the open sea. We can't have that. We expect her to berth as far in as possible, as a precaution against air attack. This will give us a very deep gauntlet to run to reach the target. However, once she's disabled in there, she's trapped.

'Her armaments comprise six fifteen-inch guns; fourteen 5.9-inch; sixteen 105mm cannon, sixteen 37mm, thirty-six 20mm; and a further twelve Oerlikon. No surface ship will get within sufficient range to do any damage, without being blown out of the water first. An air attack with fast, light bombers is the only feasible answer. B-17s or Lancs, equally, would be blown out of the sky before they could get close enough to drop their bombs. Within the confines of the fiord, they would be totally unable to manoeuvre without either hitting each other or flying into a cliff face. They would also be sitting ducks for the AA barrage that would be coming up at them.

'We can expect a standing fighter cover, as well as anti-aircraft defences all the way in, and back again. Without doubt, there'll be other surface ships in the fiord, to act as a further defensive screen. You can count on their putting up a fierce AA barrage of their own.

'Given the depth of the fiord, it was originally planned to use submarines. However, it is assumed that in addition to the surface ship defences, which would include destroyers and other depth-charge-wielding vessels, there will also be a virtually impregnable anti-submarine net system and, quite possibly, a series of nets and booms, protecting the ship.

'This armoured raider is very important to the Germans. Destroying it will be a tremendous blow to their morale. The effects of this blow will permeate down to the lowliest soldier. It could mean the difference between a wavering motivation, if we succeed, and a resolute one, if that ship escapes.

'One of our pilots is Norwegian, with a comprehensive local knowledge. He will be able to help us devise the best way to plan our attack. It is intended to attack this ship *before* she has had a chance to work up to full operational capability and while her crew is still getting to know their ship and each other. This lack of familiarity with the ship, its systems and among the crew, will lengthen their response time to attack. It may be the only leeway we have.

'It is believed that her primary task will be to hunt down all shipping within our waters. This gives her a fairly large hunting ground and plenty of room within which to "disappear", until the next attack. I am giving no secrets away when I tell you that the invasion of Europe will come eventually. Even Hitler realizes this. Therefore this *Überschiff* of his must *not* be allowed to run amok among our own shipping lanes.

'If she is as good as she threatens to be, it is not difficult to understand why the Germans planned her construction so long ago, and in such secrecy. Her formidable array of weaponry can help delay the outcome of the war, perhaps long enough to enable Hitler to recoup his losses. This could have disastrous implications. Our task, gentlemen, is a difficult one; but it is one that we must carry out. In the Mosquito, we have at our disposal the tool with which to do the job.' Smythe stopped at last. 'Questions?'

Kearns looked at the wing commander. 'Yes, sir. The bloke who planned this, is he all right in the head?'

Luwzinsky gave Kearns a startled look. The group captain's expression froze. Smythe actually smiled.

'I thought the same thing,' he replied.

'Then you can tell him from me, sir, he's nuts.'

'I'm certain he'll be interested to hear that. I'll tell him exactly what you have said.'

The group captain now had a strange expression on his face.

'The question is,' Smythe was saying, 'can it be done?'

'Anything can be attempted, sir,' Kearns said. 'It's a matter of whether or not you survive, or whether or not you get the job done. From what you've just said, neither seems possible. No survival, no target blitzed. Zero. No go.'

'So what do you suggest we do about that ship, Squadron Leader . . .'

The deep-blue eyes remained fastened on the Australian. Smythe said nothing, and seemed to be waiting.

'The way I see it,' Kearns continued, unde-terred, 'we haven't much of a choice. We can't let that ship go. Which means I'm as crazy as the bloke who planned this. But we should try to make the odds more even.'

'That's why you're here, and all the others who are coming. To even the odds. That is why we've been given the Mossie. Again, to even the odds. The enemy is already so scared of that aircraft, the mere sight of it worries him intensely. We have picked the best crews for the job. Everyone who's not already here will be by tomorrow. Training begins the day after. You and your second in command might as well start getting to know your personnel, Wing Commander Luwzinsky.'

'*Wing commander*, sir?' Luwzinsky asked.

'Yes. And your promotion to Squadron Leader is confirmed, Kearns.' Smythe turned to the group captain. 'Isn't that right, sir?'

The group captain nodded. 'It is.'

'And Kearns . . . Smythe went on.

'Sir?'

'As one crazy person to another . . .'

Kearns stared at him. '*Your* plan?'

'My plan.'

Kearns was silent for some moments. 'Then we had better make it work.'

'I agree.'

A roar of Merlins swept over the building as a pair of Spitfires took to the air.

Kearns found a pleasant surprise waiting for him in the mess.

'Any guns jammed lately?' a voice said behind him.

Kearns whirled. 'Well, well. I'll be . . . You old wombat. Where did you spring from?'

Bede was grinning at him, hand outstretched. They shook hands enthusiastically.

'Jerry moved out of Africa,' Bede said. 'Things got boring. I got fed up of wearing khaki, so when the buzz came about selection for a new unit, I put my name up. Then I heard you were deputy CO. I couldn't believe it. Just like old times, I thought. It also means I can stop getting shot down, now that we're on the same team again.'

Kearns looked at the ribbons on Bede's tunic. 'Having a good war, I see, Flight Lieutenant.'

Bede pointed to Kearns's own ribbons. 'So are you, Squadron Leader.'

'You know how it is. They throw these things away. Ranks, gongs . . .'

Bede grinned once more. 'Who would have thought we'd have wound up on Mossies?

Remember the one that flew over our old squadron?'

'I do.'

'Must have been an omen of some kind,' Bede said. 'So,' he continued eagerly. 'What's the story?'

'That, my dear Venerable, will make your toes curl.'

'They're curling already. A tough one, is it?'

'Very.'

'Should I un-volunteer?'

'It might be smart.'

'Ah well. Too late. I've had a chat with some of the boys,' Bede went on. 'All sorts of bods. Looks like we've got ourselves an international squadron. One's a Norwegian. Do you know he used to be in the resistance over there? Came over about a year or so ago, learned to fly and turned into a raging fighter pilot.'

'Where is he? We had a briefing about him. Assuming he's the same one.

'He's the only Norwegian, so he must be. See the serious-looking chap over there with the coffee? That's him. Although he hasn't been in the Norwegian air force,' Bede continued, propelling Kearns by the arm towards Ålvik, 'he apparently had some kind of civilian student licence. Anyway, he got through his flying training in record time and found himself on Spits. Interesting chap. Killed lots of Germans even before he got over here. Seems he's just continuing what he began.'

They had reached Ålvik.

'Per,' Bede said, 'Jo-Jo Kearns, deputy CO. He's a lucky man. Never been shot down. When we flew together I was never shot down either. Then I was posted, and got shot down twice. I'm glad to be here.'

Ålvik had come to attention. 'Flight Lieutenant Ålvik, sir.'

'At ease, Per,' Kearns said. 'Besides, standing to attention with a hot coffee in your hand looks a bit dangerous.' He smiled at the Norwegian.

Ålvik's own smile was hesitant, his eyes guarded.

'I hear you're quite familiar with where we're supposed to be going,' Kearns said to him.

Ålvik nodded, but said nothing.

'Then we'll be wanting to talk to you in detail at some stage,' Kearns said, watching the other closely. 'And if there's anything else you'd like to talk to me about . . . privately, feel free to do so.'

'I will,' Ålvik said. 'Thank you, sir.'

'Good-oh.'

As they walked on, Bede said, 'What was that about? Why would he want to talk to you privately?'

'There's something on his mind.'

'Really? I hadn't noticed . . .'

'The trouble with you, James, is that you think only of killing the Hun.'

'Is that such a bad thing?'

'No.'

8

The next day Smythe held the first formal briefing for the entire squadron. He did not tell them the identity of the intended target, but impressed on them the need for the intense conversion to the new aircraft. The real operational training would take place after all crews had successfully completed the conversion course.

Many pilots had come from single-seaters, but there were former heavy- and medium-bomber crews too. For the eighteen aircraft, a pool of thirty crews was available. It was expected that the failure rate and attrition due to accidents would bring that reserve down.

The three different marks of aircraft had specific roles and the crews to man them were chosen accordingly. The single-seater pilots were given the Mk 2, the bomber crews got the Mk 6, and a mixture of fighter and fighter-bomber pilots got the Tse-Tse 'Eighteen'. Their navigators, like those on the Mk 2, came from the 'nav' pool.

Bede and Kearns got the fighter version. Ålvik got the Tse-Tse. Luwzinsky also chose the Tse-Tse.

Eventually all pilots were allocated their navigators. Some got on immediately. Others had to work at it. A few didn't work out at all, and had to be changed.

Strictly speaking, Smythe was not due to fly the mission; but he insisted on being included in the training. After all, he reasoned, he needed to continuously check the feasibility of his plan. He was given a pilot called Brace. Brace was twenty-one years old.

No one was permitted to talk about any aspect of the training to anyone outside the squadron crews. The Mosquitoes flew throughout the day and into the early evenings. Then came night flying. No one crashed, but two crews washed out. One crew had no co-ordination whatsoever, and the pilot of the other simply could not get to grips with the Mosquito.

Both Kearns and Bede had drawn navigators they could work with. Bede had once again become Kearns's wingman.

Ålvik took to the Mosquito easily. He was very pleased with the Tse-Tse, and as the only person who was truly familiar with the place they would eventually be attacking, looked forward to using that formidable gun against enemy ships in his homeland.

October 1943

The weeding out of the crews was complete. After nearly a month of intense flying, exactly eighteen crews – including Smythe and Brace – were deemed fit to continue into full operational training.

When all eighteen aircraft had landed one afternoon after a cross-country sortie, Bede said to Kearns, 'I wonder how my Mossie would handle a 190.'

'You're not hungry for a fight, are you?'

'Tell you what.'

'What?'

'I'm hungry for a fight.'

'A Mossie's not a Spit, James.'

'My Mossie's got two bloody great Merlin 25 engines pumping out 1635hp each. She's got *eight* guns, four of which are cannon. She's light on the controls, and without external stores I can fling her around. You saw how that Mossie that visited us about a hundred years ago was leaping around. Wouldn't it be a good way to find out how she performs in a real fight?'

'What are you suggesting?'

'I know the Mossie's supposed to be a long-range intruder, a long-range day fighter, a long-range night fighter, and whatever else can be rigged up for it in someone's fevered mind. I know other crews have had great successes with it in these roles . . .'

'What are you *really* getting at, James?'

'You and I. A quick prowl.'

'You mean go looking for trouble.'

'Well . . .'

'I'm the deputy CO. I'm supposed to be a responsible person.'

'You are. If this target is as tough as we all believe it to be, I have a feeling we're all going to need to know how close to the edge we can take the Mossie. Some of the things we may have to do won't be in the handling notes. Shouldn't a responsible deputy CO be trying to find out?'

'Nice argument, Bede!' Kearns said drily. 'Why do I have the feeling I'm being dragged into one of your wilder . . . Does your nav know about your suicidal inclinations?'

'Bede's navigator was a former Blenheim nav, a Dutchman named Laurens Koos, from Hilversum.

'He does,' Bede said, 'and is game.'

'He probably will be game. Game that's been shot.'

'Oh come on, Jo-Jo. We might learn something valuable that we can use on the mission itself.'

'All right,' Kearns said. 'I'll talk to the CO, and Wing Commander Smythe. If they say no . . .'

'Thanks, Jo-Jo!' Bede said and hurried away, as if afraid Kearns might change his mind.

Kearns shook his head slowly. 'Mad.'

But when he raised the suggestion with Smythe, he was surprised by the response.

'Good idea,' Smythe said. 'You'll be top cover for the raid on the day. You may well have to tangle with 190s. Go high. See what she'll do. All the aircraft have the Merlin 25. It would be a good way to check performance under combat conditions.'

Kearns looked at Luwzinsky.

'I think you should,' the CO said. 'Better find out now if we've got an Achilles' heel, than over the target.'

'Since we're all crazy,' Kearns said, 'I'll take Bede on the prowl tomorrow.'

Kearns's navigator was a Frenchman called Rameau, who, unlike his eighteenth-century namesake, was totally unmusical; but he shared a great passion with Ålvik. He, too, had been a member of the resistance in his own country, before escaping to England.

Prior to joining the resistance he had been a pilot flying the Dewoitine 250, the best single-seater fighter France had produced. In the frantic time of the invasion of his country, he had been up there, taking his own toll of the invaders' aircraft. Before the surrender the fast little fighter, in the hands of the French pilots, had destroyed nearly 150 of the enemy for the loss of just over eighty. But forty-four pilots had lost their lives.

Just before the collapse, Rameau had been shot down. He had got out of the stricken aircraft cleanly, but had landed in trees, dislocating an arm. Found by the members of the growing resistance movement, he had remained to fight. Though the arm functioned properly, he sometimes experienced sharp twinges. He had been turned down for further flying duties as a pilot; but his determination to continue flying had put him in the navigator's seat. He was already an experienced Mosquito nav. Though the official name for the second crewman in a Mosquito was 'observer', Rameau, like all the other unit navs who had made the grade, hated the term.

When Kearns had told Rameau what was planned for the next day, the Frenchman had simply said, 'You are going over *France*? Fantastique!'

They were cruising at 30,000 feet.

The Focke-Wulfs made it to that height with 7000 feet to spare, but that did not worry them. All the unit's aircraft could reach 40,000. It would take any 190s some time to get to that altitude; enough time to prepare for the engagement.

Kearns glanced out of the cockpit at Bede's aircraft. Like the days when they went hunting over the Channel, Bede was once more keeping perfect station. The Mosquito, with its engines underslung in long nacelles beneath that great wing, and its slim body, looked like an elegant moth on the whiteness.

Its wingspan of fifty-four feet two inches was greater by nearly twenty feet than the Spitfire's general average of thirty-six feet ten inches, and at forty and a half feet, its length exceeded the Spitfire's by over ten feet six inches. Despite this increase in overall size and weight, Bede was still able to keep as tight a formation as ever. He was so close that Kearns could see him clearly.

Bede looked across and gave a thumbs up. Kearns responded.

'He likes a good fight, your friend,' Rameau said from the nav's seat on the right.

'He likes something. Keep your eyes peeled, Jacques, if things get hot. I want you to make sure we don't lose sight of any Huns we find.'

'I will look. Do not worry. I hope we get a few Boche today.'

'I'll be happy with one.'

They seemed to be suspended over a cloud bank that stretched in all directions. Over to their right, a high white tower billowed in static majesty, probing the lofty blue of the sky above them.

With the cloud bank a good 10,000 feet below them, they flew deeper into French airspace, but no enemy aircraft put in an appearance.

They can't pick us up on their radar, Kearns thought. They don't know we're here.

He was not certain whether this was so, but wondered whether the bonded wood construction could be the reason. But soon after, two dots appeared above the whiteness, growing rapidly.

'Looks as if we've got trade, Jacques,' he said to his companion. 'Time to get your eyes working.'

'They are ready.'

Kearns glanced across at Bede, who made a forward motion with a hand. Bede had seen them too.

Without drop tanks, the aircraft were sleek and light. Time to find out what they could do.

He reached to his left for the supercharger gear-change switch at the rear of the throttle quadrant, and switched the two-stage superchargers from MOD to AUTO. They went immediately into high gear. His left hand then moved to the top of the quadrant for the throttle levers and smoothly eased them forwards until the engines were at 2650rpm and a boost reading of 7lb per square inch. This gave him maximum continuous operation. At a boost of 18lb and 3000rpm, he would be using full combat power, but with a time limit of just five minutes.

A glance to his right showed that Bede's aircraft had also begun to accelerate. It was like their old Channel patrol days, as if Bede had never been away. The instinctive way they worked together was back.

The small dots had grown and were still climbing. Kearns reached beneath the undercarriage lever on the main instrument panel and pressed the gun master switch.

'Camera.'

Rameau reached to his right for the gun camera switch, turned that on, and set the change-over button to CAMERA.

'You have camera,' he confirmed.

'Roger,' Kearns acknowledged.

Pressing either the control column thumb trigger for the machine-guns, or the finger trigger for the cannon would operate the camera. He was ready.

The dots had become Fw-190s and, still in the climb, they began to split right and left. But Kearns and Bede were waiting for that move.

Bede barrel-rolled sharply right, losing altitude abruptly and forcing the incoming 190 to counter. Having lost momentum in the climb, it was too slow to react and Bede was already back at the top of the barrel, with the 190 nicely pinned against the backdrop of the cloud bank.

Bede brought the nose down, tracking the 190 as it tried to roll away into the cloud. But the Mosquito was dropping rapidly now, closing the range swiftly. The 190 had nearly made it into the cloud when Bede pressed the thumb trigger, then squeezed the trigger for the cannon.

The alternate chatter and thump made an

unholy chorus as the eight guns hurled their lethal cargo at the 190. The combined discharge tore into the enemy aircraft just as it plunged into cloud.

At first, Bede thought he had missed. Then a sudden billow of black erupted out of the cloud bank. No flash of flame showed, but the black plume continued to hang above the undulating sea of white.

'We got him,' Koos said. There was awe in his voice. 'I have never seen anything like this. You were so quick.' He was looking at Bede, as if seeing him anew.

'This was not one of my really quick days,' Bede said lightly. He patted the instrument panel as they turned away from the dark banner of their victim. 'She's no Spitfire, but she's no slouch either. And she bites! I think I like her. Now where has Jo-Jo got to?'

Kearns was fully occupied with following the second 190 in a spiral dive.

The Mosquito tended to become very tail-heavy when diving at speed; but the spiral kept the speed within limits and continuous forward trimming kept the controls light as they plunged. Then abruptly, the Focke-Wulf stopped spiralling and went into a straight dive.

'He wants to get away!' Rameau exclaimed.

'Or he wants to draw us into a trap where his friends might be waiting. Look out for Bede.'

Rameau checked over his right shoulder. 'Behind us, coming down also.'

'Blue Two,' Kearns called. 'Stay up and watch for fish.'

'Roger,' Bede responded. His Mosquito pulled out of the dive.

The Focke-Wulf plunged into the cloud bank. Kearns followed.

'All right, Jacques. See if you can find him on the radar. Just a brief search.'

'I have him,' Rameau said after a short while. 'He is still ahead.'

'What's he playing at?'

'Ah!'

'What? What?'

'I have lost him.' Rameau sounded mortified.

'Don't worry about it. He's not going anywhere.'

'Blue One!'

'Blue One,' Kearns said, responding to Bede's call.

'Fish just popped. Ten o'clock.'

'Blue One,' Kearns acknowledged as he hauled the Mosquito back up through the cloud.

They cleared the top just in time to see the 190 wheel round to come towards them. In the distance was Bede's Mosquito. The Focke-Wulf pilot had clearly been surprised to find the other Mosquito sitting up top, and was wheeling away only to find Kearns charging towards him.

Tracers began to stream from the 190 as it rushed for a head-on pass.

Kearns went into a high barrel roll and watched through the top of the cockpit as the smaller fighter charged through the invisible tube he'd drawn in the sky. He eased left rudder to slice downwards. Heavy ruddering was not a smart thing to do in a Mosquito.

His manoeuvre had cut into the 190's reversal as it came back at him. This had positioned him just above the Focke-Wulf's spine as he came round. He tracked into it, tightening the turn to keep the 190's cockpit in sight. He knew he had to shoot quickly before the other aircraft reversed once more to slide away, and try to get on to his tail.

Beside him, Rameau waited tensely. The Merlins sang sweetly, never missing a beat as Kearns continued to haul into the turn.

The firing, when it came, startled Rameau who had been lulled by the siren music of the Merlins. Ahead of them, the machine-guns chattered and beneath their feet the four 20mm cannon thundered. Eight streams of tracer took the 190 along its spine, slamming into it like a brick wall hurled by a giant. The pulverizing blow opened up the 190 like a fish being filleted with a blunt knife. The teardrop canopy shattered, then the engine began to belch streamers of smoke as the rounds slammed past the cockpit and into the cowling. The enemy aircraft seemed to stop in mid-air. Then suddenly, nose and tail sections parted company, the two halves dropping towards each other as if the aircraft had been punched in the belly. Then they tumbled crazily towards the cloud bank, the tail faster than the forward section, which still had its wings attached. The nose fell steeply now, marking the sky with a streaming, expanding wake of black plumes as it disappeared into the cloud.

There was no flame, and no one got out.

'I think you killed the pilot,' Rameau said quietly.

'You don't sound happy,' Kearns said as he pulled into level flight and throttled back.

Rameau was searching the sky for more enemy aircraft.

'For one small moment,' he said, 'I did not think of him as a German who had invaded my country, but as an airman dying in that burst of fire. Do I make sense to you?'

'I understand,' Kearns told him soberly.

'But also, another part of me feels good. We have won the combat, and I am glad that he is dead.'

Kearns looked across and saw Bede's Mosquito slide into place.

'I know how you feel,' he said.

Whitehall, two days later
The men in the untidy office were studying their latest information on the ship. It was on the move. They contacted Photo Recce Command, and requested reconnaissance flights to find the *Graf von Hiller*.

They didn't.

A week after that the entire squadron flew to the Moray coast in Scotland, where they were to be based for the duration of the work up to the mission. They shared their base with other units, but were to remain completely autonomous. The embargo on discussing the mission with anyone outside the squadron was strictly maintained.

Impressed by the exploits of Kearns and Bede against the 190s, Smythe and Luwzinsky

detailed them to instruct all the other crews –
without exception – in the best way to employ
fighter tactics that maximized the strong points
of the Mosquito, the most prominent of which
was its tremendous fire-power.

'Never forget,' Kearns would say to them,
'you've got a killing machine at your fingertips.
Use it!'

Bede used the same exhortation, almost word
for word.

Training for the attack on the *von Hiller* was
carried out among the lochs, with the narrowest
that could be found being used to simulate the
Sognefjord, though they were not told this.

The purpose was to give the crews experience
in manoeuvring in confined spaces, with the
high ground standing in for anti-aircraft fire.
Hitting a rock wall was just as terminal as being
'bracketed' by a lethal burst of flak. Luwzinsky
and Kearns wanted them to manoeuvre instinctively, weaving past the dangers without pause,
flying at the edge of their skill. To hesitate
was to die.

All eighteen crews flew the same schedule, so
that each would be able to cope with changing
conditions during the attack. They flew low
over the water, almost skimming the surface

with the tips of the propellers. They shot their way up steep mountainsides, and plunged down again. They threaded their way through passes, wingtips pointing straight down. They carried out air-to-air manoeuvring against each other. Frequently, Bede or Kearns would spring an unexpected attack, then assess their chances of escape.

The non-stop training continued into November, when the winter came, and on into December.

Two days before Christmas a halt was called; but no one was allowed to go off the station. After Christmas training continued and on New Year's Eve Smythe summoned Ålvik.

The Norwegian entered the wing commander's office to find Luwzinsky and Kearns there as well.

Smythe indicated an empty chair and said, 'Please take a seat, Per.' And when Ålvik had done so, he continued, 'We're all very impressed with the way you've handled your flying. It's also been noted that you have a special affinity for low flying, but we would appreciate it if you and that Kiwi navigator of yours, McLeish, would refrain from bringing back other people's washing on your wings.'

'A strong wind had blown it aloft, sir,'

Ålvik said, straight-faced. 'We . . . flew into it.'

'Flew into it. I see. Well, let's see how you handle this. How would you like to lead the Tse-Tse flight?'

Ålvik stared, scarcely daring to believe it. 'I would very much like to, sir,' he replied eagerly, then glanced at Luwzinsky. 'But isn't Wing Commander Luwzinsky . . . ?'

'I thought that as we're going into your backyard,' Luwzinsky said, 'you should have the lead.' He smiled briefly. 'Besides, you do know your way around.'

'Thank you very much, sir!' Ålvik said gratefully. 'I shall not let you down.'

'I know you won't. We're handing you one of the most dangerous parts of the mission. Your job will be to attack the anti-aircraft defences repeatedly, while the ship is bombed and rocketed. This means going after the flak guns both along the fiord *and* on the ship itself.'

'I will do it,' Ålvik said firmly.

'Good man,' Smythe told him.

'I will fly as your number two,' Luwzinsky said.

Ålvik was genuinely touched by this show of confidence in him. 'Again, I can only thank you for giving me the opportunity to strike back

at the people who invaded my country and
destroyed my family. Thank you,' he finished
in a voice that had gone very soft.

Smythe got up from his chair and went over
and patted Ålvik on the shoulder. 'We're with
you. Now, Wing Commander Luwzinsky has an
idea about the attack. You know the topography
of the area. We'd like to know what you think.
Let's go to the map room.'

They all went into a smaller, adjoining room.
A cold wind was coming off the Arctic and
hurtling down the Moray Firth. It howled
sobbingly outside.

'Let's hope we don't have this wind when
the day comes,' Kearns said with feeling.

No one said anything to that, but their faces
mirrored their thoughts. They all shared the
same hope. Things would be ferocious enough
in the fiord.

A large-scale map of the Sognefjord area was
spread out on a large table. They went over to it,
the three senior officers standing back to allow
Ålvik to study the map closely. All along the
sides of the fiord, red markers had been placed
where anti-aircraft positions were expected to
be. Various oval shapes, to signify naval units,
were placed in the fiord itself. A big oval was
at its head. This was the *Graf von Hiller*.

Ålvik scrutinized the map silently for nearly three minutes. At last he straightened and turned to face them.

'The big ship . . . ?'

'Is the *Graf von Hiller*,' Smythe replied. 'It is more powerful than the *Bismarck*, even though it's a relatively small vessel. It's specific job is to decimate the Allied invasion fleet. That's our target. I do not have to tell you what it would mean to the war effort if we fail.'

'The invader would stay longer in my homeland.'

'Among all the others . . . yes.'

Ålvik nodded slowly, understanding full well that the war could be prolonged if the *von Hiller* did succeed in wreaking havoc on the fleet.

'The flak and other AA,' he said, 'are where I would expect them to be. When I was with the resistance, the SS lieutenant colonel in command was replaced by a Wehrmacht officer who was not brutal, but very clever. A good tactician. He set up hunter-killer teams that wiped out most of the groups in the area, including mine. When I left, only four of us of my old group were still alive. I believe this same man is now in command of the defences around the fiord. Before I joined this squadron, I used to get news from home. I had to leave someone. But of course, because of our mission . . .'

'I'll have one of our people check with the Norwegian people in London,' Smythe said. 'See if there's anything for you.'

'Thank you, sir.'

'I think I may know something of the German commander you mentioned,' Smythe went on. 'What you've said confirms a little of what we do know.' He leaned over the map. 'Harry Luwzinsky believes we should make a multi-point attack, instead of running the gauntlet of the fiord. Where would you place the best points of entry?'

Ålvik again studied the map, then looked at Luwzinsky. 'How would the aircraft attack, sir?'

'In pairs, or even singly, all at different intervals, but not more than a second or two apart, and from different directions and heights. The idea is to confuse the defences. Give them so many targets, they may even shoot at each other, especially if we're low down. If there are many ships in the fiord, that may well happen as they try to track us. All attacks will, of course, be carried out at speed.'

'In that case,' Ålvik said, 'we may have many options. There will be places where the flak will be minimal. We can use the high ground to hide until the last moment. There are two places at the head of the fiord where the ship could take refuge. All the way to Årdalstangen . . . here. Or at Laerdal . . . here. They would not put it close to Laerdal but here at the junction of the Laerdalsfjord and the Årdalsfjord. They could also put it nearer the sea in that bend here, at Balestrand – but I think not. I would say one of the first two.

'If they do this, we can come at them from many quarters. As a resistance fighter I covered this whole area, and much more. There were not many soldiers, or guns. Of course, this new commander could have changed it; but I still think he will concentrate on the fiord. He will expect the attack to come from the sea, not from occupied territory. This will give us a big element of surprise. We will not be able to escape everything, but it will not be as hot as coming all the way up Sognefjord.'

Smythe nodded as Ålvik finished speaking. 'Once we've woken them up, of course, all hell will break loose. All right, Per. Draw up a plan of attack, based on your knowledge of the area.'

'I can stay in here to do this?'

'Certainly.'

'I will use this map.'

'Feel free to do so.'

Ålvik nodded. 'I will start right away.'

'Very well. Anything you need, just shout. We'll leave you to it.'

'Yes, sir.'

As they were leaving, Ålvik called, 'Squadron Leader Kearns . . .'

Kearns paused. 'I'll be along,' he said to the wing commanders.

They nodded and went out.

Kearns waited for the Norwegian to speak.

'Some time ago,' Ålvik began, 'you said if I had some private matters to discuss . . .'

'The offer still stands.'

'You heard me say to the wing commander that I left someone behind.'

Kearns nodded.

'She is someone very special,' Ålvik went on. 'She was in my resistance group. When I had to leave because the Germans were getting close, I asked her to come with me. She refused. She knew I was coming over to fly and said I had to do it, but that she should stay to carry on the fight the best way she knew how. We had all decided that the remaining four should go our separate ways, to avoid capture. The Germans were looking for a team, not individuals. They didn't know what the others looked like; but they knew me, because of what happened to my family. They tortured and raped my sister, and my fiancée . . .'

'Sweet Jesus . . .'

'Not the men of the new commander, but the SS. I feel guilty about leaving Inge. I keep thinking that if she falls into their hands, the same thing will happen to her. The SS are still there, you see, if the Wehrmacht officer is now in command of the fiord defences. Inge is not afraid of danger. She has had close shaves, but without me there . . .'

'Steady on, mate. The best thing you can do for her is to help us get that ship. Think of her when you go in to attack; but not of what you think *might* be happening to her. You've got the lead of your flight, and we're depending on you to give us the best points of entry. What would Inge want you to do?'

'Attack.'

'Precisely.'

'When they took my fiancée, I built a wall around myself. I had no feelings. Then Inge came.'

'And now you feel vulnerable.'

'Yes.'

'Tell you something, Per. There's nothing wrong with that.'

'*You* do not look vulnerable.'

'Don't you believe it, mate. One day, when this is all over, I'll tell you *my* story.' Kearns glanced at his watch. 'Oh.' He held out a hand. 'And Happy New Year.'

They shook hands.

9

Late April 1944

Smythe stood on a podium, before a huge photograph of a ship underway. Around the edges of the photo were white puffs that looked like scattered clouds. He looked at the assembled crews before him.

'Gentlemen,' he said, using a long pointer to tap at the image of the ship, 'the *Graf von Hiller*. Your target.'

There was a collective sharp intake of breath.

'As well you might,' he continued. 'Despite the quality of the photograph, which had to be taken in a hurry, those white things you see are not clouds, but a veritable carpet of flak. No doubt you'll be asking yourselves whether it's thick enough to walk on.'

There were a few nervous chuckles, but

they soon died. Most people were too stunned to react.

'You have been very patient,' Smythe continued, 'and you have worked very hard over the past months to maintain your very high standards of skill. I'm proud of you all. You will now begin to understand why you were pushed so hard during the work-up to operational capability. That ship is the most formidable vessel afloat today, barring an aircraft carrier. But an aircraft carrier's real teeth are her aeroplanes. The *von Hiller*'s teeth are with her all the time.

'We now know to a fairly certain extent that the Hun intends to turn her loose on Allied shipping before and during the invasion of Europe, whenever that is due to begin. She intends to raid from Norway to Spain, and back. Her armament is such that she can stand off and pulverize our ships without ever coming close enough to be fired upon with any effect. Our task is to stop her before she is fully operational.

'We know she has now been deployed to Norway, and is based in the Sognefjord. The head of that fiord is *127 miles* inland. From the sea to the target area, we can expect solid anti-aircraft defences, on land as well as on the surface, in addition to the *von Hiller*'s own defences. We can also expect fighters.'

There were a few groans.

'Yes, yes. I know,' Smythe said easily. 'We can't have Christmas every day.'

That brought a few louder chuckles.

'However, all is not as desperate as it might seem at first glance. The *von Hiller* is not yet a fully functioning ship. She has not yet had the time to turn her crew into a well-oiled machine . . .'

'Not like us!' someone shouted.

The laughter came more easily now.

'My thoughts precisely,' Smythe said, catching the mood smoothly. 'Further, there will be several diversionary raids mounted all over occupied Europe to keep the Hun guessing, including Germany itself, which will receive the brunt of these attacks.'

There were cheers.

'But best of all,' Smythe continued, 'we have with us Flight Lieutenant Per Ålvik, who is not only Norwegian, but knows the area like the back of his hand, so to speak. He has devised ways to let us in via the back door.'

'*Good old Per!*' they shouted.

Ålvik grinned. He had received news that Inge was still free, and in good health.

'The one thing we have not done,' the wing commander carried on, 'is to activate any resistance people in the area, or to send in saboteurs. It was imperative that no attention whatsoever be drawn to the ship. We intend to catch them napping.'

'Put the bastards to sleep for good!' came another shout.

'That will be up to us. Your flight commanders will give you the route to target. Take-off is at 0400 hours. Good luck, gentlemen. And now, the met officer.'

'*Get off!*' they yelled at the hapless meteorological officer when he had climbed the podium.

'They're in good spirits,' Smythe said to Luwzinsky and Kearns outside the briefing room.

The met officer was being mercilessly barracked.

'How many of them will be back after this?' Luwzinsky wondered. 'Or us, for that matter. Which reminds me,' he continued to Smythe. 'You said "us" during your speech. You were supposed to fly during training, but not go on ops.'

'You're not thinking of grounding me,

are you, Harry? You need every aircraft and crew.'

'You planned this from the beginning,' Luwzinsky said. 'You knew we would get to this point.'

'If I'm going to send people into a cauldron, I can hardly stay behind.'

'That's what planners *are* supposed to do.'

'Too late, Harry. I pre-empted you. I got my permission from the Air Ministry long ago.'

'You sneaky devil.'

'That's what planners are. Sneaky.'

Sognefjord, Norway

General Delsingen could see the ship clearly from his headquarters. The steep sides of the ancient flooded valley that was the fiord made it a perfect haven. He had sited anti-aircraft guns all along the route. If the enemy attacked, there would be a heavy price to pay.

But the scene was so peaceful that it was almost hard to imagine that the graceful ship out there was, in reality, little more than a representation of the zenith of naval killing machines.

Never one to take anything for granted, Delsingen had also sited listening posts at strategic points. However, he did make a mistake. He would eventually realize this far too late for him to have any hope of rectifying it.

A familiar knock on his door was followed by Geissler's entry.

'Any news of the Allied landings in France?' Delsingen asked of his subordinate, certain there would be.

Geissler shook his head. 'None, sir. There are no full-scale landings. It's almost quiet down there, by all accounts.'

'Make no mistake, Colonel,' Delsingen said. 'There will be a landing.'

'I have other news.'

'Go on.'

'There has been an escalation of the bombing at home.'

Delsingen nodded. 'The whirlwind, Geissler. It's getting closer. Look at that ship out there. It's a beautiful monster, isn't it? But it won't make much of a difference. Oh, it could probably damage the Allied fleet very badly, and the war might continue for another year or two. But what do you think our cost will be?'

'I try not to think of it, General.'

'You're a wise man, Ernst. Such things *are* better left unthought. I want you to make one of your trips to Bergen. I don't trust Mindenhof to behave himself if we don't keep him on his toes. Fröhmann's E-boat is here. Tell him he's got my authority to take you. Or would you prefer to fly?'

'I think I'll take the boat trip. Seems a nice fresh day for it. I'll enjoy the fast journey on the fiords. Fröhmann always likes to show me what it can do. We'll be there by morning.'

'All right. Do you want to take a couple of men with you? Just in case Mindenhof gives you a problem?'

'In a strange way, I don't think he'd dare. He's got what he wants. He feels he can now afford to humour you.'

'I'll give you some of your own advice, Colonel. Be careful.'

'Yes, sir.'

The E-boat powered past the *Graf von Hiller*.

'Every time I see that ship I still can't believe it,' Geissler said as they seemed to be going on and on past the battleship. It towered above their vessel, making it seem like a toy. 'It's so huge! And all those guns!'

'She's quite something,' Fröhmann agreed, 'but give me this little beauty any day. I'd hate to be aboard the *von Hiller* when she turns turtle. Imagine trying to get out from below decks. All that armour. All that weight. No thanks. I like my little sports runabout. She's fast, and she's lethal. Good enough for me.'

'But the *Graf von Hiller* is not going to turn turtle.'

'You believe she is unsinkable? Remember the *Titanic*. That was "unsinkable" too. There's no such thing.'

They were approaching the boom of the first anti-submarine barrier.

'Zuchner!' Fröhmann called to the man at the wheel.

''*Wohl, Herr Kapitän!*'

'*Beide Maschinen langsam!*'

'*Beide Maschinen langsam, Herr Kapitän!*'

The E-boat dropped its raised prow as they slowed for the passage through the boom which was being opened to let them through. They repeated the procedure through two more, then they were free of obstacles.

Fröhmann ordered the helmsman to take it back to full speed and the E-boat roared down the fiord.

They passed two destroyers, the outer screen of the battleship's defence.

As the E-boat churned throatily along, its red, white and black swastika ensign fluttering stiffly at its mast, Fröhmann said, 'This is what

I like most about this war. Sailing at speed on the fiords. I wish I could do this just for enjoyment.'

'Why don't you come back when the war is over?'

'And when might that be?'

'It must end sometime.'

'And who will give me an E-boat in which to enjoy myself?'

Geissler smiled. 'You've got me there.'

'So we enjoy it now.'

'All right, Fröhmann. You win.'

The naval officer grinned.

They would arrive in Bergen about an hour after the Mosquitoes had taken off on their mission to sink the *Graf von Hiller*.

Moray Coast, Scotland. 0400 hours

Kearns and Rameau sat in their Mosquito as the engines warmed up. Already, the first flight of six – the fighter-bombers – were on their take-off run, doing so one after the other in the dim twilight of the coming dawn.

'No turning back now, Jacques,' Kearns said.

'No. We will have some fun, eh?'

'We'll do our very best.'

The eighteen aircraft were arranged as Yellow Flight, the fighter-bombers; Red Flight,

229

the Tse-Tses; and Blue Flight, the fighters for escort. Smythe, though a navigator, had the lead of Yellow. Luwzinsky, though still in overall command of the squadron, had already passed the lead of Red Flight to Ålvik. Blue Flight was commanded by Kearns, with Bede as his number two.

He watched as the first six took off without mishap. Then it was the turn of Red Flight.

Red One, Ålvik, began his take-off run, followed by Luwzinsky. Then it all began to go wrong.

'*Burst tyre! Burst tyre!*' Kearns heard in his headphones. '*Blue One! You have command! Blue One! You have command!*'

Kearns watched in horror as Red Two, piloted by Luwzinsky, began to swing off the runway. It was going much too fast to stop safely. He could imagine the squadron commander fighting for his life and his navigator's, trying desperately to correct the swing. But the fuel-laden aircraft hit something on the ground and pivoted about a wingtip. A sheet of flame twice as long as the Mosquito suddenly shot out. It curled on itself to lick at the gyrating aeroplane. There was a sudden vivid explosion and the Mosquito seemed to vanish in the flames. There was no chance for the crew.

'Oh my God!' Kearns said softly.

Then he roused himself. He was in command now. Nothing he could do about what had just happened. Time to think about it later. The mission had to be continued.

'All aircraft. This is Blue One! You heard the man. Carry on with your take-off.' He wondered how Per Ålvik, who had been so close to the tragedy, now felt as he lifted his aircraft into the air.

There were now only five Tse-Tse Mosquitoes to take on the guns.

'Let's hope the back door works,' Kearns said to Rameau. 'Per is one down.'

'We must not think about it.'

'No.'

Red Flight were airborne.

'Our turn, Jacques.'

Bergen, 0600 hours

The E-boat cruised slowly into the inner harbour. Geissler saw the girl sitting on the sea wall and wondered what she was doing there so early in the morning. Then he saw a squad of SS men marching purposefully towards her.

'Fröhmann!' he called sharply.

Startled by the urgency in his voice, the naval officer turned quickly. 'What?'

'Get me ashore. Fast!'

'What is happening?'

'I'm not sure, but I intend to stop it.'

Geissler himself had no idea why he was behaving in such a manner. He simply had a feeling that the girl was about to get into trouble. For some reason, he didn't want that to happen.

'Come on! Hurry!'

'All right, all right! Why the sudden panic anyway?' Then Fröhmann saw where Geissler was looking. 'Aha! Pretty! Friend of yours?'

'No.'

'But . . .'

'Please! Before those SS men get to her.'

The girl seemed quite unaware that the four men were bearing down on her.

'Be careful, Colonel. These SS are a law unto themselves.'

'I'll be all right.'

The E-boat was brought close to the pier. Geissler leapt out almost before it was close enough.

'*You!*'

The girl turned, as if seeing the SS men for the first time. She did nothing else.

'*Stand up, bitch!*' the squad leader snarled in bad Norwegian. He was an *Untersturmführer*

– a second lieutenant – young, full of himself and out to impress his men. '*A German officer is talking to you!*'

She remained seated, and said quietly, 'And a Norwegian is sitting on her harbour wall.'

'*Do you want to be kicked into the water?*' he screamed at her.

'No,' she said, still calm.

The men in the squad were smiling surreptitiously. It was difficult to tell whether they were secretly laughing at her or the lieutenant. They began to eye her with more than passing interest, assessing possibilities.

'Then stand up, or you will be dragged up! What are you doing here? This is a restricted area!'

She stood up, slowly. 'Stop shouting. I'm not deaf.'

'No insolence!' He raised a hand to strike her.

'*Lieutenant!*'

He jerked in the act of striking, frozen by this unexpected interruption.

Geissler hurried up to them. 'What do you think you're doing?'

'This woman was insolent, *Herr Oberstleutnant*. I was about to teach her some manners. She is also in a restricted area.'

'You were correct in apprehending her. I shall take it from here.'

'With respect, *Herr Oberstleutnant*. I must insist . . .'

'*You what?*' Geissler roared so suddenly that all four SS men gave an involuntary jump. 'How dare you, Lieutenant! You will give me the respect properly due to my rank or you'll find yourself on the Eastern Front before your heels next touch the ground. *Is that clear?*'

The SS second lieutenant looked into Geissler's eyes, saw the coldness in them, noted the Iron Cross ribbon, and did a rapid rethink.

'I apologize to the Colonel!' he said stiffly.

His men smirked.

'Now move on!'

'Move!' the lieutenant barked at his men, his face suffused with anger and embarrassment.

'You must like living dangerously,' a voice said. 'Even though he is a little pipsqueak, he's still SS, and Mindenhof is still in charge.'

Geissler turned and saw Fröhmann. He had two armed sailors with him.

'Is that why they left?'

'No. They were doing that before we came on the scene.'

They all looked at the girl.

She was staring at Geissler. 'Why did you do that?'

'You speak German.'

'You lot have been here long enough. It's inevitable.'

'Are you crazy? What are you doing here at this time of the day?'

'I was taking a walk. I stopped. This is my country.'

'A very patriotic attitude that can get you killed.'

'So why did you stop them? You are German.'

Geissler looked at her thoughtfully. 'You're not afraid of me, are you?'

'No.'

'Or of the SS?'

'No.'

'You should be.'

'Why? Don't they die like everyone else?'

The sailors were staring at her disbelievingly, clearly thinking she was insane.

Fröhmann looked on amused. 'You can go back to the boat,' he told the sailors. 'Thank you.'

They gave the girl another bemused look, before returning to the E-boat.

'I don't know what you want here,' Geissler

said to her, 'but get away before a more senior SS man comes.'

'You are afraid of the SS?'

'No! And stop these stupid questions. Come on. Get away from here!'

She seemed surprised by his attitude. 'You really don't want them to get me, do you?'

'Move!'

'All right. I'm going.' She stared almost unnervingly at him. 'What happened to her?' she asked softly.

'Wha ... what? What are you talking about?'

'You lost someone, once.'

Then she turned and walked away.

Geissler watched her go, feeling as if a ghost had visited him.

'You seem pale, Geissler,' the E-boat captain said. 'Are you all right?'

'Yes, yes. I'm fine.'

'What did she mean?'

'I have no idea.'

Inge Jarl watched the two German officers walk away.

She'd seen all she'd needed to, and would pass the information on down the line. She had been in the area for two days. Her mission had been to observe what was going on, and report. She had no idea why this information was needed at this time. She didn't like this work and preferred to be in the field, fighting. She missed Per and hoped he was still flying and safe. The incongruity of these two wishes did not trouble her.

Had the SS men searched her, they would have found a pistol. She knew she had nearly taken one chance too many. If it hadn't been for that Wehrmacht officer . . . Strange, she thought. He had really been frightened of letting the SS take her away. Had he really let a woman down before? Someone who had loved him?

She began to make her way out of the area, resolving never to take such a stupid risk again. She would ask not to be sent on any more such assignments.

Her body ached for Per.

'Strange,' Ålvik said.

'What is?' Kiwi McLeish asked.

'Oh, I just thought of someone.'

'Is she pretty?'

'Is it so obvious?'

'Oh yes.'

Ålvik looked out of the cockpit to check

the sky about him. All he could see were
Mosquitoes.

'They look good,' he said.

'Don't they just?' the New Zealander agreed.
'You must feel good going back to the old
country to bang a few Jerry heads together.'

'Yes, I do.'

'Bad luck about the CO.'

'Yes. Very bad luck. He was a good man.
Dennis, too. The good always go first.'

'So we're going to be around for a while,
eh?' McLeish said, laughing. The sound was
bizarre in his mask.

'Perhaps,' Ålvik said.

But he smiled.

Ålvik's plan had worked – so far. He had
also been right about where the ship would
be anchored.

They crossed the Norwegian coast on opposite sides of the fiord, routeing well away from
the target area. The bombers, carrying armour-
piercing, very high-explosive bombs, some with
delayed-action fuses, would be approaching the
target from Årdalstangen.

The Tse-Tses would come from two directions: Laerdal and across from Kaupanger. The
fighters would go high, initially, then apparently

238

disappear, only to join in the fun at very low level. If fighters appeared, they would engage. The primary task was the ship and to get the bombs on.

Smythe could not believe they were still undetected and thanked every deity that Ålvik knew the area so well.

'Two minutes to target,' he said to Brack.

'Yes, sir,' the young pilot acknowledged.

'Are you all right?'

Brack swallowed. 'I'm fine, sir.'

'We go in fast and very low, drop our bombs, then break right into the valley. Just as you were briefed. We'll be in there for mere seconds, and be gone before they know it.'

'Yes, sir.'

One of the soldiers manning one of the listening posts set up by Delsingen was staring at the formation of aircraft high above him. He spoke urgently into his radio.

'They look like small aircraft. Fighters. Not bombers. How should *I* know where they're going? Am I flying up there? They're heading east. East! Yes. Pass it on anyway. Let them do what they want with it. Then they can't say we didn't relay the information. Up here? It's cold, and I want a woman. What? Fat chance out here. The Norwegians hate us.'

He ended transmission and looked up again. The fighters had gone.

Kearns, having displayed his high formation for the benefit of ground watchers, ordered his aircraft to split into pairs. Each pair descended earthwards in different directions.

Desultory flak came up at them. None of the bursts was even close.

'It seems as if Per was right, after all,' he said to Rameau. 'Hardly any AA out here.'

'Let us be thankful for small blessings.'

'I am. Believe me. The first bombs should be going down about now.'

'Christ!' Smythe said. 'Just look at the size of that ship!'

They had erupted from cover and, incredibly, the surprise was so complete, not a single gun fired at them.

'*Bomb doors!*' Brack shouted.

Smythe was already reaching for the lever next to the undercarriage selector. '*Open!*'

Brack squeezed the release button. '*Bombs gone! Let's get out of here!*'

*   *   *

The crewmen on the deck of the *von Hiller* could not believe their eyes when the twin-engined aircraft came at them from *landward*. They assumed it was one of theirs. Only when they saw the objects dropping towards them and the great planform of the Mosquito as it banked away, showing its RAF roundels, did they realize what was happening.

They then started to run.

Brack had been far more successful than he would have dared hope. Not only had he got away scot-free with not a single shot being fired at him, but his first bomb went straight down a funnel, plunging deep into the bowels of the ship before exploding. The second followed the same path, adding to the carnage.

The first wounds had been inflicted.

Delsingen, from his vantage-point, had seen the aircraft suddenly appear, heading for the ship. Like the sailors, he had at first thought it to be a German aircraft, because it had come from such a totally unexpected quarter. Then he'd seen the bombs falling, heard the roar of the aeroplane, seen the RAF roundels, and had felt both a sense of despair and of the inevitable.

He had rushed to get his binoculars and

focused on the *Graf von Hiller*'s forward funnel. A great sheet of flame had erupted from it, shooting, it had seemed, hundreds of feet into the air. A rumbling, muffled explosion deep within had sent a visible tremor through the ship, causing it to shift in the water as if it had just fired a broadside.

Why weren't the ship's guns firing? he wondered. And what of the flak batteries he had sited all along the fiord? Were they asleep out there?

Then the answer had come to him. There was nothing for them to shoot at. The aircraft that had launched the attack had gone.

In Delsingen's mind, time had stretched. What seemed like several minutes was in fact fleeting seconds. His mind had expanded the passing moments into lengths of time where even the smallest of events could be closely observed. It was thus that he was able to watch – as if in slow motion – the second aircraft go into the attack, drop its bombs: one into the second funnel, the other at its base. Again that aircraft pulled hard to the right almost immediately, to escape any possible anti-aircraft response.

Again no guns fired. Again a deep rumble shook the ship, and again it shifted in the water. Delsingen felt as if he alone could see what was happening; as if everyone else had been frozen in time.

Then time seemed to regain its natural speed.

A pall of dense smoke was now pouring out of both funnels; but this was not because the *Graf von Hiller* was attempting to conceal herself. The precious battleship was beginning to bleed.

Someone knocked on the door and rushed into the office.

'*Herr General! The British are attacking the ship!*'

Delsingen turned to the young captain who had barged in. 'That's very observant of you, Schulenheim,' he said bitingly. 'Have you discovered why the batteries are not yet firing?'

'We've already contacted them, *Herr General*. They say there are no aircraft.'

'Then tell them there'll be more! This is only the beginning!'

'Yes . . . Yes, *Herr General*!'

'Well, don't just stand there, man! Get to it!'

'Yes, *Herr General*!'

'And find out what the observation posts are doing!'

'Yes, *Herr General*!'

As the captain hurried out, Delsingen reflected on the fact that he was finished, whatever the outcome. Even if all the aircraft were shot down and the *von Hiller* not too badly damaged, the attack would be seen as his fault. It had happened, and that would be enough for them to demand his head. In the current climate there was a high demand for scapegoats.

The High Command – particularly the SS High Command – would lay the blame squarely at his feet. Not even Honnenhausen would be able to save him. And Mindenhof would have a field day.

A new sound had broken into Delsingen's thoughts. A third aircraft, this time coming from the opposite direction, but not from up the fiord.

Delsingen once more brought the binoculars to his eyes. From where he stood, the twin-engined aeroplane seemed to have curved in from the right, popping out from hiding behind high ground. Clinically, his mind observed it as a beautiful sight, the way it banked swiftly and tightly, levelled off, released its bombs, then banked hard left to rush towards Årdalstangen and the safety of the mountains. He even marvelled at the courage of the pilot, coming in so low as to appear to touch the ship with his aircraft.

He saw the bombs fly towards the deck of the ship. One bounced, before lodging itself at the base of one of the forward turrets that housed two of the big fifteen-inch guns. The other flew right through the armoured glass of the bridge. They went off simultaneously. The bridge contained the explosion, but its sides bulged and then contracted in response to the percussive force of the blast. Delsingen didn't dare think of the fate of anyone who had been within that explosion. The *Graf von Hiller* seemed to shake itself, as if shrugging off this third blow.

The bomb by the armoured gun turret tilted it off line when it exploded, but that seemed to be all. The turret, though appearing to have escaped serious damage, would not be able to swivel until repaired.

A light Oerlikon had begun to fire, but there was nothing for it to shoot at.

There was another knock on the door, and Schulenheim rushed in once more.

Delsingen turned. '*Hauptmann* Schulenheim!' he barked.

Schulenheim skidded to a halt and stiffened to attention. '*Herr General!*'

'Stop running about like a schoolboy! You're an officer, man! You are supposed to behave calmly under attack and be an example to your subordinates. Now compose yourself and tell me why you have rushed into my office.'

'*Herr General*, only one observer post has so far made a report. The observer reported high-flying fighters.'

'Delsingen frowned. '*Fighters?*'

'Yes, *Herr General*. Going east.'

'Check with that man. Ask him to describe in detail what he saw, or what he *thought* he saw, then return immediately when you've got the answer.'

'Yes, *Herr General*.

'And find me Kahler.'

'Yes, *Herr General*.'

The captain went out again, and Delsingen returned to watching the ship.

'Fighters?' he murmured thoughtfully.

The aircraft that had dropped the bombs had been small for a bomber, twin-engined, highly manoeuvrable. Though he had never been on the receiving end of their attention before, he knew what Mosquitoes looked like. He knew of people who had been on the wrong end of an attack by them. They were deadly, and remarkably accurate. Those agile aeroplanes were also *fighters*, and an observer who knew little of the type would class them as such on seeing them for the first time.

But according to Schulenheim, they'd been high-flying . . .

A feint, of course. There would be more of them, and they could be anywhere. It was time to get Mölner to send his boys up and . . .

Delsingen stopped, mouth grim. Despite the fact that his *Sondergruppe* had been astoundingly successful, someone had made a decision to remove the air element. He could no longer order Mölner into the air. He would have to go through Luftwaffe channels, and that would lose precious time.

A swelling sound made him train the glasses back on the ship. More smoke was wreathing about it, but far from forming a protective curtain, the billows of smoke and steam from ruptured pipes were effectively marking it out.

A fourth aircraft had swung into the attack, coming from the same direction as the third. This time, people on the ship were more awake. The multi-barrelled cannon were now adding their voices to the proceedings. Tracers reached for the Mosquito, but seemed to be doing it no harm. The bombs curved in an accurate trajectory from the aircraft. Both went into the bridge, yet there was no immediate explosion.

Delayed action.

The thought came instinctively to Delsingen. He continued to watch, waiting for the inevitable explosion. It was not a long time in coming. The double explosion made the bridge well until it appeared that the entire superstructure would burst outwards. But that was not what happened. Incredibly, it *collapsed inwards*. It simply caved in, as if all supporting beams and girders had been melted by an intense heat. As it went, various radar and radio masts went with it, first swaying, then toppling on top of the imploding mass.

But the gunners had drawn blood. The Mosquito that had made the fourth attack was now towing a long, bright tail of flame that ravenously ate its way forwards along the fuselage. The aircraft tried to climb, as if to get away from the flames. The fire seemed to rush even faster towards the nose until the entire aeroplane had become a rising comet. Then it turned into a starburst that spread outwards like a giant firework, sending flaming pieces over a wide area. Some fell into the water, sending erupting gouts of steam shooting upwards.

Though cheered by the success of the gunners,

Delsingen again sensed a feeling of admiration for the airmen's bravery.

But the gunners were suddenly facing a new danger. As if from nowhere, another Mosquito was approaching the ship from water-level, it seemed. The sound of a massive cannon roared within the fiord. A huge tongue of flame belched from beneath the nose of the aircraft and something pulverizing slammed into the gunners' position. They disappeared in a bright inferno.

The Mosquito banked slightly, swinging round to a new target. Another belch, and another gun position vanished.

'My God!' Delsingen heard himself say. 'They're using a flying tank!'

Even as he spoke, yet another Mosquito could be seen diving steeply down the right side of the fiord. This one seemed to have come from straight over the top. It was another of the flying tanks, for it had now engaged a flak battery that had fired just once before being engulfed in a burst from the big cannon.

More batteries were now at last opening up, but more Mosquitoes seemed to have infested the fiord, roaming along its sides, wheeling into the guns and roaring at them with that huge cannon.

Delsingen went to grab at his phone, and called for the district Luftwaffe commander. He waited impatiently until the person who finally came on the line turned out to be the deputy, who sounded harassed. All fighter aircraft throughout southern Norway were up, he was told: sent to meet massive raids that spread southwards down to the Skagerrak and into Denmark.

Delsingen had to strain to listen to what was being said, as the cacophony of guns and aircraft engines swelled appreciably.

He stifled a sigh at the man's words. 'Send me whatever you can,' he said, 'when you can. Otherwise we'll lose the *Graf von Hiller*.'

'I'll do my best . . .'

'What about Mölner?'

'He's been up twice already, dealing with these raids. He's on his third scramble right now. It's very bad, General. I don't even know if we can . . .'

'Try and have him divert at least a flight of his fighters to this area. If we lose the ship many, many heads will roll.' Mine included, he didn't add.

'I'll do my best, General,' the other man repeated, but he didn't sound at all certain that he'd be able to.

'All right. Thank you.'

'General.'

They hung up together.

Delsingen stared at the phone, then went back to his vantage-point. The ship was already lost. Of that, he was quite certain.

The attack had been beautifully executed. The unexpected first approach had achieved complete surprise. The multi-point attack was sowing confusion, and the specialist anti-flak Mosquitoes were silencing the guns so as to allow the bombers to continue their work. Nor was there any doubt that the fighter Mosquitoes were around somewhere, waiting for any German fighters that might come to attack the raid.

But those fighters had been drawn away by diversionary raids of such magnitude that they could not have been ignored, effectively preventing the dispatch of fighters to protect the ship.

Someone had also known the area well enough to have correctly judged where the gaps in the anti-aircraft umbrella would be. The attacking Mosquitoes had thus been able to make their approach without warning. No one had spotted them except the sole observer who had seen the high-flying fighters. And that had been a deliberate disclosure, to further hide the true nature of the target. For no one would seriously expect fighters to attack a battleship.

The attackers had also picked a time well before the ship was ready for operations at sea. The crew still had to be fully trained; the gunners to be drilled and finely tuned, to go into action with confidence and skill. And worst of all, the *von Hiller*, trapped within her protective, triple anti-submarine screens, was like a big fish in a small barrel.

The Allies had discovered her existence and had correctly come to the conclusion that she would be used to cause havoc with the invasion fleet. They desired her destruction at any cost. Even if this raid did not succeed completely, there would be more, and still more.

The *Graf·von Hiller* was going nowhere.

10

As these thoughts hurtled through his mind, Delsingen realized that even during the brief period that he'd been on the phone, things had hotted up considerably in the fiord.

There now seemed to be a continuing swarm of Mosquitoes, whirling and diving among the ships and guns. The flak in the fiord had grown into a ferocious barrage, staining the air with their shoals of bursts, and lacing the fiord with their tracers. Nothing, it seemed, could live through that.

But the bomber Mosquitoes were not straying far towards them. The guns were being constantly engaged by the aircraft with the tank guns and, every so often, a flak battery would be put out of action. Those further down the fiord were virtually useless, because the aircraft were not going there. They concentrated on the ship and its immediate environs, knocking out all the most threatening of guns while continuing the attack.

Flames were now springing up all over the pocket battleship. Rocket projectiles were pounding into her. It was like watching a great beast being harried by smaller, savage predators. She couldn't move and now could barely defend herself. Such guns as betrayed their presence by flashes in the ever-increasing billows of smoke, were instantly attacked and put out of action.

The tank-gun Mosquitoes were even attacking the destroyers as soon as the anti-aircraft guns on those ships opened up. But they flew so low that the gunners on the smaller ships could not bring their weapons to bear properly, or in time. Two E-boats that had come in the day before had also put up a fierce resistance with their multi-barrelled cannon. Both had been blown out of the water with a double attack by two of the tank-gun Mosquitoes. It was turning into a slaughter.

Then another Mosquito flamed into the fiord, diving straight in. At least, Delsingen thought grimly, the gunners were getting some small revenge.

He heard loud voices, then there was a loud knocking.

'*In!*'

Kahler, now a captain, entered looking exceedingly grim. He had his steel helmet under his arm.

'I got here as quickly as I could, General,' he began. 'I was attending to the guns, seeing that they put up enough high explosive to make life very dangerous for the Tommis. But, as you can see, the aircraft are keeping their attack concentrated around the ship. No one expected bombers that could manoeuvre like fighters.' The man who once had the bowel problem was radically changed. He had become every inch the confident warrior.

'You were right to get the guns started,' Delsingen said. 'As for the attack, it has been cleverly executed.'

Kahler gave a slight instinctive duck of the head as a swelling roar of engines passed right overhead. But the aircraft was not interested in the headquarters building, even though a burst of cannon fire from the nearby guns followed it.

'You should take shelter, General,' he suggested.

'Why? They're not interested in this place. Besides, I am not someone who goes into hiding.'

'They had precise information, sir,' Kahler went on. 'It's the only answer. They knew how to get into the area.'

Delsingen gave a rueful smile. 'Would you like to hear a crazy thought that has entered my head?'

Kahler was not sure how to respond to this, so he said nothing.

'Ålvik,' Delsingen told him.

'Ålvik?'

'You find that hard to believe?'

'But he must be dead by now.'

'No one ever found him. He could have gone to England. Many Norwegians go over, are trained in covert operations and return.'

'You're saying he is *here*, in Norway, General?'

'He may not be, but his extensive knowledge of this area may have been used.'

'He could not have known about the ship.'

'No. That would have come from somewhere else.'

Another aircraft, passing extremely low this time, made both of them duck. Again it did not attack the building.

'Colonel Geissler is lucky to be out of this,' Kahler said grimly, listening to the hellish noise that continued to echo round the fiord.

'That's a matter of opinion,' Delsingen said. 'There are enemies in Bergen too, and rather closer to home. All right, Captain. It's obvious you know what to do. Carry on.'

'Sir. General.'

Delsingen looked at him.

'It has been an honour serving in your command.'

'Thank you, Captain.'

'Sir.'

Kahler put on his helmet and saluted Delsingen with precise gravity.

Ålvik had ten shells remaining out of the twenty-five-round load of the big gun. The Tse-Tse could spit them at just over one a second. A two-second burst was usually enough for something like a soft-skinned boat, a gun emplacement or any target armoured like a tank.

But he was not diving on a tank. He had twice passed over a building from where streams of tracer from light guns had chased after him. He now decided to silence them, for they were on an access route to some of the other flak guns.

In the right-hand seat, McLeish was certain they were not going to make it this time. Ålvik may well know the topography of his country like the back of his hand, but the position of the anti-aircraft cannon by the squat building was too close to a steep mountainside. When they had twice flown over to attack the flak guns, they had nearly landed on the building, he'd thought. This time, they would probably hit it.

But he said nothing, not wanting to distract his pilot. He simply watched as the streams of tracer spurted towards them, wondering which of these would first punch a hole through the armoured windscreen, to be followed by the ones which would disintegrate his head.

These morbid thoughts in his mind, McLeish listened first to the machine-guns as they began to chatter, then to the single roar of the big gun as it belched, *at the building itself*. Then the Mosquito was pulling steeply away, before tipping over on a wing to come round again.

This time McLeish understood what Alvik was about. As they again approached the building he saw that a great part of it was no longer there; and only one gun, fully exposed, was still firing. A great cloud of rising dust came from where falling masonry had buried the other.

The big gun roared again, just once.

McLeish saw the explosion just as they flashed past. The anti-aircraft gun did not fire.

As the Mosquito changed course to go after

another flak battery, McLeish said, 'That was close.'

'Did you hold your breath?'

'Yeah,' the New Zealander replied frankly. 'I did.'

'So did I.'

Delsingen felt the dust in his mouth. Something incredibly heavy was on the small of his back. He tried to move, but all he could manage was a flutter of his fingers.

Had he been able to, he would have seen that most of his office had fallen on him. There was a gaping hole where one wall used to be, and the roof had disappeared. He would also have seen dust-covered people scrambling over piles of rubble to get to him.

Hearing voices faintly, he tried to turn his head. But it wouldn't move.

'I've found the General!' he heard very, very faintly, as if from a great distance.

'Get those things off him!' another voice ordered. It sounded like Kahler's. '*Hurry!*'

But Delsingen could hear nothing any more.

Jo-Jo Kearns was still keeping his flight of six Mosquitoes out of the fiord. Where were the fighters?

'It looks as if the diversionary raids have
worked,' he said to Rameau. 'There's not a
dicky-bird out there. Bede is going to get very
impatient soon. He needs a charge of action
every so often.'

Rameau peered out of the cockpit, to
where a great column of smoke rose from
below.

'The others are having fun,' he said. 'You
have brought us your great luck, Jo-Jo. We
have only lost two aeroplanes, and it seems
we have got the ship.'

'Two are two too many. Counting the CO
on take-off, that's three. I'd like to take the rest
home. How long have we been out here?'

'Ten minutes from the start of the attack.'

'My God. It feels like ten years. I'd prefer to
have them all out of there before any fighters
turn up.'

Suddenly a vast, boiling explosion lit up
the day. A great, bell-shaped, fiery cloud
rose from the fiord, expanding as it went.
From all directions, small shapes darted from
the area. The Mosquitoes were making a
hasty exit, so as not to be caught in the
shock wave.

The fiery bell ruptured and burst open, sending a fierce, bright pillar of flame reaching for the

heavens. Then a great cloud followed, boiling upwards, climbing for ever, it seemed.

Rameau gasped at the sight. '*The magazine!* They have got *the magazine! Ha-hah-hah-hah!*' he crowed with glee. 'The ship is gone! It's gone!' He was jumping about in his seat.

In the distance, the remaining Mosquitoes were rapidly heading to rendezvous with them.

'*Herr Kapitän! Herr Kapitän!*'

In Bergen, Geissler and Fröhmann were standing at the water's edge, in conversation. After the incident with the girl, Geissler had expected to see an enraged Mindenhof very soon after. But nothing had happened. Perhaps, he'd reasoned, Mindenhof had expected Geissler to come to him like some supplicant, now that he was in command of local security.

Fröhmann had turned to look at the agitated member of his crew who was running towards them.

'The ship, *Herr Kapitän!*' the man said in a rush. '*The* Graf von Hiller! *She is sunk!*'

'*What?*' both Geissler and Fröhmann shouted together.

'Yes, sir. There was an attack by British aeroplanes. E-62 was just entering the fiord when there was a great explosion. The ship just blew up, like the way the English lost the *Hood*. E-62 saw many small planes going away. They had hit the magazine. A great wave in the fiord, caused by the explosion, nearly capsized E-62. The *Graf* is gone, *Herr Kapitän*. Completely. A destroyer is also on its side. The *Alderhorst*. And we have also lost E-48 and E-25. No survivors. E-62 says it is a disaster. The explosion destroyed many buildings on land too. And sir, they think General Delsingen's headquarters has been hit. They have not yet got in close enough to check everything, but it looks very bad, sir.'

Geissler and Fröhmann stared at each other in dismay.

Just then, a voice shouted at them. '*Geissler!*' Mindenhof, accompanied by the SS men who had accosted the Norwegian girl, were coming towards them at a trot. Geissler slowly unbuttoned his holster.

Fröhmann noticed the action. 'What are you doing!' he whispered.

'Being prepared for anything.'

The sailor was still standing close, waiting uncertainly for orders.

'Forsch,' he said quietly to the sailor.

'Sir?'

'Go back to the boat. Tell the lieutenant

to get ready to leave. Issue personal arms to everyone, then send two men back to me . . . armed. Then he's to wait. Now go. Quickly.'

'Yes, *Herr Kapitän*.' The man hurried away.

Mindenhof and his men arrived just as Forsch clambered back aboard the E-boat.

'Well, Geissler,' Mindenhof began, face glowing with triumph. 'You have all had it now. You have lost the Reich its prized ship. Shooting will be too good for you!'

'We know what has happened, Colonel,' Fröhmann said. 'We're on our way back to see what can be done.'

Mindenhof gave an ugly laugh. '*Done? What's to be done? The incompetent Kriegsmarine has cost the Führer his ship!* What's to be done except shoot the whole lot of you? And as for you, Geissler. How dare you obstruct my men in their duty? You have let a terrorist escape!'

The SS second lieutenant was looking eager for revenge. He stood to one side, eyes malevolently fixed on Geissler.

'What terrorist?'

'Do you think I am a fool?' Mindenhof snarled. 'We have been watching her! These men did not know it, but they had taken the correct action and were about to bring her in as a matter of course. I have information that suggests she is one of Ålvik's gang! Do you realize what you have done, Colonel?'

'Don't be ridiculous. Ålvik's gang are finished. My own team have destroyed many . . .'

'*You are coming with me!*'

'Have you finally gone mad? Are you arresting me, Mindenhof?'

'You have no power now, Geissler. From the message we have just received, it is quite clear that your general is dead. He is not around to protect you any more!'

'I would be very careful,' Fröhmann said to Mindenhof. 'Even you cannot dare . . .'

'You can go where the hell you please, Commander!' Mindenhof again snarled. 'All you naval people will have to answer to the Führer. But Geissler stays with me.'

The starting of the E-boat engines made them all look. Geissler took the opportunity to draw his pistol and point it at Mindenhof. The SS man's eyes widened in disbelief.

'Now *you* are the one who is mad. My men will cut you down.'

'But you will be dead.'

Two of Fröhmann's crew, sub-machine-guns ready, approached quickly. One was Forsch.

The SS men unslung their own weapons.

'Trouble, sir!' Forsch said as he drew up. His eyes were on the SS men.

'I don't think so,' Fröhmann replied quietly. 'Colonel Geissler is coming with me,' he added to Mindenhof. 'Will there be trouble?'

The cold eyes regarded Fröhmann with such hatred, it was as if they were trying to burn through him.

Mindenhof continued to glare, but said nothing.

Something suddenly buzzed past, to thump Mindenhof squarely in the chest. He staggered back, cap flying off the blond head, mouth opening wide. Blood poured out.

'What . . . ?' Geissler began.

The SS men froze for a fraction of a second, then began to look at the E-boat.

But the shot had not come from there. A report sounded faintly.

'*Sniper!*' Geissler bawled. '*Move, move!*'

They all dispersed, including the SS men. They left their colonel to die alone on the waterfront as they rushed for cover.

'Let's go!' Fröhmann said to Geissler. 'The boat. No point your staying here.'

'You don't have to say it twice.'

They hurried after the crewmen, making for

the waiting E-boat. The SS men did not fire at them.

From the top of a building far enough from the waterfront to allow a certain degree of security, Inge said to Skjel, 'Did you get him?'

'Of course.' Skjel was looking through the scope.

'And the Wehrmacht officer?'

'Making for the boat with his friend.'

'Don't kill him. I'm returning a favour.'

'If you say so,' Skjel said reluctantly. 'They're all Germans. So who cares if they kill each other?'

'He saved me from the SS. Leave him.'

'And the others?'

'We should get away from here. We've already stayed too long. The SS are going to go mad.'

'All right,' Skjel agreed, discretion winning.

Mölner had detached a flight of five aircraft – including his own – from an attack on a wave of Lancasters, when he'd been relayed the desperate call from Delsingen.

Now heading at altitude for Sognefjord, he was astonished to see the sky filled with Mosquitoes, all heading in his direction.

'*Break! Break!*' he called to his four Fw-190s.

*   *   *

'Oh look!' Bede said to Koos. 'Lots of trade.'

'Go for it, Blue Two!' he heard from Kearns.

Bede flung the Mosquito on to its back and latched on to the nearest Focke-Wulf.

The pilot spotted him and rolled away, but Bede hung on, going down after his prey.

The 190 began to head for altitude once more, but Bede had caught the incipient raising of the enemy aircraft's nose and had broken early out of his dive, to counter. As a result, when the 190 was pointing skywards again, Bede was waiting and had regained level flight as it flew right past the Mosquito's nose, going up. For the barest flash of time, the 190 was pinned directly before the guns of the Mosquito. If Bede were even infinitesimally slow to squeeze the trigger, the moment would be gone.

Bede was not slow.

The eight guns of the Mosquito raked the 190 from nose to tail. The aircraft simply disintegrated. No one got out.

'Yes, yes, *yes!*' Koos cried. 'You have him!'

'That was just breakfast, Rens. Let's look for lunch.'

Bede could not know that he had just killed Mölner.

*   *   *

The fifteen Mosquitoes that had survived the raid on the *Graf von Hiller* – despite the fact that some had suffered flak damage – fell upon the remaining four 190s. In a very short space of time the overwhelming odds took their toll and the four Focke-Wulfs fell terminally to earth. No Mosquitoes were lost during the one-sided battle.

Bede did not get his lunch, but shared a second kill with Kearns. Their job finished, the fifteen Mosquitoes headed for 35,000 feet, and home.

Kearns looked about him. Mosquitoes everywhere.

It was, he thought, a lovely sight.

In Berlin, Trudi Deger entered *Obergruppen-führer* Honnenhausen's office. Overhead, the ominous drone of heavy bombers sounded. In the distance, the crump of bombs could be heard.

'Ah, Trudi,' he said. 'Another visit tonight from our friends. More news for me?'

Trudi seemed preoccupied. 'I wanted to come to you earlier, sir. But it has been very hectic.'

'I understand. There is much to do. And you do it well.'

'Thank you, sir.' She paused. 'It is a terrible thing that happened today. The *Graf von Hiller*. Lost!'

'Yes,' he said heavily. 'And I have lost a close friend too.'

'The general. I am so sorry.'

'It is war.'

She paused again, looking at him closely. In the dim lighting of the room, her face had taken on a beautiful, haunted quality.

'Who are you, sir?' she enquired softly.

Honnenhausen stared at her. 'What did you say?'

'I asked, who are you?'

'Is this a joke of some kind? Who am I? *Obergruppenführer* Honnenhausen, that's who! Are you suffering from concussion? That bomb that came close earlier . . .'

'I am perfectly all right. I know you are high in the Party . . . but who are you, really?'

'There has to be a reason for this nonsense, Trudi. I allow you great leeway, but you are putting yourself at great risk talking to me like that.'

'No I'm not. In the first place, if you were going to do anything, you would have done so already. You would have called one of the guards to drag me out.'

'And in the second?'

'It is not your way.'

'You know me so well?'

'I . . . would like to. Please. No, wait. Hear what I have to say. Remember I brought you that file on the Jews near Stolpe?'

'Yes.'

'You said you would attend to it.'

'Yes.'

'I went out there recently. They were still there.'

'What did you do?'

'Nothing. I have not reported it. I have checked other cases. Many other names that I passed to you have not appeared on the camp lists.'

'And have you reported those?'

'Of course not!' She sounded as if the very idea should not even have occurred to him.

Honnenhausen looked at her like a dangerous animal about to strike. 'Why?'

'Because I love you. You have always known it. Now I have incriminated myself because of it. At least, let me know the person who has my love.'

'A patriot,' he said.

Whitehall, London

The two men looked at the report and felt pleased with themselves. The Mosquitoes had done the job. The supership was no more. Many strands had come together to produce that success. Not the least was the source of that first piece of information.

'I wonder if he misses Devon,' one of the men said to the other.

'Bound to. He has been out there since before the war, after all.'

'Think he's gone native?'

'He gave us that ship, didn't he? That's not the act of a man who's gone "native", as you put it. Major feather in his cap when the time comes for rewards for services to the Crown, above and beyond.'

'Brave man, doing what he does. Dangerous, dangerous job. Too bad he won't get a gong when this is all over. Not publicly anyway. Deserves the VC.'

'Well, he certainly can't be publicly recognized. Not for years. There'd be a lot of people out for revenge if they ever discovered who's been hiding in their midst.'

'Indeed. They also serve who . . .'

'Quite so, quite so.'

The men went back to dealing with matters

271

concerning people in delicate and dangerous situations.

Days later, having safely made her way with Olav Skjel out of Bergen, Inge Jarl was talking with one of the senior men in the resistance.

'You have done a good job,' he told her.

'I don't want to do that again,' she said. 'I nearly got myself caught.'

'You won't have to. Your report has added to the picture we're building.'

'But I only told you about things I saw – like the behaviour of the Germans to each other. Nothing very important.'

'But that's where you are wrong. Everything is important, especially morale. Their morale is very low after what has happened to their ship. Did you know Per was on that raid?'

'*Per?*' Her eyes shone. Then a fear came into them. 'Is he . . . all right?'

'Don't worry. Your Per is safe.'

'Oh thank God!'

'You still won't see him for a while.'

'I can wait, now that I know.'

'We heard from the Norwegian network in England. Apart from that battleship they sunk, they also destroyed many German guns, E-boats, and even seriously damaged a destroyer.

There's a lot of damage to much of the German *matériel* and supplies. It is a very serious blow. Two aircraft were lost. Such brave men.

'As for your little trip to Bergen, it will all help when the time comes. And killing that SS officer was also a good blow. The worse their morale, the better for us. Although I must say, it sounds strange to me about that Wehrmacht colonel. Perhaps he risked himself like that because you reminded him of his sweetheart.'

'Perhaps,' she said thoughtfully.

'But don't make a habit of saving German lives. Most of them are not like him. What would you do if you saw him again?'

'Probably kill him.'

1945

Inge did see her beloved Per again. He arrived in style after the German surrender, landing his Mosquito, now bearing Norwegian national markings, on an airfield that once again belonged to Norwegians.

Jo-Jo Kearns and Bede both survived. Kearns decided he would return to Australia to face his family. He was proud of his achievement and if they didn't like it, tough.

Wing Commander Smythe didn't. He went

on one mission too many when he shouldn't have. Returning in a badly shot-up aircraft piloted by Brack, it crashed on landing, killing them both.

Geissler also survived the war, but Fröhmann did not.

Out of uniform now, Geissler spent months after the end of the war searching the ruined Germany for the woman he considered he had so cowardly betrayed. The months turned into a year. Two years. The terrible truth about the camps gave him nightmares; but still he persisted with his search.

A third year came and went.

Then one day, he was sitting outside a coffee shop that they had once frequented before the horrors had descended on Germany. There was a British military post near the indifferently patched-up building.

'I wondered if you would come here,' a voice said. 'If you had survived.'

He could not believe his ears. He dared not look up, afraid of what he might see. Then he made himself do so.

He got to his feet slowly in wonder. She was as beautiful as he remembered, and did not look as if she had been in the camps at

274

all. She looked as if she was not sure whether she should smile at him.

'I hear you have been turning Germany upside down looking for me,' she said. 'The British have a dossier on you. They think you are crazy.'

'I am ... I mean ... I mean I have been going crazy worrying about you all these years. I was such a coward. I cannot believe how cowardly.'

'You have the Iron Cross, First Class. That was not won by a coward.'

'But what I did. Deserting you when I should have stuck by you. That is the act of a coward.'

Her eyes were filming over. 'Did you love me so much that you carried this with you all through the war?'

He could not take his eyes off her. They gazed at her with a great hunger that was years old. He was not sure he could bear never to see her again.

'I have *never* stopped loving you. I swore if I ever got out alive, I would spend the rest of my days looking for you. And if they had taken you to the camps, I would search until I discovered where. You are my life.'

'The British know so much about you. They even know that you saved a girl in Norway from the SS, at a time when it was very dangerous for a Wehrmacht officer to do so. They found a report by an SS officer called Mindenhof, accusing you of treachery. He actually wrote down that you should be executed for deliberately allowing a known terrorist to escape.'

Geissler was stunned to realize how close he had come to death that day, at the hands of Mindenhof.

'She reminded me of you,' he said simply. 'I was trying to atone, I suppose, in some small way.'

'Not small. You could have been killed, and I would never have seen you again.'

'You . . . wanted to see me again?'

'At first, I hated you. You broke my heart . . .'

'I broke mine. But how do you know so much . . . ?'

'I escaped. I got away to England, and became an interpreter. I work for a British unit checking on the SS. That's how I came to hear about you, and your mad search.'

'If there is someone else . . . I will understand perfectly. I only wanted to know . . .' He said this, knowing if she turned away from him now, he could go quietly away somewhere and die.

'There is no one else,' she said. 'I can love only you, Ernst. Can't you see that?'

'How can you still love me? Look at what Germany has done . . .'

'Germany has destroyed itself too. *We* must not destroy ourselves.'

Geissler felt the years of hidden tears spring to his eyes.

She reached out to wipe them away gently.

Obergruppenführer Max Honnenhausen survived and made it to Australia with Trudi Deger. They married.

They have a different name and still live there comfortably. They have two children, and are now grandparents.

Max Honnenhausen, who was not born to that name, never made it back to his beloved Devon.

He got his Victoria Cross; but only Trudi knows of it.

WINGS 6

BEHIND THE LINES

Peter Leslie

1

'You're quite sure this chap, whatsisname, will fill the bill?' The red-tabbed staff officer poked a heavy finger among the papers littering the desk. 'Blake. Yes, Blake. You're satisfied . . . ?'

'Absolutely, sir,' the adjutant said. 'First-class candidate. The only choice.'

'All very well for you to say that, Hesketh, but . . .'

'Trilingual in English, German and French,' the adjutant urged. 'Spent a year at Heidelberg before the balloon went up. He even collected a wound from that FE-2b training crash that could be a duelling scar!'

'Thought him a bit of a cissie, frankly. Chap came to the interview in civvies. Trifle foppish, if you ask me. Silk handkerchief flopping out of his breast pocket, and all that.' The staff officer – he was a brigadier – drew a large handkerchief made of red cotton from his sleeve and blew his nose loudly. 'He's not one of those . . . ?'

'Good God, no!' The adjutant was scandalized. He tapped a buff booklet lying among the papers. 'Fellow got eight out of ten for gunnery. Quite out of the ordinary for these flying wallahs.'

The brigadier picked up the document. Heavy black lettering on the cover announced: 'Army Book 425: Pilot's Flying Logbook'. The first few pages were divided horizontally, each column devoted to a particular exercise

1

in the flying training programme. 'Only got five out of ten for propeller swinging,' he pointed out.

'Yes, but *nine* out of ten for Morse signalling aptitude,' Major Hesketh said. 'That's an absolute plus if the chap's to keep in touch with us from behind the lines, what.'

The brigadier grunted, ferreting among the official reports. 'I suppose so. If you people are quite sure.'

'*Quite* sure, sir.' Major Hesketh flicked a speck of dust from the green Intelligence flash on his khaki jacket. Outside the windows of the HQ hut, the sun-dried grass of Heston aerodrome stretched away towards a row of canvas hangars. Behind these were gasometers, a red-brick block of flats and a plume of factory smoke staining the blue sky.

'Patrice Blake, Lieutenant, Royal Flying Corps,' the brigadier read from the cover of the logbook. '*Patrice?* What kind of a Christian name is that?' He sounded personally affronted.

'It's French, sir,' the adjutant explained. 'His mother is descended from a Huguenot family which fled here in the seventeenth century. That's the other reason for his three languages.'

With the back of one hand, the brigadier brushed out the ends of his waxed moustache, which was modelled on Lord Kitchener's in the famous recruiting poster. He opened his mouth to reply, but the words were lost in a sudden juddering racket as mechanics outside the hut started up the radial engine of a scout plane with the metal cowling removed. In the middle distance, a BE-2c biplane lumbered across the field towards a wind-sock hanging limply from its pylon.

'How many hours' flying has your man had?' the brigadier yelled.

'Rather more than usual for a Western Front pilot.

2

Eighty-five as an observer, twelve and a half dual, twenty-six as solo pilot on patrol.'

'What's he going to fly on this madcap escapade of yours?'

Major Hesketh smiled. 'A Sopwith Pup. Partly because he's familiar with the machine, partly because the Hun has already captured several examples, so there'll be no secrets given away when he ditches it, but mainly because the RNAS use Pups and we aim to fly him off a boat.'

'Good God! But why?'

'Question of range and approach,' Hesketh said. 'Factory where Jerry is working on the device is too far inside Germany for a home take-off. But if he uses an aerodrome behind *our* lines . . . and then crosses no man's land to fly on into Hunland – well, they're going to be on to him from the start, aren't they? Supposed to be a secret foray, after all.'

'Quite.'

'If he flies in from the north and west, on the other hand – over Jutland, say – he's going to be over the river and into the trees before their observers even twig that the machine's not one of theirs.'

'And the ditched bus? No chance of him bringing it back?'

'None.'

'So what does he do when he runs out of juice?'

'We reckon he should get within twenty miles of the target. Forest in the valleys, moorland higher up. If he finds a landing place far enough away from civilization, he sets fire to the machine, which will carry no insignia anyway, and legs it into the sunset. If there's a town or a village too close, his orders will be to forget about destroying the aeroplane and set off as far and as fast as he can before the soldiery arrive.'

3

'And you really think . . . ?'

'We cannot go on having our chaps shot out of the sky at this rate,' Hesketh said. 'This is our only chance to catch up. Blake, in our opinion, is the sole candidate with a chance to succeed. For the reasons I have outlined.'

'How much of a chance?'

'Fifty-fifty,' Hesketh said.

'Hah!' the brigadier guffawed. 'Not familiar with your mount, my boy. Only met him once. But I wouldn't care to back him at those odds, by God!'

'You don't have a choice, sir,' Hesketh told him firmly. 'There's only one horse in the race.'

Heavy clouds building to an altocumulus hammerhead towered darkly above the low hills west of the aerodrome as the pilot flattened the biplane out for his tenth cross-wind landing on the undulating field.

The machine touched down briefly, leapfrogged a slight rise and staggered towards a group of canvas hangars before the 80hp Le Rhône rotary engine responded to a burst of throttle and lifted the plane high enough to circle the field and bank for a second attempt. This time there were no problems and the pilot of the single-seater scout taxied towards the group of officers standing on the strip of tarmac fronting the hutted headquarters of 200(N) Training Squadron, Royal Flying Corps. The racket of the engine wheezed into silence and the varnished propeller spun to a halt as the biplane pulled up thirty yards away in the long grass.

Major Hesketh strode forward and approached the cockpit. The pilot unbuttoned the flaps of his leather flying helmet and pushed up his goggles. Beneath the thin film of castor oil blown back from the hot engine, his young face with its precocious moustache was cheerful. 'Got it right that time, sir,' he called. 'Help us chaps if the Ministry of Whatever could make these aerodromes a mite flatter!'

'You'd better do a couple more, Blake,' Hesketh said.

'The brigadier wants to see how you handle a landing downwind.' He gestured towards the wind-sock bellying out between the hutments and the hangars. 'You won't have one of those tipping you off when you come down in Hunland, you know!'

'Just so long as the old bus herself doesn't tip the wrong way,' the pilot grinned. He looked dubiously at the sky. The storm cloud massif was spreading and there was a distant rumble of thunder. 'You don't think we've tested the old girl enough for one day?'

'It's your skill we're testing, Blake. Not the aeroplane. Two more circuits – and not so many bumps,' Hesketh insisted. 'And that's an order.'

'Right-ho, sir.' Patrice Blake slid a final glance at the hammerhead and refastened the flaps of his helmet. He pulled the goggles down over his eyes. Hesketh nodded to a rigger and two mechanics off to one side of the officer group.

The three men in their grease-stained overalls moved towards the plane. Once the disc wheels of the V-strut undercarriage had been chocked, the rigger turned the airscrew and the engine attached to it, sucking aviation spirit into each of the nine finned cylinders. Standing back, he looked enquiringly at the pilot. Blake shoved a gloved hand out beyond the padded leather rim of the cockpit and gave him the thumbs up.

The rigger nodded. He stepped up to the propeller. Grasping the higher half of the polished, sculptured blade, he swung it once with forceful, practised ease, jumping clear as the rotary caught with a shattering roar.

The mechanics pulled away the chocks. Blake kicked on full left rudder and fed power to the spinning prop. The biplane lurched around through 180 degrees and lumbered towards the far side of the field.

He throttled back the machine as a flight of slender-bodied BE-2 two-seaters planed down over the woods and hedges of Huntingdonshire to land in formation, then he turned towards the northern boundary of the aerodrome.

The wind freshened, blowing the wind-sock out horizontally. Large drops of rain spotted the tarmac in front of the headquarters hut. The thunder was loud enough now to rival the distant rumble of aero engines.

Patrice Blake's Sopwith Pup reached the airfield perimeter and turned once more through 180 degrees. The engine's stutter rose to a bellow.

'Christ!' Hesketh exclaimed. 'I told the silly young ass to try a couple of *landings* downwind – not to take off that way, dammit!'

He ran on to the grass, waving his arms frantically.

If the pilot saw him, he paid no attention. The Pup roared across the field, flattening the long grass in its slipstream. With the wind behind him, Blake was taking the longest diagonal. Even so, gathering speed, the biplane seemed unwilling to come unstuck. The tail rose, rose too high, dropped again as the pilot hauled back on the stick – too soon for take-off – then settled back firmly as the further boundary relentlessly approached.

When it became clear that the plane was not going to lift off within the confines of the aerodrome, Hesketh swore. 'What the devil is the young fool playing at?' the brigadier demanded angrily. The War Office intelligence chief, standing beside him in immaculate civilian clothes, raised his well-tailored shoulders in a shrug that was almost Gallic. Hesketh said: 'What we are seeing, gentlemen, is an example of Youth, subtly enough, flouting Authority. The actions of Lieutenant Blake – although, of course, we have no proof – could

7

be interpreted as the equivalent of what a schoolboy would call cocking a snook.'

'Sassy young blighter,' said the brigadier. 'Hope you'll tear him off a bloody strip just the same.'

'You can rely on it, sir,' Hesketh said tightly.

The Pup reached the far side of the aerodrome, skipped nimbly over a hedge punctuated by blackthorn trees and raced across a paddock beyond, scattering cows. Then, at the very last moment, it rose almost vertically, clearing by less than twenty feet a copse of sycamores sheltering a farmhouse, and soared away towards the south-east.

It returned ten minutes later, circling the aerodrome at fifteen hundred feet. Rain was falling heavily now, and lightning flashed intermittently among the massed storm clouds. A last gleam of brilliance before the sun was finally eclipsed flashed from the doped fabric of the Pup's upper wing as Blake banked to lose height in a series of side-slips.

The downwind landing was perfect . . . until a stronger gust lifted the lightweight machine and almost tipped it over on to the bright circle of its aluminium engine cowling. But Blake, feathering his controls expertly, mastered the squall and brought the scout to a halt two hundred yards from the boundary. He turned into the wind and revved up the engine immediately for his second cicuit.

The Pup raced back across the field with the Le Rhône screaming, rising steeply, dangerously, into the air in the first part of a ground loop.

When the plane was upside down, Blake threw it into a half roll, completing a textbook Immelmann turn to fly back on an even keel the way he had come. After a final circle of the field, he glided in for an effortless downwind landing, taxiing again

8

to a halt a few yards from Hesketh and his colleagues.

Snatching off his helmet and goggles, he vaulted from the cockpit and strode towards them. Beneath the dark moustache, his mouth smiled widely.

'If there were anyone else for this job, Blake,' Hesketh grated, 'anyone at all, I'd have you taken off flying duties and gated for two months. You're lucky not to be court-martialled for insolence, disobeying orders and disrespect to senior officers.'

'Very sorry, Major,' Blake said, not sounding at all penitent, 'but you did say it was my skill being tested. Thought maybe I ought to give you a taste.'

The brigadier whisked his red handkerchief from his sleeve and blew his nose. The young pilot couldn't be certain, but for a moment he had a distinct impression that the man was hiding a smile.

'No disrespect intended, sir,' he said tactfully – if untruthfully – to Hesketh. 'But I felt I had to show you that I knew what I was doing with the old bus. Especially if, as you keep telling me, I have to ferry her across the bally border and then put her down behind the enemy lines.' He stuffed his flying gloves into the inner pocket of his leather jacket and brushed a lock of rain-wet hair from his eyes. 'Any chance now of letting the cat out of the bag?'

'What?'

'Sorry, sir. Well, I mean, when am I, er, to learn exactly what's involved in this oh-so-secret caper I seem to be training for?'

'Right away, Blake.' Only partly mollified, Hesketh was curt. The shoulders of his dress service jacket were already dark with moisture. 'Two big guns from the War Office are waiting inside. You are to receive your

official briefing' – he glanced at his gold wrist-watch –
'in precisely three minutes.'

'Very good, sir. Thank you, sir.'

Blake sketched the beginning of a salute, remembered
that he was not in uniform and allowed his hand to fall.
He turned smartly and followed the senior officers into
the HQ hut.

3

It was uncomfortably close in the operations room. Rain drummed on the asphalt roof and the wooden walls still breathed a medicinal hint of creosote into the heavy air. From time to time, yellow light directed at the blackboard from an electric lamp was swamped by the livid glare of lightning flickering outside the windows.

Seven men crowded into the first two rows of chairs. Apart from Hesketh, Blake and the brigadier, the major-general in charge of the RFC's combat division, a cartographer from the War Office, a civilian representing the Secret Intelligence Service and the colonel who was Blake's station commander faced the dais in front of the blackboard.

The eighth man, a tall, languid individual with a pink face and feathers of silver hair above his ears, stood beside the desk on the dais. Despite the thundery heat of the late summer day, he wore a heavy tweed suit with Norfolk breeches. A row of pens and pencils was clipped to the breast pocket of his jacket.

'Sir Alan Ravenscraft,' the major-general announced by way of introduction. 'From the Prime Minister's economic advisory unit. Sir Alan will provide you with the background to this . . . rather special . . . operation. Lieutenant Blake may take notes, later to be committed to memory and destroyed. I'd be obliged if the rest of you would simply listen.'

Ravenscraft cleared his throat. 'I'll go right back to basics,' he said in a pleasing tenor voice, 'in case any of you chaps should doubt the necessity of the adventure we propose.'

He pulled a large-scale map of Belgium, Holland and northern Germany down from a wall hanger and turned to the blackboard to scribble two columns of figures in yellow chalk. Tossing the chalk on to a shelf below the board, he hitched up one hip on to the desk and sat swinging an elegant leg as he talked.

'I don't need to tell you,' he began, 'that the one big difference between the present show and the two previous spots of trouble in South Africa and the Crimea is the presence of flying machines. They're doing the job that observers in tethered balloons used to do: checking on the accuracy of our artillery fire and then telling the gunners where they went wrong and what they have to do to get it right. And they're doing it better because they can see further and report back more quickly. The only trouble is that the enemy are doing it too.'

He cleared his throat again. 'The obvious result is that each of us is now trying to stop the other doing it – in other words, trying to destroy his flying machines. We all know how it started. Small-arms fire: revolvers, rifles, *hand* grenades, that kind of thing.' He shook his head. 'Useless of course. The lieutenant here, who has himself been an observer, can tell you that firing a handgun from an unsteady moving base at a target that is equally unsteady and deliberately taking evasive action is, well, simply not on.'

Blake grinned. 'What-ho!' he murmured under his breath.

12

'An additional complication,' Ravenscraft said, 'is that your actual two-seater observation plane is a staid and stable old bus. Has to be, to give the chap a chance to spot his targets, take photos and that kind of thing. For stable, read non-manoeuvrable. The answer, of course, was . . .'

'Yes, yes,' the major-general interrupted brusquely. 'You can take it that we are all familiar with the progression. Use the nippier aeroplanes, the scouts, to do the firing. Which means a fixed gun – preferably a machine-gun, because of the greater fire-power – the pilot being, ah, otherwise occupied. Carry on, Alan.'

'Since the war started,' Ravenscraft continued imperturbably, 'it has become increasingly evident that each side has been obliged to concentrate on preventing its enemy carrying out reconnaissance flights, by shooting at the machines involved, either with anti-aircraft guns or from other aeroplanes. If you control the sky, you can make as many reconnaissance flights as you wish.'

Once again the throat was cleared. 'For efficient prevention, clearly, it is essential that the guns involved be both accurate and reliable. And this is where we come up against the great obstacle, and the reason for this mission.'

The major-general uttered something between a grunt and a snort. The Brigadier's eyes were closed and his chin had sunk towards the three rows of ribbons decorating his khaki chest. Blake scribbled as an extra-loud thunder crash shook the timbers of the building.

Ravenscraft went on: 'Machine-guns are not only heavy: they are also liable to jam. If one is to be fitted to a single-seat scout, therefore, it must be within reach of the pilot so that he can reach out and free the thing. This rules out wing-mounted assemblies, which are in

13

any case impossible to aim efficiently, and those on the centre section above the pilot's head. The only spot-on place is along the nose of the machine, directly ahead of the pilot, so that instead of aiming separately, all he has to do, so to speak, is point the whole aeroplane at the target, and then press the tit.'

'Hah!' The brigadier sat suddenly upright. 'There's your fly in the bally ointment, what!'

'Exactly. In theory this would be fine in the case of a pusher, where the engine and airscrew are behind the driver. But pushers like the FE-8 and the DH-2 are too cumbersome and unwieldy to be efficient scouts, because of that great cage of wood and wire joining the tail unit to the front of the machine.'

'There's another slight disadvantage,' Blake ventured. 'From the point of view of the johnny at the controls, that is. He's too damned exposed, with no engine block in front to shield him from a stream of bullets fired from dead ahead. And in the event of a crash he's going to be the first thing to hit the hard ground – with all the weight of the engine ready to flatten his back.'

'Quite. So you lay the gun along the engine cowling of a tractor machine . . . and as soon as you fire it you shoot off your own damned propeller!'

'Hoist by your own bloody petard, by gad!' the brigadier wheezed. 'Nothing like shooting yourself down in flames!'

'The French ace Roland Garros,' Ravenscraft pursued, 'who was the first man to fly single-handed across the Med, came up with a partial solution to the problem. He fitted high-tensile steel deflector plates to the lower part of each propeller blade, so that any bullets that fouled the prop as it spun were knocked out of the way instead of severing the airscrew. One disadvantage here, however, is that half your stream of bullets risk being wasted instead of homing on the target. Another is that one of Garros' modified machines was forced down on German territory – and the Hun at once seized on the idea and improved it.'

Ravenscraft eased himself off the desk and moved to the blackboard. 'Look at these figures,' he said, tapping a knuckle between the two chalked columns. 'They represent weekly aeroplane losses, ours on the left, the Hun's on the right, from the last quarter of '15 to June this year. You'll see that, within normal, acceptable variations due to climatic conditions, military requirements and so forth, the picture remains fairly stable. Here our chaps are more successful; there the Germans have the upper hand.' He tapped the blackboard again. 'Until the beginning of this month. You'll see from the last three figures that since then our losses have more than doubled – in one case trebled – against theirs.'

A murmur – of consternation? disbelief? – animated the seven men sitting below Ravenscraft, who returned to the desk.

'The reason for this is a Dutch gentleman by the name of Fokker,' he said. 'Supplier of high-class aeronautical machinery to the German Imperial High Command. Fokker was asked to examine the captured Garros monoplane and come up with something similar. In fact he went one better. The alarming increase in our recent losses is entirely due to the actions of one particular Hun scout – the new Fokker E-III monoplane.'

'Which incorporates . . . ?' the major-general began.

'Some kind of synchronization principle, so that the gun fires only when the speed of each bullet permits it to escape between successive rotations of each propeller blade.'

'So all the rounds fired are available for attacking the enemy – and the bloody prop's in no danger?'

'Exactly. The principle, of course, is easy enough. You've got one variable – the rpm of the blades, which depends on the engine revs – and two factors which can be fixed: the firing rate of the gun and the muzzle velocity of the bullets as they leave it. It's a simple enough equation to determine the right mv and firing rate for any given propeller speed, once you know the distance between the gun muzzle and the blades. Not even higher maths. It's the design of the interrupter gear that links these variables efficiently together under all conditions that gives the armourers their headaches. And the details of that, theoretical and mechanical, can be deuced tricky.'

'Perhaps,' Major Hesketh said, 'now that you have outlined the problem, it would be a good time to brief Lieutenant Blake on the manner in which he is going to solve it?'

'Oh, good Lord, yes,' Ravenscraft agreed. 'That's the simplest part of all. The brains here would solve it eventually, of course. Just a question of time. But that's a commodity in short supply this year.' He gestured towards the tell-tale figures on the blackboard. 'As you see, the matter's urgent. What you're going to do, young man' – he smiled at Blake – 'is fly yourself into deepest, darkest Hunland, submerge yourself in the local populace, locate and steal the plans of this Fokker device, and bring them back to us PDQ – preferably using an E-III as transport.'

4

The weather remained unsettled for the rest of that week.
HMS *Furious*, the first warship in the world to be defined
as an aircraft carrier – that is, equipped with a flying deck
for the operation of land planes – ran into heavy seas as
she plowed her way northwards off the coast of Holland
on the Friday evening.

The 22,000-ton vessel, converted from a battle cruiser
designed to mount a pair of enormous eighteen-inch
guns, now boasted a hangar and a flight deck along her
forecastle. With a top speed of 31.5 knots, the *Furious*
normally housed six Sopwith Pups and four seaplanes.
Tonight, however, the Royal Naval Air Service was
playing host to a cuckoo: one of the Sopwith biplanes
had been jettisoned from the nest to make room for the
specially modified machine which was to take Lieutenant
Blake through the hostile skies of Germany.

It was only weeks since the ship's Senior Flying Officer,
Squadron Commander E. H. Dunning, had made the
world's first aeroplane landing aboard a vessel under
way – side-slipping on to the deck from a forward pass
into a combined headwind of 48 knots when a crew
of two petty officers and nine men ran up to grab
straps attached to the fuselage and haul the machine
to a halt. Five days later Dunning had been tragically
killed attempting to repeat the performance into an even

stronger headwind, when his Pup had been blown over
the side into the sea. The RNAS experts were anxious
to show Blake, the landlubber, that mistakes are not
always the fault of the hired help and if the impossible
takes a little while, at least the wet-bobs are liable to do
it quicker than anyone else.

Blake himself was not over-anxious to consider the
impossible. Hunched behind the canvas dodger in the eastern corner of the flying bridge, he exchanged occasional
pleasantries with the sub-lieutenant on watch, glancing
up from time to time to meet the impassive gaze of the
steersman behind the wheelhouse windshield.

At six-thirty a chill breeze had blown in off some
distant ice-cap, whipping the crest of each swell into
crumbling foam. Half an hour later the water was more
purple than blue, and by seven-fifteen the thin silhouette
of the distant coast was awash in a platter of beaten gold.
Inside the hood of his storm coat, the sub-lieutenant's
tin-hatted features shone ruby red.

Blake listened to the hollow boom of some vibrating
structure within the hull, the deep throb of the carrier's
engines and the ringing slap of whitecaps against the
steel plates. Once the sun had plunged below the western
horizon, every shred of cloud had withdrawn from the
sky, which now lay as pale and vulnerable as a woman
naked on an operating table.

As darkness seeped in from the east, powdering an
infinity of stars above the converted cruiser's upperworks,
he wondered whether the sky would stay clear until his
hazardous take-off soon after dawn, or whether the
storms forecast would materialize before he crossed
the enemy coast. For the hundredth time he repeated
to himself the details of his final briefing.

*　　　*　　　*

It was the War Office cartographer who had provided the most illuminating details. Superseding Sir Alan Ravenscraft on the ops-room dais, he had gone at once to the map – a large, comfortable man with curling iron-grey hair and a loose uniform bearing the crown and flash of a brevet major. He was at present seconded to the Woolwich Arsenal as a ballistics expert, Ravenscraft said. Nobody explained why an authority on the trajectory of artillery shells should be briefing a would-be spy on the theft of blueprints from a German factory. Perhaps, in the corridors of the War Office, it was considered a normal progression.

The expert had picked up a small baton from the desk. 'The factory is in the Upper Hessen *Land*,' he said, 'west of the Teutoburger Wald, an extensive forest, on the outskirts of a small town called Siegsdorf-am-Lippe. The nearest centre of any size is Paderborn. Kassel's about thirty-five miles to the south-east' – he tapped the map with the baton – 'Münster about the same distance to the north-west.' Another tap.

'That's well clear of the Ruhr, I hope,' Major Hesketh interrupted.

'The headwaters of the *River* Ruhr pass through the region,' the cartographer said, 'but the actual industrial area's miles away. About sixty-five to the west. This is pretty much a rural area: woods and fields and that sort of thing. Cobbled streets and half-timbered houses in the towns.'

'And how exactly are you proposing to get my chap there?' Blake's station commander spoke for the first time.

'Somebody mentioned Jutland!' Blake himself interposed.

'Yes, well, that's a bit off the mark! We're flying you in

19

from the north, but not *that* far north. Planning wallahs in the War Office reckon the best take-off point would be somewhere off the East Frisian Islands, just past the old Dutch frontier. That gives you a southerly course past Oldenburg, between Osnabrück and Minden.'

'To within twenty miles of the target?' the brigadier said. 'In a Sopwith bloody Pup?'

'That's the thinking, sir. Remove the drums of ammo and the Lewis gun on the top wing, make up the weight with a supplementary tank and a few extra gallons. Plus, of course, the Pup's unusually generous wing surface, keeping you aloft higher up, in the thinner air, with less resistance and therefore a consequent saving of fuel. With the additional advantage' – he directed a wintry smile at Blake – 'that if you do run out of juice at that height you have that much longer a glide path before you hit terra firma. Add another five or six miles, I should say.'

The baton described a small arc on the map. 'With luck you should reach this area here, on the lower slopes of the Teutoburger Wald, somewhere between Hameln and Detmold. So far as we know, the factory's part of an industrial estate just outside Siegsdorf – one of half a dozen light engineering works installed to liven up a depressed agricultural region. A Krupp subsidiary, of course. I should add here that plans or blueprints of the interrupter gear being developed at the factory are even more important to the war effort than sight of an actual Fokker Eindekker – welcome though that would be! – because the technicians there are working on an improved version of the original design.'

'Thank you, Charles,' the major-general said. 'That gives us the broad picture, I think. You, young man, will, of course, receive very full local information, plans, maps, equipment, papers, etcetera, before you board *Furious* at Gosport.'

'Yes, sir,' Blake said. 'Thank you, sir.'

'There is one other thing,' the cartographer said, stepping down from the dais. 'Might or might not be useful to you. Still, knowing your background . . . fact is, this area, deserted in the eighteenth century, was colonized largely by French Huguenot refugees and remains Protestant today. It's one of the few Hun regions with something of a French cultural tradition. If you get really stuck – well, with Huguenot ancestors yourself you might stumble upon a family not altogether hostile to the Allied cause. You could even get a chance to air your own French!'

'I can't wait,' Blake said.

Below deck, he sat in the narrow cockpit of the Pup and slipped his flying boots under the straps of the rudder bar. *Furious* was rolling heavily in the westerly swell, and he imagined himself already several thousand feet up as the tethered biplane rocked from side to side.

Through the tiny windshield, with its padded leather rim, he stared at the aluminium engine cowling, the single shining propeller blade that was visible and the polished filler caps protruding from the oil and petrol tanks. Two large dials gleamed beneath the leading edge of the cockpit rim – one, on the left, an altimeter; that on the right an airspeed indicator, somewhat optimistically peaking, white figures on a black ground, at 140. Additional fuel and temperature gauges had been installed in this modified machine.

Blake had already, not for the first time, admired the precision engineering of the rotary engine, each cylinder machined from a solid, drop-forged ingot, each cooling fin thin enough to cut a careless rigger's hand. Behind the nine knurled screw-heads of the front-plate, which was integral with the propeller shaft, a film of burned castor oil veiled the dull gleam of metal and copper induction pipes.

'We want to offload you at first light,' the skipper had said. 'Nothing personal, old chap, but we'll be pretty close inshore and there *are* coastal batteries. That way, in any case, you'll be at operational height before sun-up. Apart from denying the Hun gunners a sitting duck offshore!'

Privately, Blake was a little more worried about the Hun gunners on land, in particular those based at Osnabrück, on the northern fringes of the Ruhr – even if they weren't expecting to see enemy aircraft this far north. One of the Western Front maxims he and his observer colleagues had quickly learned in 1915 concerned the fallibility of gunners' eyes. At that stage of the war few could distinguish the difference between an Albatros and an Avro 504, or a Fokker Eindekker and a Morane Saulnier monoplane. An aeroplane, particularly since small bombs had started to be carried, was a potential danger; it was better to shoot first and let somebody else ask the questions afterwards. The FE-2b, whose demise had produced Blake's bogus duelling scar and a deformed upper lip which was masked by his moustache, had in fact been shot down by a nest of French machine-gunners as it planed in to land at Hesdin after a reconnaissance patrol.

Things had improved slightly after RFC roundels had replaced the Union Jacks originally painted on the wings and fuselage of British machines, but pilots remained wary. Blake's Pup in any case carried no identification marks: the doped fabric surfaces had been stippled with a Halberstadt-style camouflage pattern but there were no black crosses on wings or tail. 'I don't know how the rules of war apply to machinery,' the expert seconded from the Royal College of Art had told him, 'but if *you* masquerade in German uniform you could be considered a spy and shot. Better not take a chance, what!'

Blake grinned, thinking of the rigger who had supervised the job, a grizzled veteran known to the squadron's pilots as Rigger Mortis on account of his unvarying pessimism. 'Mark my words, sir,' he had said, eyeing the multicoloured lozenges with disfavour, 'no good will come of this. Dressing the old girl in borrowed clothes just will not do. I mean it stands to reason, don't it?'

'Think of it as going to a party,' Blake had jested. 'In fancy dress.'

'You don't wear fancy dress to crack a safe,' the rigger said gloomily.

Threading his way between the shrouded shapes of seaplanes and RNAS Pups jamming the hangar, Blake returned to the bridge. The marine engines thrummed, the bows smacked sheets of spray from the swell.

The watch had changed. A bearded lieutenant commander huddled into a duffle coat stood talking to the new duty officer, a fresh-faced boy indistinguishable from the last. The lieutenant commander, who was responsible for the stowage and readying of flying machines aboard the *Furious*, nodded a greeting as Blake joined them on the bridge wing. 'Have to drag your bus into the open air in a few minutes, old boy,' he said. 'Sky should be thinning out in the east at any time, and the skipper has a lunch date in Stromness!'

'What's our present position?' Blake asked. 'Approximately.'

'About five miles off the splendidly named island of Schiermonnikoog,' the young man told him. 'Forty miles or so past the entrance to the Zuyder Zee.'

The lieutenant commander was focusing his Zeiss field-glasses on a sector a few degrees off the carrier's starboard bow. 'Right you are,' he said. 'Just right of dead ahead to you.' He handed Blake the binoculars.

It took Blake almost half a minute, but at last – each time the ship rose to a swell – he could make out beyond the streaked tumble of the sea a darker blur imposed on the dark, a thin, black silhouette that must be the Dutch coast north of Groningen. And above this indefinite, undulating line there was a definite difference in the texture of the night.

The stars had faded and died. Stealthily as a sediment draining from a glass of water, the night withdrew from the eastern sky.

Ahead of the carrier, the seas assembled themselves into parallel ridges, markers of a groundswell swinging shorewards over the shoaling continental shelf. The four thin smokestacks of the *Furious* swept across the paling sky in crazy arcs as the carrier, beam-on to the advancing tide, wallowed in the swell.

Minutes later Blake saw that the wind had freshened towards the north, stirring up small waves that raced crosswise over the swell, whipping drifts of spume from the lacework of foam whitening the troubled surface.

'Soon as we have you shipshape and ready,' the lieutenant commander told him, 'we shall wheel offshore, head directly into the wind to ride the bloody swell and give you the maximum lift.' He produced a whistle on a white lanyard and blew three shrill blasts.

Things happened fast after that. Just like the beginning of a rugger match, Blake thought. Excitement, apprehension, fear of failure, a sudden frantic desire to go to the lavatory . . . then the whistle blows, the game has started and you don't think any more, you just do.

The aeroplane, held in position by the launching crew, stood at the inner end of the flight deck, looking curiously fragile in the cold, grey light, fabric wings trembling beneath the blustering wind.

The skipper had come down to wish Blake good luck and offer advice. The LSO – landing signal officer – had last-minute instructions for the take-off. The RNAS rigger breathed encouragement into Blake's ear. He checked the magneto and carburettor inside the access hatch on the metal panel behind the port side of the engine cowling. After shaking hands all round, he clambered into the cockpit.

The skipper swung around and signalled the wheel-house. HMS *Furious* leaned into the swell and sped away from the coast, leaving a broad wake to cream among the whitecaps.

Gauges were scanned, quadrants set, levers trimmed. After an exchange of signals, the propeller was swung. The rotary engine caught with a shattering roar and the Pup shuddered in anticipation against the restraining chocks.

Five minutes before, Blake had noticed a cutter being swung outboard from one of the lower decks, ready to be lowered into the sea. A glance below and a raised eyebrow had stimulated a response from the lieutenant commander. 'In case you tip her into the drink, cock,' the bearded sailor had explained. 'Nothing to be done, in that case, for the bus. But orders are to fish you out, if living, and parcel you back to base.'

This was not an eventuality that Blake wished to consider in any way at all. He wished he hadn't seen the bloody boat.

He had made two trial take-offs from the flight deck of *Furious* when the carrier was in Portsmouth harbour, one of them when she was under way and heading for the Solent. There was no point wasting everybody's time with a deck landing when he wasn't going to be expected to make one. He had simply flown across the water to the aerodrome attached to the flying-boat base at Calshott and then returned to the ship for his second attempt.

The experience had been alarming, but not as alarming as a dawn take-off from behind the lines at Hesdin, in the middle of an artillery barrage.

Jockeying a machine into the air from a stable platform on a sunny day in port – even if the platform was a trifle short on length – had nothing in common, nevertheless, with the same exercise on a heaving battle-cruiser a few miles from the enemy coast in a North Sea gale.

Blake gritted his teeth, listening to the rotary warm up as he kept one eye on the dials and the other on the LSO, immobile in his niche at the far end of the flight deck.

The horizon sank away and then floated up again as the carrier rose, hung, dropped and then rose once more, breasting the swell. The Sopwith Pup's tail was being held up by the crew. The engine bellowed. Arms waved on every side.

The LSO was scything get-on-with-it signals into the air above his head.

The rigger nodded and the chocks were whipped away from the wheels.

Shuddering momentarily, the Pup surged forward.

Blake gave the sturdy biplane everything he had. Hunched over the control column, thighs plastered to the seat, spine in tune with the vibrations of the wood and fabric fuselage, he fed maximum power to the labouring rotary, feet and fingertips alert to every bounce and twitch of the speeding machine as he willed it into the air.

The ship's bows rose three times during the Pup's short run to the end of the flight deck. On the first heave the plane lifted for an instant, but it was still well below its stalling speed, crashing heavily down on to its undercart as the planking dropped away.

Blake was ready for the next swell, holding the machine down to allow the acceleration to build, feathering the stick as he sensed the wings' reaction to the altered wind pressure.

The final lip was terrifyingly near, a blur against the steel-grey waves. The LSO whipped backwards, with open mouth and windmill arms. The aeroplane had nothing more to give. Once more the deck rose, thrusting the Pup away. Blake eased back the stick, praying, clasping the leather top lovingly to his belly.

The Pup hopped into the void. Sank like a wounded bird.

For a deadly instant, he thought they really were going to hit the water. Then the airspeed and the elevator lift combined and they were climbing, clawing their way into the sky ahead of the dwindling carrier, banking steeply to turn south.

'Christ!' Blake yelled into the slipstream. 'Oh, *Jesus*!'

A long, low island slid into view beneath the lower starboard wing. Below and behind, *Furious* was a white arrowhead heading for Scapa Flow. Climbing still, the scout flew on towards the German mainland.

5

'I hope, gentlemen,' Field Marshal Sir Douglas Haig said to a conference of senior officers at Aldershot in July 1914, 'that none of you is so foolish as to think that aeroplanes will be usefully employed for reconnaissance in the air in any future conflict. There is only one way for a commander to obtain information by reconnaissance and that is through the use of cavalry.'

Fortunately the views of Britain's Commander-in-Chief Land Forces were not shared by everybody, and there were enough adventurous pioneers who had obtained the Royal Aero Club licence to form the nucleus of the Royal Flying Corps in 1912. The original organization was based on the Central Flying School, at Upavon in Wiltshire. The purpose of the CFS was not the basic training of pilots; neither the Army nor the Navy had funds to spare for that. Its role was to convert existing flyers into military aviators. Officers who applied to join had been required to pay their own way through flying centres at Hendon or the motor-racing circuit at Brooklands before they qualified for a course in military flying. If accepted by the RFC they received a refund of £75 towards these costs, but they remained officially on the strength of their old regiments and were only 'attached' to the new military arm.

Patrice Blake, then a junior Territorial officer in the

City of London light infantry regiment quaintly called the Honourable Artillery Company, had been one of these men. But he did not receive an order to attend No. 9 Course of Instruction at the CFS until late 1915, by which time he had been sent to France with the HAC and received a machine-gun bullet through the ankle at the first Battle of Mons.

Instruction at Upavon was tame. The commanding officer, Captain Godfrey Paine, RN, was known throughout the RFC as Bloody Paine because of his vitriolic command of foul language when scolding his pupils. But this violence of approach did not extend to the training programme. At that stage of the war stability and not getting lost were all that was required of the military pilot. The role of the flying machine in war was to provide an aerial observation platform, so most training flights took place in the early morning or late afternoon, when the prevailing winds on Salisbury Plain offered no hazards to flyers.

Suave circuits of the aerodrome, with occasional cross-country forays at a constant altitude in level flight were all that military pilots were expected to master. Abrupt or violent manoeuvres were discouraged: they might tear the wings off the aeroplane. Stunts were actively discouraged, positively forbidden below two thousand feet.

Luckily for Blake, his first posting was to 23 Squadron at Gosport. And the new Squadron Commander was Major Louis Strange, an anti-establishment rebel who got results, a man who was a passionate believer in what he called advanced training. Basic airmanship, in his view, demanded not only the ability to maintain level flight but the skill to evade attack and to launch it.

Before the war Strange had been a barnstormer touring the country with air circuses, club races, competitions to see which pilots could drop bags of flour nearest a ground

29

target from a height of five hundred feet. And he used all
the skills learned in this rough-and-tumble profession as
part of his military training programme. Strange's pilots
were not forbidden to indulge in aerobatics: they were
taught them. Instead of avoiding the problems of flight
– crosswind take-offs, spins, side-slips and stalls – pupils
were encouraged to provoke them deliberately. In this
way they should be expert enough to deal with technical
difficulties before they had the added embarrassment of
a hostile Albatros on their tail.

During his two months as a pilot on the Western Front
with 2 Squadron, Blake had profited from this instruction.
Major-General Trenchard's maxim – 'No empty seats at
RFC front-line mess tables' – had meant that as soon as
a pilot was lost he must immediately be replaced from a
Home Establishment pool, no matter how inexperienced
the newcomer or how small the number of flying hours he
had chalked up. In a situation where the RFC was losing
more pilots and machines through accidents than through
enemy action, Blake's expertise had been something of a
marvel to the young men whose expected days of survival
were too often counted in single figures. He was no ace –
his score was a modest three victories and one probable
– but he always brought his plane back. And he was
still there.

He hoped fervently, nevertheless, that he would not
be called upon to demonstrate these skills afresh during
this crazy trip over German territory in an unmarked
machine.

*Ten thousand feet below, the bleak brown wastes of
the peat moors east of Aschendorf and Papenberg glided
slowly astern. Oldenburg was a smudge of factory smoke
between the Pup's port wingtips.*

A long way ahead the flat land rose into a line of low

hills, and above these a distant cloud front drew a dark line across the entire horizon.

He stared at it with mounting concern as the biplane forged ahead through the rarefied air. The forecast had promised clear skies at least until midday, by which time, with luck, he should be back on solid ground. The only cloud formations, they had said, might be forming up behind him, blowing down from the north. The front ahead, he supposed, must be due to some freak or unexpected climatic condition over the industrial furnace of the Ruhr.

The ragged, undulating surface of the front's eastern end suddenly paled, grew a silver edge. A nimbus of glaring light seeped westward. Small drifts of cloud broke free, floated upwards in rosy light, turned white and then dissolved against the aching luminosity of the sky. A blazing arc, incandescent in the early light, hoisted itself above the sombre horizon.

Very slowly, an outsize orange observation balloon, the sun rose brilliantly into the serene, existing day.

Blake wiped the mist of castor oil from his goggles and checked his instruments. Bright shivers trembled the fabric of the wings as the headwind plucked at the stiffened surface. He had been in the air exactly half an hour.

Major Louis Strange had described himself as a 'ragtime flyer'. Blake, curiously enough, had applied the same term to himself when he first started to take flying lessons – although in his case the reference was strictly musical. He had in fact divided his time, when he left school, between the drudgery of an insurance office in the City, the blessed relief of weekend flying at Brooklands . . . and evening work with a group of friends forming a ragtime band in which he was the trap-drummer. It was the wristy skill he had acquired perfecting his rolls and paradiddles that earned him such unusually high marks for 'Morse aptitude' during his flying training. Quick, neat, separate taps at the wireless key were no problem to a man versed in the elite syncopations of *Shimmy-Sha-Wobble* and *Tiger Rag*.

'You'll find it a boon, lad, when you're on the run in Hunland,' Major Hesketh had told him enthusiastically at the end of his very first briefing. 'Particularly comforting when you make first contact with your cut-out.'

'Cut-out?'

'The agent in place. Buffer between you and us. Can't risk only a single bird with the mission at his fingertips. The cut-out forwards your stuff our way, passes on our instructions to you. Buffer between you and the Hun too, if it comes to that. If Fritz latches on to info coming in from us, traces it to the cut-out . . . well, that's only one in the bag. Leaves you free to continue. Even if . . . persuaded . . . the cut-out can't finger you. Can't tell what you don't know, eh?'

'You mean our only contact is through the wireless? We never actually meet?'

'Absolutely. Morse communication only. In code, of course.

'Well, it's nice to know one won't be totally alone,' Blake had said.

He was alone now. Eleven thousand two hundred on the clock and the spars groaning a bit, the cloud front ahead extending, reaching towers of cumulus up into the sky. A couple of teased outliers drifted across the sun, whipping sudden shadow across the wings of the machine.

It was penetratingly cold. The rotary roared reassuringly. Far below, green fields and dark woods sprawled.

He saw a small town with railway lines, a turreted castle on a hill, a loop of river glistening. Off to the east, the shadow of one of the breakaway clouds sculpted a rocky ridge from the flat country.

For the tenth time Blake felt behind his seat to check that the miniature wireless transmitter with its Morse key was there. Contacting the cut-out was all.

It was then, banking slightly to scan the sky below, that he saw the two-seater with its ring-mounted observer's gun and the black crosses on its wing.

Strange and Blake had first met on a special occasion when their two brands of ragtime coincided. It was at the Royal Automobile Club in Pall Mall on 16 January 1914. The occasion was the famous 'Upside Down Dinner' held by the brighter spirits in the flying fraternity to celebrate the exploits of two Hendon pilots – the first Englishmen successfully to loop the loop and also to fly intentionally in an inverted position.

The dinner invitations were printed upside down and back to front, the tables were arranged in the shape of a loop, with upside-down tables on top of normal ones and there was an inverted figure in an upside-down fuselage suspended above. The banquet itself was similarly 'about face'. Starting with coffee, liqueurs and cigars, it progressed through dessert and cheeses to a main course of roasted snipe. After this came lobster, soup, and finally hors-d'oeuvres.

One of the loopers – who had dared to perform his feat a second time with a brave lady passenger – drank half a bottle of champagne from an inverted glass. The other sang 'Two Lovely Black Eyes' standing on his head.

Blake's ragtime band, proudly showing off examples of the new 'jass' specialities imported from the United States aboard the *Mauretania* and other luxury liners, played suitable music in an ante-room throughout the evening.

He didn't see Strange again until he was sent on a course to the tented camp at Hythe which housed Britain's No. 1 School of Aerial Gunnery . . . and found there that the major was his new CO.

Flying alone over northern Germany many months later, he wished fervently that one of the Lewis guns with which he had proved such a fine shot was with him now.

Yes, it was an Albatros all right. One of the C.II reconnaissance versions with the upper wing mounted high above a slender fuselage. The upright engine, projecting through the nose, and the triangular rudder were unmistakable.

Blake cursed. He could out-climb the two-seater, probably outrun it, but an escape would certainly alert them; they would report an unidentified aircraft – and the whole of the north German defences would be on the lookout. All the more so because, according to the latest front-line gossip, many of the German reconnaissance machines were now equipped with wireless installations linking them to their base.

Better avoid that if possible, continue along the straight and level until the cloud cover was reached. Maybe, seeing the Idflieg-style camouflage, they'd think the Pup was a prototype, some kind of experimental machine, without crosses because it wasn't yet in military service.

If, that is, they had seen him at all.

Lowering the starboard wing, he peered over the cockpit rim again.

They had, of course. The German two-seater was climbing, fast. The observer had hauled the machine-gun around on the ring mounting and was crouched over it, squinting up into the bright sky as his pilot coaxed the Albatros aloft.

What the deuce were they doing over this part of Germany anyway, hundreds of miles from the battlefront? Blake thought irrationally. He had been tooling along practically at cruising speed, husbanding the juice in the hope of getting that much nearer the target. Better a ride than a walk in hostile country! But now . . .

Gritting his teeth, he slammed the throttle fully open. The clattering roar of the Le Rhône rose to a bellow. The slipstream punished his oily cheeks and tugged at his helmet.

Below him, the Albatros steepened its climb.

Many people, most of them experts in their own way, had contributed information, analyses, character evaluations, reports and advice on Blake's suitability for a secret mission behind German lines. Along with this wealth of personal opinion went the documentary material – the training reports, the war service, Territorial experience, a military dossier – added to by successive commanding officers – detailing his entire career in uniform. Along with this wealth of intelligence, the competent authorities considered such matters as his physical appearance, his proficiency in the right languages, his sense of loyalty, his initiative and his excellence as a gunner and wireless operator using Morse code.

Curiously, though, what was perhaps the most significant facet of all – certainly to the young man himself – had passed completely undetected through the fine mesh of this official screening. But the fact nevertheless remained: No. 1902818 Blake, Patrice D., of the Honourable Artillery Company, presently on attachment to the Royal Flying Corps, was a physical coward.

6

It was a fact that consumed Blake with self-loathing, but something he had always found it hard – sometimes impossible – to master.

Only twice had this failing been publicly exposed, once when he was fourteen years old, once, much later, at a Territorial camp. But the many hells he had been through, desperate to hide it on subsequent occasions, had scarred him almost more than the original humiliations.

In his final term at an expensive preparatory school, in front of a jeering crowd, he had funked a fight provoked by a younger, smaller but more aggressive boy – panicking to run home and fake an attack of flu that would keep him away for the few remaining days of term.

The affair at the Territorial camp was worse. It was during an exercise on Salisbury Plain. Blake and a fellow cadet were running to intercept an 'enemy' soldier driving a lightweight scout car. The driver saw them, swung the vehicle brutally around to make a getaway and tipped it over into a deep ditch, where it immediately caught fire.

Blake and his friend raced towards the blazing wreck. But once they were within reach of the scorching breath of the flames, Blake stopped dead. His friend dashed on, plunged into the inferno and emerged, smoking, dragging the injured driver.

Blake had no idea why he stopped. It was no conscious decision. He just did.

On subsequent occasions fear had driven him now this way, now that, sometimes into what appeared a logical course of action, sometimes not. But he had always contrived to conceal that basic, innate motivation – the dry-mouthed impulse to turn and run that no argument of the mind, however fierce, could overcome.

Hide it successfully, that is, from others; not from himself.

He had more than once manoeuvred himself into situations liable to provoke the craven reaction, believing until it was too late that meeting the danger halfway might annul it. He had allowed himself to be placed in positions where his activities were controlled by others, imposed upon him by authority, and not the results of his personal decisions. Joining the Royal Aero Club and forcing himself to learn to fly was an example of the first of these ploys; becoming a member of the HAC as a 'Terrier' of the second.

After the fluid, not quite believable campaigns of Mons and the Marne, he had welcomed the bullet which had invalided him home from the hell of the static trench warfare which followed. And he had volunteered to join the RFC as a panic alternative – any alternative – to avoid a return to the shell-torn desolation of the Somme.

In the air the danger was somehow not quite so personal: as an observer, control of his movements was out of his hands; as a pilot, his skills were sufficient to keep him largely out of trouble, especially in single-seaters.

And then this . . . this damnable mission. At first his fear of being thought a coward if he refused it had overcome his trepidation at the idea of actually doing it.

And then it was too late: here he was, smack in the middle of it.

Being stalked by two Huns with machine-guns. Flying an unarmed aeroplane.

Blake was already at an altitude not far short of twelve thousand feet. There was the risk that the south-westerly headwind which had proved the forecasters wrong and was piling up the clouds ahead of him could start draining fuel from the tanks. Lack of oxygen was already causing him pain in the chest. And if he did squander fuel climbing still higher there was no proof that the German might not match him. He had no information on the ceiling of the two-seater Albatros: the black crosses were widely spaced; the wing surfaces looked generous, practically as spacious as the Pup's. It was certainly possible . . .

Better to increase speed by losing height and make for that cloud.

He pushed the throttle up to maximum and eased the stick forward. The scout's bulbous nose dropped and the engine screamed. They streaked down towards the towering mountain of cumulo-nimbus.

The Albatros, perhaps no more than two hundred feet below, changed course to vector on an interception course which would bring it up under the Pup before Blake reached the clouds. The observer's ring-mounted Spandau was already canted up at its steepest angle.

The cloud mass was expanding at an alarming rate. Below the frothed white billows roiling upwards into two separate hammerheads, the colours and texture of the barrier altered dramatically. The darkest, most menacing sector, at a height perhaps of five or six thousand feet, was in constant movement, writhing from a pearly tint through slate grey to a black that was almost purple. As he watched through his tiny screen,

Blake saw blue lightning fork to the sombre landscape beneath.

Beneath the leather of his flying helmet, hairs on the nape of his neck tingled. His feet felt heavy and cold as ice. Nausea clawed at his stomach. But whether he was running because he was scared or because the priorities of the mission demanded it was a question that was purely academic now. No time here for introspection, doubts or self-interrogation. Just do it, man . . . and hope.

The storm clouds raced towards him. Strips of fabric flicked from the port wing, fluttering wildly in the slipstream. Blake looked over his shoulder. He saw holes in the tailplane, a long tear in the rudder. The Albatros, still a hundred feet below and half as much again astern, was firing at him!

He banked steeply, rolled once in the hope of fazing the Hun pilot, then dropped the Pup into a dive that was almost vertical.

Wooden spars in the fuselage behind him shuddered as a stream of bullets from the German two-seater – now level with him, now slightly above – ploughed through the stressed fabric skin.

Then wisps of teased-out grey were racing past, the darkened cumulus above blacked out the sun . . . and the visual world vanished: he was alone in a world that was totally black.

He kept the throttle wide open and continued on a compass course approximately south-west by south.

The aeroplane dropped sickeningly and then was buoyed up as arbitrarily as a ping-pong ball on a fountain jet. It was hopeless trying to keep control of it. He was completely at the mercy of the storm centre into which he had flown. All he could do was take advantage of every little chance allowed him by the elements, thróttling back when the bracing wires screamed, keeping the stick held slightly forward if there was a momentary lull.

Sometimes, when the thumping of the machine abruptly ceased, he felt as though he was floating alone in the void, with only the weight of his body thrown against his safety belt to connect him with the structure of wood and metal and doped fabric he was controlling. Then he could think of nothing but what to pull, push or swing in an attempt to roll it back on to an even keel. Once, aware of a disastrous side-slip only by the howling hurricane tearing at his left cheek, he was convinced that the Albatros had miraculously caught up with him and was peppering the plane from all sides. The thunder and shriek of the weather was momentarily eclipsed by a violent tattoo on the aerofoil surfaces as they dropped through a violent eruption of hailstones the size of frozen loganberries.

Fear was as much of an abstraction as logical thinking in this maelstrom; the will to survive, something welling up from deep in his being, had seized control of the motor reflexes, willing them to act as experience dictated.

Blake knew that they must have been losing height for an eternity, and he throttled down at last, waiting for the ground to appear through the curtain of torrential rain.

All at once he was aware of light, and the stair-rods of rain were silver. A church spire, an onion dome with a sharp steeple, upside down, appeared above his starboard wingtip. Surprise was beyond him. All he could think of was to set it back the right way up. Automatically he handled his controls.

The spire flicked out of sight and reappeared, correctly aligned, below the Pup's port wing.

He slammed forward the throttle, pulling back the stick

as the machine roared into bright light. He was less than a hundred feet above a stretch of waste ground, with a line of trees, a huddle of gabled houses beyond a river ahead. Ant-like figures scattered across a stone bridge as he zoomed up and over the steep, tiled roofs.

And then, astonishingly, above a range of low hills in the east, there was a flood of golden light, an arc of brilliance, and the sun rose splendidly into view to bathe that peaceful post-storm landscape in the luminescence of a new day.

'What-ho, what-ho!' Blake cried aloud. 'A chap for whom the sun rises twice in the same day can do no bloody wrong!' He pulled back the stick and started to climb.

The violent loss of height which had afforded him two separate views of the rising sun filled him suddenly with a confidence both in the aeroplane and in the mission as a whole which until then had been noticeably absent. Alone in the narrow cockpit as he nursed the machine back up to ten thousand feet, he began to sing.

Falling away beneath him, the lush green curves and rectangles of the summer countryside dwindled to a random patchwork sewn together by the bright threads of metalled roads and an occasional shining railway line. Once he saw dark smoke from a freight train blown across a scorched brown field dotted with tiny haystacks.

Far away to the east, blue hills rose into the sky. The Harz Mountains, he supposed. And, a little nearer, the multiple twists and turns of a broad river in a valley that must be the Weser on its tortuous way to Bremen and the North Sea.

There were more clouds ahead, but they were of the white, cotton-wool variety and there were patches of clear sky in between. It was two hours since he had left the flight deck of the *Furious*. Studying the map fixed below the windshield with its chinagraph arrows and symbols – and allowing for loss of time and wastage of fuel because of the Albatros and the storm which had enabled him to escape it – he estimated that he was probably halfway between Hanover and Osnabrück in the east–west sense, perhaps a dozen miles short of the waterway linking the Weser with the Dortmund–Ems ship canal.

And, yes, cloud shadows skipping over woods and pastures below, undulating now across the roofs of larger towns, were running into a smoky haze veiling the land to the west. Dark fumes belched from factory chimneys above the serrated glass roofs of workshops in a spider's web of railway lines. He was approaching the eastern fringe of the Ruhr.

This would be the area of maximum danger. The Ruhr, cradle of the Kaiser's entire war effort, home of the armaments industry, the Krupp complex, most of the aviation works, was Germany's most vulnerable target after the submarine pens at Kiel and the shipyards of Hamburg and Bremerhaven. It would certainly be heavily defended, even if it was far out of range of normal aircraft based on the present battlefront. And the Albatros observer would by now have reported an unidentified aeroplane flying that way, even if the burgomaster of the village Blake had so narrowly missed had not.

He didn't have to wait long to find out the truth.

He had just located the canal, a leaden ribbon, ruler-straight across the misty landscape ahead, when the Pup lurched suddenly, dropping like a stone for fifty feet as he wrestled with the stick. He hadn't heard the explosion and it was only afterwards that he remembered the smoke whipping past his face.

That near miss had been a freak chance for the gunners below, but the sky was now pock-marked with shell bursts, on either side and as far ahead as he could see – brown, white, black pricked out with scarlet, a series of cracking detonations that drowned the rotary's steady roar.

They hadn't quite got the range yet – that first one had been a lucky miss – but the way ahead was laced with spinning shrapnel. Archie, as flyers nicknamed the fire from ack-ack or anti-aircraft batteries, was flinging up everything he had.

Blake's mouth was dry. He felt as if all the blood in his body had drained to his feet. His safety belt clawed at his queasy stomach as he hurled the Pup into a dive to get up enough speed for the steep climb he needed. The murderous sky continued to erupt all around him. Air shrieked through tears in his lower wing. And after Archie, he knew, fighters would be waiting to pounce. At the top of his climb, for the second time that day, he ran for the clouds.

This time he was equally blinded, but by brightness and whiteness rather than the sombre gloom of the hammerhead. Pale scarves and streamers and ribbons of livid mist, ripped apart from the seemingly solid cloud mass by the scything disc of his propeller, flicked between the wings and past his goggled head. The engine laboured, gaining height.

And then suddenly he was drenched in warmth. Through the uppermost layer and out into the aching blue, he saw the sun, high now in the sky, dazzling the eye with the magic vision no flyer ever really tires of. Level as a marine horizon, the bubbling snowfield stretched as far as he could see in every direction.

As he skims this continent of ice-white cloud, the earth

below becomes to the flyer an abstraction, someone else's dream. Blake forgot his fear, forgot the danger, allowed the priorities of the mission to fade from his mind. The compass bearing was a shaking blur, the fuel level was menacingly low, but he lived only in the joy of his weightless existence, in the mastery of the elements granted to him by the contraption of wood and wire and metal that he controlled. The haphazard patterns of brown and blue and green visible through the occasional gaps in the cloud floor were as one-dimensional, as lacking in immediacy, as the printed symbols on his map.

Until he saw the German planes.

There were three of them, flying in close formation, perhaps three or four hundred feet below among isolated tufts of white which had torn free of the main cloud mass.

Two Pfalz D-III scouts led by a Halberstadt single-seater. The leader was unmistakable, with its single elevator and small rudder on an isolated pivot, the crescent-shaped exhaust projecting vertically above the exposed engine block. The Pfalz fighters, with their trapezoid strut formations, also had exposed in-line engines high above their pointed noses. They were silver, with thick black lines painted horizontally between the propeller boss and the cockpit, and red stripes zigzagged from cockpit to tail. The Halberstadt fuselage was pearl grey, with wings and tail in a stipple camouflage not unlike Blake's own.

The formation was flying on a course only a few degrees off the Pup's. Their bracing wires and control cables glinted in the bright sunlight . . . until the fleeting moment when the shadow of Blake's scout passed over the German leader and one of his wingmen.

Both the German fighter types had been designed with

the upper wing very low down and close to the fuselage. This restricted forward view from the cockpit, which was set fairly far back; but a semicircular cut-out in this upper wing allowed the pilot excellent upward vision.

Automatically, each man glanced above. They saw the stranger at once. The leader waved, banked and set the Halberstadt into a steep climb.

Cursing, Blake went cold all over. His machine was lighter than the Germans', but the Halberstadt was powered by a 120hp Argus engine, the Pfalz by a 160hp Mercedes and his Le Rhône peaked at no more than 80hp.

The Germans carried wing-mounted 7.92mm Spandau machine-guns.

He was two hundred, three hundred yards from the far side of the gap. Certainly he could dive down, plunge back into the clouds before they were within range, but by the time he was lost to sight they would have arrived at the same altitude. They would expect him to take evasive action once he was invisible. If he was the flight leader, Blake thought, he would direct one of the wingmen to veer left, the other right, in the hope of locating him once visibility returned. Perhaps the leader himself would keep roughly the same course, but lower down, where the cloud carpet thinned and broke up.

Playing a double bluff, Blake took no evasive action at all: he maintained his original course, height and speed.

He flew out into the next break much earlier than he expected, much sooner than he had hoped. The sun was tiresomely bright. He wiped oil mist from his goggles with the back of one glove. One of the Pfalz scouts was a speck far away on his left. There was no sign of the other. But the Halberstadt – he saw with horror, dipping the starboard wings – was immediately behind him, about fifty feet

45

below. A perfect position for the sucker kill, coming up from beneath the tail, the machine's blind spot, with guns blazing.

There was only one thing Blake could do. The next bank of cumulus was half a mile ahead. If he dived he would offer his belly to the German's Spandaus. It was too late for the classic banked turn on wingtips. On full power, he hauled the stick back and sent the Pup shooting up into the first half of a loop.

At the zenith of the manoeuvre, when the plane was upside down, he half rolled it on to an even keel and flew back the way he had come, completing a perfect example of the aerobatic stunt turn invented by the German ace Max Immelmann.

Facing this way, the clouds were much nearer. Blake put the nose down and dived.

Anticipating this, the Halberstadt pilot had wheeled steeply. Blake had an instant vision of flaming guns as he plummeted past. There was a sudden heavy jolt from somewhere amidships. And then he was shrouded again, thankfully blotted out by the merciful cumulus, gift-wrapped in cotton wool!

He emerged at about six thousand feet, the compass swinging wildly, and gazed desperately right and left in an attempt to relocate his bearings. Was that wide waterway dotted with a string of barges the Dortmund–Ems canal? There was no sun here to help. But, yes, those rolling, wooded heights on his right must be the Teutoburger Wald.

Except they should be on his left.

He swung the Pup around in a wide turn and began easing the stick back to coax it out of its dive.

Wind whistled and shrieked through the wires. The

engine roared. Tears in the wing surface flapped frenziedly. And from somewhere below the floorboards
there was a heavy thumping, punctuated at intervals
by a metallic rasp.

Blake bit his lip. The machine wasn't answering to the
controls as swiftly as he expected. She was sluggish to
react, with a tendency to yaw, the starboard wingtips
canted up.

He was sweating, a thousand feet lower down, by the
time he straightened the Pup out. It was then that he saw
one of the Pfalz scouts, a mile away on his port quarter,
heading directly for him.

And it was then that the rotary, having squandered
what was left of its fuel in the past few hectic minutes,
coughed, choked, caught again for an instant and finally
whined into silence. The airscrew spun to a halt.

For a hundredth of a second, Blake froze. Then the
experience gained through dozens of lessons, of lectures,
of mock dogfights and aerobatics, took control. The
expertise of the instructors at the Central Flying School,
Major Strange at 23 Squadron, the 2 Squadron battles
over the hell of the Somme – from the depths of his combat
memories an automatic evaluation of the situation, a
consideration of the options, a decision on the right
course of action took over.

Jockeying the control column, feet fighting the rudder
bar, he sent the powerless machine into the famous
height-losing escape known as the falling-leaf stunt –
a series of alternating side-slips, right and left, that
gained no ground but brought the earth near with
frightening speed.

Wind sighing through the struts and wires now
hummed an alto descant.

The Pfalz drew closer, preparing to circle . . .

Perhaps, seeing that the machine was crippled, the German pilot would hold his fire and simply watch it die? A kill was a kill, whether the final crash was due to the death of the aeroplane or its driver.

On one of his more violent side-slips, Blake felt an extra-heavy thump from beneath him . . . and saw with disbelief a wheel, two V struts and part of an axle whirl away below. Shots from the flight leader must have wrecked his undercarriage, and now part of it had broken away.

He gritted his teeth. A crash landing with half the undercart still in place implied a ground loop unless he was very lucky.

But a crash landing where?

He was over open country. A village with a tall church spire, sliding rapidly away on his right. Cornfields separated by twisting lanes. Woods, too many woods, carpeting the high ground on each side of a river. A stretch of moorland in the distance – but it looked as though the heath was strewn with boulders.

Nose down, the Pup was corkscrewing into a spin. With a supreme effort, the sweat coursing into his eyes, Blake flattened the machine out two hundred feet above a mill-race where a turreted manor spanned the stream. The Pfalz circled a respectable height overhead.

There was no choice now: he was into the final glide with no lift available to him. It would have to be the slanting field of cabbages . . . no, perhaps the stubbled meadow beyond. Trees, hedgerows, a weeded pond with a flurry of ducks, hurtled towards him.

Blake's hands were steady on the controls. He dropped the Pup on the far side of a blackthorn thicket. It pancaked with a rending crash, bounced into the air, nosedived with enough force to tear off a lower wing, then cartwheeled into a haystack.

Silence.

And then the small sounds, near and far, defining the time and place. The tick of cooling metal, rooks cawing in the distance, a creak of wood as the wreckage settled, wind blowing. Somewhere above, through the cloying stench of hot castor oil, he could hear liquid dripping.

And above that the regular beat of an aero engine.

Blake had to think very quickly. The briefing, dealing with forced landing, had not bargained for an enemy spectator, circling several hundred feet above.

There were two priorities: get away fast; and at the same time let the Pfalz pilot think he had perished in the crash. That way, until salvage teams called from the nearest town discovered there was no body, he might stave off a manhunt for long enough to get clear of the immediate area.

Whether or not he destroyed the Pup, they had told him, was of less importance.

Blake thought he might use that third factor, nevertheless, to help with the other two.

But first, quickly, he must have freedom of action. He was upside down in the open cockpit, hanging from his safety harness. In that situation, according to the CFS drill, the unfortunate pilot waited for rescuers to run up and free him. Suspended so close to the ground, a man fumbling with buckles could drop out on to his head and break his neck before he could reach down arms to cushion the fall.

No rescuers here, though. He had seen no workers in the fields, but the whole thing must be over before peasants or people from the manor hurried to investigate the crash.

There was a Very pistol beneath the seat. Blake reached above him to free this and allowed the heavy weapon to fall. He dropped the small rucksack which contained his maps, the proofs of his new German identity, and other necessities thought up by the intelligence experts at Gosport. Then he wedged his toes beneath the two sections of the rudder bar and felt for the buckles.

The Pfalz was still circling above.

Cramp in his left instep, agonizing in its intensity, seized the muscles of that leg. He felt the toe slipping from its hold as he wrestled with the harness. Why were these *bloody* belts always so difficult to free?

The cramp moved on, knotting his calf. He yelled, feeling the foot swing stiffly free. His whole weight was depending on the flexed muscles of his right foot now ... and he could sense the preliminary indications of cramp flickering there too.

With a gasp of relief, he felt the straps loosen and slide away. He withdrew his right foot, snatched out his arms and reached above his helmeted head.

Blake hit the ground in a shoulder roll, backing away at once in the shadow of an undamaged upper wing, dragging the pistol and the rucksack with him.

He hoped the wreck as a whole would conceal his movements. How long was it since they hit? It seemed an eternity but was probably less than a minute. They didn't always burst into flame on impact; sometimes it took time for the volatile fumes to ignite. He just hoped the Hun pilot was aware of that.

There were two rounds with the Very pistol, one green and one red. Although the tanks had run dry, he reckoned there should be enough petrol fumes still evaporating to combine with the air and form an explosive mixture – especially in the heat of a magnesium flare.

The red one, he thought. Face down at the extremity of the sheltering wing, he supported himself on his elbows and sighted the long-barrelled gun. Bristly stalks from the stubble pricked through his trousers at the knee. His left foot was still giving him hell.

Aiming up into the cockpit, between the controls, he pressed the trigger. And then swung around at once to fire the green flare into the centre of the haystack against which the remains of the aeroplane were leaning. The results were spectacular.

For an instant the cockpit glowed a blinding, incandescent crimson. Then the tanks exploded with a dual thump and the entire nose of the plane, from the smashed propeller where it had dug into the ground, erupted into a blazing fireball. Milliseconds later the fuselage was afire.

The longerons and formers of the tail, along with the struts and every single aerofoil section supporting the doped, inflammable fabric of the wings, were made of wood. All at once the Pup was no more than a fiery cross, flaming to life at the same time as the tinder-dry haystack in a crackling inferno.

From the foot of this towering holocaust, where the oily engine burned, a column of black smoke marbled with red leaned away across the meadow as the west wind blew. Beneath it, fleeing the scalding breath of the fire, Blake raced for the nearest hedgerow.

He lay flat in a ditch, watching the Pup's funeral pyre as he massaged the cramp from his foot. Soon the Pfalz overhead banked to turn north and flew away.

Blake crawled through the hedge, crossed a sunken lane and vanished into a wood. For the third time that day he ran – but this time under orders and not from a panic beyond his control.

7

'The aeroplane is – was – a Sopwith. There can be no doubt about that,' the area *Kommandant* announced.

'But, sir, how can we be sure? There was nothing left of the machine – nothing but a pile of smoking embers. And, of course, the damaged engine.'

'Precisely. A Le Rhône rotary. Favoured by Sir Thomas Sopwith for many of his designs. Two brass plates with series numbers which survived the fire relate to the Boulton and Paul factory in the city of Norwich, and to Britische Caudron of Cricklewood. Both companies are subcontracted to produce Sopwith machines – at least according to your own service, *Herr Hauptmann*,' the *Kommandant* said acidly.

The young officer who had rashly interrupted flushed. He had only recently been seconded to the foreign intelligence branch of the German secret service and had yet to learn that the wise agent told very senior officers only what they wished to hear.

'It is true that those concerns also fabricate parts for other machines,' the *Oberst* in charge of the local defence squadron observed. 'But the pilot from my No. 2 Flight who pursued the aeroplane through the clouds and eventually shot it down is convinced, despite the lack of markings, that it was a Sopwith. And an observer on a training flight in an Albatros Doppeldekker reported from a sector further north that he had sighted an unidentified intruder flying on a course approximately south-east by south. He too was convinced that the machine was an *Englander*, although he was unable to specify what type.'

The three men, together with the area police commissioner and a civilian from the Ministry of Defence in Berlin, were sitting around a refectory table in the great hall of Hohenstein Castle, a turreted fortress on a spur overlooking the Upper Weser district. The *Kommandant* had requisitioned the castle as his staff headquarters.

'A Sopwith then,' he repeated now, 'although we do not know whether it might have been the so-called one-and-a-half-strut version, an example of the new scout they call for some reason a camel, or the small dog . . .'

'The Pup,' the *Oberst* said.

'Exactly. The Puppy-dog. How absurd the *Englander* is, with his unhealthy regard for animals!'

'One of our agents reports that the Sopwith company is experimenting with a prototype that possesses *three* wings,' the *Hauptmann* put in rashly.

'Indeed. Well, here we are contenting ourselves with two.'

'But, with respect, *Herr General-Major*' – the civilian spoke for the first time – 'how can an enemy machine, an *Englander*, possibly be seen over that part of the Fatherland?' He glanced at a typed report on the table in front of him. 'Between Vechta and Diepholz, flying *south*? And then, further still, down here in Lower Saxony?'

'You have read the reports,' the *Oberst* said. 'They are factual.'

'Oh, I do not doubt that a machine was seen, that it was shot down near Detmold. But a *British* machine?

Could it not possibly be an intruder from the east, from the Russian front?'

The *Oberst* laughed. 'Your geography, my friend! From Osnabrück, where our observers first sighted the intruder and where it was fired upon by the defence gunners – from Osnabrück to the nearest part of the Russian frontier is more than one thousand kilometres. And at that point the machine still had enough fuel for a further ninety or a hundred!'

'It is not so much the damned machine,' the police commissioner objected. 'That is an academic question. It is the past. An aeroplane was here; it was destroyed. The question now is: what happened to the pilot? Did he perish with that machine, or did he somehow escape? If so, where is he and what is he doing? Why was he coming in the first place? And who was he?'

'It was a single-seater,' the *Kommandant* said. 'At least all the reports agree on that. So he was alone. It is clear, moreover, that he must have been flying to a predetermined plan, that he *intended* to penetrate the country as far – or further – than he did. This was no erring fool or overzealous scout. Particularly as the Sopwith appeared to be unarmed. No, he meant to come – and from wherever he came, whoever he was, he must have known he could never get back. What does that imply?' He looked at the *Oberst*.

'Bearing in mind that the machine bore no distinctive markings,' the aviation chief replied, 'a most ungentlemanly departure in my opinion, and remembering that the camouflage resembled our own, I would say that the purpose of the flight was indubitably clandestine. Clearly the man is – or was – some kind of spy. As my colleague points out' – he glanced at the policeman – 'the question is which. Is or was?'

'There was no body in the wreckage,' the *Hauptmann* said. 'Surely that implies that the man got away?'

'Could a man, even an uninjured one, have escaped such a blaze?' the *Kommandant* asked.

The civilian, who was an arson investigation inspector, nodded. 'It is not impossible,' he said. 'Unlikely but not impossible.'

'We are talking of the possibility of a *body* in the wreckage,' the *Kommandant* pursued. 'But there was no wreckage, not in the usual sense. Just a heap of ashes around an incinerated rotary engine. I have been to the site; I saw this myself. Wouldn't a body naturally have been consumed in such an inferno?'

This time the civilian shook his head. 'Not necessarily. Largely consumed, yes. The fire was extremely fierce . . . but it did not last long. Even if the corpse was destroyed as such, the flesh etcetera, there would be indications: bone perhaps identifiable as part of a skull, a watch case, the metal rims from a pair of goggles. Something that could positively be said *not* to be an aeroplane component.'

'And there was nothing?'

'Not a thing,' the policeman said. 'My men combed through the hot ash three times. Nothing.'

'Then we must assume,' the *Kommandant* said heavily, 'that we have an infiltrated spy in the area. A spy at large. Your dispositions, *Herr Inspektor*, must be based on that assumption.'

'The entire *Polizeikräfte*, every station, every substation, each individual agent in the region will be alerted,' the commissioner promised. 'There would be "Wanted" posters on each tenth telegraph pole – if we knew what the man looked like.'

'Exactly. If we knew. But we are only *assuming* he exists at all.'

'The population will also be warned. Every stranger, each man below a certain age, any person not known by sight must be reported. Clearly the intruder will be young: aviators are required, after all, to have a certain standard of fitness. And there are not too many able-bodied young in this region after almost three years of war.'

'Exactly,' the *Kommandant* said again. 'It must be remembered, however, that the *Englanders* are not altogether fools. They will not have gone to all this trouble without finding someone who has at least a chance of passing unnoticed. You will not, that is to say, be looking for a straw-hatted pipe-smoker carrying a cricket racket.'

The man from the Ministry of Defence smiled dutifully, and said: 'Most importantly, of course, it must be discovered *why* he is here. Militarily, this is not after all a "sensitive" area. But it is almost equally urgent to discover precisely *how* such a machine could penetrate this far, from that direction. The spy must be closely interrogated. If necessary with severity.'

'Naturally,' the police chief said. 'As soon as he is captured.'

8

Blake had watched the staff cars arrive at the castle, flat on his face in a grove of alders on the far side of the river.

Two open Mercedes 28/95 tourers led the parade, their sharp V radiators glinting in reflected sunlight as they rumbled across a stone bridge a little further downstream. The young officer lolling on the rear seat of the first was accompanied by only his driver and a steel-helmeted NCO holding a carbine upright between his knees. The second car flew from its offside front wing the pennant of 12 squadron. The *Oberst* ramrod-straight in this one had a four-man escort: one man beside the driver and two more perched on tip-up seats in the rear. The car was closely followed by a green police saloon.

It was five minutes before the last arrival appeared around a distant bend in the riverside lane: a huge black Maybach landaulette-limousine. The uniformed chauffeur behind the wheel in the open, doorless front wore polished leather buskins and a peaked cap. The single passenger in the closed rear section was a civilian.

Parting leaves, Blake noted the alacrity with which the black and gold iron gates of the castle were swung open, the crispness of the sentries' salutes as the big car swept through, and assumed the newcomer was someone of considerable importance. He had no way of knowing that the hastily called conference was in connection with his own appearance – or lack of it – in the area. But it seemed a fair guess anyway that it was an area to get out of quickly if top brass from the army, the air force and the police were meeting in what was clearly some kind of staff headquarters.

The river was not very wide here, the fast-flowing water dappled with sunlight filtering through the trees overhanging it on either side. But the castle itself, soaring above a double loop of steeply climbing drive, was iron-hard in the midday glare. Judging by the amount of military movement visible beneath its multiple turrets and pepper-pot spires, the garrison must be important. Through the arched entrance gateway he saw two squads of soldiers, and then a third, marched to roofless transport lorries. The throb of their engines carried clearly across the river. As the first truck emerged through the archway he pushed himself back from the alder clump and moved hastily further up the wooded slope of the valley.

Blake had covered twelve miles in a south-westerly direction in the two and a half hours immediately after his crash landing, mainly across fields and through sparsely forested uplands. Crouched low behind the uncut hedgerows, he had bypassed the few country folk he had seen working on the land. Only twice had he been obliged to make circuitous detours to avoid a village.

Reaching the valley, he had found an empty wood-cutter's cabin among the trees and remained there for the night. Now it was time to push on again.

Once you're in a town of any size, they had told him, come out into the open, have a meal, a drink in a bar; take a bus, a train. Your German's perfect, your cover good. But stay hidden in the country, keep off the roads, travel only at night if you can. It's there that a stranger will show up like a flashing lamp – and that's what they'll be on the lookout for.

The cover, he supposed, *was* pretty good – although he hadn't yet been called upon to test that. His stomach turned over at the thought.

He was dressed in genuine German clothes, garments that might have been worn by a minor official – a belted jacket in thick cloth, with breeches, heavy stockings and laced ankle boots. The labels in the outer garments were those of a Hamburg department store. He hadn't asked how the intelligence people had obtained them.

Because of his 'duelling' scar and his German accent, it had been thought better to give him a cover as a bourgeois rather than a worker. Beneath his tweed hat with its shallow brim, the moustache that masked the second scar was now bushy rather than clipped in the RFC fashion.

The genuine bullet wound, visible in his left ankle, which had left him with a genuine limp, sufficed as an explanation for why he wasn't in uniform. And if asked he could supply a perfectly truthful account of how he got it, for the army discharge papers with which he had been supplied were those of a soldier from a regiment in action during the first Battle of Mons.

He carried a small expandable briefcase containing documents and technical material establishing that he was one Gerhardt Ehrlich, representative of a Hamburg electrical firm, on a permitted promotional tour seeking orders from factories engaged in domestic production in central Germany. Factories whose own supplies might have been compromised by scarcities caused by increasing demands from the front.

The rucksack, the Very pistol and every non-German

item Blake had carried on his flight had been wrapped in his leather flying coat, weighted with stones and sunk in a pond in the middle of a dense wood.

He had about forty miles to cover before he reached Siegsdorf-am-Lippe. Detmold, Paderborn and Lippstadt were the only towns of any size on his route.

By far the most dangerous obstacle, however, was the miniature wireless transmitter with which he was to contact – and subsequently report to – his intelligence cut-out.

True, it was German-made, and bore on its underside a stamped intaglio serial number and the information that it had been manufactured in 1912 by Radifonik Schwerzel GmbH of Bielefeld. Certainly it fitted inside the briefcase without making it too bulky. But what was he doing with it? What did he use it for? How could he possibly explain it if he was searched or it was discovered in any other way? It could not in any way be said that it had a connection, however tenuous, with any of the equipment he was supposedly trying to sell to companies supplying installations to the domestic market, whether for the home or office.

The obvious answer would have been to find a hiding place for it, only removing the thing for the hour, early each evening, during which the cut-out would be listening in, waiting for his message.

This would have been fine if he had already arrived at Siegsdorf, or had any other static base, but was clearly a non-starter for anyone constantly on the move.

His first transmission, the important initial contact, was due that evening.

It was hard going at first, working his way upstream from the castle; the sides of the valley grew increasingly steep, the underbrush beneath the densely packed trees

increasingly thick. And there was the additional consideration, forcing his way between branches and briars, that
he must keep his clothes looking reasonably respectable
for when he did finally appear in public. This would be
at Detmold, five miles down the wooded slope of the
Teutoburger Wald, on the far side of the saddle at the
head of this damned valley. Before then, nevertheless,
the transmission must be made.

In fact he reached the saddle long before he expected.
This was because of an error in the generalized, small-
scale sketch map of the whole region supplied by the
intelligence briefers in London. He had thought the river
much less 'important' than its reputation warranted.
But it was only when he started to use the detailed,
large-scale German map that he considered it safe to
carry that he discovered the truth: this was not the
Weser at all, but a tributary west of it, running in
a parallel valley towards a confluence just south of
Hameln.

He was therefore one ridge of the Teutoburger Wald
nearer to Detmold than he had planned for. Unless he
wanted to spend another night in the open, he would
have to push on as fast as he could and send his message
from the town itself.

Ahead of schedule now, he quite enjoyed the rolling
alternations of forest and meadow which dropped
steeply down on the far side of the saddle. Detmold,
the capital of the Westphalian principality of Lippe,
lay sprawled across the lowest slope; it was a pleasant
market town grouped around a rectangular Renais-
sance castle.

Once on the outskirts, of course, he had for the first
time to use the roads, but traffic was light – farm carts piled
high with vegetables, horse-drawn drays, an occasional

bus, very few private cars. Nobody seemed to notice
the young man in the Norfolk-style suit with his neat
briefcase and heavy moustache.

The centre – narrow cobbled streets full of tall,
half-timbered houses with steep, dormered roofs – was
busier, as it was five o'clock. The railway station, he
thought, was the most believable place for a stranger to
appear. He loitered beneath a bridge until a train was
due, then left in the middle of a crowd of passengers
who had just arrived from Hanover. He went into a
Weinstübe across the street and ordered a glass of white
Franconian wine.

Not surprisingly, the gossip around the sawdust-
floored bar was largely concerned with the aeroplane
crash beyond the wooded heights the day before.

'It was between Barntrup and Bad Pyrmont – you
know: where there's a weir and that fortified mill built
across the stream.'

'Shot out of the sky by one of the aces from the
Boelke Jagdstaffel. Went up like a . . . well, like a house
on fire!'

'They say it was coming from the *north*! I must say
that's a bit . . .'

'Nonsense. It couldn't have been. I think . . .'

'Well it couldn't have got here from the *Western* Front,
that's for sure.'

'Just the same, it was an *Englander*. My nephew told
me he saw the . . .'

'There were no markings on the machine. That's
official. Frenzel was talking to the training squadron
observer who first saw it. It was definitely British
though.'

'I don't believe it. Not *here*. If you ask me, it was a
Tsarist aeroplane – a Russian spy, an anarchist.'

'*Russian?* You can't be serious! Do you know how far . . . ?'

'Fact. One of the firemen told me. It was the melted snow from their boots put out the flames.'

Laughter. And then: 'Good old Ernst! Trust him not to miss an opportunity.'

'You say *their* boots,' someone observed, 'but it was a single-seater, a scout.'

'That's what I mean: so what was it doing out here?'

'I don't believe it was a scout. It carried bombs. That's why it went up with such a bang. It was on the way . . .'

'Karl! Three more Steins, a Pils and a schnapps for doubting Thomas here!'

'. . . to one of the Krupp factories in Dortmund.'

'They'll never know. I suppose the pilot was killed in the crash.'

'That's a funny thing, my friend. An intern told me that no meat wagon went out from the hospital; nothing from the morgue. For me that means no body in the wreck.'

'Nobody could have got out of that. My God, I saw the flames across the fields. High as a church tower, they were. No, the poor devil must have been burned to a cinder, and that's the truth.'

'Even so, there'd be *something* they could scrape up and bury. There'd have to be.'

'Not at Verdun there wouldn't. Hilde's brother said the shell holes . . .'

'Anything can happen in this damned war.'

And suddenly everybody was talking at once. More drinks were ordered. Then a more authoritative voice called out: 'If the pilot didn't escape, why have the police been given special orders, top priority, to watch out for strangers? Why have a squadron of

Uhlans been sent down from Hameln to comb the woods?'

'Of course he escaped,' someone scoffed. 'Two school-girls from my village saw him. A huge bearded fellow. He chased them across a meadow.'

'With an axe?' This was Ernst, the joker. 'If the girls had been from *our* village, *they* would have been chasing *him*!'

Blake dutifully joined in the laughter this time. Thankfully, he was now well enough away from the immediate crash area. The gossip, as always, was too vague, contradictory and far from the truth to be disturbing. He paid for his drink and left the bar. It was time to find a quieter place – somewhere he could test the 'aptitude' of his Morse wrist for real.

The transmitter was halfway between an outsize desk stapler and a miniature, one-key typewriter. A single earphone, with no headband, was the only receiving unit. In a small velvet pouch in Blake's pocket were half a dozen crystals numbered from 1 to 6. Each crystal vibrated at a different frequency, and in case the German security forces somehow fixed on transmissions, he had been told to change crystals every transmission, starting with No. 1, working through to No. 6 and then using them again in reverse order.

The dry battery installed in the device would provide up to two hours' continuous transmission, rather more in the case of a series of short broadcasts, at a maximum range of twenty miles – although this tended to diminish as the power faded. Blake wondered what kind of person would be listening for him, and where. Why would they be doing it, and how would his reports be passed on?

If the cut-out was within twenty miles, why go to all

the trouble of sending a man from England? Why not have the man in place penetrate the factory at Siegsdorf and steal the plans?

Because he was too well known in the area and his presence would alert the authorities? Because for some reason he was physically incapable of moving around? Because he was psychologically unfitted for burglarious activity (a cold spasm chilled Blake's guts as the idea occurred to him)? Maybe the chap was just too old. Or was it that they felt it was a hundred per cent essential that the spy must himself be an aviator, someone who would understand the implications of blueprint designs, who could be trusted not to make off with the wrong bumf? On the whole that seemed the simplest – and the most likely – explanation.

Blake had found an ideal place to transmit: a disused timber yard surrounded by a high wooden fence, whose sagging gates had been left ajar. Stacks of rotting wood still lay piled beneath the corrugated-iron roof of a shed at the far end of the yard, and he settled himself down between two of these.

The air was spiced with the tang of ancient sawdust. Through a gap in the rear fence he could see evening sunlight gilding a row of semicircular pediments above the dormers of the Fürstliches Residenzschloss, the castle. Through a gateway below, there was a view of a courtyard with a corbelled gallery linking two of the corner towers. He took the machine from his briefcase. It took only a moment to set it up.

Suddenly everything was very real. He was a spy in an enemy country, preparing to steal military secrets. This was where the story proper began: he was about to contact another illegal, a clandestine agent in place. Everything he was doing, even the fact that he, an army officer and a pilot, was wearing civilian clothes, carried the death penalty if he was caught. Spies were executed if they were unmasked on the territory of all belligerents, including that of his own country.

Blake licked his lips. He was aware of the pounding of his heart, shaking the vulnerable ribcage. He was very much aware of the alien noises of the town too: a squeal of brakes, somebody cursing, the clip-clop of horses' hooves, the steady tramp of booted feet and guttural commands. Beyond the dilapidated fence a car or a lorry backfired, and a bird flapped heavily away from the girdered rafters supporting the iron roof over his head.

Breathing deeply, he started, cautiously at first and then with more confidence, to tap out the dots and dashes representing the four letters of the agreed call-sign.

They had decided on the word 'land' because it would announce his aerial arrival and at the same time meant something quite different in German. The cut-out would reply with 'cont', which would signify, first, that it was safe to continue, and secondly instruct Blake to proceed with his message.

He had Morsed the call-sign a dozen times at one-minute intervals according to plan, before there was a response in the small round earphone held to his left ear.

And then, scratchy, faint but unmistakable, came the dots and dashes spelling out the cut-out's reply. Pulse racing, Blake hammered out his first clandestine communication. He had been told never to transmit for more than two minutes; ninety seconds would be better, seventy perfect. For information had been obtained from the Flanders front that German counterintelligence experts had developed a system of triangulation which enabled them to home on transmissions very fast.

This, he realized, apart from the clarity of the dots and dashes, was why Hesketh and his superiors had been so impressed with the speed of his Morse transmission.

His message was brief: 'ARRIVED STOP PUP DESTROYED PILOT SAFE STOP DETMOLD.'

There was no need to sign off. He simply keyed the acronym OTY – over to you – given to him by his instructors.

His unknown correspondent shortened his replies even more by using truncated words in the manner of the cablese favoured by newspaper correspondents reporting from abroad. If the meaning was clear, why waste time and money spelling out a lot of unnecessary letters? The message Blake transcribed read: 'EXPCT YOU PADWARDS MORROW STOP THENDORF STOP TTT STOP PSE ACK.'

That was clear enough. They expected him to reach Paderborn the following day, and Siegsdorf the day after that. 'TTT' stood for 'this time tomorrow'.

He acknowledged as requested and confirmed that he would make his next report at the same hour by tapping out the single expression 'WILLDO'.

Concentrating on the correct reading of the incoming Morse, and the speed and accuracy of his own, Blake had forgotten his dry mouth and the thudding of his heart. But he was aware, dismantling the apparatus and packing the crystal away in its pouch, that he was sweating heavily.

The Bavarian fob watch supplied with his suit told him that the entire transmission had taken one minute and eight seconds.

He replaced the transmitter in his briefcase and left the yard on the far side from the entry gates, through the gap in the fence offering a view of the castle. Two uniformed policemen watched him sidle through on to the sidewalk beyond.

Blake stood stupidly staring at them with his mouth open and rivulets of sweat running into his eyes from beneath the headband of his hat. One of the policemen was tall, with a 'Kaiser Bill' moustache; the other was shorter, a plump man with a red face.

'What the devil do you think you're doing?' Redface demanded roughly. They wore holstered pistols clipped to their belts.

'I . . . I . . . I was . . .' The officers' green brimless headgear, he saw, was exactly the same shape as the hard hats worn by English postmen. What could a reasonably well-dressed man believably be doing in a disused timber yard at six o'clock on a weekday evening? Blake felt as if he was choking. 'I had to take a leak,' he said desperately. 'It . . . it was the only place I could find.'

'There are public conveniences at the station,' Moustache said severely. 'Most of the bars . . .'

'Yes, but it . . . it comes on me suddenly, you see. On account of my wound,' Blake explained with a flash of inspiration. 'I don't know the town and I had to find somewhere quickly. It was the only place I could . . .'

'Your papers,' Redface said. He held out his hand.

Blake produced them, along with his army discharge book. With luck, they might have noticed that he limped *before* he saw them.

'Where did you stop the enemy bullet?' Moustache demanded, flipping through pages.

'The left ankle. It was . . .'

'No, no. *Where?* Which *front*, God in Heaven?'

'Oh. Mons in '14. We were moving up to . . .'

'You must have been glad to get out of that, just the same,' Redface said.

'Afterwards, yes. At the time it was hell. They poured neat carbolic acid through the hole at the field dressing station.' Blake's shiver was only partly contrived, though the emotion producing it had nothing to do with the Western Front.

'Better here than there, eh? What have you got in that briefcase?'

He told them.

'Show me.' This time it was Moustache who held out his hand.

Blake started to remove promotional literature, documents, a prospectus, but the policeman took the briefcase from him. 'A salesman, eh? Got any orders yet?'

'A small one in Hanover.' He knew there was, among the papers, the carbon of an invoice confirming this.

'Rather you than me,' the policeman said. 'And what exactly is this?' He held up the chassis of the transmitter.

Breathing hard, Blake was ready for that. 'A new line,' he said. 'So new that it's not in the prospectus yet.'

'Yes, but what is it?'

'Instead of the telephone. You know how – excuse me – how the military monopolize the lines. You know how the lines available are jammed. Well, this is kind of a bypass for factory heads – not much more than a toy, really – but if they really need to contact a subcontractor, expedite an order or check on a delayed delivery, they can do so directly with this, without going through some damned operator. In their own code. It works by wireless, you see.'

'Sounds pretty far-fetched to me,' Moustache said. Privately Blake agreed. He hoped fervently that they wouldn't ask to see how it worked.

'More like something criminals would use to communicate secretly,' Redface said. 'Or spies.'

Moustache laughed. 'We're very careful not to sell them to any Russians,' Blake said as lightly as he could.

Both the policemen laughed. 'Where are you staying?' Moustache asked, handing back the briefcase, transmitter chassis and papers.

Blake swallowed. 'I . . . I haven't found a place yet. I only just arrived on the train from Hanover. I was on the lookout when . . . when I . . .' He gestured towards the fence surrounding the timber yard.

'There's the Fischerhaus,' Redface told him. 'That's where most of the commercial travellers stayed before the war. On the other side of the castle. Or the Badischer-Hof – if you like Bavarian food.'

'Thank you. I think I'll try the Fischerhaus,' Blake said.

'Which firms are you calling on here in Detmold?' Moustache asked.

'None, actually,' Blake said truthfully. 'The next ones on my list are in Paderborn and . . . and Siegsdorf-am-Lippe. I'm simply staying here because I arrived too late to go on further: the connections are not suitable.'

'But the train you were on, the Hanover train, continues to Paderborn.'

'*What!* Oh, that damned ticket clerk!' Choking back a spasm of nausea, Blake feigned indignation. 'I was in too much of a hurry to check myself . . . the idiot told me I'd have to change here and wait for over an hour . . .' He shook his head.

'That's the trouble in wartime,' Redface sympathized. 'All the efficient ones are fighting; all you get at home are the temporaries, the infirm and the dullards – amateurs seasoned with an occasional cripple . . . Oh. Excuse me, sir. No offence, I hope.'

Blake shook his head, managing to raise a smile. That stupidity about the train was the first serious mistake he had made. Check, check, check, they had urged him, before you give an explanation for anything. And he hadn't.

'There is just one thing, Herr Ehrlich,' Moustache said. 'If your . . . need . . . should take you again, be more careful where you go, eh? It may be disused, but there have been many thefts of wood from this yard. You could easily have been taken for a petty criminal.'

'Thank you, I'll remember that,' Blake said.

The policemen saluted and walked off. Blake headed for the castle and the hotel. It was only then that he realized that this – apart from the perfunctory ordering of one drink – had been the first time he had spoken German since his clandestine arrival. On the whole he thought it hadn't gone too badly. If only he hadn't allowed himself to be caught out on the question of those bloody train times . . .

The Fischerhaus was a pleasant enough hotel, a tall, narrow, five-storey building with half-timbering. Through the dormer window of his top-floor room, he could see the reddened western sky above steep slate roofs, hear the rattle of wheels on cobbles in the small square below, voices from a nearby bar and the strains of a brass band somewhere. The room had a boarded floor of scrubbed pine, a feather bed, one chair and a washstand with pitcher and basin. In the morning, he was sure, a maid would bring hot water in a copper jug.

Blake was exhausted. He was looking forward to an early night in a real bed for the first time since he had left England. His papers had, according to the regulations, been handed to the receptionist when he arrived. His luggage, he said, had been mislaid in Hanover. He was to retrieve it at the station the following morning.

It was after a dinner of rationed stewed pork with the inevitable potatoes, washed down with a litre of local beer, that he heard the familiar voice.

He was on the third landing, on the way up to his room; the voice came from the hallway below, beside the reception desk. Cautiously, he approached the wooden banister and leaned over. Yes, in the light of the oil lamp on the desk, a familiar green uniform.

'Frau Schipp, do you have a traveller from Hamburg staying with you? A certain Gerhardt Ehrlich, a man with a limp?' It was Moustache's voice.

'Why yes,' the elderly owner of the hotel replied. 'He arrived not long before dinner. Do you wish to see him?'

'No, that will not be necessary.'

Blake, whose hands had started to tremble, released the breath he had been holding.

'His papers, perhaps? They are here with the other . . .'

'No thank you, Frau Schipp. Merely a routine enquiry.' The policeman moved away from the circle of light. The front door closed.

Blake stole up the remaining flights of stairs to his room, nodding to himself. There was a lesson there for him.

Just checking.

Paderborn, according to Blake's pre-war Baedeker, had been an important stage on the ancient commercial and strategic Hanseatic route linking Flanders and Saxony. Well, that was fine by him: he was linking Flanders and Saxony himself – the war in the air in Flanders, his own aerial entry by way of Saxony. What interested him much more was the sight of a small aerodrome just east of the town. He saw hangars and dispersal huts as his train slowed to enter the station, then, through the opposite window after they had rumbled across an iron bridge, a field strewn with many different types of machine.

Glancing rapidly right and left, Blake identified Albatros scouts and two-seaters, a Pfalz D-III, several Fokker M-8s and a Halberstadt-LVG Type C-5. The machines were dispersed in no particular order, some of them with a stippled or lozenge camouflage, others painted in bands or zigzags of bright colour. The only sign of regimentation was a flight of three Fokker Eindekker monoplanes, warming up their engines in formation outside a hangar.

Before the train ran into a cutting between high brick walls, Blake glimpsed two civil aeroplanes: a Hansa–Brandenburg biplane lettered with the insignia of the Austrian postal service and a Luft–Reederei biplane with a curious five-seat cabin behind the pilot's open cockpit. Just beyond this, mechanics were wheeling out a very small scout with a rotary engine and *three* wings! Apart from the gleam of dope on fabric stretched over wings and fuselage, this machine was colourless and without insignia. Some kind of prototype perhaps?

Blake wondered if the field was being used by the Imperial German Air Service for the assembly of one of the new Jagdgeschwadern formations creating such havoc among British and French squadrons on the Western Front. These massed groups, composed of successful pilots from several different squadrons, had become known to the Allies as 'circuses' because of the vivid colours distinguishing their aeroplanes. They included such aces as Boelke, Immelmann, Ernst Udet and Werner Voss. The most successful, and the most feared, was the ex-Uhlan cavalry captain Rittmeister Manfred Freiherr von Richthofen, who started his deadly career flying Fokker biplanes and Albatros scouts.

Paderborn was no more than a stage on the route to Siegsdorf. Apart from the story he had fed to the police in Detmold, there was no reason for Blake to remain. Having seen the aerodrome and the variety of machines assembled there, however, he decided to backtrack if possible for a closer look. There might be information he could glean of use to his superiors; the Eindekkers he had seen might be equipped with the improved interrupter gear; it could be useful – possibly life-saving – to know something of the routine on the field in case he had an opportunity, or was forced, to steal a plane as a getaway ploy.

The unknown quantity in his personal equation was nevertheless the reaction of the Detmold policemen, if any, to his story.

On his way to the station that morning, he had bought a cheap suitcase at a secondhand shop and filled it with newspapers and magazines. Arriving without luggage at a hotel could be explained away once, but it would look odd if a sales rep were to leave town carrying nothing but a small briefcase!

His forethought was justified. He was ten minutes early for the train, sauntering towards the ticket barrier when he saw them. Redface and Moustache, standing idly by the door to a small kiosk where travellers could buy sausage, beer or acorn coffee – but in a perfect position to oversee everyone who came and went.

Fifteen yards from Blake, they nodded gravely and raised languid hands in salute.

Swallowing the lump in his throat, he nodded back and contrived a smile. He went through the barrier and crossed the bridge to the down platform.

Coincidence?

Were they there as part of the general alert he had heard about in the *Weinstübe*? A routine posting to keep their eyes open and check anyone they thought looked suspicious? In which case this was an advantage: they had checked him already.

Or had they decided – or been ordered – to confirm that Herr Gerhardt Ehrlich really was going to Paderborn? If so, would they have alerted colleagues to check that he did leave the train there?

There was no way of knowing, no way of telling whether or not they were there specifically for him, no chance of removing the chill which settled on his stomach the moment he saw them. He was just thankful he had thought of the suitcase.

There *were* police at Paderborn, of course, coldly eyeing everyone who passed. But again that could simply be evidence of an area alert. No direct connection with the pair at Detmold. Was it his imagination though, or did one of them murmur something and hurry to the stationmaster's office just after he passed?

He had, of course, no factories to visit. But he had a list. He thought it prudent to ask the way to one, and enquire about a hotel, in the hearing of the remaining officers.

There was a small hotel in the shadow of a massive tower pierced by many Romanesque bays which overlooked the thirteenth-century church. The restaurant was closed for the duration, but they did have a room. He booked in for one night. What the hell. It would support his story if by chance they were checking on him – and he would have more time to take that closer look at the aerodrome and the machines there. Siegsdorf would have to wait for one more day.

By the time he came out of the hotel, the sun, bright in the early morning, had retired behind a bank of cloud blowing up from the west and the huge tower no longer cast a shadow.

The company whose address he had been given was by the river, on the way out of town, but one of the others on his list was on the road to Bad Driburg and Brakel, and that he thought should pass fairly close to the aerodrome.

With his briefcase under one arm, he set out on foot in that direction. Even if he was being watched, there was after all no logical reason why he should necessarily go first to the address he had requested. *Was* he being watched? He was fairly certain that a man he had seen in the street just before he went into the hotel had still been there, across the road by the porch leading to the church, when he came out again. But there were a dozen valid reasons which could believably have explained that.

He steeled himself not to keep glancing behind as he left the town centre, but on the one occasion he did look – just before crossing the street – he experienced a thrill of alarm, thinking he saw the man threading his way through a queue of housewives with ration tickets, outside a bakery. On the other hand the follower's dress, if he was a follower, if it was the same man, resembled that of many other men in the street: a green loden jacket and paler breeches. And the bakery was at least a hundred yards away. By the time Blake had allowed a two-horse wagon piled high with hay to pass, and skipped aside to avoid being run down by a fat hausfrau on a bicycle, the possible tail was nowhere to be seen. Without increasing his pace, he continued on his way.

A.G. Wunschefabriek, according to the faded lettering on a signboard above the entrance to reception, were experts in sanitary engineering. The factory, a row of workshops with serrated glass roofs, stood on a slight rise about half a mile outside Paderborn. Below it, the white, dusty country road twisted away between fields of cabbage and ripe corn. Above the hiss of blowtorches and the hammering of metal, Blake could hear the distant roar of aero engines from the far side of a wood crowning the skyline to the north.

He looked back as he climbed the slope leading to the factory's reception. He saw a figure in the distance, apparently loitering by a farm gate, but it was too far away to make out the cut or colour of clothes. He opened the door and went inside.

An elderly woman with frizzy grey hair and spectacles sat behind a desk in a small, wood-panelled room crammed with teak filing cabinets and shelves loaded with tottering piles of documents. 'Who are you and what do want?' she snapped, glaring at him over the steel rims.

A little nervously, Blake brought out his cover speech.

No, the woman said, cutting him short, they had no need for – nor any interest in – the supplies offered by

77

an electrical manufacturer in Hamburg. They had quite enough trouble trying to make companies in the Ruhr honour their delivery dates.

She stopped him producing his promotional material and sales brochures and refused point-blank to call in a manager or even a foreman to see him.

Blake was thankful. He had been dreading the effect of his sales pitch, such as it was, on an expert. It was with a sense of enormous relief that he backed out and hurried away down the slope. At least, so far as his cover was concerned, he had gone through the motions. If he had been turned down without arousing suspicion, so much the better: in a sense it strengthened his story.

He stared back down the road. The farm gate was open. There was nobody in sight.

It was still early afternoon. Clearly the aerodrome was approaching peak activity. Above the trees, he saw a number of low-flying machines circling, rising and falling as the engines bellowed and the bracing wires sang. Halberstadt, Pfalz, Albatros, even an ancient Rumpler came and went in turn. Circuit and bumps for beginners, he thought, or perhaps in some cases experienced pilots familiarizing themselves with a new machine.

He turned again. The road remained empty. The factory still hissed and hammered.

The hell with it, he thought for the second time. It was surely reasonable enough that a sales rep, turned down and thus with time on his hands, should be interested in new-fangled flying machines in wartime. He strode off towards the wood.

A footpath led circuitously through the belt of trees. On the far side, crouched behind a screen of bushes, he looked down a long slope of meadowland, past the embankment and the railway line, to the hangars and the dispersed aeroplanes. The field was a hive of activity, with scouts and reconnaissance craft taking off and landing, it seemed, every few seconds.

Blake took notes in his own personal shorthand on the routine so far as he could make it out. He had been there perhaps fifteen minutes when there was a shattering roar and the three Fokker Eindekkers he had seen from the train began warming up in unison, surrounded by a group of mechanics and a single officer in uniform. Each of the monoplanes, he could see, was equipped with twin Spandau machine-guns, sited just behind the engine cowling.

Soon the Fokkers taxied to the middle of the field and took off, still in formation. When they had reached an altitude of perhaps a thousand feet, the two wingmen broke up the V and fell in behind the leader one after the other. They circled above an undulating stretch of moorland two or three miles to the far side of the aerodrome.

Then the leader banked steeply and dived to five hundred feet, flying in a much tighter circle above a pale scar visible between two swells of the dun moor. After four circuits he climbed again to fall in behind his two companions. The manoeuvre was followed by each of the other Fokkers in turn. After twenty minutes, the trio returned to the aerodrome.

The scar, Blake assumed, was the lip of a sandpit or disused quarry. There would presumably be a target, probably in the shape of a plane, pegged out on the floor of the pit. Certainly, from where he was, the stutter of the Spandaus was clearly audible above the roar of the machines' Oberursel rotary engines.

They were much too far away for a visual check, but he had had plenty of time to study them before they took off: there were no wing-mounted guns; *and the guns of the single-engined scouts were definitely firing forward through their propeller arcs.*

'Very interesting!' he said aloud. And suddenly his mission sprang into sharp focus in his mind, hardened into a vital imperative instead of a problem that had been almost academic.

Over the muddied desolation of the shell-torn Western Front, these machines – as the intelligence officers had told him – would be lethal for the Allied observation planes and their crews, and equally murderous opponents for escorting scouts with their antique, angled-off Vickers or wing-mounted Lewis guns.

The urgency of the task, the recognition that the responsibility of obtaining the plans of the Fokker interrupter gear was his and his alone, were all at once agonizingly acute. For the first time since he had left Gosport, self-preservation took second place to the dictates of duty.

He hurried back to his hotel.

The clouds which had been extending from the west now covered the whole sky with a lowering canopy, and before he was halfway to the outskirts of Paderborn flying from the aerodrome had stopped. A few minutes later it began to rain.

Blake's shoulders were dark with moisture and his breeches were clinging to his knees by the time he found a shop where he could buy a cheap raincoat.

There was a ruddy-faced man in pale breeches and a loden coat sheltering in the church porch opposite the hotel entrance. Blake walked straight past and found his way to the address he had asked for at the station. At this moment preservation of his cover was paramount.

The building was a converted water-mill. A huge vaned

wheel still turned slowly, channelling the swift-flowing current of a stream into the River Pader. A weathered board by the roadside bore the faded information, addressed to pre-war tourists, that this was the site of the Paderquellen – a collection of more than two hundred small springs which bubbled from the ground to form the stream powering the water-wheel.

Blake's list stated that the converted mill housed the shop-floor premises of Eberbach–Klammerhein GmbH, manufacturers of household equipment, mangles, kitchen utensils, etc. But it was evident at once that it was out of date. The windows of the two top floors were boarded up, a bare patch on the ivy-covered wall showed where a signboard had been removed, and a rusty chain barred the entrance to a loading bay. The only occupant now appeared to be a small watchmaker and repairer. Through a plate-glass window, Blake saw an old man with white hair and a leather apron peering through half-moon glasses at a table strewn with cogwheels, springs, pendulums and weights. The wall behind him was lined with empty clock cases in mahogany and bird's-eye maple. Clearly this was not an enterprise likely to be interested in the products of a Hamburg electrical supplier.

In any case there was nobody to notice whether or not he went in. He looked over his shoulder. A carter was whipping the horses of a brewer's dray across a bridge over the river. A Daimler-Benz saloon, probably a taxi, growled past in the other direction, spraying mud from the wet cobbles. No pedestrians were visible beneath the dripping trees that lined the street.

For the second time, Blake headed for the hotel.

The man in the loden coat was still there.

Blake bit his lip. Could this *still* be some kind of

81

coincidençe? Was it possible, for instance, that the fellow was indeed on the lookout, but not for him? Was he just a loiterer? Unemployed? In militaristic wartime Germany that was hardly likely. There was nothing he could do about it anyway. It was time now to signal his cut-out.

In view of the weather, he reckoned it would attract less attention if he dared to transmit from his hotel room. Heavy rain drumming on the roof above would mask the light, scarcely audible thump of the key every time he pressed it down, whereas if he set out in the downpour in an attempt to find a secluded spot, even if the man across the street was not a watcher . . .

He shrugged and went in, stamping his feet and shaking drops from his raincoat in the narrow hallway.

As soon as his call had been acknowledged and he had received the safe-to-continue acronym, he tapped out: 'DAYLATE SDORF DUE VALBLE AERO INFO PBORN STOP PSE ACK CONFIRM.'

There was a long wait before the reply came. He was distinctly uneasy by the time he heard: 'ACCEPTED BUT BASE INSISTS PPRS NEC URGENTEST STOP ACK.'

Was it because of the dangerous time-lag – he supposed the cut-out had contacted London or some superior nearer – or did he detect implied disapproval in the fact that he had been told curtly 'Acknowledge' instead of the customary 'Please acknowledge'?

That was something else he could do nothing about. It would be too complicated to explain that it was mainly to strengthen his cover that he decided to spend the day in Paderborn. He simply transmitted the word 'UNDERSTOOD', and signed off.

Before he left the hotel again to try and find something to eat, he stood inside the entrance door peering through the coloured-glass panels in its upper half. But water

streaming down the outside exaggerated the effect of
the frosted glass and he could see nothing clearly. He
opened the door and went out into the rain. The church
porch was deserted. There was no sign of the loden coat
left or right.

He found a small, down-at-heel café around the corner
where he could sit at a scrubbed table and order half a litre
of watery beer to wash down a meal of unrationed wurst
and dry bread. The place was poorly lit, rancid beneath
the layers of smoke with the odours of cheap tobacco
and acorn coffee. Three old women in black huddled
together in the far corner, screeching with occasional
laughter. All the other customers were elderly men, some
with crutches, one in a cast-off army uniform. Four of
them, conversing in low voices, were playing some kind
of game with cards.

The man in the loden coat sat at the next table to
Blake's.

He couldn't be certain that it was the man he had
seen outside the bakery or the person by the farm gate,
but it was certainly the one from the porch – a thickset
individual with heavy features and fleshy moist lips. As
Blake thumbed back the metal lid of his pottery beer
mug and raised it to his mouth, he saw that the man
was looking fixedly at him, raising his own tankard.
The man smiled.

What did this mean? Simply that the man was indeed
a watcher, that he was playing cat and mouse with Blake?
See, I have you where I want you: you cannot escape me?
Or was it that he simply happened to have noticed Blake
a couple of times that day and was doing no more than
acknowledging him? Perhaps he himself was a stranger
in town and recognized in Blake a fellow outcast.

Whatever he did, Blake couldn't ignore the approach:

the stare was too direct, the smile too personal. He nodded in a distant way, drank some beer and looked down at his plate as he ate some sausage.

The regard was unwavering. He couldn't just ignore it. The man was smiling more broadly than ever now. Blake was reminded of something he had read somewhere about the unwanted intimacy which developed between the torturer and the tortured, the executioner and his victim.

The stranger had pushed back his chair and risen to his feet. He was carrying his tankard across. He sat down at Blake's own table, next to him. 'Wicked weather if one is alone in town,' he said, the smile remaining in place.

Blake swallowed. 'Most unpleasant,' he said as coldly as he could.

'Especially for a young person. After all it is not as if there was anywhere stimulating to go – not in Paderborn anyway.'

Blake ate a mouthful of sausage. He drank more beer, making no reply.

'And in your case not even comrades in uniform to share a joke.' The man leaned closer, his beery breath warm against Blake's cheek. 'I couldn't help noticing, seeing you pass, that you walked with a slight limp.'

'I was invalided out,' Blake said shortly. 'The . . . Battle of Mons.'

'Ah. That was something for the brave ones.' The man pulled his chair even closer to Blake's. There was a slight dew of sweat on the flushed face. 'A shame that a young man – a good-looking, attractive young man such as yourself – should be deprived of the joys of youth, the companionship, the games, by an infirmity inflicted in the service of the Fatherland.'

A heavy hand descended on Blake's thigh, midway

between the knee and the hip. The moist lips were very close to his face. 'Perhaps sometimes an older man . . . someone aware of the infelicities, at times the callousness, of youth . . . can help to assuage the spiritual if not the physical wounds of war.' The fingers of the hand moved slightly higher, tightening on the resilient flesh.

Oh, *Christ!* Blake thought. Not this! This is one thing I could really do without . . .

Shoving back his chair violently, he left the remains of his meal, slapped money down on the bar and pushed his way blindly through the swing doors, out into the night.

The man had called something after him, but he was too angry to hear what it was. He ran through the heavy rain, footsteps splashing through puddles in the uneven flagstones, and burst into the hotel.

Snatching his key from the old woman behind the reception desk, he took the stairs two at a time, still panting with exasperation as he thrust the key into the lock.

The door of his room was unlocked.

Pushing it open, he stumbled across something on the floor, fumbling to find matches so that he could light the oil lamp on the bedside table.

As the light brightened and spread from the flaring wick, he saw that what he had stumbled across was his suitcase. The lid was open, and the newspapers and magazines he had stuffed inside to weight it were scattered across the floor.

For the first time in his life he experienced the sensation described as the blood running cold . . . He flung himself at the bed and hauled up the mattress.

The briefcase, containing the documents supporting his cover and the incriminating transmitter, had gone.

10

Once again there was a conference in the great hall at Hohenstein. For the second time, five men sat around the sixteenth-century refectory table. *General-Major* Rudolph von Sonderstern still sat in the throne-like chair at the head of the table.

But this time all of the participants wore uniform. Two Uhlan NCOs, with spiked helmets, thigh boots and drawn swords, guarded each pair of double entrance doors.

Oberst Klaus Frodenburg, commander of the local air defence squadron, was once more accompanied by the area police commissioner and *Hauptmann* Erich Schneider, the young foreign intelligence officer from the German secret service. The fifth man, however, rather than a ministry official, was a *Kriminalkommissar* – the equivalent of a CID Detective Inspector from Scotland Yard – brought in from Dortmund, the nearest big city.

He sat shuffling a sheaf of papers, some typed, some handwritten, others printed forms which had been filled in here and there with ticks or crosses.

'The investigations requested, *Herr General-Major*,' he said to Von Sonderstern, 'have duly been made. The Hamburg company cited did indeed have on their books as a war veteran sales representative a certain Gerhardt Ehrlich, but' – he picked up one of the forms – 'the man was killed in a car accident.' He glanced at the form again. 'In the spring of 1915. In Bremen.'

'So. We know then that the man here is an impostor.'

'Exactly. The difficulty, *Herr General-Major*, is that . . .'

'What we do not know,' the *Oberst* cut in, 'is whether this impostor is in fact some kind of domestic criminal or whether he is connected with the *Britischer* aeroplane crash.'

'Surely that is unlikely?' the *Hauptmann* said. 'At least insofar as the identity of the pilot is concerned. One would not normally fly a machine all this distance dressed as a minor sales representative!'

'Young man,' Sonderstern said acidly, 'the *Englander* secret service is not staffed by complete fools. If they are infiltrating a spy into the Fatherland, they will hardly have him running around wearing a leather helmet and goggles! If this impostor is indeed the escaped pilot, I have no doubt that everything he wears will have been fabricated in the German fashion, with suitable labels.'

'Unless of course there are two of them,' the local police chief said.

'The machine was definitely a single-seater, a scout,' the *Oberst* told him. 'There is no question of that. Five of my pilots individually confirm it.'

'No, I mean the pilot and a second man *already* here, an agent in place. This is always possible, distasteful though it may seem. In which case the bogus Ehrlich would most certainly, as the *Herr General* says, be . . . equipped . . . as a German. Even if he is not anything as unthinkable as an actual countryman, a traitor.'

'The man we are investigating is almost sure to be an

Englander – or an individual from the so-called United Kingdom,' the *Kriminalkommissar* said.

'You are sure of this?' Sonderstern asked.

'Practically certain, *Herr General-Major*.'

'How so?'

'Through a remarkably perspicacious piece of observation on the part of an officer working for my colleague here.' The detective nodded graciously in the direction of the local man. 'I have questioned this officer personally, and it seems that two of his companions in Detmold had already become suspicious after a routine identity check following the area alert.'

'Indeed? Why was this, if his cover was as good as we have been told?'

'There was an error in one of the documents he produced. An army pay book, I believe. In one place where our German text required a ß, a double S had been used. This led the officers to believe not only that the document might be a forgery but also that it could well have been fabricated by a non-German.'

'Very astute. And then?'

'Rather than arrest the man at once, the two operatives decided to keep a covert watch on him. Having spent the night in Detmold, the stranger took a train to Paderborn, and the policemen requested their colleagues there to continue the surveillance.'

'Why not arrest him at once?'

'They felt it might be more useful, if he was indeed an impostor, to find out why he was there and what he was doing first.'

'Very well. And so?'

'They decided that overt surveillance might provoke a more rapid result, perhaps frightening the suspect into making an error. And this proved to be the case. One of the Paderborn agents assumed the identity of a degenerate, one of those pests who hangs around public places and follows personable young men in the hope of . . . striking up an acquaintance. Apparently in an attempt to avoid such unwelcome attention, the suspect hastily crossed a crowded street.'

'That seems prudent enough,' the *Hauptmann* commented.

Sonderstern simply said: 'Well?'

The *Kriminalkommissar* paused for effect, and then continued: 'Before venturing into the stream of traffic, the man looked first to the right and then to the left.'

The information was greeted with a puzzled silence.

The police commissioner sighed. 'Because traffic is obliged by law to keep to the right-hand side of the road,' he explained, 'pedestrians here naturally look to their *left* before crossing a street, because it is from that direction that the nearest vehicles approach. Afterwards they look in the other direction. But a person looking *first* to the right is automatically expecting traffic from that direction – that is to say traffic keeping to the left-hand side of the road.'

Another pause.

'There is one place where that is the rule,' he continued impressively, 'and one only: England and the adjoining territories.'

Sonderstern cleared his throat. 'Excellent. Admirable reasoning. The officer is to be commended. So our man is an *Englander*, and very probably the pilot of the crashed aeroplane. Why was he not immediately arrested and interrogated?'

'Because, *Herr General-Major*, the officer did not at first make the connection. The suspect made several calls which corresponded with his assumed identity.

89

It was only after it began to rain and he repeated the manoeuvre that the officer realized the significance of what he had seen. Accordingly he followed the suspect into a café and engaged him in conversation so that colleagues could search his room in a nearby hotel.'

'What was the result of the search?'

'The suitcase supposedly containing what travellers would normally carry – clothes, additional shirts, nightwear, shoes – was stuffed with newspapers.'

'Well, that certainly proved that he could not have come from far afield, and definitely not from Hamburg!' the *Hauptmann* said.

'That in fact he was from the immediate area, perhaps no further than the field where the foreign aeroplane crash-landed?' the police commissioner added drily.

'The searcher also found a short-range wireless receiver equipped with a key which could be used to transmit Morse signals. Unfortunately he was disturbed before he could look further, because the suspect returned earlier than expected.'

'Followed, I trust, by the disguised police officer?' Sonderstern said.

'Yes, sir, indeed.' The *Kriminalkommissar* coughed. 'Alas, he was a shade too late to make an arrest: the suspect had already escaped through the window of his room.'

11

The window was a dormer, projecting from the steepest of grey, wet, slate roofs. There was a hint of the massive church tower off to the left, and between a chaos of chimneys and shining slopes a gleam of cobbles beneath the diffuse street lighting five storeys below.

Blake leaned out over the broad sill, his heart thumping wildly. From the foot of the stairwell, he had heard the harsh tones of the man in the loden coat, unmistakable now as a peremptory, hectoring voice of authority, demanding which room the receptionist had allotted the stranger. Heavy footsteps already pounded the ancient stairs.

For the first time since he had set foot on German soil, the lethal progression – arrest, imprisonment, trial, firing squad – assembled itself in his mind. What had been almost a game, a jape, a story to tell later in the mess, was now suddenly a terrifying reality. He scrambled on to the edge of the sill.

He was unarmed; the policeman would certainly have a gun. There was no chance of forcing an escape within the hotel. This was his only opportunity.

Below the sill was a short slant of tiling, then the gutter, and six feet under that a string-course – a narrow brick ledge running along the vertical face of the building. Panting, he turned, grasped the sill and began to lower himself face down across the tiled slope.

Escape now was his only priority, survival the sole target. If this was the route and there were no alternatives, he was taking the route whatever the obstacles. Blind determination, fuelled by a kind of savage, obsessive anger, obscured every other emotion, leaving no place for fright; even the fear of death was momentarily submerged.

His feet touched the gutter. He lay at the full stretch of his arms.

This was the critical moment: it was only by clinging to the gutter and lowering himself down the wall below that he could hope to wedge his toes on to the string-course beneath.

Was the gutter strong enough to hold his weight?

He shifted his body experimentally on the wet slate, loading it first on one foot, then the other. Through the lit window above, he heard the locked door of his room burst open. A familiar voice cursed in German.

Between the sole and the upper of one boot, cold rainwater soaked Blake's sock. The gutter seemed firm enough: water gurgled past his feet towards a downpipe ten yards away. He tested it one final time, allowing all his weight to pivot around one leg. He felt no evident slackening, no give in the solidity of the metal channel. Very well. This was it. He relinquished his grasp of the sill so that his body could slide.

Above his head, the shaft of light glinting through a curtain of bright rain dimmed. A man's head and beefy shoulders were blocking out half the dormer. 'Don't be a damned fool, man,' he cried. 'You'll fall to a bloody death!'

The rain drummed on Blake's sodden coat, needling

his scalp with icy points. Hunched at the foot of the slope, he clenched fingers and thumbs over the curved rim of the guttering. Water swirled around his knuckles.

'Come back; I'll lend you a hand,' the policeman shouted. 'You're twenty metres above a row of spiked railings there. You can't possibly . . .'

The rest of the sentence was drowned in a sudden, more forceful squall of rain and the slither of Blake's body scraping past the lip of the gutter.

There was an agonizing wrench at his shoulder muscles as his outstretched arms and clamped hands supported his entire weight, and then his feet found the string-course.

On tiptoe, he could still just hold on to the gutter. Very slowly, hand after hand, he began inching crabwise towards the downpipe.

The ledge was no more than three inches wide. With nothing but that strip of weathered stone beneath his toes and the cold, wet metal of the gutter above, the ten yards of that traverse was a perilous journey. He was excruciatingly conscious of the void yawning below him, the possibility of rotted stonework above and ahead. Even if the guttering held, could the iron staples cementing it into the wall pull free? Would his weight, even supported from above, risk crumbling the fragile ledge? A rising wind plucked at his clammy trousers; rain plastered his hair to his skull.

Worse was to come when he arrived at the downpipe. The policeman would have run from the hotel, rounding up reinforcements to surround the block. Blake had hoped to shin down the pipe and somehow make his getaway at street level before the cordon was in place. But if the gutter held, the pipe it supplied would not. The metal was corroded, and as he reached out thankfully to grasp the curved tube, two of his fingers sank through the rusty, paper-thin surface.

Panic suddenly seized him. There were no more dormers above the guttering. Beyond the rotted pipe, the gutter itself was discontinued. The wall of the building turned in at a right angle to circumvent the three sides of a narrow rectangular air shaft. Beyond this the steep roof, with three more dormers, continued.

Blake swallowed. Sweat mingled with the rain to run into his eyes.

He peered around the corner. The string-course continued around the air shaft and beneath the next row of dormers. But there was nothing above it except a blank face of vertical brickwork; the adjoining building was one storey higher than the hotel.

Blake's knees were trembling. Could a man edge around that narrow ledge changing direction four times, and reach that immeasurably distant line of windows? He quailed at the thought. It was impossible, it was insane, it was too dangerous even to consider.

But what were the options? He choked back a cry as he supplied himself with the answer. None.

As they used to say at school, it was do or die; in this case probably both.

He remembered the tough Scottish officer who had given him the three-day crash course in breaking and entering. There had been a special lecture on the subject of ledges.

'Oh, aye, ye could come across one,' the Scot had said. 'Sometimes the only way in, forbye. In theory there's no' a problem. A strip of stone four, three, even two inches wide should be wide enough for a man to walk along. But when that ledge projects from a sheer wall, there ye have trouble.'

There had been diagrams on a blackboard at this point, Blake recalled. 'In such a case,' the officer had continued, 'the bulk of the body becomes critical. For if the centre of gravity moves too far away from the median line of yer ledge, that body will overbalance and fall. To succeed, a man must either face the wall and move on the balls of his feet, with his heels stickin' out in space; or rest on those heels with his back to the wall.

'In which case,' the Scot said genially, with his moustached smile, 'he is shit-scared of his exposed position and will probably suffer from vertigo.'

Blake chose to face inwards. Without the gutter to support him, he was only able to remain balanced on the string-course because he was thin enough not to have much body overhang – and because he had run from his room without the voluminous raincoat he had bought that afternoon. He didn't even remember taking a conscious decision to continue: the Scottish officer had carried him around the downpipe and the right angle beyond it. Now, with arms flung wide and his lean, wet body pressed to the streaming brickwork, he inched forward, thrusting upwards and inwards with the tortured muscles of his toes and calves. With his cheek against the wall, he concentrated his gaze ferociously on the inner part of the shaft, just discernible in reflected light from somewhere below. He knew that if he looked down he was doomed.

There were two more downpipes at the far end. Without them, Blake would have been lost: he could never have transferred himself, twice, across ninety degrees of nothing without the slightest projection to grab hold of.

As it was, the fifteen feet to the first pipe were hell. Perhaps because death had never seemed nearer, he was reminded acutely of the first few seconds after the death of the Pup. Once again sounds became exceptionally important. He lived with the scrape of his soles along stone, the rasp of his jacket on brickwork, a rattle of wheels on far-off cobbles.

When at last he fell forward to grasp the first pipe, he clung to the smooth, cold casting with a sob of relief.

It was then that luck turned suddenly his way.

Dreading the next two deadly traverses, he discovered with a flood of joy that was almost indecent that they were not going to be necessary. The corroded hotel downpipe was for rainwater only; this one, linked at each floor to feeder pipes, clearly carried away waste from kitchens or washrooms. And it was solid, rock-hard and yielded nothing when he tapped it.

Blake wrapped his arms around it like a lover.

Normally, the idea of lowering himself five floors down a slippery drainpipe, lashed by driving rain and in flight from the police would have filled him with horror. After the torture of the string-course, it was almost a joyride.

Fortunately the soles of his boots were inset with cleats of composition rubber. With these clamped to the curved surface of the shiny, nine-inch pipe, he was able to halt or at least minimize the slide each time his hands slipped on the wet metal.

Cautiously, like a slow-motion frog in reverse, be began his descent.

There was no immediate danger of his falling. The pipe was ridged with iron junctions every ten or twelve feet where the outflows from each floor slanted into it, and at each of these he could wedge a foot into the angle and rest. Physically, therefore, the drain on him was relatively light. He divided the descent into five stages, at each of which he could momentarily take the weight off his hands and feet and relieve the strain on the muscles of arms, wrists and calves. Mentally, however, the problems remained, and were in fact intensified because physically he was less traumatized.

He had no idea what he would find at the foot of the shaft. He didn't know whether or not he could get out easily. He knew the man in the loden coat would have alerted colleagues, but he didn't know how far they would have got or whether the block would already be cordoned. Most importantly, he hadn't the least notion of where he could go or what he could do if he did escape the police net. The closer he got to the ground, the more these problems seemed insurmountable.

The wind plucking at his drenched clothes slackened, the rain fell less heavily. He had arrived – he could see now, glancing warily over his shoulder – in the shelter of a high wall blocking off the small yard at the foot of the shaft.

His feet rested on hard ground.

Blake was panting hoarsely. His arms shuddered. He was trembling behind the knees and one calf had locked into a painful cramp. His chest heaved as he sucked in lungfuls of air like a drowning man. Over the distant sounds of traffic he heard a tramp of heavy feet, a shouted command.

Panic again.

He stamped the cramp from his leg and ran for the wall. There was a door but it was locked. At one side of this was a row of dustbins. He clambered on to the top of the nearest and pulled himself up to the top of the wall. As he levered himself away from the bin, the lid rolled off with a deafening clang and slid noisily away across the wet yard.

Someone, somewhere threw up a window and shouted angrily. But Blake was already on the far side of the wall and running.

And now, suddenly, after the agonizing slow motion of his escape from the hotel, life moved into top gear; he seemed to himself to be moving with the accelerated jerkiness of a figure in a cinematograph film.

There was a service lane on the far side of the wall, running right and left. He turned right because as far as he could tell the sounds of pursuit had come more from the left. The lane was rough, cobbled and pitted with holes awash with rainwater. Light from a gas lamp eighty yards away, where it ran into a side-street, illuminated the shafts of rain bouncing off the polished stones and pock-marking the yellowed surface of the puddles.

Blake splashed to the far end of the lane. The street was narrow, twisting away in either direction between tall gabled houses. He turned right . . . and froze.

A block away, uniformed figures in capes and hard hats had appeared beneath another lamp where streets met. Naturally. The police were circling the block in two different directions.

Blake heard a shout, then another.

The whole group sprang into motion again, ducking out of the pool of light and clattering towards him in a single, menacing mass.

For the third time the voice bellowed, and he thought he heard the phrase 'or we shoot'.

He whirled to his left and raced away.

The street curved left and then right. Judging by the yellow light reflected up on to the low clouds, it was heading in a circuitous way for the centre of the town. Blake was out of sight of the pursuers now, but the pounding of their feet from around the last corner was terrifyingly close.

He hared between shuttered houses for the bright lights of a square a hundred yards ahead.

The square was busy. It was not yet ten o'clock in the evening. As he ran nearer he saw trams, a couple of horse-drawn cabs and a crowd of pedestrians around the brightly lit entrance to a *Weinstübe*. A convoy of canvas-topped military motor lorries was leaving the far side of the square.

In the centre of the wide space there was a triangle of wet grass surrounding a deserted bandstand. Iron railings, of which only the bases cemented into the ground remained, had been cut down to go to the smelters and aid the war effort. Blake dodged behind a Benz touring car and crossed the grassy strip.

The pavements beyond were more crowded. As he registered the sounds of pursuit erupting from the side-street, he threaded his way through a queue outside a grocer's and stepped into a dark alleyway.

Ten yards inside this, the open door of a small restaurant splashed a band of light across the alley. Just inside the door an earthenware tube acted as an umbrella stand. On an impulse, he reached inside and snatched one of the wet umbrellas. This was in fact the smartest thing he had done since he left the hotel. He was still panting but his mind, sharpened by danger, was ice cold. What were they looking for? Somebody running, someone running away. A hatless fugitive with no raincoat, a man already noticeable on a night like this.

So give them what they were not expecting.

He put up the umbrella, a large, black affair, and emerged from the alley to saunter slowly *towards* the square and the pursuit. He held the umbrella low, slanted to conceal his head and upper half. He joined the end of the grocery queue, where he was immediately joined by two housewives complaining about the rise in prices.

His back was turned, but he heard the voice – presumably that of an officer – roughly questioning passers-by. 'A man, bareheaded . . . probably wet through . . . from that direction, running hard . . .'

And amid a babble of voices, conflicting, doubting, assured, the confident assertion: 'Yes, yes. I saw him. That way: down the alley and past the restaurant . . .'

The police posse vanished into the alleyway.

After a few minutes, Blake mimed a man exasperated by an interminable wait and left the queue. Consciously mastering his genuine, frenzied impatience, he walked slowly to the far side of the square, turned into the street taken by the army convoy . . . and then hurried away as fast as he could.

At eleven o'clock he was crouched, on the inner side, at the foot of a wooden fence around a goods yard west of the station.

There was a loaded train fifty yards away, the locomotive panting wisps of steam into the rain while the engineer and fireman manhandled the trunk of a hose feeding water into the saddle tanks.

It was not until midnight that a green light glowed beside the signal-box and the train pulled slowly out of the yard and puffed away down the track in the direction of Siegsdorf, Lippstadt and Dortmund.

But by this time Blake, oblivious of the downpour thundering on the tarpaulin which concealed him, was deep in an exhausted sleep on a pile of sacking in one of the wagons halfway between the locomotive and the brake van.

12

Six trucks – flatbeds loaded with what looked like crated machinery – were attached to the freight train at Lippstadt, and two closed vans later at Siegsdorf. Blake, surrounded by what felt like sacks of potatoes or turnips, remained beneath his tarpaulin.

He had decided to make no attempt to disembark before the train arrived at Dortmund. This in any case was the destination of the truck he was in, according to the waybill pasted to the exterior. But he was convinced, first, that a city goods yard would be easier to escape from than a siding in a small town, and secondly that it would be more prudent, for the moment at any rate, to stay well clear of Siegsdorf.

Clearly, the police now knew that there was something bogus about Herr Ehrlich of Hamburg; possibly they even suspected that he might be the foreign pilot of the crashed aeroplane. There was no way Blake could know. Equally there was no way *they* could know why this suspect stranger was in the area or where he was heading. So the less he was associated with his target town the better. To approach Siegsdorf from Dortmund, in the west, would therefore give him a better chance of remaining undetected than if he arrived from Paderborn in the east, where there was already a hue and cry.

That was fine in theory. It was easy enough blithely to think of an 'approach'. But the practical details were for him quite terrifying. He still had the Ehrlich identity papers and army pay book, but unless they were used in a region where he was not known as a wanted man, they could be more of a liability than an asset. He still had money. The street plan of Siegsdorf and such information about the factory as he had been given were sewn inside his jacket. But the jacket itself was now filthy, soaked through and torn in two places. His boots were badly scuffed. He was unshaven and the palms of his hands were grazed where they had too fiercely gripped the downpipe during his escape from the man in the loden coat.

He looked in fact thoroughly disreputable, the kind of tramp unthinkable in a regimented wartime Germany. He was hungry, he had a blinding headache, and he was sure that he was getting a cold.

Worst of all, with the loss of his Morse transmitter he was now totally alone, cut off from his contact, with no means whatever of communicating his plight to cut-out or base.

It was a problem the initial stages of which he had hoped to deal with while it was still dark. But the shunting at Lippstadt took an age; there were several halts to allow what were presumably troop trains to pass; and they waited over half an hour outside a signal-box a few miles outside Dortmund. Shivering below the steady thrum of rain on his tarpaulin, Blake ground his teeth in fury as he listened to the ribald pleasantries exchanged between the engine driver, his mate and the signalman. The quiet panting of the locomotive, shining in the red glow of the signal lamp, served only to fuel his impatience each time he lifted a corner of the heavy cover.

Although the rain had by then ceased, daylight was already assembling the grey rectangles of warehouses, the long lines of shunted trucks in the yard, by the time the clatter of buffers ceased and the train finally stopped in the city.

Ten, twelve tracks away, between the lines, lorries were backing up to another train. He heard men shouting.

Blake lifted the edge of the tarpaulin higher.

Twelve tracks? Ten? With all those lines of wagons and trucks in between?

He squeezed out under the stiff sheet and dropped to the ground. Overhead, the clouds were racing. A long way ahead two figures in blue overalls – the driver and his fireman? – trudged towards a roundhouse bristling with locomotives and steam.

Doubled up, he ran the other way, stumbling among cinders. The sleepers were never the right distance apart for running.

Rounding a corner behind a pair of hydraulic buffers, he climbed to the open platform of an empty brake van. He saw a wooden hut, an oil lamp that still burned behind a window, smoke curling from beneath the conical top of a metal flue. Beyond the cabin was a wall of dark planking, a stockade, with a telegraph pole and an attached street lamp on the far side.

Blake jumped down from the van, ran past the hut and pulled himself to the top of the wall, wincing as the coarse wood bit into his damaged hands.

A door thumped open. A man shouted. Blake dropped down to a grassy bank, crossed a narrow street and started to run again.

He was in a mean neighbourhood of grimy, two-storey houses. Horse droppings littered the street. Smoke blew from only a few of the chimneys outlined against the hurrying clouds.

Over the rooftops, though, black smoke belched from a brickwork kiln visible in the distance. Blake followed a group of elderly men on bicycles pedalling slowly towards the factory. Two hundred yards further on he found a barber's shop on the corner of an alleyway. He went in and asked for a shave.

The barber, a white-haired man of about sixty with a wooden leg, settled a white sheet around his shoulders and neck. 'Just signed on at the factory, have you?' he asked, stropping an open razor as he nodded towards the smoking chimney.

Blake had allowed his cancelled army pay book to be seen as he stripped off his wet jacket. He shook his head. 'No, I was hoping to find something in Lippstadt. Not always easy, though, with this.' He patted his lame leg.

'I know what you mean,' the barber said sympathetically. 'If my old man hadn't had this business . . .' He sighed, stirring up a lather. 'The Western Front – the leg, I mean?'

Blake nodded. 'Mons. Thank God, though: it saved me from Ypres and Verdun!' He tilted back his head as the razor began to scrape.

'You want to go further than Lippstadt, just the same, if you're looking for light work,' the barber said. 'Try Siegsdorf, a few miles further on. There's an engineering company there makes spare parts for aeroplanes.' He chuckled. 'Machine-guns for the Freiherr von Richthofen to shoot down the *Englander* swine, eh?' He wiped lather from the blade. 'Good God! What happened to your hands?'

'Motor accident,' Blake said curtly. 'On the road from Essen. I was bumming a lift from an empty troop carrier and this fool of a carter . . .' He shook his head again. 'Scraped my hands getting out of the wreck, but I lost my stuff. Had to walk fifteen kilometres through the damned rain.'

'Tough,' the barber said. 'I'll put a touch of disinfectant on that for you. But you want to get out of those wet clothes. You'll catch your death. There's a secondhand shop nearby if you have the necessary.'

'Thanks,' Blake said. 'And thanks for the tip about Siegsdorf. I'll try there.'

As he limped away from the alley, the factory hooter was blaring its call to duty over the rooftops. Seconds later, further to the north, it was followed by another, shriller, more insistent. Even on the fringes of the Ruhr, Blake thought, the Kaiser's war machine was running in top gear.

The secondhand clothes shop was a godsend. The owner, a bespectacled woman wearing a flowered overall and a turban, was rolling rails of coats and suits out on to the pavement as he arrived.

Blake went straight inside. The facial blemish that resembled a duelling scar was useful as an apparent Teutonic badge, but damning as part of a wanted man's description. The less he was seen on the street the better – especially choosing a change of clothes.

In the gloomy recesses of the shop he found a table piled high with odds and ends of army uniform. He chose a high-necked tunic with the insignia and badges of rank removed, and a greatcoat of the type issued to private soldiers. Nearer the door were piles of rough cotton shirts and workmen's baggy corduroys. Blake slung the grey-green coat over his shoulders and had the rest of his purchases parcelled up in brown paper. Then he set off in search of a cheap shoe shop.

By nine o'clock he had bought thick-soled brogues, found a public baths and wash-house, and transformed himself into an out-of-work ex-soldier looking for an easy job. A worn, slightly greasy forage cap, found doubled up in the greatcoat pocket, completed the picture.

Gerhardt Ehrlich's sodden suit, boots and underclothes, packaged now in the brown paper, were discarded among dustbins in a lane behind the baths. Blake's ID, army pay book and the papers recovered from the torn lining of the Norfolk jacket were buttoned into a pocket of the private's tunic.

He walked to the railway station near the city centre and joined a queue in the booking office.

For him, this was the moment of maximum danger. Had he reasoned correctly, travelling beyond Siegsdorf and then doubling back?

There were, of course, police outside the doors leading to the platforms. But there probably were at every station in Germany. And not just because of a minor manhunt east of the Ruhr.

There was nothing for it but to go through, hoping for the best.

He was standing in front of the ticket window.

'*Eine Tagesrückfahrkarte nach Detmold, bitte,*' he told the woman clerk. A day return, he thought, might just direct their attention away from Siegsdorf if any questions *were* asked later.

The woman was piling small change on top of the pasteboard ticket.

'*Wann fahrt der Zug ab?*'

'*Halb zehn.*' It leaves at nine-thirty, she told him.

'*Von welchem Bahnsteig . . . ?*'

Platform three, she interrupted, already raising an enquiring eyebrow at the passenger waiting behind him.

Blake nodded, scooping up ticket and change. There was nothing for it, he thought again. He would have to walk past those policemen and push through the doors. Dry-mouthed, he walked.

The officers – there were three of them – scarcely glanced at him as he trudged lamely past. He crossed a footbridge to platform three and waited behind a pillar, his heart thudding painfully, until the train came in.

Perhaps fortunately, all the carriages were crowded.

Laden housewives who had been to the market, soldiers on leave, workers in overalls. Blake was ready to jump down from the footboard as the train steamed into the station at Siegsdorf.

There were police there too, but their attention was concentrated on a local arriving from Paderborn; passengers from Dortmund were waved straight through.

So far, so good, Blake thought. It was encouraging to note that his reasoning, at any rate in the short term, had been without fault.

A man in uniform was barring his way.

Momentarily, he felt the blood drain to his feet. He was unable to draw in breath.

'This ticket is a return to Detmold,' the collector said accusingly. 'That's another three stations.'

'I . . . I know,' Blake said huskily, feeling relief flood through him. 'I changed my mind, that's all. Someone . . . a man I met on the train told me I'd have a better chance of a job here.'

'A fat chance, if you ask me.' The ticket collector was dismissive. 'You won't get a refund, you know. And you can't continue later on the unused portion. No breaking the journey on a day return.'

'Yes, yes. I know. Thank you. I . . . it doesn't matter,' Blake stammered as the ticket was torn across and he was handed the return half.

The official grunted. 'People who throw away their money,' he said angrily to a colleague standing beside him.

Thankfully, Blake made his escape. Just so long as he didn't throw away his life, he thought.

The factory – a two-storey administration block and four separate workshops with serrated roofs and a lot of glass – glittered and sparkled against a background of dense woods in the sunshine which had dispersed the clouds at midday. There was no landing field attached to it, but a new Fokker Eindekker E-III still without a squadron identification stood on a motor trailer just inside the entrance gates.

Blake felt his heart beat faster. At last his goal, the physical reality surrounding the abstract paperwork he had come to steal, lay before his eyes. Finally he could begin to work out the steps he must take to overcome the ultimate obstacle barring the successful end to his mission – or examine the alternatives to those particular steps if his first plans proved unworkable.

He had wondered idly, walking the two miles from Siegsdorf, whether he might not pursue genuinely the course he had trailed as part of his cover on the way there: walk boldly right into the factory and ask for work. Even if the answer was no, he would at least get a glimpse of the interior layout.

But a single glance at the site, once he had breasted the last rise and seen the place close to, slid that one straight into the tray marked 'unworkable'.

There was a military presence, for a start. He could see armed soldiers inside the tall iron gates, a sentry box and what looked like a guardhouse. More men, walking in pairs, patrolled between the single-storey workshops, and once he thought he saw dogs.

There seemed to be no other entrance breaking the close-linked wire fence which surrounded the factory. Perhaps Mynheer Fokker's aeroplane interrupter gear was not the only military secret being developed below those flashing roof slopes of glass?

One thing, he felt, was certain. An installation requiring this amount of protection would not be left unguarded at night.

Between fields of root crops and ripening corn, he pushed on towards the wood behind the factory. The road led eventually to a village signposted as Salzkotten. He looked only once up the slope that led to the gates as he passed. He could have been a war invalid returning home, any kind of poorly paid worker. None of the soldiers paid him any attention.

Once he was out of sight, he doubled back through the wood to reconnoitre the site from behind.

From this point of view it was slightly less formidable. It was more obviously a factory, less like a military installation. No patrols were visible and shop-floor noises competed with the birdsong and creak of wind-tossed branches above his head. From the nearest building he could hear hammering, the chunter of belted machinery, a sudden screech as metal bit metal on a lathe.

Trees grew to within ten feet of the wire fence, and a ragged carpet of underbrush encroached further still.

Perhaps the military presence was routine, almost perfunctory, rather than a security imperative? If the factory was engaged in the very topmost of top-secret work, surely the ground would have been totally cleared for at least fifty or even a hundred yards all around the site, and not just in front? It was dangerous, nevertheless, to draw conclusions that happened to suit you from data that was incomplete.

Blake climbed up into the branches of a sycamore tree to watch and wait.

The information he had been given on the factory was, or at any rate seemed to be, fairly complete. He knew that the workshop where Fokker's gear was produced was the third of the four strung out behind the gates. Among the papers buttoned into his pocket was a floor plan of the building with benches and assembly lines clearly marked.

A smaller sheet – of rice-paper which could be chewed up and swallowed in an emergency – sketched the interiors of a foreman's office and design bureau at one end of the shop-floor. Here, the position of filing cabinets, draughtsmen's equipment, worksheets and drawers of planning diagrams, so far as was known, was indicated. He wondered how those who had prepared his papers *had* known. Surely, with information as detailed as this, they must have had some kind of inside access?

And if this was so, why fly out an amateur all the way from England, with all the attendant risks – to the mission as well as the amateur? Why not simply instruct the inside contact, the man already there, to grab the material required and send – or bring – it home?

It was a question he had posed before. And the only answer he could think of was a chilling one. Because if the inside man did that he would be exposed as an Allied agent, and it was more important to the people in London to keep him there incognito than to risk this one particular mission.

Whereas the amateur, if he was caught, was . . . well, expendable?

Better, Blake thought, to stop hypothesizing and get on with the job.

How, first, to penetrate the site?

It would, of course, have to be after dark, when the workforce was absent. The fence was about seven feet high. Even if it was not electrified, it could virtually be ruled out as a crossing point, particularly if the place was guarded at night, and especially if there were dogs. The trees, then, seemed the best bet.

Several of them spread low branches towards the fence; there were one or two places where an agile man – if he could find a branch that would hold his weight – might swing out and drop down on the inner side of the wire. This, on the other hand, would leave him in the same position in relation to guards and/or dogs as if he had found some way to climb over. He would have a better chance if he could somehow reach the two-storey admin block, and from there approach across the roofs.

From his perch in the sycamore, Blake allowed his eyes to rove the perimeter.

The block was just that – an industrial module, rectangular in plan, with a flat roof, two double-square and two treble-square façades. A narrow gap, spanned at ground-floor level by a covered passageway, separated it from the nearest workshop. And, yes, so far as he could see, there were at least two possible trees that might provide a jumping-off base.

From Blake's vantage point, the block was about a third of the way around the perimeter. He dropped from his branch and hurried through the undergrowth to a spot opposite the rear wall of the building. From here he was still out of sight so far as the guards on the gate were concerned, but he could see the gravelled turning area where the trailer with the Eindekker was parked.

The trunk of the first tree grew within twelve feet of the fence, with a complex of trailing branches sweeping towards the site. But the far ends of these, drooping close to the wire, offered no chance of a leap or climb to the roof of the block, even if they would bear his weight. In addition to this, the tree was some kind of pine, with a scaly bark that oozed resin – not the most suitable material to smear over the hands and clothes of a man whose life depended on undetectability.

The second tree was set much further back. But this one was a sturdy oak, taller than most of the others on the fringe of the wood, with heavy branches

111

jutting horizontally towards the site from quite high up.

Blake eyed it speculatively. From the topmost of these, was it conceivable that a man could leap to the roof of the block?

Absolutely not. Not even the finest athlete. On the other hand . . .

He stared. If a length of rope was looped from that branch, perhaps seven or eight feet of it, and a man swung out and over on the end of that, could he . . . ?

No again, so far as the roof was concerned. But he could drop right beside the wall of the building, as far as possible from the fence, without the need to cross that potentially dangerous strip of open land in between.

And from there, via two rows of arched window embrasures, it would surely be possible to climb to the roof? Blake thought it would. Whether it would be better to use the techniques of breaking and entering that he had been taught from there, or through one of those windows, was a question he would consider later, once he had worked out the logistics of the rope and the tree. For the moment it would be enough to shin up there and test the branch.

The branch was solid. But if he was going to get enough momentum to swing himself as far as the block wall, he would need more like ten feet of rope. More difficult still, if he was to work up enough back-swing on the pendulum, in the right direction, he would have to remove one of the lower branches on the tree. And that meant a sizeable saw, for the branch was more than six inches thick at the base.

Two soldiers emerged from the alley between the admin block and the first workshop. Once behind the block, they leaned against the wall to light cigarettes, shielding match flames against the wind with cupped hands. Were they in fact a nonchalant patrol? Or two men dodging out of sight for an instant to enjoy a forbidden smoke?

Shrinking back among the foliage above, Blake realized he would have to keep watch for much longer if he was to find out exactly how the factory was guarded and how often the surrounding territory was liable to be watched.

Somewhere inside one of the workshops a bell shrilled insistently. The rumble and clatter of machinery dwindled and then died away. Suddenly the late afternoon air was alive with voices. Three motor buses ground up the slope and parked beside the trailer. The day's work was evidently over.

Overalled women and elderly men in dungarees streamed out through pass doors in the tall wooden blinds closing off the loading bay in each factory block. They filed past the gap between these and the admin block and headed for the parking area.

Blake was about to climb down from his tree and take a closer look at the installation's security routine when movement around the buses froze him astride the branch.

The home-going workers were approaching . . . but as many more, mainly men this time, were crowding out of the vehicles and hurrying towards the workshops.

Blake bit his lip. Inwardly he cursed. How stupid! Of course he should have thought of this himself. In a militaristic country with insatiable battle demands for men and machines, they were not going to halt production just because darkness fell. Especially when the machines that could fly were knocking enemies out of the sky almost as fast as they could take off. The English catch-phrase 'Don't you know there's a war on?' came to his mind.

Clearly the Siegsdorf assembly lines were working round the clock, in eight- or twelve-hour shifts.

He had thought, naively, that once he had eluded any guards posted at night he could safely take his time, working inside throughout the hours of darkness until he had located the information he needed and if possible discovered completed parts of the new Fokker design. But if the factory was working full blast all night the task was going to be twice, three times, ten times more hazardous. If it was going to be possible at all.

The engines of the buses coughed into life and they rattled away towards the gates. The incoming shift, after a certain amount of ribaldry and badinage with the men and women they were relieving, had been swallowed up within the workshops. The bell was shrilling again. Soon the machinery was tapping and thumping as before. Two soldiers with rifles slung over their shoulders circled behind the buildings, glancing cursorily right and left as they walked.

There was a sick feeling in Blake's stomach. How could he be expected to find and then steal papers from a place that was guarded outside and staffed inside night and day? Why hadn't the people in London warned him? Why had they not arranged a personal contact with his cut-out, so that he could at least seek help or advice or even discuss the damned problems?

His earlier thoughts about his expendability returned, and gnawed away at his resolve. He became sorry for himself, and then furiously angry. It wasn't fair. He was a scout pilot and not a professional bloody burglar! Why should he be plunged against his will into this ridiculous, *dangerous* situation, stuck with this lethal operation which had become impossible through the incompetence of those sitting safely in London, sipping whisky and soda before they were chauffeured home to their soft beds?

Then the sense of outrage swung the pendulum of his emotions the other way. Damn them all! Very well, he would show them. They couldn't push him around all over the shop and then wash their hands of him just like that. He would get their damned plans by hook or by crook and throw them in the face of . . . well, someone with red tabs and a lot of rank!

If he was to have any chance at all, he reflected when his rage had cooled a little, the attempt would have to be made at night just the same. At least darkness would allow him, with luck, to approach the outside of the buildings unseen. The strip of ground between the fence and the factory would no longer be a danger. And, for reasons of safety and silence, he would still use the rope. Two questions, however, were vital. How often did the two-man patrol, with or without torches, circle the perimeter during the hours of darkness? And was there at any time during the night the equivalent of an English tea-break for the German workforce? If there was, that had to be the time during which he launched himself across the wire. Because it seemed to him that only if workers were eddying around away from their machines would he have a reasonable chance of getting inside the block where the Fokker gear was made.

Both questions, of course, demanded that he remain on watch until the next change of shift. Blake prepared for an uncomfortable night.

It could have been worse. He wedged himself into a fairly comfortable fork lower down the oak, with enough support at the sides to stop him falling out of the tree if he fell asleep momentarily. Discomfort in any case was not the major problem. Along with an aching

115

hunger, drowsiness was, for this was his second night without sleep.

There was no moon. Visually, there was practically nothing to attract the attention: light escaping through the slanted glass roofs of the factory cast a dim yellowish glow on low clouds scudding overhead. Only an occasional hum of conversation from the guardhouse punctuated the monotone of distant machinery, the soothing night sounds of creaking branches and the rustle of leaves.

Twice it was only a sudden freshening of the cool wind that jerked him awake as the darkness intruded and he slid into nothing. Once, as he was overwhelmed, his head snapped back to hit a sharp projection on the trunk and he felt a warm trickle of blood on his neck. The fight to keep awake was hell.

By the time the yellow glow faded against brightness spreading from the east, Blake was in possession, nevertheless, of four essential items of information.

The interval between successive passages of the patrol was on average half an hour, occasionally more, never less.

The soldiers patrolling did carry torches, sweeping them outside and inside as they marched.

The factory worked twelve-hour shifts.

There *was* a thirty-minute break – between eleven forty-five and a quarter past midnight – during which the machines were stopped and the workers flooded into the open air to smoke a cigarette, or filed into what he assumed was a canteen on the ground floor of the admin block. This might or might not coincide, he gathered, with the interval between patrols. On this particular night there was an overlap of ten minutes: the patrol passed at five past midnight. Something he could work out in advance if he took up his position early on the night he made his attempt.

It was during the change of shifts early in the morning that he climbed stiffly out of his tree, threaded his way through the wood and limped back along the road, past the workers milling around the buses, towards Siegsdorf.

It was a difficult day. Aching in every limb, Blake crammed black bread and acorn coffee into his belly at a workers' café near the railway station. He dare not order anything more substantial because he was running out of small coins and the high-denomination banknotes which could have passed without comment in the hands of Gerhardt Ehrlich would instantly arouse suspicion proffered by an out-of-work ex-soldier.

He had the same problem buying the saw he needed. The shopkeeper at once asked the direct question. Eyeing Blake, unshaven, unkempt, dressed in the clothes of a down-and-out, he demanded: 'What do *you* want with a thing like that?' as soon as Blake indicated the tool he had chosen.

'Some woman outside town offered me half a day's work cutting up logs,' he stammered. 'Her own saw's useless, rusted practically through. She gave me this with orders to buy her a new one.' He offered the man the single note he had got ready for just such a situation.

Before he reached for the saw, the shopkeeper examined the note carefully.

'And I'm to ask for a receipt,' Blake added. 'The old bitch is afraid I'll buy a cheap tool, say it was expensive and pocket the change.'

'I don't blame her,' the shopkeeper said. He counted change on to his counter and scrawled figures on a slip of paper.

'Nobody trusts anybody these days,' Blake said bitterly.

'With reason. Who is this lady anyway?'

'Frau Schneider,' Blake improvised. 'On the Belecke road.'

'Never heard of her.'

'That doesn't mean she won't need logs when it turns cold again,' Blake snapped. He snatched the saw and walked out of the shop.

His skin was crawling with fatigue, but he had to try half a dozen small shops before he could find a length of rope that was small enough not to be conspicuous but strong enough to bear his weight.

Before he left England he had been given a small bunch of flat skeleton keys, which he carried next to his skin, attached to a cord around his waist. But he still required several small household utensils which could be put to use in burglary if necessary. This again meant an odyssey involving several different shops in different parts of the town.

He was virtually at the end of his tether by the time he bought a loaf of bread and trudged away from the shops. The rope was coiled around his waist beneath the army tunic, the small tools lay inside the pockets of the greatcoat, the saw was wrapped in a piece of sacking he had found in a side-street.

So far – an extra toll on his dwindling reserves of energy – he had managed to dodge away or change direction each time he saw a policeman in the distance. But anyone who stopped him now, looking the way he did, and found what he was carrying, would have taken him instantly for a thief.

He was forced to drag himself more than a mile out into the country before he found a suitably deserted field which had already been harvested. Scrambling through a hedge, he hurried to the furthest haystack, dropped thankfully to the ground . . . and was asleep almost before his back had touched the straw.

13

Just before night fell the wind freshened again, flattening the stalks of ripening corn, roaring like distant surf through the upper branches of the trees in the wood.

The clouds, escaping into the higher reaches of the sky, moved more slowly from west to east. Blake wondered how long it was since they had crossed the English coast.

He had raised one arm to shield his face from the punishing gusts as he climbed the rise before the factory site, hoping that the suspiciously bulky bundle of sacking under his right arm would not draw the attention of the guards on the gate. The Eindekker and its trailer had gone, he noticed – presumably now equipped with the latest modification of the Fokker interrupter gear. The buses bringing the night shift should in any case be arriving at any minute.

He was almost level with the first line of trees when he heard the grinding of gears from the hill behind him. The soldiers had been too busy opening the gates to bother with the tramp on his way to the next village. By the time the factory bell signalled the stoppage, he was out of sight, pushing through the bushes towards the oak.

He would make fast the top end of the rope now, he had decided, but not allow the rest to drop until after dark. The tree was moving uneasily in the wind, the lower branches threshing as he climbed. Moving out as far as he dared beneath the tossing leaves, he uncoiled the rope from around his waist and knotted one end firmly. Then, edging back along the swaying branch, he looped the rest loosely around the gnarled wood. It was time now for one of the most delicate parts of the operation.

Extraneous noises, he had reasoned, would be more noticeable after dark; the best time at least to start sawing would be during the change-over, while the guards were occupied with the departing shift and the engines of the buses were running. There wasn't much time left, he saw: the day workers were already boarding. The moment the bell shrilled for the newcomers, he would begin.

The lower branch was crooked, with many leafy offshoots. It was going to make the devil of a noise when finally it fell, crashing through twenty feet of healthy wood. The treetop agitation caused by the wind would help to mask this, of course. But the wind would also carry the sounds of sawing, one of the most easily identifiable of all noises, more clearly to the workshops. Positioning himself carefully with his legs wrapped around a neighbouring branch, he stroked the curve of rough bark experimentally with the shining teeth of the new saw.

A pale drift of sawdust fell, and then was whisked away by the wind. The teeth bit into the bark with a satisfying ease. But once the harder wood was reached, he had to use a great deal more force and the familiar alto rasp shivered out from beneath the trees. When the buses had gone, he would have to limit himself almost to a single stroke at a time. And this would make for trouble when he was halfway through and the edges of the cut wood tended to close in over the blade. Without the impetus of continuous, forceful strokes, Blake knew, sawing through to a point where the branch was ready to fall was going to be a long job.

What the hell: he had until eleven forty-five!

The buses drove away, the sound of their exhausts swallowed in the continuous rumble of factory machinery as they coasted down the far side of the hill. Slowly, the light faded. Two soldiers circled the site, stopping behind the admin block to light cigarettes.

Beneath the restless treetops, Blake sweated, pushing his saw hard in and down, waiting until the next gust blew, withdrawing with as much force as he could muster, pushing again. After ten minutes of these single strokes, the cut was less than an inch deep. Grunting with impatience, he varied the rhythm and changed to an in-and-out pattern: one-and-two . . . pause . . . one-and-two. A quarter of an hour later, he was forced to move to the other side of the trunk and shift the saw to his left hand. His grasp on the wooden grip was rubbing the grazed palm raw. The branch was penetrated to a depth of two and a half inches.

Light splashed into the gathering dusk through the glass roof of each workshop. Another patrol passed. Thankfully there were no dogs. Through slatted shutters on the ground floor, Blake could see that the canteen was illuminated. The arched windows on the upper floor remained dark.

When the branch was sawn halfway through, he rested, panting after the combined tensions of force and restraint. The palms of both hands ached abominably.

It was completely dark now. He was marooned in a world of wind, relying only on his sense of touch to keep him from overbalancing as he thrust and pulled. All around him invisible branches creaked and swung.

121

Shafts of brilliance lanced the blackness as a patrol passed, probing the strip between fence and factory.

The work became harder with every stroke now that most of the blade was submerged in the cut. When his fingers told him that he was three-quarters of the way through, Blake rested again.

The wind, which had blown less fiercely for some time, now redoubled its force, savaging the trees in the wood with an express-train roar. Abruptly, Blake found that his saw was moving in a widening gap. The weight of twigs and foliage at the outer end of the branch, blown this way and that by each blustering gust, was wagging the whole unit up and down.

With a sudden splintering crash, the branch broke free, ripping away to leave a long scar marking the trunk. To Blake, frozen halfway up the oak, the noise as it plunged to the ground, tearing off leaves and smaller branches with it, was louder than an artillery barrage.

One of the workshop pass doors was flung open, casting a band of light across the strip. A man stood silhouetted in the gap. 'What the devil was that?' he called. There was shouting too from the direction of the guardhouse. The torches appeared, bobbing through the dark. Cowering behind the trunk of the tree, Blake stared down at the tell-tale gash, bone-white in the gloom, where the branch had torn away. In daylight it would be obvious that it had been sawn half through; at night, with foliage tossing all around it, there was a chance the clue might be missed. Clinging to the trunk, he held his breath.

The beams swung to and fro as the soldiers advanced. Reflected light gleamed from the barrels of the revolvers they held.

One of the beams halted; the other swung across, converging on the foot of the oak. The soldiers approached the fence, playing the beams up, down, left and right. 'It's all right,' one of them yelled over the uproar in the wood. 'Just the damned wind! Bloody great branch has torn away from one of the trees.'

The soldiers returned to the guardhouse. The workshop door closed. Darkness flooded the site once more. Blake breathed again.

He climbed back up to what he thought of as his own branch. Feeling for the looped rope, he unwound the whole length and allowed it to drop from the outer extremity, where he had firmly knotted one end earlier.

Thinking of his damaged palms, he had tied double knots at eighteen-inch intervals all the way down before he left the hayfield. With these to help his descent, he hoped to avoid – or at least minimize – rope burns when he let himself down to swing out over the fence.

It would be as well just the same, he thought, face down along the branch, to test it now, before the action started. He lowered himself until his feet could grip one of the knots. Then, with great care, he transferred his hands – and his weight – from the branch to the rope.

It wasn't too difficult with the help of the knots. Certainly the grazed palms still gave him hell, but soon he was clinging to the lower end a few feet above the top of the fence. Just to check that the plan was feasible, he started to shift his weight, swinging the rope backwards and forwards, confirming that the lost branch would allow him enough back-swing to work up the proper momentum.

Yes, up and over, back among the roaring branches, forward again with the dull gleam of the wire beneath his feet. A long way off, he could hear an aero engine in the night sky. Some lucky pilot – perhaps from the field at Paderborn? – learning to fly at night.

It could have been nothing but the thought of flight, the concept of being alone, in control of his own destiny, safe in a machine above the world – but suddenly, agonizingly, Blake was seized by a terrible panic. The sound of machinery was all at once unbearably loud. Nausea clawed at his stomach. His legs and arms trembled and an icy chill gripped his back.

He wasn't at the controls of an aeroplane, where he belonged. He was swinging at the end of a rope far behind the lines in enemy territory, preparing to plunge himself into an adventure as mad as it was dangerous. The mission was no longer academic, a chess game in his head. Those were real soldiers on the other side of the wire fence, real enemies with real guns; men who would shoot to kill if they even saw him. The whole thing was impossible, a joke. He must climb back at once to the safety of his branch.

He saw again the scout car turn over, the burst of flame. Saw his friend run past to save the burning driver, saw the landscape stilled as he felt the searing heat and stopped dead . . .

He didn't climb back up the rope. He let go and dropped ten feet to the ground.

Shuddering in every limb, he stumbled to his feet and turned his back to run. He ran blindly away, away from the factory, blindly through the howling trees.

14

'We lost twenty-three machines yesterday in the Somme sector alone,' the major-general said accusingly. 'Hang it all, when's your fellow going to come up with results?'

'Very soon, sir . . . we hope,' the brigadier told him.

'What do you mean, you hope? How's it going? What's his latest report?'

The brigadier cleared his throat. 'Well, sir, the fact is . . . actually we have lost touch with him.'

'Good God! What the devil happened?'

'He crash-landed his machine near the Weser valley,' the brigadier said. 'Got out from the wreck undamaged, and signalled our contact in Germany that evening as instructed. The next signal, the following day, reported that he had moved south-west. Place called Paderborn. Told the contact that he was going to spend the night there and move on to Siegsdorf the next morning. Said, apparently, that he'd come across something important that could affect the mission.'

'And?'

'I'm afraid that's the last we heard of him. Never signalled the next day. Or yesterday. Either he's been taken or forced to abandon his transmitter.'

'Good grief, man! You must replace him at once, then.'

'Think of the time that would take, sir. The contact

reports that there's reason to believe he did get to Siegsdorf. We decided to wait one more day.'

The officers were sitting on either side of a desk in a staff office on the first floor of a government annexe opposite Mudie's bookshop in Oxford Street. An RAOC corporal sat taking notes beneath a large-scale map of Germany hanging on one wall.

'And you really think the chap's worth waiting for?' the major-general demanded. 'Competent and trustworthy enough to allow him that margin?'

'To be honest,' the brigadier confessed, 'I thought meself that the young blighter was a bit on the arty-crafty side. More of a civvy really. But my adjutant – Hesketh, you know – Hesketh has a great deal of faith in him. Spent half a bloody afternoon telling me why he was the only man for the job.'

'H'm. Yes, well . . .' The senior man pushed back his swivel chair, rose to his feet and walked to the window.

There was a traffic jam on the corner below. Two hundred yards away a huge slant of rubble blocked the street where a Zeppelin bomb had destroyed half a department store. Two horse-drawn omnibuses going in different directions were locked together wheel to wheel, and a scarlet Royal Mail van, running up on to the pavement in an attempt to bypass the block, had crashed into a pillar box. A ragged urchin carrying a pile of newspapers dropped from the step of one bus and dodged, whistling, between the wheels to cross the street. He ran into an alley between two houses with boarded-up windows and vanished – for ever.

Standing with his back to the room and his hands clasped behind him, the major-general sighed.

Had the arty-crafty young man with the title Patrice

Blake disappeared as finally – and as completely – as the boy with the newspapers? Or were there more leaves inside that particular book yet to be filled before the covers were closed?

It is not wars and deaths and diseases and natural catastrophes that age and sadden us, the major-general reflected, but the way people on omnibuses look and feel, and run into alleys between bomb-damaged houses.

Then he thought of all the young men, perhaps just as arty and crafty as this beggar Blake, who would fall screaming from the sky tomorrow or die above the earth with bullets in their backs, and he shook his head.

Abruptly he swung around to face into the room. 'Very well,' he said to the brigadier. 'Twenty-four hours.'

15

Shame was not the emotion uppermost in Blake's mind: it was the only emotion there.

He had awoken at dawn lying beneath the familiar haystack, with no recollection of his flight beyond that initial panic-stricken dash away from the factory and out of the wood. He must have run blindly past the gates and on down the road to the harvested field, allowing his subconscious to convey him to the one safe haven he had found in this hostile country.

Waking up was itself a nightmare. Awareness at first filtered slowly through the clouds of a half-remembered dream, registered an agreeable sensation of exhaustion relieved, coupled with a stiff neck and a pain in his back, and then confirmed to him his own identity. He opened his eyes, to see beads of dew glistening on the rough cloth of his greatcoat and brightness in the sky above white mist blanketing the far side of the field.

It was the realization that the palms of his hands hurt that jolted him into the horror of his situation. Oh, Jesus. He had failed, let the side down, betrayed the trust placed in him. He had quit under fire – not even under fire – funking it at the last moment when everything was in place and ready to go. As the Yanks said, he had chickened out. Now, with agonizing clarity, he saw again the wire fence, the knotted rope and the soldiers' torches. He heard the insistent hum of machinery and the shrilling bell.

Never send to know for whom the bell tolls; it tolls for thee.

It tolled for cowardice, desertion and dereliction of duty; it tolled for the loss of self-respect and the compulsion to run.

Blake was overwhelmed by guilt and the dreadful knowledge that he could neither control nor master his abject, craven fear. The knowledge hit him with the impact of a blow to the stomach.

He turned over and vomited into the straw.

Before nine o'clock that morning Blake was back in Siegsdorf. He had stumbled through more fields, passed village women washing sheets on flat stones by a stream, held his breath as a squadron of cavalry – Uhlans with tall boots and spiked helmets – cantered across the country road. Now he was approaching the central square along the town's main street.

Between the burgomaster's office, the town hall and the railway station, there was a covered market with a few stalls of fruit and vegetables visible through the stone arches. Queues had already formed outside the shops that were open and there was a crowd milling around the entrance to a food office where ration tickets were issued. Blake skirted a shuttered hotel and paused outside a cheap restaurant in a row of crooked, gabled, half-timbered houses.

His mind was ablaze with a single thought: his honour, his faith in himself must be avenged, restored.

He must return to the factory and do it again – right this time. Whatever the cost.

Exhaustion, provoked by lack of sleep, hunger, stress

and the insidious effect of the head cold that was now, undeniably, taking hold of him had produced the aberration responsible for his weakness. Without these defects, he rationalized, the operation would have gone ahead as planned.

A second attempt would be – must be – successful. Certainly there was danger; it was normal to be afraid. Admittedly, there was a cowardly streak in him – lack of moral fibre, the army disdainfully called it – but such things, for God's sake, could be overcome.

Had he been in good form, the failure, the inexcusable would never have happened. To regain that form, he must eat properly, rest, and convince himself that the blackout was a bad dream.

The first step, then, had been the determination to return to Siegsdorf. Shame anyway rendered the neighbourhood of the factory insupportable. If there were police checks while he was in town, the hell with it – he would brazen them out.

The bravado was, of course, superficial, a psychological ploy enabling him to live with himself and his humiliation. It was hunger as much as anything else that drove him back. But it served to carry him through the first agonizing hours of self-hate and defeat.

He stood outside the restaurant, eyeing the police picketing the station a hundred yards away. He couldn't see inside: the morning was chilly and the windows were steamed up. He had small change now, so he would go in anyway, whether the place was deserted or full. He was moving towards the door when his eye was caught by a series of marks on the steamy window.

A passing child on the way to school, he supposed, had scrawled capital letters in the condensation, the way some people drew pictures, funny faces. He read 'DNAL' . . . and a little below, 'TNOC'.

He shrugged. The letters meant nothing, conveyed nothing to him . . . until he realized that the condensation was on the inside of the heated room, not outside in the cold. So they had been written from the inside . . .

Astonishingly a small circular space was rubbed clear on the far side of the window, and in it there appeared what seemed to be a hand with a beckoning finger.

And written from the inside, the letters would spell out 'LAND' and 'CONT'. His Morse call-sign and the cut-out's response.

He stood there dumbfounded. Those two groups of letters had been scrawled to convey a message outside the restaurant. But could it possibly, conceivably be meant for him? *Was* it an incredible coincidence? Or had the cut-out another agent in the area, with identical call-signs?

The pulses in Blake's wrists were hammering. His breath caught in his throat. There was only one way to find out. He glanced again at that ghostly, beckoning finger. Movingly slightly, it was still crooked.

He swallowed, turned to his right, walked five paces. He climbed three steps and pushed open the restaurant door. A bell clanged overhead. He strode inside.

The place was overcrowded, overheated, humid. He smelled sausage meat, sauerkraut, the acrid odour of bad coffee. There were five small tables ranged beneath the window. Advancing, he looked for the circular space in the condensation.

It was beside, and slightly behind, the middle table. There were two chairs, but only one was occupied.

He paused fractionally in mid-stride, and then continued at the same pace. There must be some mistake: the customer at the table was a young woman.

He looked beyond. Not possible either. The stout, middle-aged German sitting there beneath a pig's-bristle haircut was wearing thick woollen gloves as he gulped steaming coffee from a bowl. Even without the gloves, he was too far forward to have traced the letters or rubbed the steamy window clear.

Blake bit his lip. Was it possible that those same letters had quite a different meaning, by coincidence a risqué meaning to Germans on the home front? Was there a chance that the young woman was in fact a prostitute seeking trade?

In *Siegsdorf-am-Lippe*? At nine o'clock in the morning? With a disreputable down-and-out like himself?

Pack it in, man! he told himself.

The girl was well dressed, wearing some kind of uniform, quite pretty. She had thin hands and slender, elegant wrists. She looked out of place among the workers and small shopkeepers in that cheap restaurant.

Blake was level with her table, staring carefully straight ahead, when she spoke. 'Gunter! How nice to see you – and what a surprise!' in quite a loud voice. And then, very quietly indeed: 'Do please sit down.'

Blake stopped dead. The second sentence had been murmured in flawless French. '*Asseyez-vous, je vous en prie.*'

He dropped into the vacant chair, the sweat starting on his forehead.

'You must be famished,' the girl said in German. 'After all that travelling. Let me order something for you at once.' She raised the beckoning hand to call over a slatternly woman carrying a tray of used cups and saucers.

'Thank you,' Blake stammered as the waitress approached. 'I . . . I'll have the sauerkraut with black bread, a knackwurst on the side and a glass of beer.'

'And a large schnapps,' the girl added.

The woman nodded and went away.

Blake stared across the table, waiting for a lead. She had curling auburn hair, tucked under a close-fitting velour hat. The uniform was greenish-grey, with a high-buttoned jacket and a skirt that must have reached almost to her ankles.

'It's quieter here than Detmold or Paderborn, don't you think?' she said conversationally. 'And much less noisy than Dortmund, especially near the railway station.'

'It has its advantages,' he said, looking straight at her. Her eyes were very wide, halfway between jade green and hazel. There was some kind of military badge or cockade attached to the ribbon at one side of her hat.

For him, things had begun to fall into place. Apart from the obvious hint that she was in some mysterious way familiar with his recent movements, it was the lapse into French – clearly a signal – that did it.

He remembered that this particular area of Germany had once been colonized by French Protestant refugees after Louis XIV had revoked the Edict of Nantes in 1685. He recalled too that, during his initial briefing, the cartographer had told him that he was going to 'one of the few Hun regions with something of a French cultural tradition'. The chap had also said he might be able to exploit his ancestry. That settled it. A family with a French connection 'not altogether hostile', as he had put it – what ground could be more fertile for the recruitment of secret agents! The girl *must* be associated in some way with his lost cut-out . . .

The waitress set food and drink before him. He gulped

133

the schnapps and started greedily forking bread and sausage into his mouth.

The girl allowed him to get halfway through the sauerkraut before she said sympathetically: 'You've had a hard time of it, haven't you?'

Blake looked up from his plate. He raised his glass and swallowed some beer. 'How do you know?'

'I have been looking for you ever since you lost the transmitter,' she said.

'You mean . . . ? You're telling me that you yourself . . . ?' He was still staring. '*You* are the cut-out? You're in this part of the country already, so why the damned Morse at all, then? Why didn't they just instruct us to meet?'

'It is important – or was important – that there was no possible connection between us. As a permanent operative, you understand, I have other work to do also. But once our means of contact was removed, London decided an exception would have to be made, and I was ordered to make myself known to you.'

'Yes, but, I mean, how did you know where I was? How did you find me? How, for God's sake, did you know I would be passing this particular restaurant at this particular time today, that I would actually come in?' He shook his head. 'Come to that, how the devil did you know that I was me anyway?'

'I did have a photograph,' she smiled. 'And if one is in the know, you don't look so *very* German – even with the scar.'

'I still don't understand . . .'

'All I knew was that you were coming to Siegsdorf. I'd no idea what for: we never discuss the details of missions with agents . . .'

'Yes, they told me on no account to refer to it. They call it security.'

'. . . so I thought the best thing, after the police had taken your transmitter, was simply to come here myself and wait for you.'

'How did you know that was what happened? That the police had it?'

She touched the buttoned jacket. An agreeable curve thrust it out above the tight waist. 'This is the uniform of an auxiliary nursing service attached to the air command. I am based at the aerodrome outside Paderborn. It is not difficult to hear the echoes of what goes on – especially when it concerns a mysterious flying machine arriving from the north.'

'People talk. I know. So you learned . . . ?'

'I heard about your escape from the hotel in Paderborn,' the girl said. 'I assumed you would eventually come here. So I came too, hoping I would be able to help.'

Blake had finished his meal. He pushed away his plate. 'You must be a very good – what do they call it? – a very discreet tail,' he said.

'It was not necessary actually to follow you. You saw the hotel down the road, the one all boarded up? . . . Exactly. So. Well, it is closed for the duration of the war. But I have a key because it belongs to my aunt and uncle. All I had to do was keep a watch from behind the shutters there. I saw you arrive at the station yesterday – from Dortmund, that was smart! I saw you again later, visiting shops. And then you left, walking along the road to Salzkotten.' The girl raised one hand, signalling that she wanted the bill.

After the waitress had taken the money, she continued, still keeping her voice well down below the hubbub of voices in the crowded restaurant: 'There is only one

135

place on that road that could possibly interest you: the Krupp subsidiary where they make spare parts for aeroplanes. I assume you went there?' She looked at Blake enquiringly.

He nodded but made no comment.

'As you did not return until this morning,' the girl said, 'I wondered if perhaps your mission had succeeded, and you might not need my help after all. I thought it wise, just the same, to make contact. So I hurried here to leave my little . . . message . . . in the hope that you might stop and see it.'

'Weren't you taking a bit of a risk there? That I might not have stopped. Or gone straight to the station?'

'Not really. If you had been up all night you would need a meal . . . and this is the only eating place open in town. What shall I tell London: that you have succeeded?'

'No,' Blake said shortly. 'There was . . . a hitch.'

'What happened?'

'Something went wrong. It's a question, well, of getting inside that factory. I had to postpone the attempt, try it again another day.'

'Naturally, I shall help all I can. What exactly do you have to do?'

'Like yourself, I have been told not to discuss the details.'

'I understand.' She pushed back her chair. 'You need to rest. I think it is time we left this place.'

They left together and she led him, via a narrow alley, to the rear entrance of the closed hotel.

Her name was Kristin. 'Kristin Dony,' she told him. 'Probably a corruption of Donnée or Dounet, sometime after my family fled here in the eighteenth century.' Her parents were dead, and the aunt who owned the hotel was

136

in Berlin, working as some kind of clerk at the Ministry of the Interior.

Blake lay on a dust sheet covering a feather bed, luxuriating in the sheer comfort of a surface that accepted his tired body without an angle or a lump or a rigid plane. Kristin had gone to find ointment, bandages and disinfectant for his damaged hands – and also to make her report to London.

'In Morse?' Blake had exclaimed. 'All the way from here?'

'No, no.' She laughed. 'By wireless and then telephone. Through Switzerland. What shall I tell them?'

'Tell them that I have arrived at . . . the target.' He thought for a moment. 'Yes, tell them that there was an . . . unforeseen difficulty . . . but that I hope to leave tomorrow with . . . what is required.'

'Very well,' she said. 'Forgive me, but that sounds, well, a little vague. Will they understand exactly what you mean?'

'Oh, yes,' he said. 'They will understand all right.'

Content at last to find that he was no longer totally alone, he turned over and drifted into a dreamless sleep.

He awoke to the sound of horses' hooves clip-clopping over the cobbles, a noisy altercation between two men somewhere below and the rumble of iron-rimmed wheels along the street. In the distance, a lorry engine with one cylinder missing revved up and died, revved up and died.

Kristin was sitting by the shuttered window. She had taken off her jacket and he saw indeed that there was a generous bosom beneath the cream silk blouse tucked into her skirt. Spread out on an occasional table in front of her he saw ham, tomatoes, what looked like a jar of pickled herrings – and a bottle of Sekt, the German champagne.

'I was too late to get more bread,' she said. 'Today's ration had all gone.'

'It looks like a feast!' Blake said, pushing himself up on to one elbow. 'Did you get through?'

'Oh, yes. Message received and understood. Instructions for you were restricted to a single word: "Urgent".'

He smiled. 'As if I didn't know!'

'Part of my work,' Kristin said, 'involves the rehabilitation of returned prisoners of war and the resettlement of troops invalided out of the army. But although at the moment you could pass for either of these, I think it best that we are not seen together – at least until after dark. In case you don't agree, I have brought you a razor.'

'May you be blessed,' he said, fingering the irritation on his unshaven jaw.

'The wisest thing to do, I believe, is to stay here under cover until you think it time to return to the factory. Before that, we can eat and, so far as is possible, amuse ourselves. Does the idea meet with your approval?'

'Nothing,' Blake said truthfully, 'would give me greater pleasure.'

16

Afterwards, Blake could never remember exactly the order in which things happened, that gloomy day in Siegsdorf.

Outside the town, he supposed, the sun never pierced the clouds enough to dispel the early morning mist. Certainly, each time he peered through a gap between the shutters, he saw nothing but a uniform grey overhead. And sometime in the afternoon it must have begun to rain, for when the masked street lamps were tipped into flame by the long pole of the lighter on his bicycle, the flagged pavement and cobbles below glistened damply in the glaring gaslight.

They ate early, and when the Sekt was finished, Kristin produced a flask of schnapps which added a comfortable glow to the inner warmth produced by the sparkling wine. A little before ten o'clock they left – via the rear entrance and the alley as before – because he wanted to arrive at the factory well before the pre-midnight break and arrange the new rope she had procured for him.

In between, however – somehow, in their room in that deserted hotel – the first step was taken in the direction of what he was to remember as one of the most exciting adventures of his life . . .

It must have started, he thought later, when she was changing the bandages she had bound around his hands.

He had already shaved and bathed as well as he could in
the cold water of the bathroom. He sat on the bed in a
drowsy haze, fortified by the alcohol, determined this time
to succeed and to hell with the risks. But underlying this
euphoric bravado, scarcely recognizable but throbbing
deep within him, was a craving for reassurance and moral
support and human warmth. To sustain him on the high
he had worked himself up to, he needed appreciation and
approval.

What more reassuring, then, than a woman's arms
around him; what could be warmer – and indeed more
supportive – than a woman's body?

Yes, there was no doubt about it: the hands must have
taken, as it were, the first step. His fingers after all were
free. He had a very definite remembrance of the initial,
electric thrill he felt when the padded tips first brushed
against her flesh . . . just above the wrist, he thought.

Did he clutch? Did he stroke? Was that breath-stopping
exhilaration the result of an exploration of his own
. . . or was Kristin's response less a reaction to any
move of his than a spontaneous expression of hidden
desire? Of complicity in the face of a shared danger?
Of tenderness even?

The tips of her own fingers were cool on his forehead,
cooler tracing the line of his jaw . . . then suddenly hot
and hard as one hand clenched on either side of his chin,
hollowing his cheeks and forcing open his mouth as she
leaned down to kiss him.

That was the start of the dizzy period, what he thought
of afterwards as the ecstasy.

Her tongue, warm and wet and muscular, speared
through as his lips flew open, probing his mouth, teeth,
gums, the inner recesses of his cheeks. Dazedly, he allowed
his own tongue to be sucked into her mouth.

She was lying on the bed beside him, her arms crossed over his back to grasp his shoulders. Her breathing, fast and shallow, jetted hotly against his cheek. Through two layers of clothes, Blake could feel the heat of her belly against his hardness.

With trembling fingers, he unbuttoned the silk blouse. Beneath thin shoulder straps, the straight line of her bust bodice bulged out over the bosom whose fullness he had already admired. The breasts themselves – she must have whisked off the flimsy garment with her own hands – were a splendour of creamy flesh, swelling from her chest in ripe curves. He cradled their heavy warmth in his bandaged hands as she bent over him on hands and knees. Big nipples, hard and hot, flowered from the puckered brown circles at their tips. Some of the buttons at the side of her long skirt had come undone.

Between the waistband and these hanging delights, Kristin's body was tightly constricted by a whalebone corset inset with panels of yellow leather. Yellow, he supposed, because of the cream-coloured blouse. He reached both hands behind her waist to loosen the severe lacing, but she shook her head and reached back to remove them. 'No, no,' she whispered. 'It takes much too long to put it back on again. Unfasten the rest of my skirt.'

Except in a brothel, to a young man of Blake's background it was almost unthinkable at that time to be naked in bed with an unmarried woman. Equally rare to be able at close quarters to stare at, and revel in, the sight of female nudity. The mess, of course, was full of lascivious tales involving prurient housemaids creeping upstairs after dark to initiate the young master, and farmers' daughters in hay lofts. But nothing like this ever seemed to happen to anyone you knew, and still less to yourself. In the bedroom of the closed hotel in Siegsdorf, Patrice Blake found out for the first time what the Bible meant when it referred to 'knowing' a woman.

Kristin stood silhouetted against the street lighting which crept through the slats between the shutters. Wearing nothing but the corset, knee-length stockings and buttoned black boots with cuban heels which just covered her ankles, she seemed to him the most voluptuous, the most supremely sensual sight he had ever seen in his life.

'And now,' she said hoarsely, 'I think it is time for you to move over on that bed and make room for me, for we have things to say to each other that don't actually need words.'

Blake's heart was thumping in his chest and his mouth was dry, but not from fear this time. Not fear, at any rate, of death and pain and physical harm. A touch perhaps of apprehension at the mystery of woman, but he was much too excited to notice that.

Kristin walked over to the bed and plunged the four fingers of one hand between two of the buttons fastening his fly. Yanking open the front of his corduroys, she pulled them roughly down to his ankles. The fingers reached for him, wrapped firmly around the aching proof of his desire.

Blake thought his heart would stop.

She was straddling him, bare knees clamped to his ribs up near his armpits. Then, slowly, she lowered those padded hips and all at once he was gasping as he was engulfed in the scalding heat of her body.

Later, when the schnapps was finished, she lay on her back and took him into her again, thrusting fiercely up against him as he penetrated, breasts heaving and small cries choked in her throat. All his life he would remember the warmth of those breasts against his naked chest, the graze of damp pubic hair against his belly and the infinite suppleness of the corseted body clamped to his. When finally it was time, it felt to him like a fall from grace.

'There will be a lot of activity at the factory tonight,' Kristin said. 'They sent up three of the new Dr-1 three-winged machines on motor trailers this afternoon. I think the Fokker people are trying out some kind of modification to the original design.'

'Good Lord,' Blake said, 'how do you know that?'

'They were talking about it at the aerodrome yesterday, before I came over here.'

'Why didn't you tell me before?'

'I am afraid it slipped my mind. Why, does it matter?'

'If they're going to work on them all night, presumably in the open air, it might make all the difference – one way or the other, good or bad.'

'My dear, I'm sorry.' She tucked a hand in his arm. They had walked in silence leaving the town, until the last houses were behind them. The place was deserted, with most of the windows already dark, which made it all the wiser, Blake thought, not to run the slightest risk of attracting attention.

He was still a little dizzy from their lovemaking, not quite sure, as the alcoholic euphoria faded, whether or not to believe the evidence provided by his own memory, the tingling still in his fingers, the ache in his loins.

Kristin had been much more matter-of-fact, companionable, almost domesticated about the whole thing – but certainly a little less romantic. Perhaps it was not the first time she had plunged into such an adventure. He put the thought from his mind. They were approaching the brow of the hill beyond which the wood and the factory lay.

They were aware of the sulphurous glow some time before they breasted the rise.

'Great Scott!' he exclaimed as the view opened up before them. 'You were right about the activity, old thing!'

Yellow arc lights flooded the area between the guard-house and the first workshops with glaring brilliance, etching the small, snub-nosed triplanes against the night. Crowding the six-wheeled military trailers, uniformed riggers of the Imperial Army Air Service mingled with factory technicians working on the new aeroplanes. One of them, with its polished aluminium engine cowling removed, was being fitted with parts handed up from a trolley wheeled from one of the workshops. An officer in boots and riding breeches lounged, smoking a cigarette in a holder, against the door of an open Mercedes staff car, with one foot raised to the wide running-board.

Blake and Kristin stopped, half hidden by the branches of a hawthorn growing in a hedgerow. 'No chance tonight, I'm afraid, of sneaking past unnoticed,' he said in a low voice.

'You mean we'll have to skirt the whole site? Through the fields?'

'Don't worry,' he said bitterly. 'I'm familiar with the route.'

17

Light reflected from the far side of the factory helped them to make a rapid, virtually noiseless passage through the wood.

As soon as they arrived at the fence he saw that the broken branch had been removed. And the rope, of course, had gone. 'I'd half expected to find a sentry posted here,' he murmured.

'Did you leave a saw here?' Kristin asked, gazing up at the scarred trunk of the oak.

'Er . . . yes. Yes, I'm afraid I did.' Blake smarted again from the humiliation of the previous night's defeat.

'A good thing,' she said. 'They probably put it down to theft.'

'Theft? But that's what I was . . .'

'Theft by local people, by villagers. It's hard to keep warm in wartime winters, and there's no coal for non-combatants. Plenty of folks secretly lay in a stock of wood during the summer months, when there's less chance of being caught.'

He nodded, thinking of the mythical Frau Schneider, invented to explain his purchase of the saw. 'And the rope?'

'*You* know it was used to lower you down,' Kristin said. 'Anyone seeing it together with a half-sawn branch and an abandoned saw would assume it was there to climb *up*.'

145

'I suppose you're right,' he said doubtfully. 'In any case, I'd better push on with the replacement. I want to be over there before the break. If there is a break on a night as busy as this.' He began unwinding the new rope from his waist.

'You know our German love of routine,' Kristin said. 'There will be a break.'

'It must be something very new they are fitting,' he said, preparing to climb. 'They're not going to send up every aeroplane individually – every machine operating on the Western Front, I mean – not if it's a regular modification that could be incorporated during assembly on a production line.'

He was interested to know if she had any idea of the object of his mission. So far, although she had several times made casual references to it, he had maintained a complete discretion, revealing only that 'plans' were involved. If anything went wrong, after all, and she was caught . . . well, the Germans had brutal methods of persuasion, and what she didn't know she couldn't tell.

All she said now, however, was: 'I expect you are right.'

Stripping off the greatcoat, he stowed the workshop diagram and the tools he would need into the pockets of his corduroys. He climbed to what he thought of as his branch, edged out along it, and made the new rope fast. Then, carefully, he lowered himself until he was hanging as before just above the fence.

Kristin was perched on a thick bough ten or twelve feet up – a position from which she could give him a push each time he swung back into the gap where the other branch had been.

He was feeling confident, almost jubilant. The fact of having an accomplice, someone actually there whom he could not possibly demean himself to let down, had erased his terror – not so much his fear of the mission itself as his horror at the thought of his own weakness. For now, at any rate, that was in the past tense.

Flexing his body from the hips, bandaged hands hot around two knots, Blake began swinging the rope. When the pendulum of which he himself was the weight had sufficient momentum, he felt the first hard shove in the back as he sailed within Kristin's reach. The arc of his swing progressively increased.

Out over the fence . . . back, and shove . . . out again towards the silhouetted bulk of the admin block . . . in beneath the oak . . . out and up once more after the succeeding push . . . But the problem was that the further the swing took him, the higher he was from the ground at the end of its impetus. He had to decide between a long drop near the block and a shorter fall only halfway across the strip separating fence and factory.

There wasn't really a choice. He had to risk the long drop. He let go of the rope at the instant gravity imposed a fractional pause before the back-swing.

He fell heavily – between fifteen and twenty feet, he thought later – shoulder-rolled and staggered up with all the breath knocked from his body. Panting, he lurched the few yards to the wall of the building. Kristin would already be scaling the tree to recover the rope. Hopefully, she would be waiting with it when he returned, ready to cast it over and help him climb the fence.

Now, though, he was faced with the most difficult question of all. Which way in?

It was probable that the loading bay pass doors on his side of the workshops would be unlocked since there was so much activity outside. He had no means of telling, on the other hand, how many engineers might

still be working inside. The yellow floodlights ruled out
the gap between the buildings, the covered walkway and,
of course, anything on the far side. There remained the
two-storey block and the glass workshop roofs below
it. Again, there was really no choice.

A patrol had passed just before he climbed the oak. In
what was left of the half-hour before the next was due,
he would have to use the arched window embrasures, in
the dark, to scale the façade and struggle up to the roof
or force an entry to the upper floor. After that there were
three possible options: steal downstairs to the canteen
level and use the walkway to gain the first workshop;
re-emerge from the building – if there was a window
above the gap – and use the walkway roof to reach the
wall and then the roof of the shop; or leap down from
the roof of the block to the workshop roof. The drop
here was quite small, but the space to be crossed was at
least ten feet.

One way or the other, it had to be the façade.

Beneath the nearest embrasure, he reached up and
grabbed the sill. It wasn't too difficult to haul himself up
– except for the painful pressure on his hands. Gritting his
teeth, he raised himself upright and felt for the projections
he had memorized on his initial examination of the site.
The architect had made the two rows of embrasures
integral with the façade as a whole. Blake had reached
the summit of the arch and was feeling for the sill of the
window above when light sprang suddenly below his feet
from the shuttered windows of the ground floor.

The canteen lights had been switched on. There *was*
going to be a break – and it would be at any minute.
He would have to hurry. His feet scraped noisily on the
stonework as he scrambled to the higher level. Once on
this sill – after he had canted the first heel up, the second

148

seemed to require an interminable time and effort – he had the choice of an immediate entry, or another climb, from the top of this arch to the roof parapet. No particular difficulty there. It was only five or six feet. And he would have welcomed the chance to patrol the workshop roofs, looking down into the interior to see how the workforce was disposed. But the transfer from this roof to those could be difficult, hazardous, and he couldn't really afford the time now. The essential was to get inside.

He examined the second-floor window. This one was not shuttered, but it was closed and locked. In the instant that he felt for the tiny diamond cutter secreted in his pocket, the factory bell rang.

The hell with cutting out a circle and removing it attached to the sticky tape so that he could get his hand in. He thumped one bandaged fist against the glass, hoping that the smash of falling shards would be drowned as the bell continued to ring.

He thrust in an arm, manipulated the catch, pushed up the window and stepped inside. There was a lot of noise from below now, as workers crowded into the canteen.

Moving warily in the dark – he assumed he was in an office – he skirted desks, chairs, what was probably a steel filing cabinet, and moved towards the thread of light showing beneath a door. Very slowly, he eased it open. He saw a small landing, a stairway spiralling down into the brilliance below.

When he could hear no more traffic passing from the workshops to the canteen, he crept downstairs. In a niche by the double doors leading to the walkway, brown overall tunics hung from a rail. He took one, shrugged into it, pushed open the doors and went through into the first of the workshops.

Judging by the array of dials, small electrical windings, transformers and wired clips strewn over the benches, this was some kind of assembly shop for gauges and meters. Completed instruments – white figures on black faces in a six-inch circular shell – stood racked by the door to the loading bay, ready to be packaged.

The next twinned building – they were separated only by two doors and a short length of passageway – was clearly the one making most of the noise. He saw belt-driven lathes, overhead pulleys, banks of machinery whose purpose eluded him. The shop, deserted like the first, was heavy with the thin reek of machine oil.

He opened the door to the third. Immediately the one at the far end of the passage was flung open. Fear surged through him, savage as an electric shock.

A fat woman in a white coat, with braided hair coiled around her head, backed into the corridor pulling a trolley loaded with black bread and sausages under glass domes. She scarcely gave Blake, frozen by the second door, a glance.

'You'll have to get on with it if you want to eat,' she said crossly. 'I don't know what those admin folks are coming to – all these extra workers and no damned notice!'

Blake swallowed, holding open the second door for her. 'I . . . I'll be along in just a minute,' he said huskily.

'Well, look sharp about it,' she snorted, 'or you'll go hungry!'

The trolley rattled away among the machinery.

Blake heaved a sigh of relief. His forehead was dewed with sweat. Thank God, he thought, that there *were* supernumeraries around, unknown to the canteen staff!

The third workshop was his target. Here there were smaller lathes, trays of rods and couplings, several trains of gears on the benches. Something electrical hummed quietly in a corner.

He stole a quick glance at his plan. Yes, they had got it right. The two offices were there – behind him now – one on either side of the entrance. He moved swiftly to the loading bay. The door on this side of the platform, the pass door at any rate, was locked. But there was a key in the lock. Security during the break, he supposed, if the work was top secret. He turned the key and eased back the catch. A nearby escape route could be vital.

In the designer's drawing office he took out the large-scale plan, the one on rice-paper. That was the first disappointment. What he saw bore no relation whatever to the elements on his diagram. Banks of steel drawers stood where the filing cabinets should have been. Three inclined boards with green-shaded, counterbalanced lamps occupied the space where he expected a desk. Blake swore beneath his breath. Everything looked shiny and new: clearly the place had recently been refitted. He would have to go through it from top to bottom to find what he was looking for.

Voices.

He crouched down below the windows surrounding the room.

A door banged open. Two men walked into the workshop from the direction of the canteen – a factory overseer with a badge on the pocket of his white overalls and a uniformed under-officer in the Army Air Service. They were talking animatedly.

'. . . gear is fine for the Eindekkers and triplanes,' the under-officer was saying, 'but they are talking now of three- or even four-bladed propellers. They'll have to go back to the drawing board if they want . . .'

The door of the office opened.

Blake looked frenziedly right and left. There was no place to go, nowhere to hide, not a cupboard, a niche, the kneehole of a desk. He was crazy to have risked coming here while a double night shift was at work.

'I mean, you have to think of the tolerance,' the soldier said as they came in. 'Look at the 110hp Oberursel rotary! With a mechanism as crude as those guns, and a dwell on the cams of less than half a milli . . .'

He stopped in mid-sentence, his eyes fixed on Blake, cowering in one corner. 'One of yours?' he asked.

'I've never seen him before in my life,' the overseer said blankly. 'Who the devil are you? And what the hell do you think you're doing in here?'

Blake blanched. 'I'm s-s-sorry,' he stammered wildly. 'I must have lost m-m-my . . .'

The under-officer had a pistol in his hand. 'If there is any explaining to do,' he said evenly, 'it will be done in front of the Herr Rittmeister, in the guard-house. You will precede us through the adjoining workshops – and I may tell you that this Walther is loaded and the trigger mechanism is extremely light.'

He gestured towards the open door.

This cannot be happening to me, Blake thought. This is a bad dream; I shall wake up soon . . . Dear God, let me wake up *now*!

He moved towards the door, turned into the aisle between factory benches. A cold chill rippled down his spine as he felt the gun barrel prod him between the shoulder-blades.

'A common thief, do you suppose?' the under-officer asked.

'Out here, at this time of night? With all this activity around?' the overseer's voice was derisive. 'More likely a spy, I reckon. There's a lot of secret work done here, you know.'

'Well, we know what to do with spies,' the man from the Army Air Service said. He prodded again, harder. 'Come on, get a move on. Through that door.'

Desperation, stemming from sheer panic, fuelled Blake's action. Double swing doors sealed each end of the passage leading to the next workshop. The blind instinct of self-preservation took over as he passed through.

He was after all young, strong, lithe and quite athletic. He had learned, in a brief unarmed-combat course, about the effect of surprise on a man with a gun who came too close. And he had noticed that this particular man with a gun was left-handed.

Instead of pulling the doors towards him, he pushed his way through . . . and then exploded into movement.

He kicked violently back with his left leg, crashing the left-hand door against the menacing barrel of the pistol.

Canted slightly upward towards the nape of his neck, the barrel jerked instantly vertical under the shock. And the man's arm, bent double by the impact, was unable to suppress in that hundredth of a second the message already flashed from brain to forefinger. Taken totally unawares, he pressed the trigger and shot himself through the underside of the jaw, blowing off the top of his head.

Blake, who had thrown himself on to all fours as a continuation of his backward kick, whirled around to meet the attack of the overseer. Shouldering open the second door, the man came at him with a heavy steel wrench.

Still balanced on one knee, Blake raised an arm to ward off the assault and took a murderous blow on his left biceps, just below the shoulder. The numbing force of the stroke sent him crashing back into a sitting position, and he spun around on his seat before uncoiling himself to spring to his feet and meet the next attack with the only weapon he had.

This, one of the household tools he had been told might help in his burgling, was a metal rasp or file. The blade, triangular in section, tapered to a point, and there was a spike at the other end over which a wooden handle could be fitted if necessary. It was not necessary here.

Blake reversed the file swiftly in his hand, lunging inside the next blow which whistled over his shoulder. Before his attacker could draw back his arm again, he jabbed the tool forcefully upward into the man's face. The hardened steel spike plunged in beneath his left eyebrow with a horrifying squelch.

The overseer's mouth dropped open and a curious sound bubbled from his throat. For an instant he hung there, an obscene, deformed unicorn, with the rasp projecting from the socket. Then he crumpled slowly and collapsed to the floor. From the dreadful gash where his eye had been, fluid dribbled down over his unshaven cheek.

Blake too stood immobile for a single heartbeat, staring at the sprawling bodies. He was panting and his frame trembled all over. A fan of brains pricked out with splinters of bone slid down the wall just outside one of the doors. The metallic tang of fresh blood penetrated the cordite fumes, and there was a stench rising from below, where one of the men had evacuated himself as he died.

Cramming a hand over his mouth to stifle nausea, Blake ran back into the workshop. The corpse of the soldier had wedged one of the doors open, but he could not bring himself to move it and seal off the passageway.

His mind was in a whirl. He had envisaged a number of different scenes in which he played the role of burglar . . . discovered as he located the plans, surprised before he succeeded, taken prisoner, narrowly escaping . . . but it had never occurred to him that he might be the means of killing a man, let alone two.

Nor had he found the damned plans.

The sound of the shot had sounded terrifyingly loud. Could it have been heard outside, in the guardhouse, through two workshops, over the babble of voices in the canteen?

Perhaps not. There had been no outcry, no pounding of feet. But there could be no more than minutes left before the factory bell rang and workers crowded back into the shops.

What could he do? Chance a lightning survey – and the risk of capture? Admit defeat and abandon the mission, leaving himself a failure with a murderer's price-tag on his head? Get out now, at once, and return another night for a third attempt?

Don't be a BF, he told himself fiercely. Think.

The overseer and the under-officer had been complaining about the Fokker linkage when they arrived. They had spoken of modifications for different types of aeroplane. They had been talking technicalities, as if that work was actually in train, and they had come into the drawing office. In the middle of a break?

Wasn't it reasonable to assume that something urgent had brought them? That they had, in fact, come into that office to look at the blueprints?

And that the blueprints therefore must be readily accessible?

Blake hefted the Walther automatic from hand to hand – he must have snatched it up without realizing when he ran from the passageway. It was worth a try.

He raced back into the office. For the second time, a quick glance around.

There! A tall wooden cabinet, glistening with varnish. Wide, very shallow drawers. Off to one side of the drawing boards with their T-squares. He ran across. The drawers were individually locked.

The overseer should have keys . . . but he quailed at the thought of searching a body. Very well: use the second domestic utensil. A kitchen knife with the blade snapped off very short. He reached into his pocket.

With the stumpy blade inserted, he levered up and pulled down. Wood split with a splintering crash.

He found them in the third drawer down – plans, elevations, working drawings with all dimensions, the original blueprint: all from the Fokker works at Schwerin. Clearly, as he had thought, a contracted-out job here in Siegsdorf.

There were four sheets in all, each approximately eighteen inches by twenty-four. He slid them out, laid them on a desk. There was a reference number stencilled on the working drawings. Feverishly, he pulled open the drawers of filing cabinets, then a table, and found it finally on a card in a box file on the desk.

The number identified on which benches in which parts of the workshop different stages of the gear assembly were completed. The actual manufacturing process, the stamping and forging of individual elements, took place in the fourth building, but the fine machining was done here.

Blake took an eighteen-inch cardboard cylinder from a rack near the door, folded the sheets once, rolled them tightly and stuffed them into the tube. He hurried from the office.

Benches were identified by letters and figures suspended above them. He ran to the two marked as final assembly.

The completed train, not very large, looked a little like the outside connecting-rod system of an express locomotive. He was unable to relate it in any way to an aero engine – rotary, radial or in-line. Or, for that matter, to a Vickers or Lewis gun.

If possible, they had said in London, bring us back a sample in three dimensions. If possible! With the weight of that metal stowed about your person you wouldn't stagger ten yards without attracting attention!

Separate parts then? He wouldn't know which to take. He picked up a shining, beautifully machined helicoidal gear wheel from a tray. This looked something like part of a miniature car differential. Perhaps that was important? He dropped the part into his pocket.

There were graphs and tabulated sheets secured by bulldog clips hanging from brass nails above the bench. Both seemed to be concerned with the plotting of engine revolutions – divided by two, of course, since there were two blades to a propeller – against rates of fire and the muzzle speed of rounds from a machine-gun over given distances. He tore off one of each and managed to squeeze them into the cardboard tube.

Just samples, he thought with a crooked grin.

Abruptly, loud as a scream in the night, the bell shrilled somewhere in the rafters beneath the inclined glass roof of the workshop.

Blake froze, hands trembling and heart thumping . . . then ran.

He dashed for the loading bay, flung open the pass door

he had unlocked and hurled himself across the platform outside. He was about to drop when he realized the open door would throw light across the dark strip, pointing an unerring finger at his escape route.

Sobbing for breath, he ran back and pulled the door closed. This time, as he was preparing to jump, he heard the first outcry from inside the shop. The first arrivals from the canteen must have found the bodies.

He raced over the uneven ground.

'*Here!*' He heard Kristin's urgent voice. '*To your right!*'

Veering towards her, he reached the fence. A sudden tiny flick of a torch showed him the rope draped over the wire. 'Seize it and climb,' she hissed. 'The other end is fast around a tree.'

He grabbed the rope, hauled it tight, and 'walked' himself up the stiff chain-link surface. At the top, he perched for an instant and then dropped into freedom. She was already unfastening the other end.

There was now a hubbub of shouts from within the factory. Torchlight swept around the corner of the canteen block from the guardhouse. Several different voices shouted orders.

'I heard a shot,' the girl said.

'There was trouble. I had to act on the spur of the moment,' Blake said tightly.

'You are carrying a gun yourself!'

'I had to,' he said again. 'After the shot.' He wasn't prepared to explain in detail: the horror was still too close.

'Did you get what you wanted?'

'Yes,' Blake said. He had pushed the cardboard cylinder down inside his trousers, along the inside of his lame leg. Once again he was not going to elaborate. For a time, as they pushed through bushes and undergrowth, Kristin was silent. Then she said: 'We must get out of this area fast. Deeper into the wood and then as soon as possible across the road and into the fields. It will not take them long to work out which way you came and went – not with the floods in front and last night's evidence behind.'

'And the door I left unlocked over the loading bay,' he agreed.

By the time they had gathered up the rope, the rackety, air-cooled engine of a scout car had started up on the far side of the buildings. The brilliance of a searchlight silvered the outlines of roof and wall. When they were a hundred yards into the trees, he glanced over his shoulder. There were lights now all over the strip on the far side of the wire fence.

Minutes later they heard the scout car circling the outside of the site.

Between the densely growing trunks of trees, torch beams – perhaps a dozen of them – bobbed right and left, occasionally showing up a trailing branch, a canopy of leaves.

They were almost on the far side of the wood. Stars pricked the darkness between the interlaced boughs overhead. Blake had the sense of the land dropping away beyond the trees. He stopped, panting, to lean momentarily against the hollowed trunk of an oak. 'Are you all right?' the girl said. 'You seem to be – forgive me – but you seem to be, well, limping rather more than usual.'

'I'll be all right,' he said. 'Thanks.'

And indeed once he had regained his breath he was moving much faster, overtaking her as they came out into the open and careered down a slope of meadow towards a sunken lane.

The wood crowned a hilltop and now, towards the north, he was aware of the countryside rolling down towards two or three dimly glimmering points of radiance which marked the village of Salzkotten.

Above the lane, they had difficulty forcing their way through a hedgerow choked with brambles. Perhaps this was why they were taken so much by surprise by the long beam of light sweeping around a corner uphill . . . and the appearance immediately after of the scout car, coasting down the slope illuminated by its searchlight.

They were halfway across the narrow road when the beam trapped them.

Brakes squealed. The engine burst into life again and a voice yelled: 'Halt! Stay where you are or we fire!'

Blake thrust Kristin down violently into a ditch on the far side and flung himself prone among the long grasses. The voice shouted again.

Quite calmly, Blake levelled the long-barrelled Walther and shot out the searchlight. Glass tinkled, the aching glare dimmed, faded to a momentary red glow, vanished. Gunshots blazed out over the low sides of the car. He sensed the stirring of air as a bullet hummed through the grasses close to his head. Twigs and fragments of leaf fell on to his wrist. Aiming for the muzzle flashes, he fired two more shots.

The windscreen of the scout erupted. A choked cry from the passenger side.

Blake knew that the army-issue Walther '08 automatic had an eight-round magazine. The under-officer had fired once; he had himself now loosed off three. In a last-chance manoeuvre to make the second man in the scout car believe that he had armed colleagues, he stretched his arm wide, left and right, firing the last four as rapidly as possible in an effort to simulate a volley from several gunners.

The ploy was successful.

With a harsh grinding of gears, the car shot into reverse, wheeled crazily around to thump its rear end into the bank, and then zigzagged back up the hill in the darkness with tyres screaming.

Kristin dragged herself, squelching, from the ditch. She was soaked in stagnant water from the waist down. 'Well, you can certainly move fast enough when it's necessary,' she said breathlessly.

'Needs must,' Blake said. 'Although the devil driving that particular vehicle seemed a trifle less than satanic!'

'We must run for the village now,' she told him, 'before he comes back with reinforcements. On the other side of the hedgerow, of course.'

'Why the village? Wouldn't we be safer if we . . . ?'

'There's a school on the outskirts. A girls' school. Mainly for boarders. There are bicycles in a shed. Riding silently, we could be miles away by daylight.'

'Yes, but . . . I mean, where would we be . . . ?'

'We would be heading for Paderborn,' she interrupted.

'*Paderborn!* Why on earth . . . ?'

'There's an aerodrome there,' Kristin said. 'Remember?'

18

The airfield at Paderborn was not particularly well guarded. It was surrounded by a three-strand wire fence to stop cows and sheep straying in and interrupting the training programme. There were two sentries in front of the guardhouse at the entrance. But that was all.

Although both infantry and especially artillery commanders were conscious of the value of aerial observation, there was still a general feeling among the High Command that the air services were a bit of a luxury, the playthings of cranks, newfangled toys that had little to do with real soldiering.

Gunners could enthuse over the corrections to their aim supplied by aerial reports; officers planning ground attacks could welcome detailed information charting enemy troop movements 'on the other side of the hill'. But the Allied General Staff as a whole preferred blindly to follow the outdated precepts of Douglas Haig. And the Germans, of course, at the Kaiser's express command, placed all their faith in the machine-gun.

The British and French won back lost ground after an artillery bombardment by massed charges of infantry armed with rifles and bayonets; the Germans cut them down in thousands with cunning deployment of machine-gun 'nests'.

Most of the early – usually posthumous – VCs were

won by men who wiped out single-handedly one of these sandbagged emplacements with a well-directed grenade.

Even at battlefield level, where aerial reconnaissance was an accepted asset and the ability to shoot down your opponent's machines a necessity, the idea of an attack with 'ground support' from above had yet to be formulated. Certainly the aeroplanes had machine-guns, but they were inaccurate, the planes themselves were vulnerable – even to rifle fire – and bombs, if carried, rarely weighed more than twenty-five pounds. These again lacked accuracy, since there was no bomb-sight and in most cases they were released approximately over the target by hauling up a simple toggle lever.

There was then no foreseeable need to protect airfields. Most front-line examples were improvised from stretches of open grassland or large fields; offices, living quarters and mess were wooden huts; and the machines were garaged in canvas hangars. Many of them, close to the area of trench warfare, could be abandoned almost immediately if menaced by an attack; some, further behind the lines, were not even protected against aerial attack themselves.

Blake, having flown over the Western Front, knew all this. He was well aware of the transitory quality, the near-amateurishness, of most sites distinguished by the name aerodrome. He remembered with an inward smile a standard requirement of one English training squadron: that a pilot must be able to land and take off from a ploughed field. Yet he was surprised at the ease with which he and Kristin Dony penetrated Paderborn, not only the landing field but the command area and a concrete apron between the hangars and the headquarters block. It was a long way from the front, but what the hell

– they were training pilots to use prototype machines with new armament!

For a people known for their rigid discipline and attachment to routine, it seemed more than a little casual.

With the bicycles they had stolen from the girls' school – a barking dog had been the only interruption – they had traversed the twelve miles between Salzkotten and the outskirts of Paderborn via a maze of footpaths and country lanes which Blake could never have found, even with a map. Before dawn, they had abandoned the cycles below the railway embankment from which he had first seen the airfield. Then, on the far side of a narrow brick pedestrian tunnel, Kristin had led him to a platelayers' hut just outside the wire perimeter fence. Here, at first light, they had attempted to make themselves look a little more presentable.

Pedalling had practically dried out her drenched skirt, but she had to put up her hair and comb it, and then clean up as best she could the bramble scratches and the ravages of their escape through the wood.

Blake was still wearing the buttoned brown overall tunic he had taken from the canteen building at the factory. He was dishevelled, unshaven again and generally unkempt. His left upper arm, where he had taken the blow from the overseer's wrench, was swollen and exceedingly painful. The palms of his hands throbbed too, but the bandages were now filthy and had to be discarded. It was just possible, nevertheless, that he might pass – from a distance – for a mechanic or non-uniformed technician.

That was no less unlikely than Kristin's madcap scheme of hiding him at the base until he found an opportunity to steal one of the Eindekkers stationed there. At that moment, crazy though the idea was, he was too mentally exhausted to think of a believable alternative.

It was six-thirty when they left the hut, ducked under the wire and walked along a rough path trodden among the long grass, towards the nearest hangar. The bulk of the great canvas structure, she had explained, would hide their approach until they were less than fifty yards from the sick quarters where she had her office.

Yet that fifty yards seemed the longest Blake had ever walked in his life. It had been agreed that Kristin should go ahead as though there was no connection between them. And now here he was, an enemy alien, hundreds of miles inside German territory, a murderer in the eyes of the authorities, blithely approaching, on foot, the headquarters of what might be a secret military site without the slightest written justification of who he was or what he was doing. And no verbal excuse that he could think of that would bear the most cursory examination.

There was already a certain amount of activity on the far side of the hangar. A two-seater Albatros had been wheeled out into the open air, and several men in blue overalls were busy about the exposed engine block. Mechanics further away pushed a squat, saddle-tanked refuelling trolley towards an oversize biplane he thought might be a captured Ilya Mourometz bomber from the EVK – Flotilla of Flying Ships – on the Russian front. Beyond the headquarters block, a small squad of soldiers were marching and countermarching under the orders of a hoarse *Feldwebel*.

None of the men on duty appeared to notice Blake. With the hairs prickling on the nape of his neck, he approached the sick-bay hut. The last door but one on the right, she had said. It will be unlocked.

She herself had already vanished through the hut's main entrance. He stepped up to the door, turned the handle, went inside.

A small, bare room, with a table, two upright chairs and a framed print of the castle at Charlottenburg on one wall. The door clicked shut behind him. He swung around and, on the spur of the moment, tried the handle again. The door was now locked. Behind the table there was an inner door. He walked across and tried that. It, too, was locked.

Before he had time to register this, the second door was flung open.

Blake saw glistening boots, an impeccable uniform with a holstered revolver, a tall young officer with clean-cut features and short, fair hair.

'*Hauptmann* Erich Schneider,' he announced with a click of the heels. 'Foreign Intelligence. We have been expecting you, *Mr* Gerhardt Ehrlich. A sales representative, no? From Hamburg.' A thin smile. 'Well, no, perhaps not.'

Stupefied with astonishment, Blake blurted out the first thing that came to his mind. 'Schneider?' he repeated foolishly. 'From Paderborn? What a coincidence! I think I invented your mother! On the road to Belecke.'

The officer frowned. 'I do not understand. I am from Dresden, in Saxony. You, on the other hand, come from somewhere I imagine to be a good deal west and south of Hamburg.'

'Me, I understand only too well.' Blake's voice was bitter. He paused. Kristin, wearing a clean, freshly pressed uniform, was passing along the corridor behind Schneider. '*Bonjour, Mademoiselle Dony, et bons trahisons!*' he called. 'Good day and happy betrayals.'

The tap of her footsteps ceased. She reappeared behind the German. Her face was flushed.

'The oldest trick in the world,' Blake said before she could speak. 'And, of course, the oldest profession.'

The girl's colour darkened. 'I may be a Protestant of Huguenot origin,' she said, 'but my people have lived in this country for over two hundred years. I am German, and my duty lies with my country.'

'A pity you have not yet learned such attributes of the good German as decency, honour and loyalty to an ideal.' Avoiding her eyes, Blake spoke directly to Schneider. 'What fools we are,' he said, 'to trust them. Any of them.'

'It has not perhaps occurred to you,' Kristin said stiffly, 'that burglary and false pretences – to say nothing of killing people – could be considered by some as falling a trifle short of the very ideals you refer to. You should perhaps consider a saying I believe to be current in your country: that all is fair in love and war.' She smiled. 'Sometimes both.'

19

'I think it only fair to tell you,' Schneider said, 'that once we were persuaded the pilot of the wrecked Sopwith had escaped, a very strict control on all wireless telegraphy was instituted in the immediate area. It was thus that my engineers were able to localize the traitor who was to act as go-between linking you with your headquarters at the time of your very first contact.'

'Efficient,' Blake said drily. 'As one would expect.'

They sat one on either side of the table in the room he had first entered. He had been searched, and the helicoidal gear wheel, along with the empty Walther, the skeleton keys, the broken kitchen knife and his papers lay on the polished wood between them. An armed soldier stood in front of each door.

'It was under what we have, alas, to call "hardened interrogation" that the spy – who had been furnishing information to your masters for some time – was persuaded to reveal such details of your mission as he knew. It was then a simple matter to replace him with Fräulein Dony, one of our most experienced agents.'

'And the . . . the man you call the traitor?'

'He is no longer with us.'

'I see.' Blake's mouth was dry.

'Having first lost and then regained contact with you,' Schneider said, 'Fräulein Dony asked for further

168

instructions. Rather than bring you in at once, she was told to encourage you in the furtherance of your mission. For although we now knew who you were, where you were, and even why you had taken such trouble to penetrate this far into the Fatherland, there was one thing we did not know. And rather to our surprise Fräulein Dony did not know either. Accepting her as your cut-out, you nevertheless managed to keep from her the precise nature of the plans you wished to steal from the Krupp affiliate at Siegsdorf.'

Blake said nothing.

'We arranged therefore that she could help you to enter the factory. But although you told her subsequently that you had succeeded in your quest, you had still failed to reveal exactly what that was. Not wishing to provoke suspicion on your part, she refrained from pressing the matter, believing that the stolen plans would in any case be on your person. To our surprise, however – and hers – no trace of them has been found.'

The *Hauptmann* paused. Once again Blake made no comment.

'I have to ask you now,' Schneider said evenly, 'what plans, what papers you abstracted from which workshop at the Siegsdorf factory?'

'Under internationally agreed conditions,' Blake said at last, 'I must ask to be treated as a prisoner of war. As such, I am obliged to reveal no more than my name, number, rank and, in certain cases, regiment. They are as follows: Number 1092818 Blake, Patrice; Lieutenant, the Honourable Artillery Company; at present seconded to the Royal Flying Corps.'

The German laughed. 'Those conditions apply to belligerents taken in battle,' he said. 'Men wearing uniform. It is accepted that enemies in civilian dress, captured behind the lines, may be treated as spies – the penalty for which, as you well know, is death. A similar sentence, of course, is demanded for murder. Now, to avoid . . . unpleasantness . . . before your execution, tell me at once: where are the plans you stole from Siegsdorf?'

'I must have lost them,' Blake said blandly. 'Or dropped them on the way.'

Schneider sighed. 'A pity,' he said. 'For I admire your courage. But in that case I advise you to remember where you dropped them rather quickly; otherwise I shall be obliged to hand you over to a specialized section of the Feldgendarmerie, whose methods, although in a sense sophisticated, nevertheless lack a certain refinement.'

He prodded the gearwheel on the table with a long finger, turning it around. He cleared his throat. 'You must understand my position, Lieutenant Blake,' he said. 'People are checking at this moment from which tray in the factory this was stolen. Within hours, perhaps minutes, we shall know which plans are missing. It is only a matter of time therefore – and not much of that – before we are in full possession of the secret you strive so hard to conceal. But you must know that I am answerable to very senior officers indeed. And they, for reasons of their own, insist on knowing *now* which of the many devices manufactured at Siegsdorf your High Command is so anxious to study.'

Blake swallowed. A pulse in his throat was fluttering like a bird. 'I have nothing further to add,' he said huskily.

'Very well. So be it.' The German swung around in his chair and barked a command.

The inner door opened and a *Feldwebel* from the military police saluted. 'The prisoner is to be taken at once to Unit Twelve,' Schneider said. 'The under-officer in charge is familiar with the . . . problem. He knows what questions to ask. Just remind him that the matter is urgent.'

'*Jawohl, Herr Hauptmann.*' Two men with drawn pistols appeared behind the *Feldwebel* and stamped to attention. He looked Blake in the eye and beckoned. '*Komm!*'

Blake rose to his feet. 'It was nice meeting you,' he said to Schneider.

Unit Twelve, presumably a block used for 'hardened interrogation', appeared to be on the far side of the aerodrome. The closed van in which Blake and his three-man escort were transported there was halted in front of the third of four hangars beyond the headquarters block. Through one of the small, barred windows Blake saw that the driver had stopped to allow a group of mechanics to wheel two of the new Fokker monoplanes out through the opened hangar flaps.

He had broken out in a cold sweat. Moisture trickled between his shoulder-blades. He was familiar with the sensation. He knew, reeling with giddiness in the prison van, precisely what was causing the condition in him. The situation was certainly claustrophobic. There was no immediate escape. But claustrophobic was too polite a word for the underlying cause. It was due to sheer funk.

The first of the monoplanes had been wheeled clear. Someone was swinging the propeller. The mechanics seemed to have difficulty manoeuvring the second. The van waited, engine idling, bouncing very slightly on its long cantilever springs.

The thought of the interrogation to which he would be submitted in a few short minutes now clawed at Blake's vitals . . . Fists smashing brutally into his flesh, wire whips across his back, his head held down in a bucket of water or his fingernails ripped off . . . Saliva ran salt on either side of his tongue. He choked back scalding vomit that rose in his throat.

Why in God's name hadn't he told the man what he wanted to know? He would tell the interrogators . . . yes, before they began their filthy work, he would . . .

Then the sudden stark realization. Even if he did, he was still a spy. There would still be the firing squad.

All the blood in his body seemed to drain down to his feet. He knew that his face must have gone very white. Wooden benches ran along each side of the van. The two guards sat opposite him, the *Feldwebel* on a tip-up seat that folded down from the partition separating them from the cab. The three Germans appeared suddenly very large, swelling in his vision, which was going black at the edges.

He knew he was going to faint.

Stupidly he felt it necessary to excuse himself . . . Christ, he was going to soil his trousers! He struggled to his feet.

The second monoplane was wheeled clear. The van driver shouted some obscenity, which was replied to from the ground.

'I'm s-s-sorry,' Blake gagged as one of the soldiers started to rise from his seat. 'I'm afraid I . . . I can't help . . .'

The driver trod hard on the throttle pedal and let in the clutch with a savage jerk. The van bucketed forward as the solid tyres bit into tarmac.

Blake was hurled against the single door in the rear of the van.

The door burst open and he pitched out on to the apron.

The van had accelerated another forty or fifty yards before the hammering on his partition caused the driver to screech to a halt. One of the guards was already outside and running back.

Blake struggled up from his hands and knees. Every symptom of panic – perhaps it was the sudden rush of fresh air? – every symptom had vanished, leaving him in a one-dimensional world conditioned by a single imperative: *run like hell!*

Fear lent him wings. A phrase from a trashy novel he had read flashed into his head. He was on his feet and racing as he had never raced before towards the Eindekkers, the mechanics open-mouthed at the shouting behind. A shot rang out.

Blake dashed for the overalled group. They wouldn't shoot once he was among the men. A second slug whistled past his head and then he was scattering the workers, shouldering them violently aside, hitting out with his fists as he hared towards the first of the monoplanes.

The engine was idling, the propeller ticking over; two men held the wingtips and two more shoved, wheeling the machine towards the grassy outfield. A young man in a leather flying jacket swung his helmet from one hand as he followed them.

The instinct for self-preservation had sharpened Blake's reactions, speeded up his thinking, sent the adrenalin storming through his frame to accelerate muscular effort.

He launched himself at the pilot, sent him sprawling with a backhander and ran for the aeroplane.

It was a strange-looking machine, slightly old-fashioned visually. Square-tipped wings sprouted from the aluminium cowling just forward of the cockpit; the long, square-section fabric tail terminated in a rudder shaped like a comma. A spider's web of bracing wires ran up to the wings from the complex steel tube undercarriage.

Blake reached it as the mechanics stopped pushing, alerted by the pandemonium behind him. Sensing his intention, the one on his side of the fuselage ran for the cockpit and started to clamber in; the near wingtip man let go of the fabric-covered spars and raced to cut Blake off.

He knocked the man flat with a looping, roundhouse right as he ran, then seized the cockpit jumper bodily from behind, dragged him clear with a superhuman effort and flung him too to the ground.

He leaped for the padded cockpit rim, hauled himself up and dropped into the pilot's seat.

More by luck than instinct or knowledge, his hand found the throttle control and he pushed, hard.

The noise of the clattering rotary rose to a roar. The ticking propeller spun to a silver disc. The Fokker shuddered on its disc wheels.

Slowly at first, and then with increasing speed, it shrugged off the two remaining mechanics, yawed slightly and ran out on to the grass.

Blake glanced over his shoulder. A scout car with a machine-gun mounted above the windshield was speeding along the perimeter track. Behind him, they were swinging the propeller of the second Eindekker. Within minutes, perhaps seconds, there would be pursuit . . . and pursuit equipped with synchronized, twin Spandau 7.92mm machine-guns. Firing forward through the arc of the propeller.

He would be chased by the very machinery he had been sent to investigate!

The same guns, with their single telescopic sight, lay along the cowling in front of him. But there was going to be no foolhardy attempt at a dogfight here – not with a machine he had never even seen before, with controls

174

that were totally unfamiliar, even with an opponent who was probably only a trainee.

No nonsense either about turning into the wind. He was determined to race straight across the field the way he was facing now, taking off crosswind to save time . . . and keep away from the scout car with its gun.

He would check the manipulation of rudder and ailerons once he was in the air; all he was interested in now was lift.

The Eindekker gathered speed, bumping over the uneven ground. Blake's scarred hands grasped the two polished wood handles at the top of the control column. When he judged the aeroplane to be approaching fifty miles per hour, he began delicately easing the stick fractionally back and then forward again, feeling for the first slight reaction of the aerofoil surfaces.

The wire fence, and the hedge beyond it on the far side of the field, seemed alarmingly close – and to be approaching alarmingly fast. But the little machine was steady and it was responsive. Blake still had two hundred yards in hand when he coaxed her off the ground – the stick light now in his hands – over the fence and the embankment and the slate roofs beyond.

He wasn't even going to attempt a turn until he was at what the altimeter told him was the equivalent of two hundred feet. Nor was he going to aim at more than two hundred and fifty throughout the whole journey. Why waste time climbing when there could be a lethal pursuer closing up behind?

And, after all, he had only twelve miles to fly.

Back to Siegsdorf, to the factory, to the wood behind it . . . and the hollow tree in which he had hidden the cardboard tube containing the stolen plans.

20

Why had he done it? What could have prompted him to stow away the cardboard cylinder inside a hollow tree during their escape from the factory? With the object of his mission safely in his hands, why would he deliberately have placed it out of his own reach?

Because he feared capture, but was convinced he would be able to escape and recover the plans later? That seemed unlikely. And in any case he had no recollection of thinking that.

There was, of course, a more prosaic reason: the eighteen-inch cylinder, stuffed inside his trousers, had completely stiffened his lame leg and slowed him down dangerously as they forced their way through the undergrowth. But was that in itself sufficient for him to take such a risk? Blake thought not.

Certainly, at the time, he had had not the least suspicion that the girl was not his cut-out. With hindsight he could see that there had been pointers – little things that maybe should have at least alerted him or prompted him to ask more questions. The fact that she herself on several occasions did ask, contrary to routine, about his specific orders. The fact that she knew in advance that three triplanes would be at the factory that night – an unusually detailed piece of information for a nursing auxiliary to have. Above all that she knew just a little too much about his own movements. 'I heard about your escape from the hotel in Paderborn,' she had said.

In the time available, she could not possibly have heard that as gossip in the aerodrome mess: she could only have heard it from police or security quarters.

It was, of course, he thought bitterly, the sex which had blinded him to what should have been obvious . . . or at least worth closer attention. Because of it he had trusted her without further questioning.

And yet . . . and yet . . . *something* had prompted him to get shot of the incriminating cylinder while he was still with her. Perhaps, subconsciously, he had registered those pointers; maybe, in times of stress, the subconscious was brighter than the conscious?

At the moment, skimming the rooftops of Paderborn, he was thankful that he *had* done it, however difficult it might be to profit from that fact. And thankful too – be honest! – to the subconscious decision, the split-second determination when the opportunity arose, to grab an aeroplane in an attempt to get it back.

That was his second piece of luck. The first had been that unexpected opening of the prison van door. The third, he supposed, was the result of that dreadful night after his cowardly run from the factory.

The field of stubble where he had slept by the haystack. The harvest was in; the surface was flat enough and wide enough to land a small aeroplane.

If, of course, he survived the landing!

He was getting used to the unfamiliar Fokker controls. The rudder was stiff and the plane slow to react because of its small surface; the ailerons were stiffer when he moved the stick sideways. But otherwise he had so far discovered no vices. Apart from the inherent characteristic of all rotary engines: the fact that they tend to run only at idle or full speed, fine control being a luxury granted to few. A 'blip switch' fitted to the control column, familiar to Blake from British machines powered by rotaries, could cut the ignition to several or all of the cylinders, temporarily reducing power in approach.

Between the hand-cranked starting magneto and the fuel filler pipe there was a small switch panel with different settings marked. He assumed this was similar to one he had seen on a French Nieuport, which allowed the pilot to select different combinations of the cylinders to fire and/or cut out. But he wasn't going to experiment that far! Getting her down in one piece was what mattered now.

Whether he wished, or would be able, to take off again depended on what happened after that. And on the actions of the man piloting the second Eindekker.

He glanced back over the tapered tail. Yes, there he was, a miniature silhouette against the rising sun perhaps a couple of miles away. He appeared to be climbing steeply. Gaining height perhaps so that he could increase speed in a dive and catch Blake up. He wasn't to know how short the flight was to be!

Siegsdorf, huddled around a curve in the River Lippe, was visible ahead. Railway lines curving away below gleamed in the early morning sunshine. He banked warily over the station and the familiar square, flew over a river bridge, and headed for Salzkotten.

In front of the Fokker windscreen, an inverted steel V rose from the engine cowling. From the summit of this, four bracing wires stretched out on either side to steady the single wing, already located by a similar number slanting up from the undercarriage below. The wind sang an alto chord through the wires as he flipped the switch to cut ignition and began to lose height

... one hundred and eighty feet ... one fifty ... a hundred ...

Between the legs of the metal V Blake looked over the perforated housing of a Spandau machine-gun at fields misted by the spinning propeller. He saw the roofs and church spire of Salzkotten, half hidden among trees. He saw the hilltop factory and the woods behind. Then the village sank from sight below the wood as he dropped lower still.

He was approaching the stubble field at a height of fifty feet, thirty ... He was coming in much too fast. He blipped the switch again. The propeller feathered. Too fast, too fast – and no chance of a circuit: he would be lucky as it was to stop taxiing and get clear of the machine before the pursuer landed behind him. Or simply circled and started to shoot.

The ochre surface of the field flashed towards him. He remembered once hearing a pilot say that the average Fokker had the same glide angle as a piano.

Very well, he would *drop* the bitch down! A hedge shot past beneath the wing. He juggled with the stick. There was nothing more he could do now.

The Eindekker hit the ground with a rending crash, bounced what seemed like twenty feet into the air, thumped down once more, then wheeled into a crazy half-circle, dragging one wing like a wounded bird as undercarriage spars collapsed. It shot across the field, scoring deep furrows in the stubbled earth, and finally came to rest against the haystack with the engine stalled and one blade of the propeller snapped.

So much for the take-off! Blake thought, vaulting over the cockpit rim and running for the trees at the far end of the field.

The second Eindekker was planing in to land. They

must have told him Blake was unarmed and instructed him to take the runaway prisoner.

Throttled back severely, the monoplane made an impeccable three-pointer, lost speed, swung around and taxied toward the haystack. The pilot jumped out as the engine died. There was a pistol in his hand.

Blake heard the man shout as he ran. A single shot rang out, cracking back as an echo from a bank below the wood. He didn't even bother to start zigzagging: as something of a gunnery expert, he knew that firing a service revolver at a moving target more than fifty yards away was a waste of time and ammunition.

He scrambled, panting, up the bank. This could be a textbook exercise from the unarmed-combat course. But what he needed, first, was a suitable tree, and secondly a dense enough package of trunks and branches and undergrowth to hide him when he climbed into it. He had to force his way two hundred yards into the wood before he found the right place.

Even then it was a matter of split-second timing. The pilot had been gaining on him, and Blake could hear the thrashing of leaves a little too close for comfort as he dragged himself up on to the horizontal branch he had been looking for.

The pilot – an older, tougher man than the one Blake had floored with his backhander – ran out into the miniature clearing beneath the tree, looking right and left. He was marginally too far out for the drop Blake had planned, but there was nothing to be done about that now.

As the man started forward again, Blake launched himself out and down. His two feet crashed into him just below the shoulders, felling him to the carpet of pine needles below the tree. Before the man could get his breath back, before he realized what had happened, the edge of Blake's left hand had chopped him savagely across the side of the neck.

The pilot gagged, trying to heave himself up from his prone position. But Blake was already straddling the small of his back. With his right, he reached for the pistol, which had flown out of the man's hand, seized it by the barrel and brought the butt down once, twice, three times on the back of his head.

The German groaned, twitched once, then lay still.

Blake was sweating. He had a choice now. Recover the plans at once and deal with the problems of the pilot, the plane and his possible escape later. Or vice versa. It depended on how long the man was going to be unconscious. And over this he had no control – and no knowledge of the probabilities either.

Better, then, to go for the plans first.

It took him twenty minutes to complete his traverse of the wood, cross the Salzkotten road and retrace his steps through the wood behind the factory. If the hollow oak had not been on the far fringe, it would have taken him twice as long. Holding his breath, he plunged one hand into the fissured trunk.

The tube was still there. It was damp and a little less stiff – either from nocturnal dew or a shower – but the papers inside seemed undamaged except for a slight smudging on one of the working drawings. He re-rolled them and thrust them back inside.

Now he would have to steel himself for the difficult part. The landing of two Fokkers in a cornfield less than half a mile from the factory would most certainly have brought a patrol down from the guardhouse to find out what the hell was going on. They would expect an explanation, from one if not two pilots.

Blake aimed to provide that . . . if luck continued to be with him.

The man he had knocked out still lay on the ground beneath the tree. Feeling for a wrist and kneeling close so that he could manoeuvre one ear close to the slack mouth, Blake discovered that there was a pulse beating. The breath was stertorous and shallow, but fairly even. Very well, he could safely leave him for the time necessary. But first there were things to do.

He had never before realized how difficult it would be to remove the clothes from – or to dress – a human body that was a dead weight. The task, a disagreeable one, took him well over ten minutes. By which time the chorus of voices from the stubbled field had become frighteningly audible.

Finally, however, Blake was dressed in a German army uniform with a fleece-lined leather flying coat over his shoulders. The unconscious pilot lay in Blake's corduroys, army tunic and buttoned brown overalls.

Blake drew a deep breath. His plan, such as it was, depended on the fact that the factory guard would have seen neither him nor the pilot before. Any identification therefore would rely solely on the clothes that each wore.

Stifling the apprehension he felt, Blake picked up the German's pistol, stuffed it in the left-hand pocket of the flying coat, and hurried back through the wood.

He jumped down the bank and ran towards the group of soldiers – about a dozen of them – gathered around the undamaged Eindekker.

An officer came towards him. 'What the devil . . . ?' he began.

'He got away,' Blake panted. 'Lost him in the damned

wood behind the factory. Elusive bastard. He runs like the wind.'

'*Who* got away? What are you doing? What was *he* doing? Why are you here?'

The officer was scarcely coherent. He didn't know how to deal with situations that were not in the book.

'Escaped prisoner from Paderborn,' Blake said shortly. 'An *Englander* spy. Got away from a prison van, snaffled one of these, by God' – he jerked his head towards the Fokker – 'and took off! I was told to follow him, bring him back dead or alive.' He shrugged. 'Unfortunately he was too quick for me. Not my line, anyway: I'm not a policeman; I drive aeroplanes.'

'What do you wish us to do, *Herr Major*?' The officer had suddenly noticed the badges of rank on Blake's sleeve and epaulette. He had not, in fact, taken them in before himself. Now he allowed an authoritative note to creep into his voice.

'Throw a cordon around these woods,' he snapped. 'Block the road between here and Salzkotten. Contact your headquarters at once and double the guard on the factory. You are looking for a youngish man, about my height, dressed in workman's trousers, an army tunic and a brown factory overseer's coat. He may be armed.'

The young officer saluted. '*Jawohl, Herr Major*.' He raised a hand to summon an NCO.

'But first,' Blake pursued, 'tell your men to turn this machine around, wheel it to the far end of the field and help me ready it for take-off. I must get back at once to Paderborn and make my report.' He sighed. 'Unfortunately a negative one. I wish you better luck.'

'Yes, sir. Thank you, sir.' The German saluted again, rapped out a few terse commands to the NCO and detailed six men to manhandle the Eindekker. Four more returned to the factory at the double.

It wouldn't take them long to locate the pilot, especially if he had come to in the meantime. Perhaps rather longer before they believed his story. After all, the regional alert would by now have specified a runaway, dressed thus, who spoke perfect German but had no papers – and the man's papers were in Blake's pocket.

By the time the story was straightened out, anyway, Blake himself hoped to be over the hills and far away.

He had no idea how much fuel there was in the Eindekker's tank. There was no gauge. It didn't matter too much anyway: other than leaving the Detmold–Siegsdorf area as quickly as possible, he had no specific goal in mind. Only when he was well clear and the immediate heat was off could he begin to think of how to get himself and the precious plans back to England.

For the moment he was content to let the monoplane ferry him as far as it could – or for as long as he thought it safe to stay in the air. After that the real trouble would begin! For all the alternative suggestions mulled over with his superiors at home had been predicated on a continuing contact with his cut-out. Now that he was deprived of that advice and knowledge of the country, at least one of the possible escape routes – through Switzerland with the help of existing operatives – was definitively cut.

For the first time, he permitted himself to think objectively of Kristin's treachery and betrayal. Now that the first sick horror had passed, he found that he was less disgusted at her behaviour – after all, in a sense she was only doing, morally, much the same as he was – as he was appalled at his own stupidity. How could he have been so naive, so easily hoodwinked?

He wondered if she was continuing to send bogus reports on his progress, or lack of it, to London. By now, in any case, they would know exactly what he was after. It would, of course, be useful to the German intelligence services to have a double agent in place with the means to send false information and possibly find out more about Allied agents working in the Fatherland. But she wasn't going to last long if telephone contact with Switzerland was involved: even with all the call-signs correct, the voice would give her away at once.

Blake put the girl from his mind. He had been airborne for ten minutes. The take-off had been difficult. The soldiers hadn't understood that each cylinder of a rotary must be primed with neat petrol while the engine is turned over by hand, before it will fire. And when at last this had been correctly done, not one of them had the least idea how to swing a propeller. Finally – even if his own logbook did record only five out of ten for this exercise! – Blake had to improvise chocks and swing it himself, with the officer, duly briefed, installed in the cockpit.

Once he was back at the controls, there was no more than a momentary trauma to overcome, as he took in the slight downhill slant of the field and breathed a short prayer that the Fokker would come unstuck before the blackthorns marking its lower limit.

Fortunately he was facing into the wind and – as he had found out before – the little machine needed only a very short run. He was fifteen feet above the hedge when he cleared the far end of the stubble.

Waving a farewell arm at the soldiers below, he banked the Eindekker and set a course for Paderborn. He kept low, which was reasonable over a distance that short, so that he would be out of sight as soon as possible. When he had covered half the twelve miles, he vectored sharply right and began to climb.

He levelled out at ten thousand feet, by which time the sun was high in the sky and the misty countryside below had dwindled to a familiar map-like patchwork. At that height the air was still solid enough to make breathing euphoric rather than laborious. He was glad nevertheless to have the fleece-lined flying jacket.

He was back at last where he belonged, feet on the rudder bar, hands on a control column and the wide world empty around him. He began to sing.

Blake was in fact getting used to what had become his alternations of fear and elation, bravado and funk. If only he could be granted the power of selection . . . or at least the possibility of knowing which he would be at the mercy of in a given situation.

He was heading at the moment practically due west, edging a little southwards, when the pall of smoke rising over the industrialized sections of the Ruhr drifted uncomfortably close. Clearly the crucible of German war production would be guarded more heavily than the open country to the east.

So far as an eventual escape was concerned, Switzerland was some two hundred and twenty miles due south. The battlefields of the Western Front were about the same distance ahead. Between the two, he reckoned the front-line chaos would give him a better chance of crossing secretly into Allied territory, and thus a quick return to base, than an attempt to force the heavily policed Swiss frontier. Better still would be neutral Holland, but that was north of the Ruhr and doubtless even more strictly guarded.

He was not, in any case, expecting the monoplane to take him the whole way, whichever direction he chose.

Even if the tank had been full when it left Paderborn. He dare not risk staying in the air too long: a general alert would report that a rogue Eindekker was on the loose somewhere up there, and it would need only one keen observer to recognize the plane for them to know which way he was going. Which would mean scouts sent up to intercept him from aerodromes on his route.

If only, he thought, the machine *could* take him safely the thirty-odd miles to Holland ... This, he realized seconds after the thought had come to him, was the second 'if only' since take-off which would have no chance whatever of a satisfactory or encouraging follow-up.

Between the two legs of the bracing wire pivot, he saw them perhaps three miles ahead: four specks against the pale western sky that rapidly resolved themselves into aeroplanes with black crosses on wings and fuselage. Two Halberstadt reconnaissance two-seaters with a pair of Albatros D-Va scouts as fighter escort.

They were climbing steeply and they were coming his way.

21

Blake had not been expecting – and certainly had no appetite for – a dogfight. Nor had he anticipated, this far into Germany, that the aviation authorities would cotton on to his route so quickly or put up opposition ahead of him so fast.

There seemed, however, no alternative. The nearest cloud bank was ten miles away, uncomfortably far to the north. There was another directly ahead, but it was twice as far and the four German machines were in the way – and climbing rapidly. They would be at his altitude before he had covered a quarter of the distance.

He bit his lip. His mount was newer, faster and almost certainly more manoeuvrable than the Albatros scouts or the Halberstadts. But he was totally unfamiliar with its aerobatic characteristics, he had only just got used to the controls and his aggregate flying time in this Eindekker and the previous one was considerably less than an hour. And in any case it was four against one – two of the four benefiting from auxiliary guns fired from the rear cockpit.

Down below – the Fokker tilting fractionally to starboard – industrial smoke partially concealed a huge complex of factory chimneys, railway lines, gasometers and blast furnaces belching flame. Staring down over the padded cockpit rim Blake saw steelworks and marshalling yards stretching away to a dull grey gleam that must be the Rhine. He reckoned that he must be some way south of Essen. The interceptors had probably been put up from one of the aerodromes on the outskirts of Düsseldorf.

He swore. If he was right, he was less than thirty miles from the Dutch frontier. A hell of a time, and a hell of a place, he thought distractedly, to be faced with seasoned adversaries equipped, between them, with something like six or eight deadly machine-guns.

The two-seater Halberstadts must have taken off before the scouts – or been alerted from a nearer aerodrome. They were almost at his level, and the Albatros fighters still a mile behind and several hundred feet lower.

Very well. He would have to do what he could to disable or frighten away the slower observation planes before the escort arrived.

He reached forward and up for an experimental tug at the toggles below the twin Spandau magazine covers.

For an instant the racketing roar of the 110hp Oberursel rotary was drowned by the explosive blast hammered from the guns. The wood and fabric fuselage shuddered under the recoil of the two short bursts. Blake nodded grimly. At least he wasn't flying into a trap unarmed.

The leading Halberstadt was less than two hundred yards away. Abruptly, the pilot dipped the nose of the machine to pass twenty or thirty feet below Blake, at a slight angle. This, Blake knew, was to let the gunner in the rear cockpit have an unobstructed upward shot at the blind spot below his tail. After which the plane would zoom back up to his level, half roll and turn to come in for a frontal attack on one flank or the other.

He tipped the Eindekker on to one wing, screamed into a near-vertical dive, half rolled himself and crossed the Halberstadt's flight path fifty feet lower down. This left him free to climb steeply and fire at the belly of the second observation machine. The pilot saw him coming and veered sharply away, but Blake was happy to see a line of holes stitched across the rear fuselage and through the tailplane and rudder as the Spandaus spat fire from the blunt nose of the Fokker.

He was now directly in line with the second Albatros. Attack being the best means of defence – and surprise theoretically the best weapon of all – he decided on the spur of the moment to play the amateur card. Pulling the nose of the monoplane sharply up a hundred yards in front of the scout, he banked steeply and then dropped the machine into a near-vertical dive.

As he had hoped, the German, believing he was dealing with a beginner and not yet concentrated into a true battle awareness, howled down after him with both guns blazing.

Blake steepened his dive still more. The Albatros followed, gaining now as the range closed.

The Fokker was shuddering in every spar. Slipstream loaded with a mist of castor oil tore at Blake's goggled face. Elongated tears appeared in the wing fabric and something thumped heavily back in the tail. A stray bullet nicked one of the bracing wires and it snapped with a noise like a plucked violin string.

Blake was betting on the German pilot's eagerness for an easy kill – and on an aviation intelligence report he had read, which stated: 'Virtually all Albatros DVs suffer structural failures in steep dives, due to a flutter in the lower wing.'

The bet was well placed. The hail of machine-gun fire ceased. The biplane hurtled past . . . but it wasn't diving; it was dropping. He saw the pilot wrestling with the controls. The lower starboard wing had buckled, tearing

190

free of the V-shaped strut linking it to the wing above. As Blake watched, it broke away and floated off on its own. The crippled machine cartwheeled twice, sank tail down into an uncontrollable spin, somersaulted out of that and finally spiralled out of sight.

With sweat streaming from his brow to course through the hot oil stinging his face, Blake hauled on the control column as forcefully as he dared to coax his plane out of its dive. Once more the entire airframe juddered. Something was flapping out of sight behind. It was two thousand feet before he finally levelled out. With the height lost evading the Halberstadt, he saw that the altimeter now registered no more than four thousand nine hundred.

The remaining Albatros and the two observation planes were circling down more warily, waiting to drop on him out of the sun.

That would not do at all. Blake had to get back upstairs if he was going to come out of this in one piece. Gritting his teeth, he heaved the stick back again as far as it would come under maximum power, shooting up into the sky like a cork from a bottle as he kicked hard on the rudder bar.

The Albatros sailed past him with guns spitting as he rose.

He hung the Eindekker on its propeller above the Halberstadts, treated this as the zenith of a loop, then completed the circle to swoop down on the slower two-seater he had already damaged. With his face pressed to the rubberized fabric of the telescopic gunsight eyepiece, he opened fire with both guns.

He saw the observer, frantically swinging his weapon around on its ring mount, slump suddenly back against the cockpit rim, saw the pilot jerk forward to slide down the instrument panel, saw flame blossom from behind the exposed engine block.

The Halberstadt erupted into a seething fireball. Black debris shot out into the sky, and the carcass dropped from sight trailing a long plume of oily smoke.

Blake was trembling. He hated to see them die. But there were still two more determined to get him. He jerked the toggles again as the Albatros swam into view broadside on – a perfect kill for synchronized guns.

The engine continued its clattering roar but the Spandaus remained silent. He tugged fiercely again . . . but the scout had wheeled away. And the guns were mute.

Blake cursed. Both magazines were exhausted. They must have been partly used on one of the target runs at Paderborn. And there were no spares to be seen. He thrust the stick forward and dived again.

He hadn't noticed before, but the encounter had taken them quite a long way south, and no further towards the cloud bank in the west. The only believable cover that he could see was a blanket of industrial smoke lying over a mining area ten miles ahead and several thousand feet below him. It was, again, due south; not too far, he estimated, from Cologne.

This time, the Fokker was vibrating badly during the dive. The flapping behind had become an ugly thump. Although the second Albatros pilot was unwilling to risk structural failure in a dive this steep, the remaining Halberstadt was gamely following Blake down, shooting as he came.

Once you got used to it, Blake thought, the Eindekker really was a treat to fly, vibrations and all.

No sooner had the thought formulated itself than the

machine dropped its nose further still and threw itself into a spin.

He swore again. What the hell? He wrestled with the stick, the rudder bar. What the devil was the matter now? Why wouldn't she . . . ?

The pounding behind was reaching a climax. Over his shoulder he saw with horror that the port elevator had broken away from the tailplane. It was flapping wildly in the slipstream, held in place only by its control cables. Holes appeared in the rudder and the rear part of the fuselage as the Halberstadt circled overhead with the rear gunner firing down from his cockpit ring.

Five hundred feet above the smoke layer, the monoplane was becoming uncontrollable. Blake set his teeth, compensating for the loss of control surface with reverse rudder and skilful juggling of the ailerons. Grey wisps loaded with sulphurous fumes and the choking odour of coal gas were already whipping through the screaming stays by the time he finally halted the sickening corkscrew fall and levelled out in a shallow, stumbling descent. It was obvious, however, that the flight was over: he had scarcely any directional control, he could not climb and – just to hammer in the last nail! – the engine coughed, spat and choked into silence. The fuel tank was empty. He had to put down.

Blindly, with the propeller spinning to a standstill, he sank through the dark cloud.

It was only about two hundred feet thick. Below it, the Eindekker staggered out above a smoky wasteland of colliery wheels, chimneys and gantries carrying serpentine coils of metal piping. A little way to the west was the broad pale ribbon of the Rhine. In such a landscape, it was the only hope.

The Halberstadt emerged from a cloud a mile away to

193

the east. It was followed by the Albatros. They banked at once and headed for the Fokker.

Blake coaxed the machine towards the river, losing height as slowly as he dared while keeping as far ahead of the pursuers as he could. The swirling water leaped towards him.

He pancaked the Eindekker between a complex of ancient wharves and a tug towing a string of barges loaded with coal. It dropped twenty feet into the stream with a shattering crash and a huge surge of white foam, sinking at once in a cloud of steam.

Grasping his precious cardboard tube, Blake was already standing on the wing. He jumped as the doomed plane gurgled away beneath him, and struck out one-handed towards the tug, holding the plans above his head.

As he had hoped, the tug veered towards him. A seaman leaned out over the low stern, proffering a boat-hook. Blake grabbed it and was hauled aboard.

'What the devil was going on up there?' the grizzled skipper asked when Blake, relieved of his sodden sheepskin, wrapped in a blanket and fortified with schnapps, stood beside him on the tiny bridge.

'An exercise,' Blake said. 'Practising for the Western Front. But some dolt of a rigger had made a mistake: without knowing it, one of my colleagues up there was firing live ammunition.'

'Good God!' the skipper said. 'What will they think of next?'

'What indeed!'

'You were lucky you weren't killed.'

'That is perfectly true,' Blake said fervently. He looked up into the sky. The two planes, having circled the river banks once or twice, had flown away. Warehouses and cranes slid towards them on either side. A police launch creamed past in the opposite direction. 'The only thing is,' he added, 'I have to make my report pretty damn quick. Could you possibly put me ashore at Cologne? You wouldn't even need to tie up: just come close enough to a quay for me to jump.'

The skipper took his pipe from his mouth and spat into the river. 'You're a bit late for that, friend,' he said. 'We're heading upstream. Cologne is ten kilometres astern! I'll land you at Koblenz, though, if that would suit.' He re-lit the pipe, shielding the match flame from the breeze with cupped hands. 'In a couple of hours.'

'Perfect. And many thanks,' Blake said. 'Er . . . I'm not from this part of the country. It's a big town, Koblenz?'

The skipper chuckled. 'Big enough,' he said.

22

The brigadier and the major-general sat drinking lobster soup at the counter of Scott's restaurant in Coventry Street. Between the two white soup plates with their blue rims stood a recently opened bottle of Chablis.

'Thirty-seven yesterday,' the senior man said. 'Poor young blighters are falling out of the sky quicker than we can ship out bloody replacements. And some of those are being posted with less than a couple of weeks' training.' He shook his head. 'Life expectation of a lad like that can be a matter of hours in the sky rather than weeks or even days.'

'Yes, sir. I know. But if we can . . .'

'To say nothing,' the major-general pursued, 'of the difficulty of finding the machines they're going to fly – and probably die – in. Trenchard's really got the wind up, I can tell you.'

'If only we knew,' the brigadier said, 'for sure. I mean to say, the last signal we got from S-12 was optimistic. The last but one, I should say. Our man had actually got into the factory. And out again. But apparently without the stuff. He was to go back the following night.'

The major-general grunted. 'That got you an extension of your twenty-four hours,' he said. 'Now you're trying to wriggle out of that. What exactly did the *very* last signal say?'

The brigadier cleared his throat. He crooked a finger to summon the barman and indicated that he should pour the wine. 'It was a little odd,' he said. 'The staging contact in Switzerland – the chap who receives S-12's messages and passes them on by telephone – he said our man had got in the second time successfuly. But he didn't say – or, rather, S-12 didn't say – whether or not he had the plans.'

'Well, I must say that's a bit rum,' the major-general exclaimed. 'It's only the aim of the whole damned operation, after all! Chap gets down to the far end of the field unopposed, then doesn't say whether or not he scored a try!'

'Exactly. It leaves us in what I call a tricky situation. Do we assume yes, and wait patiently for more news? Or do we, as they say, make other arrangements?'

The major-general grunted again, then drank some wine. 'This soup's uncommonly good,' he observed. 'What is there off-ration that it's safe to eat?'

'The turbot, sir,' the barman intervened. 'Poached, with Hollandaise sauce. Arrived from Grimsby early this morning. Very popular with our regulars, sir, the turbot.'

'Very well. Two turbots then.'

The street doors swung open, letting in a gust of cool air, the rumble of wheels and the sound of motor traffic circling Piccadilly Circus two hundred yards away. Three naval officers entered and installed themselves at the far end of the bar. They were followed by a man and a woman in civilian clothes who were given a table in an alcove.

The major-general and his companion turned around on their stools, their haughty gaze sweeping over dark panelling and brasswork and crimson leather chairs – and then over the new arrivals – as if outraged by the intrusion of strangers into their private domain.

'Anyway,' the major-general said, turning back to his fish.

197

'Thing is,' the brigadier told him, 'there's actually something else deuced tricky here, sir. I can't exactly say it's another signal from S-12. But it's *about* him. Fellow in Switzerland was a shade puzzled. These Morse experts, you see, get to *know* their contacts in a way. The same way musicians can tell the difference between one pianist and another playing the same piece. Matter of rhythm and touch; way the key's handled, impact, spacing of dots and dashes. Almost like a signature.'

'So I have been told. And so?'

'Well, our Swiss wallah thought – he wasn't sure, mind, but he *thought* – that there was something rum about the last couple of transmissions. Almost as though another operator was sending the stuff. Correct call-signs and all, but *different*. Also the abbreviations, what we call the cablese, were as you might say in a different vein. As if there was another kind of intelligence at work.' The brigadier paused. He drank some wine and held up his glass for more.

'Fellow wondered at first whether S-12 was off colour or something of that sort,' he continued. 'Then, of course, he thought maybe the Hun had bagged the chap and he was transmitting under duress. Naturally we told him to check.'

The major-general was forking flakes of turbot into his mouth. 'Jolly good,' he enthused. 'We were right to take the chap's advice. What is this S-12 caper anyway?'

'Just a matter of identification,' the brigadier said. 'You know: no names, no bloody pack drill! S stands for Saxony; the number signifies that we are dealing with the twelfth agent on the list. Elderly fellow, actually. Lived there forty years.'

'What happened when your Swiss man checked?'

'Couldn't regain contact. No go. No signal at the proper time. Then – this was the queerest thing of all – a call at the wrong time, late in the evening. But before our contact could put in a special code question we have, asking for a coded confirmation that everything was all right and above board . . . before that, S-12 *himself* started to ask questions.' The brigadier shook his head. 'Most unusual. Out of court. Said our man was scot-free and heading south, *but that he wanted urgent confirmation of exactly what plans he was to filch.* I mean, I ask you!'

'What did your Swiss end say?'

'Didn't have a chance to say anything. Before he could ask why, the line was cut. Completely dead.'

'You mean your telephone line with the Swiss?'

'No, no. The wireless transmission, the Morse. Simply ceased. And nothing since, neither at the right time nor any other. The Swiss keeps trying, but the blasted airwaves remain silent. Call-sign's never answered; not a bloody sausage.'

Nodding his head slowly, the major-general laid down his fork. 'Very rum, as you say,' he commented. 'Very rum indeed.'

'I stopped Fräulein Dony sending at that moment,' *Hauptmann* Schneider said, 'because at that moment we received confirmation from the factory of what was missing. There was no need to wait for an answer we already knew. Besides, there was a risk that this kind of question might make the *Englanders* suspicious if we persisted. And it could be useful in the future, keeping the young woman in place as a supposed agent of theirs.'

Schneider was making his report at Hohenstein to Rudolph von Sonderstern. Through the pines beyond the long windows, sunlight glinted on the fast-moving water of the river below.

'So it is Fokker's interrupter gear they were after,' the *Kommandant* mused. 'Pity. But I suppose they were going to come up with something similar themselves before long anyway.' He smiled. 'At least it wasn't the rapid-fire mechanism or the new sighting machine for the delivery of bombs. It is a relief to know that they are apparently unaware of those.'

'With respect, *Herr General-Major*,' Schneider ventured, 'the unfortunate fact that the spy succeeded in stealing the plans for the Fokker gear does not necessarily mean that he will safely return with them to England. We have every hope that he will be recaptured and the papers recovered.'

'H'm. And how far, young man, or more properly how near, has this optimistic prophecy, this forecast, come to realization?'

'We know approximately where he is; we know in which direction he is heading. With an efficient collaboration between our own operatives and the police of the Cologne region, it should be possible very soon to block him ahead and catch up with him from behind.'

'As efficient as the way in which he was imprisoned at Paderborn? As the manner in which he was permitted – twice – to steal aeroplanes of the Imperial Army Air Service, and use one of them to destroy two more in the air?'

Schneider coloured. 'It must be admitted, *Herr General-Major*,' he said, 'that we are dealing with a resourceful man. And with an expert pilot. If we . . .'

'Do we too not have resourceful men, rather more of them, at our disposal? And pilots equally expert?'

'Yes, sir. Of course. It is more a matter of where they are deployed, and whether that deployment can be effected at the right time, when it concerns a quarry completely autonomous, able to speak the language perfectly and apparently equipped with plenty of money.'

The *Hauptmann* paused, staring through a window at the tree-covered hillside. The sun had vanished behind a cloud and the upper branches of the pines were tossing. Von Sonderstern, ramrod-straight in an oak chair like a throne, waited for him to continue.

Schneider, standing at attention, was at a disadvantage. 'It has to be remembered, sir,' he said awkwardly, 'that he *was* efficiently delivered to us, originally, by our female agent. His subsequent escape – and the fact that a machine was standing nearby with the engine running – were totally unforeseen.'

'In matters of national security,' Sonderstern said severely, 'the unforeseen is to be expected.'

'Yes, *Herr General-Major*. The door to the prison van should, of course, have been locked. The *Feldwebel* in charge of the escort swears that it was, that he effected this himself. It is possible that he was mistaken, is lying or even that the sudden start, the fault of the driver, threw the prisoner with such force against the door that it burst open the lock. Both men, in any case, have been disciplined.'

Schneider swallowed. He was dying to raise one hand and extend a finger to ease his tight collar away from his neck. 'With regard to the pilot who followed the stolen aeroplane,' he said, 'I feel, sir, that I should point out this was not a man trained to deal with escaped prisoners or deal with professional spies. The fact that he was mastered by the fugitive, relieved of his clothes and left unconscious while the man apparently retrieved the stolen drawings from some hiding place was unfortunate . . .'

'Most unfortunate. Go on.'

'. . . as was the fact that the soldiers who arrived had seen neither of them before, and thus were persuaded easily that that – er – one was the other. After that, it was after all a matter of aerial combat. And, as in such matters, it was skill and experience that counted. The fugitive certainly destroyed one machine, but the other was lost due to a structural failure – a defect common to the type. And the stolen aeroplane was in fact shot down by the remaining pilots.'

'Yes. Into the Rhine. And the pilot?'

'The aviators reported that he swam free. It is thought that he may have been picked up by a river craft heading upstream. But the fact that we are aware of this; the fact that . . .'

'The fact this, the fact that!' the *Kommandant* snapped. 'You deliver me nothing but what you call *facts*, young man. But every one is a *fact* connected with something that is in some way or another a failure. The next time I see you, I expect every "fact" that you present me with to concern a success. Is that clearly understood?'

'*Jawohl, Herr General-Major*,' Schneider said miserably.

Blake stood in the shadow of a buttress projecting from the wall of the Ehrenbreitstein citadel, a fortress commanding the confluence of the Rhine and the Moselle at Koblenz.

The sun, low down in the western sky, silhouetted the roofs of the city and the seventeenth-century belfries of the Liebfrauenkirche on the far side of the Rhine. The river traffic – barges laden with sand, cement, timber; a steamer transporting crated machinery; a police launch – was dense. He thought he would wait until it was almost dark before he crossed the Pfaffendorfer bridge and passed beneath the trees of the Rheinanlagen waterfront promenade on his way to the old town. It was already two hours since the tugboat skipper had put him ashore – and one hour fifty minutes since he had seen the vessel stopped in midstream and boarded by military police.

They had left five minutes later, but it was clear that

the surviving pilots had witnessed his escape from the crippled Eindekker before it sank, and reported it as soon as they returned to base. The hunt was on and the pursuers were closing in.

For the moment Blake was content to lose himself if possible in the narrow lanes of the old town. He was dressed in the uniform – not quite dry – of a German army major. Reluctantly, he had abandoned the sodden sheepskin flying jacket. In his pocket were the papers of one Bruno Früchtnicht, born in Bad Kreuznach in 1892, and what remained of the identity of Gerhardt Ehrlich, native of Hamburg, although the production of either, assuming the Kaiser's security services were efficient, would lead to a prison cell.

The stolen interrupter gear drawings, smudged a little more but still quite legible, had been removed from the cardboard tube, folded and lodged beneath his shirt just above the waistband of his uniform trousers.

The Belgian frontier, and behind it the wooded plateaux of the Ardennes, lay some fifty miles due west. Once on the far side, which was after all the French-speaking part of the country, he hoped he might be able to get help from the occupied population.

For the moment though, the problem was how to traverse those fifty miles of heavily policed, manhunt-alerted and indisputably hostile country. He would start after dark. Until then, failing a military check in the warren of the old town, he must hope that the officer's uniform would act as protective colouring.

The tugboat skipper had joked that Koblenz was 'large enough'. He hoped fervently that it was large enough to conceal the movements of a hunted man with papers that could save hundreds of lives plastered to his back . . .

23

Blake was making his way cautiously through the old town, between the market-place and the Entenpfuhl, less than three hundred yards from the Moselle. He had slunk into a narrow lane twisting away from the curving street which followed the line of the original medieval city wall, hoping to reach the river. With luck, he reasoned, there would be skiffs or rowing boats somewhere along the waterfront; if his luck held, he would be able to free one from its moorings and drift across to the far bank. After that, he could turn west and take one of the lesser roads leading to the Belgian frontier.

The lane was unlit. But the market-place behind, less crowded since the night had fallen, was nevertheless still busy enough to be a danger to a hunted man. Longshoremen and soldiers on leave mingled with drab housewives eddying around the stalls not yet stripped of the little they had to sell. Beneath the raftered roof, the long shadows of merchants packing up to go home danced in the wavering illumination of naphtha flares. A thin drizzle had begun to fall, veneering the cobbled square with reflected light.

Blake trod as quietly as he could between the ancient houses. The stench of rotting fruit and vegetables faded behind him. His shadow dwindled and died. The worn granite setts beneath his feet no longer gleamed. He turned a sharp corner and walked into total darkness.

All at once he was aware of the night sounds of the city: the hoot of a tugboat cutting through distant voices, an accordion behind one of the shuttered façades. A long way to the west, he could hear the puffing of a locomotive and the clatter of buffers in a goods yard.

He trod in a deep puddle and stumbled, cursing the water which splashed up to soak the lower part of his leg.

Footsteps from a recessed entry ahead. The sudden unexpected command: 'Halt!' A loud click and an instantaneous dazzle of white light. Frozen between two paces, he was caught in the blinding beam of a torch.

There were three of them. Throwing up an arm to shield his eyes, he had an impression of bulky figures, a gleam from buttons and boots.

'Military police,' the man with the torch announced. The beam played over Blake's still dishevelled form, his damp and rumpled uniform. '*Ach, so!* Our apologies, *Herr Major*, but we have our orders. If the *Herr Major* permits, it will be necessary to examine his papers.'

Blake was in a quandary. To say he didn't have them, that he had lost them, would be courting disaster. To pretend that he had left them in barracks or at his hotel would be equally useless: he had no idea what regiments were quartered in Koblenz and he knew the name of no hotels. Dare he on the other hand show the papers that went with the uniform, the identification of the pilot whose aeroplane he had stolen near the factory? Or would the security forces have been efficient enough, after his crash landing in the Rhine, to alert the authorities this far away that a major of that name was a fugitive with a price on his head?

'Your papers, please!' The voice of the MP was becoming more peremptory.

'I am sorry,' Blake said, having decided there was only one thing to do. 'I was temporarily blinded. You took me by surprise.' He fumbled out the papers, handed them over.

One of the men had moved around behind him. Another had stepped in very close: warm breath redolent of cigar smoke and beer fanned his cheek. The torch beam played over the water-damaged, slightly buckled pages. The MP turned back, flicked forward again, leaned down to scrutinize one particular leaf.

'So,' he said, straightening up. 'Major Bruno Frücht-nicht, eh?'

'That is so.'

'Attached to the Imperial Army Air Service?'

'Correct.'

'Born in Bad Kreuznach . . .'

'Exactly,'

'. . . in what year precisely?'

'In '92,' Blake said, dry-mouthed.

'Yes. It so happens that I am from Bad Kreuznach myself,' the MP said. 'Perhaps the *Herr Major* would be so kind as to tell us the name of the island served by the Alte Nahebrücke? And also, as further proof of his fondness for our mutual birthplace, the name of the street in which the Römerhalle can be found?'

Blake swallowed. He had, of course, no idea. Heidelberg is less than fifty miles from Bad Kreuznach, but he had never visited the spa during his year at the German university. He said nothing. There was nothing to say.

'Very well.' The MP suddenly brisk. 'This accords exactly with our instructions, our alert. If the *Herr Major*,' he said with a sneer, 'permits, I think it would be well if he accompanied us.'

'He will not be needing this.' The man behind plunged

one hand into Blake's sagging uniform pocket and produced the Walther he had stolen.

Fleetingly, Blake had thought of using it, but against three professionals, at close quarters, such a move would have been suicidal. He allowed himself to be bustled ahead along the lane, with one MP still behind and one gripping an arm on either side. There didn't seem to be any point in trying to make conversation. None of the MPs had anything to say. He had the impression that the one behind had drawn a gun.

The lane turned again, at almost a right angle. They must be heading straight for the Moselle side of the tongue of land on which the old town was built. Some way ahead, there was light. A wide square with gas lamps which thrust the façades at the lane's exit into sharp relief.

Blake examined the options open to him. They were pitifully few. Shooting was a non-starter, since he had no gun. Running for cover was out of the question. A sudden attack with fists and feet – on three heavyweights, one of whom certainly was armed – was also ruled out. He himself, on the other hand, was fit, agile and relatively strong.

From the façade of the last house in the lane, a wrought-iron bracket, perhaps once the support for a shop sign or an innkeeper's notice, projected ten or twelve feet above the ground. Immediately above the leaded panes of the bow window, there was a semicircular balcony protected by a stone balustrade. They were almost level with the house. The bracket was silhouetted against the lights of the square.

Abruptly, Blake shook off the restraining grips, took half a dozen lightning steps forward and sprang high into the air.

His outstretched hands, smarting still from the raw

palms, clenched around two of the curved bracket
supports . . . and held.

Jackknifing from the hips and knees, he arched his
body forward and up until one heel lodged on a narrow
ledge at the foot of the balustrade. A moment later, with
a titanic heave and a painful wrench of shoulders and
waist, he had projected himself upwards and scrambled
over the balustrade on to the balcony.

Panting, he heard cursing from below. A shot. And
then another. Chips of stonework stung his cheek . . .
but by then he was jerking apart the half-closed shutters
giving on to the balcony.

The French windows beyond were ajar. Blake pulled
them open and rose half upright to stumble through into
a lighted room.

'Good God!' he heard a woman exclaim. 'Usually they
pass by Madam in reception to make an appointment or
at least check that one is not actually busy with a client.
But if it's that urgent . . . well, the bed's been made and
it's just behind you!'

He stared. She was sitting in front of a dressing-table
with pink mirrors – a busty woman of about forty wearing
a semi-transparent black nightdress and a feather boa
which just managed not to conceal generous slopes of
breast. A painted smile beneath blonde curls faded as she
saw Blake's stricken face. 'What is it?' she said urgently.
'The police?'

'Military.'

'Quick, then. They're no friends of mine. Get into that
wardrobe and pull the door closed. I'll tell them you've
run through.' The smile, genuine this time, revealed a
gold tooth at one side of a wide mouth. The woman
flung open an inner door, ran to the French windows
and uttered a very convincing scream. 'Help! Help!' she

yelled. 'A man! . . . He just burst into my room . . . He ran through, towards the fire escape!'

Blake was just registering the fact that he had blundered into a brothel. Inside the wardrobe, half stifled by sequins and hanging satin, choking on the scent of cheap perfume, he heard the babble of voices below the balcony.

'All right. I'm coming up . . . Bader, give me a hand up, then run round to the back as quick as you damned well can . . .'

A scramble of boots on stone, a gasp of breath and then what sounded like a heavy fall. The same voice, the MP with the torch, panting now, much nearer: 'Schwerin, circle the block. Contact Bader behind. There's an alley . . . Yes, madam. Which way did he go?'

The woman, running from the French windows to the door, said breathlessly: 'This way . . . almost knocked me over. I think the fire escape . . .'

'Where? Quick.'

'End of the corridor. Turn right. There's an emergency door . . .'

The last sentence was lost in the diminishing clump of heavy feet.

The wardrobe door jerked open. For an instant she stood there, undecided, then hurried across and opened the windows wider. 'Could you get down again, the way you came in?'

'I suppose so. If I had to.' Blake emerged from the wardrobe.

'You do have to. Now. They'd never expect you to return the way you came in.'

'That makes sense,' Blake said. 'The escaped prisoner doubling back towards the jail.' He moved in the direction of the balcony.

The woman caught his arm. 'Listen. Which way are you heading?'

'West. Towards Belgium.'

'I thought so. Look, if you want, young man, I can help you a little in that direction. I'm leaving here in half an hour. Visiting a client out on the Mayen road. I could take you that far.'

'Well, really, that is most . . . I don't know how to . . .'

'Don't waste time on words.' She turned a small tap to extinguish the flame of the gaslight above the dressing-table. 'Listen. Do you know the Altmeier Ufer?'

'I'm afraid not.'

'It runs along the riverside. Turn left below and it's a couple of hundred metres. When you get there, turn left again, and you'll see a bridge not far ahead. There's a wall with buttresses. Wait there behind one of those and I'll pick you up in forty minutes.'

'Yes, but how do I . . . ?'

'Do you know what a hansom cab is?'

Blake smiled in the darkness. 'I think so. One of those curious horse-drawn carriages the *Englanders* use in London?'

'That's right. You sit hidden behind two flaps, with the cabbie behind you and above.' She moved closer to him. He was suddenly very much physically aware of her – the ample breasts, the big, warm body. Her breath stirred the hairs of his moustache. The sweetness of cachous, perhaps with a hint of schnapps?

'There's no fuel for motor cabs,' she said. 'Everything is back to horses. The man we use has this imported hansom. His stand is by the old flower market, just beyond the church. You'll recognize the cab at once. It's the only one – and he can be trusted.'

Soft fingers touched Blake's face. 'Go now,' the woman said. 'But I'd be telling a lie if I denied that I'd be happier if you stayed a while – a good-looking young fellow like you!' She pushed him gently towards the open French windows.

Blake transferred himself with some difficulty from the balustrade to the iron bracket. It was raining harder now and the stonework was greasy, the metal dripping and hard to grip. He lowered himself carefully until he was hanging at the full stretch of his arms, then dropped the few feet to the wet roadway.

Above him, he heard the click of closing shutters. Light suddenly gleamed again behind the slits. Somewhere over the roofs, he thought he heard the MPs shouting, but it could have been merchants in the market-place crying their wares.

Turning up the collar of his jacket, he hunched his shoulders against the rain and walked swiftly towards the river.

Her name was Birgit. He sat beside her in the cab with his thigh pressed against hers. Because of the rain, a tarpaulin screen had been rigged over the gate-like flaps and up as far as their chins. Apart from a routine '*Guten Abend, mein Herr*' when Blake stepped out from behind the buttress to flag him down, the cabbie had made no comment.

The two large wheels of the hansom rattled over the cobbles as the horse trotted briskly across the Balduinbrücke. There was very little traffic on the far side of the Moselle: an occasional four-wheeler, a solitary Mercedes-Benz landaulette with brass oil lamps flaring, a convoy of lorries crammed with soldiers on the way into town.

Birgit was discretion personified. She made no attempt
whatever to question him. It was enough that he was a
fugitive from the law; she had no wish to learn the details.
There was a warmth about her, a certain human quality
that was almost maternal, which, despite her profession,
led him to trust her implicitly.

They had left the wide western avenue and taken a
suburban by-road twisting past scattered patches of
woodland when he blurted out: 'Birgit, I can't tell you
. . . there is no way I can convey my appreciation for the
help, the kindness . . .'

'Ssssshhh!' Leaning against him, she laid a finger across
his lips. 'If I can be of assistance to someone in trouble,
that is good enough for me. Someone helped me once
– got me out of a hell of a scrape and a probable year
inside – and I've never forgotten.'

A few minutes later he heard her laughing softly over
the clip-clop of the horse's hooves.

'I've no wish to be nosey,' she said in answer to his
query, 'but I imagine they . . . the people after you . . .
will be looking for a man wearing the uniform of an
army major?'

'Only too true,' Blake said.

'Well, I just had an idea.' She laughed again, almost a
giggle, he thought. 'The client I'm going to see – not a
man I'm fond of, to tell the truth – he's an *Ober-Leutnant*.
And he's about the same build as you.'

'You mean . . . ?'

'He is lodged in a requisitioned pavilion, a self-
contained apartment in a wooden building in the garden
of a large house. After I have been there . . . a certain time
. . . he will doubtless remove his uniform. Customarily,
it is hung over the back of a chair just inside the door of
his salon. The salon is at the end of a short hallway.'

Blake was staring at her through the dark. Her profile, turned straight ahead, was visible as a darker blur against the night outside.

'If I was to keep him *very* occupied,' Birgit said, 'and if I was to arrange that the outer door was left unlocked . . .'

She left the sentence unfinished. The cab was jolting over potholes in the road. Rain pock-marked puddles glistening with light reflected from a house nearby.

'There are . . . no servants?' Blake asked huskily.

'None.'

'And you really think that I . . . ?'

'Listen,' she said for the third time. 'It would not, I am convinced, be difficult for a young, athletic man – a man who can jump up on to first-floor balconies – to open two doors without noise, creep silently ten metres down a carpeted hallway and lift a jacket and maybe trousers from a chair without disturbing a man agreeably occupied beneath a large and heavy woman!'

Blake laughed in his turn. '*Liebchen*,' he crowed, 'I love you.'

'As to that, I am hoping perhaps that you can prove it. Sometime.' He felt what he took to be a visiting card thrust into his hand. 'If ever you should happen to be this way again,' she said.

'It would be a pleasure,' Blake said. And meant it.

'*Gott in Himmel!*' Rudolph von Sonderstern smashed his fist so hard against the refectory table in the great hall at Hohenstein that the decanter and glasses rattled on their silver tray at the far end. 'The dolts had their hands on him,' he bellowed. 'The man was actually under arrest – and they let him get away *again*!'

24

Blake had no idea exactly when or where he crossed the border between Germany and Belgium. Certainly, when he was convinced that he was near, he had forsaken footpaths and tracks and taken to the woods. Perhaps the imaginary line was not continuously patrolled. Perhaps he had just been lucky.

With the sky thatched over by leaves, it had been a matter of chance maintaining a constant westerly direction in the gloom. No birds sang in the depths of the woodland. No wind stirred the branches far overhead. From time to time he was startled by a scurrying rustle as some forest creature fled before his advance. But for most of the day the swish and crackle of his own progress through the thick undergrowth – anxious though he was to avoid it – became the sole accompaniment to his escape.

It was almost dusk when he found himself at the edge of a small clearing, led there by the familiar thunk of chopping wood and the sound of distant voices. Crouched down behind a screen of bushes, he stared out from beneath the trees. He saw a grassy slope with a timber chalet on the far side. Behind the shack were neatly stacked wood piles, what looked like a fenced-in farmyard, and a horse grazing beyond a fifty-yard patch of cultivation. From a tall brick chimney at one end of the chalet, blue smoke spiralled lazily up into the darkening sky.

The woodcutter, almost invisible against the dark mass of the forest, swung his axe beside a felled pine. There was a second man beside him, loading logs as they were chopped into an ancient farm cart. As Blake watched, a woman wearing an apron came to the door of the chalet and called out something to the workers. Her voice rose shrilly over the clucking of hens. Perhaps supper was already on the table.

The woman was wearing nondescript clothes – a long skirt, a cotton smock and a scarf tied around her head. The men could have been labourers from anywhere in Europe.

It was only when he heard their shouted reply that he realized they were talking in Flemish.

That was odd, as this was the Walloon or French-speaking part of Belgium. What the hell. He breathed a deep sigh of relief – he had made it, at least the first stage of his journey to the west: he was on the right side of the German frontier!

He felt an impulse to show himself, to run across the grass and ask their help. He was physically exhausted and faint from hunger. The Belgians were reputed to be violently hostile to the occupiers ... and then he remembered that he was himself in the uniform of an occupier.

He grinned to himself. It had been ludicrously easy, snitching the jacket and breeches of the *Ober-Leutnant* of whom Birgit was 'not very fond'. He hoped she would not in any way be blamed for the loss, that it would be put down to a passing sneak-thief. And that, after all, was what Blake was.

The cabbie had been instructed to wait 'as usual'.

Blake made a pretence, after kissing the woman good-bye, of continuing along the road. Later he circled the property from behind, finding the officer's billet exactly as described. There were lights behind the shutters of the big house, but thankfully no dogs. Probably eaten, he thought, if the rationing situation in Germany was as severe as he had been told.

The outer door of the wooden pavilion was heavy and inclined to creak. He had eased it open inch by inch, pushing hard upwards on the handle to relieve the pressure on the hinges. The loudest noise he heard during the five minutes it took was the hammering of his own heart.

He could feel the sweat running down into his eyes as he slid himself through the narrow gap he had made. The hallway was carpeted, warm, with a hint of cigar smoke and the fumes of brandy. From beyond a door at the far end, he heard a murmur of voices.

Holding his breath, Blake stole towards the door.

It was ajar. Through the crack, he spied a dimly lit room with pink-shaded lamps on wall brackets. A wide, low, rumpled bed, flanked by a night table loaded with bottles and glasses, was occupied by two naked bodies. Blake saw the hairy, widespread legs of a man lying prone on his back, the swelling, rounded globes of the backside of a woman moving above him, a heavy breast in jiggling profile. The words of the couple, moaned through gasping breath, were unintelligible.

As Birgit had promised, a chair, with the uniform neatly draped over its back, was within easy reach of the doorway. He had only to push the door open another foot to grasp the smooth field-grey material. Warily, he lifted the trousers. A metal buckle on a loose leather belt swung out and hit the curved back of the chair.

Blake froze, his hand in mid-air, the garment halfway raised from the jacket. The single, sharp metallic sound had seemed to him as loud, as obtrusive, as a shot or a shout.

He was aware that the woman had redoubled her exertions, that the panting on the bed had suddenly become more urgent. But there was no direct reaction to his mistake.

Thankfully, he released the breath he had been holding. With infinite caution he completed the first part of his theft, laying the trousers beside him on the carpet. He reached in for the jacket.

This was more difficult. Knobs terminating the posts which supported the chair back had to be disengaged from the shoulders and the upper part of the sleeves. He rose upright and inserted one of his own shoulders into the gap between the door and the lintel. The added height made the task easier. The slight whisper of material as the jacket pulled free was masked by the creak of the bed.

There remained a polished cross-over uniform belt not unlike a British Sam Browne. It was looped over the nearest knob – and there was a holstered revolver attached to it. This was a prize too good to be missed. Feeling now the total unreality of the situation – the naked couple slaving away on that bed, himself as absurd as an adulterer in a French farce – Blake found within himself the mindless courage that goes with recklessness. Boldly, he stepped half into the room and unhooked the heavy belt with a single swift movement.

A pair of highly polished boots stood on the far side of the chair, but to venture in far enough to reach for those would be tempting fate. He would have to be content with the scuffed pair he had taken off the Eindekker pilot.

Silently, with a heartfelt mental thank you to Birgit,

he withdrew from the doorway, picked up the uniform and crept out of the pavilion.

For a moment, imbued with this same sense of the ridiculous – almost as though he was taking part in some juvenile university jape – he had thought of leaving the uniform he was wearing in place of the one he had stolen. He had not seen the officer's face, but he could imagine his expression when he discovered that during his exertions he had been promoted in rank from an *Ober-Leutnant* to a Major!

But no, that would never do. It might implicate the woman. It would certainly tip off the pursuers, if the officer reported the theft, that their quarry was a leopard who constantly changed his spots. As it was, there could be no conceivable connection between the *Englander* spy who had escaped from the police in Koblenz and a banal pilferer who had robbed an officer some miles to the west.

A mile away from the pavilion, he walked into a small copse and changed into the new uniform. It was a little tight across the chest and the breeches tended to bag at the knee. But it would do at a distance, especially when the belt was buckled on.

The purloined clothes were a trifle damp, but the rain had stopped now, and anyway there was nothing he could do about it. He stuffed the discarded garments beneath a low-growing bush, scattered fallen leaves over them as best as he could in the dark, and returned to the road.

He continued to walk.

During the next twelve hours a fictional story about a commandeered motor car which had broken down, and a driver who had gone to look for a garage mechanic, gained him lifts from a doctor on a night call, a carter with a two-horse wagon piled high with turnips and a

218

military transport returning to Liège with a load of fresh uniforms for troops about to be moved up into the line.

Cold fear tightened his chest during the fifteen-mile journey in the transport. He had no idea of the state of the war, the badges on his uniform meant nothing to him and he hadn't the least idea of the kind of replies he ought to give to questions of a military nature. But he needed to move west fast: the offer was too tempting to refuse.

In the event it didn't matter. The driver, a private soldier, and his NCO mate were regulars. Questioning an officer was unthinkable, and they were not going to enter into conversation unless they were spoken to first. He left them with a single word of thanks and a crisp salute at a small town called Blankenheim.

They would have taken him right through into Belgium, but he had no way of knowing whether the frontier was operated in a normal fashion, with examination of papers and questions from MPs, or whether military traffic was waved straight through into occupied territory. It was certainly not a question an officer would ask of other ranks. Equally, it was a risk he dare not take blind.

Blankenheim was between ten and twelve miles from the border. More than half that distance was through the densely wooded hills of the Ardennes.

It was only when he had left the road, subsequently renouncing footpaths and forest tracks, that Blake felt the tension of the past few days ease sufficiently to allow him time for reflection.

Paramount among three questions clamouring for response was the problem of his connection – or lack of it – with London. What was the last they had heard of him? How much truth, if any, had there been in Kristin's last transmission supposedly on his behalf? Would they know he had the plans – or would the Germans, once they knew what he had been after, have instructed her to deny this? Did London even know that he was still alive? Or might she have reported that he had been taken prisoner to account for the lack of definite news?

Forcing his way – still westwards, he hoped – through the interminable underbrush carpeting the forest floor, Blake realized that, basically, every response depended on the answer to Question Number Two. Had the German intelligence services kept her in place as a double agent, monitoring messages from the unsuspecting British and supplying false information in return? Or had they considered her usefulness, in this particular case, at an end once he had laid his hands on the Fokker drawings?

There was no way on earth that he could contact London himself, not without a cut-out, not at any rate until he reached the British side of the battle-field – and even then there would be enormous problems.

The answer to Question Two, he reasoned, would itself depend on Kristin's relation with the contact in Switzerland. If it was purely by Morse, there would be no obstacle to her continuing indefinitely. If on the other hand the liaison involved occasional telephone contact, the substitution would be revealed the moment a call was required. Or received. And whether or not the Germans knew, yes or no, if telephone communications came into it depended in its turn on how much information they had squeezed out of the original cut-out before he was executed.

It was at this point in his deliberations that Blake came across the woodcutters' glade in the forest.

Only after he had decided not to show himself – a

dog had begun barking in the yard beside the chalet – was he able to resume his analysis.

Skirting the property half a mile away in the woods, he had to admit to himself finally that, in reality, his three questions boiled down to one. Because both of the first two were intimately related to the enigma that was the third: Kristin.

It was possible, of course, that he was over-complicating things on account of his personal involvement, finding reasons to obscure his humiliation, masking the hurt stemming from his wounded pride. It was equally possible, probable even, that he was quite simply mistaken. Betrayal is a hard pill to swallow.

But the question had posed itself insistently a dozen times, a hundred times, since he had fled from the aerodrome at Paderborn. Was it a real option, or an attempt by his subconscious to rationalize an emotional defeat? He could hear the words now. She had reminded him, once the intelligence officer had made his entrance, that all was fair in love or war. Then she had added, with an ambiguity that was to torture him later: 'Sometimes both'.

The question was this. He *knew* the rear door of the prison van had been locked. He had *heard* it locked. Yet it had flown open at once when he lurched against it.

Kristin had been on the concrete apron outside the hangar when he was led out to the van. He had seen her finishing a conversation with a group of officers and start to walk his way when he was pushed inside by the MPs.

Was it possible, was it conceivable, that it was she, in some way, who had surreptitiously unlocked that door?

The most infuriating thing of all was that this was the one question to which he would never, ever know the answer.

25

The biggest, perhaps the most unwelcome, surprise Blake
received throughout his German odyssey was delivered
over a lunch table the following day, at a small restaurant
in Malmédy.

He had passed the night uncomfortably in a barn on
the westward fringe of the forest, walked out into a lush
green pastureland beneath a cloudless sky the following
morning and found a barber's shop in the first village he
approached.

Ravenously hungry, he had then wolfed acorn coffee
and an unappetizing sausage before he set out to walk
south along the network of minor roads webbing the
region.

Malmédy was eleven miles away. In normal times it
would have been considered a pretty town – still on
the wooded Ardennes plateau, a huddle of steep gabled
roofs and tall houses with slatted shutters gashed by
narrow, winding streets. Beneath the wrought-iron balconies overlooking a sloping central square, illuminated
fountains played among the flower-beds on summer
evenings, and there was a conical pavilion straight out of
a Lehár operetta housing gold-braided uniforms and brass
instruments. In the town hall visitors could be supplied
with illustrated leaflets suggesting woodland rambles and
explaining why it was forbidden to shoot deer.

None of these luxuries was available in time of war. There was a German garrison on the outskirts of town. German soldiers thronged the silent streets. The Belgian inhabitants were sullen and subdued. Most of the shops were shuttered, because there was nothing to sell and very little to eat. The brass instruments had been confiscated, along with metal parts stripped from every factory and workshop in the region, to be sent to the Fatherland to help satisfy the insatiable demands of an armaments industry invariably short of shell cases.

There were no flowers in Malmédy's square now: the only spot of colour flared from a single pot of geraniums, scarlet blooms on a fifth-floor balcony facing south near the town hall. But the woman who lived there, it was whispered, had been known to consort with German officers.

As a German officer himself, Blake felt reasonably free to wander. He was unlikely to attract attention; he had noticed men from half a dozen different formations already: infantrymen, sappers, ordnance officers, gunners, even an occasional aviator. Passing the town hall, he saw that the entrance doors were closed and locked, with a steel-helmeted sentry posted on either side. A side door was plastered with papers: casualty lists, orders from the local *Kommandant*, the official daily war communiqués – not only that of the German army, he discovered with surprise, but also copies of those issued by the French and English General Staffs. In a war that was largely static, he supposed, neither side was likely to publish exaggerated claims.

In a shallow glass case attached to the wall, a map of northern France displayed, with the use of a thin red ribbon and coloured pins, the current position of the front line. Oh, jolly good! Blake thought with a wry inward smile. From Malmédy to the nearest points on

the front it was no more than a hundred miles, a hundred
and twenty-five if you wanted the nearest British sector,
in the region of Péronne.

That, of course, was as the crow flies. Most crows Blake
had observed seemed to fly in circles, but never mind – for
an enemy alien wanted for spying, a non-crow obliged
to keep to the minor roads and show himself as little
as possible, it was clear that those distances would be
greatly increased.

The round hundred miles would take him to the French
sector on the River Aisne, north of Reims. The hell with
it: what was an extra twenty-five when distances of that
order were involved and no aeroplane was at hand!
Péronne was nearer home anyway. Apart from which
it could prove deucedly hard to get his story believed by
the French. Especially in a highly contested area morbidly
alert for German spies and dangerously near Paris. There
was an additional benefit to be gained from a route leading
west-south-west from Malmédy, a plus that could well
cancel out the extra mileage: apart from Dinant, there
was not a single large town to be passed on the way.

It was just after midday. Suffused, illogically enough,
with a sudden confidence, he walked into a small
restaurant with a sign in the window stating that it
was out of bounds to Other Ranks. He sat down at
a table. One of the advantages of being an occupier –
especially to one with no papers – was that officers were
not required to produce ration tickets. He ordered beer
with a dish of stewed pork.

Soon the restaurant began to fill up, mostly with
Germans, some of them in civilian clothes but mainly
junior officers. The food was terrible, but Blake was too
hungry to care. He was scouring the plate with a crust of
dry bread when he heard the voice behind him. '*Patsy!*

Good God, but it can't be. Yet it *is*: Patsy Blake by all that's holy! What in *hell* are you doing here?'

At the sound of that first explosive word, Blake had started like a man who has received an electric shock. One hundredth of a second later he registered the fact that the speaker had exclaimed *in English*. And with that came the horrific realization that whoever it was did actually know him, knew his real name . . .

He swivelled violently around in his chair – an instinctive, involuntary movement as rapidly executed as the abrupt halt when he was faced with danger. He hadn't even had time for the fleeting thought – brazen it out; say, 'Sir, you must be mistaken!' 'Who do you think you are?' – before he had recognized the speaker.

A young man of his own age, darkly handsome, with bright blue eyes. Hermann Gruener. They had been classmates at Heidelberg.

Gruener smiled. 'Forgive the language slip,' he said in a low voice. He was sitting alone at the next table. 'It was surprised out of me. You must admit, Patsy, that this *is* a surprise!'

Blake swallowed. He had been called Patsy at Heidelberg, not because of anything effeminate about him, but because of the American usage – a patsy was someone who always took the blame for everything. In Blake's case it might have been because he wished, as a foreigner, to ingratiate himself with his fellow students when he first arrived at the university: in all of their more exuberant rags and rebellions against authority, he was invariably the first to own up, and the name had stuck. Hermann Gruener had been his closest collaborator.

'Out with it, Patsy,' he was saying now. 'Own up again! What the devil *are* you doing here? In that uniform?'

Blake spoke for the first time. Gruener was wearing

225

the uniform of a *Hauptmann* in the Imperial Army Air
Service. 'Hermann,' he said gruffly, 'I'm not . . . I don't
know what to say to you.'

The German smiled again. 'You had better say something, old friend,' he advised. 'It is fairly obvious that
you are not here selling tickets for a Salvation Army
fête. Nor, I would imagine, have you adopted a German
uniform as part of a satirical sketch designed to amuse
the troops on the other side of the line.'

Blake shook his head wordlessly. He was totally
at a loss.

'In which case,' Gruener pursued, 'friends that we are,
this leaves me in a most awkward position. It is clear, you
see, that you must be engaged on some mission which is,
to say the least, hostile to my country. Perhaps you could
– for old times' sake, shall we say? – tell me something
about it?'

Blake shook his head again. 'There is nothing I can
tell you, Hermann,' he said wretchedly.

He was aware, beneath the banter, how much his old
friend's loyalties must be strained – between duty to an
abstract and fellow-feeling for a human being, between
simple affection and adherence to an ideal. He was
himself agonizingly conscious of the wadded drawings
burning below his shoulder-blades, plans which would
allow young men he did not know more easily to shoot
down and kill young men like Hermann, whom he
did know.

He sighed. There was nothing either of them could do
about the situation.

'In that case,' Gruener was saying, 'I have no alternative
but to ask you to consider yourself under arrest.' He
cleared his throat, producing a holstered revolver and
laying it unobtrusively on the table in front of him. He

looked around the crowded room. 'I could call on a dozen, two dozen men to help me if you were to resist. There isn't a hope in hell of your getting away, as you must know. But rather than have you hustled out publicly, I would prefer that we walk out of here quietly together, saving you the embarrassment – provided that I have your assurance that you accept formally that this arrest has in principle been made. And your word of honour that you will make no attempt to escape during the short walk we have to make to my divisional headquarters.'

'Very well,' Blake said. 'And thank you.'

Gruener inclined his head. He was looking distressed. 'First, however,' he said, 'I have to make a telephone call. May I have your parole that, to avoid any kind of disturbance, you will remain quietly here at this table, making no attempt to leave, during my absence?'

'You have it,' Blake said.

'Word of honour?'

'My word as an officer and English gentleman.'

'There is a suspicion,' Hermann Gruener said after his telephone call, 'that I may have as my prisoner a certain foreigner who flew an aeroplane an unbelievable distance so that he could rob a factory in Rhineland-Westphalia of plans that have a military significance. I don't suppose, Patsy, that you would care to comment on that?'

'I'm afraid not,' Blake said.

They were walking, in apparently nonchalant fashion, to Gruener's headquarters – it was in fact over a mile, on the outskirts of the town – two young German officers engaged in what seemed a friendly conversation. Blake had surrendered his pistol and had it returned to him minus the magazine.

'There is an additional complication,' the German

continued, 'which makes the matter a good deal more serious. It appears ·that two members of the factory personnel were killed. To say nothing of assaults on aviation staff and the theft of not one but *two* machines, the property of the Army Air Service. I need hardly tell you of the penalties this foreigner faces . . . should he be positively identified.'

Blake said nothing.

'Apart from this matter of espionage,' Gruener said, 'perhaps you could tell me what uniform you customarily wear – when you are not visiting countries abroad, that is. Or is a cloak and dagger your normal attire?'

Again, Blake remained silent.

Gruener shot him a sideways glance. 'Good God,' he said. 'That scar! You were never involved with duelling when we were together. Don't say you went back to Heidelberg for a second year?'

Blake shook his head, unable to resist a smile. 'Not a sabre,' he said. 'An FE-2b trainer. A circuit and too hard a bump.'

'Ah! So. Then we are in fact basically in the same . . . business . . . even if it is on opposite sides of the fence, no? Somehow that makes me feel better.'

Blake nodded but said nothing. They turned a corner of the road and he saw, as the land fell away to a shallow valley, a hutted camp with sentries posted by the wire gates and a number of motor transports ranged in a gravelled space outside a guardhouse. A small grass airfield was attached to the site.

'My orders,' Gruener said, 'are to fly you back to Paderborn, where those with detailed knowledge of the case can interrogate you.' He walked for some minutes in silence, then added inconsequentially, with a wave at the field: 'It was here that our first pilot to be killed on active service crashed to his death in August 1914, only a few days after war was declared. *Ober-Leutnant* Reinhold Jahnow. He was older than us. He had pilot's licence No. 80, a veteran of the Balkan campaign in 1912. He was a good instructor and a good man.'

The sentries swung wide the gates as they approached, then sprang to attention, clicked their heels and saluted. Blake remembered just in time to imitate Gruener's languid, typically Air Service, non-*junker* response.

Ten minutes later they were sitting facing one another across a wide table in one of the smaller huts on the fringe of the field. Outside the window the sun gleamed on the freshly painted lozenge camouflage adorning the top wings of two Fokker biplanes and a Halberstadt.

The room appeared at one time to have been used as a drawing office. Shallow drawers crammed an outsize filing cabinet, and two adjustable inclined boards stood on tall wooden stands against one wall. Apart from the fact that Gruener's living quarters were visible through a half-open door, Blake was irresistibly reminded both of the factory workshop and of the room in the Heston headquarters where he had received his first briefing. There was even an aero engine coughing to life somewhere outside.

The similarity was reinforced – acutely – by Gruener's first question.

'I accept that I cannot expect any kind of admission,' he said. 'Which would in any case leave me in a most invidious position. My position, as it is, I find most distressing. I am sorry I met you. But, having done so, I cannot un-meet you, any more than I can banish from my mind what I have been told. What I do not *know*, however, cannot oblige me to take any particular course of action. The question I am going to put to you

229

is thus entirely hypothetical, academic even.' He undid the three top buttons of his uniform tunic and eased his collar from his neck.

'You have told me nothing. I therefore make no assumptions,' he said awkwardly. 'But *were* you to be someone in, shall we say, the shoes of the foreigner sought by the authorities, and *had* you in fact stolen some plans, what would you think such a person would have done with them?'

Before Blake could reply he added, 'I ask only for an opinion, not for facts. Look, Patsy, I do not wish to embarrass both of us by having you submit to a body search. Other people in other places can do that if they consider it necessary. Nor do I relish the thought of sending a friend to what would almost certainly turn out to be a firing squad. Anything, any hint therefore, which might influence my . . . thinking . . . and therefore any action I might take . . . Oh, shit, man: throw me a rope! What would this man do . . . have done?'

Blake repressed a grin. Gruener was certainly leaning over backwards! 'In such a case,' he said carefully, 'I would think your man – if he happened to be in the position I am in – I think he would already have got rid of the plans.'

'I see. How would he have done that?'

'I imagine he would have passed them on to an agent in Switzerland, via a contact unknown to his original cut-out. Rolled up in a cardboard tube he would doubtless have found in the office from which the plans were . . . removed.'

'A cardboard tube. I see,' Gruener said again. 'Would your hypothetical thief, do you suppose, swear if interrogated that this was what he had done?'

'He would.'

'On his honour?'

'On his honour,' Blake lied firmly, once more acutely conscious of the wad of paper clamped to his back. He was not prepared to break his word when it came to his own behaviour, but he was if it was a question of success or failure for the mission. He felt suddenly very small, nevertheless. Gruener was sticking out his neck, not having him handcuffed in a cell awaiting the arrival of the Feldgendarmerie. And here he was, betraying his confidence as surely as his had been betrayed by Kristin. On the other hand, Kristin had not been an old friend to start with. But it was she who said 'All's fair . . .'

'Very well!' Gruener slapped the desk with his open hand, his boyish features suddenly illuminated with the raffish, devil-may-care expression which had so characterized his behaviour when they were students together. 'Patsy, I'm going to give you a chance.'

'A chance?'

'Yes. Your theoretical man, if he had already delivered his booty, would presumably have only one more thing to do: get the hell over to the Allied side of the line as quickly as possible. Am I right?'

'I would think so.'

'Right. Now I'll tell you what: we never duelled during our university days; but, given our respective services, we could very well have been duelling today – in our respective machines, over the Western Front. You agree?'

'Yes, but . . . ?' Blake frowned. What was coming next?

'Circumstances have decreed otherwise, but I intend to offer you the chance of another kind of duel, one in which you have exactly the same hopes of success as myself.'

'Hermann, I'm afraid I don't understand.'

'We are going to have a game of Heidelberg chess,' Gruener said.

231

26

Heidelberg chess was a joke, an extravagance invented by the rowdier spirits of the university town in the early years of the century. It was a game in which physical – especially alimentary – stamina was of more value than the ability to see and plan ahead. In this respect it was perhaps an intellectual equivalent of the duelling for which the place was famous.

On an outsize board, conventional chessmen were replaced by drinking glasses of different shapes and sizes – a tall-stemmed hock glass for the king, a champagne flute for the queen, Madeira, schnapps and whisky glasses for bishops, knights and rooks. The pawns were represented by normal wineglasses.

Each glass was then filled to the brim with the wine or spirit for which it was designed. Pawns, of course, were tanked up with ordinary table wine, white or red. Behind them, different chasing on the glasses distinguished one side from the other.

The point of the game, other than the banal one of winning or losing, was the rule that every time a piece was taken, the player who lost it was obliged to drink the contents in a single draught.

Gruener tore a sheet of paper from a huge drawing pad and hurriedly divided it into sixty-four squares with a charcoal stick. He summoned an orderly from

232

the officers' mess and demanded two different sets of sixteen glasses, with the seven different liquor bottles required to complete the pieces. When everything was in place, the two adversaries faced one another across the wide table. Blake chose white – largely because he thought the white wine would meld better with the other drinks each time he lost a pawn – and the German red.

A further rule of this chess variant was the necessity to call out each move aloud in a special jargon tailored for the game: *Seven – red: hock to flute two . . . Nine – white: schnapps to Madeira three . . . Thirteen: red whiskies . . .*

Frequently, after a dozen or so moves, players became so helpless with drunken giggles that the contest had to be abandoned.

'The difference about this match,' Gruener said, 'is that I have, regretfully, to limit the time in which each move is made to four minutes.' He produced an alarm clock surmounted by a bell, wound it up and set the hands. 'My instructions are to be in Paderborn before dark. Clearly, therefore, I cannot delay the take-off indefinitely.'

Blake wound and started the alarm clock and moved a pawn. 'You said something about "a chance",' he observed, intrigued but still puzzled by his captor's train of thought. 'Now you are talking about a match. Are you offering some kind of prize for the victor?'

'Certainly.'

'Namely?'

Gruener advanced one of his own pawns. He gestured towards the sector of airfield visible through the window. An Albatros reconnaissance two-seater, with a polished aluminium nose and a bolster tank attached to the top wing centre section, was being wheeled out by a group of mechanics. 'That is the machine allocated to me,' he said. 'The match is to decide who pilots it.'

Swift as a released bird, a sudden ray of hope transfixed Blake. 'Hermann,' he said, 'are you telling me . . . ?'

'In a two-seater, naturally it is the pilot who determines the flight plan, the route to be followed,' Gruener said. 'Your move, Patsy.'

27

The Albatros was not equipped with guns. It would have
been impossible anyway to mount one firing through the
propeller, for the front of the slender fuselage, with its
triangular rudder and completely flat top, was obscured
by the engine. This upright, four-cylinder in-line unit
stood, from the crankshaft upwards, totally exposed
above the aluminium nose and propeller boss. An
overhead exhaust belched out hot fumes dangerously
near the centre section fuel tank.

The pilot's view was further impeded by the head
and shoulders of his observer, who sat in the forward
cockpit.

Lowering himself into the rear seat, Blake felt as disori-
ented as he ever had in an unfamiliar machine. The cockpit
layout seemed to him aberrant. The control column had
two cylindrical, polished wood grips, one outrigged on
either side of the shaft. There was no instrument panel:
five of the six instruments were placed haphazardly, most
of them low down below the wooden frames which held
the separately formed plywood fuselage sides together.
The sixth, a large, white-faced revolution counter, was
attached to a tubular steel former just below the padded
leather cockpit rim and a plaque bearing the legend
'ALBATROS N-986 RS/C'.

The sense of unreality was emphasized by the fact that

he was convinced that he should by rights be seating himself in the forward cockpit. He did not believe Gruener had deliberately lost the chess match: the young German was too ethical a man, too firmly attached to his own moral certainties for that. Nevertheless – even if he had been playing to win – it had to be admitted that Blake's own priorities were more urgent than his.

The reasons for suggesting the game in the first place, Blake thought, were less difficult to establish. It seemed to him that, as an honourable man, Gruener's loyalties were equally divided: between the person and the state, the theory and the practice. He couldn't, as he said, un-know that he had encountered an enemy alien, masquerading in a uniform he was not entitled to wear; he couldn't just pat him on the back and wish him luck. It would be very much against the grain, on the other hand, to deliver a friend into the care of an executioner.

Torn between such conflicting imperatives, Gruener had in fact funked the positive action. He would let fate make the decision.

As in so many affairs of honour, the matter would be decided by a duel.

'The silver cylinder just below the bulkhead,' Gruener was calling from the forward cockpit, 'the one with the push-pull plunger and the word "prime" above it.'

'What? . . . Oh. Yes, right-ho.' Startled out of his reverie, Blake saw that there was a mechanic at each of the Albatros's wingtips. A third stood ready to swing the propeller. There was a red label with white lettering gummed to the iron former. He read: 'Start: full rich mixture – pump throttle three times'.

He checked switches and dials that he recognized, and obeyed the instruction.

The engine wheezed as the propeller was turned four

times. Blake wondered if the power unit was a Mercedes or an Argus. The propeller was expertly, briskly swung. He saw a puff of blue smoke. The blades revolved. The engine chattered to life with a satisfying roar. Gingerly, he manipulated the throttle.

The chocks were whisked away. Guided by the wingtip men, the Albatros trundled out towards the wind-sock at the far end of the field, rudder wagging and ailerons dipping as Blake experimented with the controls. When they were level with the perimeter fence, he turned the machine into the wind.

Gruener looked over his shoulder and nodded. The mechanics stood aside. Blake took off.

It wasn't as difficult as he expected. The engine was powerful and the aeroplane extremely light. The breeze had freshened since the morning, blowing quite hard from the west – and that was the direction he wanted to go.

Hopping at first like a magpie traversing the rough ground, the machine settled into a blustering run as Blake urged the throttle open. He felt the first hint of lift when they were less than halfway across the field, easing the stick gently back into his stomach as the speed increased.

At a little over fifty miles per hour the Albatros left the ground, soaring over the hutted camp and the grey roofs on the outskirts of town. Woods streamed past below the wings, then fields, a farm with browsing cattle, the slow loops of a river. Blake continued steeply climbing, no banks, no turns, the compass setting due west, until the altimeter registered five thousand feet.

The controls were heavy, but the machine responded quickly once they were actuated. What really got on his nerves was the noise. Apart from the racket of the naked engine, the entire framework of the machine vibrated and clattered and shook with a force that seemed to him quite deafening. Plywood panelling attached to the longerons and formers was acoustically a great deal less satisfactory than the doped fabric to which he was accustomed!

Yet again, Blake's mind was buzzing with unanswered questions. How much fuel did the Albatros carry? How many miles to the gallon did she fly? What was going to happen when the tank ran dry? Would the plane be reported missing if it failed to follow the original flight plan? Above all, what was he going to do with Gruener if he managed a safe landing?

The first question almost answered itself. Unless a refuelling stop had been planned, there must be enough fuel to take them from Malmédy to Paderborn, presumably with a little in reserve. That was a distance of approximately 135 miles. And this coincidentally – he had looked at a map – was precisely the distance to the nearest part of the front line, the British sector somewhere between Lens and Arras. Was there enough nevertheless to get them safely across the whole battlefield and avoid the possibility of being shot down – either by Allied scouts or the overzealous gunners?

One thing had been made very clear to him. Gruener himself would answer none of those questions. There had been no problems leaving the aerodrome: the *Herr Hauptmann* had been expected to take off with another officer. But when Blake had stammered, as they were about to climb into the Albatros: 'Look, Hermann, are you absolutely *sure* . . . ?' the German had at once held up a restraining hand.

'I offered you a chance,' he said. 'You won the match fair and square. So now you are the pilot. And as I said, the pilot decides everything. Everything.' And he had turned his back and clambered up into the forward cockpit.

Message received and understood. Fate had swung the pendulum Blake's way. It was up to him to take that chance. Gruener would do nothing to hinder him . . . but then again he certainly wasn't going to help.

Blake shook his head, thinking back over the game. He had played very carefully, trying as much as anything to protect the pieces filled with spirits rather than wine, so that he would not have to mix his drinks too much. Gruener had been more reckless, sacrificing two bishops (schnapps) and a knight (whisky) rather quickly. Perhaps it was the effect of these that had allowed Blake, after a Dragon Variation, to check in nine moves and mate in thirteen?

He smiled – they were flying over a lake – as another thought crossed his mind. If they had to force-land and found themselves still on the German side of the line . . . what then? Wouldn't that place the ball very neatly back into Gruener's court?

Whatever the problems, whatever the risks, Blake felt, a ride in an aeroplane was a thousand times better than the idea of walking that 135-mile route, relying on lifts or hoping to steal a car or bicycle. A passenger train behind the lines in subjugated Belgium – even 135 miles behind – was a miracle too far-fetched even to be considered.

The sky was swept clear of clouds in the west. The earth below was partly obscured now by an overall haze. Immediately in front of them, only half a dozen diameters above the horizon, the sinking sun blazed an angry red.

Shaking in every joint, the noisy biplane forged ahead. Blake wondered, staring past Gruener's hunched shoulders and leather-helmeted head, what the man was thinking. Much the same things, shot through with additional information, as he was himself probably.

What was he planning to do when they came down? It would, of course, depend on which side of the line it was ... but had he any specific action in mind, or was he going to play it by ear?

Most importantly, now that he had sobered up, did he regret his quixotic move?

It was some time since they had left the wooded plateaux of the Ardennes. A large town, spined with the bright streaks of railway lines, sprawled across the flat landscape stretching away beneath them. That would be Dinant, Blake assumed. Some way off to the north-west, smokeless factory chimneys, conical slag heaps and colliery wheels marked the shattered outskirts of Charleroi. Flying over the pale ribbon of the Meuse a few minutes earlier, he had thought they must be almost halfway there – wherever 'there' was. The needle of the fuel gauge, which was not calibrated in precise quantities, certainly trembled midway between 'full' and 'empty'.

Gruener, as a good observer should, was the first to see the single-seaters. He stabbed out an arm and pointed. Perhaps three miles ahead: four dark specks in formation, silhouetted against the glare.

Blake at once suffered the familiar chill, looked for the toggles actuating the synchronized guns ... and remembered, first, that he was in the rear cockpit with no clear view, secondly that the Albatros was in any case unarmed. An instant afterwards he remembered that he was piloting a German aeroplane. And the scouts, this far away from the battlefield, would surely be German too.

The quartet, a Pfalz leading three Fokker biplanes in V formation, approached rapidly, several hundred yards to the starboard of their course. The bulbous nose of the leading machine was painted red; the fuselage of each

Fokker sported a zigzag of black stripes and a polished engine cowling.

When they were almost abreast, the Pfalz peeled away from the other three, dived in the direction of the Albatros, then executed a neat loop with the reconnaissance two-seater as the central point of the circle. The Fokkers broke formation, soared away right and left, and banked steeply to pass above, beneath and alongside the Albatros, carefree as lambs gambolling in an upland pasture. Each goggled pilot waved as his machine shot past. Gruener waved back. And finally Blake, feeling curiously shabby, almost ashamed, raised an arm in salute.

When the bellow of unsilenced engines had at last faded and the flight, re-formed, had flown away towards the east, Blake relaxed with a sigh of relief. Stupid and unnecessary, that sudden shaft of fear, he told himself. He had drink taken, as the Irish say. Perhaps he was still a little bit under the influence. Better in any case to save the chill for what must certainly come later.

It was dusk when the engine of the Albatros spluttered and choked. The needle of the fuel gauge was jammed firmly against the end-stop. Blake swore, banking the plane to look below. A land of woods and fields, of green hills and hollows and farms and streams, could be seen to be desecrated by war, smeared with a foulness as evident as the marks from a bloodied body dragged across the floor. He shook his head. Pinpoints of light from an artillery barrage flickered through the gloom below. He leaned forward to thump Gruener on the shoulder. 'I'm going to have to put her down,' he shouted above the racket of the dying engine.

The German turned around. He was smiling. Quite

clearly he was enjoying the situation. 'You're the pilot,' he replied. 'The decisions are up to you.'

With a last explosive backfire and a diminishing rumble, the engine relapsed into silence. The bright disc of the propeller thickened, became opaque, separated into distinct blades and spun to a halt.

They started to lose height at once, wind singing through the crosswires and stays with an alto wail.

Blake bit his lip. Gruener was right. With no tractive power to modify his speed or allow him to climb, his skill as a pilot was indeed at a premium.

The German, true to his character, would be eager to see just how Blake proposed to meet the challenge. His own safety, the life-or-death options the situation offered, would remain subservient to the fascination of discovering what his one-time English friend would do with the 'chance' he had been given.

Blake himself was too busy to examine those options. With the risk of a stall always present, and no engine to pull him out of it, his choice of manoeuvres was limited. Everything depended on the normal gliding angle of the Albatros.

A large wing surface and a slender fuselage, coupled with a centre of gravity that was well forward, ensured – Blake soon found out – that this was fairly shallow.

So much the better. The furthest distance they could travel would be that at the far end of a continuous straight line: keep her dead ahead – and hope there would be a space that was not too dangerous at the end of the line. First, though, it was vital that he had some idea of what lay below. Otherwise they could be dead . . . with no ahead.

He would risk one wide circle of the immediate terrain before he settled the machine into its final glide.

He dropped the nose marginally, banking just enough to minimize the risk of a spin.

From four thousand feet, the terrain was rapidly becoming obscure.

Buildings, whole or ruined it was impossible to say, loomed here and there out of the dusk. Southwards there was woodland, almost a forest. And there were, or had been, trenches: the land was scarred with haphazard, darker streaks as far as he could see in every direction. But any action there was seemed, perhaps unfortunately, some way ahead. Flashes of artillery fire pierced the gloom and the red flowers of shell bursts bloomed miles to the west.

It was clear that he would have to lose at least another thousand feet, perhaps two, before he had any definite idea of the situation he was dropping them into.

He straightened out when the altimeter registered three thousand five hundred feet, heading a few points south of the concentration of gunfire. The Albatros, which gave the impression from time to time almost of limping in its descent, shuddered as the shadowy surface of the earth swam nearer.

It was ten minutes later that the desolation slid into view beneath the biplane's lower wing. This was land, it was clear, that had been fought over – country devastated by the German advance, far behind the lines now but still webbed with the geometric complex of communication trenches, pulverized by the duels of artillery which consumed shells more rapidly than the war factories could produce them. Roads, villages, railway lines and army camps had been obliterated by the fury of battle.

Over the wind's whine through struts and stays, some changed condition – a thermal upthrust, turbulence reflected from the combat below – was now creating a shrill descant stemming from the aerofoil sections of wings and tail. Sensing an increase in the vibration shuddering the two-seater's frame, Blake again lowered the nose fractionally. The airspeed indicator had already sunk its needle below the seventy miles per hour mark.

The darkened battlefield below rushed towards them with what appeared to be increasing speed, though the tell-tale needle continued to drop back.

Blake was now worried. Not the nail-biting anxiety of the man who is afraid but the professional concern of the expert unsure if the tools are equal to the job. In the same way that the engines used by Fokker accepted very little between the idle and full throttle, so some aeroplanes allowed a minimum of flexibility between full speed and the stall. The Albatros two-seater seemed to be one of them.

He lowered the nose further still. If they were not going to fall out of the sky, a deliberate dive – with the attendant danger brought by a high landing speed – was the only option.

The wind screamed between the wires. The wings began to shake.

Elements of the devastated landscape now began to manifest themselves, assembling a village street bordered by rubble, a smashed bridge, a lopped-off factory chimney from the murk. At a thousand feet, it was clear that the battlefield itself had moved on. Looking down over the quivering cockpit rim, Blake saw a long line of lorries and horse-drawn artillery winding through a shallow valley. Rows of tents peaked along the edge of a blasted wood. The muttering rumble of gunfire was audible, but the twinkling flashes and the blossoming shell bursts were still some miles to the west.

He changed direction slightly. There was a long slant

of open ground where the barrage was less intense ten degrees southwards. The Albatros side-slipped, dropping a hundred feet sickeningly in an air pocket. He sawed the control column, treading the rudder bar in an attempt to jockey the machine back on an even keel with elevators and ailerons. Sluggishly, they rolled back into level flight.

The earth's dark surface hurtled towards them.

Abruptly, life speeded up as dramatically as a film. Flattened hedges, craters, the pulverized remains of a farm streaked past below the wings. There were trenches down there now. A myriad points of light stitched together the almost-dark. Tracer arced up towards them, rising lazily to race past. A cracking detonation, followed by three more, rocked the plane as a group of anti-aircraft shells burst into orange flame fifty yards to the left.

Blake fought the controls once more. A high-pitched whistling shrilled from a group of holes ripped by shrapnel from the upper port wing. He freed a hand to thump Gruener on the shoulder.

'Hold on!' he yelled. 'This is it . . .'

Gruener was already holding on. His gloved hands clenched the padded cockpit rim. He ducked his head as the Albatros dropped.

At the last moment Blake yanked the stick slightly back to raise the nose, allowing the machine to plummet to the invisible ground.

For a heartstopping instant life – and the Albatros – stood still. Then there was a rending crash as they hit . . . bounced . . . grounded again to slew violently sideways . . . and started to race downhill.

Seconds later Blake and Gruener were thrown heavily forward. Trapped in a huge tangle of barbed wire, the plane groaned to a halt as the smashed undercarriage collapsed, the nose ploughed into the earth and the tail rose into the air.

The two men extricated themselves from the wreck and dropped to the ground.

'Bravo, Patsy!' Gruener said. 'I couldn't have done better myself.'

It seemed like a long time later but was probably no more than ten minutes. Blake and Gruener lay on the slope of a shell hole half filled with water. A three-quarter moon, rising into the night sky, gilded the surface and cast a wan light over the plundered land.

They had taken refuge there for two reasons. First, it was necessary to find out as far as possible where they were. Not geographically, but in relation to the ebb and flow of battle, the front line, no man's land, the artillery. Secondly, because, wherever this was, the crashed Albatros and they themselves were already targets.

They had been attacked by tracer and anti-aircraft shells as they came down. Seconds after they dropped from their cockpits there had been a blaze of machine-gun fire from further up the hill and a stream of bullets thunked into the carcass of the aeroplane. Then, hearing the once-familiar whine, Blake had hurled Gruener into the crater a heartbeat before the first mortar shell burst among the nests of barbed wire. Three more followed, shaking the ground. A trickle of earth and small pebbles broke away from the edge of the hole and cascaded into the water, fragmenting the reflection of the moon.

The fifth shattering explosion was nearer the Albatros and the sixth was a direct hit. There was a high enough concentration of fumes left in the empty fuel tank to transform the wreck into a blazing fireball.

When the hot fragments of wood and metal had stopped

pelting their backs and the flames had guttered to a fiery travesty of an aircraft outline, Blake raised his head and shoulders and looked up the hillside.

In a landscape where a forty-foot rise was an impregnable position, this miniature ridge must be something like a fortress. But where was the opposing line? And which of the combatants held the sector he could see?

He looked down the slope. A little way off to one side, perhaps eighty or a hundred yards away, the gutted remnants of a tall building raised jagged walls against the sky. It looked as if it could once have been a warehouse. Behind it was something higher still – a mill? an office block? – and here there was a suggestion of a balustraded parapet balanced above a shattered façade. At the far end, above empty windows that held no reflections, a turret and dome still stood.

Further down, the moonlight revealed the splintered stumps of trees, some kind of earthworks, an unrecognizable tangle of steel that might once have been a scout car. Blake could also make out what looked suspiciously like the bodies of several horses.

'What was that noise?' Gruener asked suddenly.

'What noise?'

The German's reply was lost in a hellish thunder of explosions. All along the ridge behind them, and out of sight beyond it, dozens, hundreds, thousands of high-explosive shells erupted in an ear-shattering cacophony. The flickering flame outlining the crest blazed into the night with redoubled fury at each successive wave of detonations.

And then, as unexpectedly as it started, the artillery barrage ceased. The scream of shells was stilled.

A star shell burst in the sky, flooding the land with livid

brilliance. That was when the chatter of machine-guns started.

'There's that noise again,' Gruener mouthed in Blake's ear. 'It sounds like singing to me.'

It did sound like singing – or at least shouting of some kind. In the distance, further down the hill. It swelled to some kind of climax. Innumerable voices. And then, 'Look!' Gruener cried. 'There!'

Blake looked, straining his eyes. He caught his breath.

In the harsh, pitiless light, the splintered trees seemed to move.

The movement coalesced, resolved itself into a long, wavering line extending far beyond the desecrated wood, separating itself from the trees.

The line was advancing. The sound of voices increased to a roar . . . and all at once that line was a flood of men, hundreds and hundreds of them, shoulder to shoulder, pounding up the slope towards the ridge with bayonets at the ready.

Machine-gun fire, punctuated now by the crackle of small arms, increased in volume. Some of the men fell.

'Christ!' Blake yelled. 'We're in the middle of bloody no man's land!'

28

The big guns started to fire again at dawn – only this time it was not a single destructive barrage but an artillery duel. Eighteen-pounders and *Feldkanone*, howitzers and trench mortars made the brightening day hideous with the reverberating fury of their cannonades.

From the top floor of the gutted warehouse, Blake looked out over the hillside where he had crash-landed the Albatros. He could see neither the field guns, the mortars, nor the heavier-calibre pieces – only the thundering hell of the shell bursts along the ridge and among the splintered remnants of the wood below. Between those two lines, around the blackened spars of the aeroplane, skewered on the barbed wire, the dead lay singly or in untidy heaps. Whoever had made the attack – and, from what he could see of the uniforms and the tin hats, it had been the British – had failed to take the ridge.

He and Gruener had simply stayed face down in the shell crater and prayed, quaking with fear as the barrage crept nearer and the advancing soldiers, scythed down by machine-guns, fell all around them.

During a temporary lull they had raced, bent double, across the battlefield towards the ruined buildings. Half-way there they had stumbled into an old second-line trench leading to what must have been a command post, destroyed in a previous bombardment. Burst sandbags here, and a savaged corrugated-iron roof, surrounded the silent witnesses to death and a hasty retreat – a smashed field telephone, mud-caked boots, the remains of a machine-gun tripod, and parts of a radio transmitter. There was an overpowering stench of putrefied flesh.

Beyond the dugout the trench had been obliterated by shell fire, but they saw in the light of another star shell, half buried by the fallen earth, several tins of condensed milk and a flat metal box packed with chocolates and cigarettes, a Christmas gift to every soldier from the Princess Royal.

By the time they had crawled the rest of the way to the warehouse, the attack behind them had been beaten off and only the groans of the wounded, punctuated by an occasional sniper's shot at the stretcher parties, broke the silence of the night.

Not daring to speak aloud, they had slept uneasily, propped up against baulks of timber on the ground floor. Far above them, stars shone between rafters where the roof had gone. The smell this time was of brick dust and charred wood.

When the dawn bombardment began they had separated – partly to see if they could spy out some relatively safe route out of the battle zone, partly to investigate the possibility of holing up in the hope that the zone itself would move.

Blake had climbed a rusted zigzag fire escape to the warehouse's top-floor gallery; Gruener was looking in the other direction. He had wormed his way across to the other building and used the domed turret at the far end of the soot-grimed, red-brick façade as a lookout post. He was kneeling behind a balustrade at the edge of a balcony circling the dome when one of the artillery batteries received orders to forget the ridge and start shelling the two ruins.

The first salvo burst against the block's ground-floor entrance, below the turret, a maelstrom of flame, brown smoke and choking plaster dust. When the air had cleared, Blake saw that half the lower part of the façade had been smashed away. Through the pall of dust hazing the narrow gap between the two buildings, the wrecked interior of the block was visible: blackened joists below a vanished floor, collapsed partition walls, a sagging stairway.

Gruener was signalling him from the balcony around the dome. Before Blake could semaphore a reply from the glassless window at the top of the fire escape, a second salvo erupted below.

One, two, three, and a thunderous reverberation as a fourth shell exploded high up against the red-brick wall. British artillery, he thought: the General Staff had recently reduced the number of guns in a battery from six to four in order to increase the number of batteries by fifty per cent and – hopefully – reduce the appalling wastage of ammunition.

There was now a huge archway blasted out of the face of the building. Bricks showered from the ragged edge at the top of the arch. Blocks of masonry fell to the growing chaos of rubble below.

The third salvo fell short, three shells only among the craters on the hillside. Even so, it was near enough to shake the foundations of the warehouse. The effect of the vibrations on the block behind was more dramatic.

The entire length of the remaining façade separated itself from the steeply pitched roof, hung for an instant in mid-air, and then slid to the ground as a single unit, to collapse on the rubble with a roar three times as loud as the detonations provoking the chute. This time the tower of yellow dust took five minutes to subside.

Coughing violently, spitting dust from his dry mouth, Blake peered through the murk. Sulphurous smoke still boiled around the base of the block. As he watched, the wall on the far side leaned outwards and fell. The dust rolled upwards again, acrid and suffocating. When the rising sun began to penetrate, he saw that the roof too had gone. Only the two end walls remained. Among the twisted pipes and charred beams projecting from the inner face of these, like the casts of fossils in a prehistoric cliff, the pale traces of cupboards, stairways and fireplaces that had been torn away bore witness to the life that had once been lived there.

Astoundingly, although the dome had gone, a sector of the terrace and balustrade, perhaps a third of the whole circumference, was still perched on a brick pinnacle above the junction of two walls.

Gruener was lying on the portion that remained.

He was alive. His back was to the warehouse, but through the balusters Blake could see him stirring, trying to sit up. There was blood on the balcony tiles beneath him.

Blake stared, aghast. No more shells had fallen. Whoever was inspecting the site through invisible field-glasses must have decided that it was no longer a danger as a possible sniper's refuge or machine-gun nest. But the artillery duel continued between the wood and the ridge. At each crescendo of the opposing barrages the column of brickwork was visibly shaking. The blast-damaged end wall was liable to disintegrate and send the wounded German five floors to his death at any moment.

Craning forward through the window embrasure, Blake saw the worst thing of all.

From among the fractured pipes and twisted conduits spining the ruin, a thick electric cable still spanned the gap to link the remains of the dome with the roof of his own building.

In other words there was a chance – at odds of a hundred to one perhaps, but still a chance – that Gruener could be rescued. And he was the only person in the world who might be able to do it.

Who *might* be able to. The electric cable was heavily insulated, undamaged, stapled to the cornice of the warehouse and the brickwork below the shattered balcony. It was just conceivable that a man in good training could reach that cable, make his way hand over hand to the parapet and return with a wounded companion over his shoulder. But it would be horribly dangerous . . . even for someone who didn't suffer from vertigo, lack of moral fibre and sheer funk. For someone, in fact, like Blake himself.

The drop must be sixty or seventy feet. The weight of even one man dragging on the wire could disturb the balance of the tottering wall, pull it out of the perpendicular and send it plummeting to the rubble below.

Gruener wouldn't know about the cable. He could turn his back, let the German take his chance, and nobody would be the wiser. Or he could take this insane, suicidal gamble: he could attempt to retain Gruener's respect – and, perhaps more importantly, his own – by balancing a rescue attempt against the probable loss of his life. The choice was his. There were no outside factors to complicate it. But the quaking wall could collapse at any moment: the decision must be made *now*.

He was on Salisbury Plain again, faced with the blazing scout car and the man trapped inside it.

In a sense, he was in a position of power. Although

Gruener didn't know it yet, his life – or death – was in Blake's hands. Perhaps it was because of the obscure feeling of superiority this gave him that he decided to take the gamble, to make an attempt to get the German off his crumbling perch. In one way he had been dealt a winning hand. But did he have the guts to play it?

The cable looked sound enough. But it was halfway between his window and the end of the building. The only way of reaching it was along a six-inch-wide decorative ledge passing above the window.

Blake swallowed. He leaned out and looked down. At once the dread signs of vertigo clawed at his diaphragm and the nape of his neck. The sheer face of the warehouse plunged dizzily into the rubble. Iron pipes and strips of planking projected from the dust cloud hanging over the jumble of masonry. He was alone with his fear and his determination. He pulled himself up into a crouching position on the window-sill. If he didn't do it now, he would never do it . . .

The window glass was long gone, but the horizontal frame of the sash was still jammed across the centre. Holding on to this, he stood warily upright on the outside of the ledge with his back to the drop. He was breathing shallowly and his forehead was cold. Now he must lean against the side of the frame, climb up until his feet rested on the sash, hold the top of the frame with one hand and reach for the ledge with the other.

For a man in good physical condition, pulling himself up on to a six-inch ledge, flexing his arms until he was high enough to cock up a leg and find a purchase with his foot, was simple enough. The difficulty was to do it without seeing what lay below. Don't look down. Never look down. Don't even *think* of what lies below. How many times had his Scottish break-and-enter tutor said that? The trick was to imagine you were doing it at ground-floor level, only a few feet from mother earth.

Like most tricks it was not as easy as it looked. Blake felt a surge of anger. It wasn't fair: he had already done this; it was the escape from the hotel in Paderborn all over again!

Getting the second leg up was the nightmare. He stretched, straightening the first, spreading his arms, forcing chest, belly and cheek against the brick ... slowly, slowly drawing up that second knee. But there was bound to be a moment, jerking the toe of his boot over the projection, when his haunches, his backside stuck dangerously far out over the abyss. He drew a quavering breath, blanked out his mind, moved smoothly, swiftly ... and did it.

He was balanced on the balls of his feet, legs spread, knees slightly bent, his arms outstretched and his two heels projecting over the void. Above him, just within reach, was a low stone coping at the lower limit of the roof. Very carefully he reached up one hand and then the other to grasp it. It was then that he realized there was no going back: the ledge was too narrow; there was no way he could scramble back to the window without overbalancing and toppling into eternity. A small sound escaped his dry lips. It was not just because of the effort pushing himself against the wall that his calf muscles were trembling uncontrollably.

He began to move. The world had removed itself, become immeasurably distant. The thunder of the artillery, the shallow whistle of his own breath, the hoarse scrape of his uniform against the brickwork and the drone of an aeroplane on the dawn patrol remained at the outermost fringe of his consciousness. He was below the dormers in Paderborn, escaping from the policeman in the loden coat, upside down in the cockpit of the crashed Pup, facing the inferno of the scout car.

He advanced his left foot, his left hand. He slid up his right. Perhaps too quickly: in his haste he snatched. The fingers of the left hand had closed over the stone right angle and held. But somehow the right slipped, and the brusqueness of the movement cast it – and with it the right leg – away from the wall and the ledge. Like an opening gate, pivoting on fingers and toes, Blake's body swung out over the gap.

Then he was desperately swivelling his left foot, exerting pressure with the scarred fingers of the left hand, to swing himself back facing the wall again.

The stone fringe of the ledge crumbled. His left foot slipped into space.

Blake uttered a despairing cry. The entire weight of his body dropped, wrenching intolerably at his left shoulder, wrist and fingers. For a timeless moment he was prevented from falling only by the frenzied clutching of those fingers over the coping.

Then, agonizingly, he scrabbled for a foothold, found it, straightened the leg, brought up the other one to relieve the load on his screaming muscles, and at last reached up to lock his right hand once more on the coping. He was gasping for breath and his eyes were streaming. Inch by inch he started to edge in the direction of the electric cable.

But his cry of anguish had alerted Gruener. The German rolled over on his tottering perch, his features caked with blood and dust. Clearly some fragment explosively displaced in one of the salvoes must have wounded him badly. He saw Blake spread-eagled against the wall at the top of the opposite façade. 'No!' he cried hoarsely during a temporary lull in the bombardment. 'Patsy, don't be a fool. You'll never make it. There's nothing you can do, man . . . leave me and get the hell out, for God's sake!'

Blake heard him but paid no attention. He had no breath to spare for a reply. In any case he couldn't go back. And having surprised himself with a positive decision in the face of danger, he was damned if he was going to be cheated out of the sense of superiority this was giving him.

The distance from the fire escape window to the staples holding the electric cable was fourteen feet. It was the longest journey of Blake's life.

The cable stretched out into space halfway between the coping and the ledge, a little below his waist. There would be no problem grasping it, but he would have to stoop a little . . . let go of the coping to transfer his other hand . . . and then push away from the ledge with his feet to allow his body to swing free below the insulated wire.

And during each of these manoeuvres it would be impossible not to look down.

He had lost all sense of time. It seemed dreadfully cold where he was, high up on the shadowed side of the warehouse. The cable brushed against his thigh. He lowered his left hand and felt it. The insulation seemed not to be perished: a black composition, not too smooth, not shiny, about half as thick as his wrist.

He gripped it hard, transferred his other hand, tested the wire to make sure it would bear his weight. He closed his eyes and began leaning outward on the swaying cable.

He couldn't do it with his eyes shut.

He opened them. Space. The dizzy void. Abyss. At the foot of the chasm, smoke still curling from the jagged interstices, the wicked mound of masonry and metal.

He saw his own body, impossibly far above this, slanting from the wire to the ledge. And suddenly the vertigo swamped him. Nausea attacked, the way an extra-large wave bowls over a bather wading in the sea. He clung there, paralysed, unable to move in any direction.

Gruener was shouting weakly. 'Go back, Patsy! There's no way you can do it. Save yourself, for God's sake.'

Blake was breathing in spasmodic gulps. An icy sweat rolled off his whole body and his teeth were chattering. He groaned aloud. If he kicked off from the ledge and hung down at the full stretch of his arms, he would be able to look up at the sky.

The wrench on his arms this time was not so severe because he was prepared for it. To a man who is young and healthy, a hand-over-hand traverse of fifteen to twenty feet of thick cable is no insuperable problem – unless he is seventy feet up in the air, suffering from vertigo and looks down. Blake looked up. His throat was tight and dry. The sky, which had darkened to an aching blue, was streaked with altocumulus in the west. Further south, a flight of three Nieuport scouts escorted an ancient BE-2c observation plane.

Halfway along the cable, Blake swung out of the shadow and into the sunlight, and the warmth washed over him like a blessing. He reached the wall below Gruener's eyrie, grasped the crumbling edge of the parapet and dragged himself up on to the tiles. It was then, gasping with relief, that he realized the artillery duel had ceased some minutes ago.

Gruener had lost consciousness. Fragments of shrapnel, one of them bloodied, lay around him. So far as Blake could see, he had been hit on the side of the head and again across the upper part of his left arm. He was still bleeding.

Time then to plan the return journey . . . and Blake

saw that this was the worst place of all. Clamped fly-like against the warehouse wall, at least he was in contact with something solid: if he fell it was from something with visible mass. Hanging from the cable, he had some control over his position in space so long as his hands could lock over the wire. But here, on these square feet of bloodstained stone, fringed by a few degrees of curved balustrade, he was totally in the void. There was nowhere to look but down. If he stared up or out, even the shaking floor supporting him disappeared; if he permitted himself to glance below, oblivion yawned on every side. And the balcony on which he was crouched, what was left of it, was too small to contain his vision: it was impossible not to look beyond it. His guts turned over and the knot behind his solar plexus tightened.

It was as well that there was Gruener to consider. The slender column of brickwork swayed with Blake's every movement; he was no longer sure if the faint shuddering transmitted to his legs came from his own muscles or the pinnacle of fissured stone; small trickles of plaster cascaded away from the broken lip and occasional fragments separated to fall – he dare not think where.

He began unbuckling the three-piece German cross-over belt that he wore. Amending the straps and fasteners to secure a casualty over the shoulder was a routine problem only: he had done it often enough in infantry training.

The transfer from the remains of the parapet to the cable was almost a relief. Somehow the fragile brick tower looked more solid as an anchor for the wire than it had felt as a platform to support them. But for one horrendous instant as he leaned out to transfer their combined weight to the cable, Blake inadvertently did look down.

He stared into the jaws of hell. For a second he thought his heart really had stopped: there was nothing left for it to pump; it felt as if all the blood in his body had drained to the soles of his feet. He froze while the sweat from between his shoulder-blades ran in rivulets down his sides.

It was then, perhaps fortunately, that the distant field-glasses focused on something unusual taking place between the ruined block and the warehouse. Blake heard the sharp crack of a sniper's rifle and a bullet smacked against one of the balusters, stinging his cheek with stone chips. A second round whined through the air a foot too high.

The new fear submerged the old and galvanized Blake into activity. With the German draped over one shoulder, he started the painful and perilous journey back along the cable.

The extra weight punished his fatigued muscles, savaging hands that were still not fully healed. There was one more shot that passed over his head, and then no more. The marksman seemed to have been downhill among the splintered trees. Perhaps the bulk of the warehouse, now that they were lower down beneath the cable, was shielding them while he moved to another position. Speed, in any case, was now more vital than ever.

The hand-over-hand progress had become automatic: he had made it once, and he could make it again, even with the added burden of Gruener. There were other problems, now that he had succeeded – yes, he had succeeded! – in removing the wounded German from his lethal position. Problems he had not had time to consider before.

Apart from the sniper, what the devil was he going to do if he got back – no, when he got back – to the ledge?

Traversing that ledge with a dead weight on his back, even if he could reach up to the coping with both hands, would be a virtual impossibility. The bulk of the unconscious man would push him too far away from the wall to maintain a solid grasp. And the thought, in any case, begged the question of how, how in God's name, could he himself clamber from the cable to the ledge and at the same time reach upwards for the coping?

Just to make things more difficult, even if that was possible, how could he lower the two of them from the ledge to the fire escape window – a manoeuvre he had already rejected as impracticable for himself alone?

Such questions abruptly became academic. Blake's stomach turned as he and his supercargo suddenly seemed to drop downwards a little. Had he imagined it? No – they sank another few inches with a jerk while he was transferring his weight from his left hand to his right. He turned his head and stared at the brick pillar they had left. There was now something like twenty-one stone dragging at the electric cable . . . and the weight had begun to pull the rusted staples out of the rotten brickwork below the balustrade.

Blake groaned again. He dare not try to accelerate his pace: he would risk pulling the old iron spikes completely free. Yet with each careful move, those staples emerged a little more, the insulated wire dropped a fraction lower. There was now a thin stream of plaster trickling, like the sands of an hourglass, from the place where the staples entered the wall. Unless they were very near – near enough to cling on – they would be smashed against the warehouse façade, or shaken off to drop into the void, when the cable pulled free.

The end came when Blake was little more than halfway along the wire.

WINGS 6

There had been the cracking percussions of anti-aircraft fire in the distance. One of the Nieuports had spun out of sight with black smoke streaming from its tail. And now there was the louder concussion of a field gun much nearer. The flat smack of the first round was followed instantly by the explosion of a shell against the brick pillar ten feet below the balustrade.

Blake never knew if there had been a second round. Pillar, balustrade and parapet disintegrated in a cloud of dust and brown smoke laced with flame. The electric cable, blown free of the shattered brickwork, swung down, weighted by its human load, towards the opposite wall.

Bracing for the final shock that would send them into eternity, Blake saw in the last tenth of a second, as they hurtled down towards the warehouse, that they would smash not into solid masonry but against a fourth-floor window embrasure that was immediately below the staples still securing their lifeline at that end. Clinging frantically to the cable, he brought up his legs an instant before the impact.

His heels exploded through splintered wood and the grimed glass of a pane still astonishingly in place as the window burst inwards.

The two men, strapped together, fell across the sill and pitched forward on to the gallery beyond.

29

The brigadier stared out of the window at Mudie's bookshop on the other side of Oxford Street. It was drizzling and the few civilians out in the lunch hour walked with heads bent and collars turned up. 'I mean,' said the brigadier, 'what the devil do you fancy your man's playing at, eh?'

'I wish I knew,' Major Hesketh said uncomfortably.

'It's deuced odd, and that's a fact. Your staging contact in Switzerland reports that he has doubts about the feller in Saxony – S-12, isn't it? He says that young Blake has been to the factory and is heading south, but he doesn't know whether or not he has the plans, is that right?'

'Yes, sir.'

'And now, thirty-six hours later, after a couple of days' silence, he signals that Blake does have the plans. That he was nabbed by the Hun but got away. Am I correct?'

'Yes, sir.'

'Very rum. So you're happy as a bloody sandboy, very bucked indeed to hear the good news . . . but when you ask for a little elaboration, such as how Blake plans to get home, you run up against another dead end.'

'It's certainly a puzzle,' Hesketh said. 'There's a lack of logic somewhere. Naturally we wanted more news. Perhaps we could set the wheels in motion to help Blake get back. The chap in Switzerland signalled S-12 to telephone him, but he never did. So the Swiss took a big risk and went into Germany himself, first Morsing a standard instruction for a rendezvous at the usual place and . . .'

'But the bugger never turned up?'

'I'm afraid not, sir. What with his previous doubts, it would seem a reasonable guess that S-12 *was* transmitting under duress. Or that the Hun had got him, squeezed the drill out of him and put a double in his place. But in that case why on earth would the double tell us that Blake had been successful? Surely that's the last thing a double's masters would want us to know?'

'Doesn't make sense, I agree,' the brigadier said. 'So what's next?'

'For the moment it's just wait and see, I'm afraid. We'll attend to S-12 later. For now, we can only hope to hear from Blake himself.'

The brigadier looked out of the window again. Outside the bookshop, a newsboy was crying a special edition of the *Morning Post*. A Zeppelin had dropped four 50lb bombs near Woolwich the previous night. Three people had been killed and seven injured. 'I think the rain's easing off,' the brigadier said. 'You better come and have lunch with me at Scott's, Hesketh. They keep me a couple of places every day and His Nibs has been summoned to Buck House to have lunch with the monarch. We can walk.'

'Thank you, sir. That would be . . . I shall be delighted.'

'Tell me one thing, Hesketh. You're a brainy kind of bird.'

'Sir?'

'Why exactly,' the brigadier asked, 'are sandboys – whatever they are – supposed to be so damn happy?'

*   *   *

Since Gruener seemed to be in a bad way, Blake did the only thing he could do: he took him to a field hospital and dressing station behind the German lines.

This was not as difficult as he expected. Soon after he had manoeuvred him to the ground floor of the warehouse, ripping off strips of clothing to staunch the bleeding and bandage the wounds as best he could, the guns started firing again. A creeping barrage this time, he saw, peering through a ruined doorway. And behind the advancing shell bursts a flood of soldiers in field-grey pouring down the hillside in a counter-attack.

Over the deafening clangour of high-explosive detonations he could hear the crackle of rifle fire, an occasional machine-gun stuttering, and above all the cacophony of human voices. Men shouting, screaming, dying; men terrified and yelling to submerge the fear; men bellowing with the lust to kill because it was the only way they knew to avoid death.

Blake knew instinctively, looking across the slope at the far side of the shallow valley and the wave of soldiers struggling there, that however animated, however ferocious the battle might seem, it would in fact be no more than a detail in the daily schedule of the front as a whole. Any ground gained by the men slaughtered amid the chaos of craters and barbed wire would be no more than a line of coloured pins on maps studied by staff officers safe in commandeered châteaux or dugouts well to the rear.

The sky was obscured by smoke drifting across the mangled hillside. When the advance had become lost in hand-to-hand combat somewhere among the trees below, a German *Feldwebel* and two men carrying a machine-gun, a tripod and two crates of ammunition entered the warehouse through a gap blown in the rear wall.

Blake assumed they had been sent to establish a nest which could cover any eventual retreat if the counter-attack was beaten off. His initial reaction was to hide . . . but at once the pride suffusing him since he had successfully conquered at last his fear and his one-time cowardice took over.

He was after all wearing a German uniform. Nobody was going to ask for identification papers in the middle of a local extension of trench warfare. He walked boldly out and addressed the astonished NCO. 'I have a wounded officer here,' he said curtly. 'How can I get him as quickly as possible to the nearest field hospital?'

'In the . . . the farm on the far side of the ridge, *Herr Hauptmann*,' the man stammered. 'Perhaps if you were to follow the stretcher bearers? I can spare one man to help you until you contact them.'

'Very well. He will be sent back to you as rapidly as convenient,' Blake snapped.

Gruener had lost a lot of blood but he was conscious again. Supported by Blake and the soldier, he hobbled out into the open air and the fumes of cordite. 'Bravo, Patsy!' he murmured as the first party they could halt loaded him on to the stretcher. 'Knight to king four – and I should imagine the move was well worth an Iron Cross. First class, of course!'

'Shut up and bleed!' Blake jested, moved by the tribute and at the same time exulting in his new-found confidence.

Surgeons and nurses sweating in the stench of blood and excrement and vomit and carbolic acid at the dressing station left their amputations and sewing among the maimed for long enough to patch up Gruener. He was a walking wounded, they said. The blood loss was important but the injuries themselves were superficial. They suggested that he report, seeing his uniform, to a temporary aerodrome three miles in the rear. Blake, who had suffered a gash on the forehead and lacerated shins when they crashed through the window, refused medical help.

An orderly driving a captured British Tin Lizzie took them away from the din of battle and deposed them, together with two infantry majors and an artillery *Ober-Leutnant*, at the hutted command post of the airfield. 'Let me do the talking,' Gruener said in a low voice as Blake helped him clamber down from the flat chassis of the Model-T Ford scout with its solid tyres and Lewis gun in place of a windscreen.

He limped into the HQ hut, leaving Blake to take stock of the different machinery the tides of war had washed up in this particular backwater.

A dozen aeroplanes were dispersed around the field – a level meadow now criss-crossed with muddy wheel tracks and the scars made by tail skids. Beyond the huts was a curious vehicle which looked like nothing more than a snail with an undercart. It was a 40-PS Panzerspähwagen, one of the earliest armoured cars, designed in 1903 by Paul Daimler and built in Vienna. All four of the disc wheels were driven, and the driver and his mate sat in an armour-plate cabin behind the 40hp Mercedes engine with only a small slit to see through. Behind them, the rear wheels were covered by the skirt of a cylindrical steel nacelle which was topped by a 360° revolving turret equipped with two machine-guns. The machine, Blake supposed, which would have been useful before static trench warfare established itself, was being kept in case a war of movement returned.

On the far side of the field a 75mm anti-aircraft gun mounted on a jacked-up Daimler-Benz truck sat in a sandbagged emplacement. Nearby, half hidden under a screen of brushwood, was a captured Renault light tank with one track missing.

Whichever combat squadron was based there, the pilots seemed to be equipped with Pfalz single-seaters. Three flights of these sharp-nosed biplanes were drawn up beyond the hutments. Blake also saw an Albatros D-III and an LVG reconnaissance plane.

Gruener reappeared, accompanied by half a dozen pilots in flying gear. There was a certain amount of ribaldry, some shoulders slapped, and then the pilots broke away to head for the Pfalz scouts. Gruener strolled over to Blake. His face was as pale as the bandages above it, but he was grinning. 'That's torn it,' he said. 'Pulled a bit of rank – socially, that is. Said I was a cousin of the Freiherr von Richthofen. Caught up in the battle with a brother officer I have to take back to Paderborn. But the bloody CO's a real *junker*: brought in his wireless operator, would you believe it, made contact with my flight commander in Malmédy, then damned well double-checked with some security officer called Schneider actually *in* Paderborn!'

'Awkward,' Blake said.

'You could say that twice again and still be underestimating it. We're being lent that old LVG two-seater – but the hell of it is, some of those Pfalz johnnies have been detailed to escort us. Security, the CO said. In case the *Englanders* jump us. But if you ask me someone has said something.'

Blake frowned. 'But if you said I was a brother officer . . . ?'

'Said you were a BO with urgent information about a spy in the Ardennes.'

'Hermann, you're going to get court-martialled if even a little of the true story gets out!'

Gruener shrugged. 'You won the chess game,' he said. 'Come on – they'll be waiting for us to install ourselves in the old bus.'

'What are we going to do?' Blake asked as they walked across.

Gruener held out a clenched fist. Two twigs projected an equal distance from between his knuckles. 'Take a twig,' he said. 'Any twig.'

Blake grasped one of the wood slivers and withdrew it.

'The longer straw. You win again!' Gruener said, throwing away the remaining twig. 'So, once we're in the plane, *you* decide what we do! Agreed?'

Blake sighed. 'If you say so.'

There was a machine-gun on a ring mounting projecting from the LVG's rear cockpit. The plane had an abnormally generous wing span, with two sets of twin struts on either side as well as N-shaped supports below the centre section. A scimitar pipe carried fumes from the exposed six-branched exhaust over the top wing.

The Pfalz scouts were already warming up. Half a dozen riggers stood around the two-seater, waiting for Gruener to give the signal to swing. Blake made a show of testing the Spandau on its ring, and settled down into the cockpit.

The altocumulus in the west now filled half the sky with cotton-wool tufts, silver-edged against the blue. 'We're heading west again, if I'm in the driving seat,' he said to Gruener, tapping him on the shoulder. 'But we'll have at least to make a pretence of going in the opposite direction at first. Perhaps when we climb to the altitude of the lowest cloud cover – well over five thousand, I'd say.'

'You tell me,' Gruener said over his shoulder.

He lowered an arm over the side of the cockpit and gave the NCO in charge of the ground crew a thumbs up. The propeller swung, the 200hp Benz engine wheezed, hiccuped and caught with a shattering roar. The NCO waved the chocks away, and the machine moved towards a wind-sock bellying out near the anti-aircraft gun emplacement.

Despite his wounds and the infernal headache he was suffering, Gruener took off neatly, effortlessly, and climbed at once to five thousand feet. The five-plane flight of Pfalz scouts followed and took up an escort formation – two on either side, one behind and below the blind spot in the tail. The nearest clouds were still several hundred feet above them.

Gruener turned round to raise enquiring eyebrows. Blake pointed upwards. The LVG continued to climb.

When the first wispy veils of white, shredded by the spinning propeller, streaked between the wings, Blake leaned out to look down. Total destruction of the green countryside was more evident from this height. From the ugly industrial sores of Lens, Douai and Béthune in the north to the fourteenth-century belfry of Bapaume in the south, the rural landscape was scarred by a swathe several miles wide of utter ruin – roads and fields and woods and villages all obliterated.

Immediately ahead of the six aeroplanes some thermal upthrust was piling the white clouds into a towering hammerhead. Gruener flew straight into it.

At once Blake was aware of the familiar weightlessness – the one-point universe with no left and no right, no up and no down: just the racket of the engine, the thin film of castor oil smarting on his face, the dense white waste with himself at its centre. Except that this time, although he was flying again, he was a passenger with another man at the controls.

Half rising in the cockpit, he leaned forward to thump Gruener on the shoulder. With his mouth close to the leather helmet he called: 'About turn, if you please, *Herr Hauptmann*. One hundred and eighty degrees should be sufficient – give or take five or ten.'

Obediently, Gruener banked the unwieldy biplane and they flew back – so far as Blake could tell – the way they came. It seemed much longer this time that they were wrapped in the cumulus. Blake was beginning to worry when they plunged suddenly into a blue so dazzling that he had to screw his eyes shut for a moment.

The sun, curiously, was beneath the lower port wing . . . until he realized, as so often occurred when flying blind, that the machine was standing on one wingtip in a near-vertical bank. Gruener half rolled on to an even course and they flew away towards the west. There was no sign of the Pfalz escorts.

Some minutes later, increasingly aware of a certain familiarity about the patchwork landscape appearing sporadically between puffballs of cloud, Blake leaned over the fuselage to stare below. Some way behind the lines, a small town on a hilltop caught his eye. Pinnacled above the huddle of grey roofs was a church with an onion-domed spire gilded with gold tiles that flashed in the midday sun.

'My God!' Blake shouted. 'That's Albert – in the Somme. Just south of Doullens and Hesdin. Hermann' – he thumped the pilot once more on the shoulder – 'turn about fifteen degrees to the north. There's an aerodrome there that I know. At Hesdigneul. It's the home base of 2 Squadron, RFC . . . There, on the far side of that rise, ten o'clock from the chalk quarry.'

He pointed down at a distant stretch of green, a brick-built headquarters block, canvas hangars, a dozen aeroplanes dispersed around the field. 'Put her down there,' he said urgently.

Gruener made no reply. He continued to fly straight ahead.

'We're on the Allied side of the line,' Blake shouted. 'You'll be treated well as an officer POW, I promise. Put her *down*, Hermann!'

'They'll be expecting you at home,' Gruener called over his shoulder. The LVG flew steadily on.

The aerodrome slid behind. Miles ahead, beyond a wilderness of dunes, a thin ribbon of blue marked the approaching sea.

Black and brown smoke clusters, some of them veined with scarlet, pock-marked the sky some way to their left. A similar rash, paler but more numerous, appeared lower down on the other side. 'We're an *enemy* aircraft now. Why don't you turn back and land?' Blake demanded.

As a reply, Gruener pointed upwards through the transparent observation panel in the centre of the LVG's top wing.

They came flashing down out of the sun, six Avro 504 fighters with Lewis guns on the top wing blazing. Blake had time to identify the long skids beneath the nose, the hoops under the lower wing – both to minimize capsized landings because of a narrow undercarriage – before Gruener stood the LVG almost on its tail and zoomed up into the first part of a loop. The machine staggered as the smoke from a near-miss shell burst whipped between the struts. There were ragged tears along the top wing and in the fuselage fabric behind Blake's cockpit, but he had no idea whether they were due to gunfire or shrapnel. Although he had no intention of shooting at a British aeroplane, he struggled up to embrace the ring mounting and cradle the Spandau. It might encourage attackers to sheer off if he looked as though he was firing.

Gruener rolled out at the top of the loop and banked steeply to avoid a flight of three RNAS Sopwith Pups with sea camouflage. He dived ... and Blake saw to his astonishment below that two pusher machines had joined the fight – slow and unwieldy with the propellers spinning within their birdcage tails, but lethal enough if you came within range of the machine-gunners exposed in their blunt noses. He had time to identify them as a DH-2 and a Farnborough-built FE-2b before Gruener was wheeling away, losing height again as the Avros re-formed for a second attack.

But now, with astonishing speed, the sky became filled with black crosses.

Manhandling the Spandau to mime a spirited defence, Blake saw a bewildering variety of German scouts, a dozen at least, maybe twenty, rallying to protect – as they thought – one of their own. He saw Eindekkers, Halberstadts, Aviatiks, an Albatros D-V, a Pfalz. Many of the top wings were camouflaged, but the fuselages were painted in all the colours of the rainbow, in bars and stripes and zigzags and even chequered. They had, he realized, run into a mass patrol of one of the German 'circuses' – the elite groups of ace pilots fighting as a combined unit. He wondered which of the near-legendary killers was spinning across his sights. Were they in contact with Fritz Holn's Jasta 21? The Boelke squadron led by Karl Bölle? Was Gruener running from Voss, Udet, Immelmann? It was encouraging, although a little disorienting, to imagine they were being protected by such men! The attackers on the other hand might include allied aces like Mick Mannock, Billy Bishop or even Roland Garros . . .

Looping, diving, banking, spinning, the machines involved in the dogfight crowded the sky from the zenith to the blue horizon. A crippled Eindekker floated past like a wounded bird with one wing detached. A Pup vanished in a ball of orange flame. Two machines which had collided spiralled earthwards trailing long plumes of black smoke.

One of the most acrobatic German fighters, only peripherally in Blake's field of vision when he first saw it, was painted a startling scarlet all over. When it climbed steeply beneath the LVG after transforming the De Havilland pusher into a blazing inferno, he realized it was a triplane, similar if not identical to the prototype he had seen in Paderborn. For an instant the machine levelled out alongside and he felt a sudden chill before he remembered that there were black crosses on his aeroplane too. A white silk scarf fluttered in the slipstream behind the triplane pilot's helmeted head. He smiled, white teeth in an oil-smeared young face, and waved a cheerful hand.

Feeling, for a second time, somehow slightly shabby, Blake grinned and waved back, wondering if he was exchanging brotherly greetings with the 'Red Baron', Rittmeister Manfred von Richthofen himself.

The red fighter veered away, closing in a tight circle on the tail of an RNAS Pup. At the same time Gruener was forced to pull the nose of the two-seater violently up to avoid ramming an Avro 504 which was shooting hell out of an Albatros. Over his shoulder, Blake saw the German single-seater roll over to show a lacerated belly and drop like a stone. The pilot, his mouth a black O in his screaming face, was frenziedly beating at the flames streaming back from his savaged engine. Blake turned away. There was nothing to do but watch the man die.

Gruener was throwing the LVG all over the sky. His aim was purely evasive, whirling them away from anything with a red, white and blue tail. But if he had been hostile, looking for a kill, he would have been a pretty formidable opponent, Blake thought.

Now the tumbling, snarling, jockeying pack of fighters were closing in as the dogfight moved out over the sea *en masse*. To Blake, on the wrong side both ways, the complex manoeuvres of these hurtling combat machines resembled more and more the antics of angry bees disturbed from a nest.

Perhaps Gruener shared the feeling; maybe it was just that he was fed up being involved. At any rate he slammed the throttle fully open, set the LVG at a shallow climb, rolled, rolled again, then rolled a third time, driving the machine into the centre of the fray like a corkscrew.

Scouts whisked away on every side, reared up like startled horses ahead, plunged past the tail. Bullets thwacked into the fuselage, tore long strips of fabric from the wings. Miraculously neither Gruener nor Blake was touched. The two-seater bored into a patch of cloud, a minor continent blowing up from the distant coastline of England.

Three minutes later, at a height of six and a half thousand feet, they flew out into the sunlit second miracle.

The sky was empty. Above, behind and below, there was not a single aeroplane to be seen. It was as if the dogfight had never been, a figment of an overheated imagination. Shimmering in the brilliant light, the sea stretched away beneath them, as static as a sheet of wrinkled silk. Southwards, where the shadow of a cloud darkened the water, a steamer – a destroyer, perhaps, on coastal patrol – engraved a fan-shaped white wake into the blue. There was white against the blue too, overhead: a twist of condensation trail, furring out of shape as a wind higher up erased this one witness to combat in the air.

Blake bent forward to tap Gruener on the arm.

He spoke close to the leather helmet. '*Herr Hauptmann*,' he said, 'I have to confess that I took your gun while you were unconscious and defenceless. I have it with me here. My own too. And this time both weapons have loaded magazines in place. In the circumstances, and considering that we are over English territorial waters, I have regretfully to ask that you consider yourself formally under arrest.'

Gruener turned completely around and pushed up his goggles. He was smiling, the blue eyes bright in the white circles above his oil-streaked cheeks. 'I'll consider it,' he said.

'It's just that, well, to establish a *status quo* I should welcome – I quote – your assurance that you accept formally that this arrest has in principle been made. I know it sounds silly, but –'

'No sillier than a similar request in Malmédy. I know.'

'Hermann, you'll be in hell's own trouble if you go back. You can't disguise the help you have been to me. Not with all those witnesses.'

'And I shall be well treated as an officer prisoner of war, correct? With real coffee and English sausages. Patsy, your request has been noted.' Gruener settled the goggles back in place and turned back to his controls.

The English coast was very clear. A few degrees to

port, perhaps ten miles ahead, the white monolith of Beachy Head rose from the sea. Beside it, the sprawl of Eastbourne was draped across the green downs.

When they had covered half the distance, the aeroplane's engine choked, coughed and missed a few beats before picking up its normal rhythm. Gruener turned again. 'I'm afraid we're running out of juice,' he said. 'Either that or the motor's about to conk out with a dud magneto.'

The nose of the LVG dropped. 'I cannot risk trying to find a suitable field,' Gruener said. 'Not among those rolling downs. I'm going to have to put her down the moment we're over land.'

The aeroplane banked steeply. A few miles to the east there was a long, sandy beach at the foot of a grassy bluff. The engine misfired again, belching a puff of blue smoke from the overhead exhaust.

Gruener flew parallel to the coast, heading for the strand.

Green slopes with bungalows, a motor bus crawling along a gravelled country road, rose rapidly towards the biplane. Gruener throttled back, raised the nose slightly and dropped them beyond a line of breakwaters to make a textbook three-point landing on hard sand.

They taxied to a halt with the engine idling.

Three men with khaki puttees and tin hats appeared from a line of dunes and ran towards the plane as Blake clambered from the cockpit – two soldiers and a lance-corporal.

'Blimey!' the NCO exclaimed, stopping dead when he saw the uniform Blake wore. 'Coupla Jerries straight from the Western Front. Fucky Nell!'

'What does he say?' Gruener called from the front cockpit.

'He is invoking a goddess of war familiar to the working classes,' Blake said.

'Not Nell Gwynn?'

'Er, no . . . not exactly. Oh, I don't know though . . . perhaps!'

'What is it, Fritz?' one of the privates guffawed. 'Missed the way to Berlin, have you? Tell him, Corp: straight ahead and turn left at bloody Wipers!'

'I am a British officer,' Blake said importantly. 'I have a prisoner . . .'

'Oh, yairss!' the lance-corporal jeered. 'And I'm Lord Kitchener. Meet my friends, the Prince of Wales and Field Marshal bloody Haig.' He produced a large, rusty service revolver and pointed it at Blake. 'Talkin' of prisoners,' he said, 'there's comfortable cells back in the camp glasshouse. So both you bleeders better come with us PDQ. Nice and quiet, eh?'

Blake opened his mouth to protest, but his words were drowned by a sudden throaty roar from the LVG's engine, which had been ticking over all the time. The machine surged forwards, tail skid slewing, as the powerful slipstream scattered a cloud of sand over Blake and the soldiers. Raising an arm to shield his face from the stinging particles, Blake thought he heard a shouted remark containing the words 'love' and 'war' and 'fair'. Then the aeroplane was hopping over irregularities in the surface of the strand, spraying out fans of water as it splashed through a rivulet running into sea, gathering speed. At the far end of the beach it lifted abruptly, soared over a low cliff and climbed into the sky.

Blake nodded to himself. Par for the course. Gruener had not in fact given his word. His rigid concept of honour had allowed him to flout convention and disobey orders when it was a question of saving a friend from the firing squad, but not permitted him to sacrifice a valuable machine and deprive his country of his possible future services once that deed was done.

Blake knew very well how easy it was to fake engine trouble when there were mixture controls and ignition switches and fuel feeders to hand. He knew too that the LVG had been fuelled for a flight from the front line to Paderborn. It was less than credible therefore that it would run out of petrol on the sixty- to seventy-mile hop from the battlefield to Eastbourne.

There was, in addition to that, the matter of the straws – the second time he had been allowed to believe that chance had helped him. Gruener had thrown away the second twig before Blake could see it, but he suspected that whichever he had chosen he would have been told it was the winner.

The aeroplane, a tiny speck in the distance now, banked steeply and turned east to fly across the Channel towards France. His personal debt of honour satisfied, Hermann Gruener was going home to face the music, whatever the cost.

As the drone of the Benz engine faded and died, Blake turned towards the NCO, who was wiping sand from his eyes. 'Very well, Corporal,' he said. 'Take me to your leader.'

It was dusk before all the necessary channels had been explored and Blake had received a reply from the secret number he had memorized. But by seven o'clock he had been re-equipped with British uniform, driven to the Royal Aircraft Establishment in Farnborough in a Crossley staff car and ushered into the presence of the civilian in charge of Experimental Research (Aviation).

279

The expert was a tall, thin man with horn-rimmed spectacles and receding hair. Somewhat distastefully, he removed the brown paper wrapping which had protected the Siegsdorf drawings during the days they were strapped, inside his underclothes, to Blake's back. He spread blueprints, plans and lists out on his desk, poring over the buckled paper with a large magnifying glass.

'Yes. Well. Actually,' he said at last, 'we have a fellow at Woolwich working on this kind of thing. Practically ironed out all the snags and got the system ready for our chaps when they have a scrap with the Hun. Captain Johnny Watts of the RAOC.' He smiled. 'Still, I dare say these will come in useful as a check, sometime or other. Pity some of the dimensions have been smudged.'

It was three hours later that Blake, who had eaten nothing all that day, was shown into the office above blacked-out Oxford Street by Major Hesketh.

Three men with red-tabbed lapels sat behind the big desk – the august figure of Lord Trenchard flanked by the major-general and the brigadier.

The brigadier raised his head as they came in. 'You took your time, Blake,' he said.